S...
is pr...

The
Romance
COLLECTION

*Three thrilling stories packed full
of passion and suspense.
Together in one volume for the first time.*

Outlawed! by **BJ Daniels**

Intrigue: Breathtaking romantic suspense

Seducing the Proper Miss Miller
by **Anne Marie Winston**

Desire: Passionate, dramatic love stories

Survive the Night by **Marilyn Pappano**

*Sensation: Passionate and thrilling
romantic adventures*

BJ DANIELS

Born in Houston, BJ Daniels is a former Southern girl who grew up on the smell of Gulf sea air and Southern cooking. But her home is now in Montana where she snowboards in the winters and boats in the summers with her husband and daughters. She does miss the good old Texas barbecue though! Her first Silhouette Intrigue novel was nominated for the *Romantic Times Magazine* Reviewer's Choice Award for best first book and best Silhouette Intrigue.

BJ loves to hear from readers. Write to her at: PO Box 183, Bozeman, MT 59771, USA.

ANNE MARIE WINSTON

loves babies she can give back when they cry, animals in all shapes and sizes and just about anything that blooms. When she's not writing, she's chauffeuring children to various activities, trying *not* to eat chocolate or reading anything she can find. She will dance at the slightest provocation and weeds her gardens when she can't see the sun any more. You can learn more about Anne Marie's novels by visiting her website at www.annemariewinston.com

MARILYN PAPPANO

brings impeccable credentials to her career–a lifelong habit of gazing out windows, not paying attention in class, daydreaming and spinning tales for her own entertainment. The sale of her first book proved that she wasn't crazy but creative. Since then she's sold more than forty books to various publishers and even a film production company. In winter she stays inside with her husband and their four dogs, and in summer she spends her free time mowing the garden and daydreams about grass that never gets taller than two inches.

You can write to her at PO Box 643, Sapulpa, OK 74067-0643, USA.

The
Romance
COLLECTION

Outlawed!
by BJ Daniels

Seducing the Proper Miss Miller
by Anne Marie Winston

Survive the Night
by Marilyn Pappano

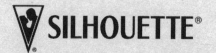

*First published in Great Britain 2005
Silhouette Books, Eton House, 18-24 Paradise Road,
Richmond, Surrey TW9 1SR*

THE ROMANCE COLLECTION © Harlequin Books S.A. 2005

The publisher acknowledges the copyright holders of the
individual works as follows:

Outlawed! © Barbara Johnson Smith 1996
Seducing the Proper Miss Miller © Anne Marie Rodgers 1998
Survive the Night © Marilyn Pappano 1996

ISBN 0 373 60272 3

055-0105

*Printed and bound in Spain
by Litografia Rosés S.A., Barcelona*

CONTENTS

OUTLAWED!

BJ Daniels

To Harry Burton Johnson,
the man who taught me to dream.
Thanks, Dad.

Prologue

The moon rimmed the tops of the ponderosas, golden in the late darkness. As Digger O'Donnel tugged his mule, Tess, up the mountain through a narrow passage between the rocks, he fought a vague sense of foreboding. A breeze danced along the back of his neck, as hot as the devil's breath. He urged Tess to move a little faster, anxious to get back to his camp.

They'd just crested the ridge, topping the band of rocks that formed a wall above the creek bed, when Digger saw the creature. At first he thought it was the moonlight playing tricks on him. A lot of people already thought he was crazy. What would they think if he told them he saw lights deep in the lake that pooled among the rocks and something dark moving around in its depths?

Suddenly the creature surfaced, and the old prospector knew he'd never seen anything like it on earth—let alone on a horse ranch in Montana. He noticed with growing fright that the strange being seemed to be attached to a small round craft that floated on the surface of Johnson Gulch Lake.

Tess sniffed the wind and let out a frightened bray. Digger hurriedly pulled at the mule. She balked as he dragged her into a stand of trees and out of sight. He stood in the shadows, afraid. Of what he'd seen. And of what he might have just imagined. What if the creature had heard Tess and was now coming after them both?

He fought the urge to run. Instead he hunkered in the pines, listening for any hint of a sound. There was nothing but the breeze stirring the tall pines. His old, tired mind told him he should leave to go tell someone what he'd seen. And yet, who would believe him? He could think of only one person— Delaney Lawson, the owner of the Rockin' L Ranch. She had always been kind to him. And the thing *was* on her ranch.

By the light of the moon, he quickly drew a crude sketch on a brown paper sack he pulled from his saddlebag. He tried to capture both the creature and its craft before he forgot the details. After all, his memory wasn't what it used to be.

When he finished, he stared at what he'd drawn. Not even Delaney Lawson would believe this, he told himself. Ordering Tess to stay put, he sneaked around the pines and took another look. The lights in the mountain lake were gone. No strange being rippled the water, no alien craft floated on the cold, dark surface. Instead the first rays of morning began to climb the back side of the Big Belt Mountains. In the distance, the ranch was as silent as the summer night.

Digger O'Donnel felt another fear—worse than when he'd seen the creature come out of the water. He crushed the paper in his fist and shoved it into his coat pocket. Space aliens! Ha! Maybe people were right. He *was* crazy, he thought as he headed back over the ridge, the new day lightening the sky to the east.

Digger and Tess had reached the outskirts of their camp, when he sensed something behind him. That same foreboding evil seemed to fill the air around him, just as it had earlier before he'd seen the creature, just as it had the night of the mine cave-in all those years ago....

"Run, Tess!" he cried, slapping the old mule on the rump. "Run!" Tess let out a startled bray and took off through the pines at a lumbering gait. "Run, old mule," Digger yelled.

He heard a branch snap behind him and turned, trying to make sense of what he was seeing. "Oh, my God, no!" He felt a sharp crack against his skull and the darkness come up to get him.

Chapter One

Cooper McLeod awoke to what he thought was distant thunder. He lay prone on a warm, flat rock, his Stetson covering his face as he napped in the shade of a huge ponderosa pine. The last thing he wanted to do was wake up. He was in the middle of a dream involving the most fascinating woman he'd ever met.

Not only was this woman beautiful, but she seemed to appreciate his finer qualities. It didn't bother her that he looked a little trail-worn or that he didn't have a roof over his head at the moment. She even liked his horse.

The thunder grew closer, and he realized it wasn't from a summer storm. Reluctantly he left the woman in his dream and sat up, his hat shading his eyes against the sun blazing in Montana's big sky. Along the valley floor below him he could see a rider coming his way, hooves pounding the sun-baked clay. The sound echoed through the rock outcroppings and the tall pines as clear as a warning.

Trouble. It was his first thought. Probably because trouble had a way of finding him. It also didn't help that he was on private property—what some might consider trespassing. Cooper squinted at the rider, telling himself he must still be dreaming, because if *this* was trouble, it certainly came nicely wrapped.

The woman rode hell-bent, her hair beneath her western

hat whirling in tight circles behind her as black and shiny as obsidian. He was enjoying just watching her, when she spotted him. She brought her horse up sharply, then spurred it in his direction. As she galloped toward him, he was reminded of the woman in his dream. Except even *his* imagination couldn't come up with a woman like this!

"What do you think you're doing?" she demanded, pulling up her mahogany bay mare. Her boots hit the ground before the horse had a chance to come to a full stop. Reins in hand, she stalked over to him.

Cooper stared up at her, too spellbound to speak. She was all curves, from her long denimed legs to the sweet promise generously filling out her blue-checked Western shirt. Her black hair spilled around her face like a storm cloud. But it was the fire in her dark eyes that made him smile as he got to his feet.

"Something funny?" she asked, her tone as steely as her stance.

Cooper figured he outweighed her by a good fifty pounds, was almost a foot taller and definitely stronger. None of that seemed to intimidate her in the least.

She stood, hands on her hips, meeting his gaze with one that would have made most men damned nervous. "When the Rockin' L takes on a man, we expect something from him," she said evenly.

He pulled a stalk of wild grass and chewed on the stem as he tried to imagine what it would be like having this woman take him on. "I'm afraid there's been a mistake." Cooper hated that he had to tell her so. He was enjoying just looking at her. She had the most kissable lips he'd ever seen. And he'd never been able to resist a woman with a little fire. This woman had enough to keep a man warm all winter.

"There's been a mistake, all right," she said. She let her gaze roam freely over him, from top to dusty bottom. He saw her stop for a moment at his belt, lingering on the All-Around

Best Cowboy buckle he'd won at Cheyenne Frontier Days, then she moved on down his faded jeans to his worn-thin lucky boots. She didn't seem all that impressed by what she saw. He fleetingly thought of the fantasy woman in his dream.

Suddenly her gaze darted past him. Her dark eyes widened. "What is *that?*"

He looked over his shoulder. "That's my horse."

"You call *that* a horse?"

Now that he thought about it, this woman didn't remind him at all of the one in his dream. "Careful now," he said, dropping his voice. "You wouldn't want to hurt Crazy Jack's feelings. He's real sensitive about his looks."

She narrowed her gaze at the horse snuffling grass beneath the big ponderosa. Cooper knew it was hard to see Crazy Jack's beauty at first. You had to get past his face. Crazy Jack was the best and worst of the Appaloosa breed. He had a head like a suitcase, just enough mane to look silly and not quite enough tail to look like a horse. Of course he had the Appaloosa spots. Everywhere. And in every size, shape and color. He wasn't the kind of horse you could miss—even at a distance.

"I suppose you named him Crazy Jack because of his eyes," she said, still staring at the horse. Crazy Jack was a little walleyed. At first glance, all you could see were the whites of his eyes. And as the old horsewife's tale has it, when you can see the whites of a horse's eyes it's a sure sign the beast is crazy.

"No," Cooper said. "Jack *is* crazy."

She stared at the horse for a moment longer, then turned back to Cooper. She appeared to be making up her mind, and not liking her decision.

"Get your...horse and come on. I'm sure Buck told you when you hired on that you were to start mending fence in the southwest pasture."

She shook her head as if she saw little hope for him.

Right then Cooper saw little hope for himself. This woman, whoever she was, was amazing when she had her dander up. She was all he could think about and he knew he should be thinking about how he was going to get himself out of this.

"The fence is over there." She tipped her hat toward a dark strip of pine and rocks etched against the blue horizon on the other side of the road. "I hope your work is better than your sense of direction."

That would probably have been a good time to tell her he wasn't lost or necessarily lazy, nor had he hired on to work for the Rockin' L. But something in the way she stood, the sun blazing in her eyes, her lips slightly parted as if needing to be kissed, changed his mind. This was an opportunity he couldn't pass up. Not only that, he didn't think she'd take kindly to the fact that he was on private property, especially if she found out why. He figured she wouldn't hesitate to have him thrown in jail for trespassing—or worse.

He dragged his hat from his head. "The name's Cooper McLeod. My friends call me 'Coop.'"

She nodded. "Fine, McLeod," she said, and swung up onto her horse.

He noticed her backside was just as intriguing as the rest of her and then he noticed she noticed him noticing.

"Is there a problem?" she asked, cocking her head as she settled those dark eyes on him.

He ran his hand along her horse's neck, pretending it was good horseflesh that had drawn his interest, and not her derriere. "Just admiring your...horse." It was a fine Morgan, bold and high-spirited like its owner.

She smiled down at him, but only a fool couldn't read the warning in her eyes just before she spurred her horse.

Cooper grinned to himself as he mounted Crazy Jack and rode after her. She *did* ride a beautiful horse, with powerful shoulders, cleanly shaped legs and a cool intelligence in its eyes. Even Crazy Jack had noticed, and he was a gelding.

As Cooper followed her, he was only a little concerned about what would happen when Buck told her he'd never seen this cowboy before—let alone hired him. Cooper had talked himself out of tight places before. He had no doubt he would again.

He thought about his last assignment, his grin fading a little as he rubbed his left thigh. He'd believed he had that one aced, and look what had happened. No, he wasn't fool enough not to know he was riding into trouble. This woman was temptation in snug-fitting jeans. He'd never seen anything like her. But, he reminded himself, he'd also never let a beautiful woman distract him so much that he couldn't do his job. This woman—no matter who she was—wasn't going to be the first.

DELANEY RODE OFF, cursing Buck for hiring an arrogant rodeo cowboy. She'd spent years avoiding men like Cooper McLeod—both professionally and personally. Long, lanky rodeo cowboys who'd ridden their share of rough stock—and charmed more than their share of women with sweet talk. She knew his kind only too well. Her father had been a rodeo cowboy. Hank Lawson had broken her mother's heart and almost lost the family horse ranch with his rodeoing.

After her mother had died, Delaney took over the place and had to watch her father, loving him, but hating the wild, irresponsible side of him that couldn't quit chasing adventure, whether it was the next untamed bull to ride at a rodeo or a beautiful woman to win over.

No, she'd learned all she wanted to know about rodeo cowboys from her father. She didn't need Cooper McLeod to remind her just how dangerous they could be. And on top of that, Cooper McLeod had to be one of the worst she'd ever seen. All denim and dimples, even with his rugged sun-browned features, he had the look of something sweet and tempting. Angel-blessed innocence, her mama used to call it.

Until you looked into his eyes. The devil jitterbugged in the depths of all that clear blue. No, this cowboy was nothing but walking trouble.

Cooper caught up with her and shot her a grin that should have been outlawed in every state in the Union. "You didn't say what I should call *you*."

Delaney slowed her horse and looked over at him. If she wasn't so badly in want of a ranch hand, she'd send him packing. This cowboy was the last thing the Rockin' L needed right now the way her luck had been running. "You can call me 'Ms. Lawson.'"

"Ms. Lawson?"

From his lips, it sounded like a caress.

"Then you must be related to Delaney Lawson, the owner of the Rockin' L."

Delaney smiled. "No, I *am* Delaney Lawson." She watched surprise wipe the grin from his face, heard him curse under his breath and realized Buck must have failed to mention the boss was a woman. She smiled to herself. This cowboy didn't know it yet, but he'd just met his match.

DELANEY LAWSON? Apprehension coiled like a rattler in Cooper's belly. Delaney Lawson was a *woman?* A young, beautiful, headstrong woman. He'd never dreamed this woman could be the owner of the Rockin' L. But he *should* have known. He should have known *everything* about the Rockin' L. His mind raced as he tried to figure out how this kind of mistake could have happened.

He'd been given the wrong information. That was the only thing that made any sense. Why else would he have been misinformed that Delaney Lawson was a man? An elderly man with one foot in the grave. He hadn't wanted to take another job so soon after the last one. The only reason he'd taken this assignment was that his employers had promised him it would be quick and simple.

Suddenly worried, he rubbed the almost healed gunshot wound in his left thigh, reminding himself how badly things had gone during his last job. And now he was getting the wrong information. Why hadn't he double-checked what Jamison had given him? Because he'd never had to before. Because he trusted his employers not to make mistakes. A mistake could have serious consequences, he reminded himself. Especially with a hellcat like this one.

He studied Delaney's slim back, quickly regaining the calm that made him the best at what he did. He could handle her. Actually, this could turn out better than he'd expected. He'd always had his best luck with women. But it did change things. Especially if his employers had failed to tell him anything else.

He considered for a moment coming up with another cover story. The problem was, he kind of liked the idea of being Delaney Lawson's hired hand. It could work into his plans quite well if he was careful. When she found out the truth, of course there'd be hell to pay. But it was a price he'd paid often enough before.

Cooper was admiring the way his new boss sat the saddle, when he noticed they were about to have company. A blue Ford pickup rattled up the dirt road, leaving a trail of dust a mile long. Delaney reined in, and Cooper did the same, hoping this wasn't the man who'd "hired" him.

The pickup rumbled to a stop beside them. As the dust settled, the driver rolled down his window. Cooper noted with relief that the painted lettering on the truck door read Kincaid Ranches. From the look of the man's expensive western suit, Cooper figured he had to be Kincaid.

"Afternoon, Del," he said, tipping his gray Stetson as his dark eyes shifted to Cooper, then settled possessively on Delaney again.

"Jared," she said with a slight nod.

Jared Kincaid looked to be hugging fifty, with a little gray at the temples and a slight paunch that strained the snaps on his western shirt. Kincaid could have been ten years younger and he'd have still been too old for Delaney, Cooper thought, but the rancher didn't seem to realize that.

"Sorry to add to the troubles you've been having, Del," Jared said, almost sounding as though he meant it. "But I was flying over the ranch this morning and I spotted about twenty head of horses I think might be yours up above Diamond Gulch. Problem is, they looked kinda…strange."

Troubles she'd been having? What was this about? Cooper wondered as he watched his new boss out of the corner of his eye. Twenty head of horses? Something told him this wasn't a cattle ranch and that he'd been given more misinformation.

She looked toward the mountains for a moment, her face appearing tranquil. But he could feel anger coming off her in waves.

"'Strange'?"

Kincaid stopped to tug at his mustache. "They were all down, Del. Didn't look good."

When Delaney spoke, her voice had an edge to it as cold and hard as a good knife. "Well, thanks for letting me know, Jared."

"It's a damned shame. Seems you've hit a real streak of bad luck."

"Seems that way, doesn't it?" she said.

"I'll get my horse and ride up there with you," he said. "It might not be pretty."

"Thanks, but I can handle it," Delaney said.

The determination in her voice and in the set of her shoulders made Cooper want to smile.

"I wouldn't go up there alone if I were you, Del," Kincaid said, biting off each word. "There's likely to be some rattlers in those rocks and I recall you're not all that partial to sidewinders." Kincaid shot a glance at Cooper. "Usually." His eyes narrowed. "*This* a new hand?"

Cooper didn't like the implication or the rancher's tone. Delaney didn't seem to take offense, nor did she seem all that excited about introducing him. He admitted he didn't look like much, but still—

"Cooper McLeod, Jared Kincaid," she said by way of introduction.

Cooper tipped his hat.

Kincaid studied him a moment, then quickly dismissed him. "You know hiring someone wasn't necessary, Del," he said.

His tone was so patronizing it made Cooper grit his teeth. Delaney looked as if her jaws were permanently locked.

"I told you I'd lend you a hand." His lips curled into a smile. "You know I'm always ready to help a little lady in need."

"Thanks anyway, but as I told you, I can take care of myself."

Delaney's tone worked as effectively as a bucket of ice water on the rancher, much to Cooper's delight.

Kincaid's smile faltered and died. Something mean flickered in his eyes, then skittered away. "You're a capable woman, all right, Del, but there're still a few things a woman needs a man for. Maybe it's been so long, you've just forgotten." He shifted the pickup into gear, touched the brim of his hat and left them in the dust.

"Seems like a nice enough fellow," Cooper said.

Delaney shot him a look. "McLeod, if I were you, I'd have the good sense to keep my mouth shut."

He doubted that, but at least he had the good sense not to say so.

She shifted in her saddle, eyeing him darkly. "You think you can find that fence now," she said, pointing to some downed barbed wire a dozen yards away. "You'll find the wire stretcher and a roll of wire in the barn."

The last thing he wanted to do was mend fence. He needed to know a lot more about what was happening on the Rockin' L. "You sure you don't want me to come along with you?" he asked.

Her expression was deadly. "McLeod, we'd better get something straight right now—"

Realizing his error, he held up his hands in mock surrender. "I just thought if there was a problem, you might want someone along, even me. I didn't mean any offense." He gave her his best grin. "I'll get to work on that fence now."

For a moment, he was worried that he'd lost his touch. But her features softened slowly. The anger eased out of her ramrod-straight back. She brushed a wisp of her dark hair back and looked over at him.

"I suppose I might need some help." She sounded resigned not only to finding her horses probably all dead, but also having to put up with Cooper. "I'll pick up my doctoring bag and meet you at the bottom of Diamond Gulch." She pointed to a narrow cut of rocks in the distance. "Try not to get lost, McLeod."

He tipped his hat at her and gave her another grin. "Whatever you say, boss." She swore as she spurred her horse. He breathed a sigh of relief. If he wanted to keep being Delaney Lawson's hired hand, he'd have to be more careful.

As he rode toward the gulch, he couldn't help wondering. Wondering about this woman. About her bad luck. But mostly wondering why Jared Kincaid seemed so happy to hear about it.

One thing was for certain, Cooper reminded himself, Delaney Lawson's luck wasn't going to get any better now that Cooper McLeod was in town.

Chapter Two

Delaney felt the air change around her as they rode up the gulch toward the east corner of the ranch. It grew thick and hot, scented with the dark aroma of death. Her mare shuddered beneath her, then snorted and tossed her head. Fear danced around the horse like electricity in a lightning storm. The mare had never been spooked around dead animals. But she was spooked now. And Delaney could think of only one other time she'd acted this way—when they'd come across a grizzly with two cubs. She brought her horse up and glanced at Cooper.

He sat astride his strange-looking beast, staring up the mountain, eyes squinted against the sun. Crazy Jack stomped the ground, ears back, nostrils flaring.

Delaney pointed to a meadow of wildflowers, high and to the left of a massive shale butte. "That's where we should find the horses." She motioned to a narrow canyon that cut through a corner of the butte. "The fastest way to get to the meadow is up that dry creek bed, but we'll have to leave our horses here and walk."

Cooper swung down out of the saddle and pulled his rifle from the scabbard. She saw him check to make sure it was loaded. He dropped his reins, ground-tying his horse, then whispered something in Crazy Jack's ear. The horse let out a whinny, as if it understood. Delaney swore under her breath. It was bad enough that Buck had hired a rodeo cowboy, but a rodeo cowboy with a crazy horse was too much.

"You want me to go take a look?" Cooper asked her. "Whatever got into the horses might still be around."

Delaney sat for a moment, suddenly afraid of what they'd find on the mountain. The steep butte shone white hot. Nearer, pines shimmered, cool, dark and green in stark contrast. Heart pounding, she dismounted and pulled her rifle. "No, I'll go along."

His gaze met hers. "You're the boss."

Right. But he seemed to keep forgetting that, she thought, as she fell in beside him.

They hiked toward the break in the rocks. Overhead the sky rode clear and blue above the mountaintop. The sun beat down, golden and hot. And yet a chill circled her neck like a noose. Something was terribly wrong.

Then it hit her. The quiet. It choked the summer day, leaving no sounds but the ones she and Cooper were making. No hawk cried overhead as it soared on a thermal. No breeze whispered in the towering pines. Not even a grasshopper rustled in the weeds.

As they followed the slim cut the creek bed had carved through the butte, the sun hammered the silence. Heat ricocheted off the rock. Each step echoed along the narrow canyon. It was hard to imagine the creek rushing with water during spring runoff just three months earlier. The dry stones reminded Delaney of the skeletal remains of something that died with summer, its bones bleached and dried from the sun.

Delaney glanced up, unconsciously searching for the familiar protected feeling the big sky over the ranch had always given her. Her heart thudded at the sight of ravens overhead.

"I don't mean to be buttin' into your business, but Kincaid mentioned you've been having some bad luck," Cooper said, glancing back at her.

She smiled to herself, doubting this man could ever keep

from butting into anyone's business. But at the same time, she was thankful to him for breaking the stifling quiet, even if it was to talk about her misfortune. "A half-dozen head of my horses got tangled up in some barbed wire during a thunderstorm. The brakes went out in the stock truck. Then some more of my horses turned up missing. And now they may be dead."

He shot her a look. "Sounds to me like you'd better put a horseshoe over your door, and quick."

Delaney rolled her eyes at his broad back as he continued up the creek bed. A horseshoe over her door! Leave it to a rodeo cowboy to come up with *that* solution. With her luck, the horseshoe would fall on her head.

But she had to admit, she was getting more than her share of bad luck. And now she had a rodeo cowboy working for her—just when she thought things couldn't get any worse. Maybe Kincaid would hire Cooper out from under her the way he had some of her other hands over the years. She smiled to herself. That would sure serve Jared Kincaid right.

They reached a short wall of boulders smoothed by years of spring runoffs. Cooper stopped, turning back to offer Delaney a hand as he started to climb up. She took it, anxious to get out of the rocks. Jared was right; she had a deathly fear of snakes. But she was also anxious to get to the meadow. And at the same time, afraid of what they'd find. With surprise, she noticed that his hand was callused from hard work. A large, strong hand that had done its share of posthole digging. She frowned, wondering if she'd been wrong about him, then saw he was limping.

"Don't tell me you've already hurt yourself," she said, remembering another rodeo cowboy she'd hired. He'd fallen off his horse the first day and slapped her with workmen's compensation for an alleged injury that laid him up for two weeks.

Cooper rubbed his left thigh. "No, ma'am. The truth is

there are some broncs in Texas a sane man shouldn't try to ride.'' He looked up at her, his eyes bottomless, and smiled. ''It makes me limp a little, but it doesn't hurt anymore.''

She nodded, realizing that must be why he'd come to work for her. And that as soon as he was healed enough to ride rodeo again, he'd be gone.

The smell of death grew stronger, the sun hotter. Birds now circled overhead. As she and Cooper topped the boulder field and started across the meadow, Delaney spotted the first horse sprawled in the tall grass. Her heart sank. Del Rio, one of her prized mares. Off to her right she spotted another carcass in the grass. A deer lay covered with flies.

Delaney shook off a chill and hurried toward Del Rio, wondering how many more she'd find dead in the grass. Suddenly the mare stumbled to its feet. Delaney let out a startled cry. She watched in horror as the mare fought to stand. Tears rushed her eyes as the mare, eyes wild, took a few awkward steps toward her, stumbled and fell over into the grass again.

Delaney stared at the horse, as fear colder than a Montana winter day settled in her bones. Other horses lay in the tall grass. Some tried to get to their feet as she approached, but fell back after a few futile attempts. When she looked up, she realized that Cooper was standing at the edge of the meadow, studying her.

''They got into something,'' she said. ''Locoweed or… something.''

''Obviously.'' He eyed her in a way that implied she wasn't as smart as she appeared.

Delaney stuck the butt of the rifle into the soft earth, settled her other hand on her hip and glared at him. ''Something bothering you, McLeod?''

''Aren't these some of your best mares?'' he asked, almost angry with her.

''As a matter of fact—'' She stopped. ''How do you know that?''

"I know good horses." He pushed his Stetson back from his face. His eyes bored into her. "So what are they doing here?"

She focused on the horse nearest her. The Rockin' L was an old-fashioned horse ranch. She didn't keep her stock in fancy arenas or barns. This was a working Morgan horse ranch. But these mares wouldn't have left the rest of the herd. And they hadn't just wandered up here by themselves. "My guess is someone tried to steal them."

He glanced around the meadow. "How were the rustlers going to get them out of here? By helicopter? There's not a road within miles. And why drug them up?"

She didn't like his tone or his attitude. And how did he know there wasn't a road within miles of here? It hit her that he wasn't lost at all when she'd found him sleeping on the rocks.

"What makes you think there isn't a road near here?" she asked, studying him.

He smiled. "If there was, wouldn't we have taken it to get here?"

She flipped a lock of errant hair back from her face. He always had an answer for everything, didn't he? So why didn't she trust him? "I suppose you have a theory on why my horses are here?"

"Maybe."

She watched him circle the meadow studying the ground as he walked, and couldn't help thinking there was more to Cooper McLeod than just some saddle-worn rodeo cowboy.

After a moment he knelt in the grass, then motioned for her to join him. "Seems that someone made a portable corral to keep the horses in. And look at this." He stuck three fingers of wet soil under her nose. She jerked back from the awful smell.

"I'd say a mixture of oats and astragalus—heavy on the locoweed," Cooper said.

Delaney swore as she looked around the meadow at her mares. "They corraled my horses, drugged them and let them loose. Why? What did that accomplish?"

She turned, surprised when Cooper didn't throw in his two-cents' worth.

He was still hunkered in the grass. She noticed he had a handful of rank soil that he was slowly letting spill through his fingers. "Oh, I think they accomplished what they set out to do." He leaned back on his haunches and squinted up at her.

"Spit it out, McLeod."

A smile turned up the corners of his mouth, setting off those dimples. His eyes burned like blue flames, but there was no humor in his look, just a deadly seriousness that froze her blood.

"It scared you, didn't it?"

She swallowed and turned away, surprised by his insight. She *did* believe that's exactly what the recent accidents were about—someone was trying to scare her. But she hadn't even admitted it to herself.

She glanced over her shoulder at Cooper, realizing he was much more dangerous than she'd first thought. He had intelligence along with all that charm and good looks. "Why would someone go to all this trouble just to…try to scare me?" she asked.

"That's a good question." He picked up a small, flat stone from the ground, his thumb making slow circles on the weather-worn surface. She remembered the feel of his hand earlier. The hand of a working cowboy, suntanned and weathered, strong and callused. She dragged her gaze away.

"Or it could be someone's out to get you," he said. "But I suppose you'd know better than I would about that."

She met his gaze. The intensity of his look startled her. Not much got past those blue eyes of his. She'd have to remember that.

Cooper dropped the stone and dusted his hands on his jeans. "Well, there's not much we can do here now. The veterinarian should be able to tell you what they were drugged with. I would imagine they weren't given enough to kill them and that this should wear off."

"Really?" she said, looking at him. While she agreed with his appraisal of the situation, she wondered where he'd learned so much about horses. And locoweed. Not on any rodeo circuit.

"You want me to help draw the blood?" he asked.

She nodded as she opened her bag, wondering why she felt Cooper McLeod knew more about her troubles than he was letting on. What did she know about the man anyway? She promised herself she'd run a check on him when she got back to the ranch. If she didn't fire him before the end of the day.

COOPER WATCHED Delaney closely as they started back down the mountain. All her bad luck sounded a little too familiar; minor accidents that frightened ranch owners but didn't devalue the stock or the land. It was the same kind of thing he'd done on other ranches. What the hell was happening on the Rockin' L? And what was the story with Delaney? Was she really as much in the dark as she pretended to be? Not that it mattered. It was obvious this job had more complications than his employers had anticipated. He needed to get to a phone and call them. And of course there was that little matter of the mixed-up information. But worse were the so-called accidents at the Rockin' L. His employers needed to know just what they'd gotten him into. And then they could damn well get him out of it.

He let her lead the way back down. He liked following her, but not just because of the view. He felt she'd be safer with him bringing up the rear. The feeling surprised him. He hadn't felt protective toward a woman in a long time. Especially one as capable as Delaney Lawson. But it also meant he thought she needed protecting. And that worried him.

They were almost out of the narrow canyon of rock, almost to their horses, when he heard the splatter of small stones, like raindrops overhead. He glanced up, caught a blur of color and lunged for Delaney. Catching her around the waist, he took her down into the gravel at the edge of the rock wall. They hit hard, Cooper absorbing most of the impact as he pulled her back under the overhang, drawing her tight against his body.

"What the—" Delaney's words were drowned out by the rock slide that whirred in front of them as loud as helicopters. Rocks hammered the creek bed in a meteorlike shower. Delaney pressed into him and he held her tighter.

"McLeod?"

It took him a moment to realize the rocks had quit falling. It took another to realize the thudding of his heart was only partially due to the near accident. He lay with Delaney spooned against him, his arms wrapped around her, his forearms against her soft, full breasts, his face buried in her hair. At every point where Delaney's body pressed against his, he felt the heat of desire. She turned in his arms, and without thinking, he sought her lips—

"McLeod." Her lips barely brushed his and were quickly gone as she slipped out of his embrace, leaving him with nothing but her hat in his hands. Fast on her feet, he decided, looking up at her standing over him.

He'd thought he might see at least a little fire of longing burning in her eyes. There was a fire, all right. But this one could have been set by an arsonist—a very mad one. Forget longing. Forget desire. Only anger burned in those dark eyes. A whole lot of anger. And all of it directed at him. She stood with her hands on her hips, eyes blazing.

"And just what was all that about?" she demanded.

Realizing he still held her hat in his hands, he got to his feet and picked up his rifle. "Ma'am?"

Angrily she dusted herself off as if she could erase the feel of him against her and picked up her own rifle from the ground. "Don't 'ma'am' me, you...you..." She waved her hand through the air.

He joined her in the rock-strewn creek bed. "You don't have to thank me for saving your life—"

"Saving my life! Is that what you were doing?"

Her ebony hair spilled around her shoulders. She threw it back as she narrowed eyes as dark as midnight at him.

"And here I thought you were just taking advantage of the situation."

He looked down at her hat in his free hand. What was wrong with him? He'd charmed his way into enough women's hearts to know better than to overplay his hand. Why in God's name had he tried to kiss her? He met her gaze. Because at that moment all he'd wanted was to kiss her. Great. "Pardon me, ma'am—I don't know what I was thinking," he answered honestly. "It was just a crazy impulse."

She took the hat he offered her, her fingers shaking. "McLeod, I have enough problems without you—"

"I'd say you're right about that. But before you fire me, there's something you might want to know. That rock slide wasn't an accident."

She glared at him. "And how do you know that?

He studied her, realizing he had nothing to lose. She planned to can him, and he couldn't say he blamed her. "I think there's something you'd better see."

They hiked back up the mountain, then across the top of the rock butte. The sun slipped toward the mountains to the west, stealing across the sky, taking the heat with it.

"See those?" He pointed to the boot tracks in the dust where he'd seen the flash of clothing. The rocks had been disturbed where someone had started the rock slide. "Right before the slide, I saw someone up here."

DELANEY FELT her legs turn liquid beneath her. She plopped down on a large boulder at the edge of the steep bluff, all her strength suddenly gone. Cooper was right. Someone had purposely started the rock slide. She rubbed the back of her neck, trying to make sense of everything that was happening, slowly realizing that like it or not, Cooper had saved her life. She looked up to find him silhouetted against the sinking sun. She didn't need to see his face to know he was watching her.

"I'm sorry. I thought you'd somehow orchestrated the rock slide just to—" She bit down on her lower lip, realizing how crazy that must sound. Almost as crazy as that split second when she'd wanted to kiss him.

He grinned. "I usually don't have to pull off such elaborate feats to get a kiss from a woman."

"I'm sure you don't." She tried to laugh, but it came out a whisper. "Thank you."

"Forget it," he said, seeming to study the dusty toes of his boots.

Delaney pushed herself up and walked toward a stand of pines, fear mixing with anger as she thought about the person who'd drugged her horses, who'd no doubt caused her other "accidents," who'd just tried to kill her. She stopped at the sight of a horse's tracks in the dirt and squatted to study them. One of the horse's shoes had been barred across the back, a corrective measure for a broken hoof, and just as individualized as a fingerprint.

She looked up to find Cooper standing over her.

"Recognize the horse?" he asked, nodding at the print.

She shook her head. "It could even be one of mine." The shoer had just been to the ranch. Buck hadn't mentioned a horse with a broken hoof, but she hadn't seen much of Buck lately. She pushed herself to her feet, fighting tears of anger, fear and growing frustration.

"Maybe I'm out of line again, boss, but I can't help thinking you know who's doing this. And why."

She took a deep breath and let it out slowly as she turned. Her first impulse was to tell him to mind his own business. But he'd just saved her life, hadn't he? Her gaze wandered across the land, then settled on Cooper. "I knew he wanted the ranch," she said quietly. "I just never believed he'd try to kill me to get it."

Chapter Three

Delaney found she was shaking by the time they reached their horses. A delayed reaction. From her near escape in the rock slide. Her near escape from kissing Cooper McLeod. She didn't know what had possessed her. She blamed it on fear, on all the bad luck she'd been having, on this cowboy's unexpected insight on the mountain.

"Is it Jared Kincaid?" Cooper asked as he put his rifle back into his scabbard.

It was a question she knew he'd been dying to ask, but she hadn't given him a chance.

She sheathed her own weapon and swung up into the saddle. "Jared? Why would you think that?"

"He seems to have an interest in your bad luck," Cooper said as he mounted Crazy Jack.

Delaney watched him, thinking the same could be said of Cooper McLeod. But Cooper had almost been caught in the rock slide with her, she reminded herself. If it hadn't been for him— "Jared's made no secret of the fact that he'd like the Rockin' L. But this isn't his style." She hesitated, having never voiced her fears before. "A man claiming to be my half brother showed up at the ranch about a month ago, about the time my so-called bad luck started."

"A half brother you didn't know about?" Cooper asked, incredulous.

Delaney looked toward the mountains, debating how much to confide in McLeod. He'd just saved her life; she owed him at least the truth. "It seems he's the son of an old...girlfriend of my father's."

"You don't sound surprised. Or convinced he's your brother."

They rode toward the ranch house, the sun melting behind the peaks. "Surprised that my father had mistresses?" She shook her head, but couldn't meet McLeod's gaze. "Hank Lawson required more attention that any one woman could give a man, not even my mother, who adored him. Ty's mother was one of many. I guess that's why I don't believe Ty Drummond is my half brother."

Cooper pulled off his hat and ran his fingers through his sandy blond hair. It was a gesture Delaney had seen her father do a hundred times.

"I heard about Hank's death while I was riding the circuit. I'm sorry."

She shook her head at the memory. "He was still riding bulls in small exhibition rodeos, even though he was too old for it and had been hurt too many times. He just couldn't quit." She glanced over at Cooper. "And I'm sure you also heard about the bull that killed him. Its name was Death Wish. How appropriate, huh?"

"Riding bulls is dangerous no matter what the bull's name. It's just something some men have to do."

"So my father told me." She couldn't help sounding disgusted. What was wrong with grown men who had to ride wild bulls or broncs? Was it the thrill? The challenge? Or did they have to continue proving themselves? Her father had never been able to explain it to her. And she doubted Cooper McLeod could, either.

They were almost to the ranch. It sat just over the next rise. Delaney quickened her pace. It was a sight she never tired of. Her grandfather, Del Henry Lawson, had built the two-story ranch house. It had weathered many storms over the years—from the worst blizzards to the loss of her mother and finally the death of her father. She hoped the house had the strength to weather more storms, because she knew it was going to have to, and soon.

As the home place came into view, she watched Cooper take it in. He nodded with appreciation.

The house seemed to fill the open landscape, stone glistening, logs glowing warm in the failing sun. Shadows lounged in the shade of a wide porch that ran the width of the house. Behind it all, ponderosas glistened like dark silk against the rocky bluffs. A small creek wound its way through the pines. Off to the side, an old barn hunkered, its horse weather vane reflecting the last of the sun. Another, newer, barn and corrals stretched to the south.

"It's beautiful," Cooper said.

She could feel his gaze on her. It warmed her face the way the sun had.

"It means a lot to you, doesn't it?"

She smiled at that. "It means *everything* to me, Mr. McLeod. I'd die before I'd let anyone take it from me."

He frowned as if suddenly hit by a sharp stab of pain, and she wondered if his leg bothered him more than he let on.

Her smile faded as they rode nearer and she saw the beat-up pickup parked off to the side of the house. "Damn," she swore under her breath. "It looks like you're going to get to meet my alleged half brother, Ty."

COOPER SPOTTED a lanky young cowboy in the shade of the porch, his feet up on the railing, his hat tipped back. His look, as well as his demeanor, oozed defiance.

"I can take care of your horse if you want to go on up," Cooper offered.

But Delaney shook her head. "Let Ty wait. It will be good for him. And I'd just as soon you not take off yet."

She seemed a little rattled. He figured Ty was to blame.

"I have some tax forms I need you to fill out, so you might as well come on up to the house."

They unsaddled the horses and Cooper cut Crazy Jack out with the others. One of the horses in the corral was still lathered up, as if it had just been run hard, he noted, hoping it wasn't Buck's horse. For a while, Cooper had forgotten about the lie he was living. But Buck Taylor would certainly take care of that once they met. Cooper wondered also when the *real* ranch hand would turn up.

"I suppose that's Buck's horse in the corral?" Cooper said, pointing at the freshly ridden dark bay.

Delaney frowned. "No, he keeps his horse, Sugarfoot, down at his place. And Buck's out of town for a few days, so he couldn't have ridden any of these horses." She glanced toward the lathered bay. "I've got a couple of college kids helping with the haying while Buck's gone. Maybe one of them took the horse out." She wasn't convinced.

Cooper climbed into the corral and checked the prints the bay was making in the dirt. No barred horseshoe.

Delaney seemed lost in thought as they walked toward the ranch house. Ty hadn't moved from his spot on the porch, but Cooper detected an agitation that belied the cowboy's apparent calm. His age surprised Cooper. Ty looked to be in his late twenties, like Delaney.

Yet there wasn't much real resemblance between the two. Ty was dark like Delaney, but lacked the striking features that made her beautiful. His eyes were a lighter version of hers, but there was no kindness in them, no compassion, no passion at all. Just an icy darkness that seemed bottomless.

"I heard about the horses," Ty Drummond snarled before Delaney reached the porch.

He sounded accusing and belligerent and Cooper suspected he'd been drinking.

"Jared said—"

"Jared?" Delaney asked, pushing back her hat to look up at him as she leaned against the porch railing.

Cooper watched the two of them from the yard.

"I ran into him in town," Ty said, avoiding her gaze.

"You didn't by any chance borrow one of my horses this afternoon, did you?"

He jerked around to glare at her. "*Your* horses?" Then he gave the idea a dismissive shrug. "What would I need with a horse?"

"I was wondering that myself," Delaney said.

Ty glanced around the ranch yard, pretending a nonchalance he wasn't pulling off. His gaze fell on Cooper. He eyed Delaney questioningly.

"Cooper McLeod is my new hand," she said with more force than she had earlier with Jared. It made Cooper feel a little better. "This is Ty Drummond."

Ty glared at her, then tipped his hat at Cooper. "I'm her brother."

"Half brother," Delaney corrected as she climbed the steps and pushed open the screen door. "Maybe." She glanced over her shoulder. "Cooper, come in and I'll get those forms for you to fill out."

He liked the way she called him "Cooper," even though he figured she only did it to make him sound more important than he was to needle Ty. Nor was he fooled by her asking him inside the house to fill out some tax forms. He figured she didn't want to be alone with Ty. He couldn't blame her. Ty made him nervous, too, but for a different reason.

Cooper followed her into the house. He'd seen photographs of the inside, but none had done it justice. A huge rock fireplace dominated the room. Pine floors gleamed golden beneath a scattering of rich-colored Native American rugs. The furniture, while rustic, looked comfortable, the cushions colorful and inviting.

Behind him, he heard Ty's boot soles slap the floor with

angry thuds. The cowboy shoved past him and into the kitchen.

"You can't keep ignoring me," Ty called, stomping after Delaney. "I have our father's will, naming me heir. The Rockin' L is mine and you know it."

Cooper swore under his breath. A will naming Ty heir to the ranch? This was worse than he'd thought. How many more surprises were going to turn up like dead bodies on this ranch? Cooper wondered.

"All I know is what my father told me a week before he died," Delaney said, her voice carrying into the living room. "He said he'd made out a will, leaving me the ranch and everything else, including his bills."

"So where is *this* will?" Ty demanded. "Show it to me."

"It will turn up, don't worry."

Delaney sounded worried, but she wasn't half as worried as Cooper. He had to call his employers—and soon. This job was starting to go sour just like the last one, he thought as he trailed Ty and Delaney into the kitchen.

Like the living room, the kitchen had the same warm and cozy feel to it. Pots hung from the ceiling. A checked red-and-white tablecloth draped the long wooden table. Wild flowers sat in the middle in an old white porcelain vase. Cooper frowned, realizing they must have been from an admirer, because Delaney Lawson seemed too busy a ranch woman to stop to pick flowers.

Ty stomped over to the table and dropped a bundle of letters tied with a ragged purple ribbon onto the tablecloth. "You wanted proof that I'm your brother—there it is."

Cooper watched Delaney pour two glasses of lemonade. She handed one to him, then looked at Ty.

"I don't want any lemonade," he said impatiently. "Well, aren't you even going to look at them?"

Cooper watched her glance toward the package of worn letters, but she didn't reach for them.

"They're love letters," he said smiling, obviously enjoying her discomfort. "From *our* father to *my* mother. I was his son. And he wanted me to have this ranch."

Delaney laughed. "Too bad you weren't around to help pay the bills when he was alive."

Anger rose up Ty's neck like a deep red rash. "I didn't know I was his son. No one bothered to tell me."

Delaney studied him for a moment, then opened the fridge and began to rummage around inside it as if she were searching for something. Cooper figured she just didn't want to deal with this and he couldn't blame her.

"The courts will decide..." Delaney said from inside the refrigerator.

"You're just trying to drag this out."

He glared at Cooper, probably since his glares at Delaney were going unnoticed.

"I'll have this ranch, and sooner than you think." He picked up the bundle of love letters, bumping the table and spilling the vase of flowers. "You can have the *copies* of the letters," he said, dropping some papers on the table before he stomped out. Cooper heard the front door slam and, a moment later, a rough-sounding engine start, then a rattling pickup sped off down the road, gears grinding.

Delaney slammed the refrigerator door and leaned against it. "So what do you think of Ty?" she asked sarcastically.

"As charming as Jared Kincaid," Cooper said, picking up the copies of the love letters and spilled flowers and mopping up the water with the towel Delaney tossed him. "But I can't help thinking he's not the one behind your accidents—or the rock slide today."

"McLeod, didn't you hear what he just said about getting the ranch, and soon?"

Cooper wished she hadn't gone back to calling him "McLeod" so soon. "I just wonder why he's trying too hard to prove to you that he's your brother, especially if he has a will.''

''Because he's not my brother, nor is his will any more legitimate than he is,'' she said angrily. ''My father died six months ago, the ranch is tied up in probate and I haven't been able to find the will he told me he wrote, leaving everything to me.''

''He didn't leave it with his attorney?''

Delaney looked at him askance. ''His attorney?'' She laughed. ''Hank Lawson was a rodeo cowboy. He didn't have an attorney. Or an accountant. Or even a safety-deposit box at the bank. He lived out of a travel trailer he dragged around the country with an old pickup truck. But I'm sure you, if anyone, would understand that.''

''Me?''

She brushed her hair from her face and looked away. ''I'm sorry. It's just that you remind me a lot of my father.''

He wasn't sure he wanted to hear this. ''Because we both rodeo?''

She studied him for a moment, her eyes dark and troubled. ''He was handsome like you.'' She smiled. ''Don't act as though you're surprised to hear that you're handsome.'' She narrowed her gaze at him as she searched his face. ''And Hank was charming, and funny, and…sexy like you.'' She laughed when he raised an eyebrow at the last. Then she looked away. ''Unfortunately, he broke my mother's heart and didn't do a half-bad job on mine.''

''I'm sorry to hear that.'' He leaned toward her and heard her breath catch in her throat. As he handed her the photocopies of the letters, he noticed a slight tremble to her fingers as she took them. It struck him that she was afraid of him. He frowned. ''You know not every cowboy who rides the rodeo abandons his family for the sport.''

She almost looked as if she wanted to believe that.

He glanced around the homey kitchen, thinking about Ty

Drummond. "A bastard son who can prove paternity could get a portion of the estate," he said quietly. "Or even if he isn't your brother, Ty could get everything if the will he has from your father is legitimate. Unless you can come up with a more recent will your father had witnessed and dated."

"You almost sound like a lawyer."

Those dark eyes of hers seemed to penetrate him.

"Who are you really, Cooper McLeod?"

He shook his head and summoned up a grin, hoping it would mollify her. "Isn't it bad enough I'm a rodeo cowboy? Now you think I'm a lawyer?"

She laughed. "What I don't think you are is a ranch hand."

He tried to appear crushed. "I guess I'll just have to work harder at it," he answered truthfully.

A movement caught his eye outside the kitchen window. "Looks like you have another visitor."

Delaney moaned and moved over to the window to see. A frown creased her brow and real worry etched itself in her expression. "Oh, no, it's Tess." Delaney bolted for the front door. Cooper ran after her. They reached the ranch yard as an old mule came trotting up.

Delaney hurried to it, running her hand along its neck, hugging the animal to her. "Oh, God." Delaney scanned the empty road and Cooper saw the same worry and fear he'd witnessed earlier when they'd found the drugged horses. "We have to find Digger."

"Digger?" He followed after her as she took the mule into the barn, gave it food and water, then grabbed her rifle from the tack room and her doctoring bag.

"I suppose you're coming with me." She didn't wait for an answer.

He pulled his rifle from the scabbard, wondering what kind of trouble hunting for Digger was going to get them in and limped after her.

"If anything has happened to Digger..." Delaney muttered as she headed for a pickup parked by the barn.

They were in the truck tearing down the dirt road, when Cooper asked, "Who's Digger?"

Delaney glanced over at him as if she'd forgotten he'd come along. "Digger O'Donnel. His camp is up near Hogback Mountain." She stared ahead at the road. Beyond it the horizon had turned lavender in the twilight. "Digger and Tess are inseparable. For Tess to come home like that—"

Home? Cooper heard the break in Delaney's voice. Whoever Digger was, he meant a great deal to her. How many men did this woman have in her life anyway? Cooper wondered.

"Digger has to be in trouble," she said quietly, not even trying to hide her fear. Or the tears that brimmed in her eyes.

Cooper watched the road ahead, worried that whoever this Digger was, he'd met with one of the Rockin' L's notorious accidents.

Chapter Four

A cool darkness had settled in the pines by the time Delaney stopped the pickup in the middle of the mountain road. With out a word, she jumped out, turned the hubs into four-wheel drive and slid back into the cab. Then she pulled onto what could only be called a Jeep trail.

Dark pine boughs closed around the pickup, reminding Cooper of the close confines of a car wash. He squirmed uneasily. ''Just exactly who is this Digger we're looking for?'' he asked, unable to take his eyes off the patch of road he could see in the headlights, for fear of what would appear around the next curve. His claustrophobia and Delaney's anxiety were making him jumpy. That and the feeling that they were riding into something nasty just, as they had the drugged horses on the mountain earlier.

The pickup climbed at a crawl, bumping over large boulders that formed the roadbed. Delaney gripped the wheel, all her concentration on the road. Worry made her eyes darker than the coming night and her expression bleak.

''Digger O'Donnel is a prospector,'' she said after a moment. She seemed to loosen her grip on the wheel a little. ''He pans for gold, but mostly just wanders the mountains with Tess.''

''Gold?'' Cooper asked, trying not to let his surprise show.

''Digger used to work one of my grandfather's claims with

a friend of his, Gus Halbrook. They were in their early twenties when they met my grandfather, Del Henry Lawson. It was the 1930s and some of the mines around here had been reopened. My grandfather, who was by then in his late fifties, hired Digger and Gus to work the Golden Dream."

"Did they strike it rich?" Cooper asked, more than a little curious.

Delaney carefully eased the pickup over two large boulders before she answered. "To hear Digger tell it. He swears they found the mother lode." She glanced over at Cooper. "But then, Digger has no money to show for it if they did."

"What about your grandfather?" Cooper asked. "He must have found some gold originally to buy this ranch."

Delaney laughed. "My grandfather married a young woman with money. Grandmother helped him start the Rockin' L after his mining claims on the land proved to be near worthless."

"But Digger says they found the mother lode?"

She turned her attention back to the road. "You see Digger is…well, his mind kind of…snapped when his friend Gus was killed in a cave-in long before I was born."

"This mine that caved in is the one Digger said was the mother lode?" Cooper asked. "The Golden Dream?"

She nodded. "I think that's the only way Digger can accept what happened. My grandfather said they found a small vein of gold but it quickly petered out. Unfortunately Gus kept working the mine on his own time, obsessed with the belief that it was the elusive mother lode. Gus didn't take the time to shore up the walls adequately and was killed in a cave-in."

She let out a sigh. "After that my grandfather closed the mine, blasting the entrance so no one else would get killed in it. The Golden Dream is gone in more ways than one. I doubt even Digger remembers where it was."

Cooper turned to stare at her. "*You* don't know where the mine is?"

She shook her head. "There are so many mines on the ranch. None of them is worth anything."

"That's interesting," Cooper said, without thinking. He tried to remember what he'd heard about the area. It had been gold country, that was for sure. Confederate Gulch and its tributaries weren't far from the Rockin' L, and they'd produced millions of dollars in gold back in the 1800s.

Delaney must have heard interest in his tone. They'd just topped a small rise, the pines dense and dark, the road nothing but rocks.

"You're not getting any romantic ideas about finding the missing mother lode, are you?"

Suspicion put an edge on her words. She sounded as if she'd expect just about anything from him, as long as it was bad.

Cooper laughed. "I'm a cowboy, not a gold miner. Anyway, there is no mother lode, right?"

"Right."

He could feel her watching him out of the corner of her eye.

"We're almost there."

Cooper stared ahead, thinking about gold, missing mines and an old prospector who swore he'd found the mother lode—and was now maybe missing himself. Everything about the Rockin' L was turning out to be a surprise, Cooper realized with growing concern.

They dropped into a ravine and Delaney slowed as the truck's headlights illuminated a makeshift lean-to built of tarps and log poles. An iron skillet hung from a nail on one of the poles. Near it a cracked mirror reflected the light from the headlights.

"My grandfather built Digger a cabin not far from here,

but he prefers *this* except in the dead of winter,'' Delaney lamented, obviously unable to understand.

Cooper stared at the camp. It resembled many he'd spent time in. "There is nothing like being able to see the stars at night," he said as Delaney brought the pickup to a stop.

She reached under the seat for a flashlight. Her fingers shook as she fumbled to turn it on. Cooper took it from her. His hand brushed her wrist and he could feel her pulse pounding. "If he's around here, we'll find him."

She nodded and swallowed. He opened his door and heard her do the same. They walked into the sparse camp. It appeared as if its occupant had just left for a moment. A worn bedroll was spread in the pine needles beneath the tarp. A striped pillow lay on top of it beside a dog-eared gold-mining book.

Cooper checked the fire pit. It was cold.

"Did you hear that?" Delaney whispered.

He listened. Night had dropped into the ravine and Digger O'Donnel's camp. The air felt cold and brittle, as if warning that fall wasn't far away.

"Over there." Delaney pointed into the dense pines. "I heard something, over there."

Cooper started to shine the flashlight into the trees, when he heard it, too. A moan. He flicked the beam across the dark boughs, then brought it back to what looked like a bundle of clothing piled next to a tree trunk.

"Digger!" Delaney cried, and scrambled toward the heap.

Cooper hurried after her, pointing the way with the light. She dropped to the ground beside the ragged bundle, speaking in a hushed tone.

Cooper shone the flashlight for her, afraid they'd arrived too late. A weathered old man lay against the tree trunk, his eyes closed. He wore a hunting cap and overalls beneath a ragged coat. His head was tilted at a strange angle, his mouth drooped open.

"Oh, Digger," Cooper heard Delaney cry as she cupped the man's ancient face in her hands. Cooper noted with shock that there were tracks in the pine needles where he'd dragged himself for some distance, obviously trying to get back to his camp.

Cooper knelt beside the pair. He was sure the old prospector was headed for the Pearly Gates, when Digger opened his eyes. His startling brown-eyed gaze fought to focus on Cooper, then Delaney. A smile worked at his lips.

"I knew you'd come, sweet Winnie."

Cooper shot Delaney a look. Who the devil was Winnie? "Yes, Digger, I'm here now," she said softly.

The old man lifted his hand to pat Delaney's cheek. "In the lake. Damnedest thing you've ever seen." His voice dropped to a whisper; his eyelids drooped. "Space aliens, Winnie. In the lake." His eyes closed, his breathing grew more ragged. Suddenly his eyes flew open again. "Tess!" he cried. "Where's Tess?"

"She's fine, Digger," Delaney assured him. "She came to the ranch, so I knew you were in trouble. I put her in the barn with some oats."

He smiled, then his eyes widened with fear. "He's back from the grave, Winnie. Back for revenge. Gus. He tried to kill me."

"We have to get him to a doctor," Delaney said, motioning for Cooper to help her lift him.

"Easy," Cooper said as he noticed the blood-encrusted lump on the back of Digger O'Donnell's head.

"He must have taken a fall," she said, swearing under her breath. "He's too old to be wandering the woods like this."

Cooper started to argue that confining him to a cabin would probably kill him. He'd seen what could happen to a man who'd lost his freedom. Instead he handed Delaney the flashlight and lifted the old man into his arms. "We can put him in the middle. You drive and I'll try to keep him as stationary as I can.''

Delaney shivered and mumbled, ''Space aliens. I wonder where he got that?''

As Cooper carefully laid Digger on the seat, his old eyes flickered open. ''Del,'' he said, his voice weak. He smiled and fumbled for Cooper's hand. He pressed a piece of crumbled paper into Cooper's fingers, then closed his eyes again. Cooper shoved the paper into his pocket as Delaney climbed behind the wheel and Cooper slid in beside Digger.

WHILE THEY WAITED at the hospital for word on Digger's condition, Delaney paced. Cooper brought her coffee and a sandwich, but she'd taken only a few bites. Like her, he was worried—just not for the same reasons.

''Digger called you 'Winnie,''' he said, trying to distract her from staring down the hallway toward Digger's room.

Delaney glanced at the sandwich in her hand, then at Cooper. ''Winifred Lawson. My grandmother. I've always suspected Digger was in love with her. They were about the same age.''

''If this Winnie was anything like her granddaughter, I can understand why,'' Cooper said.

She rolled her eyes. ''I'd say thank you, but I know charm is second to breathing for men like you.''

He laughed, not even bothering to deny it, and shoved his hands into the pockets of his jeans. That's when he remembered the crumpled paper and dug it out. ''Digger thought I was you as I was loading him into the pickup. He called me 'Del' and gave me this.'' He pressed what appeared to be a piece of paper bag flat on the waiting-room coffee table.

''More than likely he thought you were my grandfather, Del Henry.'' She stepped closer.

Cooper stared at the crude drawing on the paper bag, then up at Delaney. He let out a low whistle. ''Correct me if I'm wrong, but that looks like a space alien, complete with space ship.''

Delaney contemplated the drawing for a moment. ''I don't understand this.''

''Digger said he saw space aliens on the ranch. In the lake. There isn't a lake on the ranch, is there?''

She frowned. ''Not really. We call it Johnson Gulch Lake, but it's just a place where Johnson Gulch Creek pools in the rocks.''

''And it's near Digger's camp?''

''Just over the ridge. But he can't have seen…'' She waved her hand at the drawing.

''Extraterrestrials?'' Cooper asked, then shook his head. ''Who was this Gus he was talking about?''

''Gus Halbrook, I assume.''

''Oh, the old prospector who died in the cave-in.''

Delaney nodded. ''Obviously Gus hasn't come back from the dead, nor did Gus try to kill him. But do you think someone did attack him?''

Cooper avoided her gaze, but not quickly enough.

''You think it has something to do with my problems on the ranch?''

Cooper shrugged. ''It just crossed my mind that Digger might have seen something he wasn't supposed to.''

''Like what?'' she asked, her gaze drilling him.

He felt cornered. ''Space aliens. Or maybe someone in the process of causing one of the accidents at the ranch.''

Delaney put the sandwich down and rubbed her arms as if suddenly cold. ''I just assumed he'd taken a fall. But after everything that's been happening on the ranch—''

They both turned as the doctor came down the hall. Cooper folded the drawing and pushed it back into his pocket. ''You might want to keep this space-alien stuff just between the two of us,'' he whispered as the doctor approached.

She glanced at him indignantly. She seemed to have that

look down when it came to him. "How's Digger?" she asked the doctor.

"He's resting quietly," the doctor assured her.

Delaney pressed her fingers to her lips, tears brimming in her eyes. "He's going to be all right, isn't he?"

The doctor smiled as he laid a hand on Delaney's shoulder. "Digger O'Donnel is one tough old bird. I'd put *my* money on him. You can see him for a moment if you'd like."

She looked over at Cooper.

"I need to make a phone call anyway," he said, happy to finally get a chance to call his employers.

COOPER FOUND a phone booth at the end of the hall, closed the door and dialed the familiar number. Thom Jamison answered on the second ring.

"We've got trouble," Cooper said by way of introduction. "I got the wrong information on my ranch assignment. And that's just the beginning."

"Something's not right," Jamison said after hearing Cooper's story. "All of this should have come up in our preliminary report on the ranch. We couldn't have been that far off."

"I say we pull off this job now and that's what I intend to recommend to the agency." Cooper thought about Delaney and wondered what she would think when he didn't show up the next morning. He felt a twinge of guilt. And regret.

"Wait a minute, Coop. If someone screwed up at the agency, I want to find out before they can hide their mistake. Give me a couple of days before you pull off. I want to find the person responsible for this mess—the person who supplied me, and you, with the wrong information."

Cooper looked up to find Delaney coming down the hall toward him. Just the sight of her made his pulse quicken. He couldn't quite put his finger on what made her so desirable.

"Two days. Then I'm out of here." He hung up and opened the door.

"Where are you staying?" Delaney asked as they were leaving the hospital.

It seemed like days since he'd parked his pickup, camper and horse trailer in a wide spot off the county road and saddled up to do a little snooping around. "I'm camped on the west end of the ranch."

Delaney didn't appear surprised to hear he was camping out. In fact, he saw her shake her head and mutter "rodeo cowboys." She was probably comparing him with her father again. One of those damned rodeo cowboys, who'd rather have stars over his head than a roof. No ties. Nothing to hold him down. Always looking to see what was over the next rise.

She wasn't far from from the truth, he realized.

"I need to drop off the blood we took from the mares at the veterinarian's and then I'll take you home," Delaney said.

Home. He liked the image that came to mind when she said it. He told himself that when this job was over he'd finally have enough money to buy himself a real home. He could settle down. But as he looked up the night sky, he wondered if he ever would. Somewhere along the line he'd become hooked on the freedom. The adventure. Even the danger.

Stars brighter than any he thought he'd ever seen sparkled in the soft blue velvet. They drove toward the mountains, now etched deep purple against the sky. As they neared the campsite, the moon rimmed the Big Belt Mountains with its own kind of gold.

"What a night," Cooper said, looking over at Delaney. "But then, it's been quite a day." He couldn't help thinking about earlier in the canyon when he'd held her, when he'd almost kissed her. The sudden, overpowering desire he felt surprised him. What was it about this woman?

He smiled to himself as he realized it was more than physical attraction, more than plain-old lust. He liked her. Liked her spunk. Her determination. Her fire. She reminded him of some of the broncs he'd tried to ride.

He just hoped she was tough enough to protect herself from what was happening on her ranch. Someone was set on hurting her. Maybe Ty Drummond. But Cooper would put his money on Jared Kincaid. There was nothing about the man he liked, and he'd seen the way Kincaid looked at Delaney. Like a predator. And Cooper recognized predators; he'd been one long enough.

Delaney slowed for his campsite. "What in the world?" she cried, and hit the brakes.

Cooper swung his gaze to his camp, expecting for just an instant to see Martians waiting for him beside his weathered camper. Instead, munching grass next to the horse trailer, was Crazy Jack.

Cooper shrugged apologetically. "Crazy Jack's never been wild about being corraled for long."

Delaney laughed, shaking her head. "That's some horse you got there, McLeod. He's a lot like his owner, huh?"

Cooper smiled, opened the pickup door and stepped out. He hesitated in the darkness, thinking about the woman in the truck, wanting suddenly to warn her. But warn her about what? He didn't have the faintest idea who was behind her problems. All he knew for sure was that it wasn't him. Yet. He leaned back into the pickup.

She looked more beautiful than she had earlier that day when she'd interrupted his nap. There was a softness and a strength about her in the lights from the dash that tugged at him in a way no other woman had.

"About tomorrow—"

"We start work at five a.m. There're fences that need mending, hay to get in and those mares to get down out of the high country.'' She shifted the pickup into Reverse. ''Good night, McLeod.''

''Good night, Ms. Lawson.'' He closed the pickup door and stood in the middle of the road, watching the vehicle's taillights disappear over the next rise, until Crazy Jack gave him a good hard nudge.

''Don't say it,'' he told the horse. ''I'm not getting involved.''

Crazy Jack let out a snort and wandered off, probably in search of dinner. Cooper stood in the dark, telling himself Delaney's problems were none of his business. In a couple of days he'd be gone. And Delaney Lawson and the Rockin' L would be forgotten—just like other women he'd conned, other ranches he'd acquired.

Chapter Five

Delaney awoke with a start. She lay in bed, listening to the night sounds beyond her second-story window, listening for the one sound that had brought her abruptly from her sleep. The pines along the creek behind the house let out a sigh in the breeze. In the distance, a horse whinnied softly. No other sound disturbed the night. She closed her eyes. Instantly they flew open as she heard the familiar creak of the old barn door. She sat up, slipping out of bed to go to the window. What was someone doing in the barn this time of the night?

Through the glass, Delaney could see the old barn hunkered behind the house. The door stood open. She reached for her robe, but the soft chenille fabric fell from her fingers as the night outside the window exploded and the barn burst into flames. A dark figure hurried along the edge of the burning structure, disappearing into the darkness.

Without thinking, Delaney raced down the stairs and out into the ranch yard. The aged, dried wood of the barn blazed, hot and fiery. Flames licked up the sides. Smoke billowed up into the starlight. She stared in horror, stunned that someone had deliberately set her barn on fire. Anger made her want to chase after the shadowy figure, but common sense held her back. She didn't even have a weapon. Nor was she dressed, she realized, looking down at her nightgown and bare feet.

She grabbed the garden hose from the side of the house, knowing it would do little to save the barn but afraid the near flames would catch the side of the ranch house on fire. She turned the icy water on the log siding, praying it would do some good. Smoke and sparks showered the darkness.

Delaney wasn't sure if it was the cold spray from the hose or the memory of the figure sneaking into the night that gave her a sudden chill. With a start, she turned to find Cooper standing behind her.

"What are you doing here?" she demanded, startled to realize he'd sneaked up behind her without her hearing him. Like her, he was only half-dressed, his feet bare. Nearby, Crazy Jack stood without a saddle, his flanks sweaty as if he'd just been run hard.

"I SAW THE FIRE," Cooper said, taking the garden hose from her. "There's nothing else you can do," he said softly. The barn was now little more than a black skeleton. Flames ate up the last of the fuel, then began to die back as a portion of the barn collapsed in a pile of charred wood.

He watched her stare at the destruction, her arms at her sides. Her face was flushed from the heat. Her hair fell around her shoulders, free as the night breeze. She wore a flannel nightgown that hung to her ankles. Her muddy bare feet peeked out the bottom. All the fight seemed to have gone out of her. She looked small against the night, small and vulnerable.

He resisted the urge to take her into his arms and try to comfort her.

"I saw someone out here right after the barn went up in flames," she said quietly. "It's not going to stop, is it?"

Cooper watched the fire die away and darkness take back the night. Having orchestrated enough of these kinds of "series of accidents," he knew that once they started happening—

Slowly he dropped the hose and touched Delaney's arm. "I think you'd better call the sheriff."

Under normal circumstances, calling the sheriff would be the last thing he'd suggest. But nothing about this was normal, he realized. This job would have to be handled differently. He'd seen the suspicion in Delaney's eyes. He would have to be careful around her. Very careful.

Delaney looked over at him. Her gaze met his. He groaned softly, amazed how sexy she was even in all that flannel. "I'm not sure calling the sheriff will do any good, McLeod."

"Why is that?"

"Jared Kincaid is the county sheriff."

"WHAT TERRIBLE LUCK," Jared said as he entered the kitchen, the early-morning sun filling the room with warmth. Jared didn't appear much different from the way he had earlier. He still had that hungry look in his eye when his gaze fell on Delaney, and the sheriff's uniform, which did little to hide his growing gut, seemed only to increase his arrogance.

"Someone torched my barn, Jared," Delaney said wearily. She'd dressed in jeans, a western shirt and boots. Her fingers shook as she curled them around her coffee cup. "It had nothing to do with luck. I heard someone in the barn. When I looked out, the barn exploded. I saw a figure running away."

"Now, Del," Jared said as he reached out to pat her hand.

She moved her coffee cup, avoiding his touch. "Dammit, Jared, I don't need your sympathy," she said, her voice full of anger. "I need you to find out who's behind the vandalism on my ranch."

Jared pulled back his hand, rubbed his jaw and turned his gaze on Cooper, who stood against the wall trying to be as invisible as possible. "When did *you* get here?"

"Not until the barn was almost to the ground," Cooper said carefully. Any officer of the law made him nervous.

Jared Kincaid scared the hell out of him because Kincaid was too personally involved.

"Is that right? Can you prove it?"

"Jared! It wasn't Cooper I saw out there."

Jared lifted an eyebrow at her. "Then just who was it, Del?"

FEAR PRESSED against her heart as Delaney thought about the figure she'd seen sneaking along the side of the burning barn. She glanced toward the window. She couldn't be sure who she'd seen. So why had she defended McLeod so quickly? Because she didn't want it to be him, she told herself. "The person was smaller than Cooper and didn't move like him," she said with less conviction that she'd hoped for. Cooper moved like a big mountain cat, sure, swift and powerful. She thought of the person she'd seen from her bedroom window. If only she could be sure.

Jared must have heard the hesitation in her voice, seen the doubt in her eyes. A muscle in his jaw twitched.

"Smaller and didn't *move* like your ranch hand. That tells me a lot, Del. What I really want to know is who you think burned down your barn."

Anger bubbled up inside her as hot and fierce as any passion she'd ever felt. "Maybe the same person who's been causing all the accidents on the ranch, including setting off a rock slide yesterday afternoon that could have killed me."

Jared turned a shade of gray that didn't become him. "Why didn't you tell me about this, Del?" he demanded between gritted teeth. "I *am* the sheriff, you know."

Delaney brushed her hair back and looked toward the window again. *Then act like the sheriff,* she wanted to say. *Stop acting as if you want to own me.* "I don't have any proof, but I'm willing to wager Ty Drummond is behind it." Ty had something to gain by tormenting her. Cooper McLeod didn't, did he? she wondered, shooting him a quick glance.

"Your half brother?" Jared asked, surprised.

"Alleged half brother."

"Del, why would your brother want to burn down part of a ranch he's inherited?" Jared asked, even more incredulous.

How did Jared know about the will? Obviously Ty had been shooting his mouth off around town. Delaney started to argue that the will Ty said was from her father hadn't been proven authentic in a court of law, but decided to save her breath. "It was an old barn, Jared. We hardly used it for more than storage. Ty would know that as well as you or anyone else. And whoever is behind this seems intent on not costing the ranch too much money—just in driving me out, or possibly killing me. In my book, that makes Ty a suspect, because he's the only one who'd benefit from my death."

"Where's Buck?" Jared demanded, sounding more than a little testy. "What kind of ranch manager is he? Never around when you need him?"

She stared at Jared. Buck and Jared had always gotten along well. Where was all this animosity coming from? "Buck wouldn't have been here anyway." Jared knew her ranch manager lived in her father's old rodeo trailer down the road, several miles from the ranch. "He couldn't have even seen the fire from his place."

Jared glared at her, no longer sympathetic. "That doesn't really answer my question, Del. Where *is* Buck?"

"Surely you don't think Buck—"

He cut her off with an oath. "Tarnation, woman, *everyone* is a suspect." His gaze glanced over Cooper as if to make his point. Delaney realized Cooper was being awfully quiet, and she found that more than a little strange, since he usually couldn't seem to keep his two cents to himself around her. Nor did he seem nervous, which surprised her even more. If Jared considered her a suspect, she'd be as nervous as the devil in the company of angels.

"Buck had some personal business to attend to in Helena,"

she finally answered. Buck had been acting strange lately and she suspected he had a woman in Helena he was seeing.

"When's he supposed to be back?"

Jared was all business now and she realized she'd hurt his feelings as usual. Probably not a good idea, all things considered.

"Sometime tomorrow." Was it her imagination, or did Cooper finally seem a little worried?

"While you're looking for suspects, Jared, you might add the people who've been trying to buy my ranch," she said.

"What people?" he snapped.

Out of the corner of her eye, she thought she saw Cooper tense. "A man named Jamison, Thomas Jamison, from a company that calls itself Rattlesnake Range. They've made a couple of offers on the place."

"I didn't think your ranch was for sale," Jared said, appearing even more peeved than before. "I believe I've made you a couple of offers myself."

She glared at him. "It *isn't* for sale. That's the point."

With a curse, Jared pushed himself to his feet. "I'll get an arson expert out of Helena to come take a look at your barn. And I'll see if your brother has an alibi. I'll even run a check on this Rattlesnake Range. That's about all I can do, Del, other than come camp outside your house."

"That won't be necessary," Cooper said, making Del turn and stare at him in surprise. "If it's all right with Ms. Lawson, I'll be moving my rig out here."

She gaped at Cooper, amazed and at the same time almost relieved that the outspoken, too-bold cowboy she'd found sleeping on a rock had returned. While his pushiness had irritated her to no end, he made her even more nervous when he was silent.

"And you think that's going to make you feel safe?" Jared asked Delaney quietly as he reached for his western hat, which he'd hooked on the back of her chair. "Well, it's your life, Del. But you know what they say—crawl in a cave with a grizzly and you're liable to get eaten alive.'' He slammed the door on his way out.

She looked over again at the cowboy leaning against the wall. Jared was right. A grizzly might be far safer than getting too close to this man.

''You realize, McLeod, that was probably the worst thing you could have done,'' she said, shaking her head at him. ''He'll try to hang all this on you now for sure.''

Cooper shrugged. ''I'm not worried about me.'' He met her gaze.

She felt the shock, a surge of wild current that rushed through her veins. Something in his blue eyes pulled at her, tempting her with unspoken desires. She dragged her gaze away, fighting the sudden heat that fired her skin. ''And don't think that this show of chivalry is going to make any points with the boss.''

He laughed. ''Never crossed my mind. I just thought it would help me get to work on time.''

''Good thinking, McLeod, because we have a lot of work to do.''

COOPER CUSSED all the way back to his camping spot. Cussed Rattlesnake Range for going behind his back and making an offer. Several offers. This had never happened before, so why was it happening now?

But mostly he cussed himself for his impulsiveness. What had he been thinking, telling Delaney he'd camp next to the ranch house? Especially with Buck coming back tomorrow.

''You're acting like a damned fool,'' he told himself. Crazy Jack jerked the reins as if in agreement. ''Don't you start in on me, too,'' he told the horse.

Taking a deep breath, he looked across the Rockin' L and reminded himself how many times he'd done this sort of thing before, and successfully.

The whole idea was to get closer to Delaney, right? That's what he got paid to do. What better way than being camped right outside her door? Also, he could protect Delaney from Jared Kincaid. He didn't trust the man and wasn't convinced Kincaid wasn't behind her problems, sheriff or not. He assured himself keeping Kincaid away from Delaney had nothing to do with anything but business.

And by camping on the ranch, Cooper would have the pickup handy in case he had to make a run for it. By the time Buck got back, he'd be gone anyway. He hoped. He rubbed his thigh, figuring that the way things were going he was apt to get shot again before this was over. And once was enough.

By the time he got his rig loaded and Crazy Jack in the horse trailer, that little voice in his head that had saved his butt numerous times was telling him to hit the road and not look back. He almost had enough money to buy that little place he'd always talked about owning. Almost. All he needed was this last job.

He started the pickup and sat looking out at the valley—and the Rockin' L. He could call Delaney from town and tell her he'd quit. She couldn't expect a hand to stay at a ranch with the kind of problems she had. He'd cut his losses and walk away while he still could. He'd ask Rattlesnake Range for another assignment, one far away from here. Shifting the truck into gear, he headed for York.

At a phone outside the York Bar, he dialed the agency. York was nothing more than a spot in the road that had once been named New York, Montana, before the ''New'' was dropped sometime in the previous century. The only business in town was the York Bar, a quaint little place with log walls, a couple of pool tables, some poker and Keno machines and a few tables for eating the burgers the bar served. Houses dotted the narrow valley along Trout Creek from York seven miles up to where the road dead-ended.

Jamison answered on the second ring.

"You made two offers on the Rockin' L," Cooper said without preamble. "Behind my back."

Jamison was silent for a long moment. "It wasn't my doing, Coop. The agency wants that ranch."

Cooper's heart thundered in his ears. "What are you saying, Thom? That they're willing to do anything to get it?" It was a question he'd asked before, only back then he'd been running the scam. He'd been the one who'd decided just what it would take to acquire a ranch. Now he realized he was just one of the players on the wrong side of a deadly game. And he worried how he'd gotten there.

"The Rockin' L is just one of many acquisitions planned in the agency's overall—"

Cooper knew the agency's standard response by heart. "Don't give me that crap, Thom. What's going on? The company's sent in someone else to get this ranch?"

"There was a mix-up, Coop. You were supposed to acquire a cattle ranch in eastern Montana. Someone else was handling the Rockin' L."

"Someone from the agency?" Cooper demanded. Jamison hesitated a moment too long. "Don't tell me they hired someone local."

"The agency wants this ranch, Coop. And they plan to get it."

Cooper glanced over at a war monument someone had built across the blacktop road and noticed Ty Drummond's pickup, and wondered suddenly where the out-of-work rodeo cowboy got money to live on. "Why do they want the Rockin' L so badly that they'd hire an amateur?"

"You know the board doesn't release that kind of information."

Cooper swore. All he knew was that Jamison fronted for a group of men who made up "the agency." "I thought I could trust you."

"You can," Jamison said wearily. "I'd tell you if I knew.

It's all very hush-hush. I just do what I'm told. And I was told to tell you that since you're already there, they'd like you to stay on and keep me informed if there are any... problems.''

"Problems?" Cooper laughed. "He tried to kill her."

"What?" Jamison demanded in surprise.

"The guy the agency hired to get the ranch. He tried to kill Delaney Lawson in a rock slide yesterday."

"You know we specifically tell our people not to use excessive force—"

"Is attempted murder considered excessive force, Thom? Because that's where he's at. And he's going to take everyone down with him, including you. You're looking at prison, Thom. And you aren't going to like it—I can assure you of that."

"That's why I need you there, Coop."

He heard an urgency in Jamison's voice he'd never heard before.

"Listen, I don't know what's going on. I don't even know who they've hired. Whoever it is reports directly to the board. That's why I need you on the inside, reporting to me."

"You'll try to find out who they hired?" Cooper asked, wondering why he was doing this, knowing it was because Jamison had always been straight with him. Because if there was anyone at Rattlesnake Range he could trust, it was Jamison.

"I'll work on it from this end. You work on it from there. And Coop, I can pull a few strings and double your commission on this one."

Cooper laughed to himself. For a moment there he'd forgotten why he'd become involved with Rattlesnake Range to start with. For the money. And now Jamison was offering him a way out. After this job, he wouldn't have to work for Rattlesnake Range ever again if he didn't want to. And all he had to do was let Jamison know what was happening. Why did it feel too easy?

"Coop, I'm counting on you."

Jamison sounded scared. He should be.

"I'll phone when I've got something. If you need to talk to me before that, call me at the York Bar and leave a message." He read the number off the phone and hung up.

As he stepped away from the phone, he took a couple of deep breaths. Why did Rattlesnake Range want a relatively small horse ranch near Helena, Montana, bad enough that the agency would kill for it? It didn't make any sense. Unless a lot of money was involved. That ruled out raising Morgan horses. It had to be something else, but what? The missing mother lode?

Cooper didn't like anything about this, hadn't from the start. And now he felt double-crossed—no matter what Jamison had said about a mix-up. The agency had hired an amateur from outside, an amateur who'd almost killed Delaney—as well as Cooper himself—in a rock slide. The whole mess brought back his suspicions about Rattlesnake Range from his mishaps on his last job.

His instincts told him to get as far away as fast as he could. When this thing blew—

He got into his pickup. *It's not your problem, McLeod. You don't owe Jamison anything. Let him get himself out of this. You don't need this kind of trouble.*

Yet Cooper found himself headed for the Rockin' L, right into the heart of trouble. He told himself he couldn't leave until he found out what Rattlesnake Range wanted. And who they'd hired to do their dirty work. And of course there was the money. Going back had nothing to do with Delaney, he assured himself. Nothing to do with all that temptation in blue jeans or his fears for her life if Rattlesnake Range decided to make any more offers on her ranch. No, he was just going back to finish the job he'd started.

As he pulled his rig under some pines, not far from the house, he noticed a dark green pickup parked in front. Rockin' L Ranch, it read on the door. He got out and started toward the ranch house, then saw Delaney sitting on the porch with a man. Cooper swore under his breath as he realized who the man had to be.

"Speak of the devil," Delaney said. "Buck, you remember Cooper McLeod, that rodeo cowboy you hired?"

Chapter Six

Buck frowned and stumbled to his feet. "Rodeo cowboy?" he repeated, sounding more than a little surprised.

But he wasn't as surprised as Cooper was to see him back a day early. Buck stood a solid six feet of hard-boned cowpuncher. Cooper had seen his kind before. The kind who could pick up a half-grown calf and toss it in the air like a cowpie. And right now he looked big *and* mean.

As Cooper mounted the porch steps, his mind raced for a way out of this. He'd been so busy with all the other problems that came with this job, he hadn't really given much thought to how to handle the little problem of his hiring. Not that he usually planned things. He'd just always talked his way out of trouble. Until the last job, he reminded himself.

"I have to tell you the truth, Ms. Lawson," Cooper said before Buck could say anything more. "I wasn't entirely on the up-and-up with your ranch manager here." He shot Buck his best smile and held out his hand. "Buck, it's nice to see you again."

The cowboy hesitated, then with almost resignation took Cooper's hand in a killer grip. Cooper smiled in acknowledgment of the not-so subtle warning, withdrew his aching fingers and quickly turned his attention again to Delaney. He was about to tell her some cock-and-bull story, but didn't get the chance.

"Buck?" a honey-filled female voice called from inside the house. "Could you come in here a moment?"

"Sure," Buck said, still frowning at Cooper as he pushed back his chair, but a lot of meanness had left his features. "Del, if you'll excuse me?"

"Buck, you aren't getting off that easily," Delaney said.

"I'll be back and we'll get this straightened out," Buck said, giving Cooper the evil eye before hurrying into the house.

With relief, Cooper watched him go, then grinned over at Delaney. "Nice day, isn't it?"

"Save the charm, McLeod," she said, shaking her head. "Buck might have bought it, but I'm not."

The phone rang. She groaned. "Don't move," she ordered as she got up to go in to answer it.

Cooper let out a relieved sigh and glanced around the empty porch. Just what had Buck already told her? Did Buck's surprise indicate that he hadn't told her anything yet? Cooper sure wished he knew. Now more than ever he didn't want to get fired—let alone shot.

Voices from inside the house drifted on the afternoon breeze. Buck's. And the honey-sweet one. Cooper tiptoed over to the screen door and, standing in the shadows, peeked in. Buck and a young blond woman were standing by the couch. A bunch of photo albums were strewn across the cushions, where the woman had obviously been sitting just a few moments ago. Cooper could catch only a few words, but Buck sounded upset. Sneaking across the porch, Cooper planted himself next to the open window near the two.

"What are you saying?" the blonde asked.

She was young, only about half Buck's age, with wide green eyes and a button of a nose. Cute. But the oddest thing was that Cooper knew he'd seen her somewhere before. He just couldn't put his finger on where. He swore under his breath. This could be trouble if she remembered him from one of his other jobs.

Buck motioned for her to keep her voice down, as he looked over his shoulder. Delaney must have been in the office off the other end of the living room.

"She thinks I hired this cowboy."

"So tell her you didn't," the woman snapped.

"The point is, I was *supposed* to hire someone." He brushed his fingers down the tumbled length of her bottle-blond hair, coming to a halt just above her right breast. "I forgot because I was with you."

She giggled, wiggling a little under his touch, just enough to make Buck suck in his breath and pull back his fingers as if burned. She sobered. "You're not going to lose your job, are you? She won't give me that interview."

He looked pained. "Don't worry, I'll think of something."

"Can't you tell her you were helping me with my research?" she suggested.

"I don't think that would necessarily make her happy. I've missed a lot of work *helping* you with your...*research.*"

"Then come up with a better lie or something. Surely getting blamed for hiring a rodeo cowboy isn't as bad as forgetting to do your job."

"You don't understand—"

Delaney came out of the office and they both turned. Cooper made a quick trip down the porch to lean against the railing and pretend to study the horizon. A moment later, the screen door creaked open.

"Now, where were we?" Delaney asked.

The look she gave Cooper made it clear she remembered exactly where they were.

"Something about you not telling the truth, I believe?"

"Why, hello," said honey-sweet as she stepped through the open screen door past Buck to extend her hand to Cooper.

Cooper gazed into her baby dark greens, looking for any

sign of recognition. Zip. Either she didn't know him, didn't remember him or wasn't letting on. He took her outstretched hand. She wasn't as cute as he'd first thought. Or maybe his taste in women was changing.

"I'm Angel," she said, squeezing his hand.

"Of course you are," he answered, flashing her a grin. He knew her game. She was just hoping to save Buck. And Cooper didn't mind playing; he was just trying to save his own neck.

She giggled. "Angel Danvers. The writer."

"Cooper McLeod. The ranch hand."

Delaney let out a low oath. "Angel, if you could excuse us for a moment longer…"

Angel turned, fingers going to her painted lips. "Oh, I'm so sorry. Of course you have things you must talk to Buck about."

She shot Buck a heart-melting smile that had the desired effect. Cooper had never seen a man look more smitten.

"I'll just go back in and look at the photos until you're through."

"Yes, we need to clear up a couple of things," Delaney said.

"Then perhaps we can talk about that interview," Angel said. "It just won't be any kind of book without the history of *your* ranch in it."

"Ranch history?" Cooper asked, watching Angel's swing, trying to remember that old expression…if I had a swing like that… And at the same time, trying to place where he'd seen it—and her—before.

"Angel is a historian," Buck said with a note of pride. "She's doing a book on old ranches and I've been helping her do her…" His words died off as he realized Delaney was glaring at him. "Research."

"Okay, what's going on here?" Delaney demanded the

moment Angel was out of earshot. "And don't tell me 'nothing.'"

"Well, the truth is…" Cooper said. He looked at Buck meaningfully, hoping the old fool would go along with him. "I might have oversold myself just a little to Buck."

Delaney let out a knowing chuckle. "I can just imagine."

"And I might have told him I was damned good with horses, but I might have failed to mention I'd done a little rodeoing." He shrugged and glanced over at the ranch manager. "I needed the work."

Out of the corner of his eye, he watched Delaney. She studied him as though she'd be able to spot the truth if he so much as even moved a wrong muscle.

"And what do you have to say about all this, Buck?" she asked finally, shifting her gaze to him.

"Well, Del," Buck said, studying the dusty toes of his boots. "I know how you feel about rodeo cowboys, and under normal circumstances I wouldn't dream of hiring one—" He did a pretty good imitation of Cooper's shrug and gave Delaney a poor-ol'-boy look.

Cooper let out the breath he'd been holding. "Buck did me a favor, Ms. Lawson. And I owe him one."

Delaney searched their faces, her gaze shifting between them. "Is that right? Then why is it I'm having trouble believing either one of you?" She swore when neither responded.

"Buck, tell your…friend I'll consider that interview if it will get your mind back on your work. Have her stop by tonight," she said, heading for the barn. She waved off his gushing gratitude. "McLeod, get saddled up. We're going after those mares." She strode across the yard, stirring up dust in her wake. "And Buck, if you're of a mind to do a little work today, you could see if the haying is finished. We'll need to get that burned barn cleaned up as soon as the arson expert's done with his investigation."

"You bet, Del," Buck called after her.

The moment she disappeared into the new horse barn, he swung around to face Cooper, all that big and mean back.

"Just what is your story, cowboy?" he demanded. "You and I both know damned well I didn't hire you."

Cooper quickly told him how he'd ridden onto the ranch to look for a job but hadn't found anyone around and had been taking a nap up in the hills on the way back, when Delaney found him and mistakenly thought he was already employed.

"I meant it when I said I owed you," he assured Buck. "I really do need this job." Cooper didn't bother to point out that he had Buck over a barrel now. Cooper doubted Delaney would take kindly to the fact that her ranch manager had just lied about hiring him.

Buck made a good show of looking as if he was considering telling Delaney the truth, then nodded, clearly anxious to go tell Angel the news about the interview, as well as assure her that the new ranch hand was no longer a problem. "Well, you'd better be a damned good hand."

Cooper hustled off to saddle Crazy Jack, wondering what Angel saw in the well-preserved ranch manager. It wasn't Buck's good looks or his money, as far as Cooper could tell. And he wondered about her interest in the Rockin' L. He knew it would drive him crazy until he remembered where he'd seen her before.

DELANEY RODE with Cooper up into the high country, taking the long way around the rocky butte to avoid the narrow canyon and any more rock slides. She tried not to think about all the other recent calamities: her drugged mares, the fire, Buck's infatuation with that Angel creature, and Cooper McLeod. Especially not Cooper McLeod.

"Well, how about that," Cooper said as they topped the ridge line. Below them the horses milled in the tall grass—

an idyllic, tranquil setting so different from the one they'd witnessed the day before. ''Whatever they were drugged with seems to have worn off.''

''That call I got earlier was from the veterinarian.'' She looked over at him. His face was in shadow, but she could still see a hint of those blue eyes of his. ''You were right. The horses were drugged with locoweed. Lucky guess, huh.''

''Yeah.''

Was it her imagination, or did he avoid her gaze?

He hadn't said much on the ride. Which was just as well, as far as Delaney was concerned. She wasn't sure what had transpired between Buck and this cowboy, but none of it had rung true. She felt angry, and wasn't sure exactly why. It was probably that blamed charm of McLeod's. She'd seen the way he worked it on her. And Buck. And Angel. She grimaced, remembering how Angel and Cooper had hit it off. It was enough to make a grown woman sick.

''I've been meaning to ask you what other ranches you've worked on,'' she said now, more determined than ever to check up on her new ranch hand.

Cooper shoved back his hat. One eyebrow flicked up as he grinned at her. ''I kinda thought you might want a list, so I wrote them down for you.'' He handed her a piece of paper containing a half-dozen ranch names and phone numbers printed neatly.

''It's amazing the way you anticipate my every need,'' she said, studying him.

He grinned. ''Isn't it, though.''

She made a mental note to call a few of them and stuffed the list in her pocket. ''You don't stay in one place long, do you, McLeod?''

''Never found a reason to,'' he said, leaning on his saddle horn as he gave her a long, lazy look.

''Let's get these horses out of here,'' she said, spurring her mare and swearing under her breath. Why did she let him get to her?

"Whatever you say, boss."

But as she rode away she had to admit the man had a way with horses. And women, she thought.

After they got the mares back down into the valley, Delaney sent McLeod off to mend fence, having had more than enough of his charm for one day.

The sun was falling by the time she finished making calls to the ranches where McLeod had worked. Each gave her the same kind of response to her questions. Yes, he'd worked for them. No, they hadn't had any problems with him. They'd found him to be a good worker. Cheerful and cooperative. They'd wanted him to stay.

By the time she hung up from the last one, she wondered if maybe she'd misjudged McLeod.

Delaney showered and took the mail she'd dropped on the kitchen table the day before and a hot cup of coffee out to the porch. When she sat down in her rocker, she realized she'd also picked up the copies of the love letters Ty had left for her.

Slowly she put the mail down beside her chair and began to read the letters.

Neither the coffee nor the late-afternoon sun could chase away the hurt the letters left. Or the fear that settled itself around her heart.

The letters were damning evidence of her father's betrayal. They left little doubt Hank Lawson had had an affair with Ty's mother, Marguerite Drummond. The letters appeared to have been written in her father's scrawled handwriting and many of the phrases sounded just like him. What hurt her was the depth of emotion behind the words he'd written. He'd actually seemed to care for this woman. But who knows where Hank's charm ended and true feelings began? He'd certainly charmed Delaney's mother into an early grave. And,

Delaney thought bitterly, he'd done a pretty good job on her, as well.

Delaney reread the letters, feeling all the more betrayed by the man who'd had an affair at the same time he'd had a young wife and new baby girl at home. Why? It was something she would never be able to understand.

The letters made her wonder if Ty might be telling the truth. Not only could he be her brother, but he could be the legal heir to the ranch. Her father could have left him everything, just as Ty contended. Hank had never made a secret of his disappointment in not having a son. What would he have done if he'd discovered he had a son right before he'd died?

The love letters were all old, dating back to before Ty was born. There was no mention of Marguerite's pregnancy or Ty's birth, or any acknowledgment from Hank that he was about to become a father.

Ty hadn't known Hank was his father. Why had Marguerite waited so long to tell Ty? Had Hank known about his son? It didn't make any sense, unless of course she was lying about Ty's parentage in the hope that her son might be able to get her former lover's ranch. But if the will Ty had was legal, he wouldn't need to prove paternity. So why was he trying so hard, as McLeod had pointed out?

As unpleasant as the thought was, Delaney knew she had to meet her father's mistress and make her own appraisal of the situation. The Rockin' L was at stake and she had to have all the facts to fight Ty.

She folded the letters and put them in her jacket pocket as she spotted Jared Kincaid's pickup coming up the road. Now what? she wondered.

"'Afternoon, Del," Kincaid said as he got out of his truck.

Delaney groaned when she saw the wildflowers he clutched in his left hand. She couldn't believe the man's determination to get her ranch. And she wondered with a chill what lengths he would go to.

"Thought these might cheer you up," he said, handing her the bouquet.

"Thank you," she said, taking the flowers, "but the only thing that will cheer me up is information on who's behind my problems on the ranch."

He dragged a chair around so he could face her and sat down heavily as if she'd added several years to his age. She saw the disappointment in his expression. And the suppressed anger.

"I brought that, too, Del," he said.

She placed the flowers beside her chair, realizing she might have something to fear from Jared. In the past, she'd always figured she could handle him. But now she wasn't so sure. He seemed far more angry at what he saw as her rejections. Could McLeod be right? Could Jared be responsible for the accidents on her ranch?

"I called the state arson department," he said slowly, as if pained by this whole conversation. "They're sending a man out here this afternoon."

"And Ty Drummond?" she asked.

"He was at the York Bar until closing, then spent some time with one of the local gals before returning to his room down at Lakeside."

"Alone?" Delaney asked.

He shook his head. "The girl confirms his story."

"And gives him the perfect alibi. How handy."

Kincaid studied her, making her slightly uncomfortable. "I know you're determined he's behind this, but you have no proof. You bring me some hard evidence, Del. Otherwise I'm just wasting the taxpayers' money trying to run down your suspicions."

"I'll keep that in mind, Jared." She took a sip of her coffee. It had grown cold and bitter, but she drank it anyway,

Outlawed!

too stubborn to get more from the kitchen because she'd have to offer Jared a cup. "What about Rattlesnake Range?"

"That's the bad news, Del," Jared said. He leaned back in his chair with an I-told-you-so look that concerned her. What had he learned?

"Seems Rattlesnake Range is a company that buys up ranches. I did a little checking." He shook his head. "Buys 'em up at reduced rates after the ranches experience some 'bad luck.'"

She met his gaze. "You know this for certain?"

"If you mean, can I prove it?" He shook his head. "These guys are good. But the word is that if Rattlesnake Range wants your land, sell before someone gets hurt."

"That's ridiculous." She looked out across her land, anger and fear mixing in lethal proportions. "Why would they want my ranch? And even if they do, if Rattlesnake Range is behind my bad luck, they're wasting their time. I have no intention of selling."

Kincaid shook his head at her. "That was the attitude of some other ranchers, but they ended up selling for less than they were first offered. It seems Rattlesnake Range tries friendly persuasion first, but if that doesn't work, they're not above strong-arm tactics. At least that's what I hear."

She glared at him. "You're the sheriff and you can't do anything about this?"

He puffed up like a field mushroom that had gone sour in the sun. "Dammit, Del, these guys get away with it because they're good. They don't get caught. They don't leave evidence lying around. I'm trying to warn you for your own good. If Rattlesnake Range wants your property, then you'd better sell it to them."

"Why don't you try to find out who might be working for them, instead?" she demanded. "Or maybe I should call the county attorney in Helena?"

Jared stroked his jaw for a moment, eyes squinted in anger.

"I'm looking into Rattlesnake Range and who they might have sent to your ranch." He let out a long sigh. "What do you know about this new hand you hired, this McLeod character?"

Delaney had warned McLeod that the sheriff would try to pin this on him. "Forget it, Jared. I checked out McLeod myself."

"Then you won't mind if I do a little checking on my own," he said, pushing himself out of the chair.

"I'm sure you will anyway," she said as she followed Kincaid's gaze to a state truck coming up the ranch road.

Delaney hung around, watching the arson expert and Jared dig in what remained of her barn. It didn't take long before Jared came over to the edge of the porch with the news.

"Someone set the fire," he said. "Made a gasoline bomb out of a pop bottle. Looks like arson."

"I already knew that," she said. "The question is who?"

Jared shrugged. "Anyone can get a book at the library to learn how to make a gas bomb, for crying out loud." He stomped off in a huff.

Delaney waited until the dust died behind his pickup before she drove into town to visit Digger. She found him arguing with the doctor about when he could be released from the hospital.

"That's a nasty gash on your head, Digger," the doctor told him. "But if you're still feeling good by this time tomorrow, we'll talk about you leaving." The doctor stopped beside Delaney. "See me before you leave, all right?"

"Got to talk to you," Digger whispered the moment the doctor closed the door behind him.

For a moment, Del thought he knew who she was and might be able to tell her what had really happened to him up on the mountain.

"Gus tried to kill me again," Digger said in a conspiratorial whisper as he motioned her closer to the bed. "He blames me for the cave-in. He thinks Del Henry and I killed him.''

"Digger, Gus is dead," she said gently. "Remember?"

He nodded gravely. "I thought that, too, Winnie, but I seen him. No one has eyes like Gus. The damnedest color ever. I looked into those eyes, Winnie. Right before he tried to kill me."

Delaney took his weathered old hand in hers, sorry he was calling her by her grandmother's name again. It only made her doubt his story all the more. "How could that be, Digger?"

"I know it sounds crazy, but I think those space aliens have something to do with it. However Gus did it, he's come back from the grave." His rheumy old gaze met hers. "He was here last night, in this very room. Tried to smother me with my pillow."

Delaney blinked back the tears that rushed to her eyes. No wonder the doctor had said he needed to talk to her. Digger was much worse than she'd thought. "Are you sure it wasn't just a bad nightmare?"

Digger shook his head. "He would have killed me for sure if the nurse hadn't come in and scared him away."

"Where did he go?" Delaney asked, looking around the tiny room. There was only one way out other than the window—the door in.

"He went out the window," Digger said.

Delaney stared at the open second-story window. No screen. And the window was large enough. There was even a wide windowsill with flower boxes. She went to look out, gauging the distance between the flower boxes at the next window. She supposed someone could have escaped that way. Digger's story was feasible. It just wasn't credible. Was it?

"Did the nurse see…your attacker?" she asked, hoping for Digger's sake she had.

He shook his head. "She pushed open the door, but was talking to someone in the hall and didn't come in until Gus had gone out the window." Doubt clouded his eyes. "It was real, Winnie. The space aliens on the lake. Gus." He closed his eyes. "I know it was real. I need a little rest now."

She squeezed his hand, silently promising to call Jared and ask him to put a deputy outside Digger's room. Just in case. "I'm going to ride up to Johnson Gulch Lake and check it out, Digger." He opened his eyes in pleased surprise. She smiled at him. "I'll let you know what I find."

"Be careful, Delaney," he said quietly. "There's evil on the Rockin' L. A terrible, dark evil."

"Don't worry," she assured him, chilled by his use of her name. She agreed some terrible evil had come to the ranch. She just didn't believe it was space aliens. Or Gus Halbrook back from the grave. "I'll be careful. You be careful, too."

Chapter Seven

Cooper finished the last of the fence and went back to the ranch house to find no one around. He knocked several times before trying the front door. It opened, and he cussed Delaney for not locking her doors. Who knew what kind of scumbag would just walk in and take a look around?

He wasn't sure exactly what he was trying to find. Something that might give him a clue about who Rattlesnake Range had hired. And why. Starting upstairs, he made a quick search, keeping an eye out in case Delaney or Buck returned.

The ranch house was exactly like the plans and photographs he'd been given for the job. He found Delaney's bedroom and carefully opened the door. The room looked just the way he'd imagined it would: rich hardwoods from floors to furniture, soft cool-colored linens and drapes. The scent of her lingered on the air, making him ache in a way that confused him. With women, it had always been physical—*that* ache he understood; this was something entirely different, so different it was foreign to him.

He stepped in to examine a photograph on one wall. Delaney was about eight years old at the time of the photo. She stood beside her father and a Morgan colt. Cooper had to admit Hank Lawson was what most women would consider a very handsome man. Delaney had his good looks. And his smile. But what Hank lacked in character, Delaney seemed to have gotten in spades. Even back then she'd had that fierce independence and determination in her dark eyes. Almost defiance.

He smiled, realizing how much he liked that about her. Yet there was something else about Delaney that drew him to her. He wasn't even sure what it was, but it scared the hell out of him.

Downstairs, he made a cursory search, ending up in the office. It took only a few moments to find the letters from Rattlesnake Range. Standard offer proposals. Both signed by Thom Jamison. Both dated within the past three weeks. Nothing unusual about either.

At the sound of a pickup coming up the road, he hurried out the back door and circled around to the horse barn, where he'd left Crazy Jack eating oats.

"McLeod?" Delaney came through the barn door moments later.

He looked up to find her in the doorway. Something about the way she stood, her hands on her hips, her jean jacket open, her western hat tipped back slightly. He felt a pull toward her that was so strong it staggered him. It was followed quickly by another alien sensation: guilt.

"You're finished mending the fence?" She was surprised.

"Piece of cake," he said, trying to shake off the strange feelings.

"Then I guess you're through for the day," she said, leaning into a stall to check one of the new colts.

"Yeah, I guess so." He studied her, wondering what was up. He'd seen the list of ranches he'd given her beside the phone and figured she'd called. But he also knew the response she'd get from each. He didn't think that could be the problem. It had to be something else. "The barbed wire was deliberately cut, you know."

"I know." She looked around the barn as if making up her mind about something. Had Buck told her the truth? Not likely. Or maybe Angel had remembered him—and it *was* from some Rattlesnake Range operation.

"I thought I'd drive up to Johnson Gulch tomorrow and look around," she said after a moment.

He didn't say anything, relieved his fears weren't warranted. "I'm sure it's all just Digger's imagination but..." She looked up at Cooper. "He thinks someone tried to kill him last night in the hospital. Maybe there's something at the lake to—"

"Prove his story?" Cooper asked.

She smiled. "Yea, I don't want to believe Digger's as loco as everyone thinks."

"Yet you don't want to believe Digger's life is in danger either, huh," he said.

She nodded and smiled. "That's about it."

"Would you like me to come along just in case...you might need me?" He told himself he planned to go up there anyway to check it. Going with Delaney just made it easier. But that little voice of reason inside his head argued he was making a mistake. Because when he was around her, he tended to screw up and forget he was only her hired help. He tended to think about things that a ranch hand had no right even to think about with the boss. About kissing her. About holding her in his arms. About making love to her. *And it's going to get you shot again and this time you might not be so lucky.*

Delaney seemed to be having a battle of her own. She obviously didn't want to go alone, but she didn't seem so sure about Cooper going with her.

"I suppose it wouldn't hurt if you came along."

She didn't sound all that convinced, as if she had something to fear from him. Or as if she wasn't quite sure she trusted him. He smiled to himself; she was a very perceptive woman.

THE NEXT MORNING, Buck drove up in a cloud of dust. Delaney came out on the porch to see what was going on.

"Someone's cut a stretch of fence and a bunch of the two-year-olds are out on the country road," Buck said, his face flushed from anger.

She glanced over at Cooper's camp. He'd heard and was already saddling up Crazy Jack. "McLeod and I will round up the horses. You get the fence fixed, then ride the perimeter and see if there are any other problems."

"I just can't figure who'd do such a thing," Buck said, his face etched with worry.

"Yeah, me, neither," she said, staring at Cooper's broad back. She watched her new ranch hand for a moment, his movements sure and smooth, then she turned and headed for the barn.

THEY SPENT the morning and part of the afternoon rounding up the young Morgans and herding them to a large, fenced pasture nearer to the ranch house.

Cooper found himself studying his boss as she rode, surprised at her skills not only in riding and roping, but in doctoring the horses that had got caught up in the barbed wire. He'd known women ranchers before. But none as at home in the saddle as Delaney Lawson. She seemed as much a part of this land as the rocky buttes and the tall ponderosas. He was just as startled by her attachment to the land. It showed not only in the way she didn't overgraze her horses, but in the way she'd rein in just to look across it—the way a woman looked at the man she loved. Cooper wondered if Delaney would ever look at a man like that. He felt a twinge of remorse at the thought of her losing her ranch, but shook it off as they headed back to the house. Sentiment had no place in this business.

"I was thinking we should drive up to Johnson Gulch Lake," Delaney said, after making them both a late lunch.

"Whatever you say, boss," he answered distractedly.

"You all right?" she asked, intent on his face. "You've been awful quiet today."

He'd been quiet, thinking. A dangerous thing for a man like him to do, he realized. He grinned at her, wishing she weren't so beautiful, so intriguing. "Don't tell me you miss me minding your business?"

She laughed and shook her head. "Actually, you seem pretty capable of running your own life."

She smiled. "Why, McLeod, I do believe that was a compliment."

DELANEY NOTICED the temperature had dropped, making the warm summer evening near perfect. A slight breeze stirred the ponderosas. They shimmered, the color of green silk. She felt oddly at ease riding in the pickup with Cooper. The scent of pine and fresh water from Johnson Gulch Creek grew stronger as they drove, the windows down, a warm wind blowing in.

She reached over to turn up the country-and-western song on the radio. McLeod tapped his boot in time to the tune. She found herself drumming on the steering wheel and feeling a strange sort of contentment, which surprised her.

She took the same road they'd taken the night before to look for Digger. And Delaney noticed a change in Cooper the moment she pulled onto the Jeep trail.

"What's wrong?" she asked, suddenly worried he might know something she didn't and that was why he'd offered to come along.

He looked over at her and grinned sheepishly. "Claustrophobia. I can't stand being in tight places."

She laughed, relieved. "Then how can you sleep in that camper?"

"I don't." He met her gaze and held it for a moment. "I

sleep outside under the stars unless it's pouring rain or freezing cold.''

She raised an eyebrow. Under the stars. ''You never cease to amaze me, McLeod,'' she said as she pulled off into a clearing and drove up to the top of the ridge.

Below them Johnson Gulch Creek wound through a small, rocky canyon. The last of the sun rimmed the mountains and turned the horizon to liquid fire. The warmth filled the cab of the pickup.

''That's Johnson Gulch Lake,'' Delaney said, pointing across Cooper to a place in the creek where the water pooled among the boulders.

''And Digger's camp is on up the road not far, right?'' he asked.

She smiled to herself, remembering why she'd brought him along. True, she hadn't wanted to come alone, but she also trusted McLeod's instincts. He seemed to notice things other people didn't. She liked that about him. She told herself she didn't care that he was a drifter and would be gone before the first snowfall. Or that when she was with him sometimes she felt reckless, as if just being around him was dangerous.

''You saw Digger today?'' Cooper asked as they headed down a path between the rocks to the natural lake. ''Is he all right?''

''He's better physically.'' Delaney bit her lip, almost afraid to repeat Digger's story for fear the truth was even worse. ''His doctor's worried about him. Digger still thinks his old prospector friend Gus Halbrook tried to kill him and that the space aliens he saw in the lake somehow brought Gus back from the dead.'' She glanced over at Cooper, expecting him to laugh.

''What do you think?'' he asked as he walked down the shoreline to a pile of small rocks and sand and bent to inspect them.

What *did* she think? ''I want to believe that he fell down, hit his head and that in his confusion—'' Cooper turned and the afternoon light ricocheted off the water to catch his face in sunlight. He hadn't shaved for several days and she could see the blond stubble of his beard, rough as the land around them—and just as appealing.

''Come here,'' he said softly.

His words stirred something she'd buried long ago—desire. She walked toward him, her limbs weak, pulse fast and erratic. When was the last time she'd felt like this around a man? She laughed to herself as she realized the truth. There'd never been another man who tempted her the way Cooper did, who made her want to let go and forget all the reasons he was wrong for her.

She met his gaze. His eyes, as blue as the summer sky, filled her with sunshine, warming her in places no man had ever been able to touch.

He looked away first, breaking the spell. The breeze stirred the loose hair at her temples and cooled her skin. She brushed the hair back from her face, chastising herself. Feeling anything for this cowboy was foolish, and she wasn't a woman who could afford to be foolish. Especially now.

As she joined him at the edge of the lake, he pointed to a series of indentations in the sand.

She mocked her racing heart: *all he wanted was to show you some tracks in the sand, fool woman.* ''It almost looks like…giant ducks.''

Cooper laughed and pushed back his hat. The devil was back in all that blue just dancing up a storm as Cooper settled his gaze on her again.

''Or swim fins.''

''Fins?'' She did a couple of fast two-steps with the devil, then dragged her gaze away to stare at the tracks. ''Why would anyone swim here?'' The lake wasn't large or very deep; this was private property and so near the high mountains the water was ice-cold.

"You got me." He glanced over at her, a faint grin playing at his lips.

He knew his effect on women, she told herself. He knew exactly what he was doing to her and was enjoying her discomfort. She moved away from him, swearing to herself. At herself.

Cooper picked up a rock and chucked it out into the center of the pool. The waves circled, widening toward them. "Digger said he saw a spaceship floating on the surface, right?"

Delaney watched the ripples come closer. "What are you getting at, McLeod?"

"What if Digger is telling the truth? What if he saw something? Just not what he thought he saw. And it put his life in danger?"

She nodded, remembering that Cooper had suggested this same theory at the hospital. And that very night, someone had tried to kill Digger. Or at least, Digger thought someone had. "After what's been happening on the ranch, I'm not sure what to believe. But I can't take a chance with Digger's life. I asked Jared to put a deputy outside Digger's hospital room."

Delaney walked out on the rocks to the deeper water and scooped up a handful. It felt cold. She splashed a little on her face, chasing away all the crazy thoughts she'd had earlier about Cooper.

"But what could he have seen that would make someone want to kill him?" she asked. "There haven't been any accidents up here except Digger getting hurt."

"I don't know," Cooper said from the shore.

As she straightened, she spotted an object glistening in the lake a few yards out. "There's something in the water." She stepped closer, balancing on the bare boulders that trailed out into the water. A small piece of gray metal was wedged in the rocks. In the metal was a bright blue stone. She moved closer.

"Here, let me," Cooper said from the shore. She turned to find him pulling off his boots.

"I can get it," she said, stepping to another rock, this one just under the water. Her boot slipped as she leaned out. She tried to catch herself, but the rocks were slippery and she fell headlong into the pool. The icy water made her gasp with shock. She struggled to find her footing in the chest deep water.

"If you had just waited, I would have gotten it for you," Cooper said, standing over her, grinning. He'd rolled up his jeans, left his hat and boots on the beach and tiptoed out to balance barefoot on one of the larger rocks.

She glared up at him, shivering from the icy cold, feeling like a drowned rat, wanting to wipe that smug look off his face.

"Here, give me your hand," he said, shaking his head at her.

She handed him her hat, the felt wet and dripping. Pure stubbornness made her try to climb out over the slippery rocks by herself. After several futile attempts under his knowing grin, she gave up and reached for his hand.

In that instant, she met Cooper's gaze and glimpsed a wistfulness she recognized.

He pulled her up onto the rocks—and straight into his arms. She forgot about the cold water, forgot everything but his touch.

He groaned softly as he pulled her into him and kissed her.

She tried to resist at first, pushing against his hard chest with her palms. Then she lost herself completely in his lips, in the sweet gentleness of his kiss, in the heated hunger he tried so hard to contain. When he raised his lips from hers, she found herself trembling as she looked up into his eyes.

Then she felt something that made her heart pound even harder, that made her pulse thunder in her ears. A longing that she thought she recognized. For love. For the kind they wrote songs about. The kind she'd never let herself even dream existed.

Then Cooper seemed to back off as if he'd made a mistake. He grinned and the devil danced again in his gaze. And she wished she hadn't enjoyed kissing him, wished she'd never met him.

"Sorry, boss," he said with a shrug as he tried to move past her.

She didn't even resist the idea for a moment. Her palms were still pressed against his chest, where only moments earlier she had felt his heart beating beneath them. She took her hat with one hand and shoved him with the other. He teetered for a moment on the edge of the boulders, then toppled into the lake.

She heard him gasp as he hit the icy water, heard him swear, saw him come up dripping wet. "All you had to say is that you didn't like the kiss."

She stomped up the hill to the truck, pretending to look for something dry to put on, using the time to catch her breath, to get her balance again and run down that list of reasons she should keep her distance from Cooper McLeod. He knew damned well she liked his kiss!

It wasn't bad enough that the rodeo cowboy was her ranch hand and she his boss, but now he'd sparked something in her that she could feel starting a slow burn. Maybe Jared was right. She needed a man. But not this man, not this cowboy with the killer grin and enough charm to change the weather. Cooper McLeod was nothing but a drifter. She couldn't let herself forget that. She wasn't looking for a one-night stand.

A few moments later Cooper came up to the pickup, wringing wet, still dripping water. "Here, I guess this is what you saw in the water."

She turned to find him holding an old handmade spur. He appeared as wet and cold as she felt. She fought a smile. "It looks like an antique," she said, taking the spur from him.

The silver had darkened from age and probably years in the water. She rubbed the star sapphire embedded in the shank with her finger. "I've seen one like it somewhere," she said, gazing up at Cooper. "I wonder how long it's been in the water?"

"What is the stone?" Cooper asked.

"A sapphire. They mine them at the Eldorado Bar just down the road. You passed it on your way to the ranch."

He nodded distractedly, as if he'd lost interest in the stone. She saw him glance up the creek to where it ran down out of the mountains. She followed his gaze, wondering what he was thinking, that maybe the spur had washed down from the high country?

"We'd better get back," she said, still chastising herself for allowing the kiss. For not just allowing it. For wanting it. "About what happened down by the lake. It better not happen again. Do we understand each other?"

He looked up at her, innocence making his eyes a pale, pale blue in the dying light. "You mean the kiss or you pushing me into the water?"

She felt her breath catch in her throat as his gaze brushed her lips, sparking the memory of the kiss, of being in his arms, of feeling him pressed against her. He knew. He knew how badly she'd wanted him to kiss her. And he knew the effect he had on her!

"You know damned well what I mean," she said as she jerked open the pickup door.

"That's too bad," he said behind her.

She turned about to make a remark she'd have probably regretted, when suddenly the pickup side window next to her exploded. In the instant it took her to realize that the sound echoing through the canyon was a rifle shot, Cooper McLeod grabbed her and shoved her into the cab of the pickup.

"Stay here. Keep down," he barked. And he was gone.

Chapter Eight

Delaney lay on the seat, listening. A pine bough creaked in the evening breeze. Overhead, a hawk let out a cry. Silence. Delaney reached up and pulled her rifle down from the rack above her head. Holding it against her chest, she listened for footfalls on the dried ground outside the truck, knowing they could be Cooper's. Or the person who'd taken a shot at her. Slowly she slipped out of the pickup and crouched beside the truck.

The sun had disappeared, leaving the mountaintop cloaked in cool evening shade. Delaney looked up at the shattered window. From the angle the bullet had struck the glass, she assumed the shot had come from the other side of the creek.

But that didn't mean that whoever had fired it wasn't now headed this way. She glanced around, wondering where Cooper had gone. Darkness huddled under the pines. The trees swayed in the light breeze throwing shadows onto the forest floor.

"Damn you, McLeod, where are you?" she whispered.

Carefully she moved to a stand of pines beyond the pickup to get a better view of the creek and the opposite hillside. She knelt beneath the boughs, alert to any movement. The light had gone out of the day and the water. The lake pooled among the rocks, dark and foreboding. Delaney shivered. From her cold, wet clothing. From fear. She moved closer to

the base of the tree, hoping to make herself less of a target.
She couldn't believe someone was trying to kill her. It didn't
make any sense. Ty was the only one who would benefit from
her death. But that would also make him the number-one
suspect. Was he that foolish, or that desperate, he'd try to kill
her for the ranch?

Delaney glanced down at the ground by her feet. Her heart
thundered in her ears as she recognized the tracks. Boot and
mule prints. Digger and Tess had stood in this very spot overlooking the lake.

What had Digger seen? He'd said someone had tried to kill
him after he'd spotted space aliens in the lake. And she'd
come to investigate, only to have someone take a shot at her.
She stared at the lake, which was now bathed in twilight. It
looked no different than it ever had to her. No space ships.
No aliens. But was she seeing something she didn't realize
was important?

At the sound of a twig breaking behind her, Delaney spun
around, bringing the rifle with her, her finger sliding onto the
trigger with practiced speed. But instead of a dangerous killer,
she found McLeod in her sights.

"Whoa!" He held up both hands in surrender. An uneasiness flickered across his face as he realized just how close
he'd come to getting himself shot. "Take it easy. It's only
me."

Delaney tried to settle her heart down as she slipped her
finger from the trigger and fought to still her trembling limbs.
"Where have you been?"

"Chasing whoever shot at you," he said, sounding a little
indignant. "They're gone."

She stepped out of the shelter of the trees and cocked her
head at him as a thought struck her. "How do you know the
person was shooting at *me?*"

"What?"

He shoved back his hat to stare at her. Even in the dying light she could see the blue of his eyes.

"You were standing right next to me. Just as you were yesterday before the rock slide. Maybe it's not me they're after. Maybe it's *you*."

COOPER STARED at Delaney as her words sank in. Why hadn't he thought of that? No one had actually tried to kill her before he came to the ranch. All her trouble had been pretty much incidental and no one had been hurt. Then, within a couple of days, there had been two attempts on her life. Or had there?

He rubbed his thigh, remembering the searing pain of the bullet when it tore through his flesh after the last job had gone bad. He'd just assumed he'd been shot by an angry rancher. Now he wasn't so sure. The incident had never been investigated. Rattlesnake Range had seen to that, just as it had found a doctor who wouldn't report the gunshot wound.

He looked up at Delaney and didn't like what he recognized in her eyes. Suspicion. Fear. Two things he couldn't afford if he hoped to keep her confidence.

"Why would anyone want to kill *me?*" he asked. "I don't have anything. And I've always tried real hard not to make enemies." He gave her his best innocent look, but all the time his heart was pounding and his brain racing. Why *would* anyone want to kill him? And who? He figured it would only be someone from an old job. Or this job. Or…someone from Rattlesnake Range set on seeing he took early retirement. But why? "No one's burned *my* barn," he added.

"That could be because you don't have a barn, McLeod."

"Exactly."

Delaney shook her head at him. "But I'm sure there's a woman out there somewhere who'd like to have you in her sights right now."

He laughed softly. "I do my level best to leave women

happy." He gave her a shrug and a grin. "So far I haven't had any complaints."

Delaney swore under her breath and headed for the pickup, the rifle riding easily in the crook of her arm. "I don't know about you, McLeod. But you'd better be telling me the truth."

The truth? He didn't even know what that was anymore. But if she found out that he was in any way connected with Rattlesnake Range... And worse yet if she found out about the rest of his past.

"Stay there," she called over her shoulder. "I want to show you something."

She came back with a flashlight and shone the beam on the ground by the pines. "The tracks are fresh—in the past couple of days. And they have to be Digger's and Tess's."

Cooper leaned down and ran his fingers along the impressions in the dirt. "You're right," he said after a moment. "And look at these," he said, following the tracks away from the tree. I'd say Tess was balking. See how she dug in?"

"You mean as if she was scared?" She shook her head at him as he got to his feet. "McLeod, you amaze me," she said. "I can't help wondering *why* you're so perceptive. If I didn't know better I'd suspect you were either running *from* the law—or maybe were the law himself."

Cooper gave her a shrug. "I just notice things." He grinned. "Like your hair. It's the same color as obsidian in sunlight. And your eyes. They're like late-summer thunderstorms, dark, dangerous, mesmerizing."

She laughed and shook her head as she headed for the pickup. "I take it back. I'm more amazed that someone hasn't shot you."

He sighed, relieved to see that they were back on their usual footing. He'd deflected her curiosity about him. For the time being anyway.

Taking one final look at Johnson Gulch Lake, he went to join her in the cab of the pickup.

"So, this person you chased, I assume you didn't get close enough to see who it was?" she asked as she turned the pickup around and started back toward the ranch.

"No. But I can tell you this—he rode in by horseback this time."

She glanced over at him. "*This* time?"

"I found an old road on the other side of the creek that someone's been using."

She hit a bump, almost sending him flying through the windshield. "That old mining road? They couldn't have driven down that. It's been closed for years "

"Not anymore. Someone took a chain saw to the downed trees, widened it in a couple of places."

Delaney frowned. "Why would anyone go to so much trouble to open a road that doesn't go anywhere?"

He glanced over at her. "But it does go somewhere. Johnson Gulch Lake. In fact, *that* road runs right up to the lake."

"But why not use *this* road, the one we're on?" She narrowed her gaze at him. "Okay, let's hear it. I know you have a theory."

He picked up the spur from the seat between them. "Not far past the road I found tracks that led up the creek to an old abandoned mine. All I can figure is that someone was using the road to bring in equipment to work the mine."

She stared over at him. "I don't understand. The gold ran out years ago."

He shrugged. "Who has the mineral rights on the ranch?"

"I do." She stared at the road ahead. "Wait a minute. Didn't Digger say he saw lights near the lake?"

Cooper grinned. "I believe he said he saw lights *in* the lake."

"It could have been a reflection," Delaney said, sounding excited. "It makes sense. He *did* see something. Someone

working that old mine. And maybe he's right. Maybe someone did try to kill him to keep him quiet. And for the same
reason, tried to scare us away by taking that potshot at us."

Cooper had to agree. He just wasn't as convinced as she
was. "By the way, whoever took that shot was riding the
same horse as the guy who started the rock slide. The horse
with the barred shoe."

She drove the rest of the way back to the ranch in silence.
He figured she was scared. He damned sure was. He couldn't
throw off the notion that maybe she was right. Someone was
after him instead of her. But with Rattlesnake Range trying
to buy her ranch, Ty trying to inherit it and Jared trying to
marry it, Cooper still thought Delaney was more apt to be
the target. It just made sense for them *both* to be careful until
they could sort it out.

Delaney stopped the pickup beside his camp. "I'd like you
to ride fence tomorrow." She avoided his gaze. "Then I need
you to help bring in more of the two-year-olds. I'm going to
start working with them in the morning."

He nodded. Business as usual. Did she really think she
could just ignore what was happening on the ranch and it
would go away? "It isn't going to work."

"McLeod—"

"Your troubles aren't going to stop until you find out
who's behind them."

"How do you know that?" she asked, shifting her gaze to
his.

"I know."

She stared at him. He expected her to ask how he knew.
He debated telling her and decided it was too risky. If she
knew about him and Rattlesnake Range, she'd run him off
the ranch. And he wouldn't blame her. But he also couldn't
let her do that for reasons even he didn't understand anymore.
He just knew it didn't have anything to do with his job.

"The sheriff's looking into it and I'm sure—" She bit her lip. "You still think Jared's behind this, don't you?"

"I've seen men do foolish things for money." He looked into her eyes, feeling warmer even in his wet clothing. "And even more foolish things for a woman. Jared wants more than just your ranch, Ms. Lawson."

"Good night, McLeod," she said shifting into gear again and ending any more conversation on the subject.

He opened the door and got out. "'Night, boss."

She drove off a little too fast. He watched her park in front of the ranch house. Then he turned to find Crazy Jack dragging his oat bag around the yard beside the camper.

"Give me a minute to change clothes and I'll make us both dinner," he told the horse as he heard an engine and saw the lights of a vehicle coming up the road.

A pickup pulled up in front of the house. Buck and Angel got out. Cooper could hear Angel's laugh on the night breeze. It grated on him; he still hadn't been able to place her. Buck knocked at the front door and a moment later Delaney invited them inside.

DELANEY HESITATED in the kitchen doorway to watch Buck with Angel. He hovered over the woman, looking nervous. Now that Delaney thought about it, he'd been acting nervous for weeks. He jumped every time she said something to him; it was obvious that he didn't have his mind on his work.

The poor old fool was besotted with the woman. She felt sorry for him because he was just as obviously headed for heartbreak. Angel was much too young for him. Or maybe Buck was just too old for Angel. Delaney felt a pang of guilt as she realized she was hoping this thing with Angel wouldn't last much longer; she needed her ranch manager back.

She sighed as she carried the tray of coffee into the living room and placed it on the table in front of them. Angel had pulled a notebook out of her purse. She tapped a pen on her slim thigh as she looked around the room with appreciation, clearly anxious to get the interview over. Not as much as Delaney. It had been a long day and she couldn't quit thinking about what Cooper had said.

"This is quite the place you have here," Angel said. "You really lucked out, huh?"

"It's more hard work than luck," Buck said quickly. "Ms. Lawson saved this ranch after her father pretty near ran it into the ground."

Delaney smiled at him, knowing he was just coming to her defense and didn't realize he was telling something she would rather keep private. "I believe Angel wants to know the history of the ranch," she said tactfully. "What exactly is your book about?"

"Ranching in gold country," Angel said quickly. "Your grandfather was a gold miner, right?" she asked, flipping open her notebook.

"He was a horse breeder like his father," Delaney corrected. "My great-grandfather came west during the gold rush in 1865, hoping to make his fortune and start a horse ranch. But it was my grandfather, Del Henry, who started the Rockin' L after he met my grandmother, Winnie. It was in the early 1930s. Winnie was twenty-two. My grandfather was fifty-eight."

"Phew!" Angel said, shaking her head. "That's *old*."

Buck looked at the floor uncomfortably. Delaney knew he was fifty-two. Surely Angel realized that.

"So your grandfather's the one who struck it rich."

Delaney shook her head. "Rich? No, he quit mining when he met my grandmother. They bought this place with her dowry, built a house and started the horse ranch."

"But there were so many gold strikes back in the 1800s," Angel said. "In Helena, buildings were paid for with the gold found in just digging the foundation. Confederate Gulch and

Last Chance Gulch. Men got rich overnight. And they say the mother lode was never even found.''

Delaney laughed. ''My great-grandfather got enough gold together to start a small horse ranch in Helena, but he lost it in a poker game. My grandfather had a couple of younger friends who worked his mining claims when he got too old to work them himself. One of the prospectors still roams the ranch looking for that elusive mother lode.'' She thought of Digger with a note of sadness.

''It *does* exist?'' Angel asked in total innocence.

''With today's technology, a mining company would have found it if it did,'' Delaney said.

''But aren't there still small pockets of gold around that are worth something?''

Delaney thought about the old mining road someone had opened to one of her grandfather's mines. ''I suppose so. But with thousands of miners scouring this country for gold in the 1860s and again in the 1930s, any real gold is gone.''

Angel frowned down at her notes. When she looked up, Delaney realized the woman was disappointed.

''I'm sorry it isn't more…romantic,'' Delaney told her. ''The only thing we do here at the Rockin' L that might interest you is we raise Morgan horses the way my grandfather did. No fancy barns and stalls. We put them out to pasture. As a matter of fact, I'm going to be working with some two-year-olds tomorrow if you'd like to come out and watch.''

Angel closed her notebook and put her pen in her purse. ''I have research to do tomorrow.'' She looked up and seemed to remember her manners. ''But thanks anyway.''

AFTER COOPER FED Crazy Jack, he built a campfire and started dinner, his favorite, beans. He'd had a lot of time to think since Delaney had dropped him off. Two things kept coming back into his thoughts: their kiss—and Delaney.

The kiss had been stupid and impulsive. But as he watched the beans begin to bubble, he found himself grinning just thinking about it.

It had been one hell of a kiss. And not one that he'd soon forget. Nor would he forget her pushing him into the lake. The woman had spunk. More than was advisable in any woman.

He shook his head as he glanced up toward the ranch house. Lights spilled out onto the porch. He could hear faint music stealing out the windows. She'd turned on the music not long after Buck and Angel had left. He wondered if she was thinking about their kiss. And if she was, whether it just made her more angry with him.

The kiss had been the kind of thing he'd never done on a job before. Not that he hadn't kissed a lot of women as part of his job. But the women had come to him. They'd wanted him more than he'd wanted them. He considered it a bonus.

Delaney was different. He'd *wanted* to kiss her. He let out a laugh. No, it was much more than want. He *had* to kiss her. And he told himself at the time, it was worth it. But now he acknowledged that the kiss probably hadn't helped his standing as her ranch hand. Probably not at all, he thought, as he recalled how mad she'd been. The good news was that she hadn't fired him. Yet, he thought, as he saw her come out on the porch and look in his direction.

DELANEY STOOD on the porch, listening to the sounds of the night. She'd been antsy since they'd returned from Johnson Gulch Lake. And worried. The worry made the night feel cold. She hugged herself and looked out at the pines and Cooper's camp, remembering his kiss. She could see him silhouetted against his camp fire and felt a longing that made her ache. Who was this man who had the power to make her desire him even when she knew how wrong he was for her?

It struck her that he didn't act like anyone's ranch hand,

certainly not hers. He was much too cocky and sure of himself to have been anyone's hand for long. Maybe that's why he never stayed in one place. Or maybe he was running from something, hiding from something—here on her ranch. He'd convinced her that the rock slide and the rifle shot were more than likely meant for her. And yet, standing here now, she wondered. The feeling that Cooper McLeod wasn't who he seemed to be nagged at her.

So did the memory of Digger's and Tess's tracks beside the pines overlooking Johnson Gulch Lake. There could be something to Digger's story. Not that she believed Gus Halbrook had come back from the dead. But maybe there was an explanation for all of it. She just couldn't think of what it could be.

Nor could she explain what drew her to McLeod, she thought with a curse. It had been so long since she'd been interested in any man. Her preoccupation with McLeod had nothing to do with his good looks or that infuriating charm of his, she assured herself. It was something else, something she couldn't quite put her finger on.

In the distance, coyotes yelped. Overhead, the moon was a mere sliver among the stars. Millions of stars. She smiled as she remembered Cooper sleeping under the stars instead of in his camper. Claustrophobia. The man had an Achilles heel.

She glanced back at her house, surprised at how empty it felt tonight, and noticed that someone had put a horseshoe over her door. She smiled, shaking her head. Cooper. For good luck. The man never ceased to amaze her, she thought, as she looked out at his camp again. The tantalizing scent of his campfire beckoned her. She made a dozen excuses for what she was doing as she walked toward his fire. Only one of them was the truth: she didn't want to be alone tonight.

WHEN COOPER SAW Delaney headed in his direction, he shifted his gaze to the fire and realized he'd been so busy watching her surreptitiously, he hadn't noticed his beans were burning. He grabbed for the pot, burned his fingers, swore and dropped it. The beans started to spill out as the pot tipped toward the dirt. He hurriedly righted it with the toe of his boot.

"I hope that's not your dinner," Delaney said across the fire from him. She took a whiff and made a face.

He sucked one blistered finger as he looked up at her. Something was on her mind. He wondered what it was. He couldn't let her fire him. Not yet. "I *like* my beans a little charred."

"How about a lot burned?" she asked, raising an eyebrow at him.

He looked down at the beans, now blackened in the bottom of the pot. "I wasn't all that hungry anyhow," he said, pushing them out of the way with his boot. "I hope you weren't coming over for dinner."

She shook her head and looked around as if unsure why she'd come. "It's been a while since I've eaten over a camp fire." She smiled suddenly. He followed her gaze to where he'd laid out his bedroll near a pine and shrugged, a little embarrassed.

"Haven't you ever wanted a real roof over your head?" she asked as she picked up a stick and knelt to poke it into the coals.

"I have a roof," he said. "Clear blue by day. Black velvet by night."

She looked up. She had to admit it was one heck of a roof. "You know that's not what I mean. Haven't you ever wanted to settle down, stay in one place for a while?"

He thought of the ranch he talked about buying, wondering if it was no more than an excuse for continuing to work for Rattlesnake Range. "I'm afraid settling down has always come at a price I couldn't afford."

"You mean your freedom?"

He saw her jaw tighten. She tossed the stick into the fire and watched it burn. In the firelight, her hair was the color of a raven's wing, her eyes as dark as night.

"Freedom was the precious commodity my father revered above everything else—including his family and the ranch."

He could see angry tears in her eyes.

"At what price does *your* freedom come, McLeod?"

Cooper stepped around the fire to take her shoulders in his hands. "I can't change the way your father was," he said roughly. "And I'm not Hank Lawson. If you're thinking you might be able to break me like one of your horses, you'd best be sure you've got the right horse."

He let her go and started to turn, but she grabbed his arm. "Cooper." The sound of his name on her lips held both pleading and desire. She urged him closer. Her kiss was brazen. Fevered with abandon. Knowing what she was offering him gave him both pleasure and pain. Pleasure because he wanted her. Pain because he couldn't take her like this, knowing how he was deceiving her. It had never mattered before, with other women he'd known. But did now.

He pulled back, holding her at arm's length. "You don't know what kind of man I've been." He gently thumbed her cheek. "I've done things...."

"I don't care about the past," she whispered.

He smiled. "But I do. I can't do this, not now."

She pulled away from him; tears stung her eyes. "Damn you, McLeod." He watched her turn and walk away, realizing he'd lost a part of himself when he went to work for Rattlesnake Range—his integrity—and he wasn't sure he could get it back. Without it, he could never have the one thing he now so desperately wanted. Delaney.

Chapter Nine

Delaney was in the round corral working with one of the two-year-olds when Jared Kincaid drove up. She was still stinging from making a fool of herself with Cooper the night before. She couldn't believe she'd made a play for her ranch hand, which made his turning her down even worse. All day she'd been trying to see the humor in it. And couldn't. She'd invested more of her heart last night than she wanted to admit. She certainly wasn't in any mood to deal with the sheriff.

She finished, then cut the young Morgan out with the others.

"'Afternoon, Del," Jared said, tipping his hat. He'd taken a seat on the top rail of the fence. Now he jumped down to join her outside the corral.

"Jared."

"Del, we've got to talk about Digger. The doctor says he can leave the hospital soon and Digger is anxious as hell to get back to his camp."

She knew what was coming.

"I'm not going to be able to keep a deputy on him once he leaves the hospital. The only reason I have this long—" he looked up and met her gaze "—was as a personal favor to you."

"So you don't believe anyone's trying to kill him?" she asked, already knowing the answer.

He pulled off his Stetson and ran a hand through his graying hair. "Dammit, Del, how can I believe Martians dug up some dead prospector named Gus Halbrook and took him by spaceship to Johnson Gulch Lake?"

"Is that what Digger told you?" Maybe the sheriff was more responsible than she'd thought. At least he'd talked to Digger about it.

Jared shook his head. "My deputy told me all about it. I'm not sure what you're going to do with that crazy old man, Del, but it's just a matter of time before the county is going to catch him and put him in a home."

She gritted her teeth and fought back the series of oaths that came to her tongue. "He's not crazy, Jared. Just a little confused sometimes. It comes with age." She looked pointedly at the sheriff's graying head.

Jared stuffed his hat back on his head, covering his hair. "And we're all getting old, right, Del?"

She'd ruffled his feathers, as usual. "I just think there might be something to Digger's story." She told Jared about the tracks and Cooper's theory that Digger had seen something because of the balking mule prints on the mountainside above the lake.

"Digger and that damned stubborn mule have been all over that country. I can't see that some balking mule prints in the dirt near Johnson Gulch Lake prove anything." He held up his hand before she could protest. "And even if the craz— senile old coot had seen something, no one in this county would believe him. He thinks the mother lode is still out there and that he's going to find it. So why try to kill him? What would be the point?"

Delaney grudgingly had to admit Jared had something there. Digger was generally thought of as crazy and this latest episode certainly wasn't helping his credibility. "What if it was someone who didn't know Digger and considered him a threat? A stranger to these parts of the country?"

Jared laughed. "Like space aliens?" He turned to look back at her pickup, parked in front of the house. "Which reminds me. What happened to your side window?"

She followed his gaze to her truck. The window was a web of broken glass with a hole almost at dead center. "While I was up at Johnson Gulch Lake, looking into Digger's so-called hallucinations, someone took a potshot at me."

Jared swore, jerked his hat from his head and slammed it against his leg. "Dammit, Del, if someone's taking shots at you, don't you think you ought to at least let the sheriff know?" He wagged his head at her. "I'm worried about you. This can't go on." His gaze softened. "Have you ever thought about getting out of ranching? Maybe go to some island and sip fancy drinks in the shade beside the ocean?"

She laughed. "No, Jared, I never have."

"Maybe you should." His grave expression made her uncomfortable. He *was* serious.

"Are you warning me to sell before something worse happens?"

He chewed at his lip and squinted at the horizon for a moment. "There's only so much I can do to protect you, Del. I just don't want to see you get hurt. Or worse yet, killed."

"Jared, you almost sound like you know something I don't," she said, shaking from the worried look in his eyes.

"Dammit, Del, how do you expect me to take the news that now you've got someone shooting at you?"

"I expect you to investigate," she snapped. "Because I'm not selling, Jared. And I won't be run out. They'll have to kill me to get the ranch. And then as sheriff, you'll have to arrest them. You make this sound like it's my fault."

He stomped over to his pickup and came back with a note-book and pen. "Where did this shooting occur?"

She described it for him, stopping short of telling him about the barred-shoe tracks. If he investigated the incident, he'd find the tracks himself. And if Cooper was right and the horse belonged to Jared...

She watched the sheriff scribble down the information she gave him. He'd left little doubt in her mind that he knew a lot more than he was telling her. Her uneasiness about him jumped from misgivings to downright suspicion. Could Cooper be right about Jared?

When Jared finished, he stuffed the notebook into his pocket and shoved his hat back on his head. He seemed calmer than he had earlier, more in control again. But it was a cold kind of control that made her all the more concerned. "You know, Del, I was thinking that you and I should have dinner and talk about some things—" He stopped as Cooper came out of the barn.

The two men scowled at each other and she wondered how much of the conversation Cooper had overheard, or if it was just his general dislike for Jared coming out.

"'Afternoon, Sheriff," Cooper said. He turned to Delaney and tipped his hat. "Boss."

Just seeing him brought back the anger, embarrassment and hurt she'd been fighting all day. "Find any more fence down on your ride?" she asked. She'd just about convinced herself her behavior last night was nothing more than a moment of weakness. But as she met Cooper's gaze she knew that wasn't true. All those feelings she'd blamed last night on—everything from the scent of his campfire to the lonesome coyote's call—were just as strong in broad daylight. Damn this man for making her feel this way.

"Didn't find any problems," he said. "Any trouble here?"

Delaney knew he meant Jared, and she resented his protective tone. "No, Jared was just about to ask me out for dinner. And I was just about to accept." Cooper's shocked expression gave her some satisfaction. "How about tonight? Six sound all right to you?"

Jared broke into a smile. He was even more surprised than

Cooper, she thought. "Six sounds just fine with me, Del."
He gave Cooper a smug look, tipped his hat to Delaney and
headed for his pickup.

"I don't think that was a good idea," Cooper said as the
sheriff drove away.

"It's a good thing it's none of your business then, isn't
it?" Delaney didn't think it was a good idea, either. As a
matter of fact, it probably ranked as one of the stupidest
things she'd ever done. But she wasn't about to admit that to
Cooper. When she'd sent him out at daybreak to ride fence,
he'd acted as if nothing had happened the night before, which
was smart of him. She hoped he had the good sense not to
bring it up now.

"You're right, boss. It's none of my business."

She told herself that wasn't hurt she saw in his eyes, nor
was that guilt that pierced her heart with doubts. The man
had saved her life. And he seemed to be trying to help her.
But why? What did he want? It certainly wasn't her. He'd
made that clear last night. And yet her heart argued that she'd
witnessed her own desires reflected in his eyes. She'd felt it
in his kisses. He'd wanted her as badly as she wanted him.
So what had stopped him last night?

She cussed herself for making a date with Jared just to get
back at Cooper. But that wasn't the only reason she'd done
it, she assured herself. Jared had said they needed to talk.
Maybe he'd tell her what he knew, because nothing could
convince her that Jared Kincaid was telling her everything.
Men! Maybe he thought he was protecting her by not telling
her everything. Or, she realized with worry, maybe he was
behind her problems and only protecting himself.

Either way, she intended to find out tonight.

"Should I go help Buck with the rest of the haying?"
Cooper asked. "Or bring in some more of the two-year-
olds?"

He was all business now, generating coolness like a hint

of fall. She fought the urge to reach out to him, already missing the closeness they'd shared over the past few days. "Why don't you bring in the colts. Buck can finish the haying." He started to walk away. "McLeod." He turned, his gaze lifting to hers.

Her heartbeat did a little double time. She fought the urge to drown herself in the blue of his eyes. She dragged her gaze away, remembering what he'd said the night before. *"You don't know what kind of man I've been. I've done things...."* What kind of things? she wondered now. "Nothing. Just be careful."

He nodded. "You, too." He turned and walked away.

COOPER WAITED until Jared and Delaney had left on their date before he rode down into the ranch yard. He cussed, kicked and stomped around for a while, until he finally gave up and went down to the creek behind the house to try to drown his bad mood. The bath did little to soothe his frustration or his worry. He couldn't get his mind off Delaney. Why would she accept a date with Jared? Especially after the man had pretty much told her to sell out or else.

The mind of a woman! Cooper wasn't sure he'd *ever* understand this one. He figured she'd done it out of orneriness, something he was more than familiar with. But it had been a fool thing to do, considering who she was with tonight. He swore. Angry with himself, as well. He'd felt like a heel last night. He'd never before turned down a woman he'd wanted. And he'd regretted it all day. Now Delaney had gone and done something reckless. Jared Kincaid wasn't a man to mess with. If he was behind her bad luck—

Cooper had considered following them in his pickup, but tailing his boss and the county sheriff seemed downright foolish. And if Delaney got wind of it, she'd can his butt for sure. No, anything he did could only make things worse. Delaney had called this tune; now she was going to have to dance to the music. He just hoped the sheriff wasn't as deep in her troubles as Cooper suspected he was.

Cooper waded out of the creek, dried off and dressed in the pines that sheltered his bathing hole. He wasn't sure what he was going to do tonight, but he'd be damned if he was going to sit around the campfire, eating beans and being reminded of how foolish he'd been the previous night!

As he was saddling up Crazy Jack, Buck drove up. "She's not home," Cooper called as Buck started for the house.

"Where is she?" the ranch manager asked, disappointed he'd missed her. He walked over to Cooper, frowning.

"Out to dinner with Jared Kincaid," Cooper told him, trying hard not to sound angry. Or worried.

"Jared?" Buck raised an eyebrow. "Kinda late for a ride, isn't it?"

"Thought I'd go over to the York Bar for a beer. It's a lot shorter by horseback than pickup." It was just over the hill, a few minutes' ride. "Wanna come along?"

Buck shook his head. "I'm picking up Angel." He glanced toward the house again and Cooper had the distinct impression that Buck wanted to talk to Delaney about something important. "You think Delaney will be late?"

Cooper swore to himself. He certainly hoped not. "She didn't say. You know, I meant to ask the other night. Angel didn't mention where she was from."

"California originally," Buck said. "But she's been living in Great Falls. Why?"

Great Falls. The home of Rattlesnake Range. Cooper shrugged. "Nothing, just curious."

Buck gave him an I'm-not-sure-I-like-you look. Cooper didn't feel the least bit intimidated. In fact, he kind of wished Buck would throw the first punch. A knockdown, drag-out fight might make him feel a little better.

Buck must have recognized the challenge in Cooper's expression, because he turned and headed for his pickup. "Have a nice ride," he said, making sure it sounded just the opposite.

Cooper swung up into the saddle, disappointed. Tonight he thought he could whip Buck. He felt ornerier than hell. "Have a nice time with Angel," he called to Buck, trying to match Buck's insincerity.

The ranch manager peeled out in a cloud of dust. Cooper laughed as he rode off into the night.

DELANEY REALIZED her mistake immediately. Jared had insisted they drive into Helena for dinner instead of grabbing a burger at the York Bar. He'd complained until she changed out of Levi's and boots into a dress and pumps. Then he wanted to take her to some quiet, intimate little place in Last Chance Gulch. She couldn't stand the thought of a romantic dinner for two. She'd asked him to take her to her favorite Mexican restaurant, Rose's Cantina, saying she hadn't been there in years.

"Jared, I can't help thinking about what you said earlier," she began when they reached the restaurant. "I got the impression you know who might be behind the trouble at my ranch."

He shot her a look. "Del, I told you, I don't know."

She wasn't buying it and wondered why he wasn't being straight with her. "Jared, I'm at my wit's end," she said, trying a damsel-in-distress tack. "I need your help. As a friend. If you have any idea—"

"You're too trusting, Del," he said, shaking his head. "Things could be going on right under your nose. People you trust could be hurting you and you wouldn't even notice. You need a man around to look after you."

Oh, no, not this again. She took a breath. He was telling her something was going on, damn him. Something she was too trusting to see. "What *are* you saying?"

He smiled sadly. "That I wish you didn't have to be so

darned independent. That if you opened up to a man—'' He
looked at his menu with a heavy sigh. ''I'm starved. Let's
not talk sheriff business tonight, Del. This is the first time
we've gone out. Let's just enjoy it.''

Delaney figured she'd just have dinner and then call it an
early night. She didn't think things could get worse. She was
wrong.

''Delaney, you have the prettiest eyes I think I've ever
seen,'' Jared said after his second margarita. He pressed his
knee against hers under the table.

She moved her leg, bit her tongue, determined not to make
a scene in the restaurant. This had been really stupid. She'd
thought she might get some information out of Jared—

He leaned toward her. ''And your lips—''

''Excuse me, Jared, would you pass me the salsa?''

''DAMMIT, THOM.'' Cooper lowered his voice and turned to
look out of the ancient phone booth at the back of the York
Bar. The jukebox cranked out a twangy western tune and no
one in the place seemed interested in his conversation, but he
knew better than to take a chance. He spoke more softly into
the phone, more than a little worried and suspicious of Rattlesnake Range. ''You said you'd try to find out who the
agency had hired.''

''I have tried, Coop.'' Jamison let out a weary sigh. ''But
you know how the board operates. They don't tell me a
damned thing. It's supposed to be for my own protection.
And yours.''

And the board's protection, Cooper thought. ''Well, their
agent is taking potshots at her now.''

''I'm telling you, Coop, the board has assured me it's not
our agent on the Rockin' L job who's doing those things.
There has been no attempt on Delaney Lawson's life. None.''

''They're lying.'' Cooper pulled off his hat and ran a hand

through his hair in frustration. "How do you explain what's going on?"

"I can't. Unless someone else is involved. Someone other than Rattlesnake Range."

Ty, Cooper thought as he shoved his hat back. Or Jared. Or Buck. Or someone he didn't even know. Or— "Maybe they aren't after Delaney. Maybe it's me they want."

"What?"

Cooper laughed. "Surely you know working for the agency is a little risky."

"I'm aware of that." Jamison didn't sound happy about the fact. "There's a risk on both ends."

Cooper smiled to himself ruefully. He remembered the first time he'd met Thom. Cooper had been riding the rodeo circuit, at odds with his family and down on his luck, when Thom Jamison had come into his life with a proposition. All Cooper had had then were his saddle, his looks and the family charm. And he'd already been in trouble with the law. But Jamison had given him the job anyway. At the time, he thought Thom was doing him a favor. Now he realized his trouble with the law had been a glowing recommendation to Rattlesnake Range.

Becoming a con man for the agency had been relatively easy. He used that charm, his looks and a little friendly persuasion to talk people into selling. When necessary he was forced to use a different sort of persuasion, a little less legal one. But nothing serious or felonious. He'd convinced himself he was just making a living. If he didn't do it, someone else would. He hadn't asked any questions, hadn't wanted to know what happened to the ranches after he'd acquired them. Until recently. And he realized belatedly that the questions he'd been asking Thom weren't the kind Rattlesnake Range would appreciate.

"It could be someone from the agency who thinks it's time

for me to retire," Cooper said, testing the waters. "Permanently."

"You aren't serious?" Thom was shocked. "You make the board sound like underworld thugs. They're just businessmen. I can assure you when the day comes that you want to quit, you can."

"Oh, yeah? What if I quit right now? What would the board do?"

"Nothing." He didn't sound very convincing, Cooper thought. And he wondered if Thom Jamison was also having some second thoughts about his employers.

Cooper turned in the phone booth to look at the half-empty bar. *Tread softly,* he warned himself. *They might have already gotten to Thom. And if they think you're having second thoughts or bouts of conscience, who knows what they'll do.*

"Hell, Thom, what would I do if I quit? You know me. I'd be bored to death." It struck him that he knew an awful lot about the agency's methods and might make a pretty good witness in court. The businessmen at Rattlesnake Range had to know that. "I'm just a little paranoid. Everything about this job has gone sour."

"I can't blame you. It seems this one has a lot of complications."

Jamison sounded calm, convincing. Cooper wondered again if the agency had gotten to him. If that was true, then Cooper had already told Jamison too much.

"It's got to be someone who wants the Rockin' L other than the agency," Jamison continued.

He was so reasonable, so assured. Cooper almost felt himself being drawn back into the web. "I'm sure you're right," he said, relenting. "I'm just a little jumpy, that's all. Have you heard anything about what the agency wants with the ranch?"

"No, Coop. Nothing." The background silence changed just a little and Cooper realized Jamison had put his hand over the phone. "You know, Coop, maybe you should get out of there," Jamison said.

His voice was different and Cooper suspected one of the board members had joined Thom in his office. "Everything is under control now on that job."

Right.

"You wanted a vacation before this assignment. Why don't you take it now? We won't be needing your help there anymore."

Cooper smiled to himself. Was the board worried about him getting a conscience and maybe doing something like turning state's evidence? Or did they just want him out now that things were really going to get crazy? "Maybe you're right. A vacation sounds tempting."

"Good," Jamison said, clearly relieved. "Call me when you're ready to work again."

Count on it, Cooper thought. He knew it was just a matter of time before the board found out he hadn't left on vacation. He wondered what the agency would do, and decided he'd find out just what businessmen did in a case like that.

"I hope you get this one figured out, Thom."

"You know Rattlesnake Range. They always get what they want. And this job is near completion."

Really? Cooper hung up, shaking his head. Near completion. Did the board really believe that? Maybe they were banking on Ty Drummond. But even then, the ranch would be tied up for years in litigation, if Cooper knew Delaney. And he felt he'd come to know her pretty well. Maybe the person the agency hired was lying to them about more than just the alleged murder attempts. Maybe that person was telling Jamison he had Delaney ready to give up. Or— Or maybe Rattlesnake Range had something up its sleeve that Cooper didn't know about.

He sat back down at the bar. The jukebox was wringing out a sad country song. Cooper stared into his draft-beer mug.

What a mess, he thought. He was on the wrong job with the wrong information. He couldn't get Rattlesnake Range to back off and he wasn't any closer to finding out who was behind the attempted murders, his or Delaney's or maybe both. Now Jamison was trying to get him off the Rockin' L. And on top of that, there was Delaney. And the way he'd been feeling toward her.

He swore at the thought of her with Jared. He'd replayed last night over and over in his head, trying to get it to end differently. It always ended the same. He groaned.

"Let me guess," Ty Drummond said, joining him at the bar. "Working for my sister has put you in this mood, right? Let me buy you a drink."

Cooper watched Ty pull out a pocketful of twenties and toss one on the bar. He wondered again where the cowboy got his money.

"So, how *are* things going at the Rockin' L?" Ty asked, ordering them both an expensive import.

"All right," Cooper said, wondering what Ty wanted. Something, that was for sure. "How's life treating you?"

Ty swore. "But it'll be better when I get my inheritance." He took a sip of his beer. "It's just that I can't wait forever— you know what I mean?"

Cooper was afraid he did. He turned the import in his fingers, liking the feel of the sweat on the bottle, more interested in what Delaney was doing right now than her alleged brother's problems. "So you're planning to settle down and ranch, huh?" he asked, already knowing the answer.

Ty snorted. "I don't know anything about raising horses. And I sure as hell have no plans to raise cattle. I've done my share of cowpunching, thank you."

Cooper thought of Delaney and the ranch. Her love for the land and his captivation with her. A small fit of conscience, Jamison would have said. It will pass.

"You know the Rockin' L's been in Ms. Lawson's family

for years," Cooper said, not so sure the pang of conscience was going to pass. "But I guess you're part of that family now."

Ty made a rude noise. "They're not my family. I'm Hank's son by accident. Nothing more." He took a swallow of his beer. Bitterness distorted his features. "I would think Delaney would be sick of ranching and be looking for a way out."

Cooper wanted to laugh. Ty didn't have a clue. "I get the impression that ranch is her life."

"A substitute for a man, no doubt," Ty said with a curse.

Cooper didn't like the turn this conversation was taking. As much as the thought of punching Ty in the face appealed to him, Cooper was no longer in the mood for a fight. "What's a ranch like that worth, do you think?" he asked, hoping he could get some information out of Ty. If Ty got his hands on the ranch, he'd sell it in a heartbeat. But to Rattlesnake Range. Or someone else?

Ty smiled smugly in the mirror over the back of the bar but didn't say anything.

Cooper had wondered what was so special about the Rockin' L that Rattlesnake Range would hire someone outside the agency, something he knew was unheard of. But now another thought struck him. Maybe it wasn't the ranch that was special, but the person they'd hired. A person who was in a position to get them the ranch easier than an agent. Rattlesnake Range had to know about Ty and his claim that he was the beneficiary. Would the board hire him to get the ranch for them?

He looked over at Ty and wasn't so sure about his latest theory. He personally wouldn't hire Ty to feed his pigs, if he had pigs. It dawned on Cooper that even if Ty was dealing with Rattlesnake Range, Ty probably didn't know what the agency had planned for the ranch. But it was worth a shot.

"The Rockin' L isn't very big," Cooper said, almost

thinking out loud. "And it's not like it's in prime ranching country."

Ty played with his change on the bar. "Look, McLeod, my sister seems to like you. I was thinking—"

"Can't see that it would be very good for subdividing into lots, either," Cooper continued, ignoring Ty's attempt to change the subject. "It's too far from anything." What *did* Rattlesnake Range want with the Rockin' L? It didn't make any sense.

"Let's just say I'm going to do all right when the time comes." Ty finished off his beer. "The thing is, I thought maybe you could talk to her, tell her how stupid it would be to drag this thing out in court, tell her—"

"I'm just a hired hand," Cooper interrupted. "She wouldn't listen to any advice I had to offer. Believe me." He thought about the wisdom he'd given her on Jared. Look how she'd paid attention to that!

"Yeah, I guess you're right." Ty picked up his money, failing to leave a tip for the bartender, and stuffed it into his pocket.

"Maybe you're Hank's son," Cooper said, disliking Ty more than he originally thought he could. "But all you have to do is prove that the will you have is legit." Cooper smiled, unable to hide his satisfaction in needling the cocky fool. "But you're right. You probably won't see any money for years while the ranch is tied up in court."

Ty adjusted his hat in the mirror. "Mister, if I were you, I'd start looking for another job," he said, sliding off his barstool. "And soon. Because when that ranch is mine, you won't be needed there anymore."

As Ty left, he tipped his hat to a blond woman coming through the door. Angel Danvers. The writer. And her boyfriend, Buck Taylor. Cooper let out an oath as she made a beeline for the bar—and him.

Chapter Ten

In an angry silence Delaney knew was directed at her, Jared drove the pickup out of Helena. They left behind the houses and businesses that dotted the countryside from Helena to Hauser Lake, crossing the dam and turning onto Trout Creek Road. Tall ponderosas lined the narrow road, darker than the sky. Delaney could make out starlight above the trees and thought of Cooper. Was he lying under those same stars right now? He was probably thinking what a fool she'd been to go out with Jared. And he'd be right, she thought with annoyance. But it wasn't as if she hadn't known that from the beginning. She just hadn't expected things to go this badly.

"So, did you enjoy your dinner, Del?" Jared asked.

He sounded more than a little testy. Jared had become testy not far into the meal and hadn't improved by dessert.

"Why did you agree to have dinner with me anyway?" he demanded.

"So we could talk." Not that it had done any good. He hadn't told her anything she didn't already know.

"Talk?" he snapped. "But not about anything important."

She glanced at him, recognizing for the first time that being on the isolated road with Jared unnerved her. They hadn't seen a car for several miles now. She felt alone and a little frightened. And told herself she was just being silly. She was with the county sheriff, for cryin' out loud.

''I think what's happening on my ranch is important, Jared, but you refused to talk about *that*.''

The muscle in his jaw jumped. His hands tightened around the steering wheel in a death grip. ''Dammit, Del, you know what I wanted to talk about tonight. Us.''

Her fear level rose like a rocket. She and Jared had been over this before. He just didn't seem to want to accept it. ''Jared, you and I are neighbors. There's never been an us.''

He looked over at her, anger making his eyes dark beneath his Stetson. Suddenly he brought the pickup to a rattling stop in the middle of the road. The night seemed to close in instantly.

''Del, you know what I want.''

She stared at him, pretty sure she did, but equally sure he wasn't going to get it. ''Jared,'' she said cautiously, hoping the three margaritas he'd had would help loosen his tongue and not make him actually dangerous. ''You want my ranch.''

He looked surprised. ''No, all I've ever wanted was you.''

That surprised her. She'd just assumed that the attraction was her ranch because it ran adjacent to his. ''But I don't feel the same way and you know it.''

''Yeah. Well, that's a problem, isn't it?'' He turned off the engine.

''Jared, let's not do anything here you're going to regret,'' she said more reasonably than she felt. Normally Delaney felt she could take care of herself. But that was on her ranch, where she wore something more than a dress and a pair of pumps. And on the ranch she carried a rifle in her truck or in her scabbard. Right now she had nothing but a quarter in her shoe to call for a ride home, a trick her mother had taught her after meeting Hank Lawson.

Jared lunged for her. She elbowed him in the chest. That took the wind out of him long enough for her to jump from the pickup and slam the door in his face.

IT WAS PROVING to be quite the night at the York Bar, Cooper thought as Angel moseyed up beside him, fingered the neck of his beer bottle and whispered, "I've seen you somewhere before, haven't I?"

Cooper smiled sweetly, figuring she'd had too much to drink, and said, "I believe we met at the Rockin' L the other day, ma'am."

She laughed, filling the bar with a sound that did everything but shatter glass. "No, I've seen you somewhere before that. I never forget a face. Especially one like yours."

Cooper glanced over his shoulder to see Buck standing behind her, looking mean. "Can I buy the two of you a drink?" Cooper asked, sliding off the stool to put a little distance between Angel and him.

"No, thanks," Buck said with a snarl.

Angel bumped Cooper's beer as Buck tried to steer her away. It splashed on the bar. Buck and Angel both grabbed for the bottle, making Buck swear and Angel giggle as they finally saved it from tipping over.

"Come on, Angel, it's time to call it a night," Buck said firmly.

"Oh, Buck, you're such a party pooper," she whined.

To Cooper's relief, she went willingly enough. But at the door she stopped to call back to him.

"Don't worry, I'll remember. I always do."

That's what Cooper was afraid of.

STANDING IN THE middle of the road, a half-dozen yards in front of the pickup, Delaney felt like a scared teenager, not sure what to do next. Couldn't Jared see the foolhardiness of this? She heard his side of the pickup open. Surely the night air would bring him to his senses.

"Dammit, Del, get back here." He stood silhouetted against the lights of the truck. "This day's been coming for a long time."

Delaney pulled off her pumps, ready to run.

"Oh, come on, Del. I'm not going to hurt you."

He took a step toward her. She took two back, stepping on a sharp rock that she felt go right through her stocking.

"You going to walk all the way home?"

"If I have to," she said. "You're half-drunk, Jared. And you're acting like a damned fool."

"I'm not drunk, and fool or not, I'm in love with you, Del." He took a step closer. "I know what you need. I can make you happy, if you'd just give me a chance."

"Jared—"

"Let me finish!" he snapped. "Del, don't you see, this is an opportunity for us. We don't have to get up in the middle of the night and check calves or foals in thirty-below-zero weather. We can put all of this behind us."

"What are you talking about?" she asked, backing up.

"Leaving ranching altogether. I'm talking about selling and going away together. We'll be rich, Del. We can go anywhere we want."

Leaving ranching? Going away together? "How long have you been thinking about this, Jared?" she asked. Maybe Cooper was right. Jared was behind her problems, but not for the reason Cooper had thought. Jared didn't want her ranch; he wanted her to sell it and take off with him.

Jared shook his head. "What does it matter?" he asked belligerently. "You're not interested, right?"

She took two more steps back, hoping she could outrun him if it came to that. "And who are we going to sell our ranches to?"

He looked down at his boots. "What difference does it make?"

She had a feeling it made a big difference. He said they'd be rich. Neither of their ranches was worth *that* much. Was he just exaggerating?

"I'm sorry, Jared, but I'm not selling my ranch. Not to anyone."

"But what if you can't keep it, Del?" His voice had dropped dangerously low. He moved closer. She got ready to run. "What if you don't have a choice?"

The roar of an engine and a set of lights came up over the rise in the road. Jared swore and hurried back to move his pickup off to the side. The lights came around Jared's pickup at a snail's pace. Delaney moved to the center of the road to flag down the driver. Anyone was safer than riding with Jared Kincaid.

"Del?" Buck asked as he rolled down his window.

She got a whiff of Angel's perfume from the passenger side of the pickup. It hadn't been empty long, Delaney figured.

"Buck, boy is it good to see you. I sure could use a ride home."

He glanced back at Jared's pickup, now pulled over to the side of the road, engine running. "Jump in."

She started around the front of Buck's pickup, when Jared came roaring up beside her. As he rolled down his window, she saw that his face was an angry red, his eyes wild.

"Get in this truck right now, woman," he said through gritted teeth. "Don't you embarrass me in front of your ranch manager."

She felt her own anger simmering just below the surface. "Jared, I'm going to forget this night ever happened. But don't you ever make the mistake of trying something like this with me again."

He glared at her. "You're crossing the wrong man, Del. You could live to regret this."

She hoped it was just the booze talking, as she walked around to the passenger door of Buck's rig. She heard Jared gun his engine and roar off.

COOPER STILL HADN'T finished the beer Ty had bought him, when Jared walked into the York Bar. The couple of beers Cooper had had before to dampen his sorrows if not drown them had left him feeling even more out of sorts and a little woozy.

But when Jared slammed into the bar and ordered the bartender to pour him a Black Velvet ditch and make it a double, Cooper's mood improved considerably. Jared looked anything but happy. The date must not have gone well, Cooper thought with a grin.

"Let me buy you a drink," he said, moving down the bar with his now-warm beer to pull up a stool by the sheriff.

Jared glared at him, scooped up his ditch the instant the bartender, a guy named Dude, set it in front of him, and drained it. "Give me another one, but this time put some booze in it." Jared turned to face Cooper. "You got a problem, cowboy?"

Cooper shook his head and grinned. "Just wondering how your date went." He thought for a moment Jared was going to take a swing at him. The idea appealed to him, until he remembered Jared was the sheriff, which reminded Cooper how much he hated being behind bars.

"Better than yours," Jared said, looking around the now-empty bar.

Cooper laughed. "Yeah. You got me there. It's been pretty lonesome here."

Jared seemed to calm down by the second drink. He took a buck from the bar where the bartender had left his change and went over to the jukebox. He punched a couple of numbers, then came back and told Cooper to finish the selection off. Cooper didn't have any real interest in listening to music, let alone picking songs, but he did it because he got the idea Jared was trying to be nice to him. And that made him *real* suspicious.

He punched "Pretty Woman" and "Your Cheating Heart," then joined Jared back at the bar.

"Delaney tells me you're not a bad hand," Jared said after a moment.

Cooper doubted Delaney had told him that. Or that the two had talked about him at all.

"I could use a decent hand. And I pay more than Del."

Jared was offering him a job? Cooper wanted to laugh in the man's face. "I'm flattered, but I kind of like working for Ms. Lawson."

That didn't seem to please the sheriff. "Well, you won't be there long."

Funny, that's the same thing Ty had said. "How's that?" Cooper asked.

Jared took a long sip of his drink. "I mean I figure a man like you will be moving on pretty soon. I would imagine you'd be missing the rodeo. Am I right?"

"You sure got me pegged." He could feel Jared studying him in the mirror above the bar.

"So, were you any good?" Jared asked.

Cooper tried not to be insulted. "Good enough not to starve."

Jared chuckled and finished his drink. Cooper pushed some money across the bar and motioned for Dude to freshen the sheriff's drink. Cooper caught a look of something stronger than dislike that passed between the bartender and Jared.

"You know, I've got a horse that no one can ride," Jared said to Cooper after a moment. "He's called Hell's Fire. The meanest bronc I've ever seen. I bet even you couldn't ride him."

"How much would you bet?" Cooper asked, taking the bait.

Jared smiled. "You've probably heard about the little rodeo I put on each year at my place. It's Saturday. I'd make a substantial wager personally, if you were interested. Then there is always the prize money.''

"Let me think about.'' Cooper excused himself to take a trip to the men's room. He didn't doubt for a moment that Hell's Fire was a mean horse or that Jared was hoping he'd get himself killed riding it. But the idea of going to Jared's ranch for the rodeo appealed to him. He told himself it was just because it would give him a chance to look for the barred-shoe horse. He'd had a strong feeling for some time that he was going to find the horse on the Kincaid ranch. He assured himself riding Hell's Fire had nothing to do with the thrill of rodeoing or personal pride, although he had to admit he'd love to ride the bronc to show Jared.

On the way back to the bar, Cooper realized he hadn't eaten since breakfast. That probably explained why he felt a little light-headed. He took a sip of his imported beer, which was now more than a little warm and flat, and told Jared he'd see him Saturday at the rodeo.

The sheriff seemed too pleased, Cooper thought as he went out to find Crazy Jack waiting for him in a grassy spot by the parking lot. He let out a piercing whistle and the horse came running over to him, almost knocking him down.

"Let's go home, boy," he told Crazy Jack as he mounted the animal and headed for the ranch. Home? When had he started thinking of the Rockin' L as home? He shook his head at just the thought of Delaney and her determination to hang on to the ranch. She was going to get herself killed over nothing more than a piece of land and a few horses. It wasn't worth it. Didn't she realize that?

Chapter Eleven

"Buck?" Delaney looked over at him as he drove toward the ranch. He seemed more distracted than ever tonight, almost agitated. From the strong scent of perfume inside the cab of the truck, Delaney knew whom he'd been with and had a pretty good idea what he'd been up to.

He pulled himself out of his thoughts with a jerk. "Sorry, what?"

"Are you all right?" she asked, worried that after an amorous evening, Angel had decided to break it off.

"Just thinkin'." Buck darted a look at her. "I stopped by your place earlier."

"Something you wanted to talk about?"

He ran his hand over the top of the steering wheel. He couldn't seem to hold still. "You know I was married once."

She'd heard the scuttlebutt about his fateful marriage. Buck had married a Helena woman when Delaney was in junior high school, and after about six months, she'd taken off to become a showgirl in Vegas.

"It didn't work out," he said. "She didn't like living way out of town on a ranch. Wanted to live in a city and wear fancy clothes and go out a lot."

Just like Angel, Delaney thought. "Well, some women need that, Buck."

"I suppose." He glanced over at her. "But you don't seem to. Don't you ever wish you lived in town?"

She laughed. "No, Buck. Nor do I want to go live on an island." He frowned at her in puzzlement. "Jared offered to take me to an island."

"Seems your date didn't work out so well," Buck said.

Buck, the king of understatement. "You could say that." She looked over at him. "What makes you think it was a *date?*"

"That's what McLeod said when I stopped by the ranch."

McLeod. She should have known. And to make matters worse, he'd been right about Jared being dangerous. Delaney just hadn't realized how much until tonight. Not that she planned to admit that to Cooper.

"I've been doing some thinking," Buck said.

She studied him out of the corner of her eye. They'd never been what she'd call friends. While almost a permanent fixture on the ranch, he was a lot older and tended to keep to himself. A loner, her grandfather would have called him.

"You thinking about getting married again, Buck?" she asked, hoping he wouldn't feel she was prying. Also hoping he'd say no.

He looked surprised, then sheepish. "It crosses a man's mind sometimes, you know? It's not like I'm getting any younger."

"But this woman you're thinking about wouldn't want to live on a ranch, right?"

He eyed her as if she had ESP.

"Buck, I have to assume it's Angel."

He laughed nervously as he turned off onto her ranch road. "I'm not even sure she'd have me, mind you, and I'd have to do a powerful lot of changing to make her happy."

Delaney started to argue that if you loved someone, you didn't require them to change for you, but she realized if she were to fall for a rodeo cowboy like Cooper—not that something like that would ever happen—she would want him to quit rodeoing. "You thinking about moving into town?"

He swallowed. "That and getting a better job that pays more." He realized what he'd said. His eyes widened. "No offense."

"None taken. Buck, you've got to do what's right for you. If it's moving into town and getting a different kind of job, then I wish you the best of luck. I'd miss you and you'd be damned hard to replace, but I wouldn't stand in your way if it's what you wanted."

He felt relieved. And a little guilty. "Thank you, Del," he said, avoiding her gaze.

And she realized he'd been doing that a lot lately. Angel certainly had put this man into a tailspin.

As Buck pulled into the ranch yard, Delaney automatically looked over at Cooper's camp. No campfire lit the night. No light at all except the stars overhead. Nor did she see Crazy Jack around anywhere.

"I wonder where Cooper is?" she asked, thinking out loud.

"Angel and I saw him at the York Bar," Buck told her.

She tried not to show her disappointment as she climbed out. "Thanks for the ride."

"Are you going to be all right here by yourself?" Buck asked.

"Of course," she said with a laugh. "I've lived here for years alone." But no one has been taking potshots at her back then, she reminded herself. "I'll be fine," she assured Buck and herself.

He bade her good-night and drove away.

Delaney walked up the steps, her pumps making a completely foreign sound on the steps. She hugged herself, feeling a little cool although the night was warm. It struck her that Buck was right. She didn't feel safe here anymore. It didn't help that Cooper was gone.

Well, you'd best get used to it, because it's only a matter of time before he takes off for good, she told herself as she locked the front door.

Going through the house she turned the lights on and off as she went, feeling like a scared kid. But she had to admit, her encounter with Jared had spooked her a little. Everything else that had happened had spooked her a lot.

And what Jared had said about her selling out before she got herself killed left little doubt in her mind that whoever was after her ranch meant business. Someone out there was determined to get the Rockin' L. Someone, it seemed, who would even kill her for it.

Delaney shook her head, fighting back tears. It was becoming harder and harder not to give in to the fear.

Cooper was right. She had to do something. She was tired of feeling helpless, of waiting for the next rock slide or rifle shot. She couldn't wait for the next time the brakes went out in one of her trucks. And that meant starting with Rattlesnake Range.

She flipped on the lights in her office and dug through the papers until she found the offers Thomas Jamison had made on their behalf. She scribbled a note to herself to call the attorney probating her father's estate and ask him to check on Rattlesnake Range for her, and felt a little better. It was time she found out what was going on.

As she turned out the office lights, she decided she'd drive over to Butte and talk to Marguerite Drummond the next day. She needed to know everything she could about Ty. His mother seemed like a good place to start.

Heading up the stairs, Delaney felt her bit of confidence disappear. She'd never been afraid in this house, but she was tonight. She wished Cooper were at his camp sleeping under the stars. Maybe she *should* have had Buck stay on the couch. With some nut case out there—

A loud thump outside stopped Delaney in midmotion. She

clutched the stair railing and tried to hear over the pounding of her heart. Just the wind. Except there was no wind tonight. Maybe it was some small critter.

She heard the noise again. Louder this time. Someone was on the porch! And it wasn't a small critter! At least she'd been smart enough to lock the front door. Not that whoever it was couldn't come through a window if determined enough. Hurriedly she reached over and hit the light switch, plunging the house into darkness.

For what seemed an eternity, she stood paralyzed on the stairs, listening. There was the sound again! Whoever it was was moving around the house, possibly looking in the windows!

Shaking, Delaney moved cautiously back down the stairs and edged along the wall to the gun cabinet. The door creaked as she reached in. She felt around until she found her father's old revolver, which she kept for chasing off coyotes.

Feeling her way to the front of the house, she crept up to the edge of the window casing and peeked out. The ranch yard lay in a warm bath of yellow from the yard light. She stared out, straining to see into the edge of darkness that circled the ranch. Nothing moved in the quiet summer night.

She inched her way to a window at the side of the house and peered out, telling herself the sounds had just been her imagination. Right.

Suddenly a face appeared in the glass. Huge. Ugly. Horrible. Delaney let out a scream and fell back into an end table. The large western lamp toppled with a thud, along with Delaney. She lay on the floor, her heart hammering to get out of her chest. Gulping down a breath, she braced herself and looked toward the window. The face was gone. But not the memory of those eyes looking in at her. Crazy Jack's wild eyes.

"Damn that horse," she cried, stumbling to her feet. "I'm

going to shoot him *and* Cooper.'' It did little to still her anger at that stupid horse for scaring her half to death.

She slammed out the front door, ready to give Cooper and his horse a piece of her mind. ''McLeod!'' He didn't answer. She looked toward his camp and saw nothing but darkness. ''Damn your hide, McLeod!'' She started toward his camper but stopped, suddenly feeling vulnerable in the middle of the yard. Alone. She'd left the revolver on the living room floor where she'd dropped it. Behind her she heard the shuffled steps of the horse. He'd picked up his oat bag, which he'd been dragging around. She smiled at the horse, her pulse slowing. What a horse! As unique as his owner.

''Come on, I'll get you some oats,'' she said, motioning toward McLeod's rig.

Crazy Jack trotted toward the camper and truck. Delaney followed, wondering where Cooper was. Surely the horse hadn't come home without Cooper. A sliver of worry worked its way under her skin. With all the accidents that had been happening on the ranch, what if Cooper— She hurried toward his camp.

COOPER AWOKE WITH A start to find Crazy Jack leaning over him in the dark, whinnying softly. He pushed aside the horse's muzzle and reached for the .45 he kept tucked under his pillow. Sitting up in the sleeping bag he'd rolled out near a large old pine, he brought the pistol up with him at the sound of footfalls approaching his camp. He could see boots coming around the end of the camper. Shaking off the last of his deep sleep, he tightened his grip on the pistol, ready for whatever trouble might be coming.

The figure stepped into view. At first he didn't recognize her. Then he saw her dark silhouette against the yard light leaking around the camper. He quickly slipped the pistol back under his pillow, but not before she'd seen it.

''Do you always sleep armed?'' Delaney asked.

Her tone was cautious, suspicious, worried, almost angry. Things he didn't want her to be.

He laughed softly, grinning up at her, turning up the charm the same way he turned up the lantern near his sleeping bag. "Like Jared Kincaid said, you never know when some sidewinder will wander into your camp."

She smiled at that, but her body was still rigid, her attitude tense. He studied her face in the lantern light. She wasn't so sure he wasn't a snake who'd wandered into her camp.

He leaned back, trying to put her at ease. "Jared Kincaid seems to have staked a claim on you," he said, surprised he'd said it, since he hadn't meant to. But he was curious what role the rancher played in Delaney Lawson's life. He assured himself he only wanted to know because of business. He had to know everything about Delaney to get his job done here. "Kincaid seems a little old for you."

She laughed. "Don't beat around the bush, McLeod. Why don't you just come out and ask me if Jared and I ever were an item?"

"Were you?" he asked, surprised how much he wanted the answer to be no.

"It's none of your business," she said, shaking her head at him. "Do you always butt into other people's lives this way, or is it just my life you find so fascinating?"

"I believe you're the one who walked into *my* bedroom," he remarked as he sat up, shoving the bedroll down around his waist. Delaney quickly averted her gaze from his naked upper torso and glanced around the camp as if she wasn't sure what to look at. It was the first time he'd seen her uncomfortable, and he smiled, realizing he liked the hint of vulnerability he'd glimpsed.

"I wouldn't have come over here if your damned horse hadn't scared ten years off my life," she said angrily, turning on her heels and stomping toward the ranch house. "Why don't you feed the poor old nag?"

Crazy Jack let out a whinny. "She didn't mean it," Cooper said to the horse loud enough for Delaney to hear. "I think she really likes you."

Delaney let loose an oath right before she slammed the front door of the ranch house.

Cooper leaned back, smiling up at the stars overhead. He was enjoying this job. Then his smile faded. He might be enjoying it too much. He couldn't let Delaney Lawson keep him from doing what he had to do. No matter how intriguing the woman was.

THE NEXT MORNING Cooper went up to the house to invite Delaney over for breakfast.

"I've seen the way you cook, McLeod, and to tell you the truth, burned beans aren't my idea of breakfast."

He grinned. "How do you feel about sausage gravy, biscuits and eggs sunny-side up?"

She studied him for a moment, skepticism written all over her face. "If you can do that over a campfire, why do you eat beans?"

"I like beans."

She smiled. He could tell it was against her will.

"Well?" he asked, raising an eyebrow.

"I guess I'm going to have to see this to believe it," she said, relenting. "I'll bring the coffee."

"You're on."

They sat around the campfire, the sun at their backs, and ate in silence. In the distance, a hawk circled in the clear blue, while a few young Morgans romped playfully in a near pasture. Cooper breathed in the sweet scent of summer—and Delaney—as he ate. Sitting so close to her had made him more aware of everything—from the smooth, warm surface of the log they shared to the feathered edges of the ponderosas etched against the skyline. He felt a longing like none he'd ever known. He told himself it was just simple desire, something he understood.

"Great breakfast," Delaney said, glancing over at him as she set down her empty plate. "I take back what I said about your cooking." She searched his face. "I can't quite figure you out, McLeod. Why is that?"

"I'm a man of many talents," he said, feeling his grin slip a little. He felt his skin prickle at the thought of touching her. Of her touching him. He put down his plate, telling himself the last thing he should do was reach for her.

The phone rang inside the house.

He took a ragged breath and let it out slowly. "I meant to ask you how your date went last night," he said, feeling the need to change directions.

She shot him a look that said volumes and got up to go answer the phone. "I'd better get that. It could be something important."

"I'm going to go take a bath," he said, pointing toward the creek.

"You're welcome to use the shower in the barn," she said over her shoulder.

"I need the fresh air," he said, watching her go, wondering who'd call this early in the morning.

WHEN DELANEY reached the house, the answering machine was just picking up. She started for her office but stopped when she heard the attorney's voice and the defeat in it.

"Delaney, I just received word on the DNA tests," he said.

The tests she'd insisted on. The results she'd asked called to her immediately. She felt her heart fall, her hopes and dreams with it.

"The tests were ninety-five percent conclusive. Ty Drummond is your half brother."

Chapter Twelve

Delaney dropped into her office chair. In a daze, she listened to the rest of the message from the attorney. He explained they could run the tests again if she wanted, although he saw no reason to. With the use of her father's baby teeth, the tests had been fairly decisive. But, he went on, the will Ty claimed was from their father could still prove to be a forgery. And even if it wasn't, they could fight Ty in court for part of the ranch on the grounds that her father hadn't been himself just before he died. Or she could still find a later will, the one her father had said he'd written, leaving her everything.

Delaney couldn't believe it. She'd convinced herself that Ty wasn't her brother, that he'd made up the whole story just for the money, that the will couldn't be real—her father wouldn't have done that to her. Now she worried that she'd been wrong on all counts.

What would Hank Lawson have done if he'd found out just days before his death that he had a son? Would he have left everything, including the ranch, to his only son? It was just the sort of thing a man like Hank Lawson might have done.

She buried her face in her hands and cried, the hurt and pain overwhelming. Her father had betrayed her. All the times he'd hurt her, forgetting her birthdays, missing school events, never being around when she needed him, nothing could compare with now.

"Delaney?"

She looked up to find Cooper standing over her. His hair was still wet, making it dark blond. The cold creek bath had left a glow on his handsome face. He smiled at her, and for a moment all she saw was his irresistible charm, that cocky arrogance that came ready-made with his good looks. Then his eyes darkened with concern as he reached for her. She flew into his arms.

COOPER HELD HER tightly, afraid at first to ask what had happened. "Is it Digger?" He knew how much Delaney cared for the old prospector. He just hoped that if Digger had died, it was in his sleep and not at the hands of a murderer.

She shook her head against Cooper's flannel shirt and hugged him fiercely as if her world had suddenly dropped out from under her. "It's Ty."

She leaned back just enough that he could see her face.

"The DNA tests came back. He *is* my brother." She bit her lip. "And what if he's telling the truth about the will? My father really may have left him the ranch."

Cooper pulled her even closer, rubbing her back with his hand, as he thought about what that would mean to Delaney. If she lost the ranch— He held her, searching for words that would comfort her, knowing there were none. Maybe this was why Jamison thought they were close to getting the ranch. If he'd been in contact with Ty and knew about the DNA results, that meant Jamison also knew about the will Ty had from his father.

After a few minutes Cooper felt her strength coming back. Delaney Lawson wasn't the kind of woman to stay down and he suspected she'd come up fighting. It was a trait he couldn't help but admire. Unfortunately, with her strength would come the wall between them. She was still his boss, he her hired

hand. And the other night he'd hurt her, something he regretted.

After a moment, she pulled away and wiped her tears.
When she looked up at him, her eyes were clear and dangerously dark. "I'm not sure what's going on, but it's clear
to me that as long as you stay around here, your life will be
in jeopardy."

He stared at her, suddenly worried. "I hope you're not
thinking of firing me because I have to tell you right now, I
won't leave." He grinned at her, hoping to lighten up this
conversation—and fast. "You'll have to run me off with a
gun. And even then I'll still probably come back."

She smiled. "That's good to hear, McLeod. But why is
that?"

He met her gaze, then pulled his away. Normally he'd have
some quick, response that would appease even the meanest
of women. But Delaney wasn't just any woman. "I guess
I've gotten involved in your troubles. And I want to see them
through."

She nodded. "Good answer, McLeod. Well thought out."
She shook her head. "I know I must be nuts, but I realize I
can't save this ranch by myself. Buck's gone and fallen in
love, and Jared...well I can't depend on the sheriff for any
help, that's for sure."

Cooper nodded, seeing where she was headed. "So, since
there isn't anyone else—"

"Exactly," she said, narrowing her eyes at him.

"Well, when you put it that way—" He tried to joke about
it, but he was hurt that it would come down to this. And he
realized with regret how much it had meant to him to have
Delaney's confidence in him.

"McLeod, I have a feeling it is only going to get more
dangerous from this point on. If you'd rather pass, I'll understand," she said, watching him closely. He started to argue

that he couldn't leave, but she held up a hand to stop him. "I just need to know one thing. Can I trust you?"

He almost laughed. He didn't even trust himself. A lie came to his lips as naturally as breathing. And yet the words just wouldn't seem to come out. Instead he stared at her, seeing the strong, hardheaded, determined Delaney Lawson, but remembering the soft, vulnerable, passionate one he'd kissed. The one he'd held in his arms just moments before. He couldn't walk away now. Not the way he felt about her.

He saw her shake her head at his hesitation. "The other night you said you'd done some things," she said. "I don't care what they are or who you used to be. What I need to know, McLeod, is can I trust you *now?*"

He looked into her eyes. "Yes," he answered, hoping that for once in his disreputable life it was true.

"WHERE DO WE BEGIN?" Delaney asked as they drove toward Helena. She was sure Cooper would have an idea. He always did.

"It seems we've got two problems, finding your father's will—"

"If it exists," she added.

"And finding out who's behind the problems on the ranch and why. I thought we should talk to Digger about Johnson Gulch Lake. That's where he saw something that frightened him, where he got hit on the head and where we were shot at," Cooper said. "Do you still have that spur you found?"

She nodded. "What does the spur have to do with it?"

"Nothing, more than likely." He grinned at her. "But you said it looked familiar to you. It's obviously old. Maybe Digger will recognize it." He saw the doubt in her expression. "I thought it might jog his memory, get him talking about what he saw that night. Digger might know more than he thinks he does."

Why did she get the feeling the spur was the least of Cooper's interest in talking to Digger? "Digger thinks there were space aliens," she said.

"True. But when you add it all up—the rifle shot, the swim-fin tracks and an old road reopened—"

"Don't forget the spur." She gave him a smile. "It doesn't add up to anything, does it?"

They drove in silence for a while. In the distance she would see Lake Helena gleaming in the sun. She felt shaky and unsure, and blamed it on all her troubles—not on her feelings for Cooper McLeod.

"Are you all right?" Cooper asked as they passed the capitol building.

She glanced over at him. "I was just thinking. What will happen to Digger if Ty gets the ranch?"

Cooper figured Ty wouldn't have the ranch for long—not with Rattlesnake Range around. The days of the old prospector wandering the Rockin' L were quickly coming to an end.

THE DOCTOR LED them into a small office at the end of the hall.

"Physically, Digger is on the mend," he said. "But mentally, he's very confused. And frightened. I'd like to run some more tests on him."

"For what?" Delaney asked.

"I think this might be more than senility."

"Like what?" Cooper asked.

The doctor sighed. "Digger can't seem to tell reality from his nightmares. He's paranoid. He thinks people are after him. He's extremely agitated. These are symptoms of what could be Alzheimer's."

"Alzheimer's?" Delaney asked, her voice breaking. She looked over at Cooper. He gave her a reassuring smile.

"The tests can't hurt," he said.

"With Alzheimer's," the doctor added, "all we can do is rule out everything else."

The symptoms could also fit a person who thought his life was in danger, Delaney noted.

She looked down the hall. A deputy lounged outside Digger's room. She hoped that as long as Digger was in the hospital, he was safe.

THEY FOUND Digger in his room, sitting up in bed, yelling at a nurse. When the nurse saw her chance to escape, she scampered from the room.

"When am I getting out of here, Winnie?" Digger demanded the moment he saw Delaney.

She went to his side. "It's Delaney, Digger."

He blinked a couple of times, then smiled. "Of course it is. You just remind me so much of your grandmother." Digger motioned for Cooper to close the door. "What did you find at Johnson Gulch Lake?" he whispered conspiratorially. "You don't think I'm losing my mind, too, do you, Winnie?"

Cooper pulled up a chair for Delaney and another for himself beside Digger's bed.

"We did find odd tracks in the sand," Delaney said, trying to give Digger some hope. "They looked like swim fins, as if someone had been swimming there."

The old prospector nodded and smiled. "I told you I saw them in the water. The space aliens. I never noticed their feet, though."

The early-morning sun spilled through the window, warm and bright. Delaney realized the normalcy of it made their discussion all that much more bizarre.

"We definitely think you saw something," Cooper said.

"You remember Cooper McLeod," Delaney said to Digger. "He's my..." She started to say hired hand, but somewhere along the way he'd become much more than that. "Friend."

She saw Cooper smile at that and she looked away. Honestly, the man was incorrigible.

"Did you hear a pickup engine that night?" Cooper asked.

Digger's face wrinkled in a frown. "Can't say as I did. Can't say as I didn't. Tess was kicking up a fuss, noisier than the devil." He looked at Delaney. "How is that old mule of mine doing? Better than me, I suspect."

"Tess is fine." She started to say that the mule missed him, which she knew was probably true, but realized that would only make Digger want out of the hospital sooner.

"Gus came again last night," Digger said after a moment. He stared at the window; worry etched his face. "I told him I didn't steal his gold, but he doesn't believe me. He said he'd come back for revenge. And I imagine he'll have it."

Delaney felt pulled between her loyalty to Digger and fear that these were only the hallucinations of a diseased mind. How could Gus have gotten in with the deputy outside Digger's door? She tried to imagine Gus Halbrook. Gus had died so young. And so violently in the cave-in. It must have been horrible for Digger. She wondered if he felt guilty for what had happened and that was causing some of this.

"It wasn't your fault Gus got killed," Delaney said, taking Digger's old weathered hand.

He smiled at her, tears in his eyes. "He was my friend. I should have been there with him. Maybe—"

"Digger, would Gus go back to the mine?" Cooper asked.

Delaney shot him a look of surprise. Gus? The mine?

Digger turned his rheumy old eyes on McLeod. "You mean the Golden Dream?"

Cooper nodded. "Wouldn't he go back to the place where he died?"

"I suspect he would." He eyed Cooper with respect. "Young man, you're thinkin' that's where we'd catch him, ain't ya?"

Cooper smiled. "That's exactly what I'm thinking. Can you tell me how to find the mine?"

"Excuse me, even if you found it, my grandfather dynamited the entrance years ago,'' Delaney interjected. Why was Cooper bringing this up now? Surely he didn't believe Gus was back and on his way to the mine. He was beginning to sound like Digger.

''There's evil at that mine, Winnie,'' Digger said. His gaze flickered around the room. Agitation showed in his features. ''Pure hatin' evil. Anyone who goes near there—''

''Don't worry, Digger, I'm not about to let Del—Winnie go there,'' Cooper said. ''The mine's up Johnson Gulch, isn't it?'' Digger nodded. ''Tell me about the other entrance.''

Delaney stared at Cooper. ''Another entrance?''

''We got to stop Gus,'' Digger said, digging in the drawer beside his bed. ''What if he tries to hurt Winnie?''

''That's why you have to tell me where it is,'' Cooper said. Digger handed him a bent-up, worn photograph.

Delaney shook her head but said nothing. She knew it was the photo Digger still carried of his old friend; Gus's face was barely visible anymore. She felt a chill, although the room was unusually hot, even with the air conditioning. What if the doctor was wrong about Digger's delusions? Digger didn't sound confused. If anything, his story had been consistent from the beginning. Space aliens. And Gus Halbrook back from the dead for revenge. Now even Cooper sounded as if he believed Digger. She hugged herself, afraid there might be more truth in Digger's story than any of them had been willing to admit.

''There was a boulder, a huge thing, and a massive old pine tree, as gnarled as my old hands,'' Digger said hesitantly. ''The entrance is small. Used to be covered in brush.''

''The entrance is upstream of the lake, right?'' Cooper asked.

Digger nodded. ''Up on the hillside. But you shouldn't try to find it alone. Not with Gus out there.''

Cooper patted Digger's arm and thanked him. ''Don't

worry." But Delaney could tell Cooper was disappointed. With directions like that, he'd never be able to find the mine.

"We found something else at the lake," she said, rummaging into her bag. "It looks familiar to me." She pulled out the antique spur. "Cooper thought you might—"

Digger let out a gasp. He held up his hands as if to ward off something horrible. She looked down at the spur, the sapphire sparkling, then at Digger. But his gaze was on the window. Shadows waltzed into the room. "Gus."

"Gus?" Delaney actually turned, expecting to see an old prospector still covered with dirt from the grave. She felt a chill.

"No, Gus! Not Winnie." Digger clutched his chest. He seemed to be fighting for breath. His words came out in a hoarse whisper. "Revenge." The alarm on the monitor beside the bed went off and Delaney could hear nurses running down the hall toward them.

"What is it?" she cried.

"I think he's having a heart attack," Cooper said, moving her back as the nurses rolled a cart into the room.

"Oh, Cooper," she cried, turning into the cowboy's embrace. "He can't die."

"It was just an anxiety attack," the doctor told them a half hour later. "He's resting comfortably."

"He scared me," Delaney said. "One minute he was just fine and the next—"

"He's scaring himself," the doctor said. "He's convinced someone is trying to kill him. Someone named Gus. Do you know who that would be?"

Delaney looked down at her boots. "Gus Halbrook. He was a prospector friend. Only, Gus died in the 1930s in a mine cave-in on the Rockin' L."

The doctor nodded. "I suspected it was something like that. Well, don't worry. We'll see that he's taken care of. I'll run those tests.'' Delaney nodded. ''I'll call you when I know something,'' the doctor added.

COOPER SUGGESTED they stop at the York Bar for a beer and a burger. He wanted to talk to Dude about the night before. He'd noticed a definite animosity between Dude and the sheriff and he was curious why, and having Delaney along might help. She still seemed shaken from what had happened at the hospital, and didn't appear all that anxious to get back to the ranch.

Dude wasn't working. A petite blonde was behind the bar. She gave them a broad smile and a beer and took their orders.

Delaney sipped her beer, worry etching her beautiful face. The bartender went to play some songs on the jukebox before she started their burgers. The place was empty this time of the day. It smelled of beer, worn wood and burgers, not an unpleasant aroma, Cooper thought.

A soft, slow western song filled the barroom.

''Digger's going to be all right,'' Cooper said, taking Delaney's hand. ''There's nothing more we can do. What do you say to a dance?'' She started to resist, but he gave her his best grin. ''Look, there's only one spot left for us.''

She glanced over at the empty dance floor and smiled. ''McLeod, you could charm the wind out of the trees.''

He laughed as he pulled her into his arms. Holding her was becoming a habit he thought he could get used to. She felt so right. He wondered how he would ever be able to give her up. But he knew his past was eventually going to catch up with him and then... He looked into her dark eyes and wished he could tell her the truth.

''Why were you asking Digger about the Golden Dream Mine?''

He shrugged. ''With Digger going on about Gus and strange happenings at Johnson Gulch Lake, I thought it might all tie up somehow. And that I could put it together and—''

''And solve all my problems.'' She laughed. ''You're a romantic at heart, McLeod.''

He grinned. ''Yeah. That's me.''

They moved slowly to the music, their bodies in unison. He felt her breasts, soft and full, against his chest. Desire spread through him. He saw it reflected in Delaney's dark eyes, in the way she molded her body to his. The music drifted with them, part of them. He kissed her, then traced her lips with the tip of his tongue. She moaned softly as the song ended.

''Well, well, well, isn't this an interesting sight.''

Cooper looked up to find Jared standing in the doorway of the bar. The smile on his face couldn't disguise the meanness in his eyes. ''Let me buy you two lovebirds a drink.''

''Thanks, but we were just about to have lunch,'' Cooper said as he and Delaney returned to the bar.

''Oh, that's too bad.'' Jared studied Delaney openly for a moment. Cooper couldn't help but notice the animosity between them. He wondered just how badly their date had gone.

''You haven't forgotten about my rodeo Saturday,'' Jared said to Delaney. ''McLeod told you he's riding saddle bronc, didn't he?''

Cooper saw the look of disbelief on Delaney's face. He groaned under his breath. Damn. He'd never be able to convince her he wasn't just like her father, that rodeoing had been one of the last things on his mind since he'd met her. But he had to admit, just the thought of riding Hell's Fire excited him.

DELANEY COULDN'T believe her ears. She shot Cooper a look, expecting him to deny it. Instead he gave her a shrug and a grin. They never changed! Once they got rodeo in their blood— She kicked at the leg of her barstool and swore to herself.

"It's just a one-time thing," Cooper said, obviously thinking that would calm her down.

"And what if you get hurt?" she demanded. "Or killed? I'll have to find a new hand, won't I."

Jared laughed. "Tarnation, Del, new hands are a dime a dozen, but a man who can ride Hell's Fire, well, that's some kind of man."

"Hell's Fire?" she cried. "Isn't that the wild bronc you bought for this rodeo? The horse no one's been able to ride yet?"

Jared smiled. "That's right, Del."

He was enjoying himself. That only added to her anger with Cooper. Didn't Cooper realize he'd played right into Jared's hand?

"We've got a little wager on it, isn't that right, McLeod?"

Delaney gave them both glares, then stomped over to the jukebox. When the waitress brought their lunch, Delaney motioned for her to leave it at a nearby table. She couldn't bear sitting at the bar with Jared. Actually, the very thought of food sickened her. What was Cooper thinking? Didn't it matter that he was taking his life in his hands riding Hell's Fire?

She punched in four songs, sat down at the table and picked up her burger. No woman can take the rodeo out of a man, she told herself as she took a bite. Look how her mother had tried for all those years. It eventually killed her. She took another bite. Delaney cussed herself for ever lowering her defenses around Cooper. When was she going to learn? She looked down and saw her empty plate, surprised she'd eaten all her lunch.

Cooper sat down across from her and picked up his burger. He seemed about to say something, but probably knew she wasn't going to buy his excuses anyway. He ate in silence. Jared stood with his back to the bar, watching them, a smile on his face. Delaney glared at Cooper over her beer.

"See you Saturday, McLeod," Jared said as they were

leaving the bar. "I'm sure you'll want to see him ride, Del. I'll save you a seat."

"I wouldn't count on that, Jared," she said, and slammed out to the pickup.

"Would you like to know why I accepted Jared's bet to ride Saturday?" Cooper asked as he climbed in beside her.

He sounded so rational it made her all the more angry with him. "It's your neck, McLeod." She started the pickup and backed out, sending more gravel flying than she'd meant to. "Why should I care what happens to you? But you did say you'd help me find out who's trying to take my ranch from me. You can't do that if you're dead."

He grinned at her. "It's nice to think you're worried about me." She rolled her eyes. "I agreed to ride because I wanted to get a look at Jared's stock and it seemed like a way to do it without attracting attention," he said calmly. "As one of the participants, I'll have free run of the place."

She glared at him. "You agreed to ride a wild, unridden bronc on the off chance that Jared might have a horse with a barred shoe?"

"I'd bet this month's wages that horse is Jared's."

"You'd better hang on to your money, McLeod. You've already bet Jared you can ride Hell's Fire." She loosened her grip on the steering wheel when she noticed her knuckles had turned white. "You couldn't have come up with a better way to look for the horse than riding in Jared Kincaid's rodeo?" she asked, incredulous.

"It seemed like a good idea at the time," Cooper said sheepishly.

Men! "Jared wouldn't have bet you unless he thought you'd get yourself killed!" She slammed her fist against the steering wheel. "And from what I've heard about Hell's Fire, you probably will."

"You don't have much faith in me, do you?" Cooper asked.

She glanced over at him to see if he was serious. She hit the brakes and skidded to a stop in the middle of the dirt road. "This isn't about barred shoes or finding attempted murderers. This is about the thrill of rodeoing—admit it."

"I quit rodeoing." He met her gaze and held it. "And if I need a thrill...well, I've heard you can find that kind of stimulation in a woman." His eyes darkened. "With the right woman, of course."

An oath came to her lips, but she stifled it and got the pickup going again. He'd quit rodeoing? Then how did he explain that injury to his thigh, the one he said he'd gotten from some bronc just recently? Men. When was she going to learn not to believe anything they told her? Especially one like McLeod.

Not far down the road, Buck passed them in his truck. Angel was cuddled up next to him. Delaney wondered if Buck had popped the question yet. She groaned, thinking about what Cooper had said about stimulation and the right woman. She noticed Cooper had turned to look back at them. "Let's have it," she said. She swore sometimes she could hear the wheels turning in his head.

"What would you say to taking a look around Angel's cabin?"

She stared at him. "Isn't that illegal?"

"Not very," he lied with a grin. "I want to see if she has any reason to want to shoot at me or drop rocks on me."

"Why would a writer want to hurt you?"

He shook his head. "Why would anyone want to?" He grinned. "You seem to be the only person around here who isn't trying to kill me."

"Give me a little time," she said, and headed down the road toward the Meadows Lodge.

A young woman with frizzy brown hair, thick glasses and a mouthful of gum came out of a back room at the Meadows

Lodge. She eyed the two of them and smiled knowingly. "Cabin for two? One night? One bed?"

"We're not…together," Delaney snapped, and took a step away from Cooper. She didn't even have to face him to know he was grinning.

"Actually," she heard him say, amusement in his voice, "we're looking for Angel Danvers, the writer."

The woman chewed her gum for a moment. "Cabin twelve." She pointed down the line of cabins to one with a dark-colored van parked outside. "Except she just left with some old cowboy dude."

Delaney bristled at her description of Buck, then realized it was fairly accurate.

"Sor-ree," the woman said, and headed back no doubt to the soap opera on the television in the adjoining room.

"Angel is going to be furious that we missed her," Cooper said to Delaney. "Especially now that she's got a shot at Fabio on the cover."

Delaney blinked at him. Fabio? On the cover of what?

The woman stopped and turned at the mention of Fabio. "Fabio? I thought Angel Danvers wrote dry old history stuff?"

Cooper gave the woman a grin that Delaney recognized only too well. "That's just what she tells people. What she really writes is steamy historical *romances.*"

"Steamy" seemed to do it. "No kidding," the woman said.

"But Angel won't be writing anything without her computer," Cooper continued. He looked up at the woman as if a light had suddenly gone off in his head. "Could we leave Ms. Danvers's computer with you?"

The woman shrugged. "Just put it over there." She pointed to a dusty corner.

"I don't think that's a good idea," Delaney said. "It's an expensive laptop. Angel would have a fit."

Cooper nodded his approval. "You're so right."

"I guess you could leave it in her cabin," the young woman said. She reached up and took down the second key for cabin twelve. "You don't suppose she'd sign a book for me, do you?"

"Absolutely," Cooper said, taking the key from her. "Who knows what she'll do when I tell her how helpful you were?"

"FABIO?" Delaney asked as they left. "And what happens when that woman talks to Angel, and Angel then asks us what we were doing searching her cabin?"

"By then we'll have found out what we need and have time to come up with a good cover story."

She shot him a look. "Such as what?"

"Oh, I'll think of something," he said.

She studied his handsome face, remembering the way he'd turned on the charm—and the lies. "Why do I feel you've done this type of thing before, McLeod?"

His grin faltered as he inserted the key and they stepped into the cool, darkness of cabin twelve.

ANGEL WASN'T what anyone would call neat. It looked as if for the past week she'd simply walked into the cabin and stepped out of whatever she'd been wearing. The floor was cluttered with discarded outfits. The bed was unmade and strewn with books and papers. So was the desk in the corner.

"The sign of a creative mind?" Delaney joked.

Cooper went to the desk and thumbed through the piles of papers. Notes. Historical data on gold mines and the York area. He noticed across the creek from the original townsite of New York was a smaller one that had been Brooklyn, Montana. Both had been small, but the town of Trout Creek just down the road, which no longer existed, had a population of several thousand between 1866-1869. He glanced through the rest, surprised. It was all the same. Maybe Angel was who she really said she was.

He left Delaney digging around in the pile on the bed and went to check the bathroom. Makeup everywhere. Stockings hanging in the shower. Wet towels on the floor where she'd dropped them.

Her cosmetic case stood open on the toilet tank. He carefully sifted through the case and found nothing of interest. The medicine cabinet was empty.

As he stepped back into the main part of the cabin, he noticed the empty clothes rod in the closet. Instead an open suitcase lay on the closet floor. It looked as if a bomb had exploded inside it. Angel didn't plan to stay long, it appeared.

Cooper glanced up to find Delaney flipping through a book. "What did you find?" he asked.

"An old journal," she said, smiling at him as she closed it. "Sorry, I guess I'm not much help. It was interesting. Written by a prospector in the late 1930s about the hardships of mining for gold." The swamp cooler behind her let out a loud bang and she jumped. She gave him a chagrined smile. "All right, so I'm not cut out for this cloak and dagger stuff."

Cooper smiled back at her. "Actually, I was thinking that we made quite the team back there in the office." He glanced at his watch. "We'd better get out of here before that daytime drama ends."

As he bent to look through the contents of the suitcase, something caught his eye. With two fingers, he picked up a little navy blue dress with a white collar from a hanger at the back of the closet. Memory threw him like a mean bronc. He knew now where he'd seen Angel. She'd been wearing this dress, her hair had been pulled up into a no-nonsense style and it had been a different color, a dark auburn. Even her voice had been different. No dumb-blonde routine. No flirting. Strictly business.

"Something wrong?" Delaney asked.

He looked up. The dress slipped from his fingers. He shook his head, too stunned to speak. Angel Danvers had been a different woman the day Cooper had seen her at Rattlesnake Range.

Chapter Thirteen

Cooper had been acting strangely ever since they'd left Angel's cabin. He seemed preoccupied and anxious to get back to the ranch.

"I have a couple of things I need to do in town," he told her vaguely.

"Do they have anything to do with that dress you found in Angel's closet?" Delaney asked.

He laughed and grinned at her. "It just reminded me of someone, that's all."

Her heart tightened. "A woman from your past?" she asked, trying to keep her tone light, hoping the sudden pang of jealousy wasn't audible.

Cooper shook his head. "An old friend I recently lost."

"Oh, I'm sorry." She felt awful for being so nosy and suspicious, let alone jealous. Why did she always jump to the wrong conclusions with him? *Because he's a rodeo cowboy. Because he reminds you of your father.* Both lethal reasons not to get too close to Cooper McLeod.

She stopped the pickup at Cooper's camp. The sun rimmed the mountains to the west. Delaney felt time slipping away. "I've got to get to the bottom of this soon, McLeod. I can't keep playing detective. I have a horse ranch to run."

He nodded. "Maybe I'll find the barred-shoe horse tomorrow at Kincaid's."

She made a face. Momentarily, she'd forgotten about that stupid rodeo.

"Will you be all right here for a while by yourself?" he asked, still awfully anxious to get into town.

"I'll be fine," she answered, trying not to let her suspicious mind run loose.

Cooper nodded as if there were something else he wanted to say but changed his mind. "I won't be gone long."

COOPER STILL couldn't believe it. Angel Danvers at Rattlesnake Range. There was no doubt in his mind; he remembered her now, remembered that walk of hers—something she couldn't disguise even in a business dress.

But why was she in disguise that day? He laughed at his stupidity. She *wasn't* in disguise at Rattlesnake Range. That was the real Angel Danvers. The woman on the Rockin' L was the impostor.

Who was she and what had she been doing at Rattlesnake Range? His mind raced with theories. All of them bad. Maybe she was the person the agency had hired to acquire Delaney's ranch. He rejected that theory almost immediately. Delaney didn't like Angel. And Angel wasn't doing anything to get her to. Nor was Angel even pretending interest in buying the ranch. From what he'd seen in cabin twelve, Angel really was researching a book.

So what was she doing at the agency? he asked himself as he drove into York. Rattlesnake Range kept a very low profile. Few people even knew about it. But if you were interested in acquiring a special property on any terms, at any price, and you had enough money, you'd eventually end up at Rattlesnake Range. Angel didn't appear to have that kind of money. But he'd learned a long time ago not to judge a woman by the color of her lipstick.

He parked beside the phone booth, anxious to talk to Thom

Jamison. Cooper was desperate to find some answers before Angel remembered where she'd seen him and blew his cover.

AS DELANEY PARKED in front of the house, she noticed her front door. It stood open. Her heart quickened. Maybe the wind had blown it open. Maybe— She pulled the rifle down from the rack behind her and opened the pickup door. Hesitantly she started for the house.

As she mounted the porch steps she could see into the house. Everything looked normal enough.

She stepped in the doorway, rifle ready. And saw them. Boots. Worn, muddy boots. She peeked around the corner of the doorjamb, following the boots up the new denim to find Ty sprawled on her couch. He lay with his head back, his hat partially over his face, appearing to be taking a nap.

Fury ignited her blood—then her tongue. "What the hell do you think you're doing?" she demanded, pointing the rifle at him.

He jumped in surprise, pushing back his hat as he sat up with a start. His gaze focused on the rifle in her hands, and for a moment he looked as if he thought she might shoot him. It wasn't out of the realm of possibility.

"I was waiting on *you*," he said indignantly.

"Do you always just walk into a person's home to wait for her?" He raised an eyebrow and smirked at her. She felt as if she were dealing with a child. "It's not your home yet, Ty. Until it is—"

"I had to talk to you," Ty whined. "There has to be some way we can settle this without dragging it out in court."

She quit listening as she noticed the door to her office was also open. It had definitely been closed when she'd left. Something white lay on the floor. She stared, disbelieving. Someone had ransacked her office.

THOM JAMISON sounded more than a little surprised that Cooper hadn't started his vacation yet.

"You're still at the Rockin' L?" he asked.

Cooper thought about lying, but realized it would serve no purpose. Jamison would find out he hadn't left soon enough from the agent on the job. "Yeah. I was getting ready to leave, when I ran into someone here I had seen at Rattlesnake Range just before I came on this job. Passed her in the lobby. A little too much of a coincidence, you know."

Silence.

"She's going by Angel Danvers. Ring any bells?"

"No."

Jamison answered too quickly.

"I thought you'd be sitting in the shade somewhere by now with your feet up," he continued.

"She's a cute little redhead. Big green eyes. Stacked like a brick outhouse. Smart. And all business. The day I saw her at the agency she was wearing a little navy number with a white collar and had her hair up."

Silence. "You aren't going on vacation, are you?"

Cooper smiled; that Jamison was sharp. "No, I'm seeing this one through."

Jamison swore, something Cooper knew was out of character for him. "The board isn't going to like this."

Cooper laughed. "You don't have to tell them."

Silence.

"Or maybe you do." Maybe he'd been wrong about Thom; maybe he couldn't trust him.

Jamison swore again. "I don't remember her name, but I remember the woman. You're right. She could be trouble. She came in asking about the Rockin' L. It became obvious quickly that she didn't have the resources to buy the ranch. She asked a lot of questions about its ownership, how a person would go about acquiring it if the owner didn't want to sell. I smelled newspaper reporter and got rid of her as fast as possible, but she already knew a lot about the ranch and that the agency was trying to get it.''

''A reporter?'' Cooper asked, still wondering if he could trust Jamison, but at the same time knowing he had to. Jamison needed all the information if Cooper hoped for any help from him. ''Well, she's here pretending to be a blond bimbo historical-book writer. She's hooked up with the ranch manager romantically.''

''I see.''

Jamison sounded concerned.

Cooper shook his head as he considered the latest turn of events. ''You've got an untrained loose cannon on this job, someone else possibly taking potshots at your target, a half brother who's desperate for money and the ranch, and now a reporter who's after Rattlesnake Range.'' Cooper laughed. ''Things get any better, Thom, and you'll be doing time at the state prison in Deer Lodge.''

''You forgot one other problem the agency has,'' Jamison said softly. ''They've got you there.''

''DID YOU FIND the will?'' Delaney demanded as she came out of her ransacked office. Nothing appeared to be missing, but she couldn't tell for sure.

She turned to face her brother. Her brother. As she glared at him, she realized she'd actually accepted the fact that he *was* her brother. For so long she'd resisted any thought that they might be related. But now as she studied him, she admitted there were definitely similarities between Ty and their father. He sounded like Hank. Always making excuses. And he looked a little like Hank. In the eyes. And the cheekbones. And he definitely had that self-serving part down perfectly. ''That was what you were looking for, right, the will?''

''What are you talking about?'' Ty asked irritably. ''I could care less about any will you might have.''

''Then what were you looking for?''

Ty shook his head. "Give me a break. I ransacked your office, then took a nap on your couch to wait for you? Brilliant."

Delaney swore and leaned the rifle against the wall before she shot Ty in simple frustration. He was still standing in the living room, looking lost. "What do you want, Ty?" she asked, noticing the front door was still open as a subtle invitation for him to leave.

"I didn't even notice your office was in a mess," he said, frowning at her. "The front door was open when I got here. I just left it the way I found it." He shook his head as if he couldn't believe she didn't trust him.

Delaney eyed her brother and thought he might be telling the truth. He didn't seem the observant type, she had to admit. "All right, Ty, you didn't search my office," she said. "What did you want to see me about?" As if she couldn't guess.

"You got the results of the test, right?" he asked.

"Right." He appeared ill at ease, and she suddenly realized that maybe he wanted her to welcome him into the family. He had to be kidding. "Ty, I'll concede that we're related. But there is something you have to understand. I've worked this ranch since I was a kid. I've put sweat and blood and heart into it. My grandfather taught me to love the land. He taught me about the satisfaction of hard work over material rewards—" She could tell she was boring him.

"The point is," she said, trying not to raise her voice. "All you seem interested in is money. You don't care about this land, this ranch or this family. You don't want to work the ranch—you don't seem to want to work at all. This ranch has been in the family now for more than sixty years. Doesn't that mean anything to you?"

"I need money. Now."

He sounded scared, but at the same time threatening.

"If you could just give me some money against what you owe me—"

"That's just it, Ty. I don't feel I *owe* you anything," Delaney said carefully. "That's why I intend to fight you as long as it takes. Whatever it takes."

"This ranch is mine," he said angrily. "I have the will, dated three days before Hank died. You have no will, and even if you did find the one you said he wrote leaving you everything, it would be worthless. My lawyer says mine should supersede any others."

His lawyer. Delaney took a deep breath, trying to keep her anger in check.

"You aren't going to drag this out," Ty said, his voice dangerously low as he moved toward her. "I'm our father's only son. And he wanted me to have the ranch." Ty smiled; he knew how much that hurt her. "And I'm through waiting, Delaney." He stepped closer.

"Don't threaten me, Ty," Delaney said, standing her ground. Ty was bluffing. He just didn't strike her as a killer. Too lazy. "You'll never get this ranch by threatening me— I don't scare easily. And even if you killed me, you'd never get away with it. You'd be the number one suspect. Even Jared would know you did it."

Ty swore. "You have it all figured out, don't you? Well, I'm going to take what's mine and you're not going to be able to stop me."

"I think you'd better leave," Cooper said, suddenly filling the open doorway.

Ty looked up in surprise. "Stay out of this, McLeod. It doesn't have anything to do with you."

Cooper stepped into the room. "You're upsetting my boss, so I'm making it my business."

Ty laughed nervously, looking from Delaney to Cooper and back. "Getting involved in this could be fatal, cowboy. For both of you." He stomped past Cooper, slamming the door on his way out.

COOPER PULLED Delaney into his arms, needing to feel her safe in his embrace. On the way back to the ranch, he'd realized just how dangerous this all had become. Rattlesnake Range would push harder now, wanting to get this over with as quickly as possible. He feared what extremes they might go to. Then there was Ty. And Angel in the picture. The Rockin' L had become a powder keg about to blow.

"I'm glad you showed up when you did," Delaney murmured against his shoulder.

"Are you all right?" He pulled back to caress her cheek, his gaze on her face.

"Ty sounded a little too desperate for my liking," she said. "And someone ransacked my office. I guess I'm going to have to start locking my door."

"Delaney," Cooper said, hating what he had to do. He let his gaze run the length of her. His body stirred with desire. But the only thing on his mind was worry. About Delaney's safety. She didn't stand a chance against the people who wanted her ranch. He'd realized that on the way back from town. Ty Drummond was probably the least of her concerns. Cooper just couldn't stand the chance that something might happen to Delaney. "I think you should consider selling the ranch."

She looked up in surprise. "Not you, too."

He'd let her down; it showed in every line of her body, in the bright glint of her eyes as she pulled away from him.

"You can't win," he said quietly. "The odds are too great."

She raised a brow, her gaze locking with his. "How do you know that?"

"I've seen it happen on other ranches. Believe me, I know."

She shook her head at him. "You're a runner, aren't you, McLeod? Things get a little tough and you take off." Her gaze was rock hard and just as steady. "Well, I'm a fighter. And that's what I intend to do. With or without you."

He looked into those dark eyes, seeing a strength that made him feel weak, a determination that more than matched his own stubbornness, a fight that reminded him of himself a long time ago. What a pair we'd have made, he thought with regret.

"You're right," he admitted. "I've always run." He smiled, knowing that's exactly what a smart man would do now. Run. And not look back. Only he didn't want to run anymore. He couldn't run—and leave Delaney alone to fight this battle by herself. "But even us weak-kneed cowards have to take a stand sometime." He shook his head as he realized how good he felt, better than he'd felt in years.

She smiled at him. "I thought you said I don't stand a chance?"

"We don't stand much of one."

"'We'?" She laughed softly. "And with those odds, you're still willing to help me?"

He laughed, thinking how beautiful she looked standing there. Thinking how much he wanted her. "No one ever said I had any sense. See you in the morning."

As Cooper walked into his camp, he spotted Crazy Jack dragging his feed sack around again. "Don't you ever think of anything but food?" he demanded, giving the horse a friendly slap on the rump as he took the sack away. Crazy Jack turned to throw him a look that made Cooper laugh.

"I don't think about women *all* the time," he told the horse, but found himself glancing back at the house as he scooped out some oats. No, he hardly *ever* thought about women anymore, he realized. Just one woman.

He smiled to himself as he made dinner, cold beans right out of the can. Even with rocks and bullets flying, it surprised him how comfortable he felt here. For the first time in his life, he felt at home. The thought came as a shock. The last thing he needed was to feel content here, because it was just a matter of time before he'd have to move on. Settling in was a bad idea. And yet his gaze wandered again to the ranch house. He saw the light come on in Delaney's bedroom as he rolled out his bedroll and lay down. Just the thought of her made him ache in his loins—and his heart. A dangerous place to hurt, he realized with regret, because Delaney Lawson was the one woman he didn't dare believe he could ever have. And he'd never wanted a woman the way he wanted her.

He closed his eyes, letting sleep numb desire, memories of Delaney soothe his growing need for her.

Her scream brought him upright. The gunshot right after the scream brought him to his feet, pistol in hand. He raced toward the house. The light was still on in Delaney's bedroom, the house eerily silent.

He hit the unlocked front door, throwing it open. "Delaney!" No answer. He bounded up the stairs, two at a time, his heart in his throat. Fear made his chest hurt with each ragged breath. Fear of what he'd find. Fear that he'd just lost something he'd never really had, never even tried to have. But desperately wanted. Now more than ever.

Pistol ready, he burst into Delaney's bedroom.

Chapter Fourteen

Delaney stood in her nightgown at the side of the bed, a .45 clutched in her right hand, as she stared down at a huge rattlesnake coiled in the covers.

Cooper lunged forward, ready to kill the rattler, only to find it had already been blown away in one fatal shot. Relief rushed through his veins, making him weak. He fought to still his pounding heart as he tucked his pistol into the back of his jeans. He gently took the .45 from Delaney's trembling hand and pulled her into his arms, realizing as his chest made contact with her thin nightgown that all he wore were his jeans.

"You didn't get bit?"

She shook her head against his bare chest.

"Who—"

"It doesn't matter," he said, holding her tighter. Like hell, it didn't. When he found the person who did this— "All that matters is that you're all right." He held her until her shaking stopped, until her breathing became slow and controlled again. He leaned back to look into her face.

"I hate snakes," she said, her eyes still wide, still full of fright, her face pale.

"I know. Come on. You can't stay here."

Cooper wasn't sure where to take her, but he wasn't about to leave her alone. He led her out to his camp.

"The camper's a mess, but if you wait just a minute—" She shook her head. "Or I could take you into town." Again she shook her head, but this time her gaze came up to meet his.

"Couldn't we just sleep under the stars tonight? Together."

He nodded as he stepped to her. Rubbing his hands along her bare shoulders, he pulled her to him. "Are you cold?" Why hadn't he thought to grab her a robe or some clothes. He hadn't noticed just how sheer her nightgown was until this moment. "I could get you a jacket—"

"Cooper."

He met her gaze. "I can't do this without telling you the truth about me."

"The look on your face when you burst into my bedroom, told me everything I need to know," she said, drawing him to her. "Whatever you have to tell me can wait."

"Delaney." She silenced him with a kiss. He swept her up into his arms and carried her over to his bedroll. Trailing kisses from her lips down her neck to the hollow between her breasts, he lowered her to the sleeping bag. The moon peaked over the mountain, covering them in silver. He pulled back to see that her nipples had hardened into dark tips beneath the thin silk of her nightgown. He covered one and then the other with his mouth, teasing both to hard points with his tongue, nibbling gently with his teeth. Delaney moaned and arched her full breasts against him. He slipped one strap from her shoulder, then the other. As he pulled down her gown to expose her bare breasts to the moonlight, desire coursed through his veins, so strong it stunned him.

"You are the most amazing woman, Delaney Lawson," he said, caressing her cheek. "And the most beautiful." She traced her fingers along his chest, feathering his nipples to hard peaks before she raised her mouth to each. He felt longing ripple through his body. He kissed her, relishing in the

sweet lushness of her mouth, the sensuous ripeness of
her lips.

"Oh, Cooper," she whispered as he cupped her breast in
his hand and lowered his mouth again to its hardened bud.
Watching her face, he saw her eyes ignite with a passion that
made him groan. She buried her hands in his hair, molding
her body to his, then ran her fingers down his bare skin, over
his taut nipples to his jeans. He groaned with a desperate need
as her fingers sought out the buttons on his Levi's.

THE MOONLIGHT bathed his body in silver as Delaney freed
Cooper of his jeans. His body was just as magnificent as
she'd envisioned it would be and just as filled with desire as
her own. Kneeling over her, he slipped her nightgown down
over her hips and tossed it away. For a moment he just explored her body with his eyes, a yearning in his expression
that fired her blood and warmed her skin. He ran his fingers
over her breasts, through the hollow of her stomach, to gently
touch the swollen need between her legs. She reached up to
him, aching to feel his bare skin pressed against hers. Aching
to feel him inside her, buried deep within her. She opened
her thighs to allow his touch to explore her. He groaned as
if just the sight of her and her obvious desire for him would
be his undoing. His touch brought pleasure. And the desperate craving for more of him.

"Please," she whispered, arching her body up to tempt
his.

He smiled as she reached for him. Slowly he lowered himself to her, kissing her, teasing her. She felt his skin, hot and
smooth, then the hard fire of his desire. She cupped his buttocks with her hands, urging him deeper inside her. He filled
her with heat, fire, strength and power. He looked down at
her, wonder in his eyes. And love. Delaney wrapped her arms
around him, pressed her breasts to his chest and let him fill
her with satisfaction, again and again until the moon reached

its zenith and she felt him come to her, hot and sweet and fulfilled. She lay spent in his arms, staring up at the stars overhead, breathing in the sweet night air, smiling.

"That was...incredible," Cooper said beside her.

She kissed his bare shoulder. "Unbelievable."

He laughed and raised himself up on one elbow. His fingers gently circled her nipple. "Unbelievable." His fingers stopped. His gaze found hers and held it. "I've never felt anything like that. Ever."

She smiled, as shaken as he was by what had happened between them tonight. But equally afraid to admit just what it had meant to her. When she looked away, he turned her, spooning her against him, his arms wrapped around her.

"Sweet dreams, Delaney Lawson," he whispered against her bare neck.

She snuggled against him and closed her eyes, pushing aside any thoughts of the future, savoring instead the happiness she felt just being in his arms in the moonlight.

Delaney awoke in Cooper's arms to find the sun coming up over the Big Belt Mountains. She lay there, looking up at the blue sky through the pine boughs overhead with a contentment she had never felt before.

"Good morning," Cooper said next her.

She smiled over at him. "Good morning."

His kiss was sweet and sensuous, stirring emotions in her like a melting pot. She felt his strength and his tenderness, the smoothness of his naked skin and the roughness of his beard. The breeze stirred her hair, teasing the back of her neck as he had done with his kisses. His lips explored her body. She came to him with a willingness that made him laugh with pleasure. He smiled down at her as he satisfied her fantasies, as well as her desires, in the early-morning sunlight.

"Is there anything I can say to make you change your mind about riding in this rodeo?" Delaney asked later as she leaned on one elbow and looked down into his handsome face. Memories of their lovemaking felt as warm as the morning sun that now streamed through the pines.

"I can't think of anything." He grinned and kissed her nose. "But I wish I *could*." She thought he wasn't as cocky as he normally was. Maybe he had the sense to be worried about this ride today. But not the sense to cancel it, she reminded herself. She brushed back her hair from her face in frustration.

He gazed up at her. "I hope you won't be there to see me make a fool of myself."

She glanced at the horizon, now golden in the sunlight. "Don't worry, I gave up rodeos years ago. Along with cowboys who ride in them," she said, eyes narrowed.

He raised an eyebrow and pulled her to him. "I thought maybe a good night's sleep would help your disposition."

"You mean the way a good night's sleep helped your good sense? And there's nothing wrong with my disposition, either!" But she gave in to his embrace, letting him mold his body to hers, relishing the feel of him, the scent of his skin, the taste of him.

He grinned at her. Sometimes she forgot how handsome he was, and it startled her that just looking at him could elicit so much feeling within her. His gaze grazed her face as lightly as a kiss. He thumbed her nipple to a hard, throbbing point, then sucked at it for a moment, sending waves of desire racing through her again. Could she ever get enough of this man? She doubted it.

"Delaney, we need to talk," he said, letting go of her to gaze into her eyes.

"Buck could come up the road any minute," she lied as she pulled away from him to pick up his flannel shirt. Turning her back to him, she pulled the shirt on, hugging herself against what he might want to talk about. She'd seen the seriousness in his eyes and knew in her heart, it wasn't going to be good news.

When she glanced over her shoulder, Cooper was watching her, a frown on his face. And that's when she noticed the scar on his thigh. It seemed more like a bull had gored him than a bronc had stomped him. But either way, the scar was just another reminder of who Cooper McLeod really was. A rodeo cowboy.

"And you have to get to the rodeo if you're going to find that barred-shoe horse." She didn't like the edge to her voice but couldn't seem to control it. Just the thought of Cooper riding Hell's Fire brought back memories of the rodeos her mother used to take her to when she was a child.

"I once loved seeing my father ride," she said quietly, not understanding her need to tell him about her secret pain. "Then one day I saw him get gored by a bull. It was the first time I understood why my mother was often sick to her stomach before Hank's rides."

"Is that when you gave up rodeo? And rodeo cowboys?" he asked, shooting her a teasing grin.

"Yes, McLeod. I hated the rodeo after that. It terrifies me." The grin disappeared from his face. His eyes darkened as he realized how serious she was. "My father tried everything to get me to come see him again. But I never did." It opened a fissure between them that the years made into a canyon. And now she'd fallen for a rodeo cowboy, a rodeo cowboy with that same kind of good looks and easy charm and that same need to ride rough stock and risk his fool neck.

"I'm sorry," Cooper said softly. "I didn't know."

She turned away and finished buttoning up the shirt.

"I don't like the idea of you being here alone," he said after a moment.

"I won't be," she said, looking around for her nightgown. "I'm going to Butte to see Marguerite Drummond."

"Ty's mother?"

She nodded as she picked up her gown from where Cooper had tossed it the night before. Her skin warmed with the memory. "If my father's will leaving everything to Ty is a forgery, then I would imagine she's in on it. I need to find out for myself."

He stood up and pulled on his jeans. "And you think Ty's mother is just going to admit that to you?"

She made a face at him. "No, but talking to her should at least give me an idea of what I'm up against."

His look held both sympathy and worry. "You sure you want to meet your father's ex-mistress alone? If you wait, I'd go with you."

She nodded, realizing how much she'd like that but at the same time knowing she needed to do this alone. She couldn't depend on this rodeo cowboy. Thinking she could would be a terrible mistake. He was riding in a rodeo today. Who knows where he'd be tomorrow. Last night and this morning hadn't changed that.

"Thanks, McLeod, but I'll be all right. You'd better worry about your own neck around Jared Kincaid and Hell's Fire." She shook her head at him, fighting sudden tears. "So help me, McLeod, if you go and get yourself killed—"

He grinned and pulled her to him. Carefully he planted a kiss on her lips. "For luck." He held her for a moment longer. "Be careful."

She nodded and broke the physical connection between them as she turned and walked away. When she reached the house she touched her fingers to her lips. She just hoped he was right about the kiss. They both needed luck today.

COOPER DROVE to the Kincaid ranch thinking about Delaney. And their lovemaking. He felt shaky and unsure of himself. This morning he was all set to tell her everything about him. But she'd stopped him. And now he wasn't sure where he stood with her. He'd wanted more after their lovemaking. As much as he couldn't believe it himself, he wanted a relationship. Not some one-night stand under the stars. Yet he'd gotten the impression from Delaney this morning that's all she wanted.

He shook his head, thinking of the times that was all he'd offered a woman. And now the shoe was on the other foot and he didn't like it one bit.

The turnoff to Kincaid Ranches wasn't far past Nelson, Montana, the cribbage capital of the world. Nelson, a town of only two houses, wasn't even a wide spot in the road. Kincaid Ranches ran along the western edge of the Rockin' L. Cooper drove up into the ranch yard, not surprised to see it filled with other rigs. According to Delaney, the annual Kincaid Ranches Rodeo had begun as a little ego thing for Jared, but had grown since he started buying rough stock and inviting circuit cowboys.

Cooper recognized Ty's beat-up old pickup and Buck's rig. Angel was leaning against the front fender, looking bored. As she saw him pull up, recognition in her expression, she pushed herself off the truck and headed into the crowd before Cooper could get out of his pickup. Cooper had to smile. So she'd remembered where she'd seen him before. Maybe Jamison was right. If she was a reporter, investigating Rattlesnake Range on the Rockin' L, then she didn't want her cover blown any more than Cooper did. For the same reason, she wasn't going to say anything about him and Delaney visiting her cabin. "What a tangled web we weave," he thought as he got out of his pickup.

Cooper knew he didn't have a lot of time, so he started with the horse barn—a huge expensive thing with an arena in the center. It appeared Jared Kincaid didn't do anything halfway.

Cowboys wandered in and out of the barn. Cooper checked each stall, pretending just to be admiring the horses, but at the same time keeping an eye out for Jared. As the rodeo got into full swing, the barn emptied out. Cooper hurried, knowing he didn't have much time left.

At the second to last one, he leaned in to check a Pinto mare, when he heard a noise. The shaft of sunlight coming through the barn door at the other end of the building suddenly filled with shadows. Cooper ducked into the stall, squatting next to the Pinto. She stomped restlessly. He spoke softly to her and hoped she didn't kick him before he could get out.

"No more excuses," said a rough male voice.

"I told you—I'll get the money."

Cooper recognized that whine. Ty Drummond.

"You just have to give me a little more time."

"You've had more than enough time," said another deep voice.

Cooper edged his way up the side of the stall to peek over the side. Two large men in western wear had Ty between them. Even at this distance, Cooper recognized the threat in their voices, in their stances. He'd never seen the pair before and got the impression they weren't from around these parts.

"I can give you a little now." Ty dug into his jeans and pulled out a handful of bills. One of the men grabbed them.

Ty stumbled back. "I just need more time. You know I'm good for it."

The one man had finished counting the money. He swore and, without warning, buried his fist in Ty's stomach. Ty folded with a groan to the barn floor. The other kicked Ty in the side with his boot. Ty cried out and curled into a ball.

"Twenty-four hours, Drummond." The two turned and left.

Ty lay on the floor, sucking for breath between sobs. Slowly he pushed himself to his feet with one hand, holding his stomach with the other. He looked around to make sure no one had seen the incident, then straightened a little and walked out into the sunlight.

Gambling debts? Loan sharks? It really didn't make any difference. Ty Drummond had now become desperate and that made him more dangerous than ever, Cooper thought as he gave the Pinto a pat on the neck and stepped out of the stall. He couldn't help wondering where Ty had gotten the money he'd given the men.

He hurried down the row of stalls after Ty. At the doorway, Cooper hung back to watch Ty head straight for the ranch house—and Jared Kincaid. At Ty's knock, Jared came outside in the shade of the back porch. It was clear that the two were arguing. A moment later, Jared reached for his wallet, pulled out some bills and practically threw them at Ty.

Cooper shook his head. At least now he knew where Ty got his money. The question was, why was Jared giving it to him? Was Ty working for Kincaid Ranches? Jared always seemed to know everything that was going on with Delaney. Maybe Ty was being paid for information. Or maybe Ty was blackmailing the sheriff. But for what?

Cooper could hear the announcer in the outdoor arena as he started for the last stall. The calf roping was almost over. That meant Cooper didn't have much time before his ride. He wondered how Delaney was doing with Marguerite. He just hoped she'd find out something that would help her save the ranch from the likes of Ty Drummond.

Just as Cooper reached the stall containing a dark-colored quarter horse, a male voice asked, "Looking for any kind of horse in particular?"

"Just admiring yours," Cooper said, turning to flash Jared a grin. "This one appears fast." Unfortunately, it also didn't have a barred shoe.

Jared studied him with open suspicion. "I thought maybe you'd chickened out. You aren't hiding in here to keep from riding, are you?"

The insult raised Cooper's hackles. He laughed at the challenge he'd heard in Jared's voice. "If I was going to hide I can think of better places. The York Bar, for one. There's cold beer there and the people are friendlier.''

Jared actually laughed. ''You know, McLeod, I think I could grow to like you.''

Cooper doubted that. ''So,'' he said, turning away from the last stall with disappointment. He'd been so sure the horse with the barred shoe would be Jared's. ''Where's this bronc that no one can ride?''

Jared slapped him on the back companionably as they headed for the open doorway. ''Wait until you see Hell's Fire,'' he said, chuckling to himself. ''Just wait until you see him.''

MARGUERITE DRUMMOND worked at a place called Katie's Kut and Kurl on the hill in the center of downtown Butte, not far from the famous mile-deep, five-mile-across open pit mine.

The outside of the beauty shop was old brick much like the rest of the downtown area. But unlike the many empty buildings with their dirty windows and sad-looking interiors, the Kut and Kurl had a festive look.

Delaney stepped through the door, not sure what to expect. The walls were done in bright hot pinks and purples, the stations in striped pastels to match. The place smelled of perm solution and mint shampoo. There were six stations, but only three of them were busy. Delaney had called ahead to be sure Marguerite would be working. She was.

''I'm here to see Marguerite Drummond,'' Delaney told the young receptionist, eyeing the three women at the stations. She had an idea what Marguerite would look like based on her father's ''type.'' Her gaze stopped on a tall bleached blonde in tight stretch pants who was talking fast as she cut an older woman's hair.

''Marguerite!'' the receptionist called back.

A small dark-haired woman in her early fifties turned in

the middle of a customer's shampoo. Her hair and dress were understated; her look soft and assured. Her fingers slowed, then stopped, as her gaze settled on Delaney. She turned on the water and rinsed the soap from her hands. She said something to the older woman in the tub, then asked one of the other hairdressers to take over for her.

Marguerite smiled as she approached the counter. "I wondered when I'd finally get to meet you." She extended her hand. "I've heard so much about you, Delaney."

Delaney took the woman's hand, too surprised to speak at first. "You know who I am?"

"Of course. Come on, let's get out of here," she said, taking off her trim white uniform jacket.

They walked down the street to a small café. It wasn't until the waitress had set two cups of coffee in front of them that Delaney asked, "How do you know me?"

Marguerite looked down in her coffee for a moment. "When you were a baby, your father started showing off pictures of you. And he and I kept in touch over the years."

Delaney shook her head. He'd showed pictures of his family to his mistress?

"You were the light of his life," she said, smiling at Delaney.

She'd always thought rodeoing was the only thing that had meant anything to Hank Lawson. She tried to imagine him showing off pictures of her and couldn't. "I can't understand why you waited more than twenty-five years to tell my father he had a son."

Marguerite shook her head. "Hank would have felt compelled to do something honorable like marry me. He was already married and he'd proven he wasn't good at it." A sadness filled her brown eyes. "The truth is, I didn't want Ty coming up like his father, riding rough stock in rodeos. And I knew how much your father wanted a son—" She realized her remark had hurt Delaney. "I'm sorry."

"Everyone knows how disappointed Hank was when he didn't get a son," Delaney said, fighting the familiar anger and hurt. But that wasn't what she'd driven to Butte to talk about. "Based on Ty's age, I assume my father hooked up with you not long after I was born, about the time my mother became ill and couldn't have any more children."

Marguerite stared down into her coffee. "When I first met Hank, I didn't know about you or your mother." She smiled in memory. "Hank was so handsome and he could turn on the charm like water from a faucet. But that wasn't what appealed to me. It was the sadness in his eyes. A deep hurt that at the time I couldn't explain. It wasn't until later, when he told me about you and your mother, that I understood."

"He killed my mother, you know," Delaney said, unable to hide her anger. "When she got sick, he started staying away from the ranch even longer. My mother blamed herself for his rodeoing, for his infidelities. She believed that if she'd given him a son, he would have stayed on the ranch."

Marguerite shook her head. "Nothing could have kept Hank on the ranch, honey. Not a dozen sons. He was so young when he met your mother and fell in love with her. He thought he could change, that he could be what she needed and wanted. When you were born…" She hesitated. "He said it was the most amazing day of his life. But also the scariest. He just couldn't face the responsibility. I think that's why he wished you were a boy. He felt you wouldn't need him as much."

Delaney thought of all the times she'd needed her father and he hadn't been there. "He dumped the ranch on my mother and me. After my mother died, I almost lost the place and he still didn't care enough to come home."

Marguerite took a sip of her coffee. "He blamed himself for your mother's illness, and just the sight of her made him feel—"

"Guilty?" Delaney asked. "He *should* have felt guilty."

"I was going to say *inadequate*. He couldn't make her well and he didn't know how to make her happy."

Delaney laughed bitterly. "He didn't want to."

Marguerite reached across the table and took her hand. "You're wrong about that, honey. He loved her. He just couldn't live up to what he thought your mother expected of him."

Delaney freed her hand. "Hank Lawson was a selfish, inconsiderate man who didn't have the backbone to do anything but take the easy way out."

Tears filled the older woman's eyes as she pulled her hand back. "I'm sorry you feel that way about your father. Not that I blame you. But he loved you more than his own life."

"Is that why he left the ranch to Ty?" Delaney demanded, hot, angry tears blurring her vision. "That's how my father showed how much he loved me?" She'd finally voiced her greatest fear. That her father *had* left everything to Ty, that Ty wasn't lying about the will. "My father knew what the ranch meant to me. He knew how hard I've worked to save it. And he left it to a stranger he didn't even know. His *son*."

Marguerite cradled the cup in her hands, her eyes downcast. "I'd always hoped that Hank would never find out about Ty."

"How did he?" Delaney demanded, trying to still all the years of anger at her father.

"When I found myself pregnant with Ty, I broke it off with your father. I told Ty his father was a rodeo cowboy, a bull rider, but that he'd been killed. When Ty started rodeoing just to spite me, he met Hank and found out that Hank and I used to date. Hank and I have seen each other off and on for years. I think Ty always suspected Hank was his father—he found some old letters. Just recently he got a call from someone who had uncovered the truth."

"Do you know who?" Delaney asked, realizing it didn't really matter.

Marguerite shook her head. "I should have kept lying."

"So Ty went to my father with the truth?" Delaney said, beginning to see what could have happened. "When was this?"

"Just days before Hank was killed."

Delaney felt her heart break as she realized that for Hank, finding out he had a son would be a dream come true. "So Hank changed his will?"

"I guess so. I wasn't there when Hank made the new will, but Ty showed it to me. It was in Hank's writing. I'm sorry. I never wanted anything from Hank."

"But Ty does. He wants everything, but just for the money. I'm sure he plans to sell the ranch as quickly as possible."

Marguerite looked away for a moment as if the truth were too hard to take. "He feels cheated because Hank was never a father to him." She smiled through fresh tears. "I know, Hank was never a father to either of his children." She took a long breath and let it out slowly. "I wish Ty were different. I know now that I spoiled him and that's probably why he's never wanted to work for anything."

"Maybe he just took after his father," Delaney said, getting to her feet. "I'd hoped the will Ty had from my father was a forgery. I know now that my father could have changed his will to leave everything to his newly found son."

"I wish that weren't the case," she said, genuinely sorry. "Ty has no business with your ranch."

Delaney stood for a moment, not knowing what to say to the woman. "Thank you for telling me about my…father."

She smiled, tears in her eyes. "He loved you, Delaney. I know he did things that hurt you, but he never stopped loving you. Or your mother."

Delaney left Marguerite sitting in the café, staring down into her coffee. She'd wanted to hate the woman, but instead she'd ended up liking her. And feeling sorry for her. Marguerite had just been another one of Hank Lawson's casualties.

COOPER CLIMBED UP the side of the chute and swore when he saw the rank horse waiting for him. He'd seen his share of horses like Hell's Fire. Halter-broken rebels with a strong inclination to come apart whenever anyone tried to ride them. They were horses that just plain didn't like to be ridden. And they'd fight from hell to breakfast to throw any rider with the stupidity to get on them. The good news was that very few attempted to attack a thrown rider. But Cooper figured Hell's Fire could prove the exception. This horse was a man killer.

He stared at the horse and felt a shot of pure adrenaline. Bronc riding was one of the most dangerous of rodeo sports. Also one of the most thrilling. He felt that old pull and admitted he hadn't agreed to this just to check Kincaid's horses. He wanted to ride again. Delaney had been right about that, he realized guiltily.

He'd just finished throwing his saddle on Hell's Fire and cinching it down, when a cowboy came by to tell him Jared wanted to see him at the announcer's booth. Cooper wondered why Jared would want to see him now, not long before his ride. Probably just to goad him a little more.

But when he got to the booth, he was told that Jared had left. Cooper heard his number come up to ride. He hurried back to find Jared sitting on the side of the chute above Hell's Fire, smiling. Delaney was right. The bastard was hoping Cooper got himself killed.

"Just wanted to wish you luck," Jared said.

Cooper doubted that, but he shook Jared's outstretched hand anyway. The hand was a little clammy and Cooper wondered what Jared had to be nervous about. Losing the bet? Or having a cowboy he disliked ride his so far unridden horse eight seconds for a win?

As Cooper eased himself down on the saddle, he knew this was going to be the ride of his life. Oblivious to the crowd that had gathered in Jared's covered bandstand, he turned his attention to the horse breathing heavily beneath him. Cooper readied himself. And gave the signal. The chute opened, and just as he'd expected, Hell's Fire came apart like the wild beast he was.

Chapter Fifteen

Delaney hadn't been able to keep Cooper far from her thoughts all morning. As she drove down Beaver Creek Road toward the ranch, she glanced at her watch and realized the rodeo would still be going on. She wondered if Cooper had ridden yet. Her stomach churned at the thought of him on the mean bronc.

"Damn you, McLeod." Against her will, she turned into the Kincaid ranch. The last thing she wanted was to see Cooper ride, but the thought of going home and waiting to hear what happened was too much for her. Her fears about Cooper's welfare outweighed her fears of rodeoing. She had to know he was all right.

She parked and walked toward the rodeo arena. The crowd in the bandstand were on their feet and going wild. She hurried, fear making her heart pound and her breath come at a premium. Delaney went to the end of the arena where the cowboys hung out and climbed the corral railing in time to see Cooper being tossed around on the back of Hell's Fire. The horse twisted and turned, its nostrils flaring.

She closed her eyes, unable to stand it any longer. Then she heard the combined gasp of the crowd and opened her eyes to see Cooper hanging off the side of the horse. Something was wrong with his saddle. It had slipped and Cooper— He was hung up in the saddle. He couldn't get off the bronc!

Hell's Fire was dragging him and still bucking, tossing Cooper like a ragged doll.

"Oh, we got a problem here, folks," the announcer said over the screaming crowd. "Let's get that cowboy off that bronc."

Two cowboys on horseback were trying to free Cooper from the bucking bronc. Delaney heard the scream but didn't realize it was coming from her own throat until one of the cowboys riding alongside the bronc finally freed Cooper. He lay on the ground without moving. She stared at his prone body, hating him, loving him, praying he would survive so she could fire him and run him out of the county so she never had to see him again.

"Is he going to be all right, boys?" the announcer asked. Several cowboys had jumped down from the arena fence and run over to kneel beside Cooper.

Suddenly the cowboys stepped back. Cooper moved. First one leg, then the other. He sat up, shaking his head as if to clear it. Then he grinned and got slowly to his feet.

"It looks like he's going to be all right, folks," the announcer said over the loudspeaker. "Let's give Cooper McLeod a big hand. That was one heck of a ride."

Cooper limped toward the fence, banging his hat on his leg as he walked. Dust rose from his boots, from the hat. He spotted Delaney. His eyes widened in surprise. He smiled, then shrugged.

She glared at him, so angry that she'd witnessed him almost getting killed, so relieved he was alive. "McLeod," she said through clenched teeth. "You scared the living— I've a mind to fire you on the spot. Or shoot you."

"I'm glad to see you, too, boss," he said, and pulled her into his arms.

COOPER HELD HER, enjoying the feel of her in his arms but also needing her strength. He was still wobbly and shook-up.

But alive. Alive and unhurt. It had been a close call, one he wouldn't forget for sometime to come.

It took him a moment to realize that Delaney was crying. He held her tighter. "It's all right now," he whispered. "It's all right."

"Oh, Cooper, if you'd been killed, I'd never have forgiven you," she cried against his chest.

"I'm sorry, sweetheart." He realized then that the announcer was calling his name. He turned to listen. Delaney tensed in his arms.

"They're offering you another ride," she said, growing deathly pale. "It looks like your saddle had a weak cinch."

His saddle hadn't had a weak cinch when he'd put it on Hell's Fire. He closed his eyes, cursing his own stupidity. Jared. He'd left his rig to go find the rancher. No wonder Jared had been so nervous when Cooper had found him by the chute. The bastard had done something to his cinch!

"Well, cowboy, do you want another chance at Hell's Fire?" the announcer asked over the loudspeaker.

Cooper knew now he could ride Hell's Fire for a win, and the desire rushed through him. He wanted to show Jared up for the rat he was. But mostly he wanted to prove to himself he could ride the bronc.

Delaney stepped out of his arms. She wiped at the tears streaming down her face as she looked up at him. "You have to do it, don't you?"

He stared into her eyes, suddenly struck by what she'd given him just coming to watch him. She'd admitted to him how deathly frightened she was of rodeo. Yet she'd come to see him ride. And at what price? She'd witnessed him almost get killed on Hell's Fire. He couldn't do it to her again. Not ever. And he realized he'd just ridden in his last rodeo.

He motioned to the announcer's box that he didn't want to ride again, then pulled Delaney back into his arms, hugging her tightly as his heart swelled with love for her. Love. He didn't even put up an argument with himself. Somehow he'd fallen in love with this woman and he was tired of kidding himself that he hadn't.

One of the arena cowboys rode by and placed Cooper's saddle on the top fence rail. "Tough luck," the guy said as he rode off.

Delaney pulled free and reached up to take an end of the broken cinch. "This cinch wasn't weakened. It was cut!" She turned to face Cooper, her eyes blazing. "I knew it. Jared. Jared did this. He tried to kill you!"

"I'd be careful making accusations against the sheriff," Jared said through gritted teeth as he walked up behind them.

"Damn you, Jared. If I can prove you cut that cinch—"

"*If* his cinch was cut, anyone could have done it," Jared said to Delaney calmly. "I think you ought to take another ride," he said, turning to Cooper.

"No, thanks." Cooper circled Delaney's waist with his arm, pulling her to him. He told himself holding her was just so he could keep her quiet, but he knew he was also staking claim to her, just in case Jared had any doubts. "You come to collect on the bet?"

Jared chewed at his cheek as he let his eyes take in the two of them. Like Delaney, he seemed to be trying to contain a lot of anger. "Forget the money, McLeod. I have more important things on my mind right now." He settled his gaze on Delaney. Cooper could feel her trembling with rage.

"I think you'd better calm down, Del," Jared said, his tone condescending as usual.

Cooper felt her tighten like a rubber band about to snap. "Jared, I found out the other night just what kind of man you are, but you've outdone yourself today," she said through gritted teeth. "You could have killed Cooper."

He raised an eyebrow. "'Cooper,' is it now, Del?" He sighed. "Well, that just makes it all the harder for me to tell you what I've found out about your cowhand here."

Cooper felt his gut tighten as Delaney jerked free of his hold and fired herself at Jared.

"I don't know what you've dug up, *Sheriff,* but I don't want to hear it," she said, pointing a finger into his face. "I don't want to hear *anything* you have to say ever again." She stomped toward her pickup.

Jared smiled at Cooper. "Too bad. You didn't ride the horse for a win. And you lost the girl, as well." He turned away to call after Delaney. "I think you'd best hear this, Del," he said, raising his voice to follow her retreating footsteps. "Your boyfriend here is an ex-con. He's got a police record."

Delaney had stopped at her pickup, her hand on the door handle. Cooper saw her stiffen at the news.

"And guess what he was sent up for, Del?" he called after her. "Conspiracy to defraud. He's a con man, Del. A con man and a rodeo bum. So who do you think is behind your problems on the ranch now, Del?"

She jerked open the pickup door. Cooper fought the need to bury his fist in Kincaid's smiling face. Instead he ran after Delaney, grabbing her arm as she started to get into her pickup.

"At least let me explain," he pleaded. "I tried to tell you this morning—"

"McLeod, the best thing you can do right now is to leave me the hell alone." She shook loose of his hold on her arm and climbed in to slam the pickup door in his face.

He stepped back as she started the engine and popped the clutch, leaving him standing in a cloud of dust.

"Like I said, it just hasn't been your day, McLeod," the sheriff said behind him.

Cooper clenched his fists, weighing the options Jared was offering him. Jail time for assaulting a sheriff—but the satisfaction of cramming the bastard's teeth down his throat first.

DELANEY WAS STILL shaking as she started past Buck's place
and noticed a strange horse in the corral beside her father's
old rodeoing trailer. She stopped, surprised because she'd
thought Buck would be at Kincaid's rodeo, and even more
surprised to realize that the horse wasn't one of hers. It was
a quarter horse, and not a very good one from what she could
tell. Buck was standing beside the corral when she got out
of her truck.

"Did you buy a horse?" she asked, walking over to the
corral to take a look.

Buck's mind must have been a million miles away, because
he hadn't heard her approach. He jumped now, a startled look
in his wide eyes as if she were the last person he'd expected
to see. "I thought you'd gone to Butte."

"I did," she said, climbing up the corral railing to get a
better view of the horse. It was an older quarter horse and
had a Kincaid Ranches brand on it.

Buck joined her on the fence. "I got it for Angel."

"She could have ridden any of the horses at the ranch,"
Delaney said, a little hurt he'd bought a horse from Jared
Kincaid, especially when it wasn't necessary.

"Angel saw this horse over at Kincaid's while she was
interviewing him about his ranch and just fell in love with
it," Buck said nervously. "I tried to talk her into a Morgan,
but she just had to have this one."

Delaney looked over at him. "I didn't know Angel rode."

"She doesn't. Yet," Buck said. "I'm going to teach her."

It struck Delaney again how different Buck had been acting
lately. She blamed Angel and hoped that when this woman
broke this poor man's heart, she didn't break his spirit, as
well.

"It's not a bad-looking horse," Delaney lied. She hoped
Buck hadn't paid much for it. And wondered why a man with
such good horse sense would buy a horse like this from someone like Jared Kincaid. Because Angel had fallen in love with

it, she reminded herself. Men! Love must make them stupid. She thought about Cooper and how she felt about him, and decided there was no doubt about it—love made a person too stupid for words.

"Delaney?"

Just the thought of Cooper brought back the mix of emotions she felt for the man. She'd gone from waking up in his arms to fearing he was dead. From relief that he was all right to wanting to kill him. If this was love—

It wasn't until he'd passed on that second ride that she'd admitted her true feelings. She would never have acknowledged them to anyone, let alone herself. But in that moment when she'd seen him decide not to ride because of her, knowing how much he'd wanted to, how much he needed to prove himself on that stupid horse, she knew she loved him.

Loved a rodeo cowboy. A rodeo cowboy with a police record. Conspiracy to defraud. Cooper McLeod was not only an ex-con, he was a con man. Boy, could she pick 'em. Admittedly he'd tried to tell her something last night and again this morning, but she hadn't let him. Not that she believed he was the one who was causing her troubles on the ranch. Admittedly he could have orchestrated the rock slide and the potshot with some help, but Delaney didn't believe it, not in her heart. She just hoped love wasn't as blind as Buck made it appear.

"Delaney? Is there anything I can do for you?" Buck asked, obviously antsy. "I was just on my way into town to see Angel, but if you need something—"

She shook her head. "I just stopped to see your new horse. How long have you had him?"

"A few days." Buck scratched at his jaw. He couldn't seem to meet her gaze. She figured he felt guilty buying a horse from Kincaid and not her. Heck, Delaney would have given him his pick of horses for Angel if she'd known he was looking for a horse. She could feel her ranch manager pulling away from the Rockin' L like a teenager getting ready to move out of the family home. She wondered how long it would be before he gave notice and moved into town with Angel.

"You sure I can't do something for you?" Buck asked again. He seemed reluctant to leave her there alone. He glanced at his watch.

"Go on and see Angel," she said. She blinked, did a double take as she looked over at him. "I thought Angel was with you at the rodeo earlier," she said, thinking she had seen Angel in the crowd when she first got to Jared's.

Buck nodded, fidgeting with a button on his shirt. "She had to leave."

"Well, go on. I might take another look through the stuff my father kept in the trailer," she said, knowing she wouldn't. Buck had helped her go through it, hunting for her father's will right after Hank died. It wasn't something she wanted to do again. Nor did she think even finding the original will would probably do any good anyway. But maybe she'd search for it. She knew she was just looking for an excuse not to go back to the ranch house because she was going to have to deal with Cooper.

"I guess I'd better get going—"

Buck stood for a moment as if part of him didn't want to leave but the other part was in a big hurry to get somewhere. She couldn't remember ever seeing him this nervous.

"If you need anything—"

As Buck walked off, she watched the quarter horse circle the small corral with Buck's horse, a Morgan she'd given him called Sugarfoot. It still bothered her that Buck had purchased a quarter horse, not a Morgan, for his girlfriend.

She heard Buck drive away and thought Jared must be laughing his behind off at Buck for buying this horse. Then she realized she couldn't care less about Jared, Angel's new horse or Buck's infatuation with the woman. What really worried her was what she going to do about Cooper. Shooting him had been her first thought. Firing him and running him off with a shotgun was her second. But her heart kept arguing for clemency on his behalf.

She took one last look at Buck's new horse, promising herself she'd never let love make her *that* blind, and started back toward her truck. That's when she noticed the horseshoe prints in the dirt near the corral. She stared down at the barred-shoe track, then turned to look back into the corral. It was full of barred-shoe tracks. And Delaney knew what she was going to find before she climbed into the corral with the quarter horse. Whoever had been riding this horse the last few days was the person who'd tried to kill her.

Chapter Sixteen

Cooper drove around for a while after he left Kincaid's, not sure where to go or what to do. He'd been cussing himself since Delaney had driven off, furious with him, not even giving him a chance to explain. Not that there was much explanation to give. He just wished he'd told her the truth himself. Now he figured he'd blown it with her. It didn't make him feel any better that he'd made a halfhearted effort to tell her the truth. And now if she was to find out he worked for Rattlesnake Range— He rubbed his thigh, the gunshot wound still fresh in his memory.

His head ached. From the rough ride on the bronc. From the look in Delaney's eyes. Damn. Cooper knew he was avoiding going back to the ranch because he didn't know what to say to her. There were so many things he needed to tell her, but he knew none of them would do any good right now. She would be just looking for any excuse to get him out of her life.

He should just pack up and move on. Delaney was bound to fire him the moment she laid eyes on him anyway. Why wait and have to see her face when she did? But as Cooper drove, he knew he couldn't just ride off into the sunset this time. He'd invested too much in this job. He laughed. He'd invested too much in this woman, more than he wanted to admit. And he couldn't leave her alone now to fend off Rattlesnake Range and whoever else might be after her and her ranch.

He headed for the York Bar. The last thing he wanted was a beer. But he did want to talk to Dude. He kept thinking about Dude and the sheriff. He'd seen little more than a look pass between Dude and Jared Kincaid. There was something between them, something that Cooper recognized. Trouble. And Cooper was just curious enough to try to find out what it was.

When he pushed open the door, he found the place was empty except for Dude, who was behind the bar washing glasses. Everyone was probably out at Kincaid's rodeo, where the beer was free along with the barbecue and barn dance.

"Wanna beer?" Dude asked, and continued his glass washing.

Cooper shook his head. "Why aren't you out at the Kincaid rodeo?"

Dude stopped, a wet, dirty glass in his hands as he shot Cooper a look. "I had to work."

"Really?" Cooper said, glancing around the bar as he took a stool. "I hope you can keep up the pace."

Dude laughed and shook his head. "Hey, man, it lets me catch up on my cleaning."

Cooper nodded. "Not that you would go out to Kincaid's even if you weren't working."

The bartender put down the glass and dried his hands. "Is there a point to this?"

"Look, I don't blame you for not wanting to get involved, but all I'm asking for is a little help," Cooper said. "There are things going on out on the Rockin' L. I'm just trying to find out who's behind them."

Dude washed a few more glasses in silence. Cooper figured he was wasting his time. He was an outsider and Dude acted scared.

"I don't know what you're looking for, all right?" Dude

said after a moment. "But the other night after you left, the sheriff was pretty happy with himself. Until the guy from the mining company came in."

"What guy from the mining company?" Cooper asked, his heart pounding a little faster.

Dude shrugged. "Some guy who's been around a few times. I overheard the sheriff arguing with him."

Cooper had a feeling Dude overheard a lot of conversations. "What were they arguing about?"

He appeared hesitant and Cooper wondered if he wanted money. Cooper started to reach for his wallet, when Dude stopped him.

"The sheriff pulled me over not long ago and read me the riot act. He thought I'd been drinking, but he was the one who was drunk. The guy's a loser."

"Yeah, Kincaid does have a way with people."

Dude flipped the bar rag onto his shoulder and leaned on the bar. "I heard what happened out at his ranch today." Bad news traveled fast. "I heard you almost got killed."

"I hate to think of it that way," Cooper said. He hated to think of it at all, especially when he remembered that Delaney had witnessed the whole thing. He'd never wanted to hurt her like that. "What were they arguing about?"

"The guy said that if Kincaid didn't take care of his end, the whole deal would be off. Then he left and Kincaid was real upset. That's when I decided to investigate the guy. I'd taken a check from him as a favor the day before but hadn't paid much attention. The guy was from Burton Mining Company."

Cooper had heard of it, a large company that was remining areas of the country. They dredged gulches that hadn't been mined for fifty years or more and chemically bleached the ore from the rocks. "Is there any mining going on around here now?"

Dude shook his head. "But there's been talk. That guy

from the mining company—when he was in earlier in the week, he was asking me a lot of questions about the Rockin' L and Delaney Lawson. He seemed to think her ranch was for sale.''

ALL THE WAY down the road, Delaney argued with herself over the barred-shoe horse. Somehow Jared had tricked Buck into buying the horse to shift the suspicion from himself to Buck. It was the only thing that made sense. But Buck's strange behavior the past few weeks made her have doubts she didn't like having. She'd known Buck all her life. He couldn't be responsible for her problems. He had no motive. If she sold the ranch or got killed, he'd be without a job. It wasn't as if he had the money to buy her ranch himself. And anyway, he'd been talking about marrying Angel and moving into town.

So why had he acted so strangely earlier? And why hadn't he wanted to leave her alone by the corral? She told herself Buck was in some kind of trouble. And if that was true—She knew what she had to do.

As Delaney drove to the ranch house, she passed Cooper's camp. His pickup was gone, but his horse trailer and Crazy Jack were still there. Her sudden relief brought tears to her eyes. In that instant, she realized he could have come back and cleared out before she got home. That would be the coward's way, and he'd already admitted he was a runner at heart. She told herself that if he'd taken off without even a word, she would have tracked him down. Tracked him down and what? she wondered. Tell him that she loved him? Fear made her heart ache. The last thing she wanted was to see Cooper get into his rig and drive off. But maybe in the long run it would be better for her heart, she tried to convince herself.

The sun had burned down to streaks of pinks and oranges against the mountains by the time she'd changed her clothes, putting on a dark shirt and jeans, tying her hair back in a ponytail. Instead of her usual western hat, she pulled on a dark old western hat of her father's. As she studied her image in the mirror, she couldn't help but think about what Marguerite had told her about her father. The anger she'd felt had lost a lot of its potency. If only he hadn't left the ranch to Ty, she thought. If he actually had, she reminded herself. Having the will proven a forgery was her only hope.

She glanced at her watch, then outside at the sky. It would be dusk before long. Delaney went out to saddle her horse, figuring it was going to be a long night, wondering where in the hell Cooper was.

THE FRONT DOOR of the York Bar slammed open with a bang and Buck stomped in, an obvious black mood hanging around him like a storm cloud. Cooper groaned.

Buck was the last person he wanted to see right now. He figured the ranch manager had heard he was an ex-con and had come looking for a fight. With Delaney mad enough at Buck for hiring a rodeo cowboy, she'd be real unhappy that Buck had hired an ex-con. And poor Buck wouldn't be able to tell her the truth, that he hadn't hired anyone. So the way Cooper figured it, Buck would want to take out his frustration on Cooper. And Cooper just wasn't in the mood.

Buck strode up to the bar. He didn't even act as if he noticed Cooper. "Have you seen Angel?" he demanded of Dude.

"Angel?" Dude frowned.

Cooper wondered why Dude was pulling Buck's chain. It didn't seem like a good idea right now.

"Blond. About this high." Buck held his hand out at his shoulder. "I've been in here with her a few times."

"Oh, Angel. The writer." Dude smiled. "She was in earlier. Had a couple of drinks, then got a phone call from some guy and left."

That was definitely not what Buck had wanted to hear. He

glared at Dude for a moment. Cooper got the distinct impression he was deciding whether to pull Dude over the bar and pound him. Then Buck slammed a barstool out of his way and stomped back out, banging the door the same way he'd come in.

"Whew!" Cooper said, relieved Buck hadn't gotten into it with him.

He saw that Dude had picked up a baseball bat from behind the bar. He now put it back and smiled. "That cowboy is spoiling for a fight. He'll be back and meaner than ever when he finds out what's going on." He laughed at Cooper's puzzled expression. "Woman problem. It seems his Angel is keeping company with another man. You sure I can't get you a beer? It's on the house today."

Cooper declined the offer. "Any idea who the other guy is?"

Dude shook his head. "Voice was familiar, but I couldn't place it. Wasn't a great connection."

Cooper thanked Dude for his help.

"Just get Kincaid if he's the one," he said. "I don't trust that guy."

The feeling was mutual.

DELANEY SETTLED IN the draw above Buck's place, hiding among the ponderosas and rocks. She knew it was foolish. Buck might not be back until the wee hours of morning. And even then, he might do nothing more than go to bed for the night. Cooper galloped across her thoughts, making her groan. She couldn't help but wonder where he was and what he was doing. Maybe he was waiting for the cloak of darkness to sneak back so he could retrieve his gear. If that was his plan, she thought she would enjoy staking out his place more than Buck's. It would be worth it just to see the surprise on his face when she stepped out of the darkness and caught him.

For a moment, she wondered if he could leave that easily. She remembered their lovemaking under the pines, the stars overhead, the night breeze caressing their bodies. He'd held her so tenderly, she thought she'd seen love in his eyes as he'd bent to kiss her, his body warm and strong against hers—

She fanned herself with her hat and chased Cooper from her thoughts. Leaning back against a smooth rock, she stared up at the sky. The evening was warm. A gentle breeze stirred the pine boughs over her head. Night threatened to the east like a dark summer storm. It was summer evenings like this that made people do crazy things like fall in love, Delaney thought. Because for the life of her, she couldn't keep Cooper out of her thoughts, not the way he kissed her, not the way he held her, not the way he made love to her. Or the way he'd saved her life, the way he tried to protect her from herself, she thought with a smile, or the way he'd tried to tell her the truth about him.

Sitting up, she tried to concentrate on the corral below her. This was stupid. Surely she could have come up with a better plan if her mind wasn't so cluttered with unwanted thoughts of rodeo cowboys.

That's when she heard the pickup coming up the road. Of course her first thought was Cooper. He was finally headed home to face the music. Then she realized it wasn't Cooper at all but Buck. And he was alone, she noticed, as he pulled into his yard. He slammed the pickup door. The sound echoed up the draw. She expected him to head for the trailer. To her surprise, he headed for the corral, and instead of saddling his own horse, he saddled the barred-shoe horse.

With an aching heart, Delaney mounted her mare and followed at a discreet distance as Buck rode up into the foothills. It took her a moment to realize where he was headed. Johnson Gulch.

DAYLIGHT STILL HUNG over the treetops, but deep in the pines and rocks of the gulch, dusk settled in as Delaney followed Buck up the creek toward the lake. It didn't surprise her that he was taking a longer route that kept him hidden in the trees and rocky outcroppings. Her heart argued Buck's innocence, but her mind was busy compiling a list of suspicious facts that made him look guilty right now.

She wasn't far from the lake when she realized she'd lost Buck. Dismounting, she studied the ground, knowing it would soon be too dark in the pines to track him. That's when she heard the sound—not in front of her—but behind her. Quickly she pulled her horse in back of a large boulder and stood listening. A single rider. Coming cautiously up the mountainside. Tracking her. Could Buck have circled around? She pulled her rifle from its scabbard and crouched beside the rock nearest her trail to wait.

A few minutes later, she heard the horse approaching slowly. She waited until horse and rider came alongside her before she lunged out of her hiding place and jerked the surprised rider from the horse. The rider hit the ground with a *fffft*. She pointed her rifle at the slumped form and heard a familiar oath.

"McLeod?" she whispered angrily. "What are you doing here?"

He looked up, grimacing either out of pain or at the sight of her. She wasn't sure which. "Tracking you. What are *you* doing here?"

"I *was* following Buck until I heard you behind me."

"Buck?" He was surprised. "He's the one riding the barred-shoe horse?"

She nodded and lowered the rifle. "He says he bought the horse for Angel a few days ago—from Jared."

Cooper let out a low whistle but didn't say anything, and she was grateful. She didn't want to have to argue Buck's innocence. She really wasn't up to it.

"I've lost his trail," she admitted none too happily.

Cooper shoved back his hat and grinned at her. "He doubled back on you about a quarter mile ago."

She glared at him. "Did one of your criminal friends in jail teach you to track?" she demanded, trying to keep her voice down.

He winced as her remark hit right on target. "Actually, my father taught me." He got to his feet, meeting her direct gaze with one of his own. "You want to discuss my crime spree now, or do you want to find Buck and the barred-shoe horse?"

She glowered at him for a moment, then conceded. "Let's find Buck." She shoved her rifle back into its scabbard. "Then you and I are going to have a little talk, McLeod."

He tipped his hat to her. "You're the boss."

At least for the moment, she thought with a curse. She couldn't believe she was out there with a convicted felon. An ex-con.

As they rode, she studied Cooper's broad back, trying to convince herself he was dangerous. Dangerous to her heart—that was easy to believe. But to her ranch? To her livelihood? She refused to accept that, arguing he couldn't be trying to take her ranch because of the way he looked at her. The way he held her. The regret in his voice earlier at the rodeo, when he'd seen how much he'd upset her by his riding Hell's Fire. And the look on his face last night when he'd charged into her bedroom. She groaned, realizing she was just as besotted as Buck!

COOPER HURRIEDLY drew up Crazy Jack and swung around in the saddle at the sound of Delaney's pained groan. "Are you all right?" he whispered.

She nodded and seemed surprised that he appeared worried about her. Didn't she realize her safety was all that mattered to him right now?

"Are you sure you want to do this?" he asked. "It could be dangerous."

"Dangerous?" She laughed. "Believe me I just realized a few moments ago how *dangerous* it is."

He gave her a sideways look, thinking she was acting a little strangely. "So what do you want to do?"

"Do?" She stared at him. "What can I do now?" she asked, sounding as though she were on her way to the gallows but had to keep up a brave front.

"You sure you're all right?" He studied her for a moment, deciding she was acting more than a little strangely. Women. He'd never understand this one if he lived to be a thousand.

They circled back until Cooper found Buck's trail again. The ranch manager had dropped down into the gulch through a narrow opening in the rocks. They followed down below the band of rocks that ran the length of the gulch like a wall. Buck's trail stayed high above the creek bottom, winding through pines and rocks as if he hadn't wanted to be seen.

Suddenly a high-pitched whine filled the air. The horses danced nervously. A short distance farther, Cooper spotted the lights in Johnson Gulch Lake. He motioned to Delaney. Dismounting, he crept to the edge of the rocks to stare at the sight below him.

"I'll be damned," Cooper whispered as Delaney joined him. "There're Digger's space aliens, just as he said."

Chapter Seventeen

Delaney stared at the two creatures under the surface of the water. Illuminated by underwater lights, they seemed to be attached by hoses to a round craft that resembled a flying saucer. The saucer floated on the surface, its engine whining in the growing darkness. The whole thing looked much like the picture Digger had drawn.

"What is it?" she asked, knowing it wasn't from outer space, but equally sure it didn't belong there.

"A high-tech dredge for mining."

She looked over at him. "Mining?"

"It works like a giant vacuum cleaner," he said, the whine of the engine camouflaging their voices. Cooper pointed at the two divers. They swam beneath the water, rolling over boulders, then scouring the bedrock with a hose that was attached to the round floating dredge. "They're panning for gold, just using a little more advanced equipment than Digger."

The whine came from the motor on the floating dredge, where water and gravel spewed from the hose into what appeared to be a wire trap. "Later they'll sift through the gravel in the trap to get any color out."

"'Color'?" Delaney said, staring at the contraption. Cooper started to explain what color was. She made a face at him. "I know." The device was sucking up gold from the nooks and crannies in the rock that the old-timers like her grandfather had missed.

It wasn't that different from the dredging technique placer miners had used in the 1800s when their huge floating house dredges chomped through the nearby gulches to drag millions of ounces of gold from the creek bottoms. She knew all about that. She'd just never seen a small dredge like this one. And she was sure neither had Digger. The question was, what was it doing on her land?

That's when she spotted the barred-shoe horse some distance away in the trees. "There's Buck's new horse," she said, pointing at the poor old nag.

"Buck must be one of the divers," Cooper said. "The other one brings the gear. Buck meets him here on horseback."

Delaney nodded, finding it hard to conceive of Buck stealing from the Rockin' L under the cover of darkness. If she hadn't seen Buck ride that horse up here, she wouldn't believe it.

"Gold can make a man do stupid, dangerous, even illegal things," Cooper said, trailing her same thoughts.

"Gold. Or a woman," Delaney said, thinking of Angel.

"Yeah," Cooper agreed, looking over at her. "Or a woman."

She met his gaze and saw something that kicked her heart into gear. Love. She saw it as clearly as she'd seen the sun rise that morning. And she felt it at heart level. She warned herself that she wasn't seeing anything clearly, since she'd been bitten by that same bug herself.

"Boss, I think we should ride back to the ranch and report this to the sheriff," Cooper said. "Or someone."

Delaney stared down at the two divers. "I wonder who the other diver is." One diver moved the rocks while the other ran the vacuum system. Delaney thought of all the questions Angel had asked about mining and gold in the area, and wondered if Buck and Angel had been in cahoots from the beginning. It would explain a lot. "It has to be Angel."

Cooper frowned. "I don't know. When I saw Buck at the York Bar, he was looking for her. And making a big production of it. I suppose it could have been a cover."

"Are you thinking what I am?" Delaney asked. "That this little moonlighting venture is why someone has been taking potshots at us, dropping rocks on us? All for what little gold they could vacuum out of my creek bed?"

"I suppose," he said, unconvinced. "I think we'd better get back to the ranch and make that call."

"Go ahead," Delaney said, settling in behind the rock. "I'll stay here and make sure they don't get away."

"Sure you will," he said, looking over at her. "I'm not going anywhere without you."

"McLeod, I'm still the boss here."

He laughed. "I quit."

"You can't quit, not now," she snapped.

"Where do you think you're going?" he demanded as she got to her feet, pulled her rifle from her scabbard and started down toward the lake.

She stopped to look back at him. "I want to know who's been tormenting me."

Cooper let out an oath. "If they're the ones who've been trying to kill you, don't you think going down there and asking them could be a little dangerous?"

She smiled at him. "I'll just have to be more dangerous."

"*We'll* have to be more dangerous," he said with a growl.

"I thought you quit," she said sweetly.

"Damn you, woman."

He grabbed her before she could move and dragged her into his embrace, cutting off any further argument with a kiss. His kisses had been sweet and gentle, hard and passionate. But this one was pure possession. It laid claim to her in a way that she'd never realized she wanted to be possessed.

She would have let him take her right there in the rocks. She didn't care for the moment about anything but Cooper and his mouth on hers. Then he raised his lips and looked down into her eyes.

"We do this my way or I'll turn you over my knee right now and—"

She leaned up on tiptoes and kissed him. "You're the boss," she said, brushing her breasts against him.

He groaned. "Right."

His gaze said everything she needed to know about how he felt, but still she wished he'd say the words.

"Are you trying to tell me something, McLeod?" she asked softly, heart pounding.

"Yeah." His lips brushed hers. His tongue trailed along her lips, teasing, tempting. "I'm telling you, Delaney," he said, his breath tickling her cheek. "That if you're thinking of firing me, do it now."

"I thought you already quit?" she asked with a low laugh. "But what if I don't plan to fire you?"

He pulled back a little to gaze at her. Darkness had filled in around the boulders, under the pines. She could barely see his expression. "I'm an ex-con, Delaney, just as Jared told you. I've lied and cheated and—"

"That isn't what you want to tell me right now, is it, McLeod?"

He groaned. "I'm trying to tell you, Delaney Lawson, that—"

The engine stopped. The whine dissolved into the still night. Delaney's eyes widened. They both scrambled to look over the rock to the lake below them.

The divers had come out of the water and pulled the dredge up on the bank at the edge of the trees. For the first time Delaney noticed a vehicle waiting in the trees. It was just too dark to tell whose it was. "They're going to get away."

"Dammit, Delaney, I love you," Cooper said quietly behind her.

She whirled around to smile at him. "I know, McLeod, but it's good to hear it anyway. Maybe we could continue this later?"

She started off the mountain, determined not to let the two claim jumpers get away. Behind her, she heard Cooper cussing, but nonetheless following her. She smiled to herself. "I love you, too, Cooper," she whispered, but knew he couldn't hear her.

As she hurried down through the trees and boulders, she stepped on a rock that rolled with her weight. Cooper caught her and kept her from falling, but the rock tumbled down the hillside, crashing into the lake. The two divers, still in their drysuits, masks and regulators, turned in surprise at the sound.

An instant later a rifle shot ricocheted off a rock to Delaney's left. The shot echoed through the gulch as Cooper pulled her down behind a large boulder. "Do you think they'll try to come up here after us?" she whispered, snuggling against him.

He wrapped his arms around her and pulled her between his thighs. "I don't know. I think it's getting too dark for them to find us."

She could feel his heart beating against her back. "Cooper?"

"Yes?"

His breath on her neck was as gentle as a caress. "I love you, too."

His laugh was sweet and warm. "Your timing is amazing, Ms. Lawson. If someone wasn't shooting at us, I'd—"

An engine roared to life. Delaney leapt to her feet in time to see the lights as a vehicle rumbled off into the night. The divers and their equipment were gone. So was Buck's new horse.

THEY LED THEIR HORSES through the rocky path to the lake-shore in the darkness, going slow and easy. When they reached the lake, Cooper stood beside Delaney as she stared down into the water. Darkness had settled in, making it impossible to see even tire tracks in the dirt.

All Cooper could think about was Delaney. She loved him. The thought made him want to smile and laugh, and take her in his arms and make love to her beside the lake.

Then he remembered that she didn't have any idea who he really was, what kind of man she'd fallen in love with. He worked for Rattlesnake Range, the agency trying to steal her ranch. And until she found out everything about him, her declaration of love meant nothing.

"I can't believe Buck would do this," she said, her voice full of hurt. "I have to find him and talk to him."

Cooper followed her, wanting to settle things between the two of them rather than track down Buck, but knowing he would have to be patient. Delaney had a lot on her mind right now. She didn't need any more disappointments at the moment. He admitted he was scared. How much more bad news could she take about him, Cooper wondered, and still love him?

They mounted their horses and headed down the old mining road. The moon had come up behind Hogback Mountain. It now lit the sky over the tops of the trees, making riding easier.

"Buck has changed since he's met Angel," Delaney said, riding beside him. "Buck told me he didn't make enough money for her. I guess he could have decided to do a little moonlighting in Johnson Gulch Lake."

Cooper couldn't think of anything to say to heal the hurt he heard in her voice. Nor did he have any doubt that Angel had changed the ranch manager. Loyalty meant everything to Delaney, he thought with growing fear. What would she do when she found out Cooper worked for Rattlesnake Range?

When she found out why he'd come to the Rockin' L in the first place?

"I just find it hard to believe mining the lake would be worth it," Delaney said. "There can't be that much gold in this creek to jeopardize his job."

That was the question, wasn't it, Cooper thought, remembering Dude's story about the guy from Burton Mining Company. "Maybe there's more gold here than any of us knows," he said, and told her what he'd heard at the York Bar from Dude about Burton Mining Company and the sheriff.

"I knew it. Jared told me things were going on under my nose and I was too dumb to see them. He acted as if he was angry with Buck. Now I know why. Jared's in this up to his eyeballs."

"For once, we agree," Cooper said. "When I was in his barn looking for the barred-shoe horse, I saw two guys hitting Ty up for money. They seemed to mean business. Then Ty headed straight for Jared and demanded money."

"And Jared gave it to him," she said, shaking her head. "That explains how the two of them knew so much about what was happening on the Rockin' L. They were sharing information."

"Yeah, that's what I was thinking. But if Ty's the one shooting at you, then I'd bet the sheriff doesn't know about it. He seemed genuinely concerned about your welfare, Delaney."

"Maybe," she said quietly. "Until recently."

Cooper shoved back his hat and looked up at the stars, trying to put the pieces together. "This all has to do with gold, Delaney. It's the only thing that makes any sense."

"Don't tell me you're buying into Digger's mother lode?"

Cooper wasn't sure what he believed anymore. "Well, Digger *was* right about the space aliens. Kinda. And now we find out there's a mining company asking about your ranch— What if Digger's right about Gus, too?"

"You know, McLeod, sometimes I worry about you."
Suddenly Delaney reined in her horse. "Did you hear that?"

Cooper stopped to listen. A horse whinnied and a moment later, the barred-shoe quarter horse came trotting out of the trees, riderless.

"Why would Buck leave the horse behind?" Delaney asked as she watched the horse spook and take off down the road in the darkness.

"Maybe he decided he couldn't get away fast enough by horseback," Cooper said in answer. "Wait here." He and Crazy Jack went after the quarter horse the way Delaney imagined Cooper cut cattle out of a herd. Within minutes, he returned with the horse in tow.

"I just don't believe Buck would do anything to hurt me," she said. "I've known him all my life. But whoever's been riding that horse—"

"Buck has been spending a lot of time with Angel instead of on the ranch," Cooper said. "I guess someone else could have borrowed this horse."

Delaney was relieved Cooper was trying to help her defend Buck. But she couldn't help thinking about what Jared had said, and his obvious anger at Buck. Something was going on right under her nose, and Buck had been so odd lately. Delaney had just assumed it was Angel who made Buck act that way. And, she reminded herself, she'd seen with her own eyes Buck on the barred-shoe horse, Buck riding up to the lake tonight, skirting the lake as if he hadn't wanted to be seen. How much more evidence did she need?

"Who else would have had access to this horse?" Cooper asked.

"Angel, obviously. But Buck said she didn't know how to ride, that he planned to teach her. I figured that's why he bought her a hag like that one," she said, turning in the saddle to look back at the quarter horse.

They rode down to Buck's place in the moonlight. His

pickup was still parked next to the trailer where he'd left it earlier. Delaney dismounted and handed her reins to Cooper as she went to the door and knocked.

"Buck?"

No answer. She knocked again.

Cooper had dismounted and was holding the horses. Delaney tried the door. It was open. She reached in and flipped on a light, then cautiously stepped inside.

"Delaney?" she heard Cooper call to her.

It didn't take but a moment to see that the trailer was empty. What stopped her from returning to the yard was a large cardboard box in the center of the living room area. Onc worn leather glove lay on the floor beside the box. The glove drew her, just the way it had as a child.

"Delaney?" Cooper asked behind her, making her jump.

She'd picked up the glove, and held it in her hand, the leather rough and ragged from use. Tears brimmed in her eyes as she looked up at Cooper.

"Your father's?" Cooper asked, glancing from the glove to the box. Cooper stepped past her into the room. "Is this his rodeo gear?"

"Please, I don't want to see any of it," she pleaded. "Not now." She handed him glove and swung around to leave.

"What was Buck doing with this box?" Cooper demanded as he began to rummage through it.

She stopped and turned slowly. "I don't know. I'm not sure where it came from."

"Delaney, are you telling me you've never seen it before?" he asked. "I thought you said you went through all of your father's things."

She frowned as she stepped closer. "I thought I did."

Cooper turned the flap up. "This was recently mailed to the Rockin' L. From Texas."

"That's where my father died. You don't think—"

But Cooper was already digging through the contents. "Does Buck pick up ranch mail?" he asked.

"Yes, we both do. Why wouldn't he have told me about this box?" The moment she asked the question, she knew. Buck had helped her go through her father's things right after his death. He knew how upset she'd been.

"Delaney, from the looks of it, these were the clothes your father was wearing when—" Suddenly Cooper stopped digging and turned. He held an envelope in his hand. Her name had been printed on it in her father's scrawl. She stared at it, unable to reach for it.

"You want me to open it?" Cooper asked.

She nodded as she dropped onto the couch, and Cooper sat down beside her. The sweet scent of summer drifted in through the open door on the night breeze. Delaney pulled her knees up and studied the carpet pattern as Cooper carefully opened the envelope and pulled out the papers inside.

"It looks like a note to you," he said.

"Please read it to me," Delaney said, resting her chin on her knees.

Dearest daughter,
Writing this is one of the hardest things I've ever done. I can't tell you what goes through a man's mind to find out at this age how little he really knows about himself. But the past few days I've learned a lot. And I've had to face things about myself. I wasn't much of a father to you, Delaney, and I'm sorry. You and your mama, you were the strong ones. 'Course you know that by now. Take care of yourself.

I love you, Dad

Delaney felt tears fill her eyes and flood over onto her jeans. He'd written her the letter trying to explain why he'd left the ranch to Ty, his son.

"There's more, Delaney. It's his will. It's short and to the point, but it's dated and witnessed." Out of the corner of her eye, she watched him scan the document. "He left you the ranch."

Her head jerked up. Her heart raced. "When was it dated?"

"The day before he died." Cooper smiled at her. "He left you everything, Delaney, all his earthly possessions, except for his rodeo gear. He left that to his son, Ty Drummond."

Delaney took the will Cooper handed her and read the words for herself, still unbelieving. "He loved me," she said, unable to stop the flow of tears. "I guess I never really knew that until this moment."

Cooper smoothed her hair back from her face. "There's another note in the envelope," he said, handing it to her.

It was to Ty.

Dear son,
I thought long and hard about everything you said to me the other day. The last thing I want is to leave a legacy of pain. You never had a father. Neither did Delaney. The ranch is more Delaney's than it ever was mine. She's loved it and worked it, two things I didn't. So, Ty, I'm leaving you all that I ever owned. I hope you see fit to live a different life than I did.

Your father

She looked over at Cooper. He smiled at her and pulled her into his arms. "It's going to be all right now," she said against his shirt. "The accidents will stop. It's over, Cooper. It's finally over." She leaned back to look into his face and her smile faded. "What's wrong?"

He glanced away. "I'm just not so sure about that, Delaney."

She looked out the door into the night. "You mean Buck?

As soon as he comes back, I'm sure he'll have an explanation for what's been going on."

"Maybe you're right," he said. "I sure hope so." He released her and stood. "I'd better get that horse unsaddled and into the corral."

Delaney followed him, pressing the will and letters close to her heart. She thought of her father. All the hurts and resentments over the years. In time they would fade into soft memories like old photographs. She saw her father so differently through the eyes of Marguerite, through his own eyes at the end. She knew that for the first time in her life she would be able to forgive him. And that she had never stopped loving him.

"Delaney?"

She looked up to find Cooper standing by the barred-shoe horse, one hand on the saddle, the other resting on the horse's back.

"Delaney, would you turn on that other outside light for me?"

She stepped back to the trailer to accommodate him. The yard light came on, spilling over the corral. Delaney looked up and saw the expression on Cooper's face. "What is it?" she asked, her heart taking off at a gallop.

"I think you'd better call the sheriff," he said.

She stepped over to the horse. And saw the blood on the saddle. Too much blood.

Chapter Eighteen

"Buck could be out there, hurt somewhere," Delaney cried. "You have to go look for him."

Cooper stood in the shadows, trying hard to stay out of it. He watched Jared Kincaid glance out into the darkness. "I have men out searching, Del, but I can tell you right now, it won't do any good until we've got some daylight." He touched the blood on the saddle and studied it in the yard light. "It's warm out tonight. If he's just hurt, he'll survive till morning. If he's already dead, it won't make a difference."

"Damn you, Jared," she swore. "You knew about Buck dredging Johnson Gulch Lake, didn't you?"

The sheriff pulled off his Stetson, ran his fingers through his hair and let out a long, irritated sigh. "Del, I'm trying to be patient with you, but I'm getting real tired of your accusations." He turned his gaze on her, as steely and cold as the barrel of a gun. "You got proof, you want to file a complaint, then do it. Otherwise—"

If he thought to intimidate Delaney Lawson, he thought wrong. Cooper smiled to himself as he watched Delaney. What a little spitfire she was. He remembered the first time he'd seen her. The fire in her eyes. The determination in her stance. He'd put his money on this woman any day.

"Jared, I know you've been paying my brother to spy on me," she snapped.

The sheriff pushed back his hat. "I loaned your brother some money, if that's what you're talking about, Del." He frowned at her. "I felt sorry for him. I know what it's like to be the black sheep of the family."

"I'll just bet you do," she said, her eyes darker than the night. "You might want to tell Ty that I found my father's will. Dated just before he was killed. The Rockin' L is mine and it will stay mine."

Jared studied the ground but didn't say anything.

"You want to tell me what kind of deal you made with Burton Mining? I have a feeling the will changes your plans as well as Ty's," she said, anger making her voice break.

Jared let out a long sigh and looked again into the darkness. "Not that it's any of your business, Del, but I've been considering selling my ranch."

"And what about my ranch? Did you make a deal for it, as well?"

"Del, it's been a long day," the sheriff said. "We're all tired, so I'm going to overlook your behavior."

Delaney's eyes flashed like lightning in a bad thunderstorm. Cooper stepped over to touch her arm, afraid of what she was going to do next. She jerked her arm free, her gaze still locked on the sheriff, the threat clear in those dark eyes of hers.

"If I find out you're behind any of this—" She turned and mounted her horse. Without another word, she galloped down the road toward the ranch house.

Cooper mounted up and rode after her.

DELANEY HEARD Cooper come into the barn behind her. "I need to talk to you, Delaney," he said softly.

His tone made her heart feel as if someone were squeezing

the life out of it. She feared what he had to tell her, feared it would break her heart and leave neither of them a choice.

"You hungry?" she asked as she led her horse to a stall.

"Dammit, Delaney, food is the last thing I have on my mind right now."

"I make the best chicken enchiladas you've ever tasted," she said, unable to hide the pleading in her voice as she turned to face him. "And I never talk on an empty stomach."

They unsaddled their horses in the cool silence of the barn. Delaney watched Cooper out of the corner of her eye, loving him, wanting him. Did it matter what he'd done in the past? She didn't want to know, but he was hell-bent on telling her. Whatever he had to confess, it was bad, she knew that in her heart.

She swung her saddle up onto the stall railing and turned to find him standing, his thumbs hooked in the front pockets of his jeans, his hat tipped back slightly, his blue-eyed gaze on her. "Coop." It came out a whisper. A plea.

Cooper stepped to her and took her in his arms, crushing her to him. "Delaney. My precious, Delaney." She hugged him, her arms wrapped around him with a fierceness that frightened him.

He knew he'd never be free of the aching desire inside him to hold her. Never. Just as he knew, no matter what happened here tonight, that he'd never get over loving this woman.

"Let's go up to the house," he said, taking her hand in his.

DELANEY FELT her heart break. It snapped like a branch in a strong wind. As he told her, she listened, knowing somewhere in her heart that he'd been too good to be true right from the start.

"I was twenty-two and working on a ranch in Wyoming," Cooper said quietly.

He had insisted she sit on the couch. He'd gone to stand

by the fireplace, his body tense, and she was again reminded of a mountain cat. About to spring.

"Accidents started happening on the ranch."

She looked up at him, her eyes widening with the sudden rapid beat of her heart.

"At first they seemed like accidents," he said, his gaze avoiding hers. "Then the barn burned down and I decided to get the hell out of there." He looked up at her. "You know me. Always running. Well, I got blamed for it, and since I couldn't prove I didn't cause the accidents, I went to jail."

"Did you do it?" she asked, her voice no more than a whisper.

He shook his head. "But after that I had trouble getting jobs. I rode the circuit for a while. And then I got an offer from a company called Rattlesnake Range."

She stared at him. "Not the same Rattlesnake Range—"

He nodded. "I didn't realize it at the time, but my little brush with the law was what attracted them to me. And looking back, I think they probably set me up for the fall to begin with."

"You work for Rattlesnake Range?" she asked, her voice breaking, along with her heart. It was all so clear now. So damned clear.

He turned to face her. "Yes."

She felt her heart plummet. Angry tears rushed her eyes. "That's why you came to my ranch."

He didn't deny it, as she'd hoped he would, prayed he would.

"I came to make you an offer."

"One I couldn't refuse, no doubt." She glared at him as she got to her feet. "So you were behind my so-called accidents."

"No, Delaney."

He reached for her, but she stepped back out of his grasp.

His blue eyes darkened, just as they did when he made love to her.

"There was a mix-up. I wasn't even supposed to get this ranch assignment. I stayed on just to make sure everything went according to plan."

"And what was the plan, Cooper? Scare me out? If that didn't work, kill me?"

He shook his head. She saw the pain in his eyes but refused to let it soften her heart to him. "I'm not the first, am I, Cooper?"

"I won't lie to you," he said. "I've done things on other ranches I'm not proud of. I've persuaded people to sell. I never cared what happened to them or their ranches. But I never burned any barns or threatened anyone's life." He held her gaze. "This was going to be my last job for Rattlesnake Range. I would have had enough money after this assignment to buy my own ranch. But when I met you, everything changed. I started wondering about the ranches and the people I helped take them from. I started caring. About you. About what I was doing with my life."

She stared at him, unable to think about anything but the ranches he'd taken, the ranchers he'd conned. "So who's behind the accidents on my ranch if not you?"

"I don't know. That's one reason I stayed around at first. To find out. I didn't want to see you hurt."

"Hurt?" She laughed, unable to hide her bitterness. "Don't you know that finding out you work for Rattlesnake Range would hurt me? Knowing that's why you got close to me, just to take my ranch away from me, would hurt me?"

"Maybe that's why I did at first, but—" He slashed his hand through the air. Pain welled in his eyes. "Good God, Delaney, can't you see that I love you? That I'd die for you?" He met her gaze, not flinching as she glared at him. "Why do you think I had to tell you the truth? Don't you think it would be easier to go on lying if all I wanted was your ranch?

I'm quitting Rattlesnake Range. I'm quitting because of you. Hell, I didn't even earn my commission for this job anyway.'' He stepped closer. She moved back out of his reach, knowing that if he touched her now, she'd shatter like thin, old glass. ''I knew we couldn't go on from here, without you knowing who I really am.''

'''Go on from here'?'' she asked with a shaky laugh. ''And where is it you think we're going, McLeod?''

He stared at her. ''I don't know. I just don't want to lose you. You said you loved me.''

''I didn't know who you were then,'' she said, pain making her heart ache.

''And now that you know?''

''How could I possibly be in love with a man who came here to steal my ranch from me?'' Her voice broke. ''How could I ever trust you?'' Tears rushed her eyes; she bit her lip, desperately trying not to cry. She stared at him, wanting to hurl angry words at him, wanting to pound her fists against his chest, wanting him to take her into his arms and hold her and never let her go.

''I want you off my property by morning,'' she said. It came out a hoarse whisper. ''I want you out of my life.''

He picked up his hat with an obvious reluctance from the chair where he'd thrown it. Then he turned and walked out, closing the door behind him with a finality that broke her heart.

Chapter Nineteen

Cooper awoke the next morning, after a restless night, to find Delaney nowhere around. Her pickup was still parked in front of the house, but she didn't answer the door. When he checked the barn, he found her horse and saddle were gone.

All night he'd thought of nothing but her and ways to get her back. He'd hoped that with the morning light she'd change her mind about him leaving. But he couldn't help thinking about the defeated look he'd seen in her eyes last night. He knew he'd destroyed her trust in him. Yet there had to be a way he could get it back, that he could prove to her his love, his loyalty.

He'd lain awake most of the night, wondering how he could make things right with her. How he could make her trust him again. Just before dawn he realized he couldn't make Delaney do anything. But he'd hoped that if he could see her this morning before he left, maybe talk to her, hold her in his arms— He swore as he remembered how easily his charm had worked on other women. But Delaney wasn't like any woman he'd ever known. Or would ever know.

He packed up everything and was just about to load Crazy Jack into the horse trailer, when he heard the phone ring inside the house.

The front door was open, so he let himself in and hurried

to answer it, hoping it might be Delaney calling from the York Bar or—

"Where's Del?" Jared asked irritably.

"I don't know," Cooper said, unwilling to tell the sheriff even if he had known.

"Well, tell her Digger's taken off. He left the hospital sometime during the night. No one's seen him since he was rantin' and ravin' about Gus Halbrook coming back for revenge. Tell Del she'd best do somethin' about that old man before the county has to." He hung up.

Cooper stared at the phone for a moment, cursing Jared under his breath. He started to put the receiver back, when he remembered there was something he had to do.

"I just thought I should let you know, it's over," Cooper told Thom Jamison when he came on the line. "Delaney found the will that leaves her everything, including the ranch and the mineral rights. And she isn't selling. So call off your agent. *Now.*"

"I see," Thom said. "Can I assume that if we don't, we'll be fighting you, as well?"

Cooper smiled to himself, wishing the lie he was about to tell were true. "Yeah, you can assume that, Thom. And you might want to tell the board that I've officially quit."

"What about that ranch you were planning to buy? You won't have enough money now."

Cooper glanced around the room, seeing Delaney everywhere he looked. "It doesn't matter anymore." He was sacrificing his dream, but it was worth it. He had something more valuable, but he knew Thom wouldn't understand even if he tried to explain it to him.

"You were good, Coop."

"Too good. Goodbye Thom."

"Good luck. I have a feeling you're going to need it."

Cooper hung up, worrying what the businessmen at Rattlesnake Range would do now. Probably send their agent to tie up all the loose ends. Cooper McLeod was at the top of that list.

DELANEY RACED with the wind, her hair whirling behind her, the horse's hooves pounding the baked clay. She rode as if the devil himself chased close behind her. In truth, he did.

The devil in blue jeans. Wearing Cooper McLeod's handsome face. Grinning Cooper's grin. And calling her name. She rode faster, determined to outrun any thought of the cowboy. Riding had always calmed her, cleared her mind so she could think. It's what she did to solve problems. To get over hurts. To find herself.

But this morning all the ride did was make her think of Cooper. Of the way he looked straddling a horse; or standing against the horizon; his eyes as blue as the big sky; his body as familiar now as the land that stretched to that horizon. She brought her horse up and sat looking at her land. Once the deep green pines against the rocky bluffs and miles of reddish brown clay had offered her contentment. This morning they served only as a reminder of what the ranch would be like without Cooper in her life. She saw an emptiness she'd never noticed in the big sky before. A hollowness that echoed across the hard, dry clay. And no matter how hard or fast she rode, she couldn't seem to outrun it.

Delaney didn't even realize where she was until she heard a vehicle coming up the county road. She looked up, surprised to find she'd ridden to Cooper's old camp at the far side of the ranch. She stared at the stand of pines on the other side of the fence, remembering the night she'd driven him back here. It seemed like a lifetime ago instead of just days.

The vehicle she'd heard slowed, then came to a stop at the edge of the road. Delaney saw that it was a dark-colored van. Angel rolled down the passenger side window.

"I was just on my way to your place," the writer said.

She sounded a little shaken, and she looked as if she'd just woken up. The dark sunglasses she wore made her face seem especially pale.

"Have they found Buck?" Delaney asked hopefully.

Angel shook her head and Delaney realized why Angel looked so different. This was the first time she'd seen the woman without a mountain of makeup. Her hair, which normally was sculpted to perfection around her face, was pulled back in a no-nonsense twist at her neck.

"And they're not going to find Buck," Angel said, close to tears. "Buck sent me to get you. He has to talk to you. He said it's urgent."

Delaney felt a surge of relief. "Is he all right? Where is he?"

"He called me this morning."

Angel sounded frightened and a little breathless, Delaney realized.

"He told me to come get you and take you to him." She lifted the glasses long enough to brush at her tears. "He's in some kind of trouble, isn't he?"

"I think so," Delaney said. "The sheriff and his posse have been looking for him all night."

"Why?" Angel asked, surprised.

"His horse turned up without him and—" Delaney hesitated to tell her about the blood she and Cooper had found on the saddle or about the dredging for gold in the lake. "When was the last time you saw Buck?"

Angel frowned. "Yesterday at Jared's rodeo. I had to leave early to do some research. I was at the Helena library until it closed. Why?"

"I just thought you might have seen Buck sometime last night," Delaney said. She'd just assumed Angel had been the other diver.

"I didn't even know Buck was missing until this morning when he told me he was hiding out and that you were the only person he could trust,'' Angel said, as if she wasn't so sure about that. ''You're going to help him, aren't you?''

The desperation in Angel's voice made Delaney wonder if she'd misjudged the woman. Maybe she actually did care for Buck. ''Of course I'm going to help him.''

''He insisted we come alone,'' Angel warned. ''He sounded scared.''

Delaney nodded. ''Meet me at his place up the road. I'll leave my horse there.''

Without waiting for a response, Delaney spurred her horse into motion and took off across the pasture. As she rode, she hoped mining gold illegally was the only trouble Buck was in. She had a bad feeling it wasn't.

AFTER HE'D HUNG UP with Thom, Cooper wandered into the living room, not certain what to do about the news on Digger. He had no doubt that the old prospector was headed for the Golden Dream mine in the hope of sending Gus back to the grave. The problem was, Cooper didn't have any idea where to find the mine. Cooper smiled as a thought struck him. He couldn't leave the Rockin' L as long as Digger was missing. He knew it was just an excuse to maybe see Delaney again. But at this point, he'd take anything he could get.

Not that he wasn't genuinely worried about Digger. While he doubted Gus had returned from the grave, someone dangerous was definitely out there. And he had a feeling Digger knew who it was.

The photo albums Delaney had gotten out for Angel were still stacked on the coffee table. He picked up one and opened it. Just as he'd thought, the albums were full of old photographs of the ranch. He started looking through them, hoping to find a photograph of the Golden Dream. Instead he found photographs of Delaney as a baby. Wild dark hair around the face of an angel. Cooper smiled as he caught that familiar twinkle in her eyes. Pure mischief. He thumbed through the book, watching Delaney grow, fascinated to see her go from a child to a beautiful woman.

Seldom was she without a horse in any of the photos. Her love for this ranch and her life-style were what had first suckered him in, he realized. He cursed himself for blowing it with her and wondered where she was. Probably hiding out, waiting for him to leave.

Closing the album, Cooper picked up what looked like an older snapshot book.

Bingo. Photographs of old miners. His heart pounded with hope. Maybe there were photos of the Golden Dream, something that would give him at least an idea where to look for Digger.

He was flipping through the book, when one of the photographs stopped him. It was a yellowed snapshot of a cowboy sleeping at the base of a large gnarled old tree, his hat over his face, his clothing dirty and worn as if he'd been working. But it wasn't the tree that captured Cooper's eye or the gaping mine entrance behind him. It was the man's spurs. They were identical to the one that Delaney found in Johnson Gulch Lake. He turned the photograph over. A date was written in faded ink. Nineteen thirty-four. And a name. Gus Halbrook.

DELANEY TURNED her horse into Buck's corral with the other two horses and threw her saddle onto the fence railing. Angel waited in the van, looking worried.

When Delaney climbed into the passenger seat, she noticed Angel fidgeting with the hem of her jean jacket. The scent of her perfume reminded Delaney of Buck's pickup that night he'd given her a ride home.

"Whatever trouble Buck is in, we'll do the best we can to get him out of it," Delaney said, hoping she sounded more confident of that than she felt.

Angel gave her a trembly smile as she got the van going,

and Delaney had an odd wave of apprehension. She shook it off, blaming it on Angel's obvious nervousness. On Cooper's leaving. Cooper. By now he'd be gone. Her heart cramped with the thought. It was for the best, she assured herself. It would never have worked out. Never. And yet, suddenly she wished she'd told someone, even Cooper, where she was going. Except she didn't even know herself.

"Where are we supposed to meet Buck?" she asked.

Angel pointed toward the mountains. "Near Johnson Gulch Lake."

Johnson Gulch Lake? That was where the sheriff's posse and Jared were searching for him. How had Buck gotten himself into so much trouble that he had to hide from the law? And how much did Angel know about Buck and his double life? Delaney wondered. "Did you know that Buck has been running a small portable gold dredge in the lake nights?" she asked.

"Buck has?"

Angel seemed genuinely surprised. Maybe she hadn't known. "Someone was helping him," Delaney said. "Do you have any idea who that might have been?"

Angel stared at the road ahead. "The only person I can think of is Jared Kincaid."

"Jared?" Delaney tried to imagine the sheriff in scuba gear.

Angel shrugged. "Jared was real interested in what I found out about gold on the Rockin' L," she said. "He told me stories about the mother lode. I guess there's some gold on his property, but not the mother lode." Her painted red nails went to her lips. "What if that's it? What if Buck and Jared had been doing the dredging in your creek and Jared double-crossed him and that's why Buck's hiding now." She frowned. "Why else would Buck hide from the sheriff?"

Buck and Jared? Delaney had just assumed that Buck had been hurt last night trying to get away from her and Cooper.

That's why he'd left his horse. Now she wondered if he *had* been double-crossed. But by Jared? Could Jared be that greedy for money that he not only was making deals with mining companies, but he was dredging her creek at night?

Delaney glanced back to make sure no one was following them, and frowned. It struck her: what was a writer doing with a cargo van? That's when she noticed the floor in the back was wet with water and sand. Her heart hammered, pulse rising with more than apprehension.

Angel glanced in her rearview mirror, then smiled as she saw what Delaney was looking at. "You caught me. I've been doing a little gold panning. Jared showed me how. But all I've found so far is fool's gold." Her smile faded. "Oh, no, you don't think the buckets of gravel and sand that Jared gave me were from your creek, do you?"

"Where did Jared say he got the gravel?" Delaney asked, trying to still her growing fears. Angel had used the van to carry the dredging equipment. How much more was she lying about? Delaney watched the country whiz by, wanting out of the van, not knowing how to accomplish that.

"I didn't even think to ask," Angel admitted.

"Don't worry about it," Delaney told her, noticing that Angel had taken the old mining road. Surely Buck wouldn't hide up here so close to where the sheriff and his men were searching unless—

"You're sure Buck isn't hurt?" Delaney asked.

Angel flipped her a look and Delaney realized if Buck was hurt badly he couldn't have gotten to a phone.

"I'm just surprised he's hiding up here, so close to the lake, so close to where Jared and the posse are searching for him," Delaney said, assuring herself her fears couldn't be justified. Angel wouldn't take her to the lake where Jared and the posse would be searching if she intended to harm her. So why didn't Delaney feel reassured by that? Why was this woman frightening her so?

Through the trees, Delaney spotted Johnson Gulch Lake, glistening in the sunlight. "I'm sure Buck will explain everything," Angel said, making Delaney wonder if that was true. If they were going to see Buck. Or someone else. Jared? Angel said Jared was teaching her to pan gold. Surely Angel and Jared hadn't gotten together to— To what? Delaney thought. Steal her ranch? What would a historical writer want with the Rockin' L, a horse ranch, when she didn't even ride, didn't seem to have any interest in horses. To steal her gold? The thought hit her like a rock upside the head. That's what Angel and Jared had in common. Angel, Jared—and Buck. Gold.

As Angel brought the van to a stop, a pile of papers and books slid from under the seat. Delaney picked them up without thinking. She looked down at the papers and books she held in her lap, then toward the lake. Her fear level increased drastically. There were no other vehicles up here. Where was the posse Jared had assured her was out looking for Buck? And where was Jared?

"What is it?" Angel asked.

Delaney shook her head. "Nothing." She tried to smile but had trouble meeting Angel's gaze. Warning signals were going off in her head. Only, Delaney didn't understand why. What could she have to fear from Angel? Even if Jared and Buck had been stealing gold out of her creek and Angel knew about it, Angel had nothing to gain by hurting her.

"Here, I'll take those," Angel said, reaching for her research materials.

As Delaney handed them over, one of the books slipped out and fell to the floor. Several pages fluttered out of the worn binding.

"I'll get it," Angel cried.

But Delaney already had it in her hand. Had already seen the writing and recognized it as the old prospector's diary she'd looked at in Angel's cabin. Only this time she saw the name. She gazed up at Angel in confusion. "This is Gus Halbrook's diary."

COOPER SEARCHED the photographs, trying to find another picture of Gus Halbrook. The only other one he'd seen was that dilapidated thing Digger had tried to show him at the hospital.

As he hurried through the album, Cooper kept telling himself that finding a spur in the lake that belonged to Gus Halbrook meant nothing. Gus hadn't come back from the dead. Then suddenly Cooper stopped flipping pages. He stared down at the one semiclear photograph he could find. His heart thundered in his ears. His fingers shook as he looked from Digger's smiling face to that of his best friend's, Gus Halbrook. Gus looked up at Cooper from over the decades, his face unsmiling. "My God," Cooper breathed. Why hadn't he seen the resemblance before?

Chapter Twenty

Cooper pulled the photograph out of the album and held it up to the light. Digger and Gus stood in front of a large, old, weathered boulder. In the background, Cooper could make out a gnarled ponderosa and, to the left of it, what looked like an opening in the rocks. The Golden Dream?

He stared at the photograph, his gaze returning to Gus. A tremor of fear surged through him as he dropped the photo of Digger and Gus. It fluttered to the floor. He had to find Delaney and warn her. He only hoped it wasn't too late.

"McLeod?"

Cooper spun around to find Jared in the open doorway.

"I knocked, but you didn't answer," he said, stepping into the living room. He glanced from the scattered photo albums to Cooper.

Cooper noticed the sheriff's hand was resting on his holster.

"What's going on in here? Where's Del?"

Cooper gave him his most innocent shrug. "I've been looking for her myself."

Jared shot a brow up. "And just where exactly were you looking for her? Her pickup's parked outside and her horse is down at Buck's—saddle is on the fence. And you're in here looking at pictures." He eyed Cooper for a moment.

"And I see you're all packed up like you're planning on going somewhere."

"What's her horse doing at Buck's?" Cooper demanded, trying to imagine why Delaney would ride to Buck's, unsaddle her horse and leave it there. Unless Buck had returned. Or someone else came by—

"That's what I'd like you to tell me," Jared said.

Cooper noticed he flipped the tab off on his holster and settled his hand on the pistol handle.

"First Buck was missing. Then Digger. Now Del—"

"*Was* missing?" Cooper asked. "You found Buck?"

"That's what I came to tell Del. We've called off the search. Buck's fine. He fell off his horse last night. He's with Angel. Now, what I want to know from you is what you've done with Del."

"Wait a minute, how did Buck explain what he was doing at Johnson Gulch Lake last night?" Cooper asked.

Jared let out a sigh. "Never mind Buck. I just got a call from Del's attorney. It seems you work for a company by the name of Rattlesnake Range. I think you'd better tell me what's going on here, McLeod."

Cooper watched Jared's hand, wondering just how little it would take to provoke the sheriff into shooting him. Very little, he decided. "I used to work for Rattlesnake Range. I quit. But Delaney knows all about that."

"Sure she does. Why don't we just ask her about that when we see her." Jared pulled his pistol and pointed the barrel at Cooper's heart. With his other hand, he reached for his handcuffs. "I think you'd better come with me. Peacefully, of course."

Cooper raised his hands slowly. "We don't have time for this right now, Sheriff. We've got to find Delaney. And warn her."

"Warn her about what, McLeod?" he asked.

His trigger finger looked a little too itchy. Cooper wondered how deep Jared was in this mess. And how much it would be safe to tell him.

"Gus Halbrook," Cooper said. "Digger was right. Gus is back from the dead and after revenge. And unless I miss my guess, Delaney is his target—and always has been."

ANGEL SMILED as she took the diary from Delaney's trembling fingers. "You didn't know Gus kept a diary?" she asked, turning in her seat to face Delaney. "He wrote in it right up until the day of the cave-in. It makes for very interesting reading." She pushed her sunglasses up onto her hair and settled her gaze on Delaney. "He wrote about the people who were trying to steal his gold. He was tormented with their plots to take what he'd worked so hard for. Toward the end, he feared for his very life. And rightly so, as it turns out. He would have been seventy-seven this fall, if he'd still been alive, of course."

Delaney stared at Angel as if she'd never seen the woman before. In a way she hadn't—not this woman at least. Angel looked so different with her hair pulled back and no makeup. It was the eyes, Delaney realized. They were no longer deep green but a pale, pale green. "The damnedest eyes you've ever seen." Digger's words jarred Delaney's memory. She blinked and sat up a little straighter. Her heart rate soared as realization set in. Fear rippled through her. Cooper, her heart cried out. If she was right about this woman, Delaney knew she might never see him again. She had to do something. And quickly.

"What's Cooper doing here?" Delaney bluffed, gazing past Angel to the window behind her.

Startled, Angel spun around to look. Delaney threw open her door and ran.

"GUS?" JARED FROWNED and stepped back. "You're not going to try to tell me Gus's ghost is who's been causing all the trouble around here, are you, McLeod?'' He shook his head. ''Everyone knows how Rattlesnake Range operates. All those *accidents.* I think you'd better move away from that coffee table. Put your hands behind your head and spread 'em on the floor.''

Cooper stared at Jared. Why hadn't he realized it before? No one outside of Rattlesnake Range knew how the agency operated. Jared wouldn't know unless he had either hired them—or worked for them! It was like a light going off in his head. No wonder Rattlesnake Range had hired a local. The sheriff was the perfect person.

But right now Cooper's only concern was Delaney. If her horse was at Buck's— ''Listen to me, Kincaid, I think I know what's been going on around here—''

''Yeah? Well, I think I know what's been going on about here,'' he said, as he moved closer. ''You've been using those scare tactics, something you Rattlesnake Range people are known for, huh? But maybe this time you went too far and I got me a murderer on my hands.'' Jared kicked the coffee table out of the way. ''Get on the floor, McLeod.''

Cooper stared at the sheriff, having watched him work himself up to the point where he could—what? Kill someone? Jared didn't really believe Cooper had killed Delaney. In fact, Cooper thought just the opposite. Jared was looking for a way to get what he wanted. And what he wanted was Delaney's ranch. Unless Cooper missed his guess, Jared had made a deal with the mining company that involved Delaney's spread. Without Delaney's ranch, the deal would fall through.

But it still didn't add up. How would killing Cooper get Jared Delaney's ranch? Cooper felt a cold sliver of fear pierce his heart. Unless Delaney was dead, too. And it appeared that Delaney's ranch hand had killed her. Then Ty would get the ranch and gladly sell it to Burton Mining.

''On the floor, McLeod,'' Jared shouted, bracing the pistol with both hands. ''Or you're a dead man.''

Cooper dropped to his knees.

"All the way down," the sheriff yelled.

Cooper looked at Kincaid, saw the way his gun hand shook, saw the scared expression in his eyes and knew Jared planned to kill him. The only chance Cooper had was a slim one and the very last one he'd take under normal circumstances. But Delaney was out there somewhere, her life in grave danger from either a lunatic or a murderer. Or both. He had no choice. Cooper let out a piercing whistle as he flattened himself to the floor.

Jared jerked back in surprise. "What the hell? You dumb rodeo cowboy, son of a—"

Crazy Jack burst through the screen door in a shower of splintered wood and ripped screen. Jared swung around, pistol first, his trigger finger way beyond nervous. Cooper grabbed the edge of the coffee table and swung it around on the hardwood floor. The table hit Jared about midcalf and dropped him like a sack of grain. But not before Cooper's fears were realized. Jared got off one shot.

DELANEY'S ONLY ESCAPE was straight up. She scrambled up the rocky bluff next to the van, hoping that once she reached the top and dropped over the rim, Angel wouldn't be able to find her. She doubted the woman could climb the rocks fast enough to catch her. Running toward the lake or down the road would only allow Angel to chase her in the van.

Delaney was almost to the top of the rock bluff, when the first pistol shot ricocheted off a rock to her right.

"Don't make me kill you," Angel called from below.

Delaney climbed higher, frantically trying to reach the last few rocks that rimmed the bluff. The second shot hit closer and on the left. Rock chips stung Delaney's bare arms. Several cut her face. She felt blood trickle down her cheek as she clung to the rough boulders, her arms weak with fear and exertion. She fought to catch her breath, her heart pounding in her ears.

"Keep going and the next shot will be in your back," Angel said, anger and bitterness making her voice hard as the rocks around them. "Have you forgotten? Buck is waiting for us. You don't want to let Buck down, now do you?"

Delaney looked up at the rock bluff, estimating her chances of getting out of Angel's line of fire before the woman could get off another shot. They weren't good. And Angel knew it. "I'm coming down."

"Wise decision," Angel said. "Back down slowly," she instructed. "And please, no rock slides. They're very unpredictable and not all that reliable."

When Delaney reached the ground, she turned to face Angel, and the barrel end of the pistol the woman held pointed at her chest. Where was Jared and the posse who were supposed to be searching for Buck? Was Jared part of this, just as she'd suspected? She fought the feeling that she was alone on this mountain with a madwoman. And Buck—the traitor who'd helped Angel set her deadly trap.

By now Cooper would be packed up and off the ranch. Just as she'd ordered him. She closed her eyes, fighting tears of defeat. "Who are you? You aren't Angel Danvers—the writer."

"Actually, I am. That's how I stumbled across Gus's diary—researching a historical piece on the Halbrook family. I'm just not the blond bimbo you thought I was."

Angel frowned as Delaney opened her eyes. "What gave me away?" Her hand went to her hair. She felt the sunglasses she'd pushed back onto the top of her head and smiled. "The eyes. A family legacy. All that *my* grandfather had to leave me." She laughed at Delaney's expression. "That's right. I'm Gus's granddaughter. Angel Halbrook Danvers. Gus had a young woman hidden away in Helena. She's the one who had his diary. Unfortunately, she died in childbirth."

"It's been years since I've seen a photograph of Gus," Delaney said. But now that she'd seen Angel's eyes, she remembered that haunting look of Gus Halbrook's. "The resemblance between the two of you is remarkable."

Angel smiled. "Digger saw it right away. The old fool thought I was my grandfather. I really wish I'd known Digger was crazy, before I tried to kill him the second time. It would have saved me a lot of trouble."

"How could you do that to a harmless old man?" Delaney demanded, her heart breaking at the thought of this woman hurting the prospector. "Your grandfather was his best friend. Digger has never gotten over Gus's death."

Angel let out a snort. "And why do you think that was? Because Digger and your grandfather, Del Henry, killed Gus. Murdered him in the Golden Dream."

"That's not true," Delaney cried, feeling a little of her old fight come back. "Gus got himself killed in a cave-in. He thought he'd found the mother lode. He went crazy in that mine. Just as Digger did watching it happen to his best friend."

"We'd better not keep Buck waiting any longer," Angel said, her eyes as cold as the river ice in winter.

Delaney looked toward the mountainside. "I can't believe Buck would fall for your lies."

"Why not? You did," Angel said, jabbing Delaney in the ribs with the pistol.

Delaney took a breath, heart pounding. "You're the one who's been trying to kill me?"

"If I had wanted to kill you, I could have. No," Angel assured her, "I just wanted to torture you for a while. The way your grandfather tortured mine before he killed him. I wanted you to see what it was like to know someone was after you."

"And Buck? What part did he play in all this?" Delaney said.

"Why don't you ask him when you see him?" Angel suggested. "Come on. Let's get moving. We don't want to keep Buck waiting."

COOPER GRABBED the sheriff's pistol and turned it on him. "Blink, Jared, and I'll shoot you."

"They're going to put you back in jail for this little stunt, McLeod," Jared warned, but had the good sense to look concerned about Cooper and the gun he was holding.

"Maybe," Cooper agreed, as he checked his horse. Crazy Jack was still standing, but Jared's wild shot had left a notch in the horse's left ear. "At least I won't be in jail for murder the way you planned." He narrowed his gaze at Jared. "That is, unless you don't do exactly what I say. Slide those handcuffs over here, then let's go out on the porch real slowlike."

"You won't get away with this," the sheriff grumbled but did as he was told.

"Tell me something, Jared," Cooper said as he had Jared sit in Delaney's oak rocker and put his hands behind his back. "Did you go to Rattlesnake Range or did they come to you?"

"What are you talking about?" Jared asked.

"Rattlesnake Range. There is no way you could have found out how they work, about the small accidents they use to get ranch owners to sell. Not unless you hired them or worked for them. Which is it?"

Jared looked down at the floor. His jaw tensed. And Cooper had to laugh. How could he have been such a fool not to realize it before? The sheriff. No wonder Rattlesnake Range hired Jared. He was perfect for the job.

"What was the deal? Your ranch *and* Delaney's? And Rattlesnake Range hired you to bring in the Rockin' L. Sweet deal, except you underestimated Delaney. And now you're going to get blamed for not only the accidents, but the murder attempts on Delaney's life."

"But I didn't do it!" Jared cried. "Yes, I made a deal with

Burton Mining. I needed Delaney's property or Burton Mining wouldn't buy mine. It was Rattlesnake Range who asked me to help things along. But I didn't hurt anyone."

Cooper smiled. "Right. Been there. Done it. Jail time. Only I was innocent." He looped the cuffs through the porch railing beside the chair, then snapped one cuff on each of Jared's wrists.

"I never would hurt Del," he said angrily as Cooper took his keys. "Selling the ranch was the best thing for her. But I knew how stubborn she was—"

"So you cut her fences, drugged her horses, took a potshot at her, ransacked her office, burned down her barn—and almost got caught—and put a snake in Delaney's bed—"

"I didn't put any snake in her bed or drug her horses," Jared contended. "I looked through her office, trying to find something to help me figure out who was after her. But I didn't have anything to do with cutting the brake line on her stock truck or that rock slide. At first, when I found that barred-shoe print up at the rock slide and near the lake, I thought it had to be Buck. Then when I found out you worked for Rattlesnake Range, I figured you were doing those things. I swear to God I don't know who's behind it."

Cooper looked toward the mountains. "Unfortunately, I think I do. And if I'm right, Delaney could be in a world of hurt right now. I need to find the Golden Dream, the mine Gus Halbrook died in. If you have any idea where it is—"

Jared shook his head. "Only Digger would know. And he's run off with that blamed mule of his, probably searching for the mother lode or Gus Halbrook's ghost—"

"What?" Cooper glanced toward the barn, then back at Jared. "How do you know Digger's got his mule with him?"

"I saw the mule tracks."

"Where?" Cooper demanded.

"Down by Buck's place."

DELANEY CLIMBED UP the hillside above Johnson Gulch Lake, weaving her way through the tall ponderosas and the rocks, knowing all along that Angel had a pistol trained at her back.

"There never was a mother lode," Delaney said, desperately trying to find some way to reach Angel. She'd looked into those pale-green eyes and glimpsed the insanity there. Gus had left Angel more than a legacy of pale green eyes. "Gus died in a worthless mine, digging for something that doesn't exist."

"Lies," Angel said behind her. "That's just what Del Henry told people."

Delaney knew her only chance was to reason with the woman. "Then what happened to the gold?" she demanded, turning to look behind her.

Angel's smile was more frightening than the pistol she clutched in her hand. "The gold's still there. Del Henry only dynamited the entrance to keep anyone from getting it." She motioned with the gun for Delaney to keep moving.

"That doesn't make any sense."

"He thought he could keep the gold a secret, but it's coming out in Johnson Gulch Lake," Angel argued. "And now it's my inheritance instead of yours."

Delaney looked over at the creek, running down through the rocks and trees as it dropped to the lake. Could it be true? Delaney wondered. Gold often washed down from rich veins upstream. That's how the original miners had first discovered the larger deposits.

"Just because there's a little gold dust in the creek bed—"

"Don't lie anymore," Angel said, suddenly right behind her. "I know you were planning to sell the ranch to a mining company and cash in on the gold. But what you don't know is that Del Henry promised my grandfather one-third of anything he and Digger found in the Golden Dream. And I'm here to collect."

"Who told you I was going to sell the Rockin' L?" Delaney asked. "I'd never sell the ranch."

"It doesn't matter now."

They'd reached a flat spot beside the creek. The boulders were large. Pines towered over them. "I'm tired," Delaney said, stalling for time as she looked around for a possible weapon. A tree limb. Small rock. "How much farther is it? I have to rest for a while."

"Nice try," Angel said, prodding Delaney with the cold steel of the pistol. "You wanted to see Buck, didn't you? Well, he's waiting. Right through there."

Delaney gazed past a massive boulder to see a gnarled old ponderosa. Beyond it lay the shadow of a small opening in the rocks. Her heart quickened. The Golden Dream mine.

ON CRAZY JACK, Cooper followed the mule tracks in to the mountains, trailing Digger and Tess as they headed for the Golden Dream. Cooper had known the moment Jared told him about the old prospector taking his mule that Digger had left the hospital to find Gus. He'd be headed for the mine. But where was Delaney? She'd tied up her horse and saddle at Buck's. All Cooper could figure is that someone had picked her up. He just hoped it hadn't been Angel.

As Cooper and Crazy Jack climbed, the sun climbed Montana's big sky with him. All Cooper's fears escalated when he saw Angel's rented van parked near Johnson Gulch Lake.

Cooper looked up the mountainside, hoping to catch a glimpse of Delaney, wondering how much of a head start Angel had, hoping it wouldn't matter. He tried to rein in his apprehension. He knew running scared wouldn't help Delaney. But just the thought of Delaney with Angel—

He urged Crazy Jack up the mountainside, praying he would find Delaney and the mine in time.

"WELL, BUCK, we made it," Angel said deep in the cool, damp darkness of the mine. "Your precious Delaney was a real pain in the neck, though."

Delaney stood where Angel had left her, in the middle of the pitch black mine tunnel, wiping cobwebs from her face. The mine smelled moldy, as if it had been closed up for years. Angel had forced her through the small opening, then down a series of tunnels, with only the faint beam of Angel's flashlight to guide them.

Delaney rubbed the elbow she'd scraped on the rocks in the darkness and tried to get her bearings. She considered making a run for it, but even if she could see, she didn't know which way to run and realized she wouldn't get far in the dark, not with Angel and Buck after her.

She heard Angel strike a match. It glowed brightly for a moment before she touched it to an old lantern. Slowly the light radiated out from the lantern to fill a small section of the mine.

"Buck doesn't seem all that happy to see you," Angel noted, motioning for Delaney to come a little farther into the mine.

Delaney did, aware that she could reason with Buck. At least the Buck she used to know before Angel came into his life.

Delaney hadn't gone far, when she saw Buck sitting in the shadowy darkness. She felt her heart break as she looked at him. Buck sat against the rock wall, his head back, his feet and hands bound. He lifted his gaze to Delaney's.

"I'm sorry." The words came out in a choked whisper.

Delaney went to him, kneeling next to him. The side of his head was soaked in something dark that plastered his hair to his head. "Are you all right?"

He nodded, then grimaced as if the simple movement caused him a great deal of pain.

"He needs to get to a doctor," Delaney said over her shoulder to Angel.

"He'll live. Maybe."

Angel didn't sound as if it made a difference to her one way or another, Delaney realized.

Buck's eyes filled with tears. "I've been such a fool."

Delaney hushed him. "We all have, Buck." She thought of Buck's plans to marry Angel and wanted to scratch the woman's eyes out. She brushed angrily at her own tears and stood to face Angel. "And to think I was worried about you breaking his heart."

Angel shook her head in disgust. "At first he was so easy to control. Totally malleable, like so many men."

Delaney thought of Cooper. The opposite of malleable. Hardheaded. Impossibly determined. Totally inflexible. Her heart stopped with a jolt, then kicked back into high speed. Cooper. Had he done what she'd told him? Had he packed up this morning and left? Or had he done just the opposite and stayed? A faint glimmer of hope shone through the darkness of the mine, through the madness of the situation she found herself in. Cooper. He'd never done anything she'd told him. She just prayed he hadn't this time.

"You didn't have to hurt Buck," she said to Angel.

"He didn't give me a choice. He started snooping around in business that didn't concern him."

"I found the horseshoe tracks at the rock slide and at the spot where the sheriff said someone had taken a potshot at you, Delaney," Buck said, his voice barely above a whisper. "I knew it couldn't be Angel, though." He leaned his head back, as if the effort of talking had been exhausting.

Denver stared at the woman, confused. "Buck said you didn't know how to ride a horse—"

Angel made a face. "Or shoot a gun? Or tie my own shoes? What do you think, boss lady?"

Delaney looked down at Buck. "Then you didn't know what she was up to when you bought her the horse?"

Buck shook his head.

"He bought me the quarter horse because I insisted it was the one I wanted. The old fool thought if I learned to ride, I might marry him and stay down on the ranch."

"What a fool, huh, Angel?" Buck said, glaring up at her.

Delaney stared at the woman. "Why would you insist on such a horse? Unless— You knew we'd be able to track the barred shoe. Who were you setting up? Jared or Buck?"

Angel laughed. "Just clouding the water a little. I didn't want you to figure out who was after you too quickly."

"She's sick," Buck said, sounding as if he almost felt sorry for her.

Delaney had to agree. "I can't believe you'd go to all this trouble for—"

"Revenge?" Angel asked, her eyes bright in the lantern light. "I think of it as justice. Your grandfather killed mine. Now I will take your ranch, your life and your gold. *That* is justice."

"Killing me won't get you my ranch or this mine," Delaney said, but noticed Angel wasn't paying any attention. Instead the woman had glanced at her watch, then back down the mine tunnel. "Who are you waiting for?" Delaney asked, suddenly more frightened than ever.

Angel raised one perfect brow. "Think about it, boss lady. The perfect revenge. Who's missing?"

Delaney felt her legs turn to water beneath her and fought to keep her feet. "Digger."

"You got it on the first guess." She shot Delaney a thumbs-up sign. "I stopped by to see him last night at the hospital and told him I had his precious Winnie, as he calls you, at the mine." She glanced down the tunnel again, then back at Delaney. "Don't worry. He'll come, and then it will all be over."

Delaney tried to think of something to do as she looked over at Buck, and bit her lip to hold back the tears. And her growing terror. She was with a madwoman in a mine tunnel, a mine Digger believed cursed. And Buck was hurting and needing immediate medical attention. Her heart went out to him now. He'd fallen in love, proving just how blind it could be.

A thought whizzed past. Delaney blinked, remembering the lathered horse she and Cooper had found in the corral that day after the rock slide. If Buck hadn't been the one, and Angel was on the barred-shoe horse, then who had ridden it?

And— Delaney stared at Buck's body propped against the wall of the mine, then at the dirt on the mine floor. No drag tracks. Who had helped Angel get Buck's body up here to the mine? There was no way Buck could have gotten here by himself. Someone else was involved.

Suddenly Delaney remembered what Angel had said about having no choice but to stop Buck because of his snooping into her business. "Buck caught you and your accomplice dredging Johnson Gulch Lake last night," Delaney said, the pieces starting to fit.

"Very good, boss lady." Angel smiled. "Too bad you didn't figure it all out sooner."

So why didn't these pieces feel as though they fit together? "It *was* you and Jared in the lake last night, right?" Delaney asked. "I mean, how many other poor fools could you have suckered into your deranged plot?"

Angel turned to look back up the dark mine tunnel at the sound of footfalls on the mine tunnel floor. She smiled. "I believe that's another poor fool now."

Chapter Twenty-One

The mule tracks led up the mountainside overlooking Johnson Gulch. Then disappeared. Cooper stood in a clearing of rocks and pines, staring at the ground. Then he looked closer and saw that someone had brushed away the tracks with a limb. Cooper circled the area, knowing he must be close to the mine entrance, but wondering at the same time just what Digger O'Donnel was up to. Maybe he still believed there were space aliens who had brought Gus back from the dead and he was hiding from them.

Cooper found the boot tracks in the dust about the time he lost Digger's tracks. Small feet. Two women. Then he noticed it. The weathered old tree. The large boulder. He climbed off Crazy Jack and walked to where he thought the entrance to the mine was from the photograph. Only all he could see were thick brush and rocks. No entrance. Could Del Henry have dynamited *both* entrances to the mine?

Cooper shoved aside some of the brush where he estimated the opening should be. What he found made his heart rumble to a halt. Sweat beaded on his forehead instantly. His heart threatened to pound its way out of his chest. He swore as he gaped at the tiny, confining entrance to the Golden Dream. It was little more than a hole, just large enough for a small person to squeeze through. Behind the hole was nothing but darkness. Cooper felt his claustrophobia constrict his heart, squeezing each breath he took the way the opening would squeeze his body. He swore again. Then started moving the brush. Delaney was in there. With Angel. He had no choice.

DELANEY STARED down the dark tunnel, waiting for a figure to emerge. Ty Drummond appeared in the lantern light, dragging someone with him.

"Hello, Sis," Ty said as he gave Digger a shove. The old prospector stumbled and fell at Delaney's feet. "Look who I found on my way in."

Delaney knelt to help Digger to his feet. His eyes were wild; his voice was shrill. "Cursed. Nothin' but evil in this mine, Winnie. Pure evil." His eyes darted around the mine tunnel, then settled on Angel. "I told you Gus was back, didn't I?"

"That's not Gus, Digger. It's his granddaughter, Angel." Not that it seemed to make a lot of difference, she realized. Angel was much more dangerous than any ghost.

"I heard you found the will," Ty said.

"I figured Jared would tell you," Delaney said.

Ty nodded. "Yeah, well, it changes my plans."

"'Our' plans, don't you mean, Ty?" Angel asked.

Delaney looked from Angel to Ty and back. "So the two of you are in this together?"

"While I was doing my research, I found out about Ty being Hank Lawson's son," Angel said sweetly. "I thought it was just something else I could hurt you with, Delaney." Bitterness and hatred oozed from her words.

Delaney caught movement out of the corner of her eye. Someone was sneaking up the tunnel to her left. While she hadn't gotten more than an impression, she knew in her heart it was Cooper. She'd been right about his hardheadedness. Thank God she'd fallen for a man who didn't do anything she told him to. Angel still held a pistol trained on her and now Ty was here and probably armed, too. And there was no doubt that they planned to kill her and Digger, and likely leave Buck for dead, as well, and steal the Rockin' L. If she could just keep them talking and distracted—

"And let me guess," Delaney said. "The snake was your idea, right, Ty?"

He smiled. "Someone mentioned your fear of snakes."

"Jared," Delaney said with an oath. "And how does he fit into all this?"

Ty smiled. "Well the sheriff has come in handy."

"Why don't I believe he's been giving you money out of the goodness of his heart?" Delaney said, seeing things clearer. "Blackmail? What did you have on him?"

"He's been working with Rattlesnake Range to take your property away from you, Sis. All those little accidents around the ranch? Jared."

"Why?" Delaney asked.

"Seems he needs to sell his ranch and the only way Burton Mining will buy it is if they can get the Rockin' L," Ty explained. "I just happened to catch him in the act of cutting some of your barbed wire."

Delaney shook her head. "Angel wants revenge. But you, Ty—"

"I just want what's mine. My father's ranch," he said.

Delaney gritted her teeth. "The only way you can get the Rockin' L is to kill me, and you know it."

Ty shrugged. "You're right. You've left me no other option."

"But you'll never get away with it." Delaney moved so Cooper could get behind Ty and Angel. "You'll be the number-one suspect."

"Who's been salting the Johnson Gulch Lake?" Digger asked out of the blue. "There ain't no gold in that lake."

Angel frowned. "Salting?"

"Me and Tess seen it. Gold flakes where there shouldn't

have been none," Digger said. "Gus, you're too smart to fall
for that."

Ty groaned. "Come on, Angel, let's get this over with."

"Wait a minute," Angel said to Ty. "What's he talking
about?"

Delaney could see Cooper edging along the wall of the
tunnel, an old shovel in his hand. She needed to create a
diversion, but it wouldn't be easy, because Angel wasn't
about to fall for another "Geez, isn't that the calvary behind
you" trick.

Delaney looked over at Digger and saw that he, too, had
seen Cooper and was doing his level best to help. She glanced
down at Buck. His eyes were closed, his head back. She
hoped he'd only passed out and not died.

"Somebody put gold flakes in the lake to make it seem
like there was gold upstream," Digger said. "Only a fool
would fall for an old ruse like that."

Angel looked over at Ty, her eyes wide. "He's saying
someone tried to trick us?"

"The guy's loonier than a pet raccoon," Ty said to Angel.
"You know there's gold in this mine. It's in the diary." An-
gel appeared doubtful. "Here, give me the pistol," Ty said.
"And I'll finish this."

"I wouldn't do that if I were you, Angel," Delaney cautioned. "Don't you see what he has planned? I couldn't figure
out how Ty thought he could get away with my murder. But
he has the perfect scapegoat. You. Crazy, revengeful Angel
Halbrook."

"Don't listen to her, Angel," Ty said, stepping over to
her, his hand out. Angel retreated, waving the gun to keep
him back.

"Ty wouldn't double-cross me," she said.

"Sure he would," Delaney argued. "You think he ever
planned to split the money with you? He's too greedy. He

kills me and gets the ranch, but you get the blame and he gets all the money to himself.''

"Angel," Ty said, moving closer to her. She backed up against the rock wall of the mine and pointed the pistol at Ty's chest. "Don't you see what she's trying to do? She's trying to play us against each other."

"You said Buck would be blamed," Angel accused. "You said we'd share the money. But *you* had to be the one to salt the lake. There wasn't any color at all in the gravel Jared gave me from his place."

As Ty went for the pistol, Cooper broke from his hiding place. Cooper swung the old shovel, hitting Ty in the back just as Ty made a grab for Angel's pistol. The gun went flying. Ty fell to his knees. He cursed at Angel and swung around to slam his elbow into Cooper's knee. Cooper dropped, taking Ty to the ground with him. As the two wrestled in the dirt, Delaney made a leap for the pistol. But Angel reached it first.

"Get back," Angel said, her pale eyes eerie in the lantern light. Her gaze darted past Delaney. "Where the hell did he go?"

Delaney turned to see that Digger was gone.

COOPER SAW HIS opening. He buried his fist in Ty's stomach, then came back with a shot to his jaw. Ty's eyes crossed. He fell back with a groan. As Cooper stumbled to his feet, all he could think about was holding Delaney in his arms. He grabbed her and pulled her to him, breathing in the familiar scent of her, holding her tightly as if he'd lose her forever if he let her go. He'd forgotten about his claustrophobia the moment he saw Angel with the pistol trained on Delaney. He'd forgotten everything—the rotten timbers, the danger of being in an old mine deep in the ground. Forgotten everything but saving Delaney. He knew at that moment that he'd give his own life if that's what it took.

He looked up to see Angel, the pistol clutched in her hand, madness in her eyes. He turned Delaney, sheltering her in case Angel got off a shot before he could reach the woman.

"He tricked me," Angel cried, swinging the pistol back and forth from Ty to Cooper and Delaney. "You tricked me!" she yelled at Ty.

"Give me the gun, Angel," Cooper told her softly. "It's all over. I called the county marshal before I came up here. He and his men will be here any moment."

Angel met his gaze and smiled. "Nice try, cowboy, but you're not all that good at lying."

Cooper wondered if that was true. Since Delaney, he'd lost a lot of his old skills. They just didn't come as naturally as they used to.

"Get up," Angel said, turning her anger and the pistol on Ty. "You lying bastard, get up. That's why you suggested killing them in the mine. You were setting me up from the start."

Ty got to his feet, licking his lips as he eyed Angel. "You were already set on getting revenge when I met you. I just offered to help, that's all."

Cooper started to advance on Angel, but Delaney grabbed his arm.

"Why did you salt the lake?" Angel demanded, all her attention on Ty. "Tell me the truth, damn you!" She cocked the pistol and pointed it at his heart.

"All right," he said, raising his hands in surrender. "I put some gold in the lake. But just to get the price of the ranch up. It didn't have anything to do with you."

"You planned to double-cross me—" The pistol shot roared through the mine like a cannon blast. Dirt and gravel began to fall from the timbered shoring over head.

Ty clutched at his chest he dove for Angel and the pistol. "You're going to ruin everything!"

Cooper grabbed Delaney as the timbers groaned overhead. Dirt began to pour down in a dark shower of dust and gravel.

"We've got to get out of here," Cooper cried, pulling Delaney down the tunnel toward the entrance.

"We can't leave Buck," Delaney cried, breaking free to turn back.

Cooper reached for her, and saw that Ty had stumbled to his feet and was holding the gun. Angel was sprawled on the floor near him. As Ty advanced toward them, the pistol cocked and pointed at Delaney, Cooper saw Buck open his eyes. He nodded at Cooper, then reached out to grab Ty's leg.

"Run!" Cooper cried to Delaney as Ty's shot went wild, ricocheting through the tunnel.

DELANEY HEARD the first timbers give way behind them. Heard the roar and felt the wind as the earth caved in after them. She'd seen the look Buck had given her. "Run," he'd said. And she knew it was his way of paying her back for the pain he'd helped Angel cause her. She knew in that moment, she couldn't save Buck, could never have saved him from Angel. Or the cave-in. She ran, Cooper right behind her, for the tiny hole of light at the end of the tunnel, afraid they would never reach it in time. Just as they neared the opening, she saw Digger and Tess waiting outside. An instant later, the entrance opened like a golden door as Tess pulled a large rock from the opening, and Delaney and Cooper rushed out into the sunshine.

Behind them, the Golden Dream seemed to explode, sending dirt shooting out over them. Cooper pulled Delaney into his arms as they looked back at what was left of the Golden Dream. Nothing but a wall of rock.

"Buck. Ty and Angel—" Delaney buried her face in Cooper's shoulder and cried. "Buck saved our lives."

Cooper held her. "I've got you, Delaney. It's all right now. I've got you."

Epilogue

They rode out across the wide-open land, the sun climbing high over Montana's big sky. Cooper rode behind Delaney on Crazy Jack. The morning air smelled fresh. Tall wild grass brushed her boots as she rode. Delaney knew where Cooper was taking her long before she saw the large pine tree and the flat smooth shadowed rock beneath it. She smiled over at him. This was the spot they'd first met. It seemed like a lifetime ago.

Cooper dismounted and, taking Delaney by the waist, lifted her down from her horse. He held her for only a moment before he released her and turned to look out across the land.

The Rockin' L stretched across the horizon below them. In a far pasture, the two-year-old Morgans raced on the wind, their hides dark against the sea of tall grass and wildflowers that grew beneath their hooves.

"I heard from the county attorney this morning," Cooper said. "They're willing to drop the charges if I turn state's evidence against Rattlesnake Range. I've decided I have to do it. Not to save my own hide as much as to put them out of business for good."

Delaney nodded but didn't say anything. She'd already talked to the county attorney and knew he'd made Cooper an offer. She just hadn't been sure Cooper would take it. He'd stayed around after the mine cave-in, helping her get through the days that followed, all the funerals. He'd been there whenever she'd needed him and yet neither of them had talked about him staying.

"With Rattlesnake Range gone and Jared out of the picture...well, you shouldn't have anything to worry about," Cooper said.

Jared was now facing misdemeanor charges for the accidents he'd caused on the Rockin' L and abuse of power. She'd been surprised to learn about his financial troubles. That was why he'd made the deal with the mining company, in an attempt to keep from losing his ranch after a series of bad investments. But without Delaney's land, the mining company had said it wouldn't be financially feasible to mine Kincaid's property.

Delaney heard Cooper had made an offer on Kincaid Ranches. Jared had needed a fast sale to keep from losing everything and Cooper had picked up the ranches for a song. But Delaney wasn't sure what he planned to do with the land. For all she knew he might turn around and sell them at a profit.

"I know how you feel about this place," Cooper said, taking off his hat to turn it in his fingers.

Delaney looked across the wide expanse of pines and rocks; rolling hills and mountains; long, wide pastures and grassland as far as the eye could see. Home. The place she'd put all her dreams. All her hopes.

She shifted her gaze to the cowboy standing beside her. It wasn't until recently that she'd realized the land meant everything to her. And nothing without Cooper. But she wasn't going to make the same mistake her mother had, trying to tie a rodeo cowboy to that land. A rodeo cowboy who wasn't ready to settle down. It had to be what he wanted.

"Something on your mind, McLeod," she asked.

He grinned. "The deal I made with the county attorney is dependent on one small thing." He settled his baby blues on her, letting all that charm just pour out of him like a warm summer rain shower. "I need a job."

"A job?" she asked. "Didn't I hear that you've just bought a ranch of your own?"

He nodded. "But I was kinda hoping there still might be something for me at the Rockin' L."

"You were?" She pushed back her western hat to give him the once-over. "You look like a rodeo cowboy to me, and I make it a rule never to hire 'em."

"What about reformed bronc riders?" Cooper asked, as he closed the distance between them.

"Sorry," Delaney said, taking a spin with the devil dancing in those eyes of his. "I have only one opening on the ranch and it's not for a hired hand."

"No?" Cooper asked.

He was so close she could feel his breath against her cheek. "No."

"I thought about the ranch-manager job," he said, the devil jitterbugging away in his gaze. "But maybe I'm more upper-level management than that. And you've got Digger and Tess back at their summer camp keeping an eye on things, so you don't need me for that."

Delaney raised a brow. "So what position were you considering?" she asked with a grin. "I should tell you, when I take on a man here at the Rockin' L, I expect something from him."

Cooper grinned, but it faded quickly. A seriousness came into his eyes, into his stance. He cupped her face in his hands. "Delaney?"

His voice was soft and deep with emotion. She realized he was nervous and had to fight a smile. Cooper McLeod. Nervous.

"Yes, Coop?" she said.

"Have you ever considered marrying a former rodeo cowboy?" he asked.

"No, Coop, I never have."

He eyed her for a moment. "You're not going to make this easy for me, are you?"

She smiled. "No."

He took a breath. "Just tell me if there is anything about me that you like, so I know what my odds are."

She pretended to think for a moment. "I like your horse."

"You do?" Cooper asked in pleased surprise.

She wrapped her arms around his neck. "And I think you can tell a lot about a man by his horse."

"Yeah?" He grinned again.

"Say it, McLeod. You've never had any trouble telling me what you thought before." She leaned back to look up at him. "So just say the words. If you're sure it's what you want."

"Oh, it's what I want. It's all I want."

He met her gaze. He looked as if he thought she might run him off with a shotgun. Or worse yet, say no.

"Delaney Lawson, would you marry me?" he asked, his voice breaking with emotion.

"Yes, Cooper McLeod," she said, pulling him down for a kiss. "I certainly will."

Behind them, Crazy Jack let out a long whinny. They both laughed as Cooper lowered Delaney to the smooth, flat rock beneath the pine tree.

* * *

Look out for BJ Daniels in Silhouette Intrigue with her new mini-series, EVIL IN TIMBER FALLS— Day of Reckoning *in January 2005 and* Wanted Woman *in March 2005.*

SEDUCING THE PROPER MISS MILLER

Anne Marie Winston

For Larry

If there are volunteers in Heaven,
you must be one busy guy.
Here's to trailers!

One

WOW!

Chloe Miller froze, her gaze fixed on the window of her office in the Pennsylvania church where she was employed as administrative assistant. She'd glanced out at the April sky, hoping to see sunshine instead of showers. But the landscape was blocked by a man's body, framed in the window from hips to neck as he worked with his arms above his head on a ladder.

Her hands stilled on the keyboard, and her breath caught in a soundless "Oh-h-h," as taut pectorals stretched and flexed.

The naked male torso was lean, bronzed and packed with muscle. Droplets of sweat were caught in the curly golden *T* that bisected the chest and disappeared from sight beneath the waistband of a truly disreputable pair of jeans, a pair of jeans that embraced the heavy bulge below the zipper in a manner that left Chloe dry-mouthed and shaking her head.

So this was the carving-restoration expert the church elders had hired to repair the aging facade of the church. He looked as if somebody had carved *him*.

"That should be illegal," she muttered, tearing her gaze from the window.

The fact that she hadn't seen his face didn't matter. It wasn't often that she got the chance to fantasize about a man...in fact, she couldn't remember ever scrutinizing a male body so thoroughly before.

"You are sadly repressed," she told herself, thinking of how limited her experiences with men were compared to most other twenty-six-year-olds she knew. "Well, not just repressed," she amended. "Also too doggone busy to think about men."

Her gaze drifted back to the window and she absently appraised the torso still in full view, while her mind drifted. Did this man do carpentry work, as well? Perhaps when she got the preschool project off the ground, he could put up some sturdy shelves and cupboards that the children couldn't accidentally pull over onto themselves. There were so many safety precautions to take when considering working with young children....

In her head Chloe could see the interior of the unused rooms in the church basement, cleaned and decorated with tiny tables and chairs, the walls hung with early learning materials and shelves full of toys for little hands to explore.

There would be a rug for story time, she thought as her gaze traced the crisp line of curls that arrowed from the woodworker's chest down into his jeans. She followed the curls back up his chest, and over a rough-hewn, stubbled jaw that was nearly all she could see of his face beneath the battered cap—

Oh, glory, he was watching her!

Chloe tore her gaze from the window and attacked the typewriter keys. She could feel a blazing heat suffusing her face. *Serves you right,* she told herself sternly, *ogling the poor man. He's probably as embarrassed as you are.*

After a minute she risked another glance toward the window.

The workman had climbed down a rung or two. An unruly mess of golden-streaked curls over which he had jammed a baseball cap hid his face from full view but he was looking straight at her, and before Chloe could react again, he raised a hand and gave her a cocky salute, white teeth flashing as he laughed aloud. The sound penetrated the glass, reaching her burning ears as she ignored the wave and applied herself to the keyboard with unnecessary vigor.

She would *not* look at him again, she promised herself.

But she couldn't prevent her mind from replaying, in vivid color, the sight of him framed in her window. She didn't know his name, at least not his first name, but she assumed he was the "Shippen" of Shippen Carving and Restoration on the contract he'd submitted.

He was rumored to be wild and undisciplined, the local bad boy. Though she couldn't recall hearing anything specific, the look on the parishioners' faces when they'd learned who had been hired to do the exterior repairs had said a lot. Miss Euphorbia Bates, who helped fold bulletins for the Sunday services, had frowned darkly when she'd heard. "A devil, that one.

I bet there wasn't a girl he ever wanted who said no to him.''

Chloe took notes once a month for the congregation's meeting of the elders. Her father, the pastor, had looked apoplectic when Mr. Shippen's name was proposed. ''He's a defiler of young women,'' he'd pronounced in ominous tones.

''God will judge each of us, so there's no need for us to judge each other,'' said Benton Hastings, the elder who was in charge of getting bids for the job. ''This young man is a skilled woodworker with a reputation for fair business dealings.''

''God works in mysterious ways,'' piped up Nelda Biller. ''Perhaps we can be an instrument of salvation.'' Nelda had a way of spouting predictable Christian platitudes, and before she could get on a roll, Benton Hastings jumped back into the pause. ''Shall we put it to a vote?''

Shippen Carving and Restoration had gotten the church job despite the dark mutterings of its pastor. What in the world, she wondered, could her father have meant?

She was shaken back to the present by the sound of the office door opening. Instantly she began to type again, fixing a pleasant smile on her face. ''Good morning, may I help…you?'' The question trailed off in the sudden silence, and Chloe's fingers stilled on the keyboard when she saw who had entered the office.

It was Shippen, the Shirtless Wonder, now decently covered with a T-shirt. He'd taken off his cap and with her first clear glance at his face, Chloe nearly jumped out of her seat in shock.

It was *him.*

Oh, this was terrible. She'd wondered about him for

three years, ever since one impetuous evening of rebellion had brought her into closer contact with him than she had liked, but she never expected to see him again. Geiserville might be a small place, but she moved in an even smaller circle within it, composed largely of her father's parish. She was hardly likely to run into a wild playboy unless she went hunting him.

Which she certainly never would do. He had no scruples and fewer morals. Exactly the type of man she would avoid at all costs.

"Hi. I'm Thad Shippen. I'm the face that goes with the body outside your window." His voice was smooth and clearly amused. He was smiling at her with warm masculine interest that she couldn't miss, but what struck her forcefully was that there wasn't a glimmer of recognition in his eyes.

He didn't remember her!

Well, this certainly wasn't the time to remind him.

She looked up at him again, feeling a hot flush spread from her neck to her hairline. She couldn't sustain the eye contact, and settled for a spot just to the left of his head. Her face felt redder than ever, but she forced the pleasant smile into place again, pretending this was just an ordinary meeting. "I'm Chloe Miller. If you need anything let me know, and I'll try to find it."

"Anything?"

She glanced at him again, startled by the innuendo, and saw that he was smiling, a knowing kind of smile that made every cell in her body stand up and take notice. He looked amused, and his eyes crinkled at the corners as his smile grew wider.

His eyes were beautiful, the kind of eyes one of her friends called bedroom eyes. Chloe always noticed people's eyes. In this case she could have been blind, and still those eyes would have made an impact. They were blue, the striking unusual sky color so rarely seen, an incredibly intense blue made even more so by the tanned skin of his face. It had been dark when she'd met him, and she'd never seen him in daylight, never been subjected to the full force of that blue gaze. The eyes held an intimate smile beneath their droopy lids that made her want to smile back, but she suppressed the urge and ignored his lazy grin.

"Was there something you needed in the office?"

He nodded, still smiling. "May I use your telephone?"

"Of course. Come around the counter." She beckoned him around to her desk and set the telephone within his reach.

Thad Shippen settled one hip comfortably on the corner of her desk and picked up the telephone. His jeans were nearly white with age, stained and ragged. The fabric stretched taut over his thighs. Through a hole along one seam she could see a wedge of tanned skin and blond curl. Hastily she averted her eyes from that leg. Her stomach was tied in enough knots to satisfy a scoutmaster.

Would he recognize her? She devoutly hoped not. The memory of the night she'd met him still embarrassed her. If *he* brought it up, she'd just die.

While he dialed and spoke to someone at the local builders' supply store down on Main Street, she studied him covertly. He didn't have movie-star-handsome features, but his straight nose and the aggressively squared jaw formed a definitely masculine face. His lower lip was full and sensual, its upper mate thin and clearly defined in a manner that curled up the corners of his mouth in repose and left him looking as if he were always just a wee bit amused at the world. When combined with a high brow that invited a woman's soothing hand and those sleepy, come-hither eyes, he was a dangerous package. She could see why it was rumored that no girl ever turned him down.

Thad put down the receiver and leisurely straightened his lean frame, smiling down at her. He was at least six feet if not a little more, she'd guess. *And all muscle,* a treacherous voice inside her reminded. Seated at her desk, Chloe felt small and unexpectedly feminine, vulnerable in a way that she couldn't quite put her finger on, but one that made the knots in her stomach loosen and flutter into big butterflies.

"Thanks for the use of your phone," he said.

"You're welcome." She felt as if the knots had migrated to her tongue.

"So I guess it's no coincidence that your last name is the same as the good Reverend Miller's."

"He's my father."

The corners of his lips curled higher. "I'm glad you're not his wife."

She felt herself coloring again. For the life of her she couldn't think of an answer to that. Before she could form a coherent thought, he began to speak again.

"Well," he said. "I guess I'd better get back on that ladder or I'll get fired." But he made no move to go.

She forced herself not to sit and gawk at him. Women probably did that all the time, and she wasn't about to let him see how he affected her. "They won't fire you. You came highly recommended."

He laughed, throwing his head back and displaying strong white teeth. "I'll just bet." Then he sobered, focusing those incredible eyes on her mouth. After a silence that lasted a beat too long, he said, "If they knew what I was thinking right now, I'd be history."

Again, she couldn't reply, couldn't form a single word. He packed more experience into that single sentence than she'd had in her entire life. Her life had been spent in a quiet world of predictable routine and studying, and since her return home, all her time and energy had been thrown into her job. Oh, she'd spent the normal amount of time as an adolescent peering into the mirror, examining her features, and she'd quickly come to the conclusion that she was never going to be a raving beauty.

Nowadays, the mirror was mostly used for making sure her flyaway brown curls weren't sticking out in all directions. She knew there wasn't anything special about her, anything that would attract a man like Thad Shippen. Could he be like this with all women?

Of course, said a little voice inside. *Remember how he treated you? With his looks, he's probably had encouragement from women all his life. Flirting—and more—must be like breathing to him.*

Still, even though she knew he didn't mean it, all the heat in her body responded to his sensual teasing. He caught her gaze with his, and for a long moment she simply stared at him.

He started to speak. "Would you—"

The door banged open.

Chloe jumped. She could have sworn Thad did the same. Reverend Miller came marching into the office, his back ramrod straight.

"Chloe, did you see where that man on the ladder got to? Oh." He paused, seeing Thad standing by her desk. "Good morning, Mr. Shippen. Is there something we can do for you?"

Thad smiled widely at her father, but even from her seat she could tell that it wasn't the warm shift of facial muscles she'd received. This one was all teeth and coolness. "Hello there, Mr. Minister, sir. Thank you, but Chloe's already taken care of everything I wanted."

She was shocked by the taunting, deliberately provocative words, but her father didn't appear to notice anything out of the ordinary.

"You're not to be in the office bothering Chloe," he said curtly. "She's busy and you should be, too, if you want to keep this job."

Thad didn't move for a long moment. Then he shrugged. "If you don't want the work done, I'll just pick up my things and let you find somebody else to do the restoration."

The minister waved a hand at the door. "Don't put words in my mouth, Mr. Shippen. Just get on with your job and leave us to ours."

To Chloe he said, "If he bothers you again, let me know."

It was a clear dismissal, but as Thad winked at her and swaggered out of the office, Chloe knew who had won. Her father didn't have the authority to fire anyone and he knew it. So why had he threatened Thad with the loss of his job?

She shook her head briskly as the minister disappeared into his office. Well, whatever it was, it had nothing to do with her, and she wasn't going to fret about it.

She attacked her work with determination, and didn't stop again until almost noon, when her father stuck his head out of his office. "Chloe, would you mind picking up some lunch for me today? I have someone in my office and I can't leave right now."

"Certainly." She smiled at him, then gathered her purse and the light spring jacket she'd worn. There was no need to ask her father what he would like; she probably knew his preferences better than he did.

As she pushed open the heavy front door of the church, she realized she would have to pass by Thad Shippen, who was still working outside though he'd moved away from her window.

The elders hadn't specified what hours he was to work, but Thad knew the office opened at eight-thirty. And that meant Chloe Miller would be sliding out of that tiny car again this morning, pushing her skirt modestly down over her shapely legs and blushing when she saw him watching.

He wouldn't miss it for the world.

She was very pretty beneath all that sedate courtesy, was Miss Church Secretary, though she didn't appear to be aware of it. She must have been a few years behind him in school, but he didn't remember her. Of course, if she hadn't hung out at parties with a beer in her hand, waiting for a ride with any guy who had an itch to scratch, he doubted their paths had crossed.

He hadn't paid much attention to the good girls.

Until Jean.

His hands stilled for a moment over the chisels he was selecting, then resumed their work. His mind, however, wasn't so easily managed. It wandered back eight years in time, back to the day Jean had come banging into his kitchen, where he used to keep his business in the early days.

"I'm pregnant, Thad," she'd announced, red hair flying in agitation. "My father's going to kill me."

Jean had indeed died, he thought sadly, but it hadn't

been at the hands of her disapproving father. Thad still visited her grave occasionally, though the headstone her family had chosen, with its depiction of a woman cradling an infant in her arms was almost more than he could take. It was still startling to see "Jean Lawman Shippen" inscribed on the stone.

So what was he doing, lusting after this prim little church secretary? he asked himself. He was poison, with a woman's life on his conscience. Not to mention an unborn baby, who had never even had a chance to draw breath.

He didn't allow himself to watch as Chloe walked into the church a few minutes later, and he was working industriously when the Reverend Miller came out a while later and drove away in his gray sedan. Around ten, he could feel his fingers getting stiff, and he decided to take a short break, maybe walk down to Main Street for a cup of coffee.

He was still climbing down the ladder when Chloe banged open the front door of the church, racing over to him in a way that seemed most unlike her. As she got close, he realized that her face was white, and the wide golden-brown eyes he thought so pretty were huge and strained.

"I smell gas," she said breathlessly. "Get away from the church and call 911." He instinctively put out a hand but she shrugged it off and turned, running back into the church before he could get out a single word.

"Damn!" Suddenly his heart was thumping a hundred miles a minute. He sprinted to the street and grabbed the first man he saw on the corner. "Get to a phone and call 911," he shouted into the fellow's startled face. "There's a gas leak in the church and there are still people inside."

As the man nodded, Thad turned and ran back to the church. Yanking open the door, he plunged into the main hallway. The odor of natural gas hit him full in the face, and his pulse racheted up another notch. Sprinting down the hallway toward the office, he nearly knocked Chloe and an elderly woman to the floor as they came out of an adjacent room. Chloe gave him a brilliant smile of relief when she saw him.

"Help me get her out of here."

"Is there anyone else inside?"

"No."

Satisfied, Thad hustled the older woman out the door. As he turned to see if Chloe was all right, he realized with a sick feeling of shock that she wasn't behind him. *Dammit, she was still in the church!*

Frantic now, he ran back again. The gas smell was even stronger. He sure as hell hoped she was right, that there was nobody else in the church. Any number of tiny electrical functions could ignite gas, not to mention a match or a cigarette. He saw her immediately through the glass window in the office, grabbing computer disks and files and everything else she could find, stuffing them into a large canvas bag. He nearly pulled the door off its hinges getting in.

"Come on, we've got to get out of here!" It was a command, but she didn't even look up.

"I'll be done in a minute. You go."

"You're done *now*." He grabbed the bag from her and seized Chloe around the waist, dragging her toward the door. She struggled for a moment, then began to run with him. They cleared the office and ran down the hallway hand in hand. He kicked open the front door, and they raced through it and down the stone steps, out across the wide lawn. At the far edge of the street, policemen were pushing back the crowd of onlookers who had gathered.

Thank God, he thought, meaning it—

Behind them an immense blast shook the world. Instantaneously, what felt like a huge fist slammed into him from behind, tearing Chloe's hand from his, tossing him forward like a rag doll and rolling him across the ground. His head banged across a tree root, but he staggered to his feet, looking wildly around for Chloe.

She lay a few feet to his left, crumpled at the base of an old oak tree. Leaves and debris rained down around them, and as a stinging sensation penetrated his dazed senses, he realized that the tree was burning above them.

Dropping to Chloe's side, he shielded her body with his, feeling tiny bites across the back of his neck from the rain of fire. She had a bleeding gash at one temple, where he guessed she hit the tree, but he got a pulse in her neck. He had no choice; he had to move her.

Lifting her carefully into his arms, Thad staggered away from the tree, on toward the street and the knots of shocked people watching him approach. He could hear sirens shrieking, careering closer. Two men darted forward. One reached out and took Chloe from him, the other put a supporting shoulder beneath his arm. "C'mon, buddy, you're almost there."

But he couldn't. His knees wouldn't lock, wouldn't hold him up. As he slowly sank to the ground, his body twisted. The last thing he saw was a giant bonfire as the church was engulfed in flames.

He heard the technicians talking; before he opened his eyes he knew he was in an ambulance. One look confirmed it. He knew why, and he knew what he needed to know before he could relax. "Is Chloe okay?"

"Welcome back," said a woman in a blue medical technician's uniform. "Is Chloe the woman who was with you?"

He nodded, then was sorry as everything whirled around him.

"She's coming to the hospital with another unit," the woman said. "She wasn't conscious when we loaded you, so I can't tell you anything else."

Then they were at the hospital. To his annoyance, they carried him in on a gurney like he was severely injured, and he was poked, prodded and X-rayed about four hundred times. He was given an ice pack for his head, and some sadistic nurse cleaned and bandaged an assortment of burns and cuts he couldn't remember receiving.

He asked about Chloe at least a hundred times but nobody would tell him anything. Finally, after yet another nurse had backed out of his cubicle with a vague promise to check on Miss Miller's condition, he got off the uncomfortable bed and eased his way into the burned and bloody T-shirt they'd taken off him, then started for the door.

"Whoa, fella, where are you going?" One of his nurses, with a build and a grip like a fullback, snagged his arm.

He jerked himself free and glared at her. "I'm going to find somebody in this damned place who will tell me how Chloe Miller is doing."

The fullback scowled back. "We're checking for you. You have to be patient, Mr. Shippen."

"I've been patient," he snarled. "And now I'm done.

So just scratch me off your little list, lady, because I'm getting out of here.''

"Mr. Shippen?" Another nurse came toward them, but he was in a stare-down with the fullback. Finally, with narrowed eyes and a sniff, she looked away first.

Ridiculously pleased at the small victory, he was a little happier when he turned to the second nurse. "What?"

"Miss Miller is undergoing some tests. She's been admitted to the Critical Care Unit, room 338. That's the—"

"Tests for what?"

"Routine tests for head injury. She suffered quite a blow to the head, apparently."

"When she hit the tree," he said, mostly to himself.

The nurse looked sympathetic. "It could be hours before she is allowed to have visitors other than family. Is there someone who can take you home after you're released?"

Thad didn't bother to answer her as he turned and started toward what he hoped was the exit from the Emergency Department into the rest of the hospital.

"Wait, Mr. Shippen!" The nurse's voice was a panicked squeak. "You haven't been discharged yet."

"Tough." He didn't look back.

The nurse scurried along beside him, waving a clipboard under his nose. "You'll get me in big trouble if you leave here without being discharged."

The note of genuine dismay in her voice was the only thing that penetrated his determination. He halted. "I'll give you sixty seconds to get a signature on that."

She hesitated, then apparently realized she didn't have time to argue. Her jacket flapped behind her as she raced back down the hall.

Thad rubbed his forehead, then swore under his breath when his fingers brushed over the raised lump where he'd hit the tree root. He glanced through the glass windows of the double doors leading from the emergency area, noting a sign directing visitors to the elevators. When he turned back, the nurse was coming down the hall with the doctor who had initially looked him over striding behind her.

The man frowned at him. "We're busy people around here, Mr. Shippen. I was dragged away from a seriously ill person for this."

"So sue me." Thad frowned right back. "If you'd signed me out of here when you saw me, I'd be out of your hair."

The doctor ignored him, stepping forward to shine a small light into each of Thad's eyes. "Touch your right index finger to your nose."

"Give me a break." But he complied.

The doctor lifted the clipboard and scribbled his name across the paper. "You should be admitted for additional observation, although you don't seem to be concussed. I assume that hard head protected you. If you have any episodes of blurred or double vision, any feelings of vertigo or dizziness, call your doctor or come back. Change the dressings on those burns tonight and tomorrow. After that you may remove them. See a doctor if you suspect any infection." He handed the clipboard to the nurse, who immediately dashed away again. "Any problem with that?"

Thad grinned unwillingly. "Nope. Thanks."

The doctor grinned in return. "Now get out of here and go find your girl."

Thad didn't bother to answer as he banged through the double doors and headed for the elevators.

He had just punched the button for the Critical Care Unit's floor when he heard the commotion behind him.

"That's him! Hey, Mr. Shippen!"

"Thaddeus Shippen?"

"Mr. Shippen, give us your version of what happened in the gas explosion today." A woman with sharp features and frosted hair stuck a microphone under his nose.

Another man raised his pencil in the air. "I'm from the *Valley First Edition.* Is it true that you reentered the building to rescue the church's secretary?"

"Mr. Shippen, what were you doing at the church? Are you personally involved with Miss Chloe Miller?"

Thad sagged against the wall, wishing the elevator would hurry up. He hadn't even thought about the press, but he guessed something like this was a national story just as that plane that had crashed right into a house over in Waynesboro a few years ago had been. He might as well get this over with or they'd only get more intrusive. The last thing he wanted was this crowd following him up to Chloe's floor.

He smiled at the woman reporter. "This will have to be brief."

"Certainly." She was smooth and way too polished for him as she launched into her first question. As he answered, everyone around her was nodding and scribbling in little notepads.

"When did you first realize there was a gas leak in the church?"

He took them through a short version of what had happened. From their questions, it was obvious they had talked to the elderly woman he had escorted out before he'd gone back after Chloe.

"How does it feel to be a hero, Thad?" The newswoman lightly squeezed his arm.

Thad pulled himself away as the elevator opened. "I wouldn't know. I just did what anybody else would have done. Sorry, folks, gotta go."

He turned his back on the reporters and stepped into the elevator, then pushed the button for the third floor. When the door opened, he sprinted down the hall to where signs directed him to Critical Care. He wondered where the nurses' desk was. Hospital architects must all take the same course in How to Confuse the Public. He'd never been in a hospital yet that was easy to get around.

As he turned the next corner, he came face-to-face with Reverend Miller.

Great. Mr. Holier-than-Thou.

Behind Miller was a group of people with gravelooking faces. He recognized the man who had hired him for the job at the church, as well as the woman he'd led out of the building before it blew.

"Young man!" she twittered. She leaped to her feet with amazing speed and came over to drape herself all over him. "Thank you, thank you. You saved my life!"

Thad could feel his neck getting hot. Damned if he wasn't going to blush! "Chloe saved your life," he corrected. "I just helped out a little bit."

The lady didn't miss a beat. "Well, thank you, anyway, dear boy. If it hadn't been for you, I'm sure Chloe never would have made it out of there."

The other man, Hastings, he thought his name was, extended a hand. "Yes, thank you, Mr. Shippen. Nelda here tells me Chloe was gathering up church documents when you found her." He indicated the bag the old gal was holding up. It was the bag Chloe had been stuffing full of discs and papers when he'd dragged her out of her office.

Thad almost smiled at the memory, but he was too worried about Chloe. "Yes, she was. Can someone tell me how she's doing?"

Reverend Miller stepped forward. "We haven't heard much yet. They're doing some tests and they will let us know as soon as they know anything." He cleared his throat and glanced away, then extended his hand to Thad. When their eyes met again, Thad could see the sheen of tears in the older man's eyes. "Thank you, Mr. Shippen, for saving my daughter's life. I heard that you risked your own life to go back in after her and that you carried her to safety. Chloe's mother passed away years ago. She's all I have. If she hadn't gotten out…"

"What are the tests for?" Thad couldn't take the man's obvious grief. It reminded him too much of another time in another hospital.

"Head injuries, among other things," Mr. Hastings said gently. "Would you like—"

"Mr. Shippen has been through quite an ordeal of his own," Chloe's father said. "He needs to go home and rest."

"I'll run him home," Benton Hastings said.

"Just take me back to my truck," Thad requested. "I can drive from there."

Reverend Miller gave him a sober look. "Your truck was parked in front of the church. It was destroyed." He put an arm around Thad's shoulders and turned him toward the door. "Don't worry. Our insurance will replace it for you. Thank you again for saving Chloe. Someone will call you tomorrow and update you on her condition."

Thad started to protest, but everyone was nodding. Mr. Hastings took him by the elbow, and before Thad knew it, he'd been escorted to the man's car for the short ride home to the old trailer in which he lived.

Two

He didn't sleep well. Bumps and bruises in places he hadn't even realized he had nerve endings made themselves felt throughout the night, courtesy of the blast that had thrown him to the ground. His head ached, despite the ice pack he draped over the largest lump. The spots on his back where superheated bits of debris had burned through his clothing stung and, sore as he was, he could barely reach most of them to put on the ointment from the hospital. His favorite T-shirt, washed and worn to the ultimate in comfort, had to be tossed out.

And on top of it all, he still hadn't heard how Chloe was doing. He should have made sure she was behind him when he'd first found her in the gas-filled building. Who would have thought anybody would be dumb enough to go back into that building after a bunch of files?

Well, he had work to do. He resisted the urge to snatch up the phone and call the hospital. He'd hear soon enough how she was doing. Or maybe he wouldn't. Either way, no big deal. He was only interested because she was a fellow human being. She might have tripped his switch a bit more than any woman he'd met in a long time, but it wasn't like he couldn't live without her.

Going to the card table that served as his desk in the tiny living room, he flipped through his calendar. Now that his work on the church was a moot point, he could take on a new project.

Would the church elders still want to pay him for the work he'd done? It would probably be tacky to ask for payment, he decided regretfully. The best thing to do was to get on with another job. He called the woman who was next on his list and explained that he could start her fireplace mantel restoration sooner than expected, but she wouldn't hear of him coming over.

"Take a day or two and rest, Thad. I'm sure you must be a bit shaken up after coming face-to-face with death. How about we start on Wednesday? And if you aren't feeling up to it that soon, you just let me know, and we'll postpone a bit. I feel almost guilty taking advantage of the church's misfortune, after all."

All right. Fine. He washed up his breakfast dishes and set them in the drainer, then made a beeline for the small cinder block garage he used for a workshop. If nobody wanted him to work, he'd spend the day on his own projects.

When the telephone on the wall rang just before lunchtime, he leaped for it. Maybe it was Chloe calling.

"This is Joseph Miller. May I please speak to Thaddeus Shippen?"

"Speaking." Disappointment sliced through him and he covered it with flippancy. "Hi, Rev. I guess you don't need me to work today."

"Hardly." The minister's tones sounded cooler than yesterday, when he'd been falling all over himself to thank Thad. "I'm calling to inform you of Chloe's condition, as I promised."

"So inform me." But his heart leaped into his throat. Wasn't she okay by now?

Miller went on, though he sounded like he was speaking through gritted teeth. "Chloe regained consciousness yesterday. She's doing well and is expected to leave the hospital today. There's no need for you to make a special trip just to visit."

The message couldn't have come through more clearly. Chloe didn't want to hear from him and had sent her father to let him know. She'd woken up yesterday and hadn't bothered to let him know. He guessed he couldn't blame her. Miller had probably told her about what he did to young, innocent girls, and she'd decided to heed the warning. Oh, well. She was too much of a Goody Two-shoes for him, anyway. He preferred his women ready and willing, the kind who could look out for themselves. No more virgins for him.

"Thanks," he drawled, "but you didn't have to call. I figured I'd hear about it if she up and died."

There was a moment of shocked silence from the other end. He heard Miller draw in a breath, and in a very final tone, say, "Thank you again for your courageous assistance in rescuing my daughter and Miss Biller, Mr. Shippen. They would have been a great loss to our parish and to the community, as well as a personal loss to me."

Unlike you. The unspoken message came through loud and clear.

Thad sat for a very long time with the dial tone buzzing in his ear before he slowly lowered the receiver and moved to hang up the phone.

"I'm not even allowed to dig around a little to see if anything is left?" Chloe stood, disbelieving, on the scorched grass near the twisted rubble that had been the church. Her parents had been married here when her father was just a young seminarian. She'd been baptized here and confirmed, as well. When her mother had died, the funeral service had been held at the church. Afterward, all the ladies of the parish had contributed mountains of food for the reception.

She'd always assumed that someday she would walk down the aisle on her father's arm to her waiting groom. Her eyes burned at the thought, but she fiercely shook away the tears. A church is not the building where worship occurs, she told herself. A church is all the people who worship God together.

Thanks to Thad, no part of the true church had been lost. It was a test of faith to make herself believe that, as she mourned for the loss of the building before which she stood. The structure had been reduced to an impassable, jumbled mound of brick, blackened wiring and ash. Fire following the initial explosion had quickly decimated anything that remained, including her car and Thad's truck, which had been parked directly in front of the building. Thank Heaven the church had been set well away from the street in the middle of an enormous lot. Even so, she'd been informed that only the quick actions of the fire company had prevented the fire from spreading to surrounding buildings. Yellow tape completely encircled the jumbled mess, prohibiting the public from getting too close.

"I'm sorry, honey." Her father put a comforting arm around her. "The fire chief said everything would be too smoke and water damaged to salvage. Let me take you home to rest."

"Everything…everything is gone. I still can't believe it."

Reverend Miller shuddered. "I can. I was four blocks away when it blew, and it felt like it was right next door. The vibration knocked Mrs. Murphy's knick-knacks right off the shelves. I thank God you weren't in there."

Thank Thad, you mean, she thought. Thinking of who had dragged her out dampened her spirits even more. A sob pushed its way into her throat, and she swallowed it, fiercely narrowing her eyes to prevent threatening tears from falling. She was in shock, overly emotional, that was all. It had nothing to do with Thad Shippen.

He hadn't even stuck around to see if she was all right. When she'd regained consciousness, her first question to her father had been about Thad. He'd assured her that Thad was all right, that he'd been treated for minor burns and bruises and released already. Tears threatened again, and she swallowed hard, willing them away as her father escorted her back to his car and headed home.

She had no business mooning over Thaddeus Shippen. He might have rescued her, but deep down he wasn't a gentleman, and she had firsthand experience to prove it.

Laying her head against the back of the seat, Chloe let her mind drift back to her first days home in Geiserville after her graduation from the all-girls Christian college where she'd received her teaching degree. Coming home to live hadn't been easy after having her freedom for four years. It wasn't that she'd been wild or undisciplined, but she wasn't used to having to explain where she would be every time she walked out the front door.

Then, only weeks after she'd come home, the church secretary had resigned when a brother who lived on the West Coast had a stroke. Dear Elizabeth, who had served the church faithfully for over twenty years, went to California to nurse her brother, and Chloe had agreed when her father had asked her to fill the position on a temporary basis until the elders could find a suitable replacement.

Chloe had intended to use the summer to begin preparations for the preschool she hoped to open. Instead, weeks dragged on into months, and not much was said about hiring another secretary. Each time she mentioned it to her father, he told her how capably she had filled Elizabeth's shoes and how lucky they were to have her.

One day she had been filing documents when one of the elders walked out of her father's office. "Let me be the first to welcome you officially. I'm delighted to hear you're going to be staying," the man had said.

Chloe stared at him, wondering if he was speaking to the right person.

"Er...staying where?"

"Why, here at the church." Mr. Barlow beamed. "Your father just told me that you will be glad to continue working as the secretary, and I don't mind telling you how pleased I am. I'm sure there will be no problem making it official. You have filled Elizabeth's shoes so capably we've barely noticed she's gone." The man reached for her hand and shook it enthusiastically.

"Couldn't have worked out better, could it? You have a good day now."

As the elder sailed out of the office, Chloe turned her head and stared at her father's closed door for a moment before starting across the room. She felt like screaming, like throwing something, but she forced herself to turn the knob and step into the inner office without slamming the door behind her.

"Hello, dear. I didn't hear you knock." Her father glanced up from his desk.

"That's because I didn't."

At her tone, Reverend Miller's bushy white eyebrows lifted. "What's the matter, Chloe?"

"Daddy..." She was so angry she was shaking. "No one asked me to fill the secretary's position permanently. Why did you tell Mr. Barlow I'd accepted?"

Her father pushed his chair back from his desk and spread his hands. "Why, honey, I thought you'd be pleased. It's a measure of how well you've done that the committee is eager to have you here permanently."

"I spent four years training to teach. Just because I can do this well doesn't mean I *want* to."

Her father sighed. "This is my fault, I guess. If you want to be mad at somebody, be mad at me. I've been selfish. I missed you while you were away at school. Your lonely old father's been a happy man since you came home again, and we made such a good team I just forgot you weren't wild about the idea."

Chloe struggled with the guilt his words evoked. Oh, she recognized manipulation when she heard it, but it was hard to resist, coming from her own father. Resentment rose, as well. Every time they disagreed, her father undermined her anger with his apologies and his gently worded reasoning. Even though she knew his feelings were genuine, she still disliked the way he always made her feel like *she* was the one who should apologize.

"Well, I'm *not* wild about the idea," she said, not caring if her voice was sharp. "Whether or not I've liked working with you isn't the issue. What I want to do with the rest of my life is." She turned and walked out of the inner office, closing the door behind her. Picking up her purse, she started for the main door.

Her father's door opened behind her. "Where are you going? It's past lunchtime."

"I'm taking the rest of the day off," she had said without stopping or turning around. "I need to think about what I want to do with the rest of my life."

On Tuesday afternoon, Chloe closed the drawer of the desk at which she sat. The local business and community associations had worked long hours to arrange help for the burned-out parishioners over the weekend.

By Monday, another local church had offered to change their times of worship so that Reverend Miller's congregation could use their facilities on Sundays. A temporary office had been located rent free in an empty storefront on Main Street. An assortment of donated office furniture had been used to furnish it, and she even had a computer and a copier with a fax machine on loan from an office equipment firm.

She'd spent the day doing little but checking the disks she'd saved from the explosion, purchasing necessary supplies and planning how to reestablish an office routine. It was 4:30 p.m. now, the time the office closed, and she was so exhausted she could hardly wait to lock the door and go home.

But first she had something she had to do.

In the parking lot, she climbed into the rental car she'd picked up on Saturday. Before setting her purse on the seat, though, she pulled a slip of paper from it and examined the address she had copied from the telephone book earlier in the day.

Driving out of town through the green countryside, she told herself that a phone call simply wouldn't have done the job. Thad had risked his life to save her. She certainly owed him a personal thank-you. As she crossed the creek and turned onto a narrow road that led past a hog farm, she wondered again why he hadn't come to see her, either in the hospital or since.

Then she remembered the way her father had treated him in the office just last week. Thad probably didn't want to run into that kind of attitude again. Suddenly she felt much better. She ignored the little voice inside her head that reminded her that Geiserville was a very small town, and like most towns of its size, it would have been extremely easy for Thad to find out when her father was visiting and when he left.

Past the hog farm, she entered a small wood. She was looking for a house, so she almost missed the rusting metal trailer tucked back in a clearing. As it was, she had to reverse and check the mailbox again to be sure she had the correct address.

Could this be right?

The trailer once had been an odd shade of aqua and white, but decades of neglect had faded the white and dulled the aqua unevenly where some patches had received more sun than others. Rusty stains of orange and brown oozed dry rivulets of corrosion from every seam. The pathetic structure's only saving grace was the well-maintained landscaping that surrounded it. She recognized the swollen glory of forsythia about to bloom, the

variegated leaves of the mountain laurel, lilac, rhododendron and pussy willow catkins. Shoots poked from
the ground, signaling the advent of iris, tulips and
bushes of sweet-scented peony. Even this early in the
year it was obvious that someone cared for things that
grew.

Chloe checked the numbers on the mailbox one more
time. Yes, this was definitely Thad's address from the
telephone book.

Turning left off the road, she directed the rental car
onto the rutted lane that disappeared around the other
side of the trailer. A smaller building, hidden by the
trees, came into view. Beside it was parked a late-model
truck and she realized the pickup she'd seen Thad driving when he was working on the church probably had
met the same fate her car had.

This second building was far newer than the first,
built of sturdy cinder block. At first she thought it was
a garage, but there was no bay for a truck.

Climbing from her car, she started to follow the
driveway back to the modest front door of the trailer,
but the high whining sound of some kind of machine
caught her attention. She cocked her head to listen. The
sound was coming from the cinder block structure, so
she started in that direction.

A poured cement rectangle served as a porch. Chloe
stepped onto it and peered through the dusty panes of
glass, but she couldn't see anyone. Lifting a hand, she
rapped sharply on the door with her knuckles.

The whining motor stopped abruptly. Footsteps
clomped across the floor, and the door was yanked
open.

Thad was framed in the doorway. Despite the brisk
April breeze outside, he was shirtless again. When he

caught sight of her standing on the doorstep, his eyebrows rose in surprise. "Well, look what the breeze blew in. What brings you out this way?"

The warm greeting she had planned died in her throat. "I...I, uh, wanted to thank you for getting me out of the church." She tried a smile.

"No big deal." He grabbed a sweatshirt from the back of a nearby chair and pulled it over his head, shoving his arms through the cut-off sleeves and pulling it as far down his broad chest as it would go. "I've already been thanked. There was no need for you to drive all the way out here."

Confusion at his attitude and a depth of hurt that she wouldn't acknowledge cut into her. But she *had* driven out here, and she was determined to have her say.

"I don't believe many people would have gone back into the church after me. You saved my life, and I'm here in person to thank you because I wanted to, not because I needed to." Her gaze dropped to the ground, and she swept the toe of one polished pump restlessly across the concrete, sweeping away minute specks of mud. "You have no idea how many people have come into my office to tell me how proud they are that I managed to save so many files and records. They all tell me that was quick thinking, but the truth is, I was an idiot, staying in that building so long."

Thad was silent, and when she finally looked up at him, a half smile flirted at one corner of his mouth. "I'd have to agree with that."

Chloe smiled back, a bubble of happiness welling up inside her. "I still can't believe I did that."

"I can't believe you did, either. I won't repeat the words I said to myself while I was running back inside after you."

She giggled. "I bet the sight of you hauling me out of there was pretty funny."

Thad smiled with her. "I was too busy to notice if anyone was laughing." Then he nodded, as if in approval. "I'm sure that quick thinking you're so determined not to take credit for saved the church a tremendous amount of trouble. Just think what it would have been like to have to try to piece together all those records."

She shuddered in mock dread. "That was all I could think of. I learned early to be practical. It isn't a habit that goes away."

He straightened away from the door frame and stepped outside with her. The stoop immediately seemed too small and crowded, though she moved to one side to give him space. Thad took a deep breath of the moist spring air and loudly exhaled it. "Ah, this is great. I needed a break." Then he turned to pin her with a penetrating gaze again. "Why did you learn to be practical early? And what's 'early' mean?"

Chloe shook her head, fondly recalling her childhood. "My father spent most of his life with his head in the clouds. Somebody had to be practical."

"How about your mother? Didn't she fill the bill?"

"My mother died when I was nine. Daddy wasn't cut out for running a household, especially one with a child. He had a hard time remembering essential details like grocery shopping and paying bills. I think he simply had too many other thoughts in his head."

"Being a pastor doesn't leave room for parenting?" Thad appeared to be genuinely curious rather than critical.

"Daddy takes good care of those who need him in our congregation, even when they don't realize they need him. I was part of his team, rather than one of his responsibilities, and I liked it that way.''

Thad had sobered at her last words. Now he looked away from her, squinting at the bright light dappling the woods beyond his garden. ''Part of his team...that sounds cozy. My childhood was more of a solo flight.''

How did one respond to that? Chloe paused, searching for the right thing to say. But there was no right thing. The gossip she'd heard about him sprang into her head, that he'd run wild as a child, that his mother had entertained men on a regular basis, which was the church folks' way of saying she slept around. Chloe stood in tongue-tied silence, and after a moment he glanced back at her, his expression mocking.

''Sorry if my upbringing offends your Christian sensibilities. Unfortunately, everybody doesn't live by your high standards.''

''I'm not offended.'' She felt color springing to her cheeks. ''I was merely weighing my words. You have this prickly attitude that makes me afraid *I'll* offend *you.* I was thinking that flying solo is a really tough way to grow up.''

''It is.'' Thad exhaled, absently running a hand over his chest, but he didn't volunteer anything more. ''Sorry. I guess I'm a little defensive.''

A little? She almost laughed aloud. Thad waved his indifference to people's opinion in their faces like a matador challenging a bull. But since he'd just apologized, she supposed it wasn't the time to tell him so.

''So what are you working on now that you don't have to remodel the church?'' Perhaps a change of subject was for the best.

He glanced behind him into his wood shop. ''I have several other things lined up to start on, but today I was

just hacking around with some different techniques."
He grimaced. "I don't imagine the church will want me
to finish that job now." He chuckled, inviting her to
laugh with him.

It was good to see him lighthearted. She chuckled,
too, but after a moment the laughter died away and she
was left replaying those frantic, fearful moments when
she'd thought they weren't going to make it out of the
church in time. Thad was holding her gaze with his. His
face sobered, and she knew he was sharing the memories.

"Thank you," she whispered as her lower lip began
to tremble. If he hadn't come after her, she wouldn't be
here now, feeling the heat from his body—

"Don't think about it." Thad raised one hand and
covered her mouth with his palm, pressing firmly for a
moment. "We made it. That's all that counts." Then
he dropped his hand, reaching for her palm and lacing
his fingers through hers.

She stared at their joined hands. His curled around
her fingers, almost hiding them. His skin was hot and
dry, the palm tough from the work he did. The very
center was wet where it had pressed against her lips,
and a strange sensation tickled the pit of her stomach
as a mental image of those lips sliding onto hers slipped
into her head.

"So. Did you drive out here just to thank me, or do
you have something else to do in the area?" Thad was
speaking to her but he wasn't looking at her eyes. Instead, his gaze was fixed on her lips. Sensation magnified. She was conscious of her breath rushing in and
out over those lips, of a quivering excitement in the
muscles of her stomach. Belatedly she remembered that

she had come only to thank him, that her father would be expecting her for dinner any moment.

"I have to leave." Her voice sounded strange to her, low and strangled, but he must not have noticed. He stepped off the stoop, her hand still firmly gripped in his, and led her toward her car.

In her mind she could still feel the rough, warm press of his palm across her lips. She'd wanted desperately to lick them, to taste him so she could carry the taste with her when she left. But a combination of shyness and common sense had held her back, and she knew she would have been asking for trouble.

And of course, the last thing she wanted was trouble. Thad Shippen was trouble with a capital *T* and if she had any sense she'd get out of here right now. She'd done her duty and proffered her thanks. Her obligation was ended.

Too bad her fascination wasn't.

When Thad stopped beside the driver's door of her car she looked around, surprised. She wasn't entirely sure how she'd gotten here, but she had the awful suspicion that she might have floated. All she could think about was the way his hand cradled her much smaller one; the rough, callused warmth of his fingers where they were linked with hers; the way that hand and its mate would feel exploring her smooth, sensitive skin.

She couldn't look at Thad, afraid he might read her thoughts. Then her flustered senses jangled a warning, and she did glance up at him. He was smiling down at her as he lifted her hand to his lips. His lips. She was riveted by the sight of those chiseled male lips forming a kiss. Then he lightly pressed his mouth to the very tip of her middle finger. She wanted to jerk away—no, she wanted him to keep touching her like that. Never in her life had she been around a man who drew her as this man did. As she stared at him, she felt her heartbeat speed up. The tip of his tongue whisked across her fingertip, moistening the pad, and her breath caught in her throat, then rushed out on a sigh. Her knees felt weak. At the apex of her thighs, a warm throbbing awoke. She longed to press her body against his and...*and what, Chloe?*

Thad raised his other hand and gently lifted her chin with his index finger. She raised her eyes to his and found in them an answer to her longing.

"Would you like to stay for a while?" His voice was a low growl that made her toes curl inside her shoes.

She knew what he meant, and she knew that she shouldn't be giving this man the impression that she was the kind of girl who would—would stay. She shook her head. "I can't."

Thad smiled as if he'd expected her answer. "Then you'd better get out of here while you still have a choice, sweet thing." He dropped his hands away from her and stepped back, hooking his thumbs in the back pockets of his jeans.

Chloe stood dumbly for a minute, then mentally shook herself and reached for the handle of her car door. She wasn't interested in a fling with Thad Shippen. There was a big difference between thinking someone was attractive and deciding to engage in premarital se—*oh, my goodness!* Chloe's eyes widened. Her gaze had wandered down his body involuntarily until it reached the faded blue jeans that fit him like a second skin. The bulge distending the zipper shocked her silly, leaving no doubt in her mind what he was thinking. Her gaze flew back to his face and she could see the smirk beginning.

''Like what you see?'' Thad was openly laughing now.

Hastily she yanked open the door and slid into her car, slipping it into gear and reversing out of his driveway. As she drove away, she tried to work up outrage, anger, disgust...but all she could think was that if he had taken her inside that trailer she'd be learning right now what would assuage this anxious yearning within her.

Three

Every time he came through town the following week, she was in his way. He couldn't avoid her if he tried.

At least, that's what he told himself as he drove at a snail's pace past the storefront on Main Street where the church had set up a temporary office in the donated space. He tapped his brake, slowing a little more. She'd been seated at her desk all morning, intent on some sheaf of papers. Sure would be nice if she'd get up and sashay over to the filing cabinet so he could watch her.

The guy behind him honked his horn impatiently, and at the sound of the horn blaring, Chloe glanced up from what she was doing at the desk that looked out toward the street.

Quickly he slouched down in the rental truck, turning his face away. He hoped she hadn't seen him. She was liable to think he was watching her or something. It wasn't his fault that he'd had to make four trips to the hardware store this morning. And it sure wasn't his fault that the hardware store was two doors down from where she was working.

No, he didn't want her to get the wrong impression. He found her attractive, but she wasn't his type. No, his type wasn't afraid to show off feminine charms. He liked women with bold eyes and tight clothes, women who knew the score and the rules of the game. Jean had been the only exception to that, and she'd fooled him when he'd first met her...a nice girl posing as a party babe.

Still, he'd been interested when he first laid eyes on Chloe through that window at the old church. *Very* interested. She'd been watching him, and when she'd seen him looking back, she'd become all flustered and turned five shades of pretty pink.

Pretty. It was a good word for her. Chloe was pretty in an old-fashioned, quietly elegant, peaches-and-cream way that was rarely seen anymore, a ladylike prettiness that was distinctly less than fashionable in today's world of carefully rumpled, clumpy-shoes-and-shapeless-clothes glamour. If there was one thing Thad knew about, it was women. Courtesy of his mother, he'd been raised around women who spent big bucks and long hours trying to achieve beauty.

He could spot mascara at fifty yards and knew exactly how much time and mousse it took to create a headful of tousled curls that invited a man to dream about what they'd look like spilled across a pillow while he ravished their owner. He knew what a petite size in women's clothing was and if a perfume was musk or floral based, whether nail polish was frosted or crème and when a woman was wearing a push-up bra to help enhance what Mother Nature had skimped on.

Mother Nature hadn't skimped on Chloe, he remembered. Beneath those modestly buttoned blouses she wore with her prim suits was the figure of a goddess. The day she'd come to see him, she'd left her suit jacket in the car. He'd been so distracted by the firm mounds beneath the ivory silk of her short-sleeved blouse, he'd barely heard half of what she'd said.

For a few insane moments, he'd actually contemplated asking her out. But a few minutes into that fantasy, he'd come to his senses. Chloe was a sweet, sheltered, minister's daughter. And not just any minister, either, but the one who had conducted his wife's funeral service. She also was modest and courteous and kind to everybody—kind enough to make a big deal out of him saving her life, when she had to know her father would have thanked him already.

He, on the other hand, had never been sweet or sheltered, and he seriously doubted any woman anywhere would consider him modest, courteous or kind. A sudden vision of Chloe's face when he'd kissed her palm sailed into his head and with no more encouragement than that, his body began to respond as strongly as it had when she'd been standing right in front of him, confusion and arousal clouding her wide eyes. He'd wanted to pull up her modest skirts right there and bare every long, silky inch of her to his seeking hands—and the knowledge that he couldn't had frustrated him in a way he hadn't experienced in years. It had been rude and cruel to tease her like he had, but he'd wanted to shock her into leaving before he gave in to the inner voice shouting at him to haul her out of her car and into the trailer.

He could still see the way her pupils had dilated in shock as she'd realized she was looking at a fully aroused man. And she had been shocked, no question about it. It was just one more difference between them. Most of the women he knew would have laughed and snuggled right up.

Hell, he'd been raised watching his mother do exactly that. Chloe was the antithesis of his mother, genteel rather than coarse. He sensed that beneath her sedate surface there might be a smouldering ember waiting to burst into flame, but unlike his mother, she wouldn't allow the nearest man to feed her fire. No, Little Miss Miller would undoubtedly wait for Mr. Deadly Dull But Approved by Daddy and get a ring on her finger before she let anyone close enough to get warm. She and his mother couldn't be less alike.

But as he circled around through the high school parking lot and turned the rental truck back down Main Street one more time, he had to admit that in one way, Chloe and his mother did share something in common. Chloe was kind to everyone. That had been one of the first things he'd noticed about her. Just like his mother. She might have been easy with her favors before she'd gotten old and ill, but she'd always had a big heart.

She'd do anything for a friend who needed her, anything for him. He might have had a mother who liked the male of the species a mite too much, but he'd been loved.

As he drove past the temporary church office yet again, a car swung out of a parking space just ahead of him.

Fate.

He'd always been one to step right up when Lady Luck called. That empty parking space was a clear directive. He was supposed to stop and talk to Chloe. In fact, maybe he was even supposed to ask her out.

He considered the idea for a moment, pretending it was the first time it had occurred to him. Maybe she wasn't normally his type nor he hers, but what the heck.

Why else would that parking spot have opened up at that exact moment in time?

He sensed the exact moment she saw him. He didn't know why, but as he stepped out of the truck and popped a quarter into the meter, he knew she was watching him. He felt her...awareness of him as clearly as if she'd made eye contact.

Which she hadn't. No, she kept her head bent over her desk until the moment he stepped through the door. Then she looked up, a smile on her face. He didn't particularly like the smile. It was friendly, but professional, and too impersonal for the way he felt. He wanted her to smile at him like she meant it. Like he was someone important enough to merit an intimate exchange of expressions.

"Hi." He probably should say something else, but he couldn't quite think of what.

"Hello." Her smile did warm, then, as he stood like a dolt in the middle of her office with a big silly grin plastered all over his face.

"I...uh, was just coming through and thought I'd stop for a minute." Where was his poise, his finesse? He was pretty smooth most of the time but today, *smooth* seemed to have been replaced by *distinctly rough and bumpy.*

"I'm glad you did." Her smile warmed even more, but then she glanced over his shoulder as the door opened again, and the expression on her face faded to what he could swear was dismay, which she quickly changed as she said, "Hello, Daddy. I'm sure you remember Mr. Shippen."

Reverend Miller made a production out of hanging his raincoat up, before turning and offering a hand to Thad. "Thaddeus."

Thad extended his own, resisting the urge to squeeze the older man's hand in a handshake that would break a few bones. "Hello, Reverend Miller."

"No decisions have been made yet about when or whether the church will be restored," the pastor informed him. "Someone from the building committee will be in touch with you if your services are needed. In the meantime, Mr. Hastings can answer any questions you have." Reverend Miller stood stolidly in front of Chloe, as if she were a nineteenth-century virgin and Thad were a rake of the worst repute.

Which, come to think of it, probably wasn't all that far from the truth.

Thad merely smiled as Chloe's father attempted to outstare him. "I'm not here on business."

The minister's white eyebrows lifted. "Oh? Are you in need of spiritual assistance?"

The mere thought of that was too much to take. Thad allowed a chuckle to escape before he noticed Reverend Miller's expression, and the look sobered him suddenly. "Anyone with a dying parent is in need of spiritual assistance, Rev, but I'll take a raincheck on your offer, if that's what it was."

An awkward silence fell. Chloe and her father wore nearly identical expressions of shock that rapidly turned to sympathy. The pastor said, "Please accept my sympathies, Thaddeus. I was unaware that there was illness in your family."

Chloe's eyes were huge and compassionate. She stepped around her father and laid a hand on Thad's arm. "Is it your mother or father?"

He could have shocked her again then, but he didn't tell her he had no idea who his father was. He merely said, "My mother."

Chloe wasn't satisfied, though. "What's wrong with your mother?"

"She has cancer." Might as well be blunt, he decided. "She's been fighting it for several years, but she's about run out of options and energy. All I can do now is keep her comfortable as much as possible."

Chloe's face softened in sympathy. "I'm sorry. That's a difficult thing for a family to suffer through." Then her expression turned thoughtful. "Does she have a church affiliation?"

Thad stifled the urge to laugh again. She must not know about his mother, or she'd hardly have asked *that*. He shook his head and smiled gently at her, touched by the question in a way he hadn't expected. "No."

"Well, then!" Chloe turned to her father with a radiant smile. "Daddy, you have an opening in your visitation schedule today. You could visit Mrs. Shippen."

The minister hesitated.

Thad couldn't resist. "It's *Miss* Shippen, not Mrs."

Chloe never blinked. "Then you can visit Miss Shippen around three o'clock. Do you think that would suit?" She looked at Thad with a question in her eyes, and he realized abruptly that she was serious, that she really expected her father to visit his mother.

He couldn't do this any longer, as much as he enjoyed needling the prudish, judgmental old man. "I don't think that's a good idea," he said to Chloe. Then he looked at her father. "It's all right. No one expects you to minister to an old hooker."

Chloe gasped. "Thad! What a disrespectful way to

refer to your own mother. Of course my father will be glad to visit her.''

Reverend Miller nodded. Raising his gaze to Thad's, he said, "Thaddeus, if your mother wouldn't object to a ministerial visit, I'd be happy to see her this afternoon. We also will add her name to our prayer chain." Sincerity sounded in his tone, and his steady gaze looked almost remorseful.

Thad felt like somebody had hit him over the head. Since when had a *minister* wanted to have anything to do with his family? "I guess she'd enjoy that, sir...I think she'd like it very much."

"Good Tell her I'll be there at three, then." Recovering his aplomb, the reverend smiled at Thad, clearly waiting for him to take his leave.

Thad smiled back. He'd come in here to ask Chloe out, and he wasn't leaving without doing just that. Regardless of her father. After all, it wasn't like he was marrying her. What a thought—having that guy for a father-in-law.

Keeping the bland smile firmly in place, he waited.

Chloe turned away from the two men and plucked something from her desk. "Here are your messages, Daddy. The director of the youth conference wants you to call her this afternoon if you have time."

Her father took the sheaf of pink papers from Chloe without looking away from Thad. Finally he turned to Chloe. "Thank you. Don't forget, those bulletins have to be finished today."

"They're already done." She smiled sweetly as her father at last turned and stumped past her into the office at the back.

When the door closed behind him, she smiled at Thad

again. "I must apologize for Daddy. He's usually not so…abrupt. This change has him all upset."

He wanted to point out that her father had been rude to him since their first meeting, but he decided that might not be the best approach. "It looks like you have a pretty good handle on things here," he said instead.

"People have been wonderful." She indicated the furnished room with a sweep of her hand. "We've had everything I could possibly need donated." She cocked her head and looked at him questioningly. "What did you stop by for?"

He thought about lying, about working around to his point gradually, but he figured his time was limited. The rev might come storming out of his office any minute now.

"I want you to have dinner with me," he said baldly.

Chloe's eyes widened and she blinked. "I beg your pardon?"

Maybe he should have asked, instead of giving her an edict. "I'm asking you out," he said again. "Would you like to have dinner with me?"

She hesitated.

His heart sank.

"Well," she began, "I don't—"

"Just forget it." Sudden hurt blossomed in his chest. Unable to allow it to surface, he channeled it into anger, cutting off the refusal he could see forming on her face. "I've spent my life being ignored by half this town. I thought maybe you were different. I was wrong." He pivoted and was halfway out the door before she could marshall a word in her own defense. "Tell your old man not to bother visiting my old lady. She doesn't need to feel any worse than she already does."

* * *

It was a good thing she'd finished the most urgent work on the bulletins earlier in the day because she couldn't concentrate on a single thing after Thad barreled out of her office. She felt awful about the way he had misinterpreted her hesitation. It was all she could think about.

Why had he turned on her so fast? It was almost like he'd been *waiting* for her to refuse him.

She wished she'd thought faster. Why hadn't she simply said yes? That was what she wanted to do, actually what she'd planned to do after she'd thought about it for a second. Unfortunately he'd misread the way she'd started to reply, and before she could correct his impression, he'd stomped out.

She'd just been so stunned. She hadn't expected him to ask her out, and she knew that through the thin, temporary walls of the new office her father was listening to every word they exchanged. And then, there was her past experience with Thad...

She hardly could believe he didn't remember her at all. But then again, she knew she wasn't particularly memorable. So why was he asking her out now?

And more important, why did she want to accept? He'd been the worst kind of cad the first time they'd met. But somehow he didn't seem remotely related to that man now. Beneath the bad boy he flaunted for the world was a vulnerable core—could everyone see it as clearly as she could?

Apparently not. Her father certainly didn't appear to notice what a nice man Thad could be. She recalled her father's words about Thad taking advantage of young women, and she wondered again what he had meant.

Her thoughts were drawn back to Thad, and she knew she couldn't leave things the way they were. The clock indicated it was time to close the office. Rising from her desk, she gathered her things and locked up, heading for her car.

This time she knew where she was going.

It didn't take her long to get to the rusty trailer. Pulling into the drive, she noticed that Thad's rental truck was parked next to the trailer, rather than back near his workshop. Taking a deep breath, she walked across the grass to the door of the mobile home and rapped sharply on the metal screen.

The hum of a window air-conditioning unit masked any sound from inside. No one came to the door. She had almost convinced herself no one was home when the door swung inward and Thad stood before her.

He didn't speak, didn't open the screen that stood between them, merely surveyed her in a manner that gave nothing away.

"Hello." Her voice sounded calmer than she felt. "May I come in?"

Still without uttering a greeting, he reached out a hand and pushed open the screen, then stood back to let her pass inside. She was acutely aware of his big body only inches from her as she stepped into his home. When he closed the door behind her, she felt jittery and even more nervous than she had before. Vulnerable.

To avoid thinking further along those lines, she opened her mouth and rushed into the speech she had prepared on the drive out. "I came to tell you that you misinterpreted my words in the office this afternoon. After you asked me to dinner, I mean."

She waited a beat, but he didn't react in any way. She didn't know what she'd expected, but this wall of silence wasn't it.

"I was only thinking out loud when I started to answer you," she said. "I wasn't going to refuse your invitation."

He shrugged. "Sorry I misunderstood. It's probably just as well—it was a lousy idea, anyway." He walked around her to the tiny kitchen area of the mobile home. "Would you like a drink?"

"No, thank you." *Lousy idea for whom?* she wanted to ask, but insecurity and ingrained manners caught her tongue. He could only mean one thing, that he'd thought better of what she assumed had been an impulsive decision.

But if it had been impulse, then why had he driven past her office three times before he finally came in? Geiserville was a small town, and her office faced directly onto its main street. Did he think she hadn't noticed?

Thad scratched the back of his head. "Well, would you like to sit down?"

"No, thank you." She wanted nothing more than to leave so she could finish being utterly humiliated in private. She'd come out here expecting to right the wrong between them, and anticipating...what? That they would make plans for a date, at the least.

She walked blindly to the door. "I'll go now. I only wanted to clear up any misunderstanding."

"Wait! Would you, uh, like the grand tour before you go?"

She turned and met his gaze, wondering why he wanted her to stick around when he didn't want to take her out.

He was smiling wryly as he indicated the postage-stamp dimensions of his living quarters. She wanted to refuse, to make him feel the way she was feeling, but when she opened her mouth to say no, she found that she couldn't deny herself an extra few moments of his company.

"All right."

"Step this way, madam." He grinned, and her breath hitched in her throat for a moment before she began to breathe again. It wasn't fair that he was so handsome, that her body felt more alive around him than it did around anyone she'd ever met.

She allowed him to usher her back through a tiny hallway. "I've never been in a trailer before. They're very...compact."

"Is that a nice way of saying tiny?" His voice was in her ear, and she knew that if she turned around they'd be face-to-face in the confines of the narrow hall. She didn't dare.

"This is interesting," she insisted. "Whoever designs these squeezed in a lot of living space. I've always wondered what they looked like inside."

"This is an old one. The newer models are probably much nicer." He indicated the bath with a sweep of his hand. "The powder room." And at the end of the short hall, if it could really be called that, he opened the single door. "My office—where I also sleep."

He wasn't kidding. Built-in shelves and a desk covered most of the space that wasn't taken up by a large bed in the corner. The shelves were covered with books, some fiction, she noticed in a quick survey, but others— many others—on various aspects of the art of woodworking. The bed was a light wood with a beautifully carved headboard that boasted high posts at each side. She noticed the desk was a similar design in the same wood.

"This is beautiful." She ran her hand over the satiny

surface of the desk in one place where it wasn't covered by papers. "Did you make these pieces?"

Thad nodded. "Thank you. I like working with oak."

Chloe smiled. "I wouldn't know oak from…"

"Mahogany?" he suggested.

"Exactly." She made a wry face. "Wood wasn't one of the things I studied in school."

"College, you mean?"

"Yes." She glanced up at him, wondering what he was thinking. She doubted that he had an advanced degree. In fact, she didn't even know for sure that he was a high school graduate. Still, intelligence shone from his blue eyes and she reminded herself that a lack of education didn't go hand in hand with ignorance.

"It takes a college degree to be a church secretary?"

He couldn't know how that stung, and she tried to keep the defensiveness from her tone when she answered. "It's supposed to be a temporary position until they replace the secretary who just retired. I'm trained to teach. I hope to open a preschool at the church for disadvantaged children." Reality intruded, and she murmured, "At least, I *did*."

Thad winced in sympathy. "It'll work out. I bet they'll have that church rebuilt within two years." Then he pointed at the papers that littered his desk. She had noticed more of the same mess on a small card table wedged into a corner of his living room alongside a single couch. "I'm really bad with the paperwork. You might not have been trained to do it, but it looks like you run that office with one hand tied behind your back." He grimaced. "I can't even find time to sit down and go through this mess. Or maybe—" he grinned sheepishly "—it's that I can't bring myself to."

"I could help you." She told herself that she had no

ulterior motives, that after the way he'd saved her, it was only right that she repay him in some way.

"No! I wasn't angling for help, honest." Thad looked slightly panicked at her offer.

"I know." She smiled calmly, though her insides felt anything but calm. "You saved my life. I'd be glad of the opportunity to repay you in some way. I could help you straighten out your books or type some letters or invoices...whatever it is you need me to do most."

The words fell between them, and immediately she realized that her words could be taken in more ways than one. Thad hadn't missed it, either, she was sure. A warm blue glow lit his eyes and though he didn't move a muscle, she felt as if he'd touched her. Her breath came faster, and her knees felt wobbly. She put out a hand to steady herself on the desk, but he took it before it made contact with the wooden surface.

How could she have thought she knew what it was like to be touched by him? Slowly he drew her close, and she could feel the energy running between their joined hands, the heat his body gave off. She held her breath, unwilling to disturb the intimacy of the moment even by breathing.

And then Thad released her hand and stepped back. "I would be very grateful for your help," he said, and his voice sounded hoarse and deeper than normal. "But I'll pay you. You're not doing it for free."

She would have argued with him, but she was too busy trying to keep her knees from dropping her to the floor. Inhaling deeply, she only nodded.

Thad moved ahead of her, back into the little living room. "The most urgent stuff is out here," he told her. "You tell me when you want to start, and I'll get it organized so you know what to do."

* * *

The elders met the following week and voted to hire Thad to help with the rebuilding of the church. He met with the architect in charge of the project and the building committee twice at the office. The second time, the group concluded its meeting just before lunch on Saturday.

Chloe was working in the outer office when the group filed out. She'd had some filing she'd wanted to get done, anyway, and since she'd had to come downtown and unlock the office, she decided to stay. Although she'd insisted to herself in the morning that that had been her only motive, she called herself a liar fifty times after Thad stepped out of the conference room and smiled at her. While she busied herself with needless paperwork and tried to pretend she was unaware of every move he made, he glanced over the table of old photographs of the church.

When she looked up again, he was standing beside her desk. "Are you finished?"

She nodded, acutely aware that the others had all gone out and they were alone in the office.

"Want to grab a bite to eat?" His voice was supremely casual.

Chloe nodded while her stomach did a mad dance. He had just asked her out again! "That would be nice."

As she got her purse and preceded him out the door before turning to lock it securely, she tried to gather her careening thoughts back into some semblance of normalcy. It was only lunch. He might just want to talk business. It wasn't really a date.

But they didn't talk business. Not church business or his office work.

Instead, he made small talk until the waitress in the

downtown diner had taken their order and then asked,
"So tell me about the school you want to start."

She was surprised by his request, so much so that it
took her a long moment to marshal her thoughts. It had
been a long time since anyone had been interested in
listening to her talk about her plans for a preschool. Her
father so clearly *didn't* want to hear about it that she'd
stopped even trying to explain all her ideas to him. With
Thad, explanations were easy.

"My father means well," she said, trying to make
Thad understand. "But he needed me to help him for a
while, and I guess I made it too easy for him. He'll
never look for another secretary unless I force the issue."

"So what's stopping you?" Thad sounded almost
challenging. "It's one thing to respect your father, but
it's another altogether to let him kill your dreams."

Kill her dreams… In a way, she supposed that was
exactly what was happening. It was a shock to realize
that she had almost convinced herself she would never
have the chance to open a preschool.

"I had made up my mind to talk to him about it
again," she said. "But then, after the explosion, I just
didn't see how a new person could step into this mess.
I've settled, I suppose, for waiting until the church is
rebuilt."

"But that could be two years or more. You've got
everything reorganized *now*. There's no reason a new
person couldn't work with you for a month or so and
then take over. True, you might need to do some fast
talking to find a space and figure out some financing
until your own church has a space for you, but you
shouldn't wait."

He reached across the table and covered her right

hand with his own larger one. "I bet you'd be a great teacher. You shouldn't give up on your dreams."

She blushed. It wasn't a particularly intimate conversation, but his tone was low and seductive and his words made her feel as happy as if he'd told her she were a raving beauty. She hadn't had a champion *ever,* that she could recall.

"Do you have dreams?" She was curious. She knew so little about him, and it was suddenly important that he share some of himself the way she just had.

When he pulled his hand away and sat back abruptly, she felt like she'd been tossed into a cold lake. "My dreams all died a long time ago," he said in a tone that cautioned her not to cross the line.

"But aren't you doing what you want to do?" She thought he seemed happy with his work, fulfilled by the creative demands involved and satisfied to be doing it on his own terms.

To her surprise he relaxed again. "Yeah, I like my work. It's a good thing, too, since it's all I've ever been good at."

Then he glanced at his watch. "Speaking of which— I hate to cut this short, but I have some work waiting for me at home."

She rose, intending to pick up the bill and pay for her share, but he forestalled her effort. "I've got it."

Short of wrestling him for the tab, she didn't have a choice. "Thank you. Next time I'll treat."

He smiled, and she could have stood all day looking into those blue, blue eyes. "I'll hold you to that."

She smiled back, overly happy that he seemed ready to spend a "next time" with her, and went to the ladies' room while he paid.

As she came out of the stall, a heavy-set matron she

recognized as a clerk at the shoe store smiled and said hello. Then, without waiting for a response, the woman said, "I couldn't help but notice you had lunch with the Shippen boy. Better watch your step with that one, or you'll wind up in a bad way."

He's not a boy, he's all man, Chloe wanted to inform the woman. Even more, she wanted to know why everyone assumed the worst about him. But she did neither.

Another woman came in just in time to hear the first one's words. "You do know his mother *entertained men,*" she said with arched brows.

The first woman, delighted to have a sympathetic ear, volunteered, "Why, I hear she doesn't even know who that boy's father was."

Poor Thad. Chloe snapped her purse shut with unnecessary force. She still hadn't said a word, and the women were watching her. Well, they weren't going to have the pleasure of seeing if their words upset her. She stared back at the first woman, arching her eyebrow in a manner that conveyed silent disapproval. When the woman flushed and looked away, she turned the same stare on the second gossip, who stared back for less than five seconds before dropping her gaze to the hands she was waving under the dryer.

Chloe yanked open the door of the ladies'. No wonder Thad was so determined not to care what anyone thought. These people didn't even wait to hear the facts before spewing their nasty gossip across town.

Four

Okay, it probably was a little on the sneaky side, Thad decided, as he walked down the street toward Chloe's office on Monday a week later. Taking Chloe along to his appointment with the bank executive who could approve a line of credit for his business was a little like taking an apple to the teacher. He'd told Chloe it would be helpful to have her with him since she had helped him organize his books, but he knew her presence could only improve his chances for the loan.

He would feel bad about it if he didn't genuinely want her at his side.

She'd begun to accept him, he thought, since he'd adopted a lower-key approach. Oh, he still wanted her, and though he told himself again and again that she wasn't his kind of woman, he was drawn back to her day after day like a rabbit to a vegetable garden. He knew things were bad when he actually considered going to church just so he could see her on Sundays.

So far, he'd resisted such idiocy.

What he really wanted to do was to ask her out again. He told himself lunch didn't really count. He wanted to take her dancing. It was the only way he could think of to get her into his arms. But recalling the indecision that had clouded her eyes the first time he'd asked was enough to stop him. A man could only take so much rejection.

Yeah, she'd said she hadn't been going to refuse. Yet he didn't think he'd misread her—she might want to go out with him, but she was afraid of the idea.

Why? Okay, he knew she was…naive. His mind skirted around the *V*-word like it was a live grenade. He told himself he wasn't just interested in taking Chloe to bed, but his baser side stood up and laughed in his face. *So you don't want her in your bed? What are you dating her for, then? So you can join the church bingo club?*

A woman swept across the bank lobby, interrupting his mental wanderings. To his surprise she was smiling, though as she greeted Chloe and him he read the avid curiosity she was trying hard to mask.

Chloe was cheerful and sweet to the woman as she completely ignored the speculative glances. She was that nice to everyone they encountered, and it amused him no end. She could give a busybody absolutely no information and still make the person think they'd been awarded special treatment. He wondered how much she knew about his past, and if she'd give him the time of day if she learned about Jean.

Hell, maybe she already knew. He couldn't imagine that her old man hadn't shared all the sordid details.

Reverend Miller had handled Jean's funeral, though her family hadn't been big on church. He'd listened to the lies Jean's father had fed him and made up his mind about Thad, without once talking to *him,* the man who'd married her and whose child had died with her.

Abruptly he realized Chloe was speaking to him, and he forced his mind back to the present.

"We could go and get a pizza when we're done here…if you like."

He smiled down at her, liking the hesitancy with which she phrased her suggestion. "Yeah, that would be nice." Then a thought struck him and he smiled to himself. It was about time he had her to himself, even if it was only for a lunch hour. Excusing himself, he went to find a telephone.

The interview for a line of credit went more smoothly than Thad had expected. The banker was clearly surprised to see the summarized figures of his business, and his eyebrows rose when he saw the net profits. "Are you sure you even need this line, Mr. Shippen?"

Thad nodded, pleased and relieved at the man's professional attitude. "I want to buy a new piece of equipment that would allow me to try some new things, expand the kinds of restoration I can do right now."

The banker frowned, and Thad braced himself. "You might be better off with a straight-forward loan. The rate of interest would be better, and you would have a longer time to pay it off."

Anxiety disappeared again and he relaxed. "That would be nice, but unfortunately I need the line because I'm frequently forced to buy materials at the beginning of a job…and of course, I don't get paid until the end."

The banker nodded again. "Yes, I see…" He reached for a calculator and rapidly punched in several sets of numbers. When he looked up, he was smiling. "I believe that if you're interested, we could extend you both offers, a line of credit and the lower-interest loan."

It took a moment for the words to sink in.

Chloe turned to look at him. "That makes good sense, Thad. I think you should do it that way."

"Of course I'll need to visit your workshop, see your operation," the banker said. "But I don't anticipate that will be any problem. You have a reputation for doing good work at fair prices. Besides, you have the collateral, and your credit history is excellent."

He didn't know what to say. No one had ever extended a single extra crumb of advice or trust to him in the past, in this bank or the other one down the street. He was convinced it was Chloe's presence. It had to be.

A quarter hour later, they were climbing into his truck. He had an appointment to show the banker his workshop next week and completed copies of his loan applications in his hand.

"I can't believe it!" he exulted as he pulled into traffic. "That was great!"

"It did go well," Chloe was smiling, and he reached over and grabbed her hand, squeezing it tightly.

"Thank you."

"I didn't do anything," she protested.

"You prepared the information for me," he countered. "And you went with me." He pressed the back of her hand to his lips and smacked a lavish kiss onto it. "My good-luck charm."

She shook her head. "That's silly. Whether or not I helped, you still have the figures to show your business is solid."

He flashed her a grin, pleased that she hadn't pulled her hand away. Her skin was incredibly silky and soft, and he rubbed his thumb lightly over the back of her hand, reveling in the tactile pleasure. "You're my good-luck charm," he repeated as he swung the truck into the parking lot of the pizza place.

Chloe reached for her door handle, but he forestalled her move. "We're not going in."

"We're not?"

"Nope." He squeezed her hand once more, then released it. "Wait right here. I'll be back."

The silence was too sudden, too *loud,* in a funny way, when he cut the engine outside his trailer. She'd known since he'd reappeared with the pizza in a box to go that they were coming here, to his trailer. She felt jumpy, nervous with anticipation...which was silly when he hadn't indicated that there was anything more to this than lunch in a quiet spot.

Still, she knew that when the door of that tiny trailer closed behind them, she was going to be a nervous wreck. She was terrible at small talk. And when she was nervous, she was worse than terrible—her mind dried up like a shallow stream in a drought.

While she'd been thinking these morose thoughts, Thad had gotten out of the truck. Balancing the pizza in one hand, he came around and opened her door.

"Thank you," she said.

"Don't sound so surprised." His voice was dry. "I am capable of manners."

"I didn't mean—you're not—it wasn't meant as an insult."

"I didn't take it as one," he said, grinning. Then, as she watched in puzzlement, he walked around to the back of the trailer. "Come on—I'll get a blanket and we'll eat back here."

Behind the trailer was a small square of mowed lawn, shaded by the big trees that surrounded his home. The day was warm and the season early enough that insects weren't a nuisance yet. It was a perfectly lovely place for a picnic lunch, with flowering shrubs that surrounded the trailer displaying their blooms and wild daffodils and bluebells dancing around the fringes of the yard. Thad unlocked the back door to the trailer and took out a blanket, which he spread on the grass with a flourish.

"Please take a seat." When he offered her his hand she accepted it with a smile, bemused by his sudden whimsical manner. After escorting her to a seat on the blanket, he went back inside and returned again, with paper plates and napkins, two plastic cups and a bottle of wine which he had uncorked.

Chloe eyed the wine. Should she tell him she didn't drink? In fact, that she'd never even drunk wine other than the minuscule sip of communion wine? No, probably not necessary. After all, this was lunch. How drunk could a person get from a glass of wine with a meal? People did it all the time.

As Thad settled on the blanket beside her, her nervousness returned. "This is lovely," she said, indicating the flowers all around them. "I love spring because so many pretty things are blooming."

He nodded. "It is nice. I don't usually stop to appreciate it. All this was here when I bought it. I just try to keep the weeds in check and the trees and bushes trimmed when I get a chance."

He opened the pizza box and slid a slice onto her plate, then poured her a cup of the wine. It was a clear, pale gold and she sipped it experimentally. Hmm...not bad. It wasn't as sickeningly sweet as the communion wine. She took a bigger sip. "So when did you buy this place?"

Thad squinted his eyes in thought as he chewed. "Let's see—I guess it's been about three years. I grew up around here, but I moved away about a year after I got out of high school. I hadn't planned on ever coming back, but when my mother told me she was sick, I decided I needed to be closer."

Three years... With a small shock, she realized he must have come back right around the time she'd met him at that party. To cover her reaction, she picked up her cup and drank again.

"My mother would never ask me for help," Thad went on. "But I know she needs me. She's having more trouble getting around, and she needs help with laundry and the garbage, things like that." He swirled the wine in his cup. "I guess you've heard that my mother isn't exactly the perfect lady, but she doesn't deserve this."

"Nobody deserves it," Chloe said. "God doesn't pick and choose who's going to get ill based on the way they've lived their lives."

"The thing is, she's good-hearted," Thad said. He wasn't looking at her, but down at his food. It was almost as if he were talking to himself. "Despite her flaws, she's one of the nicest people you'll ever meet."

"I'd like to meet her," Chloe said gently. "She sounds like a very nice lady. My father enjoyed his visit with her."

"My mother enjoyed talking to him, too." Thad looked over at her. "Why did he go, anyway? Your father has never gone out of his way to do me any favors. It's easier to dislike him when he acts like a jerk all the time."

Chloe took another sip of her wine. It certainly was

a glorious day and she refused to take offense at his words. "My father is human, just like the rest of us, and certainly not perfect." She cast him a steady look. "But he surely does seem to have you pegged as a villain. Why is that, Thad?"

Thad shrugged. "Who knows? Half this community feels the same."

Silence fell as they finished their meal. Thad poured more wine into her cup. She wasn't sure she needed any more—she felt a little light-headed already. The day was warm—a harbinger of summer to come. Birds whistled and sang in the trees. There wasn't another soul around and the little garden felt intimate and cozy. Thad had stretched out his legs and was leaning back on his hands with his face tilted up to the sun.

"My father called you a defiler of young women. Why?" Good heavens, what a thing to ask a person! Chloe set her cup firmly aside. No more of that if it loosened her tongue and her mind like this. The question was intrusive, insulting. "Never mind," she said hurriedly. "It's none of my business—"

"Yes, it is." With three simple words, he changed the nature of their relationship. "It's only fair that you know what kind of man I am. You might not want to keep on seeing me."

She couldn't look at him, so she studied the blanket instead. No power on earth was going to take away her desire to be with him. But she wasn't about to tell him that.

He turned his head and looked at her, and she read bleak self-hate in his eyes. "I got a girl pregnant right before I graduated from high school. Her name was Jean—she was in my class in school but she wasn't the kind of girl I usually went out with. Jean was a *nice* girl.''

She waited, but he didn't speak more. She wondered what he was thinking, and decided he was probably waiting for her to express her horror. ''Poor girl,'' she said in a mild tone. ''I think finding out you're expecting a baby out of wedlock is probably a frightening experience for any young girl.''

''Her family threw her out when we told them about the baby.''

Chloe gasped. ''That's terrible!'' How could anyone do that to their own child?

''I thought so. Anyway, we moved in with my mother. You can imagine what people thought of *that*. My mother wasn't happy about the situation, either, but she was good to Jean. As soon as we graduated, we got married.'' He stopped for a moment, and Chloe was grateful for the pause.

Her world had just turned upside down. *He'd been married.* Somehow, she'd never considered that, and she didn't like the way it made her feel inside. Jealous and possessive, even though there wasn't a shred of doubt in her mind that he wasn't married now. Thad wouldn't do that—take her, Chloe, out to lunch if he had a wife somewhere.

She realized he was watching her.

''What are you thinking?'' he asked.

''What happened to your marriage?''

He didn't bat an eyelash. ''Maybe I'm still married.''

She tried a smile, but her lips quivered and she abandoned the effort. ''You're not that kind of man. If you were still married, you'd be sitting here on this blanket with your wife.''

"Why do you have such faith in me?" He was watching her intently.

She shrugged, twisting her fingers into a pretzel. "You're a good person."

Thad snorted. "There aren't a lot of people who would agree with you."

"Yes, there are." She did look at him then, annoyed at the way he always managed to put himself down. "That banker thinks you're a good person, doesn't he? Your trouble is, you're so determined not to give people a chance to slight you that you assume they're all the same. Yes, there are vicious gossips and judgmental individuals in this town, but there also are a lot of nice people who would befriend you if you'd stop looking for insults at every turn."

She stopped for breath. "So quit the self-condemnation. You were a young man who got into a situation all too common to young people. Lots of young people fall in love and—"

"But that's just it."

"Just what?"

"It wasn't love. At least, not for me." His face twisted. "That's the worst part of it. I wish I had loved her. God, I wanted to. Jean never made any secret of the way she felt, but I—if there hadn't been a baby on the way, I wouldn't have made any permanent plans for the relationship."

"You mean it would have been just another one-night stand."

He exhaled deeply. "Yeah, I guess that about sums it up." He turned his head, and his eyes swept over her briefly. "I told you I'm not a very nice guy."

"Would you—" She stopped, trying to choose just

the right words. "Are one-night stands still a common thing for you?"

Startled, he sat bolt upright and glared at her. "Of course not."

She smiled at his indignation. "Why?"

"Because I'm ashamed! Because it's wrong to treat women like disposable items, used once and tossed out. Oh. You think you're smart." He gave her a wry smile. "You're determined to make me a nicer guy, aren't you?"

"Not really. Just determined, maybe, to make you see you're not as despicable as you think you are. Everybody makes mistakes."

"Maybe," he muttered. "But some are a lot bigger than others."

Again they didn't speak for a few moments. Then she stirred, taking in the details of his profile, washed in a bath of strong white light. "You've managed to distract me. Finish the story."

Thad kept his face turned up to the sun. "There's not much more to tell. Jean was diabetic. I didn't know. She hid it from me." He jackknifed into a sitting position, his face contorted in pain. "If I'd known—" His voice cracked as he went on. "We didn't have much money so Jean didn't go to the doctor. She said there was no reason, that we'd need the money more when the baby came. One day I found her on our bed, unconscious. I didn't realize it, but she was in a diabetic coma."

He paused, and when he continued, his voice was flat and expressionless. "Jean never woke up. She died that night, and even though they tried a Caesarean section to save the baby, our little boy died, too. Jean's family blames me for killing her. And I did. A woman with her medical condition… She'd been told never to have children, that pregnancy could be fatal.''

"You can't believe that." Chloe reached for his fisted hands, wrapping her own over his knuckles and squeezing. "How would you have known if Jean didn't tell you? Are you a mind reader?''

"I should have known something was wrong," he muttered. "She always kept crackers in her purse, was always getting light-headed… I should have figured it out.''

"Those are common behaviors for pregnant ladies," she pointed out. "How well did you know her before you…before she—'' She stopped, not quite able to utter the words.

"We went out three times," he said. "I told you— it wasn't a long-term relationship, at least in my mind, until she turned up pregnant.''

"So you didn't really know her habits well enough to suspect she had an illness. She *chose* to hide it from you, Thad. She must have had reasons for that.''

He sighed heavily, looking away from her. "Jean wasn't very secure about our relationship. I think she was afraid I wouldn't want her if I found out.'' He looked at her and she could see the anguish in his eyes. "I wouldn't have left my child fatherless…ever.''

"I know you wouldn't," she said softly. "But I imagine she wasn't thinking very clearly.''

"I think she was embarrassed, too. She told me once that it's hard to be different when you're a teenager. At the time, I brushed it off because I couldn't see that she'd been anywhere near as 'different' as I was. Now it's easy to see she was talking about her disease.''

Chloe smoothed her thumbs across the backs of his hands. "What happened is sad and tragic, but it wasn't your fault. Her family probably just made you the target for their grief.''

"They did a great job of hitting the bull's-eye." His tone was laced with pain. "The thing I can never forgive myself for is never telling her I loved her. She was always so open, so affectionate and giving—"

"I'm sure she believed you loved her." She kept her voice low and soothing.

"God, I hope so." His shoulders slumped. "I was never big on praying, but after she died, I prayed that she never knew the only reason I married her was because I didn't want my kid to grow up never knowing his father."

Like I did.

He didn't have to say the words. They whispered insistently in the air between them.

She scooted across the blanket without stopping to think, putting her arms around his broad shoulders. His leg was pressed against hers as they knelt, face-to-face, and she put a hand to the side of his face and stroked gently. "You know what I think? I think God forgave you for all these wrongs you've stacked up in your head. You need to forgive yourself."

Thad shuddered, his hand coming up to cover hers in a convulsive, desperate grip. "You're good for me."

She smiled at him, her lips trembling despite her best efforts. His story touched her deeply, and she was determined to release him of his burden of guilt. Trying to lighten the intensity of the moment, she smiled softly at him. "You make me sound like chicken broth."

One golden eyebrow rose and she saw his shoulders relax, the corners of his mouth lift. "You don't look like chicken broth."

She returned his smile, lifting her gaze to his. Their

eyes met, clung for a long moment...a moment in which she could almost feel the sparks of attraction flying between them, like static in her hair when it was freshly washed.

"Do you taste like chicken broth?" he whispered. Their faces were so close she could feel the sweet warmth of his breath against her face. It never occurred to her to be alarmed. As he lowered his mouth to hers she closed her eyes, holding her breath in unconscious anticipation.

Then his mouth closed over hers, a soft, tender pressure. Immediately her hand slipped from the side of his face to his strong neck, and she sank against him, spellbound by the sweetness of the intimacy. His mouth left hers then, and without fully realizing the significance of her action, she tightened her arm around his neck to prolong the contact.

He hesitated for a moment, holding himself stiffly away from her, but as she continued to press her mouth against his, seeking more of his kisses, he slipped his arms around her and angled his mouth over hers.

His kiss was no longer soft, but hard and demanding, and she responded with every fiber of her being. This was what—*who*—she'd been made for, she thought in dizzy pleasure. Tilting her face more fully to his, she lay against him, overwhelmed by sensation. Her breath came in shallow gulps as her sensitive breasts were flattened against his broad chest. Arrows of unfamiliar sensation shot straight down to center at the very bottom of her torso, and she let him gather her even closer, seeking more of the strange delight. His tongue traced the seam of her closed lips, then probed gently, and she opened her mouth to admit him. Instantly he took advantage of the yielding, exploring her mouth with thorough strokes of his tongue. She moaned again and slid one hand up to clench his hair as the other wound around his neck.

Holding her tightly to him, Thad pressed her backward. She slipped her legs to one side as his weight came down across her, and she tightened her arms around him. This was what she wanted, what she needed. She was a creature of response, his to mold and shape as he willed. His kisses stoked the blaze within her until she was moaning beneath him, seeking more with restless movements of her hips.

"Thad," she said against his mouth, and his name segued into a groan of pleasure as he shifted his legs to lie fully atop her. Her body knew this man's weight, recognized his hard, muscular strength and urged her to assuage the yearning he aroused. Her hips lifted, rolling rhythmically beneath him, but as she laced her arms around his shoulders more tightly she felt his body tense over hers.

With a sudden, violent curse that scorched her ears, he rolled away from her and surged to his feet, standing with his back to her, one hand on his hip and the other gripping the back of his neck. Her body throbbed with an insistent ache and just as suddenly as he had moved, a clear image of her own abandoned behavior coalesced in her mind.

God forgive her, what was she doing?

A blinding shame rose within her as she sat up, then climbed to her feet and straightened her clothes with fingers that trembled.

She, who had always prided herself on her good sense and her ability to overcome temptations, had succumbed—no, not succumbed, she acknowledged—had invited intimate foreplay from a man. *Not just any man,* her heart insisted. *Thad.*

It didn't matter who the man was, she told herself sternly. What mattered was that if *he* hadn't stopped it, she would have let him touch, taste, take her in the most basic way a man and a woman could unite. A way that she'd always believed was meaningless without a commitment of the heart, a commitment sealed by the bonds of matrimony.

Her whole face felt hot with self-loathing and embarrassment as she reached for her purse and looked wildly around. Her car...where had she parked her car?

Then she remembered. She hadn't. Her heart sank as she realized she was dependent on Thad for a ride. She dashed tears of frustration away with an ungentle swipe of her hand as he turned to face her.

"Chloe, I didn't—are you crying?" he demanded, striding across the grass. He put his hands to her waist, and she was appalled at her treacherous body's urge to turn into his arms again.

She made herself still and stiff under his hands. "Could you please take me back to my car? I'm sorry if I led you to believe that I—that we—oh, never mind! May we please leave?"

"No."

Shocked out of her racing thoughts, she stared up at him. "I beg your pardon?"

A grim smile touched the corners of his mouth as he released her. "You can beg all you like, honey, but we're not leaving here until we've talked about what just happened."

Ohh, what she wouldn't give for the power to snap her fingers and make him disappear. "What just happened," she said through clenched teeth, "was that I nearly threw away a whole lifetime of beliefs. And if you hadn't stopped, I never would have thought to stop you. I am totally humiliated and painfully aware of my failure. Is that what you want to hear?''

"Not exactly,'' Thad said. There was a warm light in his eyes that she couldn't decipher. ''So I'm not wrong in thinking you liked it?''

"I don't tell lies,'' she said steadily, looking past him at the flowers along the edge of the grassy spot.

"Do you want to hear my take on this?'' he asked, and waited until she had raised her gaze to his. ''What happened to me was that you turned me on so quickly and so completely that I nearly forgot how much I like and respect you. There's no reason for you to feel humiliated.''

"No reason? Did you hear me calling a halt? I barely remembered my name, much less my principles.'' Her tone was bitter.

"If anything, I'm the one who should feel bad,'' he went on. ''I'm not a teenager who thinks with his glands anymore. I've had firsthand experience with the consequences of reckless sex. I know better.''

"You don't have to feel bad. You stopped, remember?''

Thad grinned. ''You sound like you're sorry.'' He took her hands again, and upset as she was, she couldn't bring herself to pull away. Just the touch of his thumbs rubbing across the back of her knuckles made her knees weaken anew. ''What happened between us was perfectly normal for two people who are attracted to each other. Taking my hands off you has to be the toughest thing I've ever done in my life.''

She tried to hold on to her outrage, even to her pique, but somewhere inside she was pleased to know that it hadn't been easy for him, either. The humor of having a discussion like this while standing in his backyard began to dawn on her and she slanted him a teasing smile. "And the noblest, too, no doubt."

"No doubt." His tone was heartfelt. Their eyes made contact for a long moment, then Thad dropped her hands. She actually could see him distancing himself from her before he spoke again. "Chloe, I'm very attracted to you. But I also enjoy being with you more than any woman I can remember. I'd like to see you again."

His gaze was earnest and his voice was sincere. Her heart skipped a beat, then returned to a rhythm twice its normal speed. She knew she would have to be insane to go out with him again, after what had almost happened here today. He definitely wasn't the kind of man she should be involved with. If she were smart, she'd get out of here fast and never see him again.

"I'd like that, too."

"Good." He leaned forward and pressed a quick kiss to her lips before she could dodge or respond, then turned away to gather up the picnic things. "Now I'm getting you out of here before my willpower deserts me altogether."

Five

The next day was Sunday. Thad had asked her to take a walk on the Appalachian Trail in the afternoon, and Chloe accepted, knowing her father would be having lunch with one of the parishioners, and that lunch would probably stretch well into the afternoon. She day-dreamed through the church service, then watched the clock like a hawk all through lunch. A minute wasn't really that long, was it?

Finally, just as one o'clock arrived, the doorbell rang. The butterflies in her stomach lifted off in a great cloud of fluttering wings. She half ran to the door, then took a deep breath before she put her hand on the knob. *Chloe Miller, this is just a date, not your wedding day! Settle down.*

Thad was standing on the porch when she pulled the door open. He was smiling, and she smiled back, struck by how handsome he was. He wore a forest green T-

shirt and blue jeans, and in contrast to the green of the
shirt, his eyes blazed more beautifully blue than ever.
She was aware of every inch of his tall, hard body,
though she had yet to look away from his eyes, and the
butterflies in her stomach winged their way to a lower
spot, bringing her body to throbbing life.

"Ready for a stroll?"

She watched his lips form the words and longed to
press her own to his, to feel his mobile mouth move as
he formed the words. The lips curved up into a smile
that spread to reveal strong white teeth. He chuckled.

With a start she realized an answer was required, and
that undoubtedly he knew exactly what was going
through her head.

She could feel the heat in her cheeks as she turned
away. "Let me get my jacket."

After retrieving her lightweight coat, she locked the
door behind her, and Thad escorted her to his now-
familiar truck. He headed for the Blue Ridge Mountains, where they would pick up the trail.

It was a warm, sunny, spring day. The section of the
Appalachian Trail they walked along wound through
forest and wandered past rushing streams filled with the
remnants of melted winter. New buds studded all the
vegetation within sight, though without the shade of
summer's leafy canopy, the May sun was surprisingly
hot. Chloe took off her jacket and tied the sleeves
around her shoulders. Thad did the same with the sweatshirt he'd donned before they'd begun to walk, but an-
chored it around his lean waist.

As they strolled over the well-marked path, he asked
her questions about the financial aspects of setting up
for a preschool. He was easy to confide in, and she
thrilled to the delight of sharing her ideas with someone

who was genuinely interested. He made suggestions occasionally and asked questions that she found she had to consider carefully. Before she knew it, thirty minutes had passed.

"Let's take a break before we start back," he suggested, pointing to a large boulder with a flat plateau on one side that leaned drunkenly a few yards off the trail.

"Sounds good. I didn't realize how pitifully out of shape I am," she confessed. The hike had been a slight uphill incline and she was breathing fast.

White teeth flashed in a quick smile. "Here's my cue to tell you what I think of your shape."

She clucked her tongue at him. "Behave."

He heaved an exaggerated sigh behind her.

"Let me check for snakes," he suggested as she clambered up onto the lichened stone surface.

"Snakes?" She froze, one leg dangling.

"There are copperheads in these hills. On a day like this, they might be taking a nap on a nice, warm rock like this."

She launched herself away from the rough gray of the boulder's face, landing less than gracefully on the ground beside him. "Don't let me stop you."

He laughed aloud as he hoisted himself up and stomped around atop the rock. "Okay."

She took his offered hand and perched gingerly on the stone, peering around her. "I don't know much about snakes. You don't think they'd come up while we're here, do you?"

He settled beside her, resting his elbows on his drawn-up knees. "Doubt it. Snakes would rather run than fight. If you give them plenty of warning, they generally leave you alone."

"How do you know all this?"

A rueful smile touched his lips. "When I was a teen-ager, these mountains were a great place to come for parties. There are so many little roads and tracks and hidden spots that we rarely got caught. I learned a long time ago that if I wanted to get a girl to relax, I'd better make sure there were no snakes around."

"So bringing girls up here to…relax, was a frequent occurrence?"

"Not that frequent." He shot her a smug smile. "Jealous?"

"No! Just wondering how many other girls you picked up that you don't remember anymore."

As soon as she uttered the words, she was sorry. She could feel an instant rush of heat surging up her neck, and she dropped her head onto her raised knees. She could almost feel his gaze on her, and she knew there was no getting out of this now.

"Other girls?" His tone was low, quiet. Menacing. "Do you have a specific girl in mind that I'm supposed to have 'picked up'?"

She took a deep breath, feeling her breasts flatten against her knees. Without raising her head, she said, "Forget it. It was a stupid thing to say."

"No, I don't think I want to forget it." His voice was harder than she'd ever heard it, and she concentrated on making herself invisible. She wondered how long it would be before anyone found her body if he strangled her and threw her off a cliff up here somewhere.

"Dammit, Chloe! You can't just make an accusation like that and then zone out. What other girls are you talking about?"

With her head still on her knees, she muttered, "Me."

"Huh?"

As reactions went, it was a bit of a dud. "I'm talking about me," she said again, lifting her head.

He was completely mystified, and it showed in his voice. "What are you talking about? When did I ever forget you?" He shifted his body toward her, forcing her to put her hands on the rock behind her to keep from falling backward. Placing a hand on either side of her, he neatly boxed her in. "Believe me, I've never thought about a woman as much as I think about you."

Her heart gave an involuntary jolt.

"So," he went on, leaning even closer. "Explain."

She could barely breathe. His face was so close she could see the splinters of gold that fractured the blue of his eyes. She averted her face, withdrawing from him in the only way left to her. "We met before. Three years ago. It was August, at a party on Frey Street. I never did find out whose home it was."

"You expect me to believe you were at a keg party? If you're talking about the party I think you are, there were more illegal substances there than there were people to try 'em. Hardly your scene."

"It wasn't. Normally. I had had...a disagreement with my father and I was feeling rebellious, I guess. I came with a friend from high school. Margie Eadams. Maybe you know her? Well, she was really more of an acquaintance. We hadn't known each other well, and I don't know what possessed me to—"

"So how did we meet?"

"Oh. Well, I was sort of out of my league, if you want to know the truth—"

"No!"

She glared at him. "Do you want to hear this or not?"

"Oh, yeah, I want to hear it. Every detail. Go on."

"I was standing alone, trying to figure out how to get home—Margie had driven and she'd disappeared—and you came over and started talking. You took me outside and we sat on the back steps and talked."

When she stopped, he prompted, "And?"

She took a deep breath. "And then you touched me." Her voice was barely audible, her cheeks flushing a deeper rose with every passing moment.

"I touched you," he repeated slowly. "Where did I touch you, Chloe?"

"You touched...you touched my breast."

She heard him inhale sharply, but he didn't speak. When a few moments had passed and he still didn't say anything, she risked a glance at him. His features were drawn into a dark scowl. "Did I hurt you?"

She wasn't prepared for the question. "No. I mean, you startled me—a lot. I got up and walked away, and then I walked home."

That got his attention. "You walked home from Frey Street? That was a crazy thing to do at that time of night."

"Well, I wasn't about to hang around at that party any longer!"

"No, I guess not." He grimaced and exhaled deeply, his shoulders slumping. "I don't quite know what to say, except that I'm sorry. I don't remember much of that night. It wasn't one of the better days of my life. If it's any consolation to you, that was the last wild party I went to. I had just come back to town that day and I knew if I wanted people to take me seriously as a businessman, I couldn't slide back into that lifestyle."

"So the first thing you did was find a party?"

"Yeah." He uttered a short bark of laughter but there

was little humor in it. "I wasn't planning on ever coming back to this town. It seemed like a good idea to start fresh somewhere that people didn't know me. But my mother had just told me she was terminally ill, and I wanted to be there for her when she needed me. On top of that, when I was coming out of the hardware store the same day, I ran into—and I mean literally—Jean's mother. She was as surprised to see me as I was to see her. I said hello, hoping that maybe the years had helped her get over Jean's death, but she was just as loving as ever." He spoke the words in a measured, detached way that told her how hard he tried to pretend it didn't matter. "She called me a murderer and said some other complimentary things that anyone within earshot could hear." He rolled his shoulders as if he were stiff. "My sole ambition at that party that night was to get drunk enough to forget."

He half turned toward her. "I've changed since then, Chloe. Grown up, I guess. I never have more than two drinks anymore. I hated waking up the next day and not being able to remember anything." Then he cast her a small smile that mocked himself. "Now I'm even sorrier."

She could still feel herself blushing, but she forced herself to make normal conversation. "That sounds like a pretty terrible day. My method might have been different, but I would have wanted to forget it, too."

They sat for a moment longer without speaking. Then she stirred herself. "We'd better start back. I have to think about getting some dinner ready."

Thad stood and stretched, then leaped down from the boulder with the easy grace of a big mountain lion. He turned and extended a hand to her. Taking his hand, she slipped off the rock beside him and they started down

the trail. He held her hand the whole way back to the
truck, where he opened her door and helped her in.

When they arrived back at her house, he didn't shut
off the engine, but got out and walked around to open
her door. She stepped out of the truck, but he didn't
move. Their bodies brushed, and suddenly, between the
space of one heartbeat and the next, she was painfully
aware of his body, of the way her nipples grew taut and
her lower body softened and throbbed. He slid his arms
around her waist and drew her against him. She gasped
and he groaned as their bodies slid into perfect align-
ment.

"Thanks for going with me today." His voice was
little more than a growl.

"You're welcome. I enjoyed it." She swallowed, and
his eyes followed the motion of her throat. "I have to
go in now."

"Okay." His lips hovered, descended, and she rose
on tiptoe to meet his mouth, knowing only that she had
to kiss him or die. This time she welcomed the thrust
of his tongue and the way his hips mimicked the se-
duction of her mouth. She welcomed the hard press of
his chest against her breasts and the way, lower down,
that his body pushed at hers, giving her a restless, waiting feeling that went along with the softening she could
feel happening to herself.

He kissed her and kissed her, right there in plain sight
in front of her house, and she kissed him back. Finally
Thad tore his mouth from hers and cradled the back of
her skull in his palm, pressing her face into his shoulder.
His hips, as if they were unconnected to the part of him
that was stopping, thrust heavily against her, retreated,
and then repeated the action twice more. Taking her by
the shoulders, he set her a step away from him.

Chloe stood passively before him. What now? She needed more. She needed his tongue and his hands stroking her all over. She needed him. She reached for him, but he grabbed her wrists and held her hands securely between them.

"Chloe."

She blinked, looking up at him.

"Go inside. I'll see you tomorrow." He turned her around and gave her a push in the direction of the front door.

She took a step, then one more before she turned sluggishly, feeling like all her limbs were so heavy she could just lie down and take a nap on the spot. No, that was wrong. She did want to lie down, but she wanted Thad to lie down with her. On her. She wanted more of this wonderful silky, slippery slowness that had seized her.

But Thad wasn't there. As soon as he'd set her away, he'd started back to his truck. He was just climbing in the door and she focused hard, willing him to come back.

He started the engine. Then, with a wave that was barely a flip of his hand, he was gone.

Monday wasn't too busy, as Mondays were prone to be. It was a good thing, too, she decided, because in the state she was, she'd be lucky to get any work done at all. All she had to do was think of Thad and her body began jumping in anticipation, all her nerve endings quivering and throbbing. And that was all she *could* do—think of Thad.

That wasn't a good sign. She was glad he'd stopped when he did yesterday—wasn't she?—because it seemed to her that all he had to do was put his hand on her, and all her common sense flew right out the window. He was a good man, an honorable man. He didn't take advantage, even though it had to have been plain that he could have done anything he wanted with her. To her. The thought brought a delicious shiver with it.

People really didn't know him at all. He had done the right thing by the girl he'd gotten pregnant when he could have walked away. He was determined to build himself a successful business, and he was going about it the right way, getting a reputation for good work and fair prices despite the things some people thought about his character. He was a vulnerable soul, still agonizing, still shouldering guilt and blame for a sad accident that he hadn't known could happen. He *was* a good man, and she didn't care what anyone else thought. She saw the real Thad…and she loved him.

She loved him. The mere idea still made her breathless. She'd had all night to think, after he'd left her standing in front of the house, and she'd finally realized what she was feeling. She was pretty sure it wasn't just sexual attraction, although that was certainly wrapped up in it. It was love.

She didn't know how or when it had happened. She did know it was one-sided, and she experienced a sudden flare of empathy for poor Jean, who'd also loved him without being loved in return.

Unfortunately, Chloe would love him until the day she died, just like Jean. That subdued the pleasurable feelings considerably. She'd always assumed the love of her life would be reciprocated, that they'd marry and settle into doing the family thing, always conscious of their love for each other.

Now that idea had been blown right out of existence. Maybe one day, she would find a man who loved her, a man she cared for and could be a wife to, a man who might never know his wife carried in her heart the image of another man.

Her hands stilled on the papers she was halfheartedly trying to organize. It was going to be hard, walking away from the perfect ecstasy she knew she would find in Thad's arms. She was going to have to be very strong. She might not be able to bring wholehearted love to her future husband, but she was determined to come chaste, unused, so that he would always know he was the only one. It didn't matter that a tiny part of her didn't care a bit about virginity, couldn't wait to give it away. She wasn't doing *it* with anyone she wasn't married to. It just wouldn't be right for her.

Unfortunately the thought of the faceless, nameless husband was mildly revolting. She couldn't imagine any other hands but Thad's on her, couldn't imagine thrilling to anyone else's touch. Maybe she'd never marry. That might be the best thing. Oh, who knew?

The only thing she did know was that she wasn't going to see Thad again. Well, she might see him around town, but she wasn't going out with him again. It would hurt too much. Besides, she knew her limitations. If he really tried, he could have her in his bed— or have her anywhere else, for that matter—and she'd never utter a peep of protest. In fact, she'd be the one turning down the sheets. No, she couldn't take that chance.

She had stopped filing altogether and was just sitting with her hands on her desk when the door opened. Expecting her father back from an errand, she looked up with a smile pasted on her mouth—and froze.

It was Thad.

A slow smile curled the corners of his mouth as he

came through the door. "Good morning. I'm relieved
to see you. Thought maybe you were still standing
where I left you yesterday."

She could feel her face burning at the reminder of
why she had been standing there. Could she never have
a conversation with him without blushing? "Good
morning."

He grinned. "You have your prim-and-proper face
on. That turns me on, knowing I can make you
look…less prim and proper." While his tone was teasing, his eyes were intent as he watched her.

"Did you come in for a reason?" She strove for a
casual note. She wasn't going to let him affect her anymore.

"Yeah. I have to go down to the lumberyard and on
my way back I'd like to take you out for lunch."

"I…I can't. I have too much work to do. I'm eating
in the office today."

"Did you bring lunch?"

He knew she'd made it up. She could tell by the
gleam in his eye. The doorbell jangled as one of the
church members opened the door to the office. The
phrase "saved by the bell" would have a whole new
meaning for her after this.

"Good morning, Mrs. Fitzworth."

"Good morning, dear. Here are the minutes from last
week's Missions meeting." The older woman shifted
and smiled at Thad. "Good morning, Mr. Shippen. I
understand you do woodwork repair."

"Yes, ma'am."

"Good. I have some wainscoting that was damaged
by the previous owners of my home. Perhaps you'd like
to look at it and give me an estimate?"

"I'd be happy to do that." Thad held the door open,

ushering her out. He gave Chloe a casual wave as he went down the steps, head cocked to listen to Mrs. Fitzworth's chatter.

She watched them as long as she could without getting up and pressing her nose against the glass window. Well. She wasn't sure what she'd expected, but having Thad accept her lie at face value and waltz out the door like he didn't even care—

Wasn't that what she wanted? Him out of her life? She should be happy, relieved, jumping up and down, joyous.

So why did she feel like a child who'd been scolded by her favorite teacher? Even though Thad was the farthest thing from a teacher she could imagine. She *had* to stop thinking about him! Resolutely, she applied herself to the paperwork in front of her, ignoring her growling stomach and the clock on the wall as it ticked past noon and on into the next hour. Her father returned from his hospital visits and several parishioners came and went. Every time that stupid bell over the door jangled, her heart hopped and she held her breath. But it was never Thad.

She was back at the copier when the bell sang its discordant notes again. ''I'll be with you in a moment,'' she called, checking the tray to be sure it had plenty of paper. When she turned around, there he was. She could no sooner stop the silly smile she felt spreading across her face than she could the sun from rising as he held up a white bag.

''Since you're too busy to go out, I brought lunch in. If you haven't already eaten?''

''No, I haven't. Thank you,'' she added belatedly. What was the harm in sharing a sandwich with him?

They were in a very public place. She was in no danger of forgetting her principles here.

He pulled a chair up across from her at the desk, and she hastily moved a bud vase, her paperweight and a stack of files. "You're good for my image."

Startled, she glanced at him as he unwrapped a ham sandwich and another of chicken and indicated she should choose one. "What?"

"You're good for my image." He pulled two cans of soda from the bag and efficiently popped them open. "Mrs. Fitzworth just hired me for her job."

"That had nothing to do with me," she said briskly. "You're a fine person. People just need a chance to get to know you."

"They're a lot more willing to take that chance now that Chloe Miller has approved my presence in the community," he said drily.

"That's ridiculous. You've gotten plenty of jobs without me. What are you working on now?"

She managed to keep the conversation light and general during the meal, and she found herself relaxing. This wasn't so bad. Maybe they could just be friends. She caught herself staring at his throat, where his shirt was unbuttoned near the top and a few golden curls peeked out. It brought a vivid image of him shirtless on the ladder the first day she'd seen him, and she swallowed. *Friends don't drool over each other, Chloe. Who are you kidding?*

She tidied up her desk, tossing away the remains of the lunch as he rose. "Thank you for the sandwich."

"You're welcome." His eyes gleamed as he walked around the desk toward her. She couldn't have moved if she'd wanted to.

He took her face between his hands and set his lips

on hers, shocking her with the sudden intimacy. She lifted her own hands to circle his wrists and push him away, but somewhere in her brain, his kiss short-circuited the command, and "Push" turned into "Hang on for dear life." His mouth was warm and firm, his tongue searching for hers, curling around it with familiar intent, and her body clamored for his touch.

Against her mouth, he growled, "Have dinner with me."

"I—"

"Yes." He had lifted one hand so that his mouth could nibble its way along her jaw to her ear, where his tongue flicked lightly at a spot near her earlobe. She sucked in a startled breath, aroused beyond belief by that small touch, and he prompted again, "Yes."

"Yes." She whispered the word.

"Good." He stepped back and linked his fingers with hers, leaving her standing dazed, aching. "I'll pick you up at six."

"Not at your house," she managed to say, recalling something about principles.

"No, I'll pick you up at your house." He grinned again, deliberately misinterpreting her words. "Relax, there'll be other people around."

He pressed a short, stinging kiss on her lips, then turned for the door. "See you tonight."

"See you tonight," she whispered as the door closed behind him. She put one shaking hand to her lips, still tingling from his kisses. Oh, my.

"Chloe!"

She jumped, turning to see her father standing in his office door. He was watching Thad's retreating back through the big window. Then he turned his gaze on her. "What is the meaning of this?"

The familiar words were probably intended to cow her into a confession, just as they had on the few occasions he'd had to use them when she was small, but they had the opposite effect. She straightened, dropping her hand from her lips. "Thad brought sandwiches and we shared lunch." She began rearranging items on her desk.

"It looks like you shared more than lunch."

"Daddy! That was uncalled for. I'm an adult and I will eat with whomever I like." She enunciated the words slowly and clearly. "And do anything else I choose."

Her father's face reddened. "The Bible tells us—"

"I know what the Bible tells us, Daddy."

"Did you know I had Jean Lawman's funeral service?" The sudden change of topic was unnerving but she refused to show it.

"Her last name was Shippen."

"Her family rued the day she set eyes on him."

"Maybe they never tried to get to know him," she said. "Did *you* know Jean never told Thad she was diabetic? Do you know how they treat him when they see him?"

Her father held up both hands. "Okay, okay. Maybe I've been as guilty as everyone else of judging him too harshly." He paused, then muttered, "I still don't trust his intentions."

She was smiling, relieved that the stand-off had been resolved without words they each might have regretted. "How about mine? You've instilled morals and values in me, and I hope you'll trust me to exercise them."

Her father opened his mouth again, flapped it once like a fish on land and closed it abruptly. "You certainly are your mother's daughter sometimes." A small smile escaped the stern face he'd arranged. "She knew how to knock me down to size when I got pompous, too."

Chloe returned the smile, grateful that he was trying not to be dictatorial. "You're not pompous. Well, not much."

Thad picked her up at six as he promised, but this time her father was home. He must have been standing there waiting for the doorbell to ring because he answered the door before she could get to it. She came rushing from the kitchen where she'd been putting on lipstick in the mirror beside the pantry door, slowing her pace to a sedate walk when she realized there was no bloodshed. Yet.

"Good evening, Thaddeus," her father intoned.

"Good evening, Reverend."

She was grateful that Thad hadn't called him "Rev," as he was fond of doing. She suspected he only used the abbreviation because he knew it irritated the minister.

"Hello. I'm ready," she announced unnecessarily. As she sailed past her father, she kissed him on the cheek. "Bye, Daddy. If you're asleep when I get home, I'll see you in the morning." *Wrong thing to say.* Now her father would think she planned on staying out half the night.

But he didn't react. And to her surprise, Thad spoke again. "We won't be late. Chloe and I both have to work tomorrow."

As they walked away toward his truck, she said, "Thank you for making an effort with my father."

"No problem." He took her hand to help her into the truck.

She wanted to ask him where they were going as the

truck drove through town and out again. But as they turned onto a familiar country road, her dismay grew. He had told her they wouldn't be alone, and now he was taking her back to his house! Well, he'd just have to take her right home again, because there was no way she was going to put herself in temptation's way.

"You missed your driveway," she pointed out in a clipped tone.

"We aren't going to my house."

"Oh."

He was silent for a moment. Then he reached across the seat and took her hand, twining his fingers through hers. "I promised you we weren't going to my house. Did you think I would lie to you?"

She felt as small as a bug, and just about as squashable. "I'm sorry, Thad." Tears hovered on the edge of her voice, and he squeezed her hand gently.

"It's okay. I haven't exactly been trustworthy around you." He took his eyes off the wheel for a moment and shot her a crooked grin. "Every time I decide I'm going to keep my hands off you, I lie to *myself.*"

That wasn't a statement she was going to address. To relieve the loaded silence that grew with each passing second, she asked him, "So where are we going?"

"My mother's."

His mother's. He was taking her to meet his *mother?* She pondered that for a moment, then decided it was too much effort to try to read anything into it. "Is she up to making dinner for us?"

"Sort of." He released her hand to turn into the driveway in front of a nicely kept rancher-style home on a large lot back from the road. "I got a casserole ready and set the table this morning so she wouldn't have much to do. It lets her have the illusion that she's still able to get around fairly normally." As he shut off the engine, he turned to her. "Don't let on that I told you."

"I would never do that," she said with great dignity.

He laughed as he opened her door and they started up the walk. "I know, I just wanted to loosen you up."

She punched him lightly in the shoulder—just to have an excuse to touch him, if she was truthful with herself—but before she could withdraw her hand he snagged it in midair and dragged her against his chest. "One to keep me going," he said, lowering his head.

He kissed her thoroughly, until she pushed his head away and gasped for air. "Stop! Your mother's going to see us."

His chuckle was wry and resigned. "Like my mother would care about two people kissing on her doorstep?" He reached past her and inserted a key into the front door, then swung it wide and swept her a bow. "*Entrez,* my lady."

They stepped into a living room quietly decorated in creams and moss shades. She didn't know what she was expecting, but this wasn't it. He left her there, telling her to make herself at home while he brought his mother out. Through an archway she could see a neat dining room in the same colors, the table set for three. Hmm...no risqué pictures, no red velvet. She was almost disappointed.

Then Thad appeared, supporting a frail woman in an eye-assaulting purple caftan, flowing and floor length. She stretched out a hand to Chloe as he seated her on the couch. "Hello, dear."

Thad waved at Chloe, saying "This is my mom," and disappeared into the kitchen. "Dinner'll be ready in a few minutes."

"Chloe. Such a beautiful name," the woman said. Two bright spots of rouge that matched her lipstick contrasted sharply with the pallor of her skin.

"Thank you." She smiled uncomfortably. She didn't even know what to call her! The older woman's white hair was confined in a bun, but a few strands had escaped and fell in gentle curls about her head. Searching the deep brown eyes, Chloe could see little resemblance to Thad, but his mother obviously had been a beauty in her youth.

"I'm Margreta, and I imagine you've heard my life story from every busybody in town. Believe about half of it, and you might come close." She laughed, a warm sound that made Chloe relax. "I've met your father. We had a delightful chat the first time he came. Last week, I'm afraid I was feeling a bit under the weather so he only stayed a few minutes."

That was news to Chloe. Her father had said nothing about a second visit to Thad's mother. "He enjoys the ministry," she said. "I'm sure he'll check back again and stay longer when you feel up to a visit."

"I hope so. Now—tell me about yourself. I'm going to be really nosy. Thad's never brought a girlfriend home before." Her faded eyes clouded. "Except, of course, for poor dear Jeannie."

"He's told me about Jean."

Margreta raised her eyebrows. "He hasn't been able to talk about her, even to me, since she died." She paused. "Now I *really* want to hear about *you.*"

Margreta was amazingly easy to talk to. Chloe found herself explaining her dreams for the preschool, even the frustrating situation with her job. Thad called them in to dinner and they talked…about the explosion, the church's rebuilding efforts, Margreta's illness and her desire to wait as long as possible before needing around-the-clock home care. Chloe couldn't believe how matter-of-fact, how frank and realistic she was about her diagnosis.

"Don't mistake me—I'm not giving up. But I know what the odds are, and I refuse to spend my last days bald and vomiting," Margreta told her. "I can think of things I'd rather do than die, like hold my first grand-child—not that that's likely to happen anytime soon." She smiled across the table at Thad, and Chloe was tickled to see a dull red creeping up his neck.

"Time to change the subject," he announced.

"Why don't you let me clean up the kitchen while you help your mother get settled for the night?" Chloe suggested, seeing Margreta grimacing in discomfort.

"Thanks," he said. "I would appreciate that."

So Chloe washed the dishes and tidied up the remains of the meal while Thad helped his mother. After seeing her settled, Thad checked the house one more time, and they said good-night.

Six

"**Y**our mother is wonderful," Chloe said as they settled themselves for the drive back to town.

Thad smiled. "She's something, isn't she?" Reaching across the seat, he took Chloe's hand and tugged. "You're too far away. Use the middle seat belt." When she did, he promptly laid her hand on his thigh, holding it in place with his own.

Under her palm, his thigh felt wonderfully warm. His flesh, covered by blue denim, was firm, and she resisted the urge to dig in her fingers, to test the muscle she could feel flexing each time his foot moved on the pedals. They didn't speak again until he pulled the truck to a halt in front of her house and turned off the engine.

"I had a lovely time tonight," she told him. "Your mother is delightful."

He released his seat belt and then hers, turning to face her in the seat. "I think she used the same word to describe you." His hand came up, sliding through the loose, silky hair around her face to the back of her neck. "You bewitched us both."

The night was dark and moonless, the inside of the truck a warm cocoon of intimacy. She could hear their breathing, could hear the blood as it pulsed through her veins, faster now that he was touching her again. When he exerted a slight pressure on her neck, she moved toward him willingly, her resolve of the morning forgotten under the magic his touch created.

He wrapped her in his arms as closely as possible, given their seated positions. "What am I going to do with you?" he murmured, almost to himself.

Her head was tilted back over his arm, her face lifted to his. She could barely make out his features, but she knew he was smiling. He was a lure and she was the helpless fish, reeled in, played out and reeled in even closer the second time. Hesitantly she lifted herself the scant distance that separated them and pressed a quick, chaste kiss to his lips.

He went still, completely motionless. His body felt like heated marble beneath her hands. Then he exhaled, a deep release of air, and his head dropped to nuzzle along her jaw until his lips met hers.

She was ready this time. She knew his taste, the way his tongue sought hers and played, the way his hands roved her body, seeking out the sweet curve of breast and hip. His fingers moved between them, and she realized that he had unbuttoned her blouse. His hand was hot against her bare skin as he dipped into the cup of her bra, freeing a breast for his attentions while his mouth left hers and moved down her throat. She barely noticed. His palm covering her breast slowly rotated in small circles, stimulating the sensitive peak until she felt an irresistible urge to shift her hips, as if that action would somehow provide relief from the heat building within her.

Then his mouth took her nipple, suckling strongly at her, and she cried out, a high, thin sound that she barely recognized as her own voice. She realized she was saying, "Please, please," pleading with him, but she didn't know what she wanted him to do.

His mouth kept up the pleasure at her breast while his other hand stroked lower, over her belly and down, bit by bit, until one bold foray traced the center seam of her slacks below her zipper. The resulting sensation almost made her jump out of her skin, and her hips lifted involuntarily against his hand. Thad groaned. He grasped her torso and lifted her, turning her so she was astride him. Between her legs she felt the hard length of him, and his hips lifted this time, pressing against her in a clear message.

"Wait." Her voice was a ragged gasp of air, but it had the effect of an enraged father with a shotgun.

Thad stopped, lifting his hands from her body as if she burned him. "Do you realize you damn near lost your innocence in the front seat of this truck?" His voice sounded as if his teeth were clenched. He also sounded furious.

"I—what?" She surfaced slowly from the storm of sexual enticement. "Yes."

"Yes *what?*" He placed his hands at her hips. "Yes, finish it, or yes, you realize what nearly happened?"

"Wait, I...can't think..." She didn't complete the thought as he lifted her ungently and dumped her on the seat beside him.

"I need a bucket of ice cubes," he announced to the roof of the truck.

She had a nearly irresistible urge to giggle, but the tone of his voice warned her that wouldn't be wise.

He opened his door and slid out, then reached in and seized her wrist, dragging her across the seat and out the door after him. "Listen to me," he said, backing her up against the side of the truck, his face in hers. "I am *not* going to have you shouting to the world that I took advantage of you, but you're making me crazy. Either we finish this or we stop seeing each other."

His words were a shock rapidly cooling the lava racing through her veins. She said, "I wouldn't accuse you of—never mind." She focused on the one thing he'd said that made sense. "You're right. We have to stop seeing each other." She put up a hand and touched the side of his face, ignoring the suppressed anger that radiated from him. "I like to think I would have stopped you, but I'm just not sure. Thad, I want to come to my marriage bed without any secrets in my past. You're the toughest test I'll ever have to pass, I guess, and I'm not all that sure of my willpower. I can't see you anymore."

He didn't speak, just turned his head, and she felt him press a kiss into her palm. "This is crazy." In contrast to the gentle touch of his mouth, his voice was harsh. "And I'm crazy for letting you get under my skin. You'd better go." He stepped away and turned his back to her.

She hesitated.

"Go," he said fiercely, and she did, tears already beginning to fall as she fumbled with the front door. Behind her, she heard the quiet growl of the truck pulling away, and she felt her heart rip out of her chest and go with it. Closing the front door, she sank to her knees against the wood, both hands over her mouth to stifle the sobs she couldn't control.

She cried until her eyes stung and her nose ran, and then she cried some more. When she finally regained enough control to drag herself to her feet, she leaned against the door and took deep breaths, trying to still the involuntary sobs that continued to choke her. Thank goodness her father's room was at the back of the house, she thought. *He'd die of shock if he came down here and found me like this.*

A knock on the other side of the door had her whirling away from it as if the wood had come alive. Her heart leaped and she yanked the door open, not even considering that it might be a stranger. She hurled herself at Thad, closing the door behind her, and felt herself become whole, healed as his arms closed around her. Unable to control herself, she began to sob again.

"Sh-h-h." He rocked her as if she were a child, using his shirt to blot her tears. "I'm sorry, I shouldn't have left that way." He sought her mouth, and she met him halfway, sharing gentle kisses of comfort, dragging her mouth over his skin as he kissed her temples, her forehead, her nose and returned to her mouth again. But he lifted his head when comfort began to turn to passion again.

"I can't take any more of this." He was panting heavily, his chest heaving up and down like a racehorse that had just won the Kentucky Derby.

"I'm sorry," she whispered, her voice hitching. Then, a moment later, "Why am *I* apologizing? You're the one who left and came back!"

"Didn't you want me to?"

"You know I did." She wrapped her arms around him, feeling the ridges of muscle along his spine beneath her palms, feeling him pressed against every part of her from head to toe and wanting him more than she wanted to take her next breath. "But nothing's changed. I wish I could be the kind of woman you need. But I can't. I'm old-fashioned, I guess."

"Then we'll get married."

"That's not what I meant!" Shock waves battered at her mind.

Rearing back, she put some space between them. She knew he'd uttered the words in jest, but the mere thought made her heart race with alarming speed, and she squelched the longing, afraid it would show in her eyes.

"I meant it, though." He grinned, his crooked smile that she knew meant he was laughing at himself. "I never pictured myself doing this, but—" Seizing her hand, he dropped to one knee before her. "Chloe Miller, will you marry me?"

Mortified, she tugged at him, trying to get him on his feet again. "Thad, you don't really want—"

He shut her up simply by pulling her onto his knee and placing a large hand over her mouth. "Yes, *I really want.* And what's more, I really want to marry you. I need you. If this is the only way I can have you, I'll take it. I can think of plenty of things worse than being married to you for the rest of our lives."

As proposals went, his stank. So did his reasoning. And his timing. A girl with swollen eyes and a runny nose was in no shape to consider a proposal of marriage. She should be insulted, but she had to restrain herself from shouting, "Yes!" and waking her father to perform the ceremony right there and then. Still, a small voice inside her cautioned her. *He doesn't love you. He was married before to someone he didn't love.*

But he wants me. He said he needs me.

Do you want to marry someone who doesn't love you on the off chance that one day he will?

Yes!

Rising from his knee, she said, "I'll consider it. But I won't rush into anything."

"I can live with that." He rose and drew her into his arms again, tucking her head under his chin. Their bodies were sandwiched together, and she could tell he was aroused, but for the moment this embrace was one of sweetness and comfort. He stroked a hand down over her hair. "Don't make it too complicated in your head."

"I'm afraid it won't work," she whispered.

"Why wouldn't it work? I'm a good provider. We're going to be great together in bed. I'd be faithful to you, and I'd love our children."

Children. He knew how to get to her, all right. Images of small, wriggling towheads with dimples danced across her mental screen. She banished them. "Why me?"

He was silent for a moment and her heart sank. She'd made him see reason. He really didn't want to marry her.

"You're the only person who's ever looked past what they heard about me. Even Jean, I think, went out with me at first to spite her straitlaced parents. You believe in me," he said simply. Then he chuckled, and she felt it through every cell in her body. "Besides, I'm afraid I'll die of terminal sperm suppression if you won't marry me."

She was glad it was dark on the porch because she was blushing again. "I still need time. Time away from you to think. You could get me to agree to just about anything if you really tried." Those words skated dangerously close to a declaration of love, and she rushed to cover them. "I won't make you wait too long for an answer."

"Twenty-four hours is too long for me," he grumbled. But she could tell he wasn't unhappy. "Right now you are going inside to get some sleep." He brushed a last kiss across her lips, lingering for a moment before pulling himself away. "This is what started all the trouble in the first place. I'll see you tomorrow."

Six days later she awoke with a feeling of anticipation. As she stretched, she remembered why. It was Sunday. Thad had agreed to go to church with her today. In fact, it had been his idea.

"If I'm marrying a preacher's daughter, I'd better get used to going to church."

"You can come to church with me, but I haven't agreed to marry you," she reminded him.

To which he had smugly replied, "Yet."

Lordy, what was she going to do? All she could think about was him. And more accurately, his body. She'd never realized how sexual excitement could cloud a person's judgment. For the first time she could understand how people could get so carried away by passion that they forgot principles, morals...their names...

How was she supposed to make a momentous decision about her future, when all she wanted was to feel him against her again. All she had to do was see him, and her breath grew shorter, her nerve endings began to twitch, and her body grew...restless. She'd told Thad she needed to be away from him so she could consider his proposal, but she hadn't realized he'd have to be on the other side of the planet before she could think rationally. She was no closer today to giving him an answer than she had been on Monday night.

Marrying a man who didn't love her was a stupid thing to do. She knew she'd be courting heartbreak. On the other hand, heartbreak would be a surety if she told him no. So why not take a chance?

Her father didn't like him. Thad didn't like her father. They were like two dogs vying for dominance when they were in the same room, circling, sniffing, calculating weaknesses and plotting attack strategies. Her father loved her, had cared for her all her life. But she wasn't considering marrying her father. If she married Thad, would she have to choose between them?

She jumped out of bed and briskly threw the covers to the foot of the bed to air out while she showered. She was making herself insane, going around and around with these questions. If only she had a crystal ball. Or hindsight. That would be a help.

Thad met her in the vestibule right before the service. She hadn't told her father he was coming, mostly because she didn't want to argue with him, and she saw his eyes widen momentarily in the middle of a conversation with one of the ushers.

Quickly, before he could approach, she took Thad's arm. "Here's a bulletin. Let's find a seat."

There was a slight ripple of interest, a wave of sudden whispering and rustling as they walked up the aisle and slid into a pew. She hoped Thad didn't realize it was unusual.

A whisper came from somewhere behind them. "...I can't believe she is dating him. Are you sure?"

"Shh." Another speaker.

And then, "You know who his mother is, don't you?"

"I know. Shh."

"Wonder when she'll start to show? There has to be a good reason he's here with her."

"Would you shut up? They'll hear you."

She could hardly breathe. A rage rose up inside her, deeper and stronger than she'd ever known anger could get. Her hands were shaking. How dare they? *How dare they?* They should be ashamed to step inside a church. She'd never been tempted, ever, to create a scene, but she had to exert every ounce of self-control she had not to turn around and blast the old biddie.

She glanced at Thad out of the corner of her eye. A muscle jumped in his cheek but that was the only sign that he'd heard. Impulsively she reached over and laid one hand atop his where it rested in his lap. For a minute she thought he was going to ignore her, and then he turned his palm up and squeezed her hand.

She ached for him. How horrible to have known this all your life, to have people *expect* you to sleep with every girl who's seen with you. After they were married, she was going to use birth control for a while, just to prove—

After they were married. Saying it, even in her head, gave her a little thrill. Why deny it, deny him, any longer? She loved him and wanted to marry him, he wanted her, and they would make it work from there.

For the rest of the service, she held on to his hand, not even letting go when they rose for the hymns and prayers. She hoped those old crones were getting an eyeful.

Her father delivered the benediction, and the organist broke into the postlude as people began to chat again.

She stood, and Thad rose with her. Around them, people were shuffling out of their pews and herding down the aisles to the exits. What better place than here? Thad had turned away from her, preparing to leave the pew so she could precede him up the aisle, but she put a hand on his arm.

He looked back, his raised brows inquiring.

"Yes."

He looked blank. "What?"

She couldn't prevent a brilliant smile from spreading across her face, so happy did she feel all of a sudden. "Yes, I'll marry you."

His eyes narrowed and beneath her hand, the muscled forearm tensed. His chest swelled visibly before he exhaled heavily. "You picked a hell of a time to tell me," he muttered beneath his breath. "Do you know what I'd like to do with you right now?"

Her breath came faster as she registered the sexual intent in his rough voice, and she whispered, "Yes."

He lifted a hand and caressed her cheek. "But I don't want to give these folks any more shocks today. Just hold those thoughts until I get you alone."

They told her father that evening after dinner.

"Daddy, I hope you'll be happy for me," she concluded, talking on and on to cover the stunned silence that followed her announcement. Thad had come in after dinner as they'd arranged, and they faced him together in the sitting room.

"Do you really know what you're doing?" Reverend Miller demanded. "You two barely know each other."

"We know each other in the ways that count," she responded steadily.

"This is for the rest of your lives. It can't be undone if things crop up that change the way you feel."

Thad cleared his throat. "We don't intend to undo it,

ever. I'll take good care of her." He hesitated. "I know I'm not what you would have chosen for Chloe, but—"

"But I'm happy with the choice I've made," she finished. "And I hope you'll give us your blessing."

The minister sank into a chair. He suddenly looked every one of his sixty-one years. He held out his hand to Chloe. "Of course I'll give you my blessing."

They drove out to tell Margreta their news afterward. She was as thrilled as Thad predicted she would be, and her bubbling enthusiasm was a joy after her father's reserved reception. They didn't stay long, though, since they both had to work the next morning.

Back in the truck he said, "What do you want to do about living arrangements? I draw the line at moving in with you and your father."

She giggled. "And here I was cleaning out the spare bedroom for you."

He put his hand on her thigh and the warm clasp made her shiver. "You don't stand a chance of sleeping in a bed without me, once that ring is on your finger, protective papa or not."

They were passing his trailer, and he suddenly swung the truck into the driveway. "I guess we can live here for a couple of months while we look for a house."

"A house to buy?"

He kissed the tip of her nose and reached for the door handle. "Come on. You can take a quick look through my cupboards so you can start thinking about what you'd like to add or get rid of."

He left her in the tiny kitchen, telling her he wanted to check something in the office. She felt strange, opening cabinets and examining the details of his life, almost like she was snooping, and she had to remind herself that one day they would be sharing everything. They still hadn't discussed a wedding date, but Thad wouldn't want to wait too long, she was sure. Neither had they talked much yet about what kind of wedding they wanted. The only thing she knew for sure was that she wanted it small, intimate and memorable. Once she'd dreamed of walking down the aisle of the old church with six bridesmaids waiting for her, the pews full of every face she knew, but she couldn't imagine putting Thad through an ordeal like that, and frankly, it sounded a lot less appealing when she was faced with the thought of organizing it all.

Quickly she made a mental inventory of the little living room. She had some furniture that her father would insist she take with her, but that might have to wait until they found a house. A house—she could hardly wait!

Two hands came down on her shoulders and she shrieked before she could control herself.

"Daydreaming?" Thad turned her around and surveyed her shining eyes.

"I'm so happy!" She flung her arms around his neck and dragged his head down for a kiss.

He staggered back a step under her exuberance, but lifted his arms to loosely circle her waist. "Remind me to make you happy often."

Laughing, she stroked her palms over his broad shoulders, down his arms and back up, her love for him welling up from the place in her heart where she kept it hidden. What a sweet luxury to be able to touch him any way she liked! Her eyes were level with his throat, where she could see golden curls peeping from the neck of his sport shirt. Acting on impulse, she leaned forward and kissed him right there, in the hollow of his throat. He didn't move and, feeling greatly daring, she kissed the spot again, this time lingering over the kiss so that her tongue slipped over the salty roughness of his flesh.

Beneath her mouth, a groan vibrated. "Woman, you're testing my self-restraint. If you want to be a virgin on your wedding day, you'd better stop that."

"Oh, come on, Thad." She was in too good a mood to be deterred. "Let's just neck a little."

"Neck a little?" he echoed. "That's like telling a bee just to sting a little." But he lifted her and sat down on the couch, holding her cradled in one arm.

She slid her arms up around his neck and tilted her head back. "I can't wait until we can do this every night."

His mouth met hers as he muttered, "Neither can I." He tasted her thoroughly, teasing her with his tongue as his free hand stroked up and down her back, circling forward until he was exploring the tip of her breast through her cotton blouse. Surrendering herself to sensation, she closed her eyes as he unbuttoned the garment, arching up as he unclasped her bra, then gasping when he took her in his mouth. For long moments he feasted on her breasts. Her toes curled, and in her abdomen a taut wanting urged her to assuage it. His lips were still at her breast when his hand slipped down, stroking her belly and dipping one long finger beneath the waistband of her jeans.

She moaned, knowing only that she liked the caress. Immediately his mouth returned to cover hers for another of those deep, drugging kisses. He traced small circles over her belly and she realized he'd unbuttoned her pants, but she didn't care. Her fingers speared through his hair to cradle his skull. The circles swept a fraction lower with each pass, brushing the nest of curls at the joining of her legs. She trembled in his arms, moaning again beneath his mouth.

He lifted his head, and his eyes glittered as he looked down over her body. A wash of color stained his cheek-bones, and then her eyes closed as he arched her back over his arm and his head descended to suckle her again. Between her legs, his fingers were sliding lower and lower, rubbing repeatedly over a spot that had her arching in his arms, quivering with tension. One long finger probed more intimately, and then her eyes flew open as that questing finger slid up inside her, pressing and retreating repeatedly. A smile was on his lips. "Relax," he whispered. "Let it happen." The sound of his hoarse voice was a trigger for her body's response. All at once great waves of rhythmic muscle spasms swept her, thrusting her body against his hand over and over again. She cried out and turned her face into his shoulder as her body completed its sensual dance, sucking in a strangled breath as his finger slipped away from her, brushing against super-sensitized flesh.

Thad's chest was heaving beneath her cheek. "Oh, baby," he whispered. "You're going to burn me alive." Slowly she realized that his body was still tense and rigid beneath hers.

Embarrassment nearly choked her. He'd touched her in ways she'd never dreamed could be so exciting, and she'd—she'd had an orgasm in his arms without even having intercourse! She'd read about it, but had never imagined the printed words applying to *her*. "I'm sorry," she said against his shirt. "I should have waited until we were married."

Above her head Thad gave a bark of laughter. "Isn't that supposed to be my line?"

She raised her eyes to his, expecting him to be sullen

and angry that she'd—gone ahead without him, but he was smiling, his eyes intense as they swept her face. "You don't have a thing to be sorry about. Did you like that?"

She felt terribly shy, answering such an intimate question. Her eyes studied a button on his shirt, but she nodded. "I liked it."

His eyes crinkled at the corners, and she relaxed, enjoying the moment and snuggling against him.

He groaned, a loud, harsh sound of pain, and she shot bolt upright on his lap. "What's wrong? Did I hurt you?"

Thad was laughing, a rueful sound as he lifted her to one side and stood up. "No, I've just got a serious case of circuit overload."

She could hardly miss it, seated as she was at eye level. A heavy bulge strained the fabric of his jeans, a bulge that she knew meant he was...aroused.

"I'm sorry," she said again, helplessly. What was she supposed to say in a situation like this? "I really didn't mean for us to end up like this."

"It's okay." He took her hand and drew her to her feet. "But we'd better get out of here before I give in to the urge to carry you in there—" he jerked his head in the direction of the office that doubled as his bedroom "—and lay you down on that bed without a stitch of clothing and—"

"Stop!" She put a palm over his mouth, feeling the hated blush stealing up her cheeks again. "I get the picture." She buttoned her jeans self-consciously and stepped toward the door, then turned and gave him a weak smile. "Thank you. For not—for waiting."

"You can thank me after we're married."

As they drove away from the little haven, she heard

his low chuckle through the dark. "If that was necking a little, I can't wait to see what 'a lot' will be like."

He deserved an A in Self-control 101. She'd been so hot and responsive in his arms last night that he'd nearly forgotten how important it was to her to wait to consummate the marriage. *Consummate the marriage?* He was starting to sound like Chloe. He'd heard that's what happened to people who spent their lives together. The thought was oddly pleasing, and he whistled as he drove through town.

It was Tuesday afternoon, the day Chloe's father was out of the office. Thad was hoping to catch him at home and it looked like he was in luck. Parking the truck, he strode onto the front porch and boldly rang the bell. *This* wasn't going to be fun, but she was worth it. A grin spread foolishly over his face as he remembered how she'd flown apart for him last night. She was definitely worth it.

The door opened and Thad quickly wiped the smile off his face. "Good afternoon, sir." He supposed it was a bit premature to start calling him "Pop."

"Thad, is something wrong?" The minister didn't invite him in.

"No, sir. I just came to ask a favor of you."

Five minutes later Reverend Miller's face drew together in a fierce scowl. "You can't plan a wedding in a week."

"We don't need a lot of planning for a small ceremony."

"I always assumed she'd be married here, in the old church." The older man paused, a fleeting expression of sorrow passing over it. "That, of course, is no longer possible, but I'm not going to deprive my daughter of a ceremony that includes all the people who have watched her grow up.''

''Chloe doesn't want a big wedding. A small, simple ceremony will make her happiest.''

''She doesn't know what would make her happiest.''

The implication being, of course, that marrying *him* wasn't going to make her happy, either. Thad took a deep breath. The old man was getting under his skin with his constant, veiled criticisms. What the hell had happened to ''forgive and forget''?

Trying another tack, he asked, ''Can you honestly say that you want a big church wedding? You want to give Chloe to me in front of a hundred of your friends?''

No response. From the look on the rev's face, the thought was less than palatable. Sensing a weak spot, Thad used his last round. He'd hoped this wouldn't be necessary, but he'd be damned if this old man was going to keep Chloe away from him a day longer than he'd planned. ''We need to be married as soon as possible, sir.''

''You need…'' Reverend Miller's face flushed a deep tomato shade. His hands closed into fists on the desktop, and he was silent for a moment. When he raised his head, there was weary resignation in his eyes. ''I see.''

Thad seriously doubted that he did see. In fact, he hoped the reverend couldn't see the carnal thoughts bouncing around in his head every time he thought about marrying the man's daughter. But since the minister didn't question him further, he let him jump to his own conclusions. It wasn't his fault, was it, if Chloe's father assumed she was pregnant? Really. He should have more faith in her. The woman's morals were set in cement.

At least, until he started kissing her.

He realized the rev was waiting for him to speak, and suddenly he had a flash of how the man must feel. "Reverend—" he hesitated "—I promise you I'll take care of your daughter. She'll be the most important thing in my life. And you'll always be welcome in our home."

The minister studied him for a moment, and Thad wondered what he was thinking. Just as he decided the olive branch might as well have been used for kindling, the pastor said, "Thank you, Thaddeus. I appreciate that." He made an effort to smile. "I suppose we'd better make this as perfect as possible. She'll never get married again."

Seven

"**W**ant to get married tomorrow?"

She smiled and glanced across the desk at Thad, who had brought a sandwich to the office again. She didn't like to leave on Fridays because her father was out until about 2:00 p.m. and there was no one else to cover. Her heart had jumped a little at his words, but she forced herself to return his teasing in kind. "That would be nice. What time?"

"The ceremony is set for four o'clock. That should give you most of the day to do all the stuff brides do." There was a ring of truth in his casual tone that got Chloe's attention.

"You *are* joking, right?"

He grinned. "Am I?"

"Of course you are." But she still wasn't certain. "Aren't you?"

He stood and came around the desk, leaning a hip

against it and taking one of her hands. "No, I'm not joking."

Butterfly wings launched a mad assault in her stomach, excitement and apprehension in equal parts. "But, Thad, we can't possibly—"

"But if we could, what would you say?"

Wide-eyed, she knew she didn't need to consider. Still, it wouldn't be good to let him know how badly she wanted to take advantage of his offer before he withdrew it. "It would be the craziest thing I've ever done."

His lips twisted in a wry smile. "Now there's a ringing endorsement."

"I didn't mean it *that* way. I—"

He leaned forward, placing a finger against her lips. "Just listen. There's a pretty little church down in Maryland reserved for four o'clock. There will be flowers and music and a minister."

She thought her heart might force its way right out of her chest, it was beating so hard. A wave of longing rushed through her. Hesitantly, searching his eyes for reaction, she whispered, "All right."

"Great." Though the word was restrained, his body seemed to lose its subtle taut-wire tension. "We can go over to the courthouse this afternoon for the license. There's no waiting period in Maryland."

"But, Thad, I can't just leave."

As if it had been prearranged, her father strolled through the door. "Chloe, I won't need you this afternoon. Take some time off. I'm sure you and Thad have things to do."

She stared at him. Her father was smiling at her. Thad had a ridiculous grin on his face. They both looked extremely pleased with themselves. It *had* been prearranged! "Are you two in cahoots?" She shook her head, slightly dazed by the thought. "I never thought I'd live long enough to see you agree on anything."

Both men had the grace to look slightly ashamed.

Thad recovered first. "So what do you think?"

She spread her hands as the butterflies changed into champagne bubbles of giddiness. "It sounds as if you two have taken care of everything." Hastily she tidied her desk and retrieved her purse. "Oh, no. We can't get married tomorrow. I haven't had the dress altered yet." Her disappointment was so keen she could feel tears at the back of her eyes.

"Oh, by the way," her father said. "Did I forget to tell you? Barbara Halteran is coming by the house in thirty minutes. She promised me she could have the dress ready for you tomorrow."

"Oh, Daddy." She embraced her father in a tearful hug. "Thank you. You don't know how much this means to me."

Reverend Miller kissed her cheek as he released her. "I only have one little girl. If you have to get married, we might as well make the best of it."

Thad cleared his throat. "Are you ready? As soon as your fitting is over we'll drive down to Maryland."

Thad stood at the altar, fidgeting while the organist played some churchy-sounding tune. The sooner this was over, the better. He wanted to get a ring on Chloe's finger before anyone talked her out of marrying him. If they waited very long, he was sure she'd have second thoughts.

The idea of living without her had become an impossibility. He hadn't looked at another woman since the day he'd met her. No other woman would ever be

Chloe, with her funny little notions of propriety in public and her astonishing habit of turning into a wild woman in private—and that was as far as he'd better take *that* line of thought, if he didn't want her father to come after him with a gun. But it was more than just the physical thing. Although "the physical thing" had a lot to recommend it. He liked the way she defended him, the gentleness with which she treated his mother, and even more, he had gotten used to the way she believed in him, totally and without question. She enhanced his life in more ways than he could count, and there was no chance he was going to let her get away.

If anyone had told him three months ago that he'd be standing at the altar, *of his own free will,* waiting for his bride, he'd have laughed himself silly. One experience with marriage had cured him forever. Until Chloe.

Just then the music changed. He looked toward the back of the church, and his breath caught in his throat as she came into view.

She had the fingers of one hand tucked through her father's arm. The other held the trailing spray of roses he'd ordered. He hadn't seen her dress before the ceremony. It had been her mother's, a delicate ivory satin that clung to her breasts and displayed her tiny waist. It had a puffy floor-length skirt and she had tucked some pretty, fragile-looking white stuff among the curls she'd pulled away from her face. She looked beautiful, and breakable.

Her face was glowing, but as he took her hand, he felt her fingers trembling. Then her father stepped up before them and began the marriage ceremony, and he felt her jolt. He gave her a reassuring smile—he hadn't told her that her father was performing the ceremony.

It went fast, faster than he'd imagined, and in the

space of a few minutes, he was a married man. As he
slipped his ring onto her finger, he thought, strangely
enough, of his mother. She couldn't make the trip, but
he'd promised to bring Chloe by later so Margreta could
see her in her gown. When he kissed his wife—*his
wife!*—he kept it light and tender, mindful of her father's eagle eye. Then it was over. They signed the marriage certificate, he paid the two witnesses—the elderly
man and woman who were caretakers of the church
property—and she clung to his arm as he led her up the
aisle to the clicking of the photographer's camera.

He'd gone to great lengths to make this day special.
The pretty little church was on the historic register—
she'd bet her father had had a hand in getting it opened
for them. And if she'd had a moment's sadness, knowing she would never say her vows in their old church,
she'd pushed it away. Her father…he'd been better,
calmer and kinder to Thad than she'd ever have believed. If he was still opposed to his new son-in-law,
he kept it to himself and did a magnificent acting job.

As she stood in the middle of the dressing room in
the luxurious bridal suite he'd booked in a nearby hotel,
slowly removing her mother's wedding dress, it hit her
fully that tonight Thad would make love to her. He'd
kept her too busy in the past twenty-four hours to think
about it.

Then her fingers stilled on the buttons of the sleeve.
She was wrong. Tonight, *she'd* be the one making love.
Thad would be having sex. She'd known that was how
it would be when she married him. She'd taken this
chance, hoping he'd love her back someday. But he
didn't love her now.

In her heart she knew the only reason he had rushed

her to the altar was because he couldn't wait any longer for the sex. All day, she'd pretended otherwise, but deep down, she was sure he never would have proposed at all if she hadn't refused to sleep with him. It took some of the joy out of her recollections of the day, but if she was honest with herself, it didn't matter what his motives were. She would have married him in a wedding chapel in Las Vegas if he'd asked her. Because she loved him.

And now, according to the laws of the state of Maryland and the vows they'd exchanged before her father, her life was bound with his. She had literally left her family to cleave to him, as the Biblical passage in the Book of Ruth said.

"Chloe? Do you need help getting out of that dress?" Thad was on the other side of the door.

She felt shy and awkward about the moments to come, but even more, she didn't want to be alone with her thoughts any longer, so she reached out and turned the knob.

Thad was still wearing the dark suit pants he'd worn to the wedding and to the restaurant afterward, but he was definitely wilting around the edges. His tie dangled around his neck, and the first three buttons of his shirt had come open. He was in his stocking feet, and his jacket had disappeared.

His eyes darkened as he looked across the small space at her. "Come here."

She came.

Under his skillful lips she forgot her reservations, her fears. This was Thad, and she loved him. Everything else would take care of itself.

They were both breathing hard when he lifted his head. "Turn around," he said, his hands at her waist·

urging her to spin. She felt the warmth of his fingers moving down her back, freeing her from the dress, and as the last button came open, he slipped his hands inside it, caressing her ribs and moving inexorably around to the front of her body. One hand cupped a breast and the other pressed lightly against her stomach, drawing her back against him. As he did so, he dropped his head to nuzzle along the side of her neck and press open-mouthed kisses along her shoulder.

Then he removed his hands, pausing for a moment at her back before he turned her again. Setting his fingers at the neckline of the gown, he eased it down as she slipped her arms from the long sleeves, until it was a bouffant puddle around her knees. Her bra went with it, and belatedly she realized he'd unhooked it. Almost reflexively, her arms came up to cross over her breasts in an age-old gesture of feminine modesty.

A small smile played around Thad's lips. Reaching out, he drew one of her hands to his mouth and kissed her fingers. She'd never thought of fingers as erotic zones before, but as his tongue swirled around each digit and gently flicked at the deep valleys between, she forgot all about her modesty as her body responded to the warm, liquid caress. Then he took her other hand, holding both her arms at her sides, exposing her body fully to his view.

Without a word, he looked at her, and she could actually feel the heat in the path his eyes traced over her. When his eyes returned to hers, they had gone a dark, stormy blue that promised satisfaction and demanded surrender.

All she wore now was a minuscule pair of panties. Silken hose were held in place by ruffled garters. She'd never felt so naked in her life.

Slowly he raised her hands, placing the palms against his lightly furred chest. Lifting his own hands, he placed them on the slender curves below her waist. "Beautiful," he said hoarsely. "You're beautiful." His eyes narrowed as he stroked a large palm over each of her breasts, slowly circling and rolling until she felt her nipples rising into taut buds beneath his fingers and her entire body vibrate with tension. A wanton throbbing spread low in her abdomen, and she closed her eyes, raising her own hands to clasp the heavy musculature of his shoulders. Just when she thought she would die if he didn't do *something,* his hands slid slowly down, over her hips and around to her bottom, curving under the tiny panties, and she gasped as he caressed the deep groove between her buttocks.

Then he sank to his knees before her. She looked down at his bright hair, trembling with new sensations. Taking his hands from her bottom, he carefully slipped her hose and garters off, one at a time, brushing the insides of her thighs as he did so and causing her to suck in a sharp breath. His eyes were intent as he hooked his thumbs in the panties and drew them down, as well.

She was nude before him, acutely aware of him kneeling before her. Lifting his arm, he circled her hips and tugged her gently forward, laying his head against her belly for a moment before turning to her and kissing her navel and lower body just above her nest of curls. She felt so strange, as if her legs wouldn't support her any longer, and as if he sensed it he rose.

He lifted her free of the dress at her feet and into his arms, carrying her to the big bed in the bridal bedroom and placing her atop the sheets. Leaving her for a moment, he quickly stripped off his shirt and tie, pants and socks. She had turned her head to watch, and she was both embarrassed and fascinated by the sight of him clad only in low-slung briefs that did nothing to hide his reaction to her. Her embarrassment faded as the passion he aroused in her blossomed, and her body recalled the peak to which he'd taken her once before.

"Hurry," she whispered through suddenly dry lips, in someone else's voice, and he laughed, the sound little more than a growl deep in his throat as he removed his briefs.

"Tonight we're taking our time," he said, placing a knee on the mattress and moving to lie on his side next to her. Against her hip, his hot silky strength throbbed. He laid a large hand on her belly as he leaned over her, his mouth taking hers in a deep imitation of possession that lasted until she thought she might die if he didn't move faster. She wound her arms around his neck, trying to pull him closer, and he allowed it. His chest felt as if it held a furnace inside where it pressed against her sensitive breasts. She twisted her torso, rubbing herself against him, and his voice was strained as he said, "Little wildcat. You make me so crazy I forget you're new to this."

She smiled against his lips, then gasped as the hand on her belly moved slowly but inexorably down, down, over her woman's mound and between her legs, cupping her heat in his palm. Unused to such intimacy, she panicked for a moment, and the sensual woman who'd replaced her vanished beneath inhibition. Instinctively, she tried to close her legs but the motion only trapped his hand more effectively. He kissed her again, using his teeth and tongue until she relaxed and forgot the hand lying between her thighs.

Then she remembered abruptly, as his stealthy fingers

began a steady, circling stroke, growing bolder with each caress. Heat flared low in her belly. As if of their own will, her thighs relaxed enough to allow him better access, and her hips began to move against his hand. Then a long finger probed her, and she arched against his hand in startlement, not able to tell whether she wanted him to stop or wanted more. It didn't hurt, it just felt so… "Ah. Are you ready for me?" Before she realized what was happening, he eased his weight onto her, lying fully atop her, covering her from head to foot with his big body.

His big, *aroused* body. She could feel the hard length of him prodding gently at the V of her legs, and excitement spiraled within her so fiercely that her hands shook where they clung to his broad back. He reached down between them and suddenly, shockingly, he was *there,* poised at the portal of her body.

His eyes blazed down at her as he slowly pushed forward, and she whimpered at the inexorable pressure. He bared his teeth and dropped his head, nipping her neck less than gently, and she arched in surprise.

As she did, he thrust his hips forward. For one long moment the pressure increased to an unbearable level, and then her body yielded and he slid past the barrier to lodge within her.

She squeaked in surprise and sudden pain, her body freezing in protest and he smiled grimly down at her. "It gets better, baby. I promise. The first time is always rough."

He held perfectly still within her. As her body adjusted to the full sensation, accepting him more easily, she could feel his heartbeat against her and within her, hear the air rushing in and out of his lungs, rub her fingers along the slick, sweated flesh of his back and feel the muscled power. As she began to relax, she realized that it wasn't terribly painful, and her confidence began to return. Her hands dipped lower, palming tight, muscled buttocks, and he groaned. "That's not such a good idea right now."

"Oh?" She tried to smile flirtatiously, but her lips trembled.

"Ah, honey." He levered his hips a fraction away from her and then flexed again, pushing back into her. "I have to... I can't wait."

She started to tell him it was all right, that it only hurt a little bit, but his body began to move against her again, more urgently and more powerfully than anything she'd been expecting, and suddenly it hurt a lot. He was too big, moving too fast. She squirmed beneath him, trying to push him away as tears sprang to her eyes. Why had it felt so good before?

Against her sensitive flesh, his body moved faster and faster, sliding in and out of her in measured strokes as his breath whistled in and out. Then, just when she thought she couldn't bear being split asunder like this for another second, he arched against her, embedding himself as deeply as he could fit, and she felt the small pulses of his release against her inner walls, an intimacy greater even than what had just occurred. A few more times, less and less violently, he arched again, until he was lying limp over her, his dead weight pressing her into the mattress.

And even in the discomfort she felt, she still was moved to raise her hands and cradle his skull, to run her fingers over his blond hair, feeling somehow as if *he* were the one who needed comforting.

Finally, he stirred. "I'm sorry."

She wanted to tell him it was all right, but she

couldn't. It *wasn't* all right. *She* wasn't all right. She settled for "I know."

Still nestled snug within her, he raised himself on his elbows and said through his teeth, "No, you don't. You don't know one damn thing." He lifted himself away then, sliding off the bed and padding naked into the bathroom.

She lay watching as he walked away, confusion and unhappiness a sudden tight ball in her chest as she took in his tight, round buttocks and the ropes of muscle that rippled across his back, the long, firm legs and the way his shoulders tapered to his trim waist. His occupation certainly kept him fit. A wave of weariness washed over her, and she yawned. It had been an eventful, draining day. Reaching down to the foot of the bed, she had just pulled the sheet over her when Thad returned, carrying a washcloth in his hand.

She watched without comprehension until he flipped the edge of the sheet back, baring her body. Automatically she started to cover herself with her hands.

"Don't." The single word stopped her hands in mid-air.

She knew he was right. It was silly to be shy in front of him now that they were married, particularly given what had just occurred between them. But that didn't stop the hated feeling of heat, the blush, from rising to her cheeks.

Thad's face softened, and he reached out, tracing the curve of her cheek with a gentle finger. "I can't believe you're blushing *now*."

Her face grew even redder as his gaze swept down over her exposed body. "I know. It's a little late for modesty."

Then she gasped as he gently parted her thighs and

cleaned *there* with the washcloth. He was careful, and it didn't hurt, but she turned her face away. It might be silly, but it was going to take some time before she got used to his casual attitude about nude bodies.

"How do you feel?" He tossed the washcloth in the general direction of the bathroom.

"Fine." She moved experimentally. It wasn't a lie, she did feel fine, although she wasn't about to explore to see where she might hurt. At least her body felt fine, she amended. Her mind was still whirling with disappointment despite her exhaustion.

He crawled back into bed and reached for her, pulling the sheets up over them both and settling her in the curve of his arm, one hand resting low on her belly. "It'll be better next time."

She hoped so. She really hoped so. But she wasn't holding her breath.

His arms were warm around her, and despite the soreness in her body, she enjoyed being cuddled and coddled. She was almost asleep, still in his embrace, drifting away into slumber, when a disturbing thought burst into her mind.

"We didn't use any birth control tonight."

Instantly she felt the tension in his body, in the way the arm beneath her stiffened, and she sensed he was wide awake—he must not have thought about it, either, until she said something.

"Is that a problem?" His voice was in her ear, sounding strangely cool and remote, not like his usual lazy, teasing self at all.

"Well, isn't it?" She was suddenly uncertain. "We need time to get used to living together."

"We have the rest of our lives for that." He paused,

and his tone was softer when he went on. "I wouldn't mind if you got pregnant tonight."

She considered his words for a while. "I think I'll mind. I'm barely used to being a bride, let alone a mother."

The hand on her belly flexed, then relaxed. "We can worry about it if it happens."

"And from now on, for a little while, at least, we'll use birth control. I'll go to the doctor—"

"No." His voice was as hard as she'd ever heard it. "I'll take care of it for a while. We can talk about it again in a few months and decide." Levering himself over her on his palms, he dropped his head and kissed her, and even knowing what she might provoke if she aroused him, she couldn't keep herself from responding. As he lay back, he urged her onto her side so that her back was to him, pressing her against his chest, his thighs cradling hers. How strange. She shouldn't feel so comfortable. She'd never slept with another person in her whole life. And yet—this felt *right*. She felt safe and protected, and as another wave of weariness swept over her, she forgot her concerns and closed her eyes.

He opened his eyes slowly, immediately aware of the sweet warmth of feminine flesh at his side. Chloe. His wife. He was on his stomach, head buried in the pillow, and carefully he raised himself to his elbows so he could look down at her.

She slept on her side, facing him, her hands curled up beneath her chin in loose fists. One leg was stretched straight, the other drawn over it with the knee bent. Her skin looked soft and rosy, her lips smiling the faintest bit even in repose. The sheet had slipped down across the curve of her hip, leaving her upper body bared to his view. One breast was hidden by her arms but the other peeked out from beneath them, the pink nipple capping it soft.

He could watch her all day. And he did, for a long time, as the room grew lighter with the approach of dawn.

It seemed like a miracle. Every morning he could wake like this and find her sleeping by his side. The only flaw, he thought, thinking critically of what he was taking her home to, was the trailer. She deserved better, and as soon as she could find a house she liked, he'd buy it and move her into it. One more little tie to bind her to him.

He honestly hadn't thought about birth control last night, because it didn't matter to him. Well, that wasn't strictly true. As far as he was concerned, the sooner she was pregnant, the better. He'd been unprepared for the surge of longing that shot through him when she mentioned having a child. Maybe then he'd stop thinking that she was going to look at him—*really* look at him— one day and wake up to realize she didn't want to spend her life with him.

But it was more than that. He wanted kids. He wanted to come home to shrieking, giggling chaos, to sticky fingers and stuffed animals. He wanted to watch his child grow and change, to look for Chloe's features, or his own, in a tiny face, to celebrate milestones like first words and first grade.

Until she was really and truly pregnant, until he could put his hands over her belly and feel his child moving within her, he would harbor a small knot of fear deep inside. Maybe she really didn't want his child and was just putting off the decision—

"Deep thoughts this morning?" A warm hand reached out and stroked his cheek.

Without thinking, he turned his head and kissed her fingers, then lost his balance and fell atop her as she put both arms around his neck and yanked him down.

"Hey!"

"Hey, yourself." She smiled up at him, looking immensely pleased with herself, then squeaked in surprise when he wrapped his arms around her and rolled so that she lay atop him, every sweet inch of her aligned with his own body.

"This is more like it," he pronounced.

"Umm-hmm." She wriggled her hips, effectively sandwiching his morning erection between them, and the feel of her silky flesh made him stiffen even more.

He groaned. "You're torturing me."

"No, I'm not." She propped herself up on his chest and circled one flat bronze nipple with her index finger.

"Yes, you are. I wasn't going to do anything this morning. I was going to be noble, let you have time to heal."

She dropped her head and licked his nipple experimentally with her tongue, and he almost jumped out of his skin with pleasure. "I don't need time to heal," she said in a husky voice.

He didn't need a second invitation. Rolling again, he switched their positions, then slid to one side so he could caress her warm, willing flesh.

In the early-morning light, her skin looked luminescent, as if it were lit from within by the smallest suggestion of light. He traced the line of her jaw, sliding over her heart-shaped chin and moving down her throat, stopping to lay his fingers over the place where her pulse fluttered beneath the fragile covering of skin. The

flesh of her breasts was pale as porcelain, underlaid with
a delicate webbing of blue veins.

He bent his head and gently kissed the closest nipple,
then suckled lightly, feeling it draw into a tight bead
beneath his attentions. Her fingers dug into his scalp.
Repeating the action with the other breast, he used his
fingers to roll and pluck at the sensitive tips. She was
beginning to breathe faster, and she shifted her hips
once on the bed. He doubted if she even knew she did
it.

"Do you like that?" He raised his head to examine
her face.

Her eyes were closed, but her lips curved up a bit at
the corners and she breathed, "Yes."

He bent again to his task, until her chest was heaving
and she clutched at his back and biceps with damp
hands. "Please…"

"Please what?" His own flesh had responded to the
scent and feel of her in its predictable way, and he
surged against her hip once, trying to ignore the throbbing ache that begged him for release.

She grasped his wrist and swept it down across her
body, whispering, "Touch me. Like you did before."

She had picked the damnedest time to remind him of
that. He was so hard he actually hurt, but he forced his
mind away from his pulsing flesh, spreading his fingers
wide to comb through the nest of curls she'd directed
him to. Her legs moved restlessly and she opened them
the tiniest bit, inviting him in. With the lightest of caresses, he drew a single finger down, tracing the seam
that lay between her legs, then retracing the path back
up to circle lightly over the small nub he found at its
beginning.

Her back arched. She rolled her hips and he used the

motion to place his palm against the shadowed cleft, bathing him in slippery, steaming heat. He groaned. She was ready. He could take her now without hurting her. He shifted over her, lay himself between her thighs and let the taut head of his swollen flesh rub gently against her. She moved her hips in a new way, helping him continue to please her, but he knew he wasn't going to be able to wait much longer if he stayed in this position, and he wanted her to enjoy it this time, so he started to move away again so that he could use his hand.

"No!" Her legs drew together around his hips, surprisingly powerful, holding him in place. "Don't stop."

"I don't want to hurt you," he panted.

She didn't answer but spread her legs and dug her heels into the mattress, sliding down so that she caught him with the clasp of her body. Poised to enter her, he used every ounce of self-control he possessed to move forward steadily, slowly, letting her feel his size as her body stretched and accepted him.

"What are you doing?" Her eyes were open now, and he could swear she sounded irritated.

"I'm trying…to take it…easy. I don't want…to hurt you again." Beneath his chest, her breasts pushed against him, making his own nipples tighten into tiny buds of need.

She dug her heels into his buttocks now, inexorably shoving him deep within her. "Don't wait. Please don't wait."

And suddenly, he couldn't. Not for another second. His hips flexed, sheathing him within her until they were pressed together, belly to belly. But he didn't take time to savor the sensation. He couldn't. His head pounded, blood rushing through it as his body began the primitive, driving rhythm that would lead him to climax. Her heels climbed his back as he thrust, and she threw her head back, her body arching like a drawn bow. A high keening tore from her throat as he felt the ripples of her release begin, shaking her like a leaf in a high wind and milking him in intense, repeated pulses that stroked the flesh fitted within her. At the back of his neck, a shiver began, working its way down his backbone in a lightning flash of command, and his body obeyed, taking him into his own frenzied, jolting, tooth-grinding finish.

When the storm passed, he wanted to do nothing more than close his eyes and sleep, right there on and in her. But perhaps she didn't. Dread coiled in his stomach as he raised himself over her and looked into her face. He hadn't meant to lose control like that. He'd hurt her again—

She was smiling.

Cautiously, he said, "You look…happy." *Happy* didn't cover it, though he wasn't about to tell her she looked wanton, satisfied.

Her smile grew wider. "You were right." Her hand moved from his back, sliding up to caress the fine hairs at the back of his neck.

"About?"

"It is easier after the first time."

"If it's done right, it should be. Otherwise, how would a man ever coax his woman back for more?"

She laughed, and it struck him that he was enjoying this as much as he did the sex. He'd never known this cozy intimacy before, and he liked it.

He liked it a lot.

Eight

The first thing she saw when she pulled into the driveway was Thad. He was mowing the grass in a pair of ragged cutoffs. His only other clothing was his sneakers, the old ratty ones that looked like they'd been through a war. She'd almost thrown them out last week, but he pitched a fit, insisting that they were the most comfortable shoes he owned for yard work. She guessed he hadn't been exaggerating.

He smiled when he saw her. She waved at him and went on into the trailer. Her knees were shaky and her pulse raced from no more than that wordless exchange. Lordy, what that man did to her system!

Surely it was sinful to lust after a man's body like this, even if he was your husband. She had walked around in a daze of sensuality throughout the whole past month. Even when she wasn't with him, her mind replayed vivid fantasies of their lovemaking, fantasies that made her body ache with need. At the office, her father had to speak twice before she heard him. It was embarrassing, darn it. If women didn't go into heat, then this must be the next thing to it.

Outside, she heard the mower cut off. She filled a glass with ice water and walked out the back door. Thad was standing in the shade of the big tree beside the trailer, mopping his face and chest with a T-shirt he must have discarded earlier.

"Ah-h-h. Thanks. It was hot today." He took the drink and lifted it to his lips. As he drank, the strong muscles in his neck worked, and she forced herself to look away. A woman could only take so much temptation.

"I guess I'd better start supper."

"Forget supper. It's too hot to eat." He grabbed her hand and began to pull her away from the house. "We can put a cold meal together when we come back."

"When we come back from where?" He was leading her into the woods behind the house, and she protested as she realized she was still wearing her office clothing. "Wait a minute. I have to change my clothes."

"Your clothes will be fine, I promise." He ignored the first question as he moved with easy familiarity down a well-marked path ahead of her.

It was a little bit cooler beneath the trees. She could hear water burbling somewhere nearby, and the full force of the late-day sun didn't penetrate the dense canopy of leaves. She gave up questioning and just followed him. She knew him well enough by now to know that she wouldn't get a single scrap of information out of him unless he chose to enlighten her.

The sound of water was very near now, and in another moment they emerged into a small clearing near the stream. Less than thirty feet from bank to bank, it meandered around a sharp curve at the place where they stood, creating a little point that sloped gently to the water's edge.

"Oh, this is pretty. I didn't even know this stream was back here." Though now that she thought about it, she realized it must be the Antietam Creek, which cut through the southern part of the county before wandering away into Maryland, passing through battlefields that had been saturated with blood almost a century and a half ago. She crossed it every day on her way into town, driving over a scenic stone bridge left from an earlier era.

"I've been coming down to this old swimming hole since I was a kid." Thad stopped on a grassy verge near the water's edge. He pried his sneakers off one at a time, balancing on the other leg like a big stork. "Nobody comes here anymore. There are other spots that are bigger and a lot easier to get to, I guess." His shoes removed, he placed his hands at the worn waistband of his jeans and opened the snap with a small popping sound. "Gonna take a dip with me?"

No wonder he'd been so sure her clothes would be all right. She stared at him, then at the water. Obviously he didn't expect her to *wear* any clothes.

"Um, I don't…think so." She couldn't imagine taking off her clothes outside. Just the thought made her feel exposed. She pointed to a large boulder a few feet away. "I'll just sit and relax over there."

Thad shrugged. His face was a blank mask; she had no idea what he was thinking. "You don't know what you're missing." Ignoring her completely, he shucked out of his jeans and briefs and walked toward the water.

She stared at him, dry-mouthed, as he waded into the

stream. Oh, yes. She knew exactly what she was missing. His shoulders were bronzed already from the sun. The breadth of them when he took off his shirt never failed to surprise her all over again. Her hands itched to stroke over those shoulders, to feel the play of the long, corded muscles of his legs, which flexed and shifted as he walked. His sex hung heavily against his thighs, cushioned in a thicket of hair as golden as that on his head.

They'd explored each other's bodies thoroughly in the weeks since the wedding, but she'd never watched him so openly before. In the trailer, no matter if they were in the bedroom or the kitchen or the tiny living room, she was a creature of sensation. She knew her way around his body blindfolded by now, but if he was in a nude line-up with a bag over his head, she wondered if she'd be able to pick out his body. The outrageous thought made her giggle, and he turned his head to survey her as he waded into the creek.

"Are you laughing at me?" He looked down at his body, definitely as unaroused as it could get in the cold water. "I guess it is pretty laughable."

"That's not it!" She was giggling openly now as she perched on the edge of the rock after giving the surface a cursory swipe with her hand to clear away any dirt.

"Well, if it isn't that, then what is it?"

"Nothing." No way on earth could she explain to him what she was thinking. In his arms she didn't feel shy very often anymore, but she still couldn't talk about sex without blushing. Which she was doing right now, darn it.

"The day a woman is thinking nothing is the day the world ends," he predicted darkly, just before he submerged himself in the deepest part of the stream, near the tree roots at the far side.

She propped herself back on her hands and tilted her face up to the sun, still warm during these long early-summer days. The water looked cool and tempting, and she would love to take a dip. Why not? But as much as she wanted to be the kind of woman who wouldn't worry about stripping off her clothes in broad daylight, she *would* worry. What if someone came by?

A splash caught her attention, and she saw Thad stroking through the rippling water, the muscles of his arms gleaming. She still couldn't believe she was married to him. She, Chloe Miller—Chloe Shippen, she corrected—could touch that gorgeous male splashing in the creek anytime she liked. It was like a dream from which she hadn't awakened.

A dream marred only by the knowledge that her husband liked her and desired her, but didn't love her.

A voice near her right side said, "The water feels great."

She sat up with a start, pressing her hand to her heart. "You scared me!" Her body sagged in the automatic relaxation produced by relief.

"Sorry." His grin flashed, white and insincere, as he crossed his arms on the edge of the rock and rested his chin on the back of one, allowing his body to float in the water. "So…what did you do today?"

She shrugged. "Same old, same old. Most of the records that we saved have been restored in the new computers."

"Are you enjoying it?"

She cast him a sideways glance that clearly asked after his sanity. "I'd rather be working with children. *That* would be a challenge I'd enjoy."

"We can remedy that in about nine months." He traced one wet finger from the inside of her knee up her inner thigh, brushing her skirt aside as his hand moved higher.

Children of their own. She wanted them, definitely, could almost see chubby little boys with golden hair tearing through the house. But she wasn't ready to change this idyllic time when just the two of them made their family complete. Before she brought children into the world, she was going to be sure their parents shared love.

His fingers found the edge of her panties and slowly explored, and she almost relaxed and let him touch her—and then she remembered where they were. She pressed her legs together, preventing him from any more intimate touch. What if someone came along and saw them? "Not here," she said. "I wasn't talking about our family and you know it."

"Right. You meant your preschool." Abruptly he removed his hand. "If it's so important to you, what are you waiting for? Quit your job and get started." His voice was cool, almost challenging, as he pushed off the rock and let the current carry him away from her.

She sat up and pulled her skirt over her knees, no longer enjoying the warmth of the day. Why had he gotten so distant all of a sudden? They'd been talking about her work, and all of a sudden he was cooler than iced tea. What had she said? Then it hit her. It wasn't what she had said, it was what she had done. He was miffed because she hadn't let him entice her into love-making out here by the stream.

He wasn't really interested in talking. When they were together, he was thinking about making love. Or recovering from making love. She'd known when she married him that he didn't love her the way she loved him, but she'd counted on proximity drawing them together, forging common bonds they shared.

As she stood and dusted off her skirt, she thought sadly that the only bonds they were forging were the physical kind. And much as she liked that, she needed more.

It's only been a month, she told herself. *Meaningful relationships take time to grow. Be patient.*

He watched her walking back up the trail to the house as he pulled his shorts on and stuffed his briefs in his pocket. What if she didn't want children at all? He knew her well enough to know that if she bore children, she'd never break up their marriage. Maybe she was afraid he wouldn't be a good father. Hell, he wondered that himself. It wasn't like he'd had a role model or anything.

He sprinted up the path. To hell with it. He was probably wasting a lot of good brain cells on this. Relationships never lasted a lifetime. He'd seen enough men come and go through his mother's life to know that monogamy—and love—were myths.

So what if he'd been thinking both were possible since he'd met her?

As he emerged from the woods, he could see her. She was almost back at the house. Her head was down, and she walked without her customary lilt.

What did she have to be upset about? Other than the fact that her damned school was still a dream.

Her father, surprisingly, didn't kick and scream like she thought he would when he read the letter of resignation she handed him at the end of the workday the next day.

"This was temporary. We both knew it," she said.

Reverend Miller snorted, though the sound was good-humored. "Some of us knew it faster than others." He laid the letter to one side. "I guess you're going to be busy soon enough, anyway."

"That's for sure. Did I tell you we think we've found a house? Thad's having a contractor look it over with him this afternoon. It's an old farmhouse. There's a shed behind the house that Thad can renovate for a workshop, and the kitchen is huge. It has two fireplaces and five bedrooms and—" she grimaced "—a bathroom that will have to be modernized before we do anything else!"

"That's good. You'll want to be moved in and organized before the baby comes."

"And I—*what did you say?*"

He only smiled at her. "It's all right. I've known since before the wedding."

She couldn't find her voice for a moment. This wasn't quite the kind of discussion she'd ever imagined having with her father, for heaven's sake! Finally she managed to speak. "You think I'm pregnant?"

"I'm delighted," he assured her.

"You're delighted. And the fact that you assume I got into this condition before the wedding doesn't bother you?"

"I was very disappointed." He shot her a stern look over the tops of his glasses. "You had strong moral guidelines that I had hoped —"

"Well, it bothers me! I am *not* pregnant." She stopped, feeling sheepish. "Well, I could be, now, but I wasn't when we got married."

Her father's brows rose in question. "You weren't? But when Thad came to see me, he said—"

"Thad came to see you?" she repeated. "When was this?"

"When he came to ask me for your hand."

"He *asked* you for my hand?" She was overwhelmed by facts that didn't compute. This whole conversation was beginning to make her feel like Alice must have felt when she first saw the Mad Hatter race by.

"Well, strictly speaking, he didn't ask. He told me that you were marrying, and he asked me to help plan the ceremony."

"And he told you I was pregnant?" She was going to have quite a chat with Thad. And while she chatted, she was going to pull out every soft, curling hair on his chest, one by one by one.

"Actually, he said you needed to be married right away. I suppose I assumed…but he definitely wanted me to believe—"

"I see."

"So I'm not going to be a grandfather yet?"

"Not yet." Her face felt frozen; she had to consciously relax her jaw. "I have to go. I'll write a job description for you as soon as I get a chance."

Her drive home to the trailer was fueled by fury. It was almost dinnertime, but when she pulled into the driveway, she didn't see his truck. She slammed drawers and banged pans as she threw together a casserole for dinner. What reason could he possibly have had for leading her father to conclude… Oh, thinking about it just made her angry all over again. She tossed the casserole into the oven and was heading for the bedroom to change her clothes when the door swung open.

Thad stepped into the room, and the small interior of their home immediately seemed even tinier.

"Hello," he said, reaching for her. "We have a green

light on the hou— Hey!'' He grabbed her wrists as she shoved against his chest.

It had been almost a reflex; she hadn't been expecting him right at that moment, and when he'd walked right into her path, she hadn't wanted to be touched. "You…you rotten, lying *rat.*" It was the worst insult she could come up with. "Why did you make my father think I was pregnant?"

He stared at her as if she'd gone mad. Which probably wasn't too far from the truth. Slowly he straightened away from the door, keeping his eyes on her. "I didn't lie to him," he said. "He jumped to that conclusion all by himself."

"Don't you split hairs with me." She stepped forward again and poked him in the chest. "You *led* him to believe we had to get married fast, and then you *allowed* him to keep believing it. You knew how important it was to me to come to my marriage, *untouched,* and now my own father is going to think I didn't—I wasn't—"

"You *didn't* come to this marriage untouched." His tone was angry, too. "The way I remember it, I touched you pretty damn near everywhere before I ever put a ring on your finger. And you enjoyed it."

She ground her teeth together so hard she'd probably damaged the enamel. "Thank you so much for reminding me. I forgot what a *gentleman* you are." She started to brush by him, intending to go back to the bedroom and grandly slam the door in his face and stay there for the rest of the evening, but he reached out and caught her by the arm.

"Let go of me!" She tried to wrench her arm away, but he used both hands to wrestle her up against his body, holding her wrists behind her in one hand and roughly taking her chin in the other.

"If you're going to be mad at me, I may as well give you something to be mad about."

She twisted, trying to wrench her head away as he set his mouth down on hers but he simply hitched her higher against his body and lifted her off her feet. One of her kicking feet caught him solidly on the shin, and he grunted, lifting his head.

They glared at each other for a few taut seconds. She was furious with him. She really was. But her body, pressed intimately against his and coursing with adrenaline, communicated another message. Between them, his growing length told her that he was as aroused as she suddenly was. Heat pooled between her legs, and she felt herself going soft and wet. She struggled to remember why she was angry, but her mind drew a blank. His expression changed, and his gaze dropped to her lips. She could swear she felt him touching her.

This time when he lowered his head, she didn't try to get away. Her mouth clung to his and her tongue met him, demanding more. He had set her back on her feet, and she lifted one leg, wrapping it around the back of his thigh and rubbing herself against him. He released her hands and grasped her buttocks in both big palms. She hadn't started a fight with this result in mind, but she couldn't wait for his possession. Reaching for him, she ripped at the buttons on his shirt, and he glanced down in astonishment as one popped off and flew across the room. Then, almost instantly, her urgency communicated itself to him. He burrowed under her skirt, lifting handfuls of fabric out of the way until he could reach her. Stripping her panty hose and the panties beneath them down her legs, he peeled the hose away until

she could kick out of them. She was fumbling with the
front of his trousers and he shoved her hands aside,
opening his jeans and freeing himself from the briefs
beneath. She grasped him in one small hand, murmuring
with pleasure, and he groaned. He couldn't wait long
enough to take her to the bedroom. He had to have her
now. He lifted her by the waist, turning so that she was
braced against the door. He didn't bother removing the
skirt, and she lifted it out of the way, then clutched at
his shoulders as he used his body to spread her legs
wide, entering her in one mighty thrust.

Her back arched, and she yanked his head up to hers
by simply pulling on his hair; her mouth was ferocious.
He held her in place against the door, silently thrusting
in and out of her as their mouths mated. She felt like
her skin was electrified, every sensation magnified by
her heightened emotions. She loved the feel of him between her legs, his body pounding against her most sensitive flesh, his tongue matching the rhythm of his hips.
Abruptly she realized her body was beginning its surge
toward satisfaction. She could feel her climax gathering
into a tight fist within her, only to explode, shattering
her into shards of mindless sensation. She tore her
mouth away from his, crying out as her body shuddered
and bucked against him. He didn't let her rest but continued his assault, baring his teeth in what might have
been a smile. "My turn."

Her body was so sensitive that she felt as if she'd
received an electric shock with each stroke of his flesh,
each meeting of his torso against hers. She cried out as,
incredibly, she felt herself rushing to a second peak, and
he gave an involuntary groan as his body stiffened and
shook, surging against her in the throes of his own climax.

When he was finished, they both hung against the door, chests heaving. She reached up and caught a drop of sweat with her thumb as it trickled down his temple. He staggered to the couch, slipping from her body as they sat, and sank down with a grateful sigh. His legs couldn't have carried him another step. Chloe lay on his chest, her breath coming hard and fast against his neck, and despite the lethargy that invited him to simply drop his head back and close his eyes, he lifted his arms and wrapped them around her, holding her close as their breathing steadied and their pulses returned to a less frantic rhythm.

He stroked a hand down her hair, a chuckle rumbling up from the depths of his chest. "I vote we always fight like that."

Her lips curved into a smile against his neck. "Was that our first fight?"

He shrugged, running his palms up and down her slender back. "You prefer *disagreement?*"

She brushed the tips of her fingers lightly across the hairs on his chest, and he felt ripples of goose bumps spring up. "I don't know what to call it." Sitting up on his lap, she gave him a long, sober look. "I'm sorry I shouted at you." She shook her head. "I don't know what happened. I just got so *mad.*"

He sighed. "I'm sorry, too. I shouldn't have implied that to your father."

"Why did you?" She didn't sound angry anymore, just curious.

He hesitated. How could he explain the compulsion that had driven him? *I was afraid you wouldn't want to marry me if you had time to think about it?* He settled for "I wanted you too much to wait."

She didn't say anything in answer, simply lifted her

hand to his cheek, but he noticed she didn't meet his eyes.

Turning his head, he kissed her palm. "Am I forgiven?"

She nodded. "It doesn't really matter what my father believes. I just hate the idea of people thinking you took advantage of me, when we both know that's not true."

Deep in his chest, the icy sense of unease thawed. As usual, she was more concerned with what people thought of him than she was of herself. It sounded as if she was planning on being with him for the long haul. It was a pleasing thought.

"This isn't great, but I can live with it for a while." Chloe stood in the middle of the kitchen in the house they'd just bought. They'd signed the final papers that morning. It had given her a warm feeling to see her name underneath Thad's on the deed. A good feeling.

She looked around the enormous old room. It hadn't been renovated for at least fifty years. There were no counters, few cupboards, and the sink was one of the wide, shallow kind that she'd seen in some of their oldest parishioners' homes.

"You don't have to live with it at all," Thad said. "We can afford to renovate the upstairs bathroom, put one in down here and still redo the kitchen. The rest of it, we can work on ourselves."

She shifted, uncomfortable with the idea of him using all his savings on the house. "I really don't mind waiting. We can set aside a little bit at a time for—"

"Chloe."

Her name on his lips stopped the flow of words.

"What's bothering you? I want to get this all done at one time. The thought of living with workmen traips-

ing in and out for months on end doesn't appeal to me."
He crossed the floor to her, placing his arms around her
waist and pulling her back against him. Bending his
head, he blew a warm stream of air against the spot
right behind her ear that he'd discovered got to her
every time, and, as always, she relaxed, letting her body
soften against him in surrender.

"I feel *funny,* using your money for all this."

"It's not *my* money. It's *our* money."

His lips nibbled down the side of her neck, and a
wave of heat rushed through her. "Thad, wait!"

She could feel him smile against her skin. "For what?
We're alone for the first time in our house. Don't you
think we ought to celebrate?"

"Seems to me we've celebrated an awful lot since
we got married." She was smiling now, too. His lovemaking was as fierce and devastating each time he
touched her as it had been from the beginning. In his
arms, she became someone new even to herself, matching his passion with her own. She floated through her
days waiting for evening and his return home, feeling
as if she were only half alive until he walked through
the door and touched her.

"We have a lot to celebrate," he said in her ear.
"Your last day at the church is tomorrow. Then you
can work on the house to your heart's content."

"While I work on my preschool proposal."

"Whatever. You know you don't have to work. If
you want to be home with the children, I can support
us."

Children. Another troubling thought. But his words
reminded her of something. "Um, we can't "celebrate"
for a few days. I found out this morning that I'm not
pregnant."

His hands stilled in their exploration of her body, then slowly dropped away from her. "All right. Let me know when—"

"Okay," she said hastily. Her body suddenly felt chilled. Was it unreasonable of her to want to be cuddled even when they couldn't make love? *He didn't marry you for love,* she reminded herself with brutal honesty. *He married you for your body.* Thad had seemed a little reserved, a bit distant for the past few weeks. The only time she felt like he was completely with her was when they were making love. Which, she acknowledged, was almost all the time when they were together.

He already had stepped away from her and was looking critically around the kitchen. "Why don't we talk about what we'd like the finished room to be like."

As he began to tell her about traffic patterns and the triangle that made the best workspace, she felt her enthusiasm fall away. "You decide what will work best. I'm sure I'll like it."

Thad accompanied her to church on Sunday as he'd done every week since the first time she had brought him. Outside, it was a glorious June day, but inside the church where the congregation was still meeting, it was sticky. By the time her father's sermon ended, women were fanning themselves with their bulletins and the men's starched shirts were wilting.

As Chloe preceded Thad out of the pew, a wave of dizziness rushed up over her. She clutched at the corner of the pew for support, but the world continued to spin. Thad caught her by the elbow.

"What's the matter?"

"I'm a little dizzy," she said.

He put his arm around her and drew her back into the pew.

"Sit down."

She did, and immediately began to feel a bit better.

"How about some water?" Thad was hovering over her.

"That would be nice," she replied, more to give him something to do than because she really wanted a drink.

"Stay right there. Don't try to get up until I get back."

"Okay, boss."

It was evident that he wasn't amused, by the dark look he cast her before he turned away.

She watched him sprint out of the rapidly emptying sanctuary. She just didn't understand him. He was solicitous in public, passionate in private. But since their marriage, he'd avoided sharing any personal moments.

"What's the matter, dear?"

She turned to see one of the other parishioners bearing down on her. "Nothing," she said. "Or not much. I felt a little dizzy, so Thad went to get me a drink. It's just this heat."

"It certainly is hot." The matron fanned herself vigorously. Then she leaned forward, focusing on Chloe's hands. "I never did get to see your engagement ring, dear."

Chloe sighed inwardly. Another busybody. "I don't have one," she said. "But my wedding band is lovely. Thad picked it out himself." She shoved her ring finger under the lady's nose.

"It's just darling! My, weren't you a surprise. I don't believe anyone even knew you were dating seriously, and here you go off and get married!"

Chloe smiled.

The woman looked a bit disconcerted at this lack of response. She released Chloe's hand. "Of course, we all wish you the very best." Her voice dropped to a whisper. "I knew his first wife. Poor little thing. I hope you have better luck than she did."

Chloe sat up a little straighter. "Mrs. Goode, I'm surprised at you." She pitched her voice to carry just a little, so that the only people who could hear her were the ones in danger of spraining their necks trying to eavesdrop. "If that's your way of expressing your congratulations on my marriage, then perhaps you shouldn't say anything at all."

The woman's face was as red as a fat, juicy tomato. "I...I—"

As soon as the words had left her mouth, Chloe had felt bad. Gently, she tried to soften her tone. "I come into this place of worship to unburden myself of the unkind things I say and do. I have trouble sometimes with not judging others, but it's a flaw I try to work on. I'm sure you do, too." She smiled directly into the woman's eyes, willing herself to let go of her annoyance and heed her own words.

Mrs. Goode had recovered her aplomb by the time Chloe finished speaking. "Sounds as if your father isn't the only preacher in this congregation. You've missed your calling, young lady. I apologize." But there was a twinkle in her eye and she was smiling as she turned away.

"Chloe." Thad's voice startled her, and she turned to find him standing behind her. He'd come up the other side of the aisle. "Here's your water."

She smiled at Thad. "I feel better. I'm ready to go home."

Thad's mouth was compressed into a tight, angry

line. What in the world was the matter? He hadn't heard her exchange with Mrs. Goode, she hoped. She didn't linger to chat with anyone else, but headed directly for the parking lot, aware that the wrong word could cause an explosion.

He didn't speak all the way home. After he parked the car beside the trailer, he killed the engine before turning to her. "Do you still feel dizzy?" It was more a demand than a question.

"No." She looked at him wonderingly.

"Good." With that he slammed his door shut and mounted the step to the house with a leashed tension coiled in him so tightly she could see it from where she sat.

He was in the house before she even left the car.

What was wrong with *him?* Chloe unfastened her seat belt, struggling to control her own rising ire. Even if he was furious with Mrs. Goode, he shouldn't be taking it out on her. Besides, she was sure the woman hadn't meant to be cruel. She simply hadn't considered the brashness of her words.

She headed for the bedroom. Thad was just pulling a worn T-shirt over his head when she entered.

"I'm going out to the shop," he muttered, brushing by her. "I have some work to do."

"I thought we were going to start papering the walls in the dining room at the new house."

"It'll have to wait."

Wait? *Wait?* "Are you going to tell me what your problem is, or do I have to guess?" she inquired, sarcasm coating each syllable.

Halfway down the stairs, he whirled.

"I know I've made some stupid mistakes in my life. But I've paid for them and paid for them, and I'm damn sick of it! I don't care what other people think. And I don't need you to defend me!''

"You never objected to it before. I thought that was exactly why you married me.'' She was hurt beyond belief at his words, and angry now, too. How was she supposed to know that had bothered him? It was human nature—well, *her* nature, anyhow—to help anything in distress.

"Maybe it was! Is that any worse than you marrying me because you were too hot to wait?''

His words were so unfair they staggered her, slicing a deep gash in her heart. She was stunned, groping for a response. Before she could come up with something coherent, he was gone, slamming down the steps and out the back door.

Nine

The words that had been thrown between them hung in the air around her, a thick, black cloud that obscured her vision. Or maybe it was the tears that had begun to flow, regardless of how hard she pressed the heels of her palms against her eyes.

She groped for the edge of the bed and sank down, shaking. His words had shattered the illusion of normalcy she'd woven around their marriage. She'd told herself over and over again that he would come to love her, that there had to be something more than simple physical attraction between them, that they could build a life together.

But she'd been wrong. If only she'd had more experience, been more worldly. She would have known not to mistake simple chemistry for love. He'd told her he wanted her too much to wait through a long engagement, and she'd dared to hope he meant it in a deeper sense than the physical.

She'd thought they'd been sharing themselves with each other, while he'd been resenting every minute they spent together outside the bedroom.

Throwing herself down on the bed, she sobbed for what felt like hours, releasing all her hurt and disappointment. When she finally got herself under control, she knew she couldn't stay with him any longer. Their marriage had been a mistake that she would remember for the rest of her life. *The rest of her life without Thad.*

The thought brought more tears to her smarting, swollen eyes. Going to the closet, she pulled a suitcase out and opened it on the bed, then set about packing as many of her things as she could fit into it. Fortunately a lot of her possessions were still at her father's house, packed up and waiting to be moved into the new house.

"Where you lodge, I will lodge...."

Unbidden, the words of her wedding vows whispered through the room. Her hands stilled among the folded clothes.

Her head drooped, and she sank to the floor. What was she thinking? Thad was her husband now. She'd chosen him of her own free will. She couldn't run back to her father's house simply because her marriage wasn't working out the way she had hoped.

"Until death do us part."

That pretty much said it all. Slowly, she began to return clothing to drawers. Refusing to allow herself to replay the hurtful words he'd flung at her, she emptied the suitcase and returned it to the closet. She was married. That was all she needed to remember.

And if the love she had brought to the union wasn't enough to nourish their relationship, then she would live with the consequences of her hasty actions for the rest of her life. "Marry in haste, repent at leisure." It might be an old cliché, but whoever said it first said it perfectly.

Blowing her nose one final time, she went to the kitchen. She was going to prepare lunch. After that she was going over to the new house and start wallpapering the dining room. While she worked, she could compose a letter to several area churches and recreation centers asking about the possibility of starting a preschool.

"You don't know a damn thing—"

No! Don't think about it.

Let's see, she'd need a letter to the local businessmen asking for sponsorship for the first year or two until the program began to pay for itself. The furniture, toys and supplies would have to be outright donations....

He stayed in the workshop until early evening, until his stomach was growling. What was the point in going back into the house? Chloe had climbed into her car and left about an hour after he'd ruined any chance he'd ever had of keeping her. He'd noticed from the workshop window that she didn't take any bags with her, but it didn't make him feel much better. He knew she had left plenty of her own things at her father's home. She wouldn't be back.

And it was all his fault. He'd wanted her, been determined to have her, from the first time he'd seen her perching on that little chair with such ladylike posture in her office at the church. Her skirt had ridden up a little, but she hadn't pulled it down because she didn't think there was anyone else around, and he'd practically had to wipe drool from his chin looking at those long, slender legs and her pretty feet slipped into high heels. Did she have any idea how sexy those shoes were?

She did now. The thought was sobering, crushing. He'd pursued her, pestered her, petted her until he'd caught her. He'd taught her everything she knew about her own passionate nature, about responding to a man.

And he had driven her away. He'd known from the beginning that she was too good for him, that it couldn't last. He'd heard it spoken aloud time after time, heard her defending him—and he had taken out his frustration on her.

Other men would take one look and pursue her just like he had. And when she made a new life for herself with one of them, another man would be fixing up a home with her, sitting beside her in church, sharing stolen kisses over a picnic lunch.

Another man would realize he didn't want babies quite yet, because he wasn't ready to share her, even with their children. Another man would be holding her close at night, loving her, thanking his lucky stars she loved him and cherishing her the way she deserved to be cherished.

Cherishing her...loving her...loving her just like he did.

If he hadn't just used the last board he had in stock, he would have hit himself over the head with a two-by-four.

He hadn't allowed himself to even think it before, hadn't allowed the word *love* to surface in his mind. Sex was sex. Love was love. Great sex didn't mean lasting love. He'd had plenty of practice observing *that* little axiom. He would have died before telling anyone he was in love. Even the woman he loved.

But now...now, it didn't seem so important to hold

on to his pride and his independence. Not when the only woman he'd ever wanted to spend his life with had slipped through his grasp.

Slowly he replaced his tools and swept the floor before heading for the house. The silence inside the trailer seemed dark and oppressive. He flipped on the light in the kitchen, half expecting to see a note.

No note. And none in the bedroom, the only other logical place she would have placed it.

His stomach growled, reminding him it was feeding time. He put the remains of the chicken-corn soup Chloe had made in a bowl and nuked it while he peeled an orange and ate it standing at the sink. He was just checking to see if the soup was ready, when he heard her car crunch into the gravel of the driveway. Her car! Was he hallucinating?

Nope. She parked and got out. Her clothes were dirty and she had a hole in the knee of her pants.

As she dragged herself to the door, he saw her wince, and he had it open before she could reach for the knob. Had she been in an accident? "What the hell happened to you?"

She glanced at him quickly, then looked away. But he'd seen wariness in that glance and knew he deserved it. Why was she here after the things he'd said?

"I was wallpapering." She said it in a matter-of-fact tone, and before he could absorb that, she wandered over to the microwave and peeked into the bowl. "Mmm. Smells good. Did I miss supper?"

He shook his head, mimicking her casual tone, because he wasn't sure how to respond. "I was just getting ready to eat. I'll set two places."

"I can mix up some biscuits and throw a salad together."

What was going through her head? She was perfectly pleasant, and she actually smiled at him as she washed her hands. It was a fake smile, not her usual warm one, but at least she was looking at him.

He didn't know what was going on, but he didn't want her to leave again. He searched for something neutral to say, but couldn't come up with anything brilliant. "You sit. I'll make biscuits and salad."

"Oh, thanks." She sank into a chair with a grateful sigh. "I got almost two walls of the dining room done. Tomorrow I might be able to finish it. Wait till you see it—the paint looks fantastic with the paper. I'm glad you insisted on the lighter color."

Whatever she was thinking, she was offering a peace pipe and he grabbed at it. "I've learned from my own mistakes that paint always looks darker than the sample chips."

They didn't speak much throughout the meal. Beneath her surface calm, he sensed something unsettled, something wary. He could understand that.

But she seemed determined not to mention anything personal. Why? He wanted to ask her, to apologize for the hurt he'd put in her eyes earlier, but the woman before him wasn't the kind a guy could apologize to. If he tried now, his words would slide right off the slick surface of the wall she'd built around herself.

When the food was gone, she stood. He noticed how carefully she moved, and guilt pricked at him again. If he'd helped her with the papering like he'd promised, she wouldn't have worked herself so hard.

"I'm going to take a hot bath," she said. "You can leave the dishes in the sink, and I'll do them after breakfast."

But he didn't. While she was in the bathroom, he

cleaned up the kitchen, then turned on a ballgame. The Orioles were ahead by two runs, but they were struggling to hold on to that lead. It was a tense game, the kind the fans loved—and he had to force himself to watch it. Every two minutes he checked his watch.

She must really be sore, he thought, thirty minutes later. She would turn into a prune if she stayed in the water much longer.

When thirty more minutes had passed, he couldn't stand it anymore. He went to the closed bathroom door. "Chloe?"

No answer.

He turned the knob, half-expecting that she had locked him out, but the door opened easily. "What are you—"

The room was humid and warm. Chloe lay in the small bathtub—sound asleep. His heart twisted as he looked at her features, soft in sleep and utterly relaxed. She was so beautiful, so perfect. If she left him, nothing in his life would be right, ever again.

He bent over the tub and called her name. When her eyelids fluttered, he said, "Put your arms around my neck." Automatically, more asleep than awake, she obeyed. As he lifted her out of the water, he stood her on her feet long enough to snag a bath sheet and bundle it around her. Her pretty breasts flattened as he wound the towel around her, but he wouldn't allow himself to linger over the soft curves. Then, regardless of the water that was soaking into his own clothing, he lifted her again and carried her into the bedroom.

She didn't resist when he unwrapped her from the towel and laid her in their bed, covering her before he turned away to lock the door and turn off all the lights. But when he had shed his own clothes and slipped into bed beside her, he hesitated. They'd fallen asleep in the position she called spoons since their first night together, but he didn't feel free to touch her tonight. Or maybe it was that he wanted to respect her space, if that was what she needed.

She already had turned onto her side facing away from him, as usual. Reaching out, he touched a hand to her waist. She immediately scooted back against him, and a warm rush of relief filled him. He pillowed her head on one arm and draped the other over her, flattening his palm over her stomach and pulling her snugly against him. As always the feel of her silky warmth made him hard and ready, but he ignored his arousal.

She couldn't possibly miss it, lying as she was with her buttocks pressed against his thighs, but she didn't acknowledge him. In any case, he couldn't imagine any less likely time to start lovemaking.

He just wanted to hold her.

She dreamed he was making love to her. His clever tongue teased the sensitive spot behind her ear. His fingers plucked and rolled her nipples; his hands stroked her all over. As his lips moved down her neck, his hand slipped between her thighs, preparing her for his entry, and she willingly opened, welcoming him into her body.

But then, before she could begin to enjoy the intimate coupling, his voice shattered the quickening silence.

"I married you for sex."

She began to cry, hot, scalding tears that rapidly pooled on the floor and made a small lake of the bedroom—

"Chloe? Come on, honey, wake up."

Gradually her mind began to grasp at reality as the dream world receded. She opened her eyes to find Thad leaning over her with a concerned look on his face. He raised a hand to her cheek and stroked his thumb across her skin. "What's wrong?"

She realized she was crying. That part hadn't been a dream. She struggled into a sitting position and reached for a tissue. "Nothing. I just had a bad dream."

"Want to tell me about it?"

Yes, she wanted to say. She wanted him to laugh and tell her how silly it was, that he loved her, that he had married her because he needed her on all levels, not just for physical release. But he hadn't, and she knew he didn't really want to hear about her nightmare. "No, but thank you for your concern."

He went still for a moment, then said, "Okay," but he didn't lie back down.

She sat for another minute, crumpling her tissue into a small, soggy wad, then set it aside. But as she began to recline, Thad put a hand on her arm. When she turned toward him, he slipped his arms around her and pulled her down, cradling her against the hard planes of his chest. His embrace held her closely to him, her head tucked under his chin. Their legs tangled; against her belly she could feel him stirring, growing to full tumescent arousal.

"Stop." She pushed at his chest. "I can't—tonight."

"It's all right. I just want to hold you."

"You never 'just want to hold me.'" Her voice wasn't angry, just weary.

Seven small words. He opened his mouth to deny their truth—and stopped, speechless as he recognized the accuracy of her remark. He'd been so busy protecting himself that he'd never thought of how his actions seemed to her.

Cautiously, he said, "I do now."

No response.

Finally she made a small sound, a mere sigh of breath. Her body relaxed against his, and he realized how tense she'd been holding herself. He wanted to talk, but he sensed she wasn't ready to listen. If he made so much as a peep, she'd tense up, clam up, maybe even *get up* and leave for good this time. Although she hadn't spoken in an accusatory tone a moment ago, he felt as if he were treading on a very narrow ledge; a single misstep would dislodge him. And he knew if he fell, he'd never manage to reclaim the ground he'd lost.

The morning sun was heating the bedroom to an uncomfortable temperature when he awoke the next morning. He knew before he opened his eyes that he was alone.

Chloe wasn't in the kitchen, but there was a fresh pot of coffee waiting for him. On the table was half a grapefruit, already sectioned the way he like them best, and a plate with several slices of the cinnamon bread she had made. He sniffed the pleasing aromas absently, wondering where she could be. Then a flash of movement outside caught his attention and he saw her, kneeling in the flowerbed beside the mailbox. It looked like she was trimming around the edges of the bed.

Why was she bothering with that when they would be moving in a few weeks? He eyed her lithe shape as he wolfed down cinnamon bread and sipped at coffee that was entirely too hot to drink in big gulps. Would she treat him with the same careful courtesy that she had last night? All things considered, he thought he'd rather have her scream and throw things. At least he knew how to respond to that.

When he'd cleaned up his dishes, he opened the door and stepped out into the June sunshine.

"Good morning." She turned and waved an arm in his general direction before turning back to her work.

"Good morning." He ambled across the lawn. "You got an early start today."

"I woke up early and couldn't get back to sleep, so I thought I might as well be useful."

A vivid image of what they usually did when they woke up early drifted into his mind. From the blush that was creeping up her neck, she was thinking of the same thing. His body stirred at the thought of those lazy, sensual morning encounters, and he quickly banished the thoughts. He didn't need sex complicating what he wanted to say to her this morning.

But as he looked down at her hands, he realized he didn't want to talk out here, where she could pretend to be busy or distracted. He extended his hand. "Would you take a walk with me?"

She glanced up at him again, squinting in the bright light as she rose to her feet and dusted off her hands against the old shorts she wore. "All right." She hesitated for such a brief moment that he might have missed it if he were less tuned in to her, then took the hand he was offering.

Satisfaction coursed through him at the feel of her small, soft palm sliding against his. He spread his fingers wide and linked them with hers before she could initiate a less intimate clasp.

He didn't really have a destination in mind. He just wanted her undivided attention. As they crossed the backyard and turned onto the wooded path leading to the old swimming hole, he was uncomfortably aware of the invisible shield she had erected around herself. She was with him, but not with him.

They walked for a few minutes in silence, until the glint of sun on water told them they were approaching the clearing where he'd tried to entice her into swimming nude.

He cleared his throat. "I owe you an apology."

"No, you don't." She smiled at him impersonally.

"Well, then, just pretend I'm doing this for fun," he said testily.

"I'd rather not." She broke free of his hand and headed for the water, stooping down to test it with her fingers. "It feels great. Let's go swimming."

"I don't think—" He broke off, his voice failing him at the sight of his wife unbuttoning the sleeveless blouse she wore. Before he could oil his vocal cords enough to make a sound, she had stepped out of every stitch of clothing she wore. "What are you doing?"

"Going swimming." Her tone was casual but he noted that she glanced around nervously. This wasn't as easy for her as she wanted him to believe. As she waded into the stream, he decided that her back view was as enticing as the front. A long, slim line marked by the slight ridge of her spine stretched from her slender neck to the heart-shaped curve of her bottom. The skin there was pale as porcelain and he knew from experience how soft it would feel under his hands. He could feel himself getting aroused; for once he was annoyed rather than amused at the effect she had on his senses. Dammit! He wanted to clear the air. To apologize for his unreasonable anger yesterday and hear her say she had forgiven him. He *needed* to hear her say it.

"Whew! It's chilly." She splashed on in until she

was submerged up to her neck. "Once you're wet it feels great. C'mon in."

It was almost funny. He'd dreamed about having her naked in the old swimming hole, been disappointed when she'd been too inhibited last time—and now he was the one who didn't want to take off his clothes. Reluctantly, his hands went to his belt.

She didn't watch him enter the water, but turned and swam upstream with a strong, steady crawl. It struck him that they knew so little about each other; he hadn't even known if she could swim. Maybe she was right about the kid thing. They *did* need a little time together before they enlarged their family.

She had flipped over onto her back and let the current carry her slowly downstream. As she reached the spot where he stood, he caught her by one ankle and pulled her toward him. The movement of the water pushed her toward him and she spread her legs and caught him around the waist. The sudden shock of her soft woman's flesh pressed against his abdomen ignited a fire deep in his belly. Looking down, he saw her soft brown nest of curls mingling with his own bush of hair; heat raced through him. He could feel himself quickening, pulsing, no longer minding the water's temperature, growing harder and harder until his aroused flesh brushed against her buttocks. She was pink and white and pretty, framed by the cool water rippling around her, and her breasts were buoyant, bobbing gently as if begging for his attention.

He had automatically put his arms around her back to support her; she linked her hands behind his neck and pulled his head down, thrusting her breasts at him.

"Wait." He resisted her with the last of his strength. "We need to talk."

She laughed, and it was the siren's song that had lured men for centuries. "No, we don't. We need to do something about this."

Using the weightlessness the water provided, she slipped away from him far enough to capture his erection against her. He gasped, a harsh sound of shock and pleasure, and he was lost.

He thrust himself into her in one long stroke, and the heat of her body compared to the coolness of the water seared him. Forcing himself to hold still within her despite the urgency licking at his nerve endings, he let her guide his mouth to her breast. She liked to be touched there, he knew, and he suckled, circled and fondled until she was writhing against him and his body wouldn't let him be still any longer. Gripping her hips, he started to move, but the weight and motion of the water slowed him too much. She uttered a sound of dismay and he put his mouth on hers, kissing her deeply as he began to make his way toward the creek bank. Without releasing her or himself, he surged toward the bank, coming down with her onto the sweet, spongy grass at the water's edge. Their legs were still in the water but he was blind to everything other than her. His world was beneath him, around him, hot and tight and matching the frantic pace he set. She lifted her hips to him over and over, and he looked down at her face. She was close, he could tell, her breath rushing in and out and her cheeks flushed with color. Her eyes were open, watching him, and he held the contact, deepening the intimacy. Gripping her bottom with both hands, he angled her up higher and doubled his rhythm.

Never taking her gaze from his, she whimpered and jerked as her climax rolled over her, and he groaned, giving in to his own release as her inner pulses squeezed his swollen length. It seemed forever that she milked him; when it was finished he dropped his head and let his weight settle slowly onto hers as his chest heaved and his heart rate steadied. Finally they were both quiet. Her hands smoothed gently over his back, sliding down over his buttocks. He propped himself up just enough to see her face, then dropped his head and kissed her. "My campaign must have been successful."

"What?"

"I voted for ending all our fights like this, remember?" He smiled down at her.

And just that fast, she was gone. The warm, willing woman with the intimate smile who lay beneath him, still harboring him within her, became the cool, friendly but not approachable woman she'd been since she returned last night. And equally fast, his patience vanished. He wasn't going to let her shut him out again, dammit.

"Hello in there. Anybody home?"

Her gaze came back to his, clearly startled. "I beg your pardon?"

God, he loved the way that phrase rolled off her tongue. He was tempted to give her permission to beg, but he had something other than a double entendre on his mind today. "You were a million miles away. Where did you go?"

"Nowhere." She shrugged, and the movement of her silken shoulder caused one breast to slide up and down against his chest. Delightful as the sensation was, he wasn't going to let himself be distracted this time.

"Yes, you did. You've been putting me on one of your mental shelves since you came home last night. I want to know why."

"I'm sorry." Her voice was quiet and even.

He gritted his teeth. "Don't be sorry. Be truthful."

"I'm not lying!"

The flash of irritation was the first real emotion he'd seen, other than the way she'd lost herself in lovemaking. "I didn't say you were. If you're still mad about yesterday, just come out and say it."

"I'm not mad." She looked away. "I was hurt, at first, but I'd rather know how you really feel than be walking around in a daze, thinking we have a normal marriage."

"I'm sorry I yelled at you." He caressed the ball of her shoulder and traced a line across her collarbone. "I didn't mean what I said. You know how much your 'running interference' for me has helped. I was fed up with people always forcing you to defend me, and mad at myself for being the kind of man you have to defend."

Then the rest of what she'd said penetrated. "What do you mean by that crack about us not having a normal marriage? It seems pretty normal to me."

Beneath him, she sighed, and he lifted his weight onto his elbows more fully so she wasn't uncomfortable. He was vividly aware of their joined bodies, pleasantly so, but it suddenly occurred to him that making love to her might not be the same act in her mind that it was in his. The thought chilled him. He might not have said the words, but surely she could tell how much he cared by the way he treated her, by the way he touched her.

Couldn't she?

"Don't pretend you don't know what I mean, Thad." At least her indifference had vanished. "We got married for one reason."

"Well maybe you'd better clue me in," he said, uneasiness beginning to writhe deep within him.

He was so close that he clearly read the decision in her eyes, and a cold foreboding dimpled his arms with gooseflesh. He'd wanted to know what she was thinking, and he was about to have his wish granted.

Chloe hesitated. Thad's body had gone stiff and angry on hers; she could feel the thin control he had on the imminent explosion of his temper as he pulled away from her and sat up. She sat up, too, hugging her knees to her chest and looking out over the water. Before, she would have been terrified that someone might come along and see them. Today...well, today, worrying about what someone else might think was beyond her.

But she might as well be truthful. She would tell him everything—except that she loved him so much it destroyed her to think of leaving, even when she knew he didn't return her love. That just sounded too pitiful to put into words.

Taking a deep breath, she said, "You told me when you asked me to marry you that you couldn't wait any longer. I knew when I accepted, that...sex...was important to you. That if I wanted to be with you, we'd have to get married."

He rolled away from her and sat up, then turned and looked at her, and she felt scorched by the sizzling anger in his blue eyes. "And you think that's the only reason I asked you to marry me?"

She didn't really have an answer to that, so she didn't say anything.

Thad exhaled, a long, windy gust of frustration, and reached for their clothing. In silence, they dressed. It took her a bit longer than it took Thad, and she was still slipping her sneakers back on when she realized he was standing in front of her. He didn't look angry anymore, but there was a puzzling intensity in the blue gaze he directed at her.

He took her hands in his and stood there, running his thumbs back and forth over her knuckles. He didn't speak, just continued to hold her hands loosely in his, searching her eyes for something. Finally she couldn't take the silence. In a near whisper, she said, "What?"

Thad's fingers stopped their restless dance across the backs of her hands. "You're important to me. Whether or not we make love every day, I still want to be married to you. Yesterday I thought...I thought you were leaving for good when you drove away."

Her pupils dilated, and he knew he'd struck close to the truth. She hesitated, as if to choose the right words. "I never left with the intention of abandoning our marriage. I thought about it. I even started to pack. But then I remembered my wedding vows. 'For better or for worse.' I said those words and I meant them." She looked away from him then, fixing her gaze on some inner vision.

"I meant them, too." He waited, but she didn't respond. "Is that it?"

"Is what it?"

"Is that the only reason you came back?" He was pushing her, but he had to know. He hoped he was right—God, he *had* to be right—but he needed to hear her say the words before he could believe them.

She still hadn't looked at him again. Her hands trembled in his and with a sudden, swift movement, she withdrew them from his clasp and crossed her arms over her breasts, tucking her hands close to her body as if she were cold. It struck him that it was an extraordinarily defensive gesture.

"Please tell me."

She heaved a deep sigh. "All right, Thad. You want to know what I'm thinking? I'm thinking that I was terribly unwise to marry you so quickly. We needed time to get to know each other, time to explore our relationship and decide—"

"I made my decision the day I looked through that window and caught you staring. You blushed, and I was hooked."

She hadn't been expecting *that*, he could tell. Her mouth hung slightly open, and she had a distinctly dazed look on her face. "The first day we met?"

He smiled wryly. "Well, it was technically our second meeting. Which brings me to another question. If you remembered me as the cad who manhandled you at that party, why are you married to that cad now?"

"First impressions can be wrong," she said primly.

"And you think you've gotten out of answering the original question. Did you only come back because it was your duty as a wife?"

She wouldn't look him in the eye. "No. Not only because of duty."

He took a deep breath and let it slowly out. "One day we're going to need something more than sex to hold us together."

Finally she looked at him. And in her eyes he saw the depths of a despair greater than anything he had imagined. The sadness that overlay it slumped her shoulders; tears welled in her eyes. "I know."

Gently he put his hands on her shoulders, massaging the tension away. "Why are you crying?" If he were the kind of man who prayed, he'd pray he knew the answer.

She shrugged; her shoulders felt fragile and delicate beneath his hands. "Reality and expectations collide in everyone's life, I suppose."

"And our marriage hasn't lived up to your expectations." He knew he deserved every lash of the mental whip with which he was flaying himself.

"It's just…" Her eyes filled with tears and she squeezed them tightly shut for a minute. "You are *not* going to do this," she said, and he realized the comment wasn't directed at him, but at herself.

He couldn't take her tears. Encircling her waist, he moved to pull her against him in comfort.

"Don't!" She tore herself away and stood beyond reach.

He was so shocked it took him a moment to recover. "Why not?"

"Because…because I don't want charity. I've accepted the limits of our relationship." Her eyes overflowed as she turned and stood with her back to him.

"*Charity?* How can putting my arms around the woman I love be charity?" He spread his hands in bewilderment and exasperation. This was going all wrong. He'd wanted to—

She had whirled around again. Her eyes were huge and serious in her face. "Did you mean that?"

It took him a moment to realize what she was talking about. "That I love you? Hell, yes, I meant that!" He took her by the shoulders, caressing her upper arms. "Why else would you be wearing my ring?"

Her eyes were shining and incredulous. "But you never said—"

"I didn't even say it to *myself* until recently." He

folded her close, and this time she came willingly, fitting against him the way only she could. "But I'm telling you now. I love, you, Chloe. And starting right this minute I'm going to tell you how much you mean to me every single day for the rest of our lives." There. It hadn't been as painful as he'd expected.

Her shoulders were shaking, and he looked down at her, alarmed. "Stop crying. You're supposed to be deliriously happy now." He couldn't prevent the note of anxiety that crept into his voice. He'd just bared his soul to her; now he realized she hadn't said a word about love yet. Had he been mistaken?

Then she raised her face to his, and he saw she wasn't crying. Well, yes, she was. But through her tears her smile was brilliant. "You asked me a question that I still haven't answered."

For a moment, he went blank. Then he remembered. "I think—I *hope*—I know the answer, but you tell me, anyway. Why did you decide not to leave me yesterday?"

As he rocked her back and forth, she played with the curling hairs that escaped the neck of his T-shirt. "I decided to stay because I love you. Because I wanted to spend the rest of my life with you even if you couldn't love me the same way." She pressed a kiss into the hollow of his throat, making him shiver.

He tightened his arms around her and swung her in a wide circle, holding his world in his arms. He might not have much experience with "forever," but he recognized it now. She humbled him and delighted him, and he thanked God she'd looked past the man she'd met initially, the man who'd been trouble with a capital *T*. His name might still start with that letter, but his lady loved him. It made all the difference in the world.

Epilogue

"What if it's a girl?" Thad rubbed his hand gently over the swollen mound of his wife's belly. "Should we call her Luke-retia?"

"Very funny." Chloe shook her head definitely. "This is Luke. A mother knows these things. But if the next one is a girl, she's going to be Ruth Anne. Ruth is the Biblical woman in the story that kept me from walking out on you."

"Thank God you didn't." It was a fervent prayer. He leaned forward and gently touched his lips to hers.

A crash from the kitchen had both of them whipping their heads around in alarm. "You'd better get in there and see what's keeping Matthew and Mark so fascinated. The last time they were quiet for this long was the day they flushed my pearl earrings down the potty."

Thad laughed as he got to his feet. "I notice you

haven't left your jewelry lying around in the bathroom anymore.''

As he walked into the kitchen to see what his sons were up to, her heart flipped in her chest just like it had that day, the day she'd seen him standing in her window at the old church. After almost two-and-a-half years of marriage, she felt luckier than any woman had a right to be.

They'd waited just long enough to ensure that anyone who could count would know she and Thad hadn't ''had'' to get married. The twins would be seventeen months old next week, two precocious terrors with their father's blond curls. They moved through life like miniature tornadoes, leaving everyone in their path gaping in disbelief and thanking God the damage wasn't worse.

They'd been only ten months old when she'd realized that she was going to be a mother again. So much for the rumor that breastfeeding women didn't get pregnant. Thad had been delighted. She was, too, after she got over the shock.

Her father was the epitome of the doting grandpa, and he'd taken the news of the new baby better than she had. Thad's mother had passed away two weeks after Chloe learned of her second pregnancy, but their grief had been tempered by her happiness at having the chance to see her first two grandsons. Margreta had refused to let them mope in her presence. She had never expected to live long enough to see one grandchild, much less two, she said, and it was cause for joy rather than sorrow.

Four of her former lovers came to her funeral and wound up consoling each other, much to Chloe's amazement. Her own father had performed a beautiful and touching service that celebrated Margreta's life; and the twins, whom they hadn't been able to bring themselves to leave in the hands of a baby-sitter, had slept through the entire thing. Which had amazed them all.

And in about two weeks, another little Shippen would enter the world. Life came full circle, she thought.

Another louder crash made her jump in the recliner where she sat. Thad's voice sounded harried, and although she couldn't make out the exact words, the tone told her that Daddy needed reinforcements.

Letting down the footrest, she scooted herself forward to the edge of the chair just as Thad appeared in the doorway, a squirming toddler in each arm. All three of them wore liberal coats of what appeared to be flour, and she struggled to keep a straight face as she slowly rose to her feet and waddled toward them.

An unexpected popping sensation warned her, mere instants before a gush of fluid spilled down her legs and created a spreading puddle on the polished wood floor of the family room. Her slippers were soaking wet and the puddle inched precariously close to the Oriental rug they'd purchased only a month ago.

"Your water broke!" Thad leaped forward, then lurched to a halt. "But it's two weeks too early."

"You want to explain that to Luke?"

He wheeled and ran back into the kitchen, returning with a roll of paper towels, which he tossed at her. "Here. Let me call your father to manage these monkeys, and I'll take you to the hospital."

"Mommy tinkled!" Matthew crowed.

"Tinkled onna f'oor," pronounced his brother.

Paper towels. She was giggling helplessly as she caught the roll just before it hit her in the face. Only a man would use paper towels at a time like this. She hoped he had about a hundred more rolls ready.

Thad had promised her the rest of their lives together, but he hadn't warned her about the wild ride along the way. She should have known, she thought, as love swelled within her. With a man like Thad, nothing would ever be predictable.

She smiled to herself, then sucked in a breath as a contraction tightened her belly with surprising intensity. It would be in keeping with the unorthodox Shippen family character if this baby were born on the floor, or in the car on the way to the hospital.

Oh, well. She'd resigned herself to raised eyebrows long ago. It was a small price to pay for love that would last a lifetime.

* * * * *

If you've enjoyed this story, look out for
Anne Marie Winston's The Marriage Ultimatum
in Silhouette Desire in February 2005.

SURVIVE THE NIGHT

Marilyn Pappano

Prologue

The first thought in Dillon Boone's mind when the car stopped its violent side-over-side roll at the bottom of the ravine was that he had to escape. Maybe the men on the roadway up above would assume that the crash had killed him; maybe they wouldn't bother making their way down the steep, rocky slope and would instead leave the scene as quickly as possible to avoid detection, but he doubted it. Not when they'd chosen the spot for their attack so carefully. Not when they had ignored the deputy with him. Not when they had apparently decided that killing him would be worth killing a cop.

The cruiser lay upside down now, its wheels still spinning, one side lodged against a barrier of fallen trees, rocks and other debris that darkened the interior and made escape from the passenger side impossible. Another small tree blocked the rear door on the driver's side, and a solid steel-mesh screen prevented him from climbing into the front seat and exiting the driver's door, which had come open and broken off in the wild ride. His only chance was to kick out the window, already marked with a web of cracks, and wriggle through the small

space. The way the roof was compressed, he wasn't sure he
could make it. He wasn't sure he had the time. He wasn't sure
he could endure the attempt.

But he had no choice. It was either try…or wait here to die.
Damned if he was going to make it easy for the bastards. They
still might succeed, but they were going to have to work for
it.

Turning onto his back, he raised his feet, drew a breath, then
slammed them hard against the glass. Jolts of pain traveled up
his legs, becoming knife-sharp and hot as they moved through
his ribs. If his ribs weren't already cracked, the shock wave
just might finish the job, he thought with a grimace; then, pushing the pain to the back of his mind, he kicked again. This
time the weakened glass popped out, falling without sound to
the wet, mossy ground outside. He twisted around, working his
way out headfirst, swearing silently, viciously, to keep the pain
under control.

For one precious moment he simply lay there, barely able to
breathe, feeling the mist soak through his clothes and trickle
down his neck, then he forced himself to his knees, forced
himself to look above for signs of danger. He could see the
ragged scar of downed saplings, scraped rock and disturbed
earth where the car had tumbled its way to the bottom, but
from here, he couldn't see the roadway where the men had
been waiting for them. He couldn't see the black van that had
been pulled across the lanes on a hairpin curve, leaving the
deputy nowhere to go but down. He couldn't see the three men,
two of them strangers, the third vaguely familiar, who had
opened fire on them as they'd skidded across the blacktop and,
finally, over the side.

But they were still there. He could hear voices, low, the
words indistinct, the tones threatening. They were coming after
him, and they intended to kill him.

As he summoned the strength to get to his feet, his gaze
settled on the deputy in the front seat. His name was Coughlin,
and he was about Dillon's age and probably twice his size—
beefy and muscular. His seat belt still held him in place and

had likely saved his life when the door had snapped off under the car's weight. He was unconscious, his breathing labored, his green uniform shirt stained with blood. If he left the deputy here alone, the man might die, Dillon acknowledged. It wasn't likely that the men responsible for his condition would summon help for him, and passersby probably wouldn't notice the skid marks or even see the damaged hillside unless they were out of their cars looking.

But if he stayed, he couldn't help Coughlin.

If he stayed, all he could do was die with him.

From overhead came the squeal of tires, then the slamming of car doors. Maybe help had arrived...but for him and the deputy? Or the men trying to kill him?

"Wow, look at that!" A child's voice drifted down into the ravine. "Did someone have a wreck? Is there a car down there? Jeez, do you think they're okay?"

Another one, this one a girl's, maybe a few years older, joined in. "My mom's calling the sheriff from her car phone. They'll be here any time now. Are you guys hurt?"

Maybe Coughlin would be all right, after all, Dillon thought. Surely Russell's men wouldn't try to finish the job with two curious children and their Good Samaritan mother standing by, and there was no way they would stay around and wait for the sheriff to arrive. Any minute now they would return to the van and drive away, and more than likely, neither the kids nor their mother would be able to provide a tag number or even a decent description of them or their van.

Reaching inside the car, he removed the deputy's pistol from its holster and tucked it into the waistband of his jeans. He took a moment to lean past the deputy, close enough to hear his uneven breathing and pull the keys from the ignition. If he was going to survive, he needed the small key dangling next to the car keys, the key that would open the handcuffs fastened around his wrists. Sliding the keys into his pocket, he rose to his feet and made his way awkwardly around the car and over the pile of debris. He headed deeper into the mountains. The handcuffs could be dealt with later, but his first priority was getting out of there alive.

His second was staying that way.

Chapter 1

With a glance at the clock, Ashley Benedict removed the last of the reeds from the tub filled with gallons of strong tea, checked the color against the last batch she had dyed, then began hanging them from the line suspended the entire length of her workshop. By tomorrow morning they would be dry, and she could begin making the oversize market basket Seth was giving his mother for her birthday. Mrs. Benedict would love the basket, would love that her son had gone to the trouble to have something specially made for her, would love that he'd listened all those times she had complained about keeping her knitting yarns neat and convenient, but she wouldn't be at all happy with the idea that the basket had been made by her former daughter-in-law. Although she hadn't minded Ashley and Seth's friendship when they were growing up, she had seriously disapproved of their marriage.

That was all right, though, Ashley mused as she hung the last of the pliable strips. Marriage to Seth had been a mistake from the beginning, and for the past four years, it had been over and done with. Now they were just friends, which was all they ever should have been.

Reaching for a towel on the worktable, she dried her hands, then opened a jar filled with pale pink cream and scooped some onto her hands. Her own concoction, the lotion was satiny, cool and smelled of roses. It kept her skin soft, and the aloe it contained helped heal the scrapes and cuts that were a hazard of her work.

While she rubbed it in, she leaned against the sturdy table and stared out the window. It was a little after five on a dreary March afternoon. Yesterday had been beautiful, with temperatures in the seventies and a definite hint of spring in the air. Even this morning the sun had been shining brightly, warming the air, filling the workshop with its light and heat, and she had allowed herself to wonder if winter truly was past. Then the sun had disappeared, the temperature had dropped a good twenty-five degrees and the rain had started. It had been a good day to snuggle beneath a quilt in front of a roaring fire, to drowse away the hours and weave nothing more than dreams.

It had also been a good day for weaving baskets and blankets, for mixing potpourris and herbal concoctions, for making soap or baking bread or any of the other hundred and one chores that kept her in food, clothing and money.

With a soft sigh, she shut off the lights and stepped outside, pulling the door firmly shut behind her. The only locks were hook and eye, one on the inside, one on the outside, to secure the workshop against the door blowing open, not against intruders. She never had intruders up here. Surrounded by parkland on three sides, more than five miles from her nearest neighbor and ten miles beyond that to the nearest town, she was too far off the beaten path for wanderers or drifters. Seth came by at least once a week to check on her, and she had occasional business-related visitors, but no one else ventured so far. Her friends were hours away in Raleigh and Durham, and her parents and sisters lived on the California coast, selling pottery by the sea. She was alone.

And she liked it that way.

She had taken her first steps from the workshop's sheltering stoop when movement in the clearing caught her attention. A man was coming around from behind where her van was parked, his head bent low against the rain and the piercing wind. It took only a second's glance to tag him a stranger, only a second longer to identify him as an outsider. No local would be out in weather like this wearing nothing but jeans, sneakers and a stained T-shirt. Even though the sun had been shining this morning and the temperature had been on the mild side, no one who had lived more than a season in these North Carolina mountains would make the mistake of wandering far from home without a jacket.

Maybe he was a hiker who'd lost his way in the park...but no serious hiker would take to the rugged trails around here in worn tennis shoes. Even a novice on a day hike knew to wear sturdy boots with ridged soles.

She felt a moment's uneasiness brought on by his presence, but she shook it off. Living the way she did, isolated and with no one but herself to depend on, she couldn't afford to let every unusual occurrence frighten her. She couldn't acquaint herself with easy fear, or she would start thinking that every bump in the night was the bogeyman come to get her. When that happened, she would have to give up her solitude, her peace and her easy way of living and move into town.

Besides, this wasn't such an unusual occurrence. She'd had unexpected visitors before, and all they had ever wanted was a little neighborly assistance. This man wasn't likely to be any different. In fact, she was pretty sure she had seen him before, probably in town. He didn't live nearby—she knew all her neighbors—but maybe he was visiting one of them. Maybe he was a relative of one.

"Can I help you?" she asked, folding her arms across her chest, wishing she'd grabbed the jacket she kept in the workshop, wishing she hadn't planned on a quick dash across the clearing when she'd walked right past it.

His head came up, and his steps slowed. Coming to a stop a half-dozen feet away, for a moment he simply watched her in the thin light. He looked tired and battered, with a few raw scrapes and bruises that darkened his face, and he was obviously weakened. However long he'd been out in the cold rain, it had been too long. He was suffering, probably a little from shock and a lot from exposure.

"My car..." His voice was raspy and rough, perfectly matching the appearance he presented. "I hit a slick spot and ran off the road back there. Do you have a phone?"

At least that explained his face, the awkward way he stood and moved and his lack of warm clothing, she thought as she shook her head. "Sorry, I don't."

"Is your husband around? Maybe he could help...."

She smiled. "I don't have one of those, either. But I can give you a ride into town or down to the Parmenters' place about five miles down the road. They have a telephone, and they would be happy to let you use it. Wait here, and I'll get my keys." Still hugging herself for warmth, she hurried across the clearing, taking the half-dozen stairs to the porch in three steps. Under the shelter of the porch roof, she opened the unlocked door, switched the lights on and went inside and to her purse on the kitchen table. She was digging through it when the floorboard right in front of the door creaked and the man stepped into the open doorway.

The uneasiness she'd felt briefly outside reappeared. *Wait here,* she had said. Instructions couldn't get any simpler. So why had he followed her? Why was he standing there blocking the door, making the hair on the back of her neck stand on end, making her feel very unsafe?

Her fingers closed around her car keys, but she continued to dig through the deep shoulder bag. "I keep telling myself I should get a smaller purse. I'm forever losing things in here," she said, hearing the beginnings of fear in her voice, hoping he didn't recognize it as that. "What's your name?"

He was looking around the cabin, paying it far more attention than it deserved. Was she about to be robbed? Ashley wondered, the thought sending chills down her spine. Surely not. Even the most inept thief could find a better target than this primitive little cabin with her inexpensive furniture, aged. appliances and minimal personal belongings.

After a long, still moment his gaze settled on her. "What does it matter?"

"Just trying to be friendly." She tried for a casual shrug. "I thought maybe I'd seen you before."

"Where would you have seen me?"

"In town. In Catlin."

He shook his head. "I never met you there."

No, she knew that. She never would have forgotten such a handsome face...or such an unsettling manner. But she *had* seen him. She was sure of it. Maybe in a store, maybe on the street, maybe even in a photograph or...

A photograph. Yes, that was it. A grainy black-and-white photograph underneath a red heading: Have You Seen This Man? For a few months last year those flyers had been prominently displayed in every business in town. Bill Armstrong, president of Catlin's only bank, had paid for the printing and had distributed them himself. It was a waste of time, Seth had confided in her. After weeks of investigation and intensive searches, there was one place the Catlin County Sheriff's Department was sure the man wasn't: in Catlin County.

Neither was the four hundred fifty thousand dollars he'd stolen from Armstrong's bank.

The caption underneath the photo and the lines directly following it came clearly to mind: Dillon Boone. Wanted for bank robbery. If you have any information regarding his whereabouts, please contact the Catlin County Sheriff's Department. Reward.

It was Dillon Boone. Dear God, what was he doing back here in Catlin County, where everyone knew his name, where practically everyone knew his face?

He stood absolutely motionless, watching her watch him. He knew, she saw—knew that she had remembered. He read it in the shock that had turned her face pale, in the trembling that swept over her as if she'd just stepped into a frigid wind.

Slowly he stepped inside the cabin, then closed and locked

the door behind him. He moved stiffly, as if each motion were painful. He was badly hurt, she realized. In addition to the cuts and bruises on his face and arms, she would guess from the way he was breathing that he had a few broken ribs, and that rusty stain spreading across his shirt she recognized now as blood that might have come from something as innocent as a cut or as sinister as a gunshot wound. Toss in his inadequate clothing, the rain and the chill—the temperature outside was hovering in the high forties now, she estimated, with a stiff breeze out of the west—and he was in seriously bad shape.

Watching him, Ashley ran through a mental checklist of anything in the cabin that might be used as a weapon against a man in an obviously weakened state: the butcher knife and the rolling pin in the kitchen, the scissors in the sewing basket at the end of the sofa, next to the door the solid length of hickory that she took on her walks into the woods and the logs stacked next to the hearth. Most of the logs were too short and fat to be of any use, but there was an occasional slender piece that could do some damage if she got close enough. It wasn't much of an arsenal, she admitted grimly. Not that it mattered much. The mere idea of stabbing someone with a butcher knife or scissors or of swinging that hickory stick or a sturdy length of firewood against unprotected flesh was enough to make her cringe.

Get a gun, Seth had counseled when she'd moved up here, but she had protested. It was a less intimate means of defense, true—it could be used with the safety of distance between shooter and target—but it was also such a final one. She couldn't risk killing someone to protect her property; she wasn't sure she could do it even to protect herself. If she tried and couldn't, she would simply wind up giving a possibly unarmed intruder a weapon to use against her and any other poor unfortunate who crossed his path in the future.

But Dillon Boone wasn't unarmed. When he faced her again, he was holding a gun in his left hand—holding it as if he were comfortable with it, as if he were comfortable with the idea of using it. "Put the purse down and move over there," he instructed, waving the gun toward the braided rug in front of the fireplace.

Withdrawing her hand, she let the keys drop to the table, then backed away as he'd directed.

"Do you live here alone?"

She considered lying, but she had already been foolish enough to tell him that she wasn't married—*and* that she had no phone she could use to call for help. She had already let him into her house, where the only jackets that hung on the coatrack next to him were obviously hers, where the only shoes lined up next to the bed in the corner were women's shoes, where the only items scattered across the dresser top were perfume bottles and a lacy, flowery fabric box filled with earrings. Biting her lip, she nodded.

"What's your name?"

"Ashley."

"You know my name."

"A person can't live within fifty miles of Catlin and not know who you are." Softly she added, "Especially a person with money in the First American Bank and Trust."

"And did *you* have money in the First American Bank and Trust?"

"I don't have money, period. So if you're planning to rob me..."

He made an impatient gesture that caused him to sway unsteadily. Taking a few steps forward, he leaned against the table for support, the gun hitting the wood with a hollow thunk. The exertion made his voice thinner, his breathing raspier. "I don't want your money or your van or anything else. I just need a place to rest. As soon as I can, I'll be on my way."

She wanted to believe him, wanted to believe that he would stay, get warm, get dry, maybe eat and sleep a little and then be gone. She wanted to believe that he wasn't going to steal anything, that he wasn't going to hurt her. But Dillon Boone was a bank robber, a fugitive on the run from the law for nearly a year, living in the shadows, desperate to avoid jail. He was a criminal who had forced his way into her house and was now holding her hostage. How could she believe *anything* he said?

His gaze moved past her to the fireplace behind her. The ashes were cold. The morning had held such promise that she hadn't bothered with the fire when she awoke; she had let the embers from last night's fire burn themselves out. It wouldn't take much to coax a flame from the kindling stored in the rough-woven basket on the hearth, wouldn't take long for the well-seasoned hickory logs to blaze into the bone-warming sort of heat that he obviously needed—that *she* was starting to need. Still, she didn't offer to build a fire. She remained silent, watching him warily.

After a moment he redirected his glance toward the kitchen, where a pot of stew was simmering on the back burner. He was cold, but he didn't ask her to build a fire. He was hungry, but he didn't ask to share her food. Instead, he said, "Your clothes are wet. Go change."

With a shiver, she realized that he was right. The rain had been blowing with enough force that those brief moments she'd spent in it had been enough to turn her faded jeans dark, enough to streak her shirt and to dampen her canvas shoes.

She made her way around the foot of the bed to the small armoire that served as her closet. There she pulled out a heavy chambray skirt and a navy blue sweater, then, eyeing him cautiously, she started toward the bathroom. He was still standing next to the table, his head bowed, his hands spread wide to support him. He looked miserable and just barely able to stay on his feet. If she could make it into the bathroom, she could lock the door; she could open the window, pry the screen off and climb out in no time. Before he even realized that she was taking too long, she would have retrieved the jacket she kept in the workshop and would be halfway down the driveway to the road. She would be cold and wet, but she was in good shape. She could easily make it to the Parmenters'.

If she could make it into the bathroom.

She was halfway there when a creaking board brought his head up. He shoved himself away from the table and once more brought the gun up. "Out here," he commanded, closing the distance between them more quickly than she would have thought him capable of. "You change right here."

Seeing her chance to escape slipping away, she faced him, only inches between them, intending to inform him that there was no way she was changing clothes in front of him. But when she opened her mouth, no words came out. Her voice failed to materialize; her brain failed to give the command.

Dillon Boone, so the talk went in town, was a dangerous man, but Ashley had never quite believed it. He had worked in Catlin for several weeks before the robbery, and the people who had met him had liked him well enough. Seth had met him and hadn't found him worthy of suspicion or scrutiny. His crime hadn't been violent; no one had been hurt. The bank's money had been insured. He had used his brains instead of brutality, had used his inside knowledge of the bank's security system—which he had helped install—rather than a weapon, hostages or threats.

But now, in an instant of eye contact, she had become a believer. Standing there, face-to-face, looking into those empty eyes that were colder than the iciest winter wind, she *knew* he was dangerous. Just that look made her heart rate increase, made her breathing grow quick and unsteady, made her muscles quiver. Just that look made her realize what a precarious position she was in. Just that look put the fear of God into her.

A sensation feeling distastefully like defeat—acceptance, resignation—swept over her. It was Boone's lucky day. She was a reasonable woman. She wasn't going to fight him. She wasn't going to anger him. She wasn't going to give him a reason to hurt her. She intended to follow his every order, to see to his every need, to fulfill his every wish. She intended to be the best little hostage any fugitive could wish for.

And she intended to come out of this alive.

How quickly the woman could change, Dillon thought bitterly. Her expression when she had faced him had been mutinous. She hadn't liked the idea that he was giving orders,

hadn't liked that he was going to make her undress in front of
him. Most of all, she hadn't liked that she wasn't going to be
allowed to lock herself in the bathroom, with its two big windows offering a chance to escape.

But she had taken one look at him, one really good face-to-
face, up-close-and-personal look at him, and it had scared her
in a way that his sudden appearance outside, his barging into
her cabin and his gun hadn't. What was it she'd seen that had
frightened her? What was it that made him capable of terror-
izing an innocent woman with no more than a look?

Tearing her gaze away, she turned and laid the clothes she
carried on the hearth. He retreated once more to the table, giving her plenty of room. He'd told the truth when he'd said that
he didn't want anything from her. If he'd had his way, the
cabin would have been empty and he wouldn't have been
forced to take a hostage. The less contact he had with anyone,
the better.

The less contact he had with a *woman,* the better, he
amended as she turned her back to him and began removing
her T-shirt. Her skin, as it was revealed, was smooth, pale,
probably soft, probably sweet smelling. She was naked underneath the shirt, he realized as she drew it over her shoulders,
then up over her head. That long expanse of bare skin somehow
seemed vulnerable, made *her* seem vulnerable...which, of
course, she was. She was his prisoner, his hostage. She had to
respond to his whims, had to do whatever he commanded.

He wished he could command her to disappear. He wished
he could remove her from this place and time, wished he could
remove himself from her life. Of course, he couldn't. For now
they were stuck with each other.

Raising her arms over her head, she pulled the sweater on.
The movement gave him just a glimpse of the soft swell of her
breast, fuller than a man might have imagined, swaying unre-
strained as she tugged the sweater down. When the ribbed hem
was in place somewhere high on her thigh and she began working her jeans off, he swallowed hard and looked away, muttering a silent curse.

He had never known such misery as he'd felt today. His clothing had been soaked within minutes of leaving the wrecked patrol car, and the temperature had gone into a steady downhill slide. Around midafternoon he had considered making a shelter of some sort, but he knew that, without heat and dry clothes, he would never survive the night. Sheer desperation had kept him moving, and sheer luck had brought him here. He had been stumbling through the woods for hours, thinking numbly that death couldn't be worse than what he was already enduring, when he had smelled the woodsmoke coming from her workshop. He had forced his way through thick undergrowth to the clearing, praying that he would find no more than a place to get out of the rain, a place to recuperate just a little, a place where he could be alone, as he'd been his entire life. He hadn't asked for this. He didn't *want* this. God help him, he couldn't deal with this.

Forcing himself to concentrate, he gave the cabin another slow, searching look. It was one big room divided into distinct areas. There was a kitchen in one corner with appliances older than their owner. Through an open door just beyond the kitchen, he could see the bathroom with its windows and a big claw-foot tub, the absence of a shower curtain indicating the absence of a shower. In the opposite corner was the sleeping area with a bed, dresser and night table. The center of the cabin was her living room, with a sofa, two chairs and the big stone fireplace. The *cold* stone fireplace.

There was no television. No telephone. No stereo. No microwave. No dishwasher. No washer and dryer. Who lived out in the middle of nowhere like this without any conveniences beyond electricity and running water, a refrigerator and a stove? What kind of person—what kind of *woman*—thought that was a sensible way to live? Hadn't she ever realized that her isolation placed her in danger? Hadn't she known there were people in this world who would take advantage of it? Mean people, desperate people. People like *him*.

The acknowledgment made him feel sick. So this was how low he had sunk. This was what his old friend Russell had brought him to. As of today, he deserved undeniably every derisive and scornful insult he'd ever been given.

"I—I have a pair of sweatpants...."

Slowly he shifted his attention back to her. She was dressed now in a pale blue skirt that reached practically to her ankles and that sweater, its sleeves long enough to warm her hands, its weave heavy and nubby, its fit big and loose...but not loose enough to make him forget that she was naked underneath.

"Th-they belong to Seth, my ex-husband." Her voice was softer, less steady, more frightened. "H-he left them when he did some work out here. You can wear them while your clothes dry."

Dry clothes. Damned if that didn't sound good...and damned if even the idea wasn't enough to make him feel weak. With the hand that still clutched the gun, he gave her silent permission to return to the armoire. "He come out here often?"

"Usually every Saturday."

Today was Tuesday. He would be long gone before Saturday rolled around. He intended to get some rest, spend a night— maybe two—and then he was going to head west. Last time he had stopped running in his hometown of Atlanta, but this time, he vowed, he wouldn't stop until he was hell and gone from Catlin, North Carolina. Maybe he would head for Mexico, or maybe Canada. At least he spoke their language.

Whatever his final destination, he was never coming back to North Carolina. He was never going to let them take him to trial.

God help him, he was never going to spend another night in jail.

After a moment she returned with a pair of gray sweatpants. Loath to approach him, she laid them across the arm of the sofa, then took a few steps safely away. Hiding a grimace of pain, he crossed to the sofa and picked them up. They were soft and well-worn, the fleece incredibly warm around his frozen fingers as he measured their waist against his own. It was a pretty good fit, maybe an inch or two looser than he preferred, but the drawstring that ran through the elastic waist would take care of that. They were going to feel good…*if* he could manage to get them on. *If* he could bully her into helping him undress. *If* he could frighten her into coming that close.

Gripping the sweats as if someone might try to rip them from him, he raised his head to look at her. ''I—I can't….'' His face grew warm with embarrassment. He was thirty-four years old, on the run and trying to hold a hostage, and he was so helpless that he couldn't undress himself. He couldn't even kick off his shoes.

She stared back, her blue eyes rounded, her blond hair frizzing a little as it dried. She was afraid to help him, afraid to come close enough to touch him. No matter how much he might hate it, he *needed* her fear. He was in no condition to stop her if she tried to escape. Except for its ability to frighten her, the pistol was worthless; it was for damned sure he would never use it. He hadn't been in the greatest shape when the deputy had picked him up at the Sylvan County Jail this morning for transfer to Catlin, and the gunshot wound, the car crash, the new injuries and seven hours in the cold and rain had left him pretty useless. If she decided to walk away from him right now, to turn her back and leave, he couldn't stop her. He couldn't go after her. He couldn't make her stay.

Part of him wished she *would* go. All he wanted was a fire, some food and a night's rest, wrapped in one of her quilts and huddled on the stone hearth, as close to the flames as he could get without being singed. He *didn't* want a hostage. He didn't want any more regrets, any more guilt, any more complications.

He smiled grimly. His life, from the moment of his conception, had been nothing *but* complications. There had been the mother who had never wanted him and the father who had always denied him, the kids who had made fun of him and the adults who had looked down on him. And his failures… He'd failed at everything he'd ever tried—his jobs, his relationships, his affairs. It was a failed relationship that had brought him here. Nearly eleven months ago the best friend he'd ever had had set him up. Just this morning the same friend had tried to have him killed.

He wondered how much it cost to buy such a betrayal. How much of that four hundred fifty thousand dollars had Russell required to ease his conscience?

The woman took a reluctant step toward him. "Sit down," she requested, her voice little more than a whisper, and he did, sinking heavily onto the nearest chair. The muscles in his legs, relieved of his weight for the first time all day, cramped, then eased and grew warm. He hadn't realized how exhausted he was, hadn't let himself feel the fatigue that now coursed through him.

The woman. *Ashley.* He silently tried her name and liked it—liked its softness, its gentleness—and because he *did* like it, he didn't use it.

She knelt in front of him and reached for his foot. The muddy laces were soaked and didn't want to release their loops. He watched as, with trembling hands, she tugged the laces free, removed one shoe and dripping sock and then repeated the process with the other.

Setting the shoes aside, she reached for the hem of his T-shirt. She had to lean closer to him, close enough that her trembling increased, close enough that he could identify the faint fragrances—roses and sweet honeysuckle—that clung to her hair and skin. Closing his eyes so he wouldn't have to watch, he gritted his teeth as she began tugging, sending agonizing little waves of pain through his entire body, until finally he groaned aloud and she stopped.

Her fingers, soft and warm, gently probed his rib cage. "I think you've cracked some ribs."

Feeling queasy from the pain, he didn't respond.

"I can tape them for you, but most people find it doesn't help."

"Don't bother."

"I'll have to cut your shirt off. I don't have any of Seth's shirts here."

"Fine." If worse came to worst, when he was finally able to leave, he could take that sweater she was wearing. It was big enough to make, at worst, a snug fit on him, and it would keep him warm and, until the scent of her faded from its fibers, it would remind him of her, standing in front of the fireplace, arms upraised, naked to the waist, pulling it over her head. It was safe to indulge in such thoughts, since nothing would ever come of them. Right now he hurt too badly to even contemplate intimacy ever again, and when he left here, when he was trying to make it out of the South, staying alive and uncaught would require all his energies.

Using scissors from a nearby lidded basket, she began cutting away his shirt. When she was finished, she dropped the tattered pieces on the floor with his shoes, then, with a reluctance he could feel deep in his bones, she reached for the button at the waistband of his jeans. Wrapping his fingers around her wrist, he lifted her hand away. "Build a fire, would you?" he asked, his voice shakier than he would have liked. "I'll do this."

Relief easing the tautness of her features, she got to her feet, placed a pile of kindling on the grate over a small waxy glob, then set a match to the starter. The pieces caught fire almost immediately, as did the narrow lengths of old, seasoned wood she laid over them. She gave them a minute or two to burn before adding longer, thicker cuts. When the sap was crackling and the flames were curling over and around the top log, she dusted her hands and sat back on her heels. She didn't look over her shoulder at him. She didn't check to see what progress he'd made. She simply sat there and stared into the flames.

Dillon wasn't sure he could finish the job she'd started. Every breath was agony, and moving, bending, tugging and wriggling were all going to hurt like hell. But what were his alternatives? Spending the night in clammy, wet jeans? He would never get warm enough to rest. Letting her undress him? He would never get *relaxed* enough to rest.

Sliding the gun deep between the seat cushion and the side of the chair, he forced himself to his feet. He unfastened his jeans, then began working the tight, wet fabric down his hips, his body protesting every movement. His breathing grew heavy and labored as pain swept over him, bringing with it fiery heat.

By the time he'd stripped, then stepped into the sweats she'd given him, his face was flushed and damp, his stomach was churning and his muscles were quivering uncontrollably.

Taking breaths too deep to be painless but too shallow to fill his lungs, he removed an item from his jeans pocket, then made his way carefully to the bed. It was neatly made and turned back, a pink blanket sandwiched between white sheets and a pastel-hued quilt. He stacked the pillows against the headboard, then lowered himself to the mattress, groaning aloud as he settled in. "Do you have a first-aid kit?"

Still kneeling in front of the fire, she nodded without looking at him.

"Do you have any objection to using it on me?"

She was still for so long that he knew she wanted to refuse. The only concern she had for his injuries was that they weren't serious enough. She would have preferred it if he had been hurt too badly to escape the deputy's custody, if the gunshot wound had been a few inches lower and a few inches to the left, if one of the bumps on his head had been hard enough to leave him unconscious. She certainly wouldn't choose, of her own free will, to take care of him.

Well, *he* certainly wasn't choosing, of his own free will, to be taken care of. The last thing he needed—besides jail—was her closeness. Her nursing. Her touch. But he had no choice. The longer he stayed in Catlin County, the greater the risk of discovery. He couldn't leave until he was in at least a little better shape, and she was his best—his only—chance at getting better.

Finally she got to her feet and went to the kitchen, filling a basin with water, collecting towels from a cabinet. She set them on the night table, then left again, this time getting a basket from the hook where it hung near the bathroom door. He saw when she returned that it was filled with bottles and jars, with sterile dressings, scissors and tape.

As she sat down on the bed beside him, he tilted his head back and focused his gaze on the ceiling and the massive beams that crossed it. A half-dozen baskets hung from one beam; a variety of flowers and stalks with dull green leaves were hung upside down to dry from another.

God, he was tired. He had never wanted sleep as badly as he wanted it now, had never needed oblivion the way he needed it now. His body was about to give out on him. Unless what she had in mind for him was particularly excruciating, he had no doubt that being in her bed, underneath her covers, leaning back against her pillows, would soon put him to sleep for the rest of the night.

And then she would be free to go. Free to summon help. Free to lead the sheriff and his deputies straight to him.

He couldn't let that happen. He knew how to stop her—was prepared to stop her—but he found the idea distasteful. He knew all too well how violently *he* hated being handcuffed and utterly helpless. He knew how vulnerable those thin steel bracelets made a man feel. He couldn't even imagine how threatening they would feel to *her*.

He had no choice, but at least he could delay it. He could let her doctor his injuries, could let her get something to eat. He could put it off as long as possible, but the woman—Ashley, he reminded himself. Her name was Ashley, and she was going to have one hell of a miserable night.

For once, Ashley thought, Dillon Boone had gotten lucky. Seth considered her interest in herbs more than a little odd, but there were plenty of people in the surrounding mountains who considered her something of a healer. She knew practically every plant that grew in the region, knew its healing properties and its harmful ones. She knew what could prevent infection, what could aid healing, ease pain and soothe discomforts. She knew what was harmless, knew what would help and what would hurt.

Unfortunately she had nothing accessible right now that might hurt the man who'd made himself comfortable in her bed.

The thought brought her a flush of guilt. Even if she had some deadly herb available to her, she wouldn't make use of it. Boone was suffering enough. She could never do anything to add to that.

Dipping a cloth in the crockery bowl filled with warm water, she began bathing dirt and blood from his face and arms. None of his injuries there was serious—scrapes, bruises, some minor lacerations, a split lip. He sat motionless for her ministrations, still as a statue, not looking at her. It was as if he found the situation too personal, too intimate to acknowledge; the only way to endure it was stiffly, impassively.

Funny. The man was a fugitive. He had forced his way in here, had used his gun and his absolute soullessness to frighten her into helping him and yet he didn't *want* her help. He hadn't wanted to ask for the fire whose warmth he badly needed. He had refused to ask for food. Instead of worrying about exchanging his own soaking clothes for something dry, he had suggested that *she* get out of her wet clothes. Even now he didn't want her to touch him. He didn't want her to come close to him. Very odd.

Needing to break the uneasy silence between them, she asked the first question that came to mind and found that her voice was steady for the first time in too long. "Why did you come back to Catlin County?"

"Believe me, it wasn't by choice." As if sensing that she found the answer lacking, he scowled a little and continued. "I caught the attention of a deputy with a good memory for old Wanted bulletins."

"Then you were in custody when you came back." He offered no response, but she didn't need one. So he had been arrested, but had somehow escaped. Now he was not only a fugitive, but an escaped fugitive. Now he faced additional charges—as if the original charge hadn't been serious enough. Now he was likely more desperate than ever to get away.

Rinsing the cloth, she moved to his chest. His skin was icy cold, and he was shaking, as much from the cold as from his injuries. There were plenty of those: more cuts and scrapes, a number of bruises—some recent, the others older and healing—and a furrow cut across the top of his right shoulder.

Anything from a cut to a gunshot wound, she had thought earlier, and she had been right on the last guess. The bullet had penetrated from the back, entering at a downward angle and scooping a deep V out of the flesh in its path. If the angle had been a few degrees sharper, the injury would have been much more serious, a through-and-through wound that would have required threading a gauze wick through his shoulder. It would have been much more painful, much slower to heal and much more susceptible to infection.

The nature of his injuries disturbed her. The split lip and the bruising around his right eye seemed indicative of being on the losing end in a fight. Of course, maybe he had struggled with the deputy before he'd escaped, but she knew all of Seth's deputies. There wasn't one of them who didn't dwarf Boone in size, who couldn't break him in half without even breaking a sweat. And there was the gunshot wound. Obviously he'd been shot from behind. Granted, he *was* a fugitive, but to shoot a man in the back seemed cold, almost vicious. Surely there had been other ways to stop him.

But maybe not. After all, he *had* escaped, even with getting shot in the back.

"Who shot you?" she asked as she laid the basin on the floor and put the basket in its place.

Finally he looked at her, his scowl deeper, his eyes emptier. She'd never seen eyes so intensely brown—or so utterly blank—before. "Does it matter?"

"Was it Sheriff Benedict or one of his deputies?" Seth was an expert shot. If he had shot a fleeing prisoner, it was pure luck that Boone had survived to tell the tale.

"No."

"Then you weren't in Catlin County's custody when you escaped."

"Yes, I was."

His answers confused her. She had assumed that he'd been captured elsewhere—that he was too bright to come back to the county on his own—and was being transported to the Catlin County Jail when he escaped. She knew from conversations with Seth that if Boone had been caught in another jurisdiction, it was up to Catlin County to go after him and bring him back, and the man had just confirmed that he'd been in their custody. So if he'd been under escort by a Catlin County deputy but it wasn't a Catlin County deputy who'd shot him, then who had? A dutiful citizen, perhaps? Had someone witnessed his escape? Had he stumbled onto someone else's property before he'd made his way here?

Selecting a bottle of antiseptic from the basket, she dampened a thick gauze pad, then began cleansing his open injuries. "You *were* shot when you escaped," she stated, just to clarify things, but she couldn't keep a faint questioning tone from her voice.

"No," he answered softly. "I was shot *before* I escaped."

The implications of that sent a shiver up her spine. Shooting a prisoner to stop an escape was one thing. Shooting him when he was doing nothing, when he was basically helpless and at his escort's mercy... That was criminal.

That was attempted murder.

If it was true.

Finishing with the rest of his injuries, she turned her attention to the gunshot wound. He watched as she blotted the blood, bathed the wound with antiseptic, coated it with ointment and covered it loosely with a sterile dressing. It was nasty and painful, but there was nothing else she could do for it. The tissue was destroyed, leaving too wide a gap to bring the edges of the skin together and suture. In a few days' time it would start to heal, the tissue granulating in from side to side and bottom to top. Tomorrow she would find a square of fabric to fashion a sling from, and, barring complications, within a week to ten days the wound would be healed enough to allow him some use of his arm again. Another two to three weeks after that, and nothing would remain but the scar.

He was waiting for her to ask more questions, waiting to see whether she would believe him. Finally done, she folded her hands in her lap and quietly asked, "What happened?"

"Does it matter?" he asked again, closing his eyes, wearily letting his head roll back.

"Yes."

"Why?"

"It just does. Where were you arrested?"

"Sylvan County."

That explained his more minor injuries, Ashley thought, her expression turning somber. Sylvan County was right across the Tennessee state line from Catlin County. There were a lot of ties between the two counties; they had a lot of things in common. Fair and humane treatment of prisoners by their sheriffs' departments, though, wasn't one of them. People who ended up in Sylvan County's custody seemed to fall a lot, to suffer a lot of mysterious injuries while locked alone in cells bare of everything but cots and toilets. There had been a number of complaints filed and investigations conducted, but few, if any, changes. Seth hated picking up prisoners there almost as much as he hated transferring his own prisoners there. As pleased as he must have been to hear that Catlin's one and only bank robber had been arrested, he also must have been dismayed to find out by whom.

"How long were you there?"

"Three days, four nights."

Three days was about the right age for the oldest of his bruises. "Who picked you up to take you to Catlin?"

"A deputy named Coughlin."

"I know Tom Coughlin. He never would have shot you unless he had absolutely no other choice, and he never would have stood by and let someone else shoot you."

After a long, still moment he opened his eyes just a bit and looked at her. "I told you it wasn't a Catlin County deputy." He started to heave a sigh, but winced and blew his breath out gently instead. "We were ambushed on our way to Catlin. We came around a curve, and there was a black van and three men blocking the road. They opened fire, Coughlin swerved and we went over the side and down into a ravine."

She stared at him in dismay. "Was Tom hurt?"

"He'd been shot."

"And you left him there?" Her voice rose a few notes. "You just walked off and *left* him?"

"Some people came—a woman and her kids. I could hear them talking from down below. They called the sheriff from their car phone. They got help for him." His dark eyes turned even darker. "Damned right I walked off and left him. Those men were trying to kill *me,* not the deputy. He was unconscious. He was of no use to me, and there was no way in hell I was going to wait around for them to finish the job. I took his gun, and I took off."

"Why would anyone want to kill you? What you did was wrong, but it's not worth dying for."

"No," he agreed. "But to a couple of people out there…" Grimness settled over his features. "It's worth killing for."

Chapter 2

She was staring at him. Dillon knew it without looking. He could *feel* the weight of her wary blue gaze. She was looking at him and trying to figure out whether or not to believe anything he'd just said.

He knew what her decision would be: that he was unreliable. Untrustworthy. That anything he said was more than likely a lie. That naturally he would try to put himself in the best light and so he would claim that he'd been forced to escape from custody in order to save his own life.

He didn't give a damn whether she believed him. He was used to not being believed, to not being trusted. Since the time he was nine years old and had gotten the devil beaten out of him by Alex Waters and no one had believed his side of the story, he had known that he would always need proof. Well, he didn't have any proof to give this woman, and he wasn't sure he would offer it if he did. He was tired of always having to provide verification. He was tired of never being believed on nothing more than his say-so.

He was just tired, period.

Beside him the mattress shifted as she moved to stand up. Moving far too quickly for the comfort of his shoulder and ribs, he caught her wrist. He felt her tremble beneath his fingers, but he didn't release her. Instead, he pulled her back down and held her there.

"I was just going to put these things away," she said, her voice unsteady once again and tinged with fear, "then fix dinner. You could use some food."

After a moment he let go, and she rose to her feet. Before she walked away, though, she hesitated, then bent to draw the covers up to his shoulders, tucking the edges between his back and the pillow to hold them in place. It was a little gesture. It didn't mean a thing. No one else would have even noticed.

But *he* did. He noticed it and appreciated it like hell, and it made him feel even guiltier about his plans for her and the steel handcuffs he'd hidden beneath the covers and out of her sight.

Settling back against the pillows, he watched as she returned the basket to its hook, then emptied the heavy bowl in the sink. She washed her hands, took down dishes from the cabinet and cut thick slices of homemade bread all with the same easy, familiar movements. These were tasks she had performed hundreds of times, mindless jobs that she did without thought. So what *was* on her mind? he wondered. Maybe she was sending silent prayers to God for her safety. Maybe she was asking why *she'd* had the bad luck to get trapped with an escaping bank robber, or maybe she was planning an escape of her own. Maybe she was cursing the day he'd set foot in Catlin or regretting the day she'd decided to make her home all alone at the top of an isolated mountain.

He didn't blame her for that decision, even if, thanks to him, it hadn't turned out to be a great one. For all his negative feelings regarding the area, he had to admit that Catlin County was the most beautiful place he'd ever seen. He fully understood the desire to make a home there, especially all the way out here, where she had no neighbors, no intrusions and very little contact with the everyday world. If it weren't for the small matter of money to pay the bills, he could be perfectly happy living off away from other people like this.

He had never had much skill in the art of getting along with others.

But he was a man, fully capable—most of the time—of taking care of himself. The very virtue of being female made her less physically capable, more vulnerable, more at risk. If she wanted to live like this, she should at least have a gun to protect herself and a telephone to call for help. What she really needed—with no apology for the chauvinism—was a man to do the protecting for her. If he'd seen any sign of a man around, Dillon would have kept on going. If she'd answered affirmatively when he'd mentioned a husband, he probably would have stolen that beat-up old van of hers and tended his wounds himself once he got someplace safe. He wouldn't have followed her into the house. He wouldn't have taken her hostage. He sure as hell wouldn't be lying in her bed, watching her fix dinner as if he were a guest.

Wearily he slid a little lower beneath the covers. His shivers were slowing, his misery slowly easing. Powerful heat from the fireplace radiated into the room, and the heavy blanket and quilt she'd tucked around him were trapping the heat and keeping it comfortingly close to his body. After hours in cold, wet shoes, his feet were thawing; he could wiggle his toes and actually feel them respond. He was starting to feel human again—except for the hunger. And the pain. And the grim future facing him.

Her bare feet making little noise on the floor, she came across the room to the bed, bringing with her a tray fashioned from twigs and lengths of narrow rope. He assumed she had made the tray herself; in the long minutes that he'd stood beside the van and watched her through the workshop windows, he'd noticed a table full of similar items. That must be how she supported herself—with baskets and twigs, with the weaving loom and the quilting frame that filled half the workshop, with the soaps and the candles and the flowers drying overhead.

She was never going to get rich, but if it paid the bills and made her happy, what else mattered?

She set the tray across his lap, and he studied it for a moment. It was well made, the legs sturdy and level, the twigs that formed the top smooth, uniform in size and tightly lashed. It held a cloth napkin in faded red gingham, a soup spoon, a salt shaker filled with some seasoning that wasn't salt and a pottery mug filled with a fragrant, steaming liquid.

"What is that?"

"Chamomile tea. It'll make you feel better."

He looked at it suspiciously. It hadn't escaped his notice that she was into herbs. There were pots of them on the windowsills all around the room, there were bunches hanging overhead, and the antiseptic and ointment she'd used on his injuries hadn't come out of any commercially prepared tube or bottle. Anyone who knew the good about herbs had to also be aware of the bad. Maybe the pale brew in the cup was no more harmful than the iced tea served by the gallons in restaurants all across the South. Maybe it *would* make him feel better...or maybe it would put him to sleep. Maybe it was beneficial.

Or maybe it was poison.

"Oh, for heaven's sake..." Picking up the mug, she blew gently across the surface, then took a drink, followed immediately by another. Then she put the cup down again, took a step back, folded her arms and watched him.

Working his left arm free of the covers, he reluctantly picked up the mug and sniffed. The fragrance reminded him that he'd had nothing to eat or drink since the breakfast of soggy cereal, dry toast and weak coffee a Sylvan County deputy had served him shortly after dawn and that he'd eaten none too well the three days before that. For a short time out there in the woods, ignoring the emptiness in his stomach had been even harder than ignoring the pain in every part of his body. Then the thirst had kicked in, and the hunger had been immediately forgotten. All that water around, and not a drop to drink. A couple of times he had been convinced that he would gladly give up food forever in exchange for a cup of hot coffee.

He tasted the tea and found it warm on his tongue and sweetened with honey. It wasn't coffee, but it was good, and she was right. Even that one small drink made him feel better. It made him feel a degree or two warmer and a degree or two more human.

At last she turned away, making another trip to the kitchen while he finished the tea. She brought back a basket—the gingham napkin inside wrapped around warm slices of bread—and a pottery plate holding a bowl filled with vegetable stew and set both on the bed tray.

When she sat down once again on the edge of the mattress, he scowled at her. "What are you doing?"

She paused in the act of picking up the spoon. "I was going to feed you."

"I can manage."

"You shouldn't be using your arm. Tomorrow I'll fix a sling for it, but tonight—"

"I'm left-handed."

With unmistakable relief in her eyes, she stood and returned to the kitchen. Some small part of him regretted her retreat; there was something vaguely comforting about having her so near. The larger part of him was glad for the reprieve. He didn't need a reminder that—right now, at least—she was by far the stronger of them, and *she* didn't need a reminder that he was disgustingly weakened. He didn't need to be fed like a baby, taking food from a spoon that *she* held because he couldn't. He didn't need that helplessness, that embarrassment. That intimacy.

Like hell he didn't.

His face warm, he reached for the spoon and, keeping his gaze down, began eating. The stew was rich, heavy with tomatoes, carrots, potatoes and onions, but he would have eaten just as appreciatively if it had come in a can from some unimaginative company. By the time she returned with her own bowl to sit on the hearth near the fire's warmth, his bowl was empty. He laid the spoon inside carefully so it didn't clatter. "That was good."

Acknowledging his words with no more than a nod, she set her bowl aside on the stones, refilled his and brought it back, then seated herself again. They ate in silence, her gaze directed into the distance, his traveling around the room but all too often returning to her.

When he had literally stumbled out of the forest and into the clearing, he had first noticed the darkened cabin and had thought he'd found the perfect place—dry and empty. Even when he'd seen her van—probably thirty years old, its dominant color gray primer and missing body parts—his first thought was that the vehicle had been junked long ago. Then he had moved closer, and he had seen the lights on in the workshop. After only a moment he'd caught a glimpse of her—young, blond, vulnerable. For a while he had simply watched her, feeling sneaky and shameful. Even now, every time his glance strayed her way, he felt guilty for it.

But he could live with guilt. What he couldn't live with was prison. Being locked away for much of the rest of his life. Living up—or down—to the expectations of everyone who knew him. Taking the blame, as he so often had in his life, for something he hadn't done.

"Why do you live up here?" he asked, awkwardly peeling the golden crust away from a slice of bread with one hand, then taking a bite from it.

She looked startled, almost as if she had forgotten that he was there, then abruptly her expression turned blank and she shrugged. "I like my own company."

"You can be a loner in town, where it's safer."

"I lived in town. In Raleigh. You want to talk about how safe life is in the city?"

"You could live in Catlin."

"I've lived there, too. I prefer it here."

"Don't you get scared?"

She gave him a long, steady look that made him want to squirm. "Only when I have good reason."

"You should at least have a gun."

She shrugged again. "I would never shoot anyone."

"That's nice to hear," he said dryly.

She stood up, her skirt falling in swirls almost to her ankles, and came to the bed, adding her soup bowl to his dishes on the tray, picking all of it up. Before she walked away, though, she spoke again, her voice as soft as a whisper, sending a chill up his spine. "I don't need a gun. There are easier, simpler, subtler ways of stopping someone."

Facing her reflection in the uncurtained window, Ashley filled the sink with hot, sudsy water, then slid the dishes in. Across the room, Boone was still puzzling over her last remark, wondering if she had been teasing, no matter how unexpectedly or more ominously, giving him a warning. She would know what he'd decided when morning came and she served him breakfast. If he refused to eat, no doubt he would have decided that she wasn't to be trusted.

He would have decided wrong. He could trust her. She wasn't going to do anything foolish that might result in her getting hurt or worse. She wasn't going to race across the room, grab her keys and dash out the door, even though she could probably be halfway to the van before he even managed to get to his feet. She wasn't going out into the rain that was streaming down now, beating a steady rhythm on the roof, wasn't going out into the cold dark night.

However, that didn't mean she intended to do absolutely nothing. He would surely fall asleep soon. His body had been taxed to its limits; only sheer determination had brought him this far. He was warm and dry, his injuries had been treated, his stomach had been filled, he was as comfortable as he was going to get outside of a hospital, where pain-relieving drugs could give him peace. Exhaustion was going to take over any minute now, and he would sleep soundly enough that nothing she did would disturb him.

So what would she do?

She could find his gun wherever he'd hidden it…but after her comment—*I could never shoot anyone*—how much impact would it have?

Better still, she could tie him to the bed. She could make him her prisoner. She had some cord in one of these baskets, and if there was one thing hours of crafting had taught her, it was how to tie a strong knot. The bed was sturdy and had both a headboard and a footboard; there was no way he would be able to pull free. She would have to be careful of his shoulder, of course, but she could rig up something that would cause him no harm and would do her a world of good. Then she would drive down to the Parmenters' and use their phone to notify Seth that he could pick up his escapee at his convenience. Within an hour, two at the most, Dillon Boone would be out of her house and out of her life. He would be in jail, where he belonged.

He *did* belong there...didn't he?

"How long have you been divorced?"

She rinsed the last bowl and placed it in the drainer before turning around. He was pale, almost as white as the sheets, and he looked miserable enough to make her feel more than a twinge of sympathy. He needed better care than she could provide, but not even the best M.D.s in the state could make things right for him. They couldn't keep him out of prison. They couldn't fix a life that had long ago gone wrong.

Drying her hands on a tattered towel, she answered his question. "Four years."

"How long were you married?"

"Four years."

"And you're still friends."

She hung the towel over the front of the sink, then began turning off lights. "Best friends."

That was what she and Seth had always been—*all* they had ever been. If they hadn't found themselves in Raleigh at the same time, Seth finishing his degree at the state university there when she had started, if they hadn't both felt out of place, if they hadn't both been homesick and lonely, they never would have married. They never *should* have married. It had taken them no time at all to realize that they'd made a mistake, that friendship was no basis for a marriage—at least, not the sort that they both wanted—but nearly four years had passed before they were able to admit that marriage was destroying their friendship, which was far more important to them both. She was glad that they had managed to save it. They were closer now than ever before.

Still, she couldn't help but wish briefly that they *were* still married. Then Seth would be coming home tonight. Then she would have told Boone yes, she had a husband, and he was due home any minute. Then she probably wouldn't be in the situation she was in.

But she would find a way out of it, and she would do it without Seth's or anyone else's help. She was strong. Independent. Capable. She could take care of herself. She could take care of Dillon Boone.

"Why does he come out every Saturday?"

"To check up on me." She sat down at the far end of the hearth where she could lean back against the warm fireplace stones and tucked her skirt around her legs. "To make sure I haven't fallen from the roof and broken my neck or had trouble with Bessie, my van."

"Or to make sure you haven't been taken hostage by an escaped prisoner."

Thinking about his words, she nodded. *Of course.* With an armed and dangerous fugitive loose in the mountains around her home, Seth wouldn't wait until Saturday to warn her. If he didn't take time this evening, he would surely come first thing in the morning. She might be rid of Boone sooner than she'd hoped.

"That van..." His voice sounded weaker, fading. "I wouldn't take that van even if I were desperate."

"I thought you *were* desperate."

"Something that ugly and beat-up would draw too much attention."

"Bessie suits my needs just fine. She gets me and my stuff where we need to go, and all she asks in return is a tank of gas, plenty of oil and a kind word now and then."

That last made him smile just a bit. He wasn't a man smiles

came easily to, she thought, and that was a shame, because
they made a handsome face more so. That one little beginning
of a smile softened the hardness, warmed the chill and lessened
the sense of danger swirling around him. "All of us do better
with a kind word now and then," he murmured. "But sometimes they're damned hard to come by."

And that was a shame, too, she silently acknowledged.

He shifted in the bed, making the springs squeak, then, almost immediately, he grimaced. Even across the distance that
separated them, Ashley could see the sweat bead across his
forehead as he tried to find a position where the pain was tolerable. It wasn't fair that he should be suffering so, wasn't fair
that after nearly a year on the run—nearly a year that he had
passed presumably unscathed—he should suffer so many injuries as soon as he was taken into custody. Police custody was
one place where a person should be safe, one place where he
should be able to count on being treated fairly, on being protected.

Obviously it wasn't.

"Put some more logs on the fire, then come over here, will
you?"

Although the room was warm and certainly didn't need more
heat, she did as he asked, placing another four logs at angles
to those already burning, then crossing to the bed. She sat down
next to him and raised her right hand to wipe the perspiration
from his forehead. That was how he caught her off guard when
he snapped one half of a pair of handcuffs around her left wrist.

For a moment Ashley stared uncomprehendingly at the
bracelet that now circled her wrist and connected her, via pathetically few steel links, to the other bracelet that he'd fastened
around his own wrist. Then, with a surge of anger, she tried to
yank free. "Let me go!" she demanded, twisting her wrist,
trying in vain to force the wider part of her hand through the
small opening. "Get this off of me *now!*"

Her struggle made him groan with renewed pain, but she
didn't care. Her sympathy was gone, disappeared inside an
ever-growing panic. He couldn't do this! He couldn't chain her

to him, couldn't make her, in every terrifying aspect of the word, truly his prisoner. Damn him, he couldn't take away her options and leave her totally at his mercy!

She tried to rise from the bed, but he caught her with his free hand, tugging her down again so that she sprawled half across the mattress and half across him. "Ashley, damn it—" His face contorted with every shallow breath he drew, with every move she made. "Jeez, don't do that," he whispered. "You're killing me."

Very carefully she pushed away from him and sat on the bed, utterly still, glowering at him. "Take this off right now," she demanded, her voice low and threatening and trembling.

"I can't. I'm sorry."

"What do you mean you can't? Where's the key?" If he didn't have a key, if they were stuck together until *someone* managed to separate them... Oh, God.

"It's over there." He gestured vaguely toward the rest of the room.

She twisted around to look behind her. The most likely place was the pocket of his jeans, still lying on the rug where he'd undressed earlier, but she knew from living with Seth that a handcuff key was small; Boone could have hidden it anywhere. He'd stood at the door, where baskets were stacked on a small half-round table. From there he'd moved to the dining table, with more baskets, a dried flower centerpiece and a tatted lace runner. He had walked past the sofa, had sat in the armchair and passed close to the fireplace, where the mantel was filled with pottery and wooden boxes. He could have dropped the key behind the logs stacked on the hearth, could have slipped it into the drawer of the table next to the chair or the one next to the bed. He could even have the darned thing in bed with him. She hadn't watched him closely enough, had been all too willing to turn her back on him.

She faced him again. "You can't do this," she pleaded, the words broken by a hiccup that sounded suspiciously like a sob. "You just can't—"

It was the look in his eyes that stopped her. Just a short

while ago, when they had stood face-to-face in front of the fireplace and he had commanded her to undress right there, the complete emptiness in his eyes had frightened her into compliance. Now there was emotion in that deep brown. There was guilt. Shame. "I have to," he whispered. "I can't let you go. I can't let you turn me in."

"I won't—" Once more she broke off.

He waited a moment, but seemed to know that she wasn't going to continue. "Go ahead, Ashley. Tell me that you won't try to escape. Tell me that you'll sit there while I'm asleep, and you won't do anything to get away." He paused. "Go ahead. Make me believe you. I would *love* to believe you."

She sat silent, her mouth clamped shut.

"As soon as I'm able to travel, I'll be out of here. I won't make you go with me, and, I swear to God, you won't be hurt. I know you don't believe me, but it's the truth. But because you don't believe me, and because I can't afford to trust you, I have to do this."

He raised his right hand, and the cool steel tugged uncomfortably at her hand, sending a shudder of revulsion through her. "I *can't* spend the night like this."

"*I* can't spend it any other way." He sighed grimly. "Get comfortable. It's a long time till morning."

Scowling, she turned away and slid off the mattress to sit on the floor. Her back was supported by the bed, her bottom cushioned by the handwoven rag rug beneath her. Her right arm dangled awkwardly in midair, suspended by the steel cuff. He was right: it *was* going to be a very long night, and she didn't intend to sleep through one bit of it. How could she, when she was chained to the side of a wanted felon? How could she possibly relax enough to sleep when every move brought discomfort, when every brush of the metal on her skin brought a new sense of helplessness?

"Ashley?"

She stared hard into the fireplace, concentrating all her energies on the flames that would surely go out and leave them cold before morning, trying desperately to ignore the drained voice above and behind her.

"Ashley." He jangled the chain that connected them, making her arm twitch. "You don't have to spend the night on the floor."

"Oh, yeah?" she responded belligerently. "Are you going to sleep down here instead?"

"The bed is big enough for two."

His voice was as gentle as hers was caustic, and it fed the anger she needed to remain in control of the fear seeping through her. "Not even in my worst nightmare."

"I *am* your worst nightmare, aren't I?" There was a moment of silence before he spoke again—or, at least, she thought he did. The words were so soft, so hesitant, so insubstantial that they might have been nothing more than the whisper of the wind. "I'm sorry."

Dillon awakened Wednesday morning, feeling cold, stiff and worse than half-dead. The pink blanket was heavy, but not heavy enough to combat the early-morning chill by itself, and he'd given up its accompanying quilt right after the fire had gone out sometime during the night.

Rubbing his hand over his face, then over his hair, he felt the stubble of beard and hair standing on end. Ignoring that, he closed his eyes and did a rather uncomfortable assessment of his condition. Breathing still hurt like hell, but he thought he detected a slight improvement—or was that merely wishful thinking? His legs were stiff, his muscles taut, his joints sore. His shoulder was hot and so tender to the touch that he didn't bother trying to move it. He wondered if it was infected, or if some of that herbal stuff Ashley had used on it had caused further damage. Last night it had been sore; after her ministrations, this morning it was sore *and* his right arm felt unusually heavy, his hand unusually numb.

Then he looked down and saw the reason for the discomfort: sometime in the past few hours, Ashley had fallen asleep deeply enough to seek whatever comfort she could find. What she had found—*all* she had found—was the slight pillow of his hand. Her cheek was pressed against his palm, her chin tucked into the curve of his fingers. His arm felt as if he'd held a bowling ball all night, deadening the nerves, stiffening the joints. But he had never touched a bowling ball so soft, so smooth. Even with his hand half-numbed, he could feel every place her skin touched his, could feel the differences between his own callus-roughened skin and hers, as delicate and fine as anything he'd ever touched.

Moving cautiously so he wouldn't disturb her, he flexed his fingers, touching the tips to her jaw. Squared off, it gave her a stubborn look and kept her just barely from crossing over from mere attractiveness into prettiness. Better than pretty, though, her face was interesting. It showed character. Personality. She was strong. Generous. Kind—and he had known so little kindness in his life that he recognized it instinctively when he saw it. Her eyes were bright, clear, probably filled with trust for everyone in the world but him, and her mouth seemed to want to curve into a smile as naturally as *his* didn't. Altogether it was a good face, one that would age with great grace. When she was eighty years old and her blonde hair had turned white, when fine wrinkles had replaced the smoothness of youth, she would surpass prettiness with uncommon beauty.

With a heavy, suddenly almost forlorn sigh, he fixed his gaze on the kitchen window and wished he had the keys that were in his jeans pocket halfway across the room. She was sleeping so soundly that he was sure he could unfasten the cuff from his wrist and secure it for safety to the bed frame. Then he could get up, build a fire, see about breakfast. He could make rather urgent use of her bathroom, could wash his face, brush his teeth, maybe even shave. All that would go a long way toward making him feel human again.

Setting her free would go even further.

Who was he kidding? He was still weak, still feeling some serious pain. He would be lucky if he could even get to his feet without help. Building a fire, fixing breakfast, finding a steady hand for a razor? Not likely. And setting her free? Letting her go, when he knew the first thing she would do was turn him in, when she hadn't even bothered last night to deny that she would? Letting the only thing that stood between him and a jail cell walk out of his reach? Not a chance in hell.

Not even if refusing did make him feel like the lowest of bastards.

Outside, the sky was dreary and dark, although it looked as if the rain had stopped, at least for a while. Had the weather slowed the search party yesterday as much as it had hindered him? Had they continued through the night, or had they taken a break so they would be well rested this morning? How long would it take them to follow his trail here? He didn't kid himself that they wouldn't. There were men up in these mountains who could track a sparrow flying too close to the ground. There was no way they could possibly miss the tracks he'd left for them—the footprints in the mossy ground, the scarred places where he'd slid down hills, the broken foliage, the overturned stones, the unmistakable signs of passage. He might as well have painted signs pointing to Ashley's cabin and proclaiming Here I Am.

He had to get out of here today, even if he did feel like death warmed over. Even if another day or two in this bed would go a long way toward physical healing. Even if another day or two in this place—with this woman?—might go a long way toward spiritual healing.

He could use some spiritual healing.

No doubt the North Carolina prison system would be happy to provide him with many long months where he could concentrate on just that.

So what were his options? There was no way he could leave here on foot. Hadn't he just admitted that he probably couldn't even make it twenty feet to the bathroom without help? He could steal her van, but the piece of junk was a stick shift, and he was pretty sure that, with this shoulder, shifting gears was out of the question. He was also pretty sure that there was no way he could drive that van through the town of Catlin without being noticed, and that was a risk he couldn't take. Besides, taking the junk heap— What had she called it? Bessie? Taking Bessie would leave her stranded up here all alone. If something happened to her... That was another risk he couldn't take.

That left only one choice. He would ask her to take him outside the county, maybe even outside the state. They weren't far from the state line; maybe the Tennessee cops weren't looking for him yet. He would have her let him off somewhere outside the immediate area, and he would do something to temporarily disable the van—let the air out of the tires, maybe— so that she couldn't notify the authorities right away. He would get a head start, and she would be rid of him. They would both be happy.

He could actually remember the last time he would have described himself as happy. It had been nearly a year ago, and his good friend Russell had sent him to Catlin to install an alarm system in the local bank. He had liked the town, had liked the people. He had thought it must be a nice little place to live, and he had enjoyed the few weeks he had lived there.

Then everything had gone more wrong than it had ever been in his entire life, and it wasn't ever going to be right again.

On the floor beside the bed, Ashley stirred, drawing his attention back to her. A shiver rippled through her, and she huddled deeper into the quilt he'd wrapped around her during the night. Its warmth wasn't enough to reverse the waking process, though; gradually her sleep lightened. Her eyes moved restlessly behind closed lids. Her breathing changed, becoming more measured, and her jaw tightened against his hand.

At last she opened her eyes. Dillon looked down at her, and she gazed up at him. Already there was wariness in her expression. There was no moment of confusion, no drowsy bewilderment, no lack of awareness. One moment she was asleep, and the next she was looking at him with such distrust and resentment that for a second he thought it actually hurt. But it was just his ribs, he told himself, and a breath taken the wrong way.

She raised her head from his hand and used her free hand to rub her face. Her hair stood high on top, was crushed flat on the side that had rested in his palm and curled in wayward wisps all over. She looked about ten years old, innocent and defenseless.

But she was closer to thirty. She was no child, but a woman. Very much a woman.

It had been a long time since he'd felt like much of a man. "I need the key."

He knew exactly what she needed; it had been a long night. "You'll have to help me get it."

Shrugging off the quilt, she awkwardly got to her feet. She rolled her head to ease the kinks in her neck, then started to stretch her arms over her head. The handcuffs stopped her. "Can you stand up?"

He pushed the covers back, then swung his feet to the floor. The rug where she had spent the night was warm beneath his toes, but that was the only warmth he found. The room was cold, and Ashley's gaze was even colder. Holding his arm to his ribs and taking the deepest breath he could manage, he pushed himself to his feet. His vision dimming, his knees threatening to buckle, he muttered a savage curse that ended in a sound too close for comfort to tears.

Cool hands closed around his upper arms, lending support. "Try to relax and breathe evenly. It'll pass."

Not before it killed him. How was he ever going to get out of here today if he couldn't even manage standing on his own feet without assistance?

With more will than he'd known he possessed, he forced the pain to the back of his mind, forced it under control. When he thought he just might survive, he carefully moved her out of his way and, one awkward, agonizing step at a time, he made his way, Ashley trailing at his side, to where his jeans lay on the rug. She bent and picked them up, patted the pockets and found the keys, then offered them to him.

For the second time in less than twenty-four hours, he unlocked the handcuffs, removing them from his own wrist, then hers. "You can go first."

She started toward the bathroom.

"But you have to take your clothes off."

That stopped her in her tracks. For a long moment she stood motionless, then, very slowly, she turned to face him. Her voice was as unforgiving as the wintry mountains outside. "Excuse me?"

He shifted uncomfortably. "You have to take your clothes off out here first. I can't let you climb out the window, and I'll be damned if I'm going to keep you company in there, so taking your clothes seems to be the only choice."

"But I'm not wearing anything under—" She broke off, and he briefly squeezed his eyes shut. He knew. As if by magic, the image from last night popped into his mind: Ashley, standing in front of the fireplace, all soft, bare skin backed by rugged stone, arms raised to reveal a tantalizing glimpse of breast. Sweet damnation, he *knew*.

As she realized that he was serious in his demand, expressionless ice turned to mutiny. "I won't."

"It's the only way you're getting out of my sight," he said, hearing the regret in his voice. "If you're worried about your modesty, don't be. I'll look the other way. If you're worried about your virtue... Hell, even if I could get hard, which I seriously doubt, it's for damned sure I couldn't do anything about it."

In an instant her face flushed from pale shock to the fiery heat of... What was it? he wondered. Embarrassment over his crudity? Anger that he wasn't going to give in? Revulsion at even the mere idea of being intimate with him? Probably a combination of all three, he admitted, the acknowledgment accompanied by a stinging bitterness.

"Take your clothes off," he ordered, his words sharp, his tone defensive, "or sit down so I can cuff you to the leg of the sofa so *I* can go in there."

She stared at him for a moment, pure hatred contaminating the blue of her eyes, then she walked to the bathroom door, where she stopped and faced him once again. With slow, deliberate, precise movements, she reached beneath her sweater to the waistband of her skirt. She unfastened the top three or four buttons, opening the skirt enough that she could slide it down her hips and step out of it. Next she grasped the ribbed bottom of the sweater in both hands and peeled it up and over her head, and the whole time, except when the fabric covered her face, she never took her eyes off him.

Wearing nothing but lacy little panties—he wasn't looking; he swore he wasn't—she bent to pick up the skirt, bundled it together with the sweater and flung both pieces at him. An instant later the bathroom door slammed shut, followed by the unmistakable click of a lock.

Wondering how he could suddenly feel so feverishly warm when only minutes ago he'd been close to freezing, Dillon clutched the clothing he'd caught. The sweater was warm with her body heat and fragrant with her scent. Simply holding it made his fingers itch to hold *her*. Simply smelling it made him wonder how much sweeter, how much more enticing those scents were on *her*.

Muttering a curse, this one no less desperate but far more vicious than the earlier one, he threw the garments away from him, sending them sailing across the room, bouncing off the closed, locked door. He was a fool. He should have taken one look at her yesterday through the workshop window and known that this was no place for him. He should have listened to the first sound of her voice—*Can I help you?*—and kept right on going. He never should have come inside here. Never should have made her undress in front of him. Never should have made her touch him. Never should have looked at her just now.

He was such a liar. He wouldn't look, he'd said. He wouldn't threaten her virtue, he'd promised. He couldn't even get hard, he'd assured her. But he *had* looked, and if he thought there was any chance he could sweet-talk anything at all out of her, he would damn well try. And, as if he didn't have enough problems, as if he weren't already suffering enough, he *was* hard. As a rock.

He'd made it a habit over the years to avoid exercises in futility. Trying to change people's opinion of him, trying to prove that he wasn't a total failure, trying to convince anyone at all that he wasn't guilty of the crime he'd been accused of—those were all lost causes. They weren't worth the breath he would expend arguing.

Wanting this woman…

That was the biggest lost cause of all.

Chapter 3

Ashley was so damned cold that her teeth were chattering and goose bumps had popped out all over very private parts of her body. Mouthing silent curses, she tried wrapping up in the only bath towel that hung on the bar, but it was too small to provide decent coverage, and the robe that usually hung on the back of the door was gone—tossed into the washing machine three days before. She had never bothered, she remembered, to transfer the load to the dryer, which meant it was still wet and quite possibly growing all sorts of nasty mildew.

For the first few minutes after she'd taken care of business, she had been smug. Maybe she was practically naked and cold, but at least she'd gotten to use the facilities. *He* was half-naked and cold, too—although he did have the option of wrapping up in one of her quilts—and he had the added misery of being unable to heed Mother Nature's call. But about five minutes ago, she had smelled woodsmoke, and her smugness had disappeared. He'd built a fire, and she wanted to be in front of it, absorbing its heat until she sizzled. She *needed* that warmth,

almost as much as she needed her clothing and the false sense
of security it gave her.

She had to admit that he'd made the best choice. If she were
in his position, she would have made the same decision. She
certainly couldn't escape this way, and being naked was a sight
better than having his company in here.

But she was still angry. And *cold*. She didn't tolerate cold
well. Hot, muggy summers didn't faze her, and the mountains'
frigid winters were fine, too, as long as she was prepared.
Coats, scarves, gloves, fires, blankets, quilts. She believed in
staying warm.

Reaching out, she laid one hand flat against the door. Was
the wood warm? Could there be such a tremendous difference
between the room temperature out there and the chill inside,
or was she simply so cold that even the slightest warmth felt
like a heat wave to her blue fingers?

This was ridiculous. She couldn't stay in an unheated bathroom all day. So she was naked and there was a man on the
other side of the door. It wasn't the first time, and—she fervently hoped—it wouldn't be the last.

But it *was* the first time with a man like Dillon Boone. The
other men in her past—Seth and one other—had been lovers;
they had been a part of her life, invited in, cared for. Boone
had simply barged in, pointed a gun at her and made threats.
He had chained her like an animal, had forced her to sleep on
the floor at his side, had demanded not once but twice that she
strip in front of him.

But once he'd gained her cooperation, she felt compelled to
admit, he had put the gun away and she hadn't seen it since.
He had offered to share the bed with her, and when it had
gotten cold during the night, although he'd needed all the warm
covers for himself, he had given up the warmest of them all to
tuck around her. And although he *had* made her undress, he
had been as uncomfortable with her nudity as *she* was.

She simply had to gather whatever dignity she could find,
open the door, walk out and find her clothes and put them on.

Then she would huddle on the hearth until the fire's heat had seeped into every bone in her body.

Discarding the skimpy towel, she walked to the door, drew a deep breath, then stepped into the outer room. Before she'd taken more than a few steps, she reached her clothes. Hastily, gratefully she pulled them on, burying her hands in the sweater's long sleeves, padding barefoot to the fireplace, where Boone was standing. He gave her another of those oddly regretful looks, this one not quite reaching her face, and gestured toward the couch. Biting her tongue on the protest that bubbled up, she sat down where he indicated, on a rug in front of the old sofa. One end of the handcuffs was already attached to the left sofa foot; bending cautiously, he fastened the other around her wrist.

Instead of going straight to the bathroom, though, he picked up a quilt from the chair. It was the Shoo Fly off her bed, the first quilt she'd ever made. He held it close to the fire, warming the layers of cotton, batting and muslin, and then he brought it to her, stooping, gathering it around her.

Then *he* went into the bathroom and closed the door.

Barely moving, barely breathing, Ashley stared into the flames. Damn these little gestures of his! He wasn't supposed to be this way. He was a crook—a bank robber, an escaped fugitive, a hardened criminal. He had forced his way in here with a gun, scaring her senseless, and had made her his prisoner. He cared about nothing but himself—*his* escape, *his* needs, *his* freedom. He didn't give a damn about anyone else, didn't give a damn whom he scared or whom he hurt.

But he didn't want her to be cold. He hadn't wanted her to sleep on the floor, hadn't wanted her to wear wet clothes. He had offered her every assurance possible, had promised that he wouldn't hurt her, had *sworn* that he wouldn't hurt her. He wasn't supposed to be that way, not if he was everything people said he was.

So maybe he wasn't.

Maybe he wasn't such a loser. Maybe he wasn't a hardened criminal. Maybe he wasn't a sociopath, unburdened by conscience or guilt, as Bill Armstrong would have everyone believe.

But he *was* a bank robber, and he *was* holding her hostage. He *was* a wanted man, and she had seen in his eyes last night that he *was* a dangerous man.

But maybe he wasn't dangerous for her. Maybe he saved his ruthlessness for people who threatened him, and she certainly didn't fall into that category. She couldn't hurt him, couldn't do anything that might bring harm to him. She couldn't get to a phone to notify Seth of his location. She couldn't—so far—outsmart him. She couldn't get him recaptured. She was no threat at all, and maybe, because of that, he presented no danger at all.

Her stomach growled, distracting her from her thoughts. On a normal day she would already be eating breakfast by now. Of course, it was too much to hope that Boone might have bothered to fix her a bowl of cereal or a cup of tea while he'd waited for her to give up her refuge in the bathroom. She was lucky he had built a fire. Knowing the toll his injuries had taken on him, she was surprised that he had managed even that task.

On a normal day… This undoubtedly was *not* going to be one of those. On a normal day she got up between six and six-fifteen, built a fire and got dressed. She fixed her tea first and if it was even remotely comfortable outside, she drank it on the porch, sitting in an old hickory rocker, listening to the birds, looking for deer, squirrels and other wildlife that often wandered out of the woods, watching the sunrise and gathering wool as the fog slowly drifted across the valley. Breakfast came next—whole-wheat pancakes with butter and syrup, a frittata heavy with vegetables from her own garden, biscuits floating in a platter of cream gravy or, if she was short on time or just plain lazy, a bowlful of granola with nothing but fresh yogurt for a garnish.

On a normal day she was in the workshop by eight. She followed no set routine there, unless she had an order to fill or an upcoming craft show to attend. She might spend the morning cutting reed for baskets, make eight dozen rose-scented, heart-shaped bars of soap after lunch and blend potpourri, work on her latest quilt, sketch a design for a new shawl to weave, tie together a twig tray or dip candles until quitting time. Lunch was always leftovers from last night's dinner, and dinner was usually something easy—a pot of stew that would yield several days' worth of meals, a meat loaf that could be sliced for sandwiches or frozen and reheated next week or a roast that would be wonderful tonight in thick slices, even better tomorrow in cold sandwiches with spicy mustard and best of all the next day chopped and cooked in gravy with potatoes and carrots.

In the evening on a normal day she would work on her counted cross-stitch samplers, or she would make herself comfortable on the rug while she fashioned the miniature sweetgrass baskets that commanded amazing prices from people familiar with such baskets in the Lowcountry of South Carolina. If her fingers grew tired, she might read or put a tape in the little deck on the night table, and she would fall asleep to music.

Normal days might be gone forever. Even if Boone kept his word, even if he left her physically unhurt, there were other harms that he would be responsible for. She might never again feel safe in her own home. She might need weeks or even months to forget the fear he'd caused. She would probably never again look without suspicion at a stranger who wandered her way.

She would have lost some of her innocence, and after a lifetime in *this* world, she didn't have much of it left to lose.

The bathroom door opened with a creak, and he came out, looking cold, pale and miserable, as if all he wanted was to crawl back into bed and sleep for a week. That was probably the best thing he could do. Sometimes the body needed to simply shut down all nonessential functions in order to handle the injuries dealt it. Twenty-four, thirty-six, forty-eight hours of sleep would do wonders for him, but she wasn't going to suggest it. Whenever he slept, no doubt, she would be handcuffed nearby. She didn't care to spend any more time than absolutely necessary wearing these bracelets.

He knelt beside her, leaning forward to unfasten the cuffs. There was a faint lavender smell about him, from the soap he'd used to wash up. His hair was wet and slicked back, and he had no doubt made use of one of the extra toothbrushes in the medicine chest—she could smell the minty toothpaste when he made a pained exhalation—but he hadn't tried to shave. The heavy stubble that had covered his jaw yesterday was going to soon become a full-fledged beard that gave him a slightly sinister look.

As soon as her hand was free, Ashley slid away from him and got to her feet. "I'm going to fix breakfast," she announced, giving him a chance to stop her before she turned away to the kitchen. She was putting water on the stove to boil when she finally spoke.

"Do you have any aspirin?"

"No, but I have some white willow bark." Without glancing his way, she knew the look he was giving her. Seth gave her those same looks, as did most of her friends, but she'd learned to ignore them. She had come by her faith in alternative treatments legitimately. Her mother, her grandmother and all the women before them had believed in natural remedies. She'd grown up using licorice for sore throats, ginger for upset stomachs and evening primrose oil for PMS, along with a host of other herbal concoctions taken daily as a preventive measure. She couldn't remember the last time in her adult life that she'd been bothered by even anything so minor as a stuffy nose.

After filling a glass with cold water, she took a bottle from the cabinet and carried both to him at the table, where he'd taken a seat. For a moment he didn't move, but finally he extended his hand, palm flat, and accepted the two capsules she shook from the bottle. He didn't take them right away, though. Instead, he looked at them as if he might rather suffer the headache instead of the cure.

She gave an exasperated sigh. "I'm not going to poison you, Mr. Boone. It wouldn't do much for my reputation if I did."

He glanced up at her. "What reputation?"

"Some people on the mountain don't have much faith in

doctors or much money to pay them. They prefer the old ways, the natural ways. I put remedies together for them.''

"You're an herbalist."

"Or a quack, depending on who you ask."

"You 'put' this together." He held up the capsules.

"You buy the capsules, and you can fill them with anything you need. For myself, I generally prefer to take herbs in tea form, whenever possible, but sometimes a capsule is better," she said with a shrug. Before returning to the stove, where the water was starting to steam, she hesitated long enough to speak again. "Besides, if I were going to poison you, I would have done it last night, *before* you got too comfortable in my bed."

Back in the kitchen, she added tea bags to two cups and poured hot water over them, then took a bag of baking mix from the cabinet. She wanted biscuits this morning, she decided, hot and flaky, with apricot preserves and honey and the butter that old Granny Tompkins had churned herself and traded for one of Ashley's egg baskets. Humming to herself, she prepared the mix, rolled it out on the floured counter and was in the process of hunting for her biscuit cutter when, unexpectedly, Boone appeared behind her, grasping her arm tightly.

"What—" Breaking off, she followed his gaze outside. A truck was slipping and sliding its way up her muddy driveway. She didn't need to see the blue light bar on top or the Catlin County Sheriff's Department seal on the door or to hear Boone's savage, almost frantic curse to know who was driving it: Seth.

"Son of a bitch!" Boone dragged her back a few feet from the window. When she looked back to tell him that he was hurting her, to insist that he let go, she saw the reason his grip was hurting so: he held the pistol in the same hand he had wrapped around her, and her tender skin was pinched against it. The sight of it, and the absolutely palpable panic emanating from him, made her heart skip a beat.

"You don't need the gun," she said quickly. "Please, just

put it away. I swear, I'll get rid of him, but you have to promise
not to do anything, *please!*''

"What is he doing here?" he hissed.

She swallowed hard and glanced out the window. The Blazer
was coming over the last small rise. In another moment it
would be parked behind the van, and another moment after
that, Seth would be at the front door—unless she stopped him
first. "It's my ex-husband," she admitted. "I told you he
comes by to check on me."

"Your ex—" Dismay and disbelief made his eyes even
darker. "Sheriff Benedict? Sheriff Benedict is your *ex-
husband?*"

She gave a small nod. "Please... He just wants to let me
know that a prisoner has escaped. He'll want me to move into
town until you're caught. He'll tell me to be extracareful.
That's all, I swear it is. Please just let me talk to him, and I'll
send him away. I won't tell him anything. I won't make him
suspicious. *Please,* Dillon, please let me talk to him."

He looked out the window, then back at her. "If you try to
warn him—"

"I swear to God, I won't."

He glanced out again, then released her. "Go on. But don't
forget—if you can't get rid of him... *I* will."

She took a quick look. Seth was still inside the truck, pulling
on a jacket. It was raining again, she realized numbly, a heavy
mist that seemed to fall in slow motion. Twice she'd looked
outside and hadn't noticed. Then, giving herself a mental shake,
she went to the counter. She carried the mugs to the table,
setting them down, removing the tea bag from one as she slid
her feet into a pair of stretched-out loafers kicked underneath
the table. She was about to turn toward the door when a set of
keys, half-hidden in the folds of a lace runner, caught her attention—*her* keys, dropped there last night when he'd closed
the door and pulled that gun on her.

Seeing that his attention was still on Seth, she slid the keys
into the deep pocket of her skirt, then took her tea to the door,
pausing only long enough to take down a heavy woolen shawl

from its peg and wrap it around her shoulders. With one last look back at Boone, she opened the door and stepped outside, leaving the door open a few inches behind her. "Morning."

Seth came to the top of the steps and stopped, the width of the porch between them. He was wearing his uniform, khaki trousers with a green shirt and a shiny green jacket. His boots were muddy, the uniform was wrinkled, as if it had been slept in, and his face was lined, as if he hadn't slept at all. "Good morning."

"What brings you out on a day like this?"

He drew a pair of black gloves from his pocket and tugged them on, reminding her of just how chilly it was and how poorly dressed—cotton skirt, sweater, shawl, bare legs—she was. "We lost a prisoner yesterday morning. The deputy who was transporting him, Tommy Coughlin, apparently lost control of the car and went into a ravine over near Sadler's Pass. The prisoner then somehow got his gun, shot him and escaped."

Ashley's throat went dry, but her expression didn't change. Had Boone lied to her? Had it happened the way he claimed—an ambush, an accident that was no accident, three attackers who'd shot both men—or was Seth's version correct? She didn't know, and she desperately needed to. "Jeez, I'm sorry, Seth. Is Tom okay?"

"He's in a coma. Besides being shot, he got pretty banged up in the accident. Apparently he suffered some head injuries. I talked to his mother this morning, and she said the doctors are guardedly optimistic—whatever that's worth." He removed his green baseball cap, bearing the county name over an embroidered sheriff's star, and shook the rain out of it, then hung it over the hand-carved wooden pineapple that decorated the railing there. "Anyway, I came to help you pack."

She kept her gaze even and cool. "I'm not going anywhere."

"You've got to get out of here, Ashley. You can't stay up here alone with that criminal on the loose. I won't be home much until Boone's in jail again, so you're welcome to stay there. Just get your stuff, and I'll follow you back into town."

She ignored the part about leaving—as she knew he would expect her to—and focused instead on what he would expect her to find interesting. "So you've caught—or almost caught—Dillon Boone. Bill Armstrong must be delirious with joy. What about the money?"

"It wasn't on him when they arrested him over in Mossville," he said dryly.

"Mossville. That's Sylvan County." She pretended she hadn't already known that that was where Boone had been captured. "Dillon Boone is an extraordinarily unlucky man."

"He's a *desperate* man. That's why you're going to do what I say. Pack whatever you need for the next four or five days and get the hell off this mountain."

She wrapped both hands around the mug to keep them from trembling and lifted it for a hot sip. Feeling only slightly fortified, she lowered it again and gave him a reproving look. "You expect me to drop everything and leave my home on the remote chance that some convict might come by here? You know me better than that, Seth. There's nothing here that Boone could possibly want—no telephone, no weapons, no money. Only poor Bessie. Besides, Sadler's Pass is miles from here. What are the chances that he could make it this far without getting caught?"

"It's only five miles over the mountain."

"*Only* five miles over the mountain?" she repeated, exaggerating the words and rolling her eyes. "What are the chances that he could even find his way here? You and I grew up in these mountains, and we still get lost from time to time. Boone's an outsider. A flatlander. He's from Georgia, for God's sake. He's a city boy." After another sip of tea, she grew serious. "What are the chances he could even survive the weather last night? He must have been hurt, bouncing around in Tom's car when it went into the ravine. Hell, coming from the Sylvan County Jail, he was probably hurt *before* the car went into the ravine. I don't know if you had it any better in town, but up here it was pretty darned cold last night, and the rain didn't stop till morning. You know how quickly exposure can kill a man.''

Seth's expression turned grim. ''We're considering that possibility, but until we find him—or his body—we have to assume that he's still out there. The first thing he'll want is shelter, then transportation.'' He gave the van a derisive look. ''I'm not sure even Boone is desperate enough or crazy enough to believe Bessie qualifies. Not that transportation will do him any good. The county is pretty much sealed off. The highway patrol has roadblocks on the only roads in and out.''

''Seems like a lot of effort for a bank robber.''

''A bank robber who shot a cop,'' he corrected her. ''A bank robber who nearly *killed* a cop.''

She leaned her shoulder against the doorframe, feeling the rough wood prick at her shawl. If Boone *had* lied, if he had shot and almost killed a good man like Tom Coughlin, then she was a fool to protect him—even if protecting him also meant protecting Seth. But he'd told a different story—*We were ambushed.... There was a van and three men.... They opened fire....*—and he'd told it convincingly. Last night she had believed him. This morning—this morning she thought she still believed him.

What was Seth's explanation for Tom losing control of his car? she wondered without asking. Tom was a good driver, never reckless, certainly not with Catlin County's Most Wanted in his back seat. Yes, it had been raining, but not hard; it hadn't started to come down hard until after lunch. Yes, the road might have been a little slick, but like her and Seth, Tom had grown up in Catlin. He'd logged tens of thousands of miles on the county roads. He would have been prepared for that.

Also Seth apparently thought Boone had taken the gun and shot Tom after the accident. *Why?* If the deputy had suffered serious head injuries in the wreck, there was no reason for his prisoner to shoot him. He could have simply walked away. And Seth's assumptions left no room for one other small detail that she knew and he didn't: Boone's own gunshot wound. If he'd stolen the gun from Tom and shot him, then *who* had shot Boone?

There was a van and three men....

"I really am sorry about Tom," she said. "I hope he's all right. But I can't run away every time something happens in the county, Seth. This is my home. This is where I belong. I can't be afraid of everything, or I won't be able to live here anymore. We've had this discussion often enough, Seth. You understand."

He looked anything but understanding. "This is different, Ashley. We're talking about an escaped fugitive who shot an injured cop! God only knows what he might do to you if you get in his way."

She remembered waking up this morning to a cold cabin and the warm quilt Boone had covered her with. She thought about him taking the time just a short while ago to heat that same quilt and tuck it around her before he went into the bathroom. Those didn't seem like the actions of a man who could cold-bloodedly shoot an already injured man and leave him to die.

She gave Seth an apologetic smile. "Sorry, sweetheart, but I can't go. The gift shop over near the parkway has an order in for more trays, and I've got to get six dozen candles in the mail to South Carolina this week, and there's that market basket I'm making for a certain person's grouchy mother's birthday. I've got too much going on to waste even a minute of time packing or moving into your house or moving back out here."

"Ashley—"

"Seth." She mimicked his strained-patience voice, then smiled.

He stared at her for a long moment, his eyes dark, his entire face dark and handsome and dear. She kept her smile in place by sheer force of will, wishing all the while that he would simply leave, praying that he would leave before Boone's patience ran out or his fear grew unmanageable. Finally, running his fingers through his hair, Seth grudgingly asked, "You'll be careful, won't you?"

"I'll keep the doors locked and the windows barred and my hickory stick at my side."

"I'd prefer that you keep my shotgun at your side." He added hopefully, "It's in the truck, loaded and ready to go."

"I've never handled a gun in my life, Seth, and I don't intend to start today. I'll be careful. I'll stay inside. I'll keep the doors locked. If any escaped prisoners happen along, I'll cower and hide until they've gone on their way."

"Don't joke about it, Ashley," he said sharply. "If anything happened to you—"

"Nothing will. I'm safe here. Dillon Boone, if he makes it this far, will take one look at this place and at Bessie, and he'll keep on going." Reaching out, she gave his hand a squeeze. "*You* be careful, Seth. You're the one who's going off into the mountains in the rain and the cold to track down a desperate fugitive. You're the one who will be out there with a bunch of nervous, trigger-happy cops. Take care of yourself, and don't worry about me. I'll be fine." She was counting on that.

He held her hand and her gaze for a moment, then, releasing her, he turned to look out across the valley. With the low clouds, the mist and the fog, visibility was at a minimum. Tramping around in the forest looking for signs of Boone was going to make for a miserable day, and Ashley felt guilty that she couldn't spare Seth the discomfort. But how could she try to give him any sort of message when the man he was looking for was on the other side of the door at her back and holding a gun? When he was prepared to use that gun?

After a moment Seth faced her again and, changing the subject, tried to lighten up. "That wouldn't be hot coffee you're drinking while I stand here and freeze, would it?"

"When have you ever known me to drink coffee?" she asked chidingly. "This is green tea. I have more inside. Would you like a cup?"

His answer came quickly and was delivered with conviction. "No, thanks."

"Are you sure? It's good for you."

He didn't look convinced.

"I can fix you some ginger tea—it'll warm you up from the inside out. Or chamomile to ease your stress. Or how about some cayenne—"

"How about I wait until I stop by the Parmenters' on the way back down? Nell will have a pot of strong coffee on the stove."

"Strong enough to melt iron," she said with a touch of scorn. "It'll destroy your stomach lining, but suit yourself." She swallowed the last of the tea, then dangled the mug from one finger by its handle. "I appreciate your coming by, Seth."

"But you're not going to reconsider my request."

"Your *request?*" she echoed. "I must have missed that. All I heard was orders."

He put his cap on, pulling it low over his eyes. "Go in and lock up."

"I will."

"Stay inside."

"Absolutely."

"Don't do anything foolish."

Too late, she wanted to reply, but she smiled brightly and gave him the answer he wanted. "I promise I won't."

Coming forward a few steps, he bent to kiss her forehead. "Be careful."

"You, too." Tugging the shawl tighter, she watched him move down the steps and sprint across the saturated ground to the truck. She watched him climb inside, start the engine and back away, and all too soon she watched him drive out of sight. As his taillights disappeared down the hill, she gave a sigh. Seth was safe, for the time being.

But *she* still had to deal with Dillon.

Inside the cabin, Dillon was watching, too, his fingers tightly gripping the pistol, as the sheriff drove away. He didn't breathe a sigh of relief as the Blazer disappeared from sight. Benedict could change his mind and come back, could get to the bottom of the driveway and decide that he would *make* Ashley leave.

She might be stubborn, but acting in his official capacity as sheriff, her ex-husband was probably just as stubborn.

Her ex-husband. Jeez, how bad could his luck get? Of all the women in Catlin County, the one he took as hostage was the sheriff's ex-wife—an ex-wife whom, judging from that exchange on the porch, the man was still quite attached to. He'd just given Benedict reason to make this whole thing personal, and when cases got personal for cops, they could also get deadly.

But this case was already deadly. Russell's men had tried to kill him once; they wouldn't miss on their second chance. Every cop in this part of the state believed he had shot an injured deputy; if they found him, they weren't going to be inclined to exercise much restraint in dealing with him. The fact that Ashley's ex-husband and best friend was the county sheriff was just the icing on a very bad cake. If anything happened to her, Benedict would surely see that the person responsible was punished for it.

And so much for his plans to have Ashley take him outside the area today. They would never get through the roadblocks, and he would prefer not to involve her in his capture. It could get nasty.

He wished he had never met Russell Bradley, wished he'd never heard of Catlin, North Carolina, and had never set foot in the First American Bank. He wished that son of a bitch on the highway had been a better shot, wished that the ravine had been deeper, that his miseries had ended at Sadler's Pass.

He wished like hell that he'd never met Ashley Benedict.

Wondering why she was dawdling so long in the chill weather, he pulled the door open just in time to see her reach the bottom of the steps. Her head was bent against the rain, and her hands were clutching the edges of the shawl together. Her right hand was also clutching something else: keys. He had forgotten about the keys she'd dropped on the table last night. He had seen them this morning, had noticed that there were only two—one to the cabin, presumably, and one to the van—and then he had promptly forgotten them. *Fool.*

Switching the gun to his right hand, he stepped outside, the cold hitting him with a vengeance. The porch, at least, was dry, but only a few strides took him to the steps, icy wet, and into the rain. Looking ahead, he saw that Ashley had reached the van, had climbed inside and was probably trying to still her shaking long enough to get the key into the ignition. He reached the bottom of the steps, and mud, squishy and frigid, closed over his bare feet. He ignored the discomfort, though, the pain and the chill, and made his way, limping and awkward, to the driver's side of the van.

She was trying to start the engine and having no luck. Jerking the door open, he leaned inside, grabbed the keys and threw them as hard as he could into the weeds that separated the house from what had once been tilled fields. Catching hold of her upper arm, he hauled her out and to the ground, fighting to maintain control when she resisted, when she struggled against him. He lost that control when she shoved him hard, both hands banging on his chest, over his ribs, sending bolts of pure agony shooting through him.

Doubling over, he released her and turned away, his knees buckling. Sinking to his knees in the mud, he tried to breathe, but his lungs refused to expand, refused to accept even one particle of oxygen that might increase the pain radiating through him. Oh, God, he'd never known what it was like to hurt so bad, to feel such torture. For a moment he couldn't breathe, couldn't see, couldn't hear anything but a loud rush in his ears; then there was a voice, soft, feminine, frightened.

"Are you all right?"

Rain was dampening his hair, running down his back, and the mud where he knelt had quickly stolen the last of the warmth that had taken him all night to find. The pain was gradually receding, though, the edges dulling, the sick churning in his stomach calming. He was going to survive.

She touched him, her hands cold but infinitely warmer than he was, but he pushed her a few feet back and held her there with the pistol, pointed level at her throat, as he staggered to his feet. She swallowed hard. The fear was in her eyes once again, exactly where he wanted it. "I—I'm sorry," she whispered. "I didn't mean—"

"Move." He gestured toward the cabin, and she started hesitantly in that direction. Together they climbed the steps, then went inside after she'd paused to remove her shoes. He paid no attention to his muddy feet, made no effort to wipe them on the mat outside the door or the rag rug just inside.

When she came to a stop near the table, he nudged her with the barrel of the gun. "Go over to the bed."

There she stopped again and waited silently, not turning to look at him. She couldn't see the handcuffs he'd picked up as they'd passed the table, but he had no doubt she knew what was coming. That was why, when he moved around her, she was so pale, why, when he shoved the nightstand aside and reached for her hand, she was trembling. She opened her mouth, but no words came out on the first try, and by the time she tried again, he already had one half of the cuffs fastened around her wrist.

"Please don't," she whispered. "I had to try. You would have done the same thing. Please…"

The headboard of the bed was wood, solid, and there was no place where the remaining cuff could be secured. Pushing the covers back, though, he found that the metal side rail supporting the mattress and springs on wooden slats was more than adequate. He closed the cuff around it, locked it down tight, then moved to the warmth of the fire and drew a calming breath.

Laying the gun on the mantel, he faced the fire and braced his hands on the rough-hewn wood. Bearing only a small portion of his weight made his arms tremble, and his legs were also unsteady. He hadn't been in great shape before the sheriff's arrival, and that little exertion—down, then up, one short flight of steps, across thirty feet of rain-saturated ground, pulling her out of the van—left him almost too weak to stand. And he'd had hopes of being able to move on today, he thought scornfully.

Behind him there came the scrape of wood on wood, and he

turned his head to see that Ashley had pushed the nightstand farther from the bed and was now sitting on the floor between the two pieces of furniture, her back against the wall, her face dark with anger as she scowled at him. She'd discarded the woolen shawl, tossing it onto the rug. Her skirt was stained with rain, her legs splashed with mud, but he didn't offer her a chance to change clothes. The shawl should have kept her sweater dry, and it was only the bottom few inches of her skirt that had gotten damp. She wasn't going to suffer for wearing it until it dried.

He, on the other hand, felt wet from head to toe, and it was definitely adding to his misery. "Do you have any more of Seth's clothes here?"

The gruffness of his voice made her mouth thin into a narrow white line as she shook her head.

Great. The sweats were wet and caked with mud from the knees down, and his jeans, left in a heap all night, were also still wet. Modesty be damned, he was going to find comfort somehow.

Turning away from the fire, he spread his jeans out to dry, then grabbed the quilt from the sofa, carrying it along with the gun into the bathroom. He didn't bother closing the door; he had learned quickly this morning that the fireplace was the only source of heat for the entire cabin, and he wasn't going to freeze in the name of privacy. Bending over the tub, he turned the water on, waited until it got warm, secured the rubber plug, then stripped off the sweats and carefully lowered himself into the tub.

The first rush of liquid heat sent a muscle-relaxing shudder through him. The water was hot enough to steam, rising up to warm his still-exposed skin, carrying with it a familiar fragrance. Honeysuckle. A bottle on the window ledge was labeled Honeysuckle. There were others alongside it, fanciful glass shapes filled with jewel-toned gels and labeled in flowing script. Tea Rose. Chamomile. Lavender. Vanilla. He reached for the honeysuckle, removed the glass stopper and started to pour a thick stream under the faucet, but stopped before the first drop escaped. Returning it to the ledge, he took down the vanilla and added it to the water instead. It was better, he thought with a scowl, that he smell like a vanilla bean than like Ashley.

Leaning back in the tub, he closed his eyes and was about to settle down so that as much of his body as possible was underwater when a grudging warning came from the outer room. "Don't get your dressing wet."

With a grimace, he resettled so that his shoulder with its white gauze bandage was well above the surface of the water.

"I don't suppose I'm going to be allowed to take a bath this morning."

He didn't suppose so. In fact, he didn't plan on leaving the tub until every last drop of hot water had been sacrificed for his comfort.

"What about fixing breakfast? Or changing your dressing?"

He didn't answer. Eventually, of course, he would have to let her go, but until that moment came, he would find relief in knowing that, for *this* moment, he was safe. He didn't have to worry about her, and he didn't have to be close to her. He didn't have to fear that she might try another escape. He didn't have to breathe in her scent. He didn't have to spend hours only inches away from her. He didn't have to worry about what she might do.

He didn't have to fear what *he* might do.

As the water neared the top of the tub, he leaned forward and shut it off, suppressing a groan of discomfort. He didn't think his ribs were broken, after all. Cracked, maybe, or perhaps he'd just torn some ligaments in the accident. As painful as their little struggle had been outside, he assumed that getting hit the way she'd hit him, directly above a broken bone, would have been even worse.

If her escape attempt had taken him by surprise, that blow she'd dealt him had left him shocked. He had begun to believe that he could trust her, he realized. It didn't take much to sucker him—a few tender touches, a little genuine concern and a pair of innocent blue eyes. She could never shoot anyone, she'd

insisted, and she had passed up more than a few opportunities
to do him harm. She'd had a number of weapons in her hands
last night—the scissors with which she had cut away his shirt,
the logs she'd added to the fire, the knife she'd used to slice
the bread for their dinner. She could have cracked open his
skull with that heavy crock she'd used when she had cleaned
him up, scalded him with hot tea or poisoned him with one of
her herbal concoctions. He had believed that he was safe with
her, that she wouldn't deliberately hurt him.

Once again he'd been wrong.

How many times did he have to get knocked to his knees
before he learned to quit trusting? How many times did he have
to get let down hard? He was a reasonably smart man; he
should be capable of learning from his mistakes. But he just
kept repeating them, and he kept falling harder.

Ashley Benedict could be the hardest fall of all.

Sliding a little lower in the water, he yawned. She had mentioned breakfast a few minutes ago, and it had sounded like a
good idea, but right now all he wanted—all he really needed—
was sleep. As long as he was asleep, he couldn't worry,
couldn't be bothered by the mess he'd gotten himself into. He
couldn't wonder how in God's name things had gone so bad.
He couldn't brood over whether they could ever be set right.
His body could continue the healing processes, and he could
escape to some dreamland where Russell Bradley, Catlin,
prison and Ashley Benedict didn't exist.

Finally he pulled the plug, then stood up, stretching slightly
less sore muscles, drying much warmer skin. When he was
done, he wrapped the quilt around him, returned to the fireplace
and added several logs to the fire, then, in a carefully controlled
move, dropped down on the sofa.

"You need to eat."

He glanced across the room at her. She was probably hungry
herself. Maybe it would do her good to miss a meal. Maybe
she would think twice next time about trying to run off before
she'd eaten.

"You can take these off now." She rattled the cuffs against

the metal rail. "Obviously I'm not going anywhere. I don't have an extra set of keys to Bessie, and, as you heard, she wasn't about to start. Sometimes she gets cranky when it's wet. Seth says it's the distributor cap and I should get it replaced, but I just tend not to drive her when it's raining."

The sofa was old and well-worn. The fabric, an ugly green weave, was threadbare in places, and the cushions were lumpy underneath him. Still, he could easily see why she didn't throw it out. With one of her quilted throw pillows under his head, he was almost as comfortable there as he'd been last night in her bed.

On the floor, she lost her patience with his silence. "Damn it, Boone!"

"Dillon." The fire was burning brightly, filling the cabin with heat and soft yellow-red light, and he was sinking into the drowsy, otherworldly land of sleep, his eyes closing, his breathing evening out, his voice husky and distant. "When you were pleading for Seth's safety, you called me that." He finished in a yawn. "You called me Dillon."

So she had, Ashley silently acknowledged. *Please, Dillon, please let me talk to him.* She hadn't meant to. He was a bank robber, for heaven's sake, who might have shot a wounded deputy, who definitely had barged in here and taken her hostage. His name had slipped out only because she'd been afraid for Seth, not because she'd wanted to be on a first-name basis with him.

She had never heard anyone call him by his first name, she realized. In all the talk she'd heard about him in town right after the robbery, people had called him Boone or Dillon Boone. They had called him thief, liar, lowlife and bastard, but not once had anyone called him simply Dillon. Not Seth, who had liked him, or Bill Armstrong, who had—through the security company—employed him. Not Daphne Meadows at the boarding house, who'd rented a room to him, or Harry Lightfoot at the diner, who had served him dinner every day for weeks, or any of the people at the bank who had worked with and—presumably—liked him. No one had wanted to claim that little intimacy.

She wasn't thrilled with her first name; given a choice, she would have been Rachel or Sarah, Katherine or Anna. Still, she *liked* being called Ashley, not simply Benedict or, worse, Ms. Benedict. She liked the friendliness of first names, the acceptance. She wondered if *he* missed it. If Dillon missed it.

He was asleep now, his face turned away from her, his breathing even and just a little ragged. She hoped that raspy sound was just a variation on a snore and not the first symptom of an oncoming cold or flu. The last thing he needed in the condition he was in—especially with the rib pain—was a coughing-and-sneezing cold.

No, the *last* thing he needed, she admitted with a scarlet face, was getting hit in exactly the spot where he'd displayed such tenderness last night. She hadn't meant to hit him there, hadn't meant to hit him at all. She had only wanted to push him away, to gain a moment's freedom and possibly make her escape. She hadn't wanted to hurt him.

When he had fallen to the ground, the color in his face had disappeared, leaving him a sickly, ghastly gray. For a time, she was sure, he had stopped breathing, and his voice, half curses, half agonized groans, had been raw. She'd had terrible images of serious injuries made worse, of cracked bones fracturing, of broken bones puncturing lungs. She honestly hadn't meant to hurt him.

With a sigh, she pulled a pillow from the bed, slid it behind her back and settled more comfortably. She couldn't blame him for cuffing her here. If she had to be restrained while he slept, she preferred it like this, across the room from him. In some crazy way, she didn't feel as vulnerable, sitting on the floor and handcuffed to the bed, as she did when she was handcuffed to *him.* Over here she felt safer, more comfortable. A little damp, maybe, and definitely hungry, but less at risk.

Less at risk for what? she wondered. He'd had plenty of chances to hurt her or even kill her, and outside she had definitely given him reason, but he hadn't touched her. She hon-

estly believed that she wasn't in physical danger from him.
Maybe from the people looking for him, but not from him.

So why was she afraid?

Maybe because, next to Seth, he was one of the handsomest
men around. Because he was a dangerous man, in ways that
had everything—and nothing—to do with his alleged crimes.
Because his story of being arrested and probably mistreated in
Sylvan County, ambushed at Sadler's Pass, shot in the back
while unarmed and most likely handcuffed, roused her sympathies. Because he had little reason to smile and found kind
words from others difficult to come by. Because he hadn't
asked for a fire when he was cold, food when he was hungry
or dry clothes when his were soaked. Because he had been
ashamed of his actions last night when he'd fastened the hand
cuffs around her wrist. Because he wasn't the lawless, unprin-
cipled, psychopathic criminal he was supposed to be, but an
apparently decent man who'd gotten himself into the sort of
trouble that just might get him killed.

She wished he would wake up, wished she could ask him
why he had robbed the bank in the first place. He'd had a job
that he was apparently pretty good at. Maybe he hadn't made
a lot of money, but a person could live on very little and be
happy; she was proof of that. With his aversion to prison, why
had he stolen so much money that a jury would be more likely
to put him under the jail rather than in it? Had the temptation
just been too great—seeing all that cash, knowing that, with
his inside knowledge, he could simply waltz in, pack it up in
a bag and walk out again?

And what had he done with the money? That was the big
question, the one that would interest everyone in town. Where
had their four hundred and fifty thousand dollars gone? He
didn't look as if he'd spent much of it living the good life. If
the lines on his face and the expression in his eyes were anything to judge by, the last year had been a tough one. He'd
had little comfort and no peace.

He didn't seem to have spent the money on material goods.
His jeans had probably cost less than twenty bucks new and

were long past new; his shirt was a simple white T-shirt, three to a pack for six dollars anywhere; and the tennis shoes drying over near the fireplace were inexpensive, an off brand, and had seen many better days.

Pulling another pillow from the bed, she rested it against the nightstand and laid her head on it. Sometimes life just wasn't fair. Many mornings she had awakened from a restless night's sleep and wished for the opportunity to stay in bed and snooze the morning away, but she'd never allowed herself to do it. When she had made the decision to move out here to the cabin and try to become self-supporting, she had also determined that discipline was the key. If she didn't work, she didn't eat, get paid or pay her creditors. She had to keep fairly regular hours, had to treat her crafting as a regular job and not the hobby it had been for so many years.

Now she had the chance to sleep in and be lazy, and she was wide-awake and handcuffed to the bed frame while an escaped prisoner lay snoring on her couch. Lay *naked* on her couch.

A blush warmed her face as she recalled the instant she had realized that he was going to strip down for his bath without closing the door. The thought had popped into her mind that a proper young woman would close her eyes or look away, followed immediately by the acknowledgment that she just must not be as proper as she'd believed, because she had looked enough to see that he was lean, muscular and the same smooth golden brown shade all over. But then he had stepped into the bathtub and out of sight before she'd seen anything else.

Outside, a gust of wind rattled through the house and drew her attention to the windows. The rain was coming down hard again, the sky dusk dark. Poor Seth and his men, out beating the brush in this weather for someone who was safe and warm by a fire. She wished she could have talked to Seth privately, wished she could have told him to call off his search and his roadblocks. All he needed to do was post a few deputies at the bottom of her driveway and wait a few days, and she would send their quarry to them. It wouldn't have been hard, if Dillon hadn't heard about the roadblocks, to persuade him to take Bessie and leave the county. After all, he desperately wanted out of North Carolina as quickly as possible, and in this terrain, on foot *wasn't* the way to go. She would have offered him Bessie, and knowing that it was his best choice, he would have accepted. He would have left her behind—he had promised he would—and he would have driven down her narrow driveway, and when he cleared the grove of oaks and hickories growing so close that their branches blocked out the sun and scraped Bessie's roof, he would have been in perfect position for another ambush, only this time without the shooting. Angry as Seth was about Tom Coughlin's injuries, he would see to it that no harm came to Dillon.

But she hadn't had a moment's private conversation with Seth, and Dillon had heard about the roadblocks. So what would he do now? Stay for the days, weeks or even months it would take for the urgency of the search to calm? Stay only long enough to regain his strength, then set out once again through the mountains? Either plan was impossible. If Tom Coughlin died from his injuries, the Catlin County Sheriff's Department would *never* let up on their search. Seth would be back, probably in a day or two, just to check on her, and sooner or later the trackers would make their way to her cabin. As for Dillon trying to get out on foot, if the cops didn't get him, exposure and the mountains, combined with his injuries, would.

Maybe she could provide him with a third option. Thanks to Seth and the better part of a lifetime spent in this county, she knew virtually every law-enforcement officer in the area, including those troopers with the highway patrol. If she loaded up her van with baskets, blankets, quilts and boxes that could provide a hiding place to anyone who didn't mind the cramped quarters, she could probably talk her way right through any roadblock using friendship and Seth's name, no questions asked. She could drive Dillon Boone out of Catlin County, out of North Carolina and out of her life.

But she would be helping a fugitive—a dangerous man—escape. Could she live with that?

Better than she could live with *him*, she thought grimly.

Far better than she could live with watching him walk into the mountains to almost certain death.

Chapter 4

The rain was coming down with a vengeance, blowing against the windows, beating a steady cadence on the roof. Dillon lay on his back, propped up by pillows, and gazed out the window. If he hadn't found this cabin yesterday, if he had managed to survive last night, today definitely would have killed him. This rain would have made him so miserable that he would have simply stopped. He would have waited to die or get caught, with little preference for which came first. In his situation, getting caught was as good as dying.

He wondered what time it was and how long he'd been asleep. Through the workshop windows yesterday, he'd seen the big clock on the wall, round, white with sharp black numerals. If Ashley kept one inside, he hadn't seen it anywhere; there wasn't even an alarm on the bedside table. He liked the idea of being able to live without timekeepers, of setting his own pace and answering to no one, of not worrying over hours and minutes, about being late or having enough time. Unfortunately he couldn't imagine many places where such a life was possible. Everything was regimented, with hours to keep and schedules to maintain.

Everything except Ashley's life up here.

From over by the bed came a restless sigh, soft and barely audible but registering instantly. When he'd first awakened, he had sneaked a look at her. She had been sitting exactly where he'd left her, between the bed and the night table, her head tilted to one side, her eyes closed. It had been impossible to tell if she was sleeping or simply resting. He certainly hadn't given her many possibilities for getting comfortable. He could have at least put her on the bed...and then he could have crawled in beside her.

Then neither of them would have gotten any rest.

Now he slowly turned his head until his gaze connected with hers. Her hair was mussed again, her skirt dry once more, her expression telling him nothing about her mood. She simply looked at him as he sat up, gathering the quilt close. "You said something about food," he said after it became apparent that *she* wasn't going to break the silence.

For a time he thought she would continue the mute act, then she gave a sardonic reply. "About six hours ago."

No wonder his stomach felt so empty. But in general he felt better. A few more days of rest like that, and he would be up to taking off again. There was just one little problem: he had nowhere to go and no way to get there.

Sliding to the edge of the sofa, he stood up and retrieved his jeans from the hearth. The denim was stiff, but as dry and warm as if he'd taken them from a dryer. He made a trip to the bathroom, got dressed, then came out and got the handcuff key before approaching her. He was a half-dozen feet away when she straightened, pushing the pillows away, drawing her feet together, anticipating being free again. He stopped and studied her distrustfully. "You aren't going to try something stupid again, are you?"

A blush coloring her cheeks, she glowered at him. "I'm sorry I hit you."

"Uh-huh. I got an apology more sincere than that from one

of the deputies over in Mossville after his fist connected with my eye.''

''If you were in my place, you would have done the same thing.'' She sniffed haughtily. ''You *did* do the same thing.''

Balancing with one hand on the mattress, he crouched in front of her. ''There were people trying to kill your deputy and me. If I wanted to stay alive, I had no choice but to escape.''

Her gaze didn't waver. ''Seth says *you* shot the deputy.''

''Do you believe him? Is that why you ran?''

Clearly she didn't want to answer. She caught her bottom lip between her teeth, looked away, then sighed heavily. Was she afraid her answer would anger him? She needn't worry. He was used to being distrusted. He was accustomed to people thinking the worst of him, expecting the worst from him. Under the circumstances, she was entitled to it.

But her answer, when it finally came, surprised him. ''No,'' she said quietly, looking at him once more. ''I don't believe you shot Tom.''

For just a moment he sat motionless, hearing her words echo in his head, feeling the warm rush of pleasure they brought him. It was an amazing thing, being believed by someone who had no reason to believe him and every reason in the world not to. If there was one little bit of trust inside her, then maybe he could find more; if he could, maybe he could get her help in leaving North Carolina.

The rattle of the handcuff chain against metal brought him out of his thoughts. Moving forward, he leaned close to her and opened the cuff, freeing her. At first she didn't move, didn't even seem to breathe, then she raised her right hand and began an even, steady massage of her left wrist. He watched as her fingertips made slow circles over her skin, pushing with enough pressure to reach deep into the muscles. His stiff joints and strained muscles could use a little of that kind of attention. Hell, *he* could use any kind of attention she had to spare.

''You need a new dressing, and we both could use some food.'' Her voice was cool. The moment of trust was gone, the wariness back. ''If you'll move...''

He stood up and backed away. She stood, too, stiff, stretching before she started toward the kitchen. "Sit at the table," she ordered over her shoulder as she began washing her hands.

He obeyed, pulling out the same chair where he'd sat that morning, settling in. Scents that he recognized but couldn't identify—vanilla, he thought, and spices, maybe cinnamon—came from a basket of potpourri that shared the center of the old table with another basket of dried flowers. Underneath them was a piece of lace, diamond shaped, one point dangling over the center edge of each side. "Is this your work?"

She glanced his way. "Yes."

"The baskets, the flowers or the lace?"

"All of it, including the table. I made it from an old shed that Seth and I tore down."

He fingered the lace, pretty, delicate, the color of old, old ivory. "There was a lot of lace in the house where I grew up—curtains, tablecloths, doilies, sachets."

Bringing the basket of first-aid supplies, she sat down in the chair on his right. "Your mother liked lace?"

He shook his head. "My grandmother did, or so I was told. She died before I was born."

"You lived with your grandfather?"

"Until I was eleven. Until my mother didn't have much choice but to move us to Atlanta." He felt rather than saw the curious look she gave him, but he didn't explain. Telling her what his childhood had been like—the looks, the whispers, the gossip, the hostility, the fights—would earn him nothing but her pity, and he'd had enough pity back there in Waterston, Georgia, to last a lifetime. "You grew up around here?"

She paused in removing items from the basket to glance around the cabin. "In town. This was *my* grandparents' place. My grandfather farmed those fields out front, and my grandmother cooked, cleaned, quilted and sewed, raised five kids and buried three babies and worked alongside him when he needed the help. He died just before I got married, and she died eight months later. She had always said she couldn't get along without him. I'd never guessed how much she meant it." Scooting her chair closer, she leaned forward and loosened the tape that held the bandage to his shoulder. It pulled on the tender skin, making him wince. "Is your grandfather still alive?"

He realized he was holding his breath and blew it out. "No. He's dead, too." After a moment he grimly admitted, "If he had still been living, this last year would have killed him."

"I imagine he had higher hopes for you."

"He was a farmer, too. He worked hard all his life and never had much of anything. He wanted better for my mother. When she let him down, he was hoping for better from me." And he'd let the old man down, too, in ways far worse than his mother had ever managed. As much as he missed his grandfather, sometimes he was glad he was dead. It truly would have broken Jacob Boone's heart to see all that Dillon had accomplished, to see what his only grandson had become.

"It looks good."

He glanced at her, then followed her gaze to his shoulder. She had the dressing off now and was using some cool, tinted liquid to clean the wound. It didn't look good to him; it was raw, red, hot and tender. About the best he could say was that it was no longer oozing blood. But he was no expert. What he knew about medicine began and ended with Band-Aids and iodine. *She* was the herbalist. The healer.

And he sorely needed healing.

"So you grew up in Catlin and moved to Raleigh," he said, seeking—needing—a change of subject. "Why?"

His question was followed by a moment of silence. He suspected that she didn't want to answer, that she didn't want him to know anything about her, that she certainly didn't want to know anything more about him. Then the moment passed and, with a hint of resignation, she replied. "I wanted to do something with my life, to live someplace else and meet interesting people and do exciting things."

"What went wrong?" At the questioning look she gave him, he shrugged. "You're living in your grandmother's cabin on top of a mountain only miles from the town you'd wanted to leave, without a telephone or neighbors, and supporting yourself weaving baskets and making lace. That's about as far from interesting people and exciting things as you can get.''

Opening a jar of salve, she used a narrow wooden spoon to scoop some onto a pad of gauze. She laid it over his shoulder, then used two long strips of tape to secure it. ''I make the lace only for myself. It's not cost efficient to sell.''

She was entitled to avoid answering his question. Nothing in her past was any of his business. Nothing in her *life* except for these few days together was any of his business. But he wanted to know all the same, and so he pressed on. ''Was it the divorce? Is that why you hid away up here?''

She picked up yet another jar and twisted the lid off. ''I'm not hiding,'' she corrected. ''I live up here because this life-style suits me. I was young and foolish when I thought I wanted something else.'' After a moment she set the jar aside and leaned back. ''The Catlin County sheriff's job came open about the same time Seth and I divorced. He was with the Raleigh Police Department at the time, but he wanted to come back home, so he applied for and got the job. I stayed in Raleigh, kept my job as a teacher and tried not to feel so out of place. I had plenty of friends there, but I was lonely. My grandparents were dead, my parents and sisters had moved to California after I got married, my marriage had ended and my best friend had moved back to Catlin.''

Best friend. He could buy that description of her ex-husband. He hadn't seen Benedict while he and Ashley talked, but he'd heard all the words and the intimate little silences. He'd heard the concern in the sheriff's voice. He'd seen the fear in Ashley's eyes when she had pleaded with him to let her send Seth on his way. There was no shortage of love and caring between the two.

So why had their marriage failed?

''It wasn't the happiest time of my life,'' she went on, ''but I was making it. Then one day I went to school, and a fourth-grader in the class across the hall got angry with the teacher and pulled a gun on her. A *fourth-grader.* He wasn't even ten years old, and he was threatening his teacher with a gun. I decided that same day that I was giving notice and coming home to live in Granny's cabin."

Where she could be threatened by a man with a gun, Dillon acknowledged guiltily. Given a choice, she would probably prefer the fourth-grader...but she was safer with the man. *He* wouldn't hurt her. "How long ago was that?"

"Three years."

"Any regrets?"

She shook her head.

"Not even about the divorce?"

With a sweet smile that he wished was meant for him, she picked up the jar again. "I love Seth. I always have. But we weren't meant to be married—at least, not to each other."

It seemed that *he* wasn't meant to be married, period. He had never been against the idea. Most people he knew—his mother excepted—were married, or had been, and he'd always thought it would be nice to have that sort of relationship, that sort of commitment to someone else. But he'd never met the right woman, and then his life had gone sour, and any possibility of settling down had gone right out the window. If he got caught by the sheriff, he would spend the next twenty-five years in prison. If he got away, he would spend the rest of his life on the run, and if he got caught by Russell's men...he would be dead. What woman in her right mind would settle for a future like that?

"Where do your ribs hurt?"

He looked at the jar and the hands that held it. Small hands, fine boned, with long, slender fingers. For all their delicate look, they were strong; they had to be to manage all the work she did to support herself. Although marked with calluses, small cuts and faint scars, a legacy of all that work, they were soft. Gentle. Soothing. Arousing.

He didn't want them touching him any more than was necessary.

But after a lifetime of living alone, if he gave it a moment's effort, he could convince himself that even the slightest touch was necessary.

When he didn't answer, she brought one of those small, delicate hands to his chest, probing until her lightest touch made him wince. Marking the place, with the other hand she scooped up a dollop of cream and began rubbing it into his skin with the same easy, sure movements she'd used a short while ago to massage her own wrist. He wanted to believe that it was the coolness of the cream that made him shiver, that it was the discomfort her fingers were causing that made his breath catch, but he knew neither was the case. It was Ashley, touching him in a way he hadn't been touched in months. In years. In his lifetime.

"This is comfrey," she said, her voice soft, her tone conversational. "It's been used for centuries to treat wounds and skin irritations, to reduce inflammation, to heal damaged ligaments and tendons and to help heal the tissue damage caused by bone injuries."

"Where did you learn about all this stuff?" he asked, pretending he didn't notice that she was so close, that he couldn't smell the honeysuckle that lingered on her skin, pretending that there was nothing intimate about her touch, that his muscles weren't tensing, that his hands weren't shaky.

"From my mother and some of the other women in the area." She dipped into the jar again, bringing out more salve. "Mostly from my granny. She knew every plant that grew in the mountains and all its uses. She knew as much as any doctor."

He cleared his throat; his voice had gotten a little husky. "Did she teach your sisters, too?"

She shook her head, and a strand of soft blond hair fell to brush his arm. "Deborah and Gail weren't interested. Just me." She continued to massage the salve in, her fingers moving in slow circles, starting small, then widening. Did she notice, he wondered, that her attempt to provide comfort was making him *un*comfortable? Did she feel the change in his skin temperature, from cool to warm and well on the way to hot? Did she hear the change in his breathing, shallow as before but unsteady now? Did she see that his muscles had gone taut or feel the trembling that rippled through him?

Closing his eyes tightly, he tried to concentrate on the slight jarring pain every time her fingers passed over a particular point above his ribs, but that little bit of pain was nothing compared to the pleasure. The need. The hunger. It had been so long since anyone had touched him without causing pain, so long since a woman had touched him....

Abruptly he opened his eyes and clumsily brushed her hand away. His body hard, his face hot, his voice shaky, he said, "I'm kind of hungry. What about lunch?"

If she noticed anything brusque about his manner, she didn't show it. She simply drew back, screwed the lid on the jar, wiped her hands on a gauze pad and got to her feet. "I'll get it now," she said, gathering her supplies together in the basket again, then walking away. She was calm, collected and completely unaware—or uncaring?—of the effect she'd had on him. Worse, she was completely unaffected herself. *He* might be dealing with an incredible desire for *her,* but *she* didn't feel a thing for *him.*

Damn her.

Damn them both.

Making bread was one of Ashley's favorite tasks. It supplied her with food and—in the spring, when she sold fresh-baked loaves at the Hatfields' vegetable stand on the edge of town—money. It filled the cabin with its warm, rich, homey scent and reminded her of childhood days whose innocence and goodness she would like to recapture, when she had stood on a three-legged stool right at this counter and learned to measure, stir and knead from her granny.

It also provided her with a few minutes of hard work, kneading and manipulating the stiff dough, that were guaranteed to ease any tension affecting her. She needed that release now.

She hadn't meant to become so absorbed in tending to Dillon's injuries. She hadn't meant to lose her perspective, to forget the situation they were in, to forget that theirs was no normal association—that at best they were patient and practitioner, at worst captor and hostage. She hadn't meant to let the professional task of providing medical treatment somehow slide into pure personal pleasure.

She certainly hadn't meant to arouse him…or herself.

It didn't mean anything, she silently insisted as she began gathering ingredients on the counter. It was just that she'd been alone too long. Since the divorce, she'd made only one effort to revive her all-but-absent social life, and that relationship had died a natural death a few short months later. She was too young to live so all alone, her mother kept warning her. When she found herself attracted to a man like Dillon Boone—a man who had taken her prisoner, a man with a disreputable past, a man with no future—no doubt, her mother was right. She needed people in her life, needed friends and a lover.

She *didn't* need Dillon.

Even if he was the only person available.

With a deep, cleansing sigh, she forced her attention to the ritual of bread making. She measured each ingredient precisely, then ran the water in the sink until it was exactly the right temperature. She oiled the loaf pans, only two this time, and the big pottery bowl the dough would rise in. Next she returned the flour and sugar canisters to their place in the corner, put the milk back in the refrigerator and the shortening, yeast and salt back in the cabinet. While the yeast softened in warm water and the milk heated on the stove, she put a pot of water on for tea—also part of the ritual—then sorted through the various herbal varieties stored in Mason jars in the cabinet. Already feeling the slightest bit more relaxed, she took two bags from one jar and placed one in each of the two mugs on the counter.

"Isn't it easier to buy bread from the store?"

At the sound of his voice, the muscles in her neck tightened again. They hadn't spoken through lunch. He'd eaten two bowls of stew and thick slices of bread spread with the strawberry preserves she'd put up last summer, and he hadn't looked at her or talked to her or even seemed to notice that she was there. But now he was talking to her. Now he was looking at her. She felt his gaze.

"The nearest store is fifteen miles away," she commented, her tone chiding. "It's raining, so Bessie doesn't want to run, and even if she wanted to, someone threw my one and only key into the weeds, where it will probably get buried so deep in the mud that I'll never find it again."

From the corner of her eye, she caught the beginnings of a flush as it crossed his cheeks. Was that a little regret for his actions this morning? Had he realized too late that if *she* couldn't drive away in the van without the keys, then neither could *he?* Would he be out there in the weeds when the rain stopped, searching for the keys? Maybe he would simply hotwire Bessie. He was a criminal; surely he knew how to do that.

If he didn't, once the rain stopped and Bessie's distributor cap dried out, maybe she would show him how.

Turning back to the stove, she checked the milk, found it ready and stirred it together with the sugar, salt and shortening. The recipe she used was her great-grandmother's, passed down through the generations. Like the herbs—and the quilting, the weaving, the needlework—her sisters had displayed little interest in baking. They shared Dillon's opinion that it was easier to simply buy. Someday she hoped to have a daughter to share all her knowledge with. Otherwise, when she was gone, her grandmother would be finally gone, too.

While the milk mixture cooled, she removed the kettle from the burner and filled the mugs with steaming water. She thought about leaving his there on the counter, where he could get it or not, and taking hers over to curl up on the sofa and enjoy the fire. But when she moved from the counter, it wasn't toward the fireplace with only one cup. She carried them both to the table, sat down in the chair opposite him and returned to the conversation. "'Easier' isn't always better, you know. Some things are worth the extra effort, and bread is definitely one of them." She drew a deep breath, savoring the aromas of the steeping tea: roasted grains, carob, chicory and spices.

"Wouldn't it have been easier for you if you'd learned to live within your income instead of breaking into the bank?"

For a long time he simply looked at her, his eyes unreadable. Then he shrugged. "Breaking into the bank had nothing to do with money."

"Then what *did* it have to do with?"

"Proving a point. Learning a lesson."

"Proving to whom? Learning from whom?"

Again he looked at her without speaking; again he shrugged. "It doesn't matter."

Oh, but it did. It mattered to Seth and to Bill Armstrong. It mattered to the company Dillon had worked for in Asheville and to every single person who'd had money in the First American Bank. It mattered to the district attorney, and it especially mattered to the government, which had made good on every depositor's funds.

It mattered to her, too. She wanted to hear that he wasn't guilty, that he hadn't done anything wrong, that it all had been a terrible mistake. She wanted to think that he was running and hiding to avoid a miscarriage of justice and not simply to avoid paying for his crimes. She would like to think that he was a better man than that. She wanted to believe that she was attracted to a better man than that.

Even though the evidence indicated that he wasn't.

Picking up one cup, she used a spoon to remove the tea bag. After sliding the cup to Dillon, she removed the bag from the second, stirred in a squirt of honey, then took a sip. "Did you learn the lesson?"

His smile was humorless. "I certainly did."

"What was it?"

"Never trust anyone."

She studied his face for a moment and saw that, yes, he had indeed learned the lesson well. There was nothing even remotely resembling trust in his expression, nothing that came close in his eyes. Looking away to hide the sadness that knowledge brought, she quietly commented, "That's no way to live."

"No," he quietly disagreed. "In prison is no way to live. Dead in a ravine is no way to live."

"Neither is on the run," she argued. "Why don't you turn yourself in?"

"I can't do that."

"They're going to catch you. You heard Seth say that the roads out of the county are all blocked. There are people out there searching for you now. Sooner or later they'll pick up your trail, and they'll follow you here."

"Maybe not. Maybe the rain will wash away enough to throw them off."

That wasn't likely to happen. She knew it, and she suspected that he did, too. Even if the signs were all washed away, rather than give up, the search parties would simply forget about picking up and following his trail and would instead focus on canvassing the entire area. They would make their way to every house in the mountains, would ask questions and look around. They would make their way *here*. "If you turn yourself in and get a good lawyer—"

He interrupted her. "And how would I pay for a good lawyer?"

She met his gaze evenly. "With the money you stole."

"When I got arrested, I still had most of the money from my last job—about two hundred and eighty bucks. I don't know where it is now. I assume the Sylvan County sheriff turned it over to your deputy and your sheriff has it, but it's all I have in the world."

"What about the four hundred and fifty thousand dollars you took?"

His grin was cynical. "I've never even seen four hundred and fifty thousand dollars, and I never will."

She toyed with her cup. Not once had he actually admitted that he'd robbed the bank—but not once had she actually asked. Nobody that she knew of had asked. He had been so easy to blame. He'd been a stranger in town, and he had helped install the very alarm system that had been bypassed in the break-in. He knew the system, the bank, the operations. He had known that the money would be there, had known how to get in and out. His fingerprints had been found inside the bank, in places where he'd worked and they were expected, and in places where they shouldn't have been. Blueprints and notes detailing how to circumvent the security system had been found in his room over at Daphne Meadows's boarding house. He'd been in trouble with the law before—although a long time ago, his boss had offered in his defense. He had even talked to his co-workers at the security company about how easy such a robbery would be.

No, there had been no reason to ask him if he was guilty. But she asked anyway. "Did you break into the bank?"

He didn't look away, didn't avoid her gaze, didn't back down from his guilt. "Yes," he said grimly, "I did."

"And you stole the money."

"I took *some* money. Not four hundred and fifty thousand dollars."

"Then what happened to it?" The money had been there in the vault when the bank closed for business that afternoon, and it was gone late that night when, after the robbery had been reported, Armstrong opened up the bank for Seth's investigation. It hadn't magically disappeared. *Someone* had taken it, and since Dillon had admitted to the break-in, to stealing *some* money, it seemed most likely that he had taken it all.

His expression made it clear that he knew the conclusion she had reached. Skeptical, mocking, sardonic, he shook his head. "Honey, you wouldn't believe me if I told you."

"Try me."

With a gesture toward the counter, he said, "Your milk's getting cold. You're supposed to add the flour while it's still warm." At her look, he raised one eyebrow. "My mother used to bake bread."

Because he was right, Ashley returned to the kitchen. She stirred the flour into the milk, adding extra to make up for the day's humidity. "So what are your plans?"

"Beyond staying alive, I don't have any. I don't know how

I'm going to get out of here, don't know where I'll go or how I'll get there or how I'll live when I get there.''

"Didn't you plan ahead? Didn't you think to put some of the money aside? Didn't you realize you would need a way to survive?''

There was the scrape of wood on wood, then he came into the kitchen, moving with care, his right arm bent and immobile against his chest. He rinsed his empty cup, set it in the sink, then leaned back against the counter to watch her. ''There wasn't any money to put aside.'' His voice was strained. ''I only took five thousand dollars, and I left that—''

She turned the dough out on the floured counter as she waited for him to continue. When he didn't, she began the job of kneading and considered the possibilities. He hadn't left any money at the bank; Seth would have found it there. He hadn't left any in his room, either. In fact, Seth didn't believe he'd even gone back to his room; if he had, surely he would have taken the blueprints and the notes detailing how he'd intended to accomplish the robbery—the strongest evidence, along with his fingerprints, against him. The authorities in Asheville didn't believe that he'd gone back to his apartment there. The manager hadn't seen him, and the girlfriend upstairs claimed—quite believably, Seth had thought—that she hadn't, either. Everything there had appeared untouched. His belongings had still been scattered about when they'd searched it; his clothes were still in the closet, and a few personal items—photographs, she recalled—had been left behind.

So where might he have left the money? Perhaps with an accomplice? There had been no evidence that anyone else was involved, but that didn't make it true. Maybe he'd had a partner, and he'd given the money to this person whom the police didn't know existed to hold until the heat was off. Maybe they'd had plans to meet up somewhere and split the take, but this person had never shown. After all, why should he—or she? He or she had nearly half a million dollars that Dillon was receiving all the blame for stealing. No one would ever connect him or her to the robbery.

Or maybe it hadn't been an accomplice but simply a woman whom he'd trusted. Maybe he'd thought her affection for him would outweigh the temptation of a half-million dollars.

Then she looked at him and reconsidered that last theory. She couldn't imagine him trusting *anyone*. But hadn't he said that to never trust anyone was the lesson he'd learned?

"Where did you go when you left here?"

"Back to Georgia. I stayed in Atlanta awhile, then did some traveling—Georgia, Mississippi, Tennessee."

"How did you support yourself without the bank's money?"

"The old-fashioned way. I worked."

She felt the skepticism cross her face. "You just applied for a job and got hired and worked like anyone else, and the police never caught you? Why didn't they check with Social Security, find out where you were employed and arrest you?"

His sigh started out heavy and impatient, but with a wince at the movement, it ended hushed. "No, I didn't just walk into a place and apply for a job. I worked the kind of jobs where you get paid in cash and no one worries about taxes, withholding forms or things like that."

He was talking about day-labor sort of work, drudge jobs where a man worked very hard for very little pay. It was a tough way to earn a living. She couldn't imagine anyone who had any other choices at all choosing to live that way. But surely it beat going to prison, which was all he'd been facing.

Giving the dough one last turn, she formed it into a ball, placed it in the oiled bowl and coated it, then washed her hands. She dried them, then carried the bowl to the hearth, set it a fair distance from the fire and covered it with a towel. Next she took a piece of fabric from the tall lidded basket that sat in one corner, got pinking shears and a safety pin from her sewing kit and laid everything out on the clean counter next to the stove.

"What is that for?"

"A sling. You shouldn't be using your right arm."

"I'm not using it."

"You're moving it a little, even if you don't mean to. A sling will more or less immobilize it and your shoulder, and it'll help your shoulder to heal more quickly.'' She measured out a piece of cotton, about forty-five inches square, cut it, folded it on the diagonal, then approached him. He watched her warily—no more so, she suspected, than she was looking at him. She wished he could fashion the sling for himself. It was possible, of course, with a lot of trial and error, tying, trying on, adjusting, retying. It was also silly to even suggest.

She slid one short side underneath his bent arm, then brought the ends up around his neck. It wasn't possible to reach high enough to tie them, though, without asking him to sit down…or getting very close.

For reasons she couldn't begin to understand, she chose to get close.

She took one step, then one more, until the only way she was going to get any closer to him was in his embrace. Her feet were between his, her thighs only a millimeter from his. She swore she could feel the heat radiating from his body…or was that her own warmth? She certainly had gotten hot in the past few seconds.

Rising onto her toes brought her a fraction nearer. She could smell the vanilla bath gel he'd used this morning, could feel his breath on her forehead, could hear each measured intake and each slow breath out. She could feel his skin—warm, smooth, her fingers lingering over each small touch.

This was ridiculous, she scolded herself as she fumbled with the cloth. She had nursed other men and had done far more intimate things with two of them. Heavens, she'd been nursing *this* man for nearly twenty-four hours now. Touching him now was no different than touching him all those other times had been.

Oh, but it was. This time he was standing up, looking strong, vital, virile. He wasn't lying in bed, so miserable that he might rather be dead, or sitting in a chair, pale with pain. He wasn't so weak that he couldn't remove his own shoes, so cold that he couldn't stop shivering, so tired that he could barely hold his head up. This time she wasn't seeing him as just a patient, an unwanted visitor, a criminal to be feared. This time she wasn't afraid—although she had no doubt that, if he wanted her fear, he could easily provoke it.

This time was definitely different.

She tied the two corners into a neat, square knot, adjusted it on the side that wasn't injured, then began gathering the excess fabric over his elbow, folding, tucking, securing it with the safety pin. When she finished, she took a step back, smoothed a wrinkle from the cotton and cleared her throat. "Is that comfortable?"

Still looking uneasy, he nodded.

For his peace of mind, as well as her own, she moved farther away, busying herself with cleaning the counter. She imagined she heard a sigh of relief as the distance between them increased, but she couldn't say whether it came from him...or her.

She'd had plenty to worry about in the past twenty-two hours—whether he might mistreat her, force her to flee with him or maybe even kill her. Those concerns, it appeared, had been groundless. He'd promised he wouldn't hurt her, had promised he would leave her behind when he left, and she believed him. But now she had another worry, one that could potentially be as big a threat to her well-being as any of those others.

God help her, what if she was falling for Dillon Boone?

Moving each log with care, Dillon stoked the fire, then rested his good arm on the mantel, leaned his head on it and closed his eyes. He was tired and expecting a better night's rest than he'd gotten last night. He didn't know if it was the comfrey that Ashley had used or the natural healing process—or if he was gullible enough that simply being told that the herb would help had made him believe it as fact—but his ribs weren't quite so tender this evening. He could even manage an occasional deeper breath without feeling as if he might pass out from the pain.

"Are you ready for bed?"

Ashley's voice came from the chair behind him. She'd been

curled up there since dinner, a wooden frame holding a piece of needlework in her lap. He had lain on the couch most of the evening and watched her work, lit by the harsh yellow light of the lamp on one side and the softer golden glow of the fire on the other. That was all he'd done for the better part of two hours, just watched her, and he had enjoyed it in ways he'd never imagined.

It had been such a homey scene, one that would have appeared so normal to someone looking in: the well-lit room, the blazing fire, the freshly baked bread on the counter, the man stretched out on the couch, the woman bent over a cross-stitch sampler a few feet away. The only things missing were the kids at play and the dog curled up on the rug. And the conversation. The connection. The caring. The intimacy.

He'd never had many normal, homey scenes in his life. The closest he'd come had been in his grandfather's house, where they'd had the woman, the kid, the dog, but the man—the father—had been missing. As much as Dillon had loved his grandfather, Jacob hadn't quite taken the place of the father he'd never had.

Even though that father was one hateful son of a bitch.

"Yeah," he said at last in response to her question. "Do you want to change into a nightgown or something?" A flannel nightgown, he hoped, something with a high neck and a hem that dragged on the floor when she walked, something that not even his long-unsatisfied lust could find attractive.

He seriously doubted that such a garment existed.

She was quiet for a moment, then she softly, hesitantly replied, "Yes, I do."

He turned around and watched as she went to the dresser and took a cotton gown from the top drawer, shaking it out. So much for hopes. The gown wasn't flannel, the hem wouldn't come within six inches of the floor once it was on and as for the neck... He couldn't see its line, but he could tell it wasn't anything high and substantial. Damnation. He'd be better off if she slept once again in that skirt and shapeless sweater.

Clearing her throat, she asked, "Do I have to change out here…with you…?"

Sweet damnation, that was all he needed. Not trusting his voice enough to answer, he simply shook his head instead. With a quavery smile brought on by gratitude, she hurried across the room to the bathroom.

Muttering soft curses, Dillon went to the bed. She'd made it that afternoon, folding the covers down invitingly. He sat down on the edge, then leaned forward to reach the handcuff that was still fastened to the frame. He wished like hell he could leave it there, wished he could trust her not to try anything during the night, but he had trusted her this morning and look what it had gotten him. She had almost escaped, and he had suffered for her attempt. He couldn't risk it again.

So what would they do? Pass another night as they had last night, with him in the bed and Ashley handcuffed to him and on the floor? Maybe tonight she would be brave and would choose to share the bed with him. Yeah, right, and then *he* would be the one sacked out on the floor. Last night he could have slept beside her. He had been so cold, so weak, so exhausted from the pain. Tonight… What a difference a day had made.

She came out of the bathroom, wearing the gown. It had no sleeves, a V-neck that dipped too low and was made from a fabric almost sheer enough to see through. God, why hadn't he kept his mouth shut? Why hadn't he left her in wrinkled chambray and heavy knit?

At the couch she scooped up the afghan there and wrapped it around her shoulders. "My robe's in the washer out in the workshop," she said apologetically, uncomfortably. "It has been for days." Her gaze focused on the handcuffs he held, and her mouth thinned as revulsion tempered by resignation slid across her face and flattened her voice. "Where do you want me?"

He almost groaned aloud. *Right here in bed,* he wanted to say. *Underneath me, on top of me, however I can manage it.*

Instead, he forced some steadiness into his voice and asked, "Where do you want to sleep?"

She glanced at the bed where he sat, then at the sofa, then dug her bare toes into the rug she was standing on. "Here."

"You won't be very comfortable." He swallowed hard and made the offer that just might kill him. "You're welcome to half the bed. I won't bother you. I won't touch you."

Without even a second's consideration, she shook her head. She didn't want to be that close to him, he realized bitterly. "Do you have some extra blankets?"

She went to the far end of the room, where a large wooden quilt rack stood in one corner. A moment later she returned with an armload of quilts and started to dump them on the bed. "Not for me," he said, laying his hand on the top one to steady it. "Make a bed for yourself."

After a moment's hesitation, she set the covers on the chair, then began spreading them out, each one folded in half lengthwise, on the braided rug. She laid two aside to cover up with, then brought the last one to the bed. "I won't be able to keep the fire going," she said, her voice subdued. "It may get cold."

She laid the quilt, neat geometric shapes with sharp corners and rounded sides, across the foot of the bed, then returned to the pallet in front of the fireplace. He followed her, standing back as she laid the afghan aside and stretched out. Once she was settled in, the covers snug around her neck, only her left arm remaining uncovered, he knelt beside her and secured the handcuffs, one around her wrist, one around the ball-shaped foot of the sofa. He moved the afghan so she could use it to cover her arm once the room cooled down, then stood up, switched off the lamp on the chair-side table and returned to the bed.

The entire time she never stopped looking at him, her gaze disappointed, faintly accusing.

He removed the sling, sliding his arm free and lifting the cloth over his head, then unfastened his jeans. Getting them off was easier this time, but it was still painful, still slow going. By the time he'd finished and swung his legs underneath the bed covers, he'd broken into a sweat and raised his heart rate substantially. He had made himself weak again...though not so weak that he could sleep right away. He lay back against the pillows, weary but not yet sleepy, and stared up at the ceiling, at the strange swaying shadows there created by the fire's dancing flames.

"Can I have a pillow?"

There were five or six on the bed, most of which he was using, but he took one of the others and started to push the covers back.

"Just throw it, if you can." Her voice was soft in the dimly lit cabin, too feminine to be comfortable, too sweet to be uncomfortable.

Sitting up, he swung the pillow into the air. She caught it, stuck it under her head, then settled in again. She was so quiet that he thought she'd fallen asleep, but when he looked, he saw that she was staring into the fire. Only this morning he'd thought that she wasn't quite pretty, that there was strength, character and generosity clearly defined in her face, but not beauty. But he'd been wrong. In this light—warm, yellow gold—and this pose—thoughtful, subdued, serene—she was very definitely pretty. There was such softness in her face and yet strength, too. Such fragility. Goodness. Hopefulness.

Such faith.

"When the weather has cleared and Bessie will run—" she shifted her glance his way for only a moment "—I can get you out of here."

"How?"

"My crafts are sold at a number of shops in western Carolina and eastern Tennessee. I make deliveries, pick up supplies and go to craft shows on a fairly regular basis. No one in Catlin gives a second look to Bessie loaded to the max with stuff."

Stuff that could provide him with a place to hide. "What about the roadblocks?"

"I know all of the deputies around here and most of the state troopers. They would never dream that I might voluntarily help you escape."

"You think you can talk them out of searching the van?"

"If I make it difficult enough. If I make it appear that there's no room to hide anything. If I fill it with boxes and baskets." She smiled faintly. "If I mention Seth's name often enough."

And what if they did search the van? he wondered, watching a bunch of dried sunflowers sway in the hotter air above. What if she happened to approach a roadblock manned by cops she didn't know, strangers who couldn't care less that she was Sheriff Benedict's ex-wife? What if they wanted him so badly that they refused to overlook the slightest possibility? Not only would *he* get caught, but the circumstances would certainly make them look closely at *her*. The fact that he was armed might be enough to protect her, but there was a chance that it wouldn't, a chance that they might suspect her of collaboration and not forced cooperation.

There was a chance that they might arrest her. Seeing her in handcuffs here was bad enough. Seeing her arrested, chained and taken away and knowing that he was solely responsible... That was too much.

But what choice did he have?

"Where would you go?"

"I don't know."

"Isn't there someone who could help you?"

Once before he had accepted help—from Russell Bradley. He and Russell had lived in the same poor neighborhood in Atlanta, had come from the same background and had faced the same future. They had played together, raised hell together, fought together and grown up together, only somewhere along the way Russell had straightened himself out. He had left Georgia for a hitch in the navy, where he'd learned a few things about electronics. Once he got out, he'd begun working in that field, moving up every few years to a better job while Dillon had simply kept moving on to a different one. By the time they'd met again two years ago, Russell had settled in Asheville and was running his own company and he'd offered Dillon a job.

It had seemed to Dillon at the time that his life had been on one long downhill slide, and he'd seen Russell's job as a chance to stop it, to turn things around, to quit being the failure everyone had always expected him to be and maybe make something of himself. Even though he'd known nothing about alarm systems, he had accepted the offer, moved to Asheville and gone to work installing the alarms and learning the business. Eleven months ago he had discovered the hard way—for him, wasn't it *always* the hard way?—that he'd learned entirely too much about the systems…and not nearly enough about his old friend.

So was there anyone who could help? "No," he said, disliking the flatness in his voice, hearing the disappointment and the utter *aloneness* that formed it, hoping she missed it.

"What about your mother?"

"What about her?"

"Is she still living?"

"I suppose."

"Where?"

"I don't know. Marietta, Smyrna, Conyers—somewhere around Atlanta, I guess."

"When was the last time you saw her?"

He had to give the answer a moment of serious thought. He knew in an instant the last time he had talked to Carole—he had called to tell her that her father had died—but the last time he had actually seen her… "I guess it's been about ten years. I don't really remember."

It took some awkward maneuvering, but she managed to roll onto her side and face him. With the covers pulled high, most of her face was in shadow, but that was all right. He didn't need to see her dismay and censure; he could clearly read them in her voice. "How can you not remember the last time you saw your *mother?*"

"When's the last time you saw *your* mother?" he asked defensively.

"Christmas, three years ago. But it's a matter of logistics that keeps us apart. She lives on the other side of the country, and neither of us has the money to be traveling back and forth.

But she and Daddy are coming to visit this summer, and we write at least two or three times a month, and I call her from Seth's house on all the holidays.''

''Well, my mother and I are different.'' Hostility edged into his voice. Carole had never been an average mother. If she hadn't honestly believed that a baby on the way would force his father to make good on all the promises he'd given her, she wouldn't have chosen to ever *be* a mother. But instead of divorcing his wife, leaving his family and thumbing his nose at everyone in Waterston, Alexander had left Carole. He had denied paternity, had refused support and later had even denied their affair. He had led the entire town in scorning her and her illegitimate brat.

The first job Dillon had ever been given to do—bring his father together permanently with his mother—and he had failed. He smiled bitterly. Jeez, he'd been a failure from the moment of his conception.

''Do you have any brothers or sisters?''

''No.''

''Will your father help you?'' Her voice was softer, more subdued, as if she thought that she'd hit a nerve in talking about his mother. He considered telling her that it didn't matter, that he'd never had a mother in the real sense of the word, that he couldn't miss what he'd never had, but it wasn't true. He'd never had a woman like Ashley, either, but when he left here, he would miss her. He would regret that he had nothing to offer her but trouble, fear, inconvenience and discomfort. He would regret that there was no future for them, and he would especially regret that he wasn't the kind of man a woman like her got involved with.

''My father has never claimed me as his son. He has, however, made a fool of my mother, shamed my grandfather and made my life hell. He always said I would wind up in prison someday. If he knew the trouble I'm in now, he would no doubt subsidize the search and offer a generous reward for my capture, preferably of the dead-or-alive variety and preferably dead.''

Out of the long silence came her voice, softer than ever, sweeter and with enough pity in two little words to make his jaw clench in revulsion. "I'm sorry."

"I'm not." He said it forcefully, so she would understand that, while he wanted many things from her, pity sure wasn't one of them. Then, wanting to bring the conversation to an end, he added in a brusque, strained tone, "It's late. Go to sleep."

There was a soft rustle as she rolled over, her back to him now, a long slender form under a pile of covers. Intending to follow his own advice, he slid down in the bed, seeking a position he could bear for the rest of the night. He'd just found it when she spoke again, little more than a whisper in the still night.

"Good night, Dillon."

He sighed grimly. She had just ensured, with no more than the voicing of his name, that sleep wouldn't come easily tonight.

So much for a good night's rest.

Chapter 5

Ashley had heard of cabin fever, but she had never experienced it. She always had plenty to do and had never, in her three years on the mountaintop, seen weather so bad that she couldn't make the journey between the cabin and the workshop. But this dreary, rainy Thursday morning, she was restless, edgy and fairly certain she would go crazy if she didn't get a breath of fresh air and find *something* to do with her time.

The only problem was the work that needed doing was out in the workshop. Somehow she didn't think Dillon was going to let her go out there alone, not even just to get a few projects and bring them back. She could ask that they both spend the morning over there, but it wasn't the most comfortable place for someone recuperating from the injuries he'd suffered. She didn't have even one decent chair in the place—just the tall stool she used when she was working at the table and Granny's old ladder-back chair that was just the right height for the quilt frame and the loom.

She sighed heavily. If she were home alone, on this third day of rain and fog, she would forget about work, put on her heaviest sweater, add her yellow slicker, gloves and rubber boots and go for a hike. Seth hated when she did that. What if she fell? he argued. What if she got hurt and couldn't make it back home? How slim were the chances that anyone would find her—or even miss her—before exposure took its toll?

Still, she'd been tramping around the hills in all kinds of weather ever since she was a little girl, and she loved them best in the rain. She had seen the peaks wreathed in frothy, cottony fog, had seen the trees and hillsides drenched and washed clean, had smelled the rich, refreshing scent of rain and lush earth. She had watched the thin rays of gold pierce the clouds as the sun broke through and had seen, heard, even *felt*, thunderclouds rumbling in. Not even for Seth would she give up those vistas, those smells and feelings, for the dry, warm safety of her cabin.

But if Dillon wouldn't trust her alone in the workshop, he certainly wouldn't trust her to come back from a hike into the woods.

"What is it you're so anxious to do?"

She turned from the window to find his attention on her. He had been quiet most of the morning. Moody. She disliked moodiness in herself and had learned in the last months of their marriage to dread it in Seth. His moods had usually led to arguments that had left her feeling abandoned and utterly alone.

As Dillon was.

She knew he'd misinterpreted her apology last night. She hadn't meant anything by it. She had simply meant to say that she was genuinely sorry that he wasn't close to his mother and had never gotten along with his father. She certainly hadn't meant to make him feel pitied.

She couldn't imagine not being close to her parents. Even though they lived on the California coast, they were—and always had been—the anchors in her life. They, along with her grandparents, had taught her everything important she needed to know. They had shaped her into the woman she was today.

Dillon's parents, she supposed, had shaped him into the man he was: a bank robber, an escaped criminal, facing a lifetime in prison if he was caught, a lifetime of fear and uncertainty if he managed to flee. Surely some of the blame for that lay on a mother who lost touch with her only child, on a father who always told that child that one day he would end up in prison. What great expectations the man had had for his son.

"Ashley?"

She shrugged. "I'm just bored. I'm not used to sitting around doing nothing all day."

"What would you like to do?"

"Go for a walk."

The look he gave her was scornfully dry. "Right."

"Or I could go to the workshop and work for a while."

"Uh-huh." More derision.

"You think I would make a beeline for the nearest neighbor, don't you?"

"Or the nearest search party."

"I wouldn't. If I were going to turn you in, it would be to Seth, no one else."

"Why? So he would get the credit for my apprehension?"

"No. Because he would keep you safe."

He put down the book he'd been reading the better part of the morning and leveled his gaze on her. "Safe from what?" he asked evenly.

"From angry cops who believe you shot an injured deputy." Her gaze was just as level, her voice just as even. "From whoever shot you. From whoever believes that robbing the bank is worth killing for." Those last were his own words, the only explanation he'd offered Tuesday evening for his own gunshot wound. She hadn't pressed him for more that night; he'd been too weakened from exposure and pain, and she had been afraid for her safety. She wasn't afraid now, though, and he was getting stronger, it seemed, with each passing minute. "Who would that be?"

He studied her for a long time before shaking his head slowly from side to side. "You don't need to know that. *No-body* needs to know. Keeping my mouth shut just might keep me alive."

"Or it might mean that if they succeed in killing you, they get away scot-free. But if you tell me…"

"Then they'll kill you right along with me. I don't want to die with your death on my conscience. And, yes," he added sarcastically, "I *do* have a conscience."

She tried to ignore the ominous little shiver the mention of death sent dancing up her spine. "I know. I've seen evidence of it."

"You have, have you?" He almost smiled then. It was a pretty dismal attempt, but the corners of his mouth did lift and his eyes lightened about a dozen shades. Then he seemed to remember that he wasn't supposed to be relaxed or amused or friendly, and his eyes went dark again and his mouth compressed once more into a thin line.

"Well, since you won't let me go to the workshop, I suppose I could spend the rest of the morning shaving you," she said, her voice determinedly lighter.

Giving her an owlish look, he blinked once, then scratched his chin, a habit she'd noticed for the first time this morning, one that seemed to have developed as his beard grew heavier. "Shaving me," he repeated blankly.

"You don't ordinarily wear a beard, do you?"

He shook his head.

"I didn't think so. It makes you look rather sinister, and when you're wanted by the police, the last way you want to look is sinister. I could shave it off for you."

"You and a razor and my throat? I don't think so."

"You don't trust me, do you?" She wondered what it would take to earn his trust. How many promises would she have to make and keep? How many times in how many different ways would she have to prove that she was reliable? How many months and years—if he had months and years to spare— would she have to pass how many tests before he would judge her worthy of his trust?

The answers were too depressing to even guess at.

"It's nothing personal. I told you, I don't trust anyone."

"Because of what happened with the robbery."

He looked at her for a moment, then pointedly opened the book to the page he had marked.

"What did happen, Dillon?" she persisted. "You said you didn't do it for the money but to prove a point. What point, and to whom? The people who tried to kill you?"

"The people who will kill *you* if they think it's to their advantage," he said heatedly. "Drop it, Ashley. You don't need to know more than you already do."

He was wrong. She needed to know a whole lot more. She needed to know *everything*.

And she wasn't even sure why.

What kind of point could a person prove by breaking into a bank? That he could do it. That he was smart enough. That he was capable enough. That he could outwit the security experts and the electronic systems and make it in and out without getting caught. Obviously Dillon *was* smart and capable, and according to Seth, in his time with Bradley Electronics, he had become something of a whiz with the systems. The owner of the company had given him a job as a favor—they were old friends—but all he had expected, again according to Seth, was a day's work for a day's pay. He had never imagined that Dillon would have such a knack for electronics, alarms and codes. In no time at all, he had taught himself everything there was to know about the high-tech security systems Bradley Electronics installed. Including how to disarm them.

To prove a point.

To his boss and old friend?

Watching him closely, wanting—needing—to see every bit of expression that crossed his face, she asked, "Was it Russell Bradley?"

The look he gave her should have killed the last bit of curiosity she could muster. The tautly controlled anger made his eyes darken to almost black, and narrow white lines formed around his mouth. He closed the book, very carefully, very quietly, and leaned forward to lay it on the table, then he looked at her, simply looked. It was like that look two nights ago that had convinced her more thoroughly than anything else could have that he was a dangerous man...but worse.

From somewhere she found the courage to go on, but her voice shook just a bit and her hands, shoved into the hip pockets of her jeans, were curling tightly. "It *was* him, wasn't it? He was the one you were trying to prove a point to. The one who taught you not to trust anyone."

His voice was low, intense, a warning for all its softness. "This is none of your business."

She swallowed. "You said you didn't take the four hundred and fifty thousand dollars. Did he?"

"*I* was the one who was there. *I* was the one whose fingerprints were all over the place."

"And were *you* the one who stole nearly half a million dollars? Did you lie yesterday when you said you didn't?"

His smile was cool, unpleasant. "Funny you should ask, since you didn't believe me when I said I didn't."

Ashley shifted her weight from one foot to the other. He was right. She had reached the conclusion just yesterday that he probably *had* stolen the money, even though he'd denied it. Had she changed her mind so quickly? Had she really come to believe that, while he might be guilty of many things including the break-in at the bank, he was truthful when he said he didn't take the cash?

Or did she simply *want* to believe that because she thought he was handsome, because she was attracted to him, because she felt sorry for his lack of family, because she felt his loneliness?

"If you were set up—"

"I wasn't."

Ignoring his interruption, she went on. "Maybe Seth could help prove it."

"There's nothing to prove."

"Then what happened to the money?"

He looked away. He didn't have a lie prepared for her last question. That was what his previous two responses were: lies, short, simple but none too convincing. He *had* been set up, she believed, by Russell Bradley. There was nothing to make you lose faith in people like being betrayed by an old, good friend.

But if that was the case, who had taken the money? Dillon had made a valid point: *his* fingerprints had been all over the place. Not Russell Bradley's or anyone else's. In fact, there was nothing she was aware of that might point to anyone else. All the evidence led back to Dillon, and only to him.

"You don't know, do you? Or if you do know, you don't want to say."

"It's none of your business," he repeated stiffly.

"If you'd tell the truth, maybe I could help you."

He rose from the couch and approached her, stopping a few feet away. "You? Help?" he repeated, a touch of scorn in his voice. "How? You live in a log cabin at the top of a mountain with nothing but deer for neighbors. Your only form of transportation is a piece-of-junk van that won't even start when it's raining. You don't have any money. You peddle little baskets and candles and stupid twig trays to support yourself. You play with your roots and fruits, you make god-awful tea and you pretend that this is a reasonable, rational way for a woman to live. You don't even have the good sense to protect yourself. How could you help me?"

Biting the inside of her lower lip, Ashley dropped her gaze to the floor. She was used to being considered a little odd. Weird, others said; eccentric, she preferred, or unconventional. Her mother called her a free spirit; Seth's mother called her a hippie. Her friends back in Raleigh thought she was crazy, and even Seth insisted that this was no way to live. But she had never minded the judgments and the names. She had never cared much what others thought, except her family, and as long as they loved her, what did it matter if her father described her to their California friends as his little Bohemian?

But she cared what Dillon thought. She cared that he obviously thought she was foolish. She cared that he found her life-style—and therefore *her*—deserving of mockery and scorn.

Drawing a deep breath, she looked up, though her gaze went no farther than his jaw. "You're right. The only help I can give you is to get you out of here, and I promise, as soon as the rain stops, that's exactly what I'll do.''

She turned to walk away, but suddenly his left arm snaked around her from behind, crossing her shoulders, stopping her short. ''Ashley—''

Stiffness shot through her, making her voice cold and flat. ''Don't touch me.'' After one still moment he let go, and she headed for the door. ''I'm going over to the workshop. You can come, you can stay here or you can go straight to hell. Either way, it doesn't matter to me.''

Expecting him to stop her at any moment, she took her woolen shawl from its peg, wrapped it around her shoulders and opened the door. Her mud-caked loafers were on the porch where she'd left them yesterday morning, cold and damp but comfortable enough for now. She slid her feet into them, walked down the steps, then, when the rain hit her, lifted the shawl over her head and dashed for the workshop stoop. A glance back from beneath its shelter showed the front door still open but no sign of Dillon. She couldn't believe he had let her walk out, couldn't believe she wasn't now sitting on the hard floor beside the bed wearing those handcuffs.

Lifting the latch, she went inside and flipped the lights on. The first order of business was to get a fire going in the pot-bellied stove. The second was finding some interest in working. Yes, just a short while ago, she had been craving something to do, had thought that working sounded like a fine idea, but now all she wanted to do was curl up in front of the fire in one of her ready-for-market quilts. Now all she wanted to do was brood.

Over Dillon.

Sinister.

Dillon studied his image in the bathroom mirror and saw that Ashley had been right. The beard did make him look sinister. Shifty. Unworthy of trust. Maybe it wasn't his usual look, but this morning it seemed an accurate reflection.

Her razor rested on the windowsill between bottles of cham-

omile and lavender bath gel, and a can of shaving cream—
Specially Formulated For A Woman's Skin—was on a trian-
gular shelf in the corner above the tub. He squirted a bit of the
cream into his hand and sniffed it. Specially *scented* for a
woman's skin, too, but it would have to do. Besides, what
could it possibly matter how he smelled? He didn't have a
snowball's chance in hell of getting close to anyone around
here.

Turning the hot water on, he leaned against the sink and
stared out the window at the workshop across the clearing.
Through the big windows the lights gleamed yellow, two lone
bright spots—three, if he counted Ashley—in yet another bleak
day. He'd stood at the kitchen window for nearly an hour,
watching her work. She'd been perched on an unpadded stool
before the tall worktable, assembling the materials for a tray,
putting them together, weaving the thin cord over and underneath the twigs. The work seemed to go quickly, not because
she hurried but because her movements were so sure, so exact.

Stupid twig trays. For the hundredth time in an hour, he
cursed himself. All he'd wanted to do was make her back off
and quit pushing for answers he couldn't give her. He hadn't
meant to be so snide, hadn't meant to insult her work or mock
her choices. And he sure hadn't meant to hurt her.

Or maybe he had. Maybe his subconscious had figured that
the best way to be with her was at a distance. Maybe he'd
thought that if he angered her, he would be safe from her.
Maybe he'd believed that if he hurt her, she would quit caring
what had happened that April night a year ago; Russell would
have no reason to suspect anything, and maybe she would stay
safe.

Feeling the faint warmth of the steam rising from the sink,
he turned, bent and splashed warm water over his face. Lath-
ering up with only one good hand was awkward, but he managed. It would have been easier if the scent of the shaving
cream was minty or medicinal instead of sweet, light and very
feminine. It would have been much easier if he hadn't taken a

deep breath that made him wonder if this same fragrance clung to Ashley's skin after she used it.

It would have been easier by far if he'd had sex sometime in recent memory so that everything he did, saw, smelled and touched didn't make him think about sex—and not just sex, but sex with *her*. That was what he wanted. Just her.

He finished and rinsed his face, patted it dry on her towel, then stared into the mirror again. It wasn't much of an improvement, he conceded. Maybe *sinister* was gone, but *shifty* and *untrustworthy* remained.

He had never cared much for his own looks. From the time he was old enough to notice, he'd known that the opposite sex found him appealing, but he'd seen too strong a resemblance to Alexander Waters to find much appeal in himself. After a lifetime of being denied by his father, he'd been tempted a few years back to visit Waterston, just to show everyone that neither blood tests nor an admission from Alexander was necessary to prove his paternity. Genetics had put the proof right there on Dillon's face for all the world—all the town, at least—to see.

But he'd gotten a job offer, and there was really nothing to gain by showing up in Waterston after all these years. There was nothing he wanted from the Waters family, nothing he wanted from the town. And so, instead, he had come to North Carolina. If he'd had any idea of the trouble he was walking into, he never would have set foot across the state line.

And he never would have met Ashley Benedict.

One last glance out the window showed that she was still seated on the stool, still bent over her work. He turned off the light and, knowing he shouldn't bother, knowing it would be better for both of them if he stayed over here and she stayed over there, he made his way around the furniture to the armoire near the bed.

From a rod across the top on the right side hung a few summery dresses and a number of skirts similar to the chambray one—long, full, casual. Shelves on the left side held lingerie, socks and a variety of T-shirts, sweatshirts and sweaters.

The first one he picked up—a sweatshirt, black and bearing the teal-and-purple logo of the Charlotte Hornets—looked adequate. Removing his sling, he carefully tugged it over his head and *very* carefully slid his right arm into the sleeve. The movement tugged at this morning's dressing and made his wound throb, but by the time the shirt was on and his arm was back in the sling, the pain had subsided.

The shirt was a snug fit, washed until the colors had faded, until the cotton had gotten soft, and it smelled of her. For months after he left here, he was going to live with her scent. It was going to infuse every waking breath and haunt him every night. *She* was going to haunt him.

Scowling, he sat down on the hearth to put his tennis shoes on. They were mostly dry and stiff. Rather than trying to tie the laces with his one good hand, he yanked them out, then left the cabin. He walked as quickly as he dared across the muddy ground, breathing a sigh of comfort as he stepped onto the small porch, out of the rain, then another as he opened the door and felt the first rush of heat.

Ashley didn't even look at him, but she was obviously aware of him; her scowl matched his own. She had finished with the trays in the past few minutes and was now measuring lengths of cotton wicking. Boxes of candles sat in front of her, hand dipped, rich colors—red, green and deep translucent blue. The reds and greens, when he picked up their boxes, smelled simply of wax, but the blues... They had a fresh, clean, wintry scent that he couldn't begin to identify.

"You told the sheriff that you have to send six dozen of these to South Carolina. To sell?"

For a long time she ignored him, concentrating harder than necessary on the easy task of measuring and cutting. Hell, this was the woman who could effortlessly lace together a rustic tray, weave a basket, dress a wound or whip up a few loaves of bread. This little job didn't need even a fraction of her attention. She just didn't want to give *him* any of it.

And suddenly, foolishly, perversely he wanted it. *All* of it.

As he moved slowly around the table, she finally answered.

"They're used in some of the historic house museums down around Charleston and Beaufort."

"The blue ones smell nice. What is that?"

"A combination of roots and fruits."

Inwardly wincing at the cold disdain in her voice, he reached the end of the table, where basketry supplies were gathered, turned the corner and started up the other side. Toward her. "My grandmother quilted," he remarked, studying the quilt in the frame on the opposite side of the room. "I have—I *had* some of her quilts in Asheville. I guess they're gone now."

He had asked the deputy only one question before they'd reached Sadler's Pass: what had happened to the personal belongings left behind in his apartment when he'd fled the state? He'd broken the lease, Coughlin had explained, and under the law, the landlord was entitled to box up everything left behind and dispose of it however he wanted. Dillon hadn't had much and had cared about little of it, but he would have liked to have his grandmother's quilts, the family Bible that had passed to him on his grandfather's death and the family photographs. He wondered what the landlord had done with it all—kept or sold the quilts, probably, and tossed the rest. Who wanted a Bible documenting a family of strangers or snapshots of people they'd never known?

He stopped right beside Ashley. She pretended not to notice, but he saw the faint tremble in her hands. Was she uncomfortable because he was invading her space? A little nervous because she sensed that something was going to happen? Or uneasy because she meant what she'd said in the cabin? *Don't touch me.* It wasn't the words that had made an impression on him so much as the emotion behind them. Anger. Insistence. Revulsion?

She continued to work, continued to ignore him until he reached out and laid his hand over hers. Instantly she went still, as motionless and lifeless as the slab of wood in the middle of the table. She didn't move, didn't blink, didn't even breathe. For a moment he forgot to breathe, too. When the tightness in his chest reminded him, he drew a breath that was fragrant with her varied scents—honeysuckle from this morning's bath, almond from the shampoo they had both used, roses from the lotion on her hands. They were simple scents, homemade every one of them, and they were sweeter, more intoxicating, more enticing than the most expensive designer fragrance in the world.

He moved a step closer, so close that when he spoke, his breath stirred a strand of pale blond hair above her ear. "Ashley." He flexed his fingers, pressed them against hers, drew his fingertips across her hand. He felt the little shiver that rustled through her, starting in exactly the spot where his finger stroked the web of skin between her thumb and index finger and intensifying as he slid his finger between hers, over that skin, into the hollow formed by her loosely clenched fist.

This was crazy. Didn't he have enough fantasies to torment himself with without touching her? Didn't he already want her more than he could remember ever wanting anything? Did he have to add sensation to fantasy, to lust, to need? Did he have to torture himself further?

Why not? He'd learned as a kid that life was hard. Just once he wanted it hard in a way he could enjoy.

Finally she breathed, a quavery little sound as erotic as any he'd ever heard, and her eyes fluttered shut. Watching her, he moved his caress from her palm to her arm, feeling her pulse, rapid and erratic, when he brushed across her wrist. Her arms were slender, tanned, strong, the muscles swelling and rounding to soften the straight lines. The few women he'd shared serious relationships with had all been petite and very feminine, and he had assumed that fragile, delicate and helpless was his type. In the past few days, he had discovered that strong, muscled and independent had an appeal all its own.

His fingers curved over her shoulder, glided across soft fabric to softer skin, followed the line of her throat to her jaw. It took just a slight pressure—and ignoring the voice in his brain suggesting that he stop—to turn her head toward him. Just the slightest bending to bring his mouth into contact with hers.

He half expected her to flinch, expected her eyes to fly open,

her feet to hit the wood floor with a thud and her demand—
Don't touch me—to echo through the room with more loathing
than he'd ever been treated to. But she didn't flinch, didn't
stare at him, didn't jump to her feet and flee. She didn't do
anything at all but open her mouth to him and raise one hand
to his chest, bringing it gently to rest on his ribs, then letting
it slide down until her fingers hooked in the waistband of his
jeans.

So long. It had been so long since he'd kissed a woman, so
long since he'd touched a woman, so long since he'd been
intimate with a woman. So long that the sweet taste of her
mouth was something new, never experienced, as intoxicating
as the best aged whiskey, as full of promise as a spring morning. So long that her fingers, snug against his stomach, stirred
an ache that spread until it threatened to engulf him. So long
that he felt every bit as weak as she was strong. So long—and
so good—that he had to stop.

For one brief moment she clung to him, seeking more of his
mouth, tightening her fingers around his waistband. When he
pulled, though, she let go. She let him go.

He wished to God that she hadn't.

She was looking at him now, her blue eyes curious, a little
surprised, a little disappointed. He knew that if he kissed her
again, that disappointment would go away, and sweet damnation, he wanted to make it go away. But if he kissed her again,
he might not stop, not until it was too late. Not until they'd
traveled to hell and gone beyond what was safe. Not until he'd
learned all sorts of new meanings for the word *torment*.

As he forced himself to take the first step back, then the next
and the next, her gaze never left him. It followed him the length
of the table and back up the other side, where he'd started out,
where he leaned against the solid table and finally returned the
look.

After a time she spoke. She had to clear her throat first.
"Well...that was interesting."

The droll evenness of her comment forced a choked laugh
from him. "Interesting?" he echoed. "That's all?"

"How would *you* describe it?"

There were a hundred ways to put that moment into words, but he settled on the easiest and simplest of them. "Nice. Very nice."

"I'd rather be interesting than nice."

"You're both," he said, suddenly serious. "You're a better hostage than I deserve."

"So that's your way of saying thanks?"

"No. My way of saying thanks will be to walk away from here and never look back. To leave you the way I found you—unharmed. Safe. Too trusting, but out of danger." Damned if he wasn't sure he could do it. Two days ago he'd *known* that he could. All he'd wanted was shelter from the rain, heat to ward off the cold and a little precious rest to deal with his injuries. Today... Today he wanted Ashley.

And he couldn't have her. She wasn't the sort of woman a man could seduce, then forget, wasn't the sort a man walked away from. She and the sheriff had been divorced as long as they'd been married, but Benedict hadn't yet walked away from her. He still loved her, was still part of her life.

The only way Dillon could begin an affair with her was if he stayed long enough to let it run its course, to come to a natural end or go on forever, and he couldn't do that. He couldn't put her in any more danger than he already had. He couldn't risk getting caught for her. He couldn't risk getting both of them killed simply because he harbored this incredible lust for her.

She gathered the wicks and laid them off to one side, then rested her arms on the table and laced her fingers together. "You know, you could stay awhile," she said quietly.

"Don't say that." *Don't tempt me.*

"You could. You talk about running and hiding. Once they move their search out of this area, what better place to hide than right here?"

"Anyplace where they've never heard of Catlin, North Carolina." Someplace where all the women had dark hair and dark eyes, where the only tea they drank was iced, where the bread came in plastic wrappers from the store, where herbs were for cooking and never for nursing. Someplace where he wouldn't be enticed, where he wouldn't find hope, where he wouldn't have a future. Someplace where he would never fit in, where he could never belong. Someplace where he wouldn't even want to try.

He could belong here. He could live on this mountaintop, could till those fields, chop firewood and keep the van running. He could spend his days doing the kind of hard work his grandfather had always done, and he could spend his nights...

Heat flushed his face as he turned away from the words that would naturally complete that sentence. He would spend his nights in hell if he even contemplated making a future here. Making a future with her.

"Right now you can't get to someplace where they've never heard of Catlin, North Carolina," she observed, sounding cautious and a little off balance. "But you're safe here."

"And what about when the search parties come? You know they will. It's just a matter of time."

"You're right. They may come today, maybe tomorrow, maybe even the day after. When they come, chances are good that you'll still be here. Once they're gone, they won't come back, so there's no reason you should leave, too."

She was the best reason he had to leave. The way she had nursed him. The way she had lied to Benedict to hide him. The way she had touched him, looked at him, listened to him, kissed him. The way she was looking at him right now. If he stayed, he might forget the lesson Russell had gone to such pains to teach him, and he might start trusting someone again. He might start believing he could have a normal life, with a home, a family, a future. He might start thinking he could make things right, with the sheriff's help, with Ashley's help. He might tell the truth, and it very well might get him killed.

He very well might get Ashley killed.

"What's wrong, Ashley?" he asked softly, seeking to avoid temptation in the only way he could manage. "Been alone too long?"

Her eyes widened, and her breath caught. Then she breathed deeply and offered him a chilly smile. "Yes, I guess I have."

"Since the divorce?" Stupid question, he warned himself. Her sex life was none of his business. He didn't need to know that maybe she'd been celibate since the breakup of her marriage, didn't want to know that there might have been men other than Benedict in her life, men who had kissed her, men who had done with her the things that he'd spent much of the past day—and especially the past night—aching to do.

"Not quite."

In thirty-four years he'd never had occasion to discover that he was a jealous man. Now, in only an instant, he knew. He was. Feeling hot, frustrated and just a little mean, he asked—demanded, "Who was he?"

"A man in Raleigh. His sister was a teacher at my school. He was an accountant who certainly destroyed every preconceived notion *I'd* ever had about accountants." She stopped, then added, "He was much easier than you are."

Easier to seduce? Dillon wondered. Easier to be around? Easier to want? Damn her, easier how?

Sliding off the stool, she went to the deep cubbyholes that lined one wall and selected a few items: loose coils of reed, oval hoops, a gracefully curved handle. She laid them on the table, picked up a bucket and came around to his side to fill it with water in the small bathroom behind him. When she came back, she stopped close to him, lifting the bucket onto the table in front of him, then giving him a steady look. "But you know what, Dillon?"

He didn't speak but simply looked at her as she leaned closer, close enough that he could sort out all her scents, close enough that he could feel her heat, close enough that he could hear her words even though they were merely whispered.

"'Easier' isn't always better."

Ashley looked up at him and waited for him to back off. She knew he would, just as she'd known he would end that sweet, unexpected kiss, just as she'd known he would shy away

entirely from the possibility of an affair. She didn't have long
to wait—just a minute, maybe two. After about ninety seconds
by her estimate, he took a long step away, removing himself
from what he surely perceived as imminent danger, then moving another dozen feet for good measure. As she returned to
her stool, he pretended great interest in everything in the workshop except her.

Maybe his sarcastic little remark had been right on target,
she thought with a suppressed sigh. Maybe she *had* been alone
too long. First she'd gotten turned on doing nothing more than
rubbing comfrey salve over his ribs; then she'd given her car-
diovascular system quite a workout with the simple task of
fitting a sling to support his arm. Now after one kiss—one
simple little kiss, one nothing-special, shared-by-millions-
every-day kiss—she was willing to make room for him in her
life on a permanent basis. She was offering to live a life of
deceit, to lie to Seth and everyone else in her world in addition
to breaking who knew how many laws, just so Dillon could
stay.

Oh, but that kiss *had* been something special. She wasn't
the most experienced woman around, but she knew a good kiss
from a so-so one; she knew a sizzle-and-burn kiss from the
gee-that-was-nice variety. And it didn't matter, anyway, because Dillon didn't *want* to stay. He didn't *want* to be a permanent part of her life.

Resting her chin on her cupped hand, she considered the
materials she'd gathered. She needed to mark the middle of
each of the reeds before putting them in the bucket of water to
make them more pliable; then she would lay out the bottom of
the small market basket, weaving over and under the handle to
secure it. Or she might sit here, watch the weather, listen to
Dillon prowl and pray for the longest, heaviest rains since Noah
built his ark.

What she needed was physical activity—*real* activity. Something like stacking firewood under the shelter of the porch
roof...but the porch already held all the firewood it could hold.
After running out of wood nearby in her first heavy snow up

here three years ago, she'd become almost obsessive about keeping a good supply handy.

She could always go back in the house and bake more bread...but there was no room for it in the freezer, and she would hate to see it grow old and stale before they could eat it.

Maybe she could...

"You do nice work."

Slowly she shifted her gaze to Dillon, standing beside the quilt frame, tracing one fingertip over the stitching that secured the three layers together. He sounded grudging and looked annoyed, but she accepted his compliment anyway. "Thank you."

"How long does it take to do one of these?"

"For me, months, but I do them along with everything else. If I devoted my time exclusively to a quilt, I imagine it would take me three or four weeks."

"How much do you sell them for?"

"It depends on the size, the fabric, the intricacy of the pattern and where it's sold. Anywhere from a few hundred dollars to a thousand or more." She gestured to the partial quilt over on the sewing table. "That one will go to the most upscale of the shops I sell in, and it will probably bring fifteen hundred, maybe more."

He circled the frame to look at the unfinished one. "I don't like it as well as this one," he said, comparing it to the one in the frame. Then he gave her a quick, sheepish look. "I mean—"

"I don't, either, but it's not for me." The quilt in the frame was a Jacob's Ladder, a series of squares and triangles placed to create a crisp geometric pattern in sharply contrasting colors. It was bright, clean, pleasing to the eye. The other was a Cathedral Windows. Each window consisted of two squares of fabric, one soft ivory, the other varying. Once each piece of ivory was folded, pinned, stitched and reduced to half its original size, the second fabric was slipped underneath and the four outer edges were slip-stitched to create the effect of looking through a window. Each window was time-consuming, and the entire quilt required hundreds of windows. It was going to be a *long* time in the finishing. "Fifteen hundred dollars for a bed cover sounds like a lot, but when you consider the time invested, it's not much of a return."

"So why do you bother?"

"Quilts are never a bother," she chided. "They're folk art. Americana. A piece of history." Then she shrugged. "I started out making them for myself. I never intended to sell them, but one day the owner of an antique shop in Durham came to buy some baskets. He saw the quilts stacked on the rack in the cabin and said he could sell as many as I could make. I agreed to make a few for him, and I've been doing it ever since."

Finally he faced her again. "You should have been born a hundred years ago."

"So I've been told. My chosen life-style and I are throwbacks to an earlier time." She made no effort to temper the sarcasm that crept into her voice, even though, once again, his face turned a deep red.

"I shouldn't have said…"

She mimicked the shrug that followed his trailing words. "Why not? Everything you said was true." It wasn't *what* he'd said that hurt, but the *way* he'd said it. With derision. Scorn.

Dragging his hand over his face, he muttered a curse. "Hell, who am I to criticize the way anyone else lives? I've screwed up every thing I've ever done. I'm hiding from the cops because I can't face twenty-five years in prison. I don't have a place to live. I don't even know *how* to live except on the run. I should be—I *am* grateful that you've chosen to live up here, because without you, I don't think I would have made it through that first night."

Before she could think of a response, a sound outside drew her attention. Slowly she rose from the stool and started toward the window.

Halfway there, though, she stopped and abruptly stepped back. "Oh, no."

Dillon moved away from the quilt frame toward the opposite

window, but she quickly stopped him. "It's one of the search parties. You've got to hide."

"Where?"

"In the bathroom. Go on, hurry." She didn't wait to watch him, didn't wait to hear the click of the door as it closed behind him. Instead, she grabbed her shawl, went to the front door and stepped outside. "Good morning."

There were four men coming into the clearing. Two were civilians, the Briggs brothers. They had lived all their lives in these mountains; they were skilled hunters, trackers and expert shots. She recognized the state trooper following them and was fairly well acquainted with the Catlin County deputy bringing up the rear. Steven Vickers was a few years younger than her— Gail's age—and had been one of Gail's many boyfriends their last year of high school. After school her sister had moved to California with the rest of the family, finished college and started her own business. Steven hadn't done much of anything at all before he'd been hired a few years ago as a deputy, but he seemed to enjoy the job and Seth said he did it well.

All four men looked cold, tired and grim.

All four of them were armed.

"Mrs. Benedict." The trooper spoke first. Jess Briggs's greeting was less formal. "Miss Ashley."

She drew her shawl tighter. "Any luck yet with the search?"

"A little bit," Steven replied. "We tracked him as far as that bluff a couple hundred yards back of here, then lost his trail again. Have you seen anyone suspicious around here?"

Ashley forced a smile, hoping it appeared somewhere close to natural. "Steven, I live five miles from my closest neighbor. *Anyone* around here would be suspicious." Then she let the seriousness she was feeling take over. "Seth came by yesterday morning to tell me about the escape, but he's the only visitor I've had in weeks. So…you think he came that close to my house."

"We *know* he came that close," the younger Briggs answered. "Those were his tracks, all right. He was walking with a bit of a limp, which makes a difference in the footprints, and there was a cut on the sole of his left shoe. Easy tracks to pick up. Easy to follow."

"Except when he goes across two hundred feet of rock," his brother added.

Ashley's breath was trapped in her chest. Just a short while ago, Dillon had walked from the cabin to the workshop, minus the limp but wearing the same shoes with the same cut on the sole. Surely his footprints were still there, clearly visible for all the men to see. What if they *did* see? They would insist on searching the workshop—how could she tell them no?—and they would find Dillon. There was no way they couldn't.

Then what would she do?

Quickly she did a mental scan of the cabin. The dishes from a breakfast for two had been washed, the bed was made, and the quilts she'd slept on were all folded over the back of the couch. Dillon's shirt was in the wastebasket under the kitchen sink, he was wearing his jeans and shoes, and Seth's sweatpants were in the bathroom hamper. There was nothing in there that might give him away…except the handcuffs. What had he done with the handcuffs this morning?

Unable to remember, she clenched her fists over the edges of the shawl and moved to the edge of the stoop, one step away from the rain. "I don't drink coffee, gentlemen, but I do have a wide assortment of herbal teas in the cabin. I'd be happy to fix you some—although I'll warn you that I *have* been told it's god-awful. How about it?"

There was a moment of collective hesitation, then Jess Briggs grinned. "After six hours out in this weather, *anything* hot sounds good, Miss Ashley."

Out of habit, she reached back and secured the door of the workshop; then she led the way to the porch steps. Every stride was longer than usual, every step landing squarely in the center of a bigger and—according to the Briggs brothers—distinctive step. When they reached the cabin, she stifled a sigh of relief and instead offered a silent prayer that Dillon's other footprints—when he'd arrived Tuesday evening and when he'd followed her to the van Wednesday morning—had apparently been obliterated by the rain.

Stopping in the cabin door, she paused to hang up her shawl, dawdling, subjecting the cabin to a quick look. There was nothing out of place, nothing to indicate that she hadn't been alone, as usual, the past two days. She needn't have worried, though; all four men refused to come inside. Their clothes were wet, their boots muddied, they explained. She didn't mind; they could get warm, and she could clean the floor later, she insisted, but they still refused. Just the tea on the porch, Steven requested.

Inside she put a pot of water on to boil, placed tea bags in four mugs and watched nervously out the window. The men were talking, their voices a low rumble through the glass, their words indistinguishable. There was no sign of life in the workshop. *Be patient,* she silently pleaded of Dillon. *Don't get nervous, don't wonder what's going on, don't come out to check. Trust me.*

At the first sign of a bubble in the pot, she switched off the burner, poured the water into the cups, then nervously tapped her fingers on the counter. When the tea had steeped barely ninety seconds, she fished out the bags, gave each cup a squirt of honey, placed them on a tray and carried them outside, serving each man in turn. "Maybe I should have taken Seth's advice and moved into town."

"You probably don't need to worry, Mrs. Benedict," the trooper said. "The boys think he passed through here at least twenty-four hours ago. If he'd thought he could stay around awhile, he would have made his presence known by now. Still, it might not hurt to think again about staying in town. Boone's a dangerous and desperate man. While he's never used violence before this incident, there's no telling what he might resort to now. After all, he *did* almost kill Tom Coughlin."

Poor Tom, she thought, feeling guilty that she'd let him slip completely out of her mind. "How is Tom?"

Steven answered, his expression grim, his eyes cold. "He's

still in a coma. The doctors say the longer he stays that way, the less his chances are of coming out of it okay.''

''If you talk to Mrs. Coughlin, tell her my prayers are with them.''

In the silence that followed, each man finished his tea—and she saw more than one grimace. Maybe Dillon was right, she mused, leaning against the doorframe and watching them. Maybe it *was* awful, and she'd just been drinking it too long to notice.

''We'd best get going,'' the trooper said, handing his cup to her. ''Would you like us to look around before we go?''

''I appreciate the offer, but the only place to check is the workshop, and I've been in there all morning. If anyone were hiding in there, believe me, I would know it.'' She collected the last cup. ''Steven, if you see Seth, let him know that I'm okay—but don't tell him I was in the workshop when you came. He seems to think I should stay behind barred-and-locked doors in the cabin until Boone is caught.''

The young deputy looked at her. ''He might have the right idea. I'll tell him that you were, that you wouldn't open up even for us.''

''Thanks.''

They trooped down the steps, one behind the other, and headed south across the clearing, toward the forest there. Ashley stood exactly where they'd left her and watched until they were out of sight. When the last glimpse—the bright yellow cap Jess Briggs wore—disappeared from sight, she gave a heartfelt sigh of relief…and promptly developed a case of the shakes so bad that she dropped the tray and all four cups in a glass-breaking crash.

Chapter 6

If there were room to pace in the tiny, closed-in space of the bathroom, Dillon would be doing it, but he could hardly turn around without banging his head or his elbow or some other portion of his anatomy. He couldn't even see what made the room so cramped. The light was off, there was no window and the door was extraordinarily tight fitting. He was in pitch black—couldn't see anything, couldn't hear anything, couldn't *do* anything.

That was the worst part—being unable to take action—that, and not knowing. When the door opened, it could be Ashley coming to tell him that it was safe, or it could be a cop. An angry cop. One who believed that Dillon was far worse than just an escaped prisoner. One who would hold him responsible for the misfortune that had befallen Tom Coughlin. Just this morning Ashley had said that she would turn him over—if she were so inclined—to Seth and only Seth, that her ex-husband could be trusted to keep him safe from other officers. She *knew* those other officers. She believed they presented a threat not to be considered idly.

Maybe, though, she had lied. Maybe she was out there right now, telling her rescuers everything that had happened the past two days, telling them exactly where he could be found. Maybe when that door opened, it *would* be a cop, led straight to him by the woman he was trusting to…

The thought trailed off, and he sank down on the only seat in the room, replaying the last words in his mind. *The woman he was trusting…*

Trusting…

Oh, God, he was in trouble.

He had trusted Russell Bradley, and now his good buddy wanted him dead. How much more dangerous could Ashley be to him? She could get him arrested. She could get him killed. Worse, she could make him believe in things he'd never believed in. She could make him want things he'd thought he would never have. Love. Respect. Acceptance. A family. A future.

She could break his heart.

She could destroy him.

But only if he let her, he insisted uneasily. Only if he let himself trust her. Only if he let her get too close. He knew how to avoid it. He'd been running, in one way or another, all his life. He knew how to avoid involvement, how to keep people at a distance. He had learned by example from his mother, from his father and the entire town of Waterston. He could do it with Ashley.

Couldn't he?

From the outer room came the sound of a door opening, followed by soft footsteps. Quickly he stood, moving the two steps necessary to reach the door. If it was one of Catlin County's or North Carolina's finest on the other side come to arrest him… Hell, he'd rather end it here than bother with the farce of a trial that was sure to follow and prison. And if it was Ashley…

She opened the door, then stepped back so he could leave the small room. "Are they gone?" he asked before taking that step out.

"Of course they are."

"It took you long enough to get rid of them."

"I made them a cup of tea."

"You're just little Miss Hospitality, aren't you?" he asked sarcastically as he left the bathroom's close, dark shelter. "First you invite the sheriff in for a cup of tea, then the search party."

"It's what they expect of me. If I didn't offer, they would think it was strange." Her voice was strained but soft, controlled. "I think we'd better go back to the cabin and stay there."

"Why?"

"Jess and Toy Briggs are good trackers, but they're not the best. They lost your trail back in the woods at the bluff, so they had no reason to believe you might be here. If they don't find something soon, they'll bring in one of the best—Dub Collins, Zeke Henderson or Mac Haney. If even the slightest sign still exists out there, they'll find it."

"So what does that have to do with staying inside? If they catch me there, I'll be just as screwed as if they catch me out here."

She shot him an impatient look. "You've been outside three times already. Every time you go out, you leave new footprints. *That's* why I offered them tea—so I could blur the latest set. I guess it worked. They didn't seem to notice a thing."

"What was it you were telling me just a little while ago? That once the search party comes here and doesn't find me, they won't come back?" He muttered a curse. "Now you're saying they *will* be back."

"Possibly. Probably."

"To try to pick up a trail they lost?" He lowered his voice. "Or because you told them to come back?"

She stared at him for a long time, her blue gaze softened by disappointment, then abruptly she turned away. Taking a big handled basket from a shelf, she began neatly placing materials into it: basket-weaving supplies, bolts of cloth, a gallon jug of something clear, small plastic bottles, smaller glass vials. When she was done, she left it all on the table, checked the fire, then picked up the basket, switched off the lights and waited at the door.

He knew he should let it drop, knew in his heart that she hadn't betrayed him to those men. But it would have made perfect sense if she had. She could have confided in the searchers, could have told them to get reinforcements, to come back when they could take him by surprise. For all he knew, she could be leading him into a trap. The men could be outside, just waiting for him to step into the clearing. They could be in the cabin, ready to ambush him when he walked in the door. "Ashley." Her gaze met his, but he couldn't read anything in her eyes. "Did you tell them to come back?"

She studied him for a moment, then slowly, coolly smiled as she approached him. "Yes, I did," she replied. "I told them to get Seth, to get all his men and all the troopers and all the guns they can carry. I told them to come back late tonight, when you're asleep. I told them I would slip into the bathroom and light a candle in the window when you were snoring away, that I would leave the door unlocked for them so they could sneak in and capture you before you knew what was happening."

She was lying. Dillon knew it as surely as he knew he wanted her. She was telling tales to alarm and frighten him, and, damn it all, he deserved to be alarmed and frightened. "And how did you plan to get out of the handcuffs so you could light a candle in the bathroom window?"

"I wasn't planning on wearing the handcuffs tonight." Now she was standing right in front of him, only the big basket separating them. She leaned across it, close to him, too close, and murmured, "I wasn't planning on wearing anything at all tonight."

That was a thought too tantalizing to consider. Just the brief image that formed before he stopped it was enough to make him squeeze his eyes shut and bite down hard on a groan. "Just for that, you *will* be wearing the cuffs tonight," he warned her. "I had been considering leaving you free, seeing that you've been so good lately, but now..." He shook his head.

Her smile this time was also slow and cool, but it was a totally different proposition from the last one. In fact, Dillon feared, that was *exactly* what it was: a proposition. She proved him right when she said, "You put me in handcuffs tonight, it'll be in bed, not on the floor."

With that, she turned and walked out. Forgetting about search parties, guns and possible ambushes, he followed her. She latched the door, then set the basket down once more and walked out into the rain, checking to the south first, then the west, north and east. Raindrops staining her red sweatshirt crimson, she motioned for him to move and, head ducked, he made the short trip to the cabin. She followed more slowly, squishing in the mud, leaving nothing in each place he'd stepped but tiny hills and valleys that quickly filled with water.

He stepped over one of her woven trays and a pile of broken glass near the door, then removed his tennis shoes at the door. He hesitated just a moment, though, until, with a knowing, chiding look, she came up behind him, reached around and opened the door, then slipped past and entered the cabin.

"Look, Dillon," she said, turning in a circle, spreading her arms wide. "No cops."

He went in, closing and locking the door. "What happened to the cups?"

"Nerves," she said carelessly. "It's not every day I lie to the good guys."

He leaned back against the door. If the cops were the good guys, then that left only one role for him: the bad guy. He always had been. The Boone bastard. The punk kid. The budding juvenile delinquent. The loser. The failure. The sucker. The fugitive. The target. The prey. They were roles he knew well, roles he played well. He was used to them.

So why did it hurt to be cast in them by Ashley?

She laid the basket on the table and began unloading it. "It wouldn't be a bad idea to figure out a hiding place in here," she remarked, not noticing his silence. "Seth will come back whenever he's got time, and the next time he might expect to come in."

"So you'll have to stop him."

His curt response made her look sharply at him. "If he asks to come inside, I can't very well refuse without arousing his suspicion, which is the last thing you want me to do."

No, the last thing—and the first—he wanted her to arouse was *him*. "Fine. If he wants to come in, invite him. He can keep us company for a while."

"You wouldn't take him hostage. You're not that stupid. He's the sheriff, for God's sake. He's trained to deal with this sort of thing. He's an expert shot, an expert at self-defense. You would be lucky if he didn't kill you."

"He wouldn't do a thing." Joining her at the table, he stroked his hand lightly over her hair. "Not if he believed *you* would be punished for it."

A shudder rippled through her and into his fingers. "You won't hurt me. You promised."

"He already believes I would hurt you," he explained. "That's why he was so anxious to get you out of here. He expects the worst from me. He thinks I'm a dangerous man, a desperate fugitive who almost killed a cop. God only knows what I might do to you if you get in my way." Those last were Benedict's words, merely rephrased.

She was supposed to feel at least a little threatened, to stand utterly still, unable to move, or to tremble with fear. Well, she was trembling, all right, little shivers that intensified each time he drew his hand down her hair to her shoulder, but instinct told him there was nothing the least bit fearful about it. Her soft blue eyes, hazy now and barely open, confirmed it.

"Let me get in your way," she murmured, "and let's find out what you'll do."

He jerked his hand back and took a half-dozen steps away from her. "Ash, I'm not going to seduce you."

She smiled. "Actually I thought *I* might seduce *you*."

His breath locked in his chest, depriving his brain of the oxygen desperately needed to argue that point with her. Reason failed him, but imagination didn't. Without closing his eyes, without making even the slightest effort, he could see her, naked, lean, beautiful. He could feel her, soft and hot. He could smell her fragrances, light and erotic on her skin, between her breasts, on her belly, scenting her hip. He could taste her mouth, could savor the exotic forbidden flavor of her. He could…

He could die an early death from wanting her.

He could die a slow and very painful death from having her.

"Not counting your precious Seth, how many men have you been with?" he asked harshly, already sure he knew the answer.

"One."

"Your friend's brother the accountant. Were you in love with him?"

"No."

"But you cared for him. You thought something might develop with him. You thought he might be the next great love of your life."

Her head tilted to one side, she looked curiously at him. "Why do you think that?"

"Because that's the kind of woman you are. You don't have sex with men. You have *relationships* with *suitable* men. You've never gone to bed with someone you picked up one night in a bar. You've never had sex with someone whose name you never bothered to find out. You've never had sex for its own sake, because you'd had too much to drink or you'd been alone too long." His smile was thin and bitter. "Well, *that's* the kind of man I am. I don't have relationships. I don't meet *suitable* women. I meet women in bars, women whose names I sometimes never knew to forget, women who are interchangeable, who are just there for the using. You're not that kind of woman, Ashley. You're not *my* kind of woman."

"So you're saying that you don't want me."

He gave a short laugh. "I've done without a long time, and I've been alone even longer. Of course I want you. But—no offense, sweetheart—I'd want just about any woman under these circumstances."

"So what's the problem?" she asked stubbornly. "We're

both adults. We're both capable of weighing the consequences and making the right decision.''

Swearing silently, Dillon crossed the room to tend the fire. There, with more than half the length of the cabin between them, he felt a little safer, but not much.

God help him, she was going to kill him. She was absolutely going to destroy his good intentions, his resolve and, ultimately, *him.* He never should have touched her this morning, never should have kissed her...but he would sell his soul to the devil to do it again.

He just might sell it to the sheriff for a chance to make love with her.

''The problem, Ashley,'' he said, his patience severely tested, ''is common sense—your lack of it. Women like you don't have affairs with men like me. Women like you don't have affairs, period.''

''What do we do?'' she asked dryly. ''Live alone and unsatisfied all our lives?''

''You have relationships with men like your precious Seth. You get married. You have children and grandchildren, and you devote yourself to your family. Like your mother. Like your grandmother.''

She came closer, stopping at the sofa, sitting on its overstuffed arm. ''Is that what your mother did?''

''No. My mother picked up men in bars, men whose names she didn't bother to learn, men she used to help her forget the pain of falling in love with a *suitable* man.'' He stared at her for a moment, then exhaled heavily. ''You're not my kind of woman, Ashley.''

After a pause to let that sink in, he felt the bitterness cross his face in a smile again. ''And I'm damned sure not your kind of man.''

Their *problem,* Ashley thought as she got ready for bed that evening, had nothing to do with her lack of common sense. Maybe it was bad timing. Maybe if they'd met a year ago, when he had first come to Catlin to work at the bank, he would have decided he had too much to lose to risk the bank job.

But a year ago he'd had a woman in his life, and not of the pick-her-up-in-a-bar-and-never-know-her-name variety. She had been his neighbor, a nice woman, in Seth's judgment, one who'd had no idea at all what kind of man she'd gotten mixed up with. She'd had a silly name—Calla? Cilla? No, Pris, short for Priscilla.

After pulling her nightgown over her head, Ashley made a face at herself in the mirror. Could she simply claim an extraordinary memory for details, or had she been fascinated by Dillon Boone eleven months before meeting him? Was that why unimportant little things—like the photographs left behind in his apartment, the name of his former lover and the fact that the woman had red hair—were so clear in her mind?

So what was the big difference between her and Pris, other than the fact that Ashley wouldn't be caught dead answering to a nickname that, in other usage, was less than complimentary?

Other than the fact that, while Ashley wasn't Dillon's kind of woman, Miss Pris obviously was?

As she picked up her brush from the rim of the sink, a flash outside caught her attention. Switching off the light, she peered out the window into the darkness. There were often hunters in these woods, both in season and out, along with the hikers. She stayed locked up tight and ordinarily paid them no attention. After all, it wasn't as if she owned the mountaintop; her acreage was on the small side. The rest was private property or public parkland.

But this wasn't an ordinary night, and the scene in the next room wasn't an ordinary sight, at least not in *her* house. That light could be a hunter or a hiker, or it could be a search party or a lone tracker hoping to bag a reward.

Leaving the bathroom, she took the extra sheets from the armoire near the door, grabbed a hammer and a box of nails from under the sink and, giving herself a boost, climbed onto the counter that ran under the kitchen window.

Dillon, lying on the couch and reading, looked up. "What's wrong?"

"Nothing." Kneeling on the counter, she tacked a corner from the first sheet to the window frame, scooted across and nailed it again in the opposite corner. "When I moved in here, I always intended to make curtains—yellow gingham, just like my granny had. But there was so much work to do that I never got around to it. In the first year I was terrified that I wouldn't be able to stay, that I couldn't earn enough money, that I couldn't barter enough services, and so I worked ten, twelve and fourteen hours a day, seven days a week. I figured nonessentials, like curtains, could wait. I mean, the place is so isolated. It isn't as if there are neighbors around to peek through the windows."

Taking the sheets and tools with her, she moved to the next window and repeated the process. "After a while I got used to not having curtains. I thought maybe someday I would buy some gingham, or maybe I would make enough yards of lace to cover them all, but it wasn't any big deal."

"But now it is."

"Well, it occurred to me tonight—" Just a random thought, she hoped he believed; there was no sense in worrying him about the light she'd seen. It had been way off in the distance and probably didn't mean a thing, but he would surely believe it was a posse of angry, gun-toting men out looking for him. He might even begin to believe her lie this morning about instructing Steven Vickers and the others to come back tonight with Seth. "With the lights on in here and all these uncurtained windows, to anybody outside looking in, we may as well be in a spotlight. And since there very well *might* be people outside, why take a chance?"

By the time she'd finished, she had covered all the windows in the main room and used her last sheet. Without giving it much thought, she took one of the quilts from the back of the sofa and headed for the bathroom.

"Hey, what are you doing?" There was a thump as Dillon dropped his book to the floor, then the shuffle of footsteps behind her. She was holding a nail to the upper right corner of the quilt, the hammer poised in her other hand, when he yanked it away. "Stop that. You can't put holes in this."

"I don't have any more sheets."

"So keep this door closed."

Still holding the corner of the coverlet above her head, she scowled at him in the dim light. "Maybe you haven't spent enough time in this room to notice, but icicles form in here when the door is closed. When porcelain that cold comes in contact with human flesh, it can do some painful damage."

"You can't put nails in this. It'll ruin it."

"It'll put a few holes in it," she said with exaggerated patience. "Look, *I* made it. If I want to hang it as a curtain, I can. Besides, I think it'll look kind of nice—brighten the room. Give it a homey effect." Pulling the hammer from his hand, she stretched onto her toes and hit the first nail squarely on the head, sinking it with three strikes. Smoothing the fabric as she went, she added more nails, one every six inches or so, until she reached the corner. There, she climbed into the bathtub and affixed the other half in the same manner over the front window.

Climbing out again, she turned on the light to study her handiwork, then smiled. It *did* look nice. The bright shades of the fabric added color that the plain wood walls badly needed, and the straight, rectangular lines of the Log Cabin pattern nicely echoed the lines of the wall boards.

Then she glanced at Dillon again. He was staring at the quilt, a dismayed look darkening his face. "Hey," she said softly. "It's just a quilt. I've made dozens of them. I'll make dozens more."

He shook his head. "You've ruined it."

"Of course I haven't. Don't you know quilts aren't supposed to be perfect? All of the good ones have some rips, tears, lumpy batting or whatever. It gives them character. I bet your grandmother's quilts weren't in pristine condition." The look he gave her at that last part made her wince. He didn't have any idea what kind of shape his grandmother's quilts were in now.

Someone else had them now, probably someone to whom they meant nothing, someone with no emotional connection. Heavens, for all he knew, they could have been thrown in the garbage with the rest of his stuff when he failed to pay his rent the month following his disappearance.

Moving past him, she smoothed the fabric in the corner. "This quilt will become a family heirloom now," she said lightly. "When I'm old and gray, I'll still have it, and I'll tell my grandchildren and great-grandchildren how those holes came to be there. They'll be intrigued that *their* granny once helped an escaped bank robber hide from the police. It'll probably make me a minor legend in their eyes." She turned to grin at him, but her expression soon turned sober. He was staring at her, his gaze as intense as any she'd ever seen, as hard and troubled as any she might ever see. "Dillon—" She reached out, but he turned and walked away.

She stood there a moment, then, taking a deep breath, joined him in the outer room. He had turned off all the lights and was now adding fuel to the fire. She returned the hammer and nails to their proper place, reclaimed the brush she'd forgotten earlier and went to sit on the pallet in front of the fireplace.

Finished with the logs, he went to the bed, removed the sling, stripped and slid under the covers. She didn't exactly watch him...but she didn't turn away, either. Sitting cross-legged on the thick pad of covers, she began drawing the brush through her hair. "Do you ever miss Pris?" she asked conversationally.

"How do you know about her?"

She smiled into the fire. "You forget, my ex-husband and best friend is the sheriff. By the time his investigation into the bank robbery was completed, he probably knew everything about you, and he told me the interesting stuff. So...do you?"

He was quiet a long time, then the bedsprings squeaked. "In a way. She was a nice woman. You would probably like her if you knew her."

"No, I wouldn't."

"How can you be so sure?"

"We can't possibly have anything in common."

"Why do you say that?"

"Because you slept with her. You won't even let me touch you." She thought back to that moment in the bathroom, how close her fingers had come to his shoulder, how quickly he'd avoided her touch, how hurriedly he'd put distance between them.

He fell silent. What kind of response could a man make to a comment like that? She didn't blame him for not even trying.

"What would I like about her?"

An impatient sigh. He didn't want to continue this conversation. She didn't blame him for that, either. "She's nice. Funny. Generous. She's a lot like you."

"How is she different from me?" She had to be, since he'd found her perfectly *suitable* for an intimate relationship.

"Come on, Ash..."

All right, so *all* nicknames weren't bad, she acknowledged. She could warm right up to "Ash," especially when it was Dillon saying it. His name didn't lend itself to shortening—"Dill" was definitely out of the question—but she could easily see herself calling him darlin'. Sweetheart. Baby.

"Satisfy my curiosity." *Since you aren't willing to satisfy anything else.* "How is she different?" When he didn't answer, she supplied her own answer. "I know she has red hair and that she lived upstairs from you. I assume she's prettier than me."

"Why?" He sounded as if he were scowling again.

"Because men like pretty women. Pretty faces, big boobs, long legs..." She laughed, but it wasn't with good humor. "At least I've got the legs."

"Yes, Pris is pretty, but you..." He sighed wearily. "Jeez, Ash, do we have to do this?"

"No," she whispered. That was enough of an answer. *Pris is pretty, but you have character, Ashley. You have inner beauty. You have so many talents.* So it wasn't the answer she wanted. It was exactly what she deserved for asking.

She was an enlightened, independent woman of the nineties,

and *she* thought she was pretty. She liked her face. She realized
there was more strength than daintiness, more character than
conventional beauty, but she liked her looks anyway. What did
it matter if he found his old girlfriend more attractive? *She*
didn't find *him* as handsome as her ex-husband…at least, she
hadn't in the beginning. Funny— the more time she spent with
him, the better she came to know him, the more handsome he
was.

So maybe, if the reverse was also true, in another…oh, fifty
or sixty years, he would find her prettier than Pris. She could
wait. She didn't have any plans for the rest of her life…but *he*
did. He had his own plans, and Seth and the D.A. had their
plans for him. Bill Armstrong had lots of plans for him.

Gazing into the fire, she continued to draw the brush slowly
through her hair. When she was little, she had spent countless
nights sitting right there, brushing her hair while, beside her,
her grandmother did the same. For as long as Ashley could
remember, the old lady's hair had been snow white, fine and
long, reaching almost to her waist. During the day she'd worn
it up, wound around her head into a bun and secured with long
rippled pins. She had covered it with a scarf when she went
outside, a simple square of calico folded into a triangle, the
ends tied under her chin, or with an old straw hat adorned with
one floppy, yellow cloth daisy. But at night, every night, whatever the season, she had sat on the braided rug in front of the
fireplace—not this rug, but very nearly the same—and let her
hair down, and she had brushed it, long gentle strokes gliding
all the way to the ends, over and over, slow and easy. ·

While she had brushed—and Ashley followed suit—she had
talked. She had told stories about her parents, had repeated tales
her mother had told her. She had talked about herbs and flowers
and the phases of the moon, about moonshine stills and soap
making and the seasons of her youth. Ashley had learned much
in those regular talks about living and dying, about love and
joy, heartache and great sorrow.

In spite of the failure of her marriage, Ashley knew she'd
been unusually blessed. She had her family and their unswerv-

ing love. She had a strong sense of who she was and a sure knowledge of what she wanted. She was living a life that she loved, a life that she wouldn't change one thing about...except for the fact that she was living it alone. She had never gone hungry, had never been broke, had never been afraid. She didn't know what hard living was. Her only sorrow had been losing her grandparents, and she had never experienced heartache, not even with Seth. She had, indeed, been fortunate.

But her luck, she suspected, had changed Tuesday evening when Dillon Boone walked into her cabin. Unless he left now—walked out of her life *right* now, right this very instant— she feared that she was going to find herself on a first-name basis with heartache. She was going to drown in sorrow, and she didn't have a clue how to save herself.

She wasn't even sure she wanted to save herself.

Dillon lay in bed, his eyes gritty and sore, his hands clenched tightly at his side. The cabin was quiet except for the crackle of the fire. Except for the softer crackle—real or imagined?— of Ashley's hair as she slowly pulled the brush through it. Except for the urgent pleas he'd been making for several miserably long moments.

Put the brush down.

Move away from the fire.

Find some clothing more substantial.

Go to bed and, please, God, don't ask me to join you.

Did she know that that flimsy little gown of hers, when backed by the flames, was nearly transparent? Did she know that, every time she raised her arms, he could see the curve of her breast almost as clearly as if she were naked? Did she know that he could think of few things more erotic than watching a woman brush her hair in the firelight?

Did she have any idea that she was killing him?

He wished he could believe the answer was yes. Yes, she knew her gown revealed as much as it concealed. Yes, she knew what a tantalizing sight she presented. Yes, she knew that she was arousing him, tormenting him, teasing and taunting him. If he could believe that, if he could believe that everything she was doing was calculated to seduce, then maybe he could find the strength to resist.

But there was nothing calculating, nothing manipulative about her. Hell, she was a grown woman, married and divorced, and she didn't even realize how pretty she was. She had no idea why he hadn't wanted her to touch him earlier. She didn't even begin to understand why he couldn't have an affair with her.

In all honesty, he was having a few doubts himself. They *were* both adults, as she'd pointed out, both capable of weighing the consequences and making the right decision. Wouldn't that make it all right? If she came to him, fully understanding that it wouldn't be a relationship but an affair, that there wouldn't be anything between them but sex, that it might last a day, three or four at most, and then he would be gone... If she knew all that, wouldn't it save him from burning in hell?

No. She didn't have affairs, and he couldn't have a relationship. There was a lot more between them than just sex, and three or four days would be plenty of time to figure out what it was. It would be more than enough time to damn him.

But he was damned anyway, wasn't he? Since he was going to pay for these few days here with Ashley with every bit of longing he'd ever known, with his peace of mind and just a little of his sanity, would it be so wrong if he made love to her before he left? If he had to suffer the torment anyway, couldn't he experience the pleasure first?

She laid the brush on the hearth—*thank God*—folded back the top quilt, fluffed the pillow, then glanced around. "Where are the handcuffs?"

"I put them away." While she'd been in the bathroom changing for bed, he had unhooked them from the leg of the sofa and tucked them, along with the key, underneath the cushion. He wasn't going to need them anymore...unless he had to chain himself in the corner to keep himself away from her.

"Does this mean that you've decided I'm worthy of your trust?"

"I don't trust anyone," he answered automatically as he watched her settle on the pallet. She didn't have a pretty face or big boobs, she'd said earlier, but at least she had the long legs. Damned right, he thought as he caught a glimpse of her legs, long, strong, the thin gown sliding up to reveal more, now at the knee, now the thigh, the hip.... Catching his tongue between his teeth, he squeezed his eyes shut and swore.

"Maybe you don't, maybe you do. How do you know I won't sneak away during the night?"

Dragging in a breath, he forced his jaw to relax enough to answer. "Where would you go? It's cold out there, and it's not going to stop raining until we drown. Bessie won't run, and your nearest neighbor is five miles away. Getting there in the dark, in the cold and the rain wouldn't be the easiest hike you've ever taken, and, honey, I promise you, most of the people out there looking for me are much more dangerous than I am."

"You trust me not to leave," she said simply.

"I believe you have the good sense to weigh the consequences and make the right decision."

"Which is the same as trusting me."

"It's got nothing to do with trust," he insisted, exasperation shading his voice.

She sat up, the quilt falling to her waist. "You're afraid to admit it, aren't you?"

"The last person I made the mistake of trusting set me up for a major fall, then tried to have me killed. I'm not afraid of anything except him." And getting caught. Going to prison. Dying in prison. Wanting Ashley. Needing her. Making love to her. Not making love to her.

Russell, it seemed, was the *least* of his fears.

She stared at him, her gaze compelling even though her face was mostly in shadow. "It *was* Bradley, wasn't it?" she asked softly, and Dillon cursed aloud. "*He* was involved in the robbery. *He* took the money."

He swore again.

"What happened? How did he convince you to break into the bank? Did you take the money and take it to him?"

Why couldn't he learn to keep his mouth shut? The less she knew about what had happened that night and who was involved, the safer she would be. And he *needed* her to be safe. That was the thing he feared most of all: Ashley getting hurt because of him. Ashley being punished because of him. God help him, Ashley dying because of him.

"Forget it, Ash," he said—pleaded—wearily.

"In your dreams." She scrambled to her feet and came to sit on the bed. He drew aside so quickly that a sharp pain shot through his ribs. "Did he pay you? Bribe you? Blackmail you?"

He tried to ignore how close she was—always too close, never close enough—and focus instead on her last question. "What could I possibly have done that Russ could use to blackmail me?"

She shrugged. "You robbed a bank. Surely there must be other secrets in your past."

"Not one."

She allowed herself to be distracted for a moment. "You've never done anything you're ashamed of?"

He also allowed a brief distraction as he reached out and drew his fingers over the curve of her knee, making her shiver before he lifted his hand and tugged the hem of her gown down to cover her legs. "There's a lot that I'm ashamed of," he answered quietly. "Things I did, things I didn't do. But most of it isn't a secret, and none of it's worthy of blackmail."

"What sort of things?"

There were so many to choose from that he couldn't, starting with the trouble he'd caused when he was a kid—the fights he'd picked, the mischief he'd created, the embarrassment and pain he'd caused his grandfather. There was the sorry state of his relationship with his mother; granted, Carole had never been prime parent material, but then he'd never given her any reason to try. He had been more trouble than he was worth since before he was born, she had often declared to whoever would listen, and he had been determined to prove her right. She had been a bad mother; he had deliberately been a bad son.

There were all the failures in his life: the jobs he'd lost, the women he'd known, the disappointments he'd caused. As much as he'd loved his grandfather, and as much as Jacob had loved him, Dillon hadn't even been able to keep that relationship healthy. Weeks, months or—on a few occasions—entire years had gone by when he had refused to return the old man's calls, had tossed his letters in a drawer unanswered, had found it too much a bother to drive the few hours necessary for a visit. Only a few days before Jacob's death, Dillon had turned down a request that he drive out to the old farm for an afternoon. He hadn't wanted to go to Waterston, hadn't wanted to risk running into any of Alexander's family—at least, that had been his official reason, and partly true. The real reason was that he'd lost another job and another woman in the same day. He hadn't been able to face his grandfather, hadn't been able to bear seeing the disappointment in the old man's eyes every time he looked at him. Selfishness and pride had cost him one last meeting with the only person who had always loved him.

"Dillon?" Ashley's voice was gently prodding and as soft as her hand settling over his.

He looked down in the dim light, comparing, contrasting. His skin was dark and brown; hers was painted gold by the fire. His hand was big and strong; hers was deceptively delicate. His palm was callused from years of hard work; hers bore the traces of hard work, too, but was softened by cream that felt like powdered silk and smelled of roses. His hands could cause great pain. Hers could bring great peace.

He needed peace.

"Why are you always touching me?" Immediately she started to draw her hand back, but he surprised both her and himself by turning his hand, catching hold of hers.

"People need to touch and be touched." Her voice was throaty, unintentionally provocative, and her fingers were stroking his palm. "It gives us a connection to each other, makes us feel less alone.'' She slipped her hand free of his and raised it to his jaw, drawing her fingers along it, then down his throat, making him shiver. ''It allows us to get closer, to build intimacy. It can comfort, soothe, reassure and encourage.'' Her fingers teased and tickled their way across his chest, skirting around the tender place on his ribs, turning away when they reached the covers and returning once more to his hand. ''It can heal…'' Her voice was softer now. ''And hurt…'' Breathier, too. ''And bring great pleasure…''

And it could arouse. *He* was aroused, his body throbbing, and if she *wasn't*, it surely wouldn't take much to remedy.

But she was. If he needed proof, he got it in the next instant, when she lifted his hand to her mouth. Cradling it in both of her hands, she kissed his palm, her tongue moistening his skin, then she pressed his hand to her throat, holding it there, molding it to fit before slowly sliding it down.

He couldn't breathe, couldn't speak, couldn't find the words to stop her or the strength to stop himself. He simply lay there and let her guide his hand across warm, satiny skin, over delicate lace and thin cotton. He let her slide his hand along until it was cupped over her breast, cradling it in his palm, feeling the hard peak of her nipple like a brand.

For a moment he remained still and compliant. Then, no longer needing her guidance, he began stroking her, simple little movements, not much but enough to make her eyes close, enough to make her breath catch and her lips part on a silent sigh. He rubbed her, bringing each stroke slowly, deliberately over her nipple, creating friction with the heat and pressure of his palm and the barely there fabric, and he tried to remember one reason, just *one* reason, why he shouldn't do this. His mind was thankfully blank.

''Is that pleasurable, Ash?'' he whispered.

Eyes still closed, she gave him a smile of such satisfaction and raised her hands, not to push him away but to fumble with the tiny white buttons down the front of the gown. He watched as she unfastened the top one, then the second, the third and the fourth. Holding on to him, she used her free hand to push the fabric aside, then clasped his hand to her breast, naked now, so smooth, so soft and hot. So beautiful.

She was right. He needed this—needed to touch her, needed to be touched by her. He needed her hands on his body, anywhere, everywhere. He needed to be stroked and petted until he died from the pure pleasure of it. He needed to kiss her breasts, to hold her, to explore and taste and savor her. He needed her body against his, her breasts flattened against his chest, her belly rubbing his, her hips sheltering his, her legs twined with his. He needed it all.

And what did *she* need?

Anything in the world but him.

She needed Seth, or someone just like him. Someone respectable, someone she could be proud of, someone who wasn't likely to end up dead or in jail before his thirty-fifth birthday. Someone who knew what it meant to love, who knew how to give it and receive it, how to care for it and keep it growing. Someone who would be there for her not just right now but five weeks and five months and five years from now. Someone whom the children she needed to provide the grandchildren and great-grandchildren she wanted wouldn't be embarrassed to claim as their father. Someone who could protect her and keep her safe and never, ever cause her a moment's harm, a moment's pain or a moment's shame.

Someone *else. Anyone* else. Anyone else but Dillon.

Giving up that touch was the hardest thing he'd ever done. His fingers literally ached, curving toward her, reaching in silent plea. His entire body ached, too, with disappointment, with regret and desire.

It took her a moment to realize that he was stopping. Her eyes slowly fluttered open, and she drew a deep, noisy breath. She didn't plead. If she had, he probably would have given in, and she would have made the biggest mistake of her life. But she simply looked at him, her eyes dazed, her expression hazy, her body all soft and invitingly warm.

He copied her earlier act, lifting her hand to his mouth, pressing a kiss to the center of her palm. ''I want to make love to you, Ashley,'' he whispered, his voice not quite steady. ''I want to pull you over here and slide inside you and stay there forever. I want to see you naked, to kiss you and touch you. Oh, God, I want to touch you…but it would be wrong, Ash. Can't you understand that?''

She shook her head.

Silently swearing, he squeezed his eyes shut on the tempting picture she presented, sitting there with her hair mussed from the moment she'd spent in her bed and her face flushed from the moments she'd spent in *his* bed, with her gown unbuttoned and her breasts uncovered.

When he opened his eyes again, he pulled the top edges of her gown together and, making a concentrated effort not to actually touch her, he buttoned it up. It didn't help, though. He had already seen, and he wasn't likely to ever forget. ''You don't even know me.''

''Yes, I do.''

He wanted to argue, wanted to insist that she was wrong. In spite of the close quarters they had shared these past few days, in spite of the intensity of the relationship—the alliance, the companionship, whatever the hell it was—they had built, they were still strangers. She couldn't possibly have learned enough about him to believe that she wanted to have an affair with him, because knowing him should convince her of exactly the opposite.

But he couldn't argue a lie. These past few days probably *were* enough for her to reach that decision, because they had sure been long enough for him to reach it.

''I *can't* make love with you.''

She treated him to a long, slow, appraising look that didn't stop until it reached evidence—still very strong evidence—to the contrary. Feeling stripped bare and frustrated, he shifted positions and pulled the covers higher.

''I *won't* make love to you,'' he amended, his voice sharp. ''I've got to leave here in a few days, Ash, one way or another. Whether I get away free or go to jail, one fact doesn't change. There's no room in my life for you.''

After a long moment she smiled the cool sort of smile she chose when she was hurt. "You have a high opinion of yourself."

He scowled at her. "Why do you say that?"

"You think a few days as your lover is going to be so meaningful that it will change my life, that I won't be able to live without you, that I'll pine away the rest of my life because you aren't here."

She waited, but he couldn't respond. To agree that, yes, that was exactly what he was afraid of was too arrogant, and to admit that, no, *he* was the one whose life would change, *he* was the one who would have trouble getting along, *he* was the one who would die missing her, would be too painful.

With a sigh, she rose from the bed. "We could have been good together, Dillon. You'll never know what you've missed."

Oh, he would know. Every lonely minute of every lonely day would remind him. Every empty night would torment him. Every image of her would haunt him. But instead of admitting that to her, instead of giving her something more to use against him, he echoed her sigh. "And you'll never know what you've escaped."

Chapter 7

"Do you have a map?"

At Dillon's question, Ashley looked up from the dining table. He'd been restless all afternoon, pacing the cabin, stopping occasionally to lift the corner of a sheet and peer out the window. She'd wanted to tell him a dozen times to calm down, to take it easy, read, relax, try to sleep, but she'd known instinctively that he wouldn't listen. He was fidgety. Nervous. Eager to be on his way.

Eager to leave her behind.

She pushed away from the table. "There's one in the van. I'll get it."

He started to protest, then shrugged. After putting on her loafers, she hurried out to the van. The rain was still coming down, but it was gentler this morning, warmer, a typical spring shower. The sun was trying to break through the clouds, and try as she might, she couldn't make out any more rain clouds to the west. A day or so of dry weather, and Bessie would be ready to go.

Dillon was already ready.

Leaning across the passenger seat, she pulled out the tattered atlas, then returned to the cabin and silently handed it over to him. While he flipped through the pages to the North Carolina map, she reseated herself at the table and went back to work. For small-ticket items, shower gels were among her more profitable enterprises. She bought the clear soapy gel by the gallon, colored it in rich jewel tones or soft pastels and added scents with essential or fragrance oils. She had a large collection of the oils, each in a small vial, but her own personal favorites were tea rose and honeysuckle. She hoped that wherever he went, whatever he did, Dillon never smelled either of those scents again without thinking of her. Without missing her. Without regretting her.

Just as she would never again breathe in the fragrance of vanilla without being reminded of him. When he left, she would send her last two bottles of the ivory-hued, vanilla-scented gel with him…and maybe a bottle or two of the deep red honeysuckle, too.

"This atlas is over ten years old." He tossed it on the table, nearly knocking over the round plastic bottle she was filling with the last of the jasmine-scented gel. Dragging out the chair across from her, he turned it around and straddled it.

"So?"

"So things change. New roads get built. Old ones get closed down."

"Not around here. I doubt that Catlin County's gotten a new road in my lifetime."

"So how do we get out of here?"

"That depends on where you want to go." She used a narrow spatula to scrape the last of the gel into the jar, removed the funnel, then capped it with a small white lid. Later she would label the jars with the pretty gummy labels her sister Deborah had had designed and made up for her last Christmas, but for now she was simply setting them aside. She wouldn't forget what they were and, if she did, she needed only a whiff to remember. "If you want to head into South Carolina or Virginia, we should probably take this road." Reaching across the table, she tapped one finger on a thin north-south line on the upside-down map. "If you want to go to Tennessee, Georgia or points west, you need to take this road to the interstate."

He studied the map a moment. "Those are the two major roads out of the county."

"Those are the two *only* roads out of the county," she corrected him.

"Surely there are some secondary roads."

"There are lots of secondary roads, but those two are the only ones that leave the county. Catlin's a small county, and a lot of it is too rough for travel. We have plenty of little meandering country roads like the one I live on, but—like the one I live on—they dead-end after a while or they circle around and run into one of those highways. That's how we have to go."

He stared at the map a while longer. Wishing he'd escaped in Asheville, maybe, where he knew his way around and Miss Pris would have helped him? Or maybe in a city like Raleigh or Charlotte, where the possibilities for getting out of town were endless, where there were so many roads that trying to close off the city with roadblocks would be impossible. Maybe he was wishing he'd never heard of Catlin, that he'd never left Georgia, that he'd never trusted his buddy Russ.

Maybe he was wishing he'd never met *her.*

Finally he looked up at her. She was measuring drops of oil into a bowl filled with gel in a rich translucent red, and the scent of honeysuckle drifted up between them. Reaching out, he caught the next drop on his fingertip, rubbed it together with his thumb, then sniffed it. "This smells like you."

Her smile was hard to find, but she managed a faint one.

He drew his hand back and rested his arms on the back of the chair. "Once the rain stops, how long will it take Bessie to dry out?"

"A day, maybe two. It depends on how humid it is."

"Why don't you get the thing fixed?"

She gave him a dry look. "That van is nearly thirty years

old. You don't just walk into an auto-parts store in a place like Catlin and pick up a new part off the shelf.''

''Why don't you get something safer?''

''Bessie's perfectly safe.''

''Something more reliable.''

''Who's got the money to spend on a car?''

He scowled and muttered, ''This is no way to live.''

''This is exactly how I *want* to live,'' she responded quietly. ''If you find it so unappealing, well, in another day or two, you won't have to endure it any longer. Whatever happens, in jail or on the run, you'll be living in a way that's much, much worse.'' That turned his mood a few degrees darker, prompting her to go on quickly. ''Which way do you plan to go?''

''West.''

''I have family in California. If you make it that far, look them up.''

He disregarded the flippancy in her voice. ''Why did they move there when their roots are here? When their daughter is here?''

''It was Daddy's dream to live someplace else.''

''To meet interesting people? Do exciting things?'' He almost smiled. ''I guess you came by the desire honestly. Do you miss them?''

''More than you can imagine.'' After all, he'd never been close to his mother, and his father had never acknowledged him. He'd never had the sort of normal upbringing that she'd taken for granted—the typical family, the working father and stay-at-home mother, the annoying siblings, the rivalry, the vacations, the big holiday get-togethers. She would like the chance to include him in a few of her family's affairs.

Fat chance. Slim chance. *No* chance.

''Where is your father?'' she asked, giving the gel one final stir, then setting up the first bottle with the narrow-necked funnel in place.

His scowl returned. ''He lives in Georgia.''

''Atlanta?''

"No. A little town called Waterston. He's one of the Waterses for whom the town is named."

"There's nothing quite like small-town aristocracy, is there?" she asked lightly. "In Catlin, the Benedicts are the most aristocratic of them all. Seth's mother was tremendously disappointed by our marriage. I was one of the riffraff, my father worked in the mill that used to operate over on Tompkins Ridge." Waiting for the thick gel to ooze into the bottle, she sobered again. "I take it your parents weren't married."

He shook his head.

"You want to talk about it?"

He stared at the atlas for a moment before finally shrugging. "My mother was eighteen when she began her affair with Alexander. He was twenty-six, married and already had one kid and another on the way. He told Carole—my mother—that he loved her, that as soon as the baby was born, he would divorce his wife and marry her, and she believed him. She honestly believed that the only son of the Waters family, the richest family in town, with the oldest money and the bluest blood, was going to divorce his wife—from the second-richest family with the next-to-the-bluest blood—to marry the high-school-dropout daughter of a poor dirt farmer and take her away to a better life. She was a fool."

"Being in love can make you crazy," Ashley said softly. "It can make you do foolish things."

She felt his glower even though she wisely wasn't looking. "How would you know?"

Because *he* was teaching her. But she didn't say that. "What happened?"

"After four or five years, she got pregnant. By then Alexander had three legitimate heirs to the throne. He wasn't pleased with the prospect of an illegitimate one. As her pregnancy became obvious, there were rumors, of course. There had always been speculation about their affair, and people were apparently pretty curious about the new development. Alexander didn't like the gossip, and his mother and his wife especially didn't like it, so he denied being the father. He denied ever having been with Carole, and he cut her off—socially, financially, emotionally. All the years we lived there, he treated her worse than anyone should ever be treated. He despised her and made certain that everyone, especially my mother, knew it. It didn't help any that, to get back at him, she named me after him—Dillon Alexander Waters Boone.'' He gingerly touched his eye, where little sign of the bruising courtesy of the Sylvan County Sheriff's Department remained. ''The name alone got me about a dozen bloody noses and twice that many black eyes from Alexander Waters, Jr. Alex didn't like sharing his name *or* his father with me.''

Either Carole Boone had had a cruel streak running through her, Ashley thought grimly, or she had been too much a fool to consider what she was doing to her son with that name. If Alexander Waters had despised his ex— What had Carole been to him? Lover? Mistress? Plaything? Amusement? Whatever role she had filled for him, if he had come to despise her for the gossip and the notoriety, he surely must have despised their son as much. Giving Dillon the man's name—particularly when Alexander's legitimate son already had a claim to it— must have been like rubbing salt into an open wound. It must have made Dillon's life in Waterston, Georgia, pure hell.

''How long did you live there?''

''Until I was twelve. Things had gotten kind of tough by then. Alexander's family was determined to run us out of town so they wouldn't have to face the product of Alexander's indiscretion every day, and I was determined to help them. I hated it there. I hated the talk. I hated the way they treated my mother and especially my grandfather, just because the almighty Waters family decreed that they should be treated that way. I hated Alex beating the hell out of me every time I left the house…although I have to give him credit.'' He grinned sardonically. ''He taught me how to fight dirty, and that surely did come in handy in Atlanta.''

She set aside the filled bottle, then reached for another empty. ''You've either been looking for trouble or running away from it most of your life, haven't you?''

Sometimes she thought his face should be permanently etched with a scowl. In less time than it took to blink, it chased away his grin and the faint softening that had accompanied it and left him looking hard and unforgiving. Ignoring her question, he returned his attention to the atlas, flipping open to a map of the United States. "If I want to head out west, we pick up the interstate and cross into Tennessee. How far can you take me?"

Swallowing a sigh, she glanced at the map. "You want to try for California?"

The scowl deepened. "Be serious."

"I *am* serious. I told you that I haven't seen my family in over three years. I wouldn't mind surprising them."

"You think Bessie could make it all the way across the country?"

The scorn in his voice turned her smile sad. "Stranger things have happened." In spite of her insistence, it *hadn't* been a serious offer, she told herself. She couldn't just lock up and leave. If she wasn't here, she wasn't making money, and without money, she couldn't hold on to this place. It wasn't much, but it was all she had. It was her life. The offer had been a joke, all in jest.

So why did it sting just a little that he hadn't jumped at it? That he hadn't found anything the least bit attractive about it? That he no more wanted to take her with him than he wanted to stay here?

"How about Nashville?" It was four, maybe five hours away. The city was large enough that he would have some options, close enough that she could make the trip there and back without too much cause for concern.

He located it on the map, stared at it for a moment, then silently nodded.

"It would be in your best interests to wait at least a few more days."

"Why?"

"The roadblocks will have to come down pretty soon. It costs a lot of money to have officers assigned exclusively to one location, doing only one job. Frankly I don't think you're important enough to justify the expense for too long."

"You said you could get through the roadblocks."

She acknowledged that with a shrug. "There's also the risk of recognition. I imagine your face has been plastered all over the newspapers and TV stations for miles around. It's not an easy one to forget."

"And what am I supposed to do while I wait for the roadblocks to come down and for something more important to bump me off the front page of the paper?"

She could tell from his expression that he expected her to repeat yesterday's invitation, to say, *You could stay here. I could hide you.* Of course, that was what she wanted to say. She wanted to ask, beg, plead. She wanted to argue with him, wanted to insist, wanted to somehow convince him that *here* was exactly where he belonged. Instead, though, she shrugged carelessly and repeated an earlier suggestion.

"You could turn yourself in."

Turn himself in.

For the first time in more than eleven months, Dillon gave the matter serious consideration. Always before, he had dismissed it out of hand as utter foolishness, a mistake he would pay for with the rest of his life. After all, who would believe anything he had to say? When he was pointing fingers at people like Russell Bradley, when he had a history of unreliability and minor run-ins with the law, when he had fled town that night last April like the guiltiest of the guilty, who would even listen?

Ashley believed Seth would. Maybe she was right. Maybe he would not only listen but actually even believe…but could Dillon stake his life on it?

What life? a mocking voice asked. On the run was no way to live, she'd once told him, and she was right. It was the loneliest, most miserable life he'd ever known…and growing up as Alexander's bastard son and Alex's punching bag, he'd known some miserable times.

But surrendering wouldn't give him any other choices. Instead of being miserable and free to go where he chose, he would be miserable and behind bars.

Unless Ashley was right. Seth could help prove that he'd been set up, she'd said. If he told Seth everything, if he revealed the entire story that he'd never shared with anyone, if Seth believed him and agreed to reopen the investigation... Dillon could clear his name and be free to live wherever he wanted, however he wanted, with whomever he wanted.

He could stay here. With *her.*

If there was evidence to clear him. *If* Seth believed him.

"What happened that night, Dillon?"

Those were mighty big *if*s. Besides, he knew better than to want what he couldn't have. That was one lesson he'd learned when he was a kid. He was wrong to want Ashley. To want to stay here. To want to make this old farm into a viable proposition once more. To want to spend his days working in the fields, the way his grandfather had, and his nights making love with her. He was wrong to think about watching a lifetime's worth of sunrises from that front porch with her, about sharing just as many sunsets.

He was wrong to think about marrying her, having children with her, growing old with her.

"I can't tell you."

"Why not?"

"Because there are people out there who want me dead! Have you forgotten that?"

Her gaze shifted to his shoulder, to the dressing that was hidden underneath the sweatshirt he wore. Though still tender, the gunshot wound was healing. Sometimes, if not for the sling, he could forget it was there—and that was dangerous. As long as he was here, as long as he was around Ashley, he needed to always remember that there were a lot of people out there who would be better off if *he* were dead.

"So tell me again what happened *then*—when they tried to kill you. You said the first night that you and Tom Coughlin were on your way to Catlin when you got ambushed at Sadler's Pass, that three men opened fire on you."

He made no response.

"Did you see them very well? Did you know any of them?"

When he still said nothing, she left her chair and came around to crouch beside him. Her fingers, very delicate and feminine in spite of their short, unpainted nails, rested on his thigh. "Dillon, you aren't protecting me by keeping silent. Someone tried to kill you because of the bank robbery. You believe they're out there looking for you along with the police. If they find you here, what will they do?"

"They'll probably take me into custody to turn over to the sheriff. Unfortunately, somewhere between here and town, I'll try to escape, and they'll have to shoot me. No one will even question their story because I *did* get away twice before."

"*I'll* question it, and when I do, what will *they* do?"

Sliding back on the seat, he rested his head on his arms and stared down, seeing nothing. If Russell and his accomplices were willing to kill to keep *him* quiet, would they balk at using the same deadly force to silence Ashley? He would give his soul to believe that the answer was yes—that, while they had no qualms about murdering someone who had been part of their plans from the start, they would draw the line at killing an innocent woman who'd been dragged into this mess through no fault of her own.

But try as he might, he couldn't believe it. Russell and everyone else involved had a lot to lose, and who better to put them in jeopardy than the investigating sheriff's ex-wife and best friend? They weren't fools. If they found him here, they would kill them both. Whether Ashley knew the truth would be irrelevant.

Tilting his head to the side, he met her gaze. "Two of them were strangers. The third one—the one who shot the deputy... I'd seen him before, but I don't remember where."

"Could it have been someone who worked for Bradley Electronics?"

He shook his head. "Not while I was there. I knew everyone."

"A friend of Bradley's? Someone you saw with him in Asheville?"

"No." That meant it was probably someone he'd seen around Catlin the weeks he'd lived there. An employee of the bank, maybe, or a regular customer at the diner where he'd eaten.

Her muscles growing tired, Ashley drew back, pulled a chair over and sat facing him. He immediately missed the touch of her hand on his leg. "What did he look like?"

He thought back to that morning in the cruiser. When the Sylvan County deputies had turned him over to Tom Coughlin, they had cuffed his hands tightly behind his back. Without a word to them, Coughlin had removed the handcuffs, then refastened them just tight enough to keep Dillon from slipping free, and he'd done it with his hands in front. Having ridden in a Sylvan County car with his hands behind him and the cuffs tight enough to make his fingers turn blue, Dillon had appreciated the small consideration.

The drive, for the most part, had passed in silence. The deputy had been all business, no chitchat or small talk. Dillon had asked him about the belongings he'd left behind in Asheville, and the deputy had told him that the law allowed the landlord to dispose of them as he saw fit. That was the extent of the conversation until they'd reached Sadler's Pass. Coughlin had slowed down for a tight curve, then suddenly hit the brakes and muttered, "What the…" and all hell had broken loose. Dillon had had only seconds to take in the scene ahead—the black van, its windows tinted, the three men. They had been all business, too—so cool, so collected, so deadly. As if this sort of thing came naturally to them. As if violence came naturally to them.

With a deep breath, he tried to focus on the man he'd recognized. He'd stood apart from the other two, right out in the middle of the lane, as if he'd had no fear. It was his shot, Dillon was pretty sure, that had hit Coughlin. He had no idea who'd shot *him* because the car was already going off the side of the mountain; the shot had come from behind, and he was being tossed around like a rag doll.

He had believed at that moment that he was going to die.

It still might happen.

"He was young, probably in his mid-twenties," he said at last, his voice flat. "He was about six feet tall, maybe a little taller, with black hair, kind of shaggy, a mustache, kind of cocky. He was wearing jeans and a green-and-yellow jacket— you know, a high school letter jacket."

More than a little of the color drained from her face, but she tried to hide her shock with a smile. It didn't work. "You just described Steven Vickers."

"Who is that?"

"My kid sister's ex-boyfriend. The star quarterback for the Catlin High Wildcats eight or ten years ago." That sickly little smile reappeared. "A member of the search party that came through yesterday. And one of Seth's deputies."

For a moment Dillon felt nothing. He sat there, leaning on the back of the chair, hearing her words in his head but not understanding them. Then he realized that his fingers were gripping the chair tightly enough to hurt, that his stomach had gotten queasy and his lungs felt as if they just might burst. The man who had tried to kill him had been right outside the cabin yesterday morning, and he was a cop. He wasn't sure which frightened him more.

A cop. He hadn't expected that. He'd known that there was more than enough corruption in this mess to go around, but he hadn't thought that it might have reached the sheriff's department. He hadn't considered that Russell might buy himself a cop, but really, it made perfect sense. If Dillon had been arrested eleven months ago, a deputy on Russell's payroll could have kept his old friend informed. He could have passed on every bit of inside information on the case. He could have told Russell and the others things like what Dillon was telling the sheriff. Things like if and when he was being transported, and by what route.

A cop. Even worse, a cop who had shot another cop, who

had been willing to kill a fellow officer, a friend. It seemed the stakes had gone even higher than Dillon had imagined.

"You can't be sure that the guy with the gun is your deputy," he said stiffly. "Vickers can't be the only man in the county with shaggy black hair and a mustache."

Ashley gave him a chastising look. "Haven't you heard about the death of small-town America? Young people want excitement, education, opportunity, so they move away to the city. There aren't more than two dozen men in Catlin between the ages of twenty and forty, and only one who fits that description *and* has a Wildcats letter jacket." She drummed her fingers agitatedly on the tabletop. "I have to tell Seth."

"Like hell you do." Reaching out, he grabbed her hand and held it tightly in his. "What are you going to tell him?"

"That he might have a dirty cop working for him!"

"And he'll want to know where in God's name you got that idea. *Then* what are you going to tell him?"

"The truth. Dillon, he can help you!"

"I don't *want* his help. All I want is to get out of here." But that wasn't true. In the best of all worlds, accepting help from the sheriff would rank right at the top of his priorities. Getting help, clearing his name, staying here, making a life, loving Ashley—those would be his goals.

But this was far from the best of all worlds. If the sheriff knew he was here, Benedict would arrest him. He wouldn't believe his story about Russell and the money. He wouldn't make an effort to clear Dillon's name. He would lock him up in a cell guarded by the very man who had tried to kill him. Dillon would be lucky to live long enough to go to trial.

"So you're just going to run away without even a look back." The accusation in her voice made him uncomfortable, made him feel weak and cowardly. He wasn't weak—the fact that he could walk away from her proved that—but he *was* a coward. He was afraid of going to prison. Afraid of failing in exactly the way that Alexander and so many others had expected of him. Afraid of losing his freedom, his dignity and whatever was left of his pride.

Running away without looking back. "That's what I do best," he replied grimly.

But that was a lie, too. He would be looking back. Until the day he died, he would look back with great regret on this place, this time and especially this woman.

Chapter 8

The dinner dishes were done and night had fallen when Ashley took her shawl from the peg near the door. "I'm going outside," she announced, then, at Dillon's sharp look, she hastily added, "Just to the porch. Just for a few minutes."

He didn't offer her permission, didn't respond at all except to watch with a scowl as she stepped into her shoes, then wrapped the shawl tightly around her shoulders. She gave him a quick, reassuring smile before she went out and closed the door behind her.

It was chilly, the sort of crisp, sharp cold that made her think winter was coming, not leaving. It felt good, though. Refreshing. The icy air chased away the heat that seemed to have seeped into her very bones, cleared the cobwebs from her head and cleaned the pungent woodsmoke from her lungs. It made her feel stronger. More alert. More alive.

She also felt incredibly alone.

With a heavy sigh, she moved a few inches closer to the steps. If the moon weren't so bright, she would go to the top step to sit, to breathe and brood. Tonight, though, she stayed in the shadows, nothing more than a darker shadow to anyone who might be out there looking.

She wondered whether Seth was out there somewhere, hoped and prayed that he was nowhere near Steven Vickers. She hoped the man Dillon had described wasn't Steven, but either way, she had to tell Seth. She couldn't let him continue working closely with a man who might be dangerous, who might have almost killed another deputy. She *had* to tell Seth, the sooner the better.

She just didn't know how she was going to manage.

She sighed so deeply that it made her shiver and, for just a moment, gave her a sense of lightness, of eased burdens, of peace. It was the night, of course. If days were peaceful up here in the mountains, nights were nothing less than heavenly. There were no lights to cast their reflections into the sky and block out the stars, no highways with traffic to break the night stillness, nothing man-made at all to disturb nature. The sounds were soft—crickets, the occasional rustles of wild creatures in the woods—and the scents—pine, flowers both wild and cultivated, clean, clear air—were soothing. Nighttime was a healing time. It was a time to relax, to rejuvenate, to refocus.

She was going to need a great many nights once Dillon was gone. A great deal of healing.

The door behind her opened, then closed again, so softly that if it weren't for the prickly little sensations racing down her spine, Ashley would have thought she'd imagined the sound. But it wasn't imagination. Without looking, she knew that Dillon had come out, knew that he was standing at the door, only a foot, maybe two, behind her. She knew that he, like her, needed the night's healing, too.

The boards creaked, alerting her that he had shifted. "Don't come out into the light," she said, her voice as quiet as the air.

The boards creaked again, then the door gave a faint groan as he leaned back against it. "Nice night."

"Hmm." She wrapped the ends of the shawl over her hands to warm her fingers, then tugged it tighter. "When I first considered moving here, I knew I'd be fine during the day, but I wasn't sure about the nights. I thought they would be so lonely. So scary."

"Were they?"

"No." Gazing out over the untended fields, she smiled. "There was a full moon when I moved in. I was a little edgy and couldn't sleep, so I came out here, wrapped myself in one of Granny's quilts and curled up in the rocker. It was so bright, so clear and quiet. I could see easily all the way to the woods. Everything was sharper, more intense—the light, the smells, the air. I fell asleep there in the rocker and didn't wake until dawn. After that, I was never afraid of the night again."

"Until I came."

Finally she glanced over her shoulder at him. He was even more in the shadows than she was. She could barely make out the pale colors that were muslin in the quilt wrapped around him. She couldn't make out his face at all. "Until you came," she quietly agreed. "Now, when you leave, the nights *will* be lonely."

"But not scary."

She turned her back to him again. "No, not scary." She would have her fears; they just wouldn't be tied in any way to the cycles of the sun, moon and stars. She would worry about him, would wonder where he was and how he was getting along and whether he ever thought about her. She would be afraid that someday he would get caught, that Bradley's men would track him down and finish the job they'd started. She would spend the rest of her life worrying and wondering, and she would never have any answers, because she knew without asking that he would never try to contact her. He would never let her know that he was safe. Of course, if Bradley's men caught him, he would never be able to let her know that he wasn't.

It would be hell not knowing. She thought she could let him go, thought she could say goodbye to him and get on with her life, if only she could know that he was all right. That he'd found someplace safe to stop running. That he'd settled into the sort of life he deserved to be living, a normal life, with a job and a home, with friends…and family? Could she accept that he'd married someone else, had children with someone else, that he'd found someone else suitable for sharing his life when *she* wasn't?

She could, she thought with a thin smile. She might hate him for it, but at the same time, she would be grateful for knowing.

"Will going to Nashville be a problem for you?"

She swallowed over the lump in her throat. "No. The only person who keeps track of me around here is Seth, and he's too busy looking for you. I do a fair amount of traveling to shops and shows and to buy supplies, so no one will think twice about it."

"Can you get there and back in one day?"

"If Bessie and the weather cooperate."

"Maybe we shouldn't try for Nashville. Maybe we should go only as far as Knoxville or just some little place in Tennessee."

"Knoxville is too close. You've surely been in the news there. Nashville's big enough that they won't have much, if any, interest in Catlin news, not even if it involves a bank robbery."

He blew his breath out in a hollow sound. "I don't want you to drive that far in Bessie alone. What if she breaks down? What if it rains? I can't even give you the money for a motel room or gas."

"I've got a little money." She'd told him his first night here that she didn't have any money, not in the bank, not at all, but it had been a lie. Granted, her savings account in Bill Armstrong's bank was on the paltry side; no self-respecting bank robber would touch it. But like her granny before her, she kept a little stash here in the cabin, all the money she'd earned in the past couple of months, tucked away neatly in a round basket with a lid that she'd woven specifically for that purpose.

"Why don't you let me take Bessie? You can stay here where you're safe."

Her back still to him, she shook her head. "You wouldn't

get past the roadblocks. Besides, your shoulder isn't healed yet. A few days working her gearshift will just make it worse."

She knew from his silence that he knew she was right on both points; otherwise, he would have argued them with her. Instead, he stood there behind her, quiet and still.

A light breeze moved up the valley, rustling through the trees, making her shiver. "Want your jacket?" he asked.

She thought of the coats hanging on the wooden rack behind the door—some water-repellent, the others not, one long, most of them shorter, all of them chosen for function and not style. There was one, a heavy quilted parka in olive drab, that would feel wonderful right now. Even the black-and-blue nylon windbreaker would be warmer than the shawl, but she didn't ask for it or any of the others. "I'd rather share your quilt."

For a long time there was silence, then she heard a rush of breath and the rustle of fabric. "Come here."

It took only two steps to reach him. One arm was spread wide, the quilt falling like a cape toward the floor. She snuggled in, taking a place not at his side, as he clearly expected, but in front of him, the back of her body fitting nicely along the front of his. He hesitated a moment, then lowered his arm, drawing her closer, enfolding her in his embrace, both arms clasped around her waist.

Closing her eyes, Ashley breathed deeply and smelled spices, flowers and vanilla. The scent was warm, sweet and intoxicating, a heady contrast to the cold, clean smells of the night.

"I'm sorry I came here."

"I'm not."

"You'll be safe when I'm gone."

"I suppose I will." Safe. Lonely. Sad. But she would survive. She was strong. She'd made a satisfying life for herself alone before he'd come, and she would eventually manage to do so again once he was gone. She would get up early, have her tea out here in the rocker and spend her days in the workshop. She would still go to craft shows, resupply the shops with her goods and see Seth every Saturday. It wouldn't be different at all…except that she would be missing Dillon every moment that she was awake.

"Will you ever tell Seth?"

"I don't know."

"Have you ever considered trying with him again?"

"Trying what?"

"Marriage. Trying to make it work this time."

She twisted just enough to get a faint glimpse of his face. "Would you like that? Would it make you feel better if you knew that Seth and I were married again, that I was living with him and sleeping with him?"

He scowled. "Yes. No. Oh, hell, forget I mentioned it."

With a private little smile, she turned forward again, clasped her hands over his and rested her head on his shoulder. "You could ask me to go with you."

"No, I couldn't."

"Why not?"

"Because you would say yes."

"Would that be so bad?"

"You need a home, Ash. You need to stay here, where your work is, where your roots are, where your heritage is. You belong here every bit as much as I don't."

"I could adapt." She said it quietly because she wasn't entirely sure it was true. He was right: she *did* belong here. This was her home, her life. This was who she was. But he was also wrong: *he* belonged here, too—or he could, if he would let himself. If he would trust her. If he would turn himself in, face his problems squarely and deal with them once and for all.

"Living with me wouldn't be fun or romantic or exciting. It would just be hard. You can't stay anyplace. You can't trust anyone. You can't do anything. All you can do is run, be scared and wish for something better."

"You don't sound too fond of the life-style."

"I hate it. And you'd hate it and you would hate me for making you live it."

She couldn't imagine anything that would truly make her hate him…but she could see herself simply stopping one day, no matter where they were or what they were doing, and saying, "I have to go home."

She drew a deep breath. "You know, you could always—"

Before she could finish, he laid his fingers over her mouth. "Don't say it. We had this discussion just this afternoon, and nothing's changed. I can't surrender, and you can't accept that, so let's forget it."

His fingers were warm, callused, rough against the tender skin of her lips. She savored the touch for a moment before drawing his hand away, holding it tightly in hers and softly inviting, "Make me forget it."

He was still, barely breathing, as if he suspected that he was about to walk into a trap but couldn't avoid it. "How?"

"Kiss me."

"No way."

"You did it before, and I do believe you enjoyed it." In the tight cocoon of the quilt, she turned to face him and realized for the first time exactly how intimately close they were. "You did enjoy it, didn't you?"

"More than you can imagine."

She laughed. "Oh, Dillon, I can imagine plenty."

"Ash—" Whatever protest or argument he'd been about to offer died unsaid as he raised his hand to her. He touched her gently, so gently—her hair, her forehead, her cheek, her jaw. Then he found the words again. "It would be wrong."

She became as serious as he was. "We've both been alone a long time, Dillon. We've both been lonely. I admit that I would like for you to stay, that I can look ahead years from now and easily see the two of us together right here, but I know that's not going to happen. I know you're going to leave. I know that, if you have any control over it, I'll never see you again. I can accept that. What I can't accept is not being able to touch you, not being able to make love with you, not being allowed to have any part of you at all. That's all I'm asking for, Dillon. Until you leave, I just want to be a part of you."

He lowered his head until his forehead rested against hers. "It's only going to hurt," he whispered.

Her voice was just as soft and a lot shakier when she answered. "Saying goodbye is going to hurt, no matter what the circumstances. You can't make a commitment. You can't give me a future or make any promises or even give me any hope. At least give me this much." She had to stop to take a breath, to force air into her lungs and to banish—or at least try to—the tears from her voice. "Please, Dillon. Give me just this one night."

Closing his eyes, Dillon swore a silent curse.

One night. She made it sound like a generous gesture. *You can't give me anything else, so please do this for me. You can't stay with me, can't love me, can't marry me, can't give me a family, can't be here when I need you, can't live with me, can't grow old with me, can't die with me, but, hey, you can make love with me, so please give me that little bit of nothing.*

One night. Just one night. Maybe she would be satisfied with that. Maybe it would be enough for her. It would be enough to drive *him* crazy. Enough to haunt him for as long as he lived. Enough to guarantee that he would spend the rest of his miserable life longing for this place and this woman. Enough to kill him, little by little, every day that he wasn't here and every night that wasn't spent at her side.

He couldn't do it. He couldn't spend just one night with her and then spend hundreds—thousands—of nights without her. If he made love to her, he would never be able to leave her until they took him away in chains. He would be damned for wanting her.

And maybe even more damned for not having her. Wouldn't it be easier living among strangers, always alone, with the memory of one night to sustain him? Wouldn't it be better just once to ease the loneliness that sometimes threatened to destroy him? Wouldn't all those hard miles and all that hard living be more tolerable if he had one good, sweet, pure moment to carry him through?

One night doing the one thing he'd wanted desperately to

do practically since the first time he'd seen her. Was that so much to ask? So much to need?

Ignoring the discomfort in his shoulder, he raised both hands to her face, cradling it in his palms. "Tell me to go to hell."

"Not unless you take me with you."

His smile was bitterly sad. "That's one of the things I'm afraid of."

Her responding smile was utterly sweet. "That's not going to happen. We're no different than a lot of couples out there, Dillon. They know that their relationships are likely to end sometime. We just happen to know when."

When. Tomorrow or the next day. Sunday seemed like a heartbeat away. If he hesitated, if he blinked, Friday would be gone, Saturday skipped over and Sunday would arrive.

Or it could be part of another lifetime. They could hold it at bay, if they moved slowly enough, if they tried hard enough, if they loved long enough.

"We can't have everything," she said softly. "We can't have much of anything. But does that mean we have to settle for nothing?"

He'd been settling all his life, it seemed. Settling for whatever affection he could have. Settling for the low expectations everyone except his grandfather had saddled him with. Settling for a second-class life as a first-class failure. Now she was offering him exactly what he wanted—not for as long as he wanted, but for a time. For a day or two—and that was a day or two more than he'd ever thought he would have.

He would be a damned fool to agree.

But he would be a fool to turn her down.

"Just promise me one thing."

He sensed rather than saw her sweet, satisfied smile. "What's that?"

"That you won't regret this." He could live with almost anything, but not her regret. Not knowing that, later, she might wish this night had never happened. Not knowing that she might be sorry she had asked him to kiss her, sorry she had shared such intimacies with him.

"Not as long as I live."

Still holding her with one arm, he reached behind him and opened the door with the other, then backed inside, drawing her along with him. He took a moment to secure the door before letting the quilt slide to the floor, taking her shawl with it. She was wearing a denim skirt, another long one that came almost to her ankles, buttoned, belted and buckled at the waist over a plain cotton shirt. He wondered what she was wearing underneath that shirt—a bra or nothing at all—then realized that in a moment he would find out. He would unfasten every one of those buttons, slide the shirt off her shoulders and down her arms and see her, touch her, kiss her, stroke her. He would remove the skirt, too, and lay her down naked on the bed. He would memorize the feel of her skin against his fingertips, would commit to memory forever the taste of her and all the different scents of her. He would arouse her, satisfy her, then do it again. And again.

Just thinking about it aroused *him.*

She reached for the big metal buckle at her waist, but he stayed her hands. "I want to undress you."

Her only response was a soft smile, then she turned and took a circuitous route to the bed, shutting off the lights as she went. Only the glow from the fireplace lit the room as she kicked off her shoes, turned down the covers, then waited, hands folded demurely together, for him to join her.

As he approached her, he tried to think of a single reason why he shouldn't do this, a single argument that could stop him, but his brain was incapable of cooperating. He *wanted* this, wanted *her,* more than he'd ever wanted anything in his life, wanted her so badly that he was willing to suffer for it later. Right or wrong, good or bad, sweet passion or intolerable pain, he had to do this. *Had* to. He just might die if he didn't.

Sliding his arm free of the sling, he lifted the fabric over his head and tossed it on the night table, then reached for her, hooking his fingers around her belt, using it to pull her to him. She didn't hesitate or hang back but came willingly, right up to him. "I've waited all my life for a woman like you."

She started to respond, then thought better of it and simply smiled instead. What had she been about to say? he wondered. That she'd waited all her life for *him?* Or maybe that she would wait the *rest* of her life for him? What a waste that would be, because she would be waiting for nothing. Once he left here, he could never come back.

Unless he did as she asked. Turned himself in. Went to prison. Served his time. One day in the distant future—if he lived long enough—they would let him go and he could come back here. *If* she waited. *If* she still wanted him. Hell, he wouldn't even have to wait that long to see her. They had visiting days in prison; a lot of them even made arrangements for conjugal visits. Ashley could take her chances on the road with Bessie every month or two or three, get herself all prettied up and drop in at the prison for a few hours' stilted conversation and a desperate fumble and grope behind bars. Wouldn't that be a terrific offer to make to a woman like her?

He would rather never see her again than see her in a shameful place like that.

Shaking away the grim thoughts, he unfastened the big brass buckle, then drew the belt from its loops and laid it on the night table atop his sling. Next he pulled her shirt free of the denim skirt, the cotton gliding smoothly along her skin. The shirt was white, a nice contrast to the pale golden hue of her skin, and the style was masculine, copied from a man's dress shirt, emphasizing the very decidedly feminine curve of her breasts and the narrowness of her waist. The buttons opened easily; in only a moment the two sides of the shirt were separated, revealing a strip of soft bare skin all the way down to her waist.

He had the answer to his question. She was naked underneath the shirt.

Now he owed her an answer that he couldn't give last night. Sliding his fingers over that strip of skin, he brought his hands to her throat, then her face. "You're a beautiful woman, Ash, more beautiful than any woman I've ever known."

Her smile was bright, teasing and just the slightest bit unsteady. "More beautiful than Pris?"

"I told you—Pris is pretty. You—you make a man feel weak. You're the strongest woman I've ever known, but just looking at you makes me want to protect you. You're sweet and lovely and delicate and tough, and you take my breath away."

Leaning forward, she kissed him. There was nothing tentative or hesitant about it. Her mouth connected with his; her tongue stroked inside. He was feeling little shocks all through his body when, as quickly as she'd begun, she ended the kiss. "You could have told me that last night when I asked."

"Last night?" He buried his hands in her hair, feeling it settle cool and silky around his fingers. "When I was lying in bed praying that you would quit tempting and tormenting me while I still had some small measure of willpower left? When I was seriously considering using the handcuffs on myself because *maybe,* just maybe, they would keep me away from you?"

"Tempting and tormenting..." Vague bewilderment was replaced by shameless satisfaction. "You mean when I put your hand on my breast."

"I mean when you sat in front of the fire and brushed your hair. The way you looked. The way you moved. Even the way you breathed." He chuckled softly. "You were seducing me then, and you didn't even know it."

"I'm trying to seduce you now, but you don't seem to know it."

He sobered. "I know, Ash. God help me, I know." Sliding his hands down, he caught the shirt and guided it along her arms until it was free and fell to the floor, a puddle of bright white on the dark woven rug. *Beautiful.* He hated to overuse the word, but he couldn't think of any other to describe the way she looked standing there, her hair mussed, naked to the waist, the firelight gleaming on her skin. So beautiful.

He reached out, almost touched her but not quite, his hand hovering only a fraction of an inch from her breast. "You know, don't you," he began, his voice so hoarse that it scratched his throat, "that this is going to destroy me."

The certainty in his voice made Ashley's heart ache. She longed to protect him, to draw him close, to hold him tight and keep him safe for the rest of their lives. All she did, though, was touch him, brushing her fingers just barely across his jaw. "Maybe not," she whispered. "Maybe it will heal us both."

For a moment he stood there, his hand less than a breath away, then he touched her. Her nipple hardened instantly, with no more than his light caress, and the ache around her heart seeped out in every direction, making her tremble. She wanted to let her head fall, to close her eyes and lose herself in the sweet sensations he was creating, but even more she wanted to look at him while he touched her. They would have so little together—tonight, maybe tomorrow, maybe even, if she was very lucky and fate was feeling kindly, tomorrow night. She wanted to remember every detail about every moment. She wanted to see every expression that crossed his face and softened his dark eyes. The desire. The need. The hunger. The pain. She wanted always, for as long as she lived, to remember his face.

With gentle touches, he guided her to the bed, laid her down on her grandmother's Double Wedding Ring quilt, then joined her there. Supporting himself on his left arm, with his right hand he stroked her, tender caresses that, because of the stiffness and pain in his shoulder, should have been awkward and clumsy but were nothing less than exquisite. They spread heat through her body, made her breasts swell and her nipples ache, stirred a desire deep in her belly that was unfamiliar in its intensity. The acts were nothing new—Seth had touched her, and so had the only other man in her life—but the results... They were different. Stunning. Breathstealing.

"Your skin is so soft," he murmured.

Her smile trembled. "Aloe and evening primrose oil."

"You smell so sweet."

"Honeysuckle." Now her voice was trembling, too, and her breathing had grown unsteady.

He ducked his head, placing kisses between her breasts, then breathed deeply. "Chamomile," he disagreed. "Every time I take a bath, I reach for the honeysuckle because it smells like you, but I always put it back because smelling like you would surely drive me insane. Now you've switched to chamomile and that will also drive me crazy."

Raising her hand to stroke his hair, she shook her head dazedly from side to side. "No, it would relax you. The scent of chamomile brings tranquility."

"I've been many things since the minute I walked into your clearing, but, honey, tranquil isn't one of them."

His teeth closed around her nipple in a tender bite, bringing a gasp of sharp pleasure from her and, at the same time, a low groan from him. He suckled her breast, drawing hard on her nipple, and her muscles twitched and tightened. Lower, his leg was hooked over hers, his hardness pressing against her thigh. Heavy denim separated them—her skirt, his jeans—but she could feel the heat, the length, of him. She could feel that simple, strong evidence of his need, and it made her greedy. It made her throb.

His kisses moved from one breast to the other, then across her ribs, lower, slower, until the skirt blocked his way. She watched as he slid down on the bed, finding the hem of the skirt, then working his way up, unfastening each button, pushing the fabric aside, frequently diverting his attention to a light touch across her thigh or her hip or drawing his fingers, just the very tips, across the pale cotton of her panties in an achingly intimate caress.

At last he opened the final button. Rising to his knees, he pulled the denim out from underneath her, dropped it over the side of the bed, then removed her last bit of clothing, following his progress with a trail of damp kisses—on her stomach, her hip, her thigh, the inside of her knee and all the way down her calf. Sitting back, for a moment he simply looked at her, and in the heartbeat and ragged breaths that filled her ears, she thought she heard him murmur one soft, gratifying word. "Beautiful."

She reached for him, both arms stretching out. "Please, Dillon…"

Grasping the hem of his sweatshirt, he started to strip it off, but stopped halfway through the motion. His expression was a mix of pain, impatience and embarrassment as she sat up and pushed his hands away. "Let me." But she didn't go straight to the task. She glided her hands underneath the fabric, bunching it, then bent to kiss his chest, bruises, scrapes and all, pausing only briefly to flick her tongue across his nipple, wondering if her mouth felt as heart-weakeningly good to him as his mouth had felt on her body.

Reaching his shoulders, she eased his left arm free of the shirt, then carefully worked it over his head and off his other arm. The dressing on his right shoulder was a reminder that his arm couldn't support even a fraction of his weight, that his bruised ribs, though much improved, also required special consideration. But that was all right. Though there was something tremendously appealing about lying underneath him—her body sheltering his while his, in turn, sheltered hers, his weight pressing against her as they moved together, arms and legs entwined—the options were terribly erotic, too. It didn't matter *how* they did it. All that mattered was that they did.

Advancing on her knees, she nudged him toward the edge of the bed. "Stand up," she whispered, her hands seeking and finding the button, then the zipper, of his faded jeans. Her fingers were suddenly clumsy, resulting in a great deal of fumbling that made him suck in his breath, then groan aloud.

"Ash…" There was a note of warning in his voice. "Don't play games or you're going to make me—" He groaned again as she opened his jeans and slid one hand inside. The muscles across his belly quivered as she explored lower, finding his arousal with a feathery light caress. Suddenly he grabbed her wrist, but he didn't pull her hand away. Instead, he pressed her palm hard against him. "Now, Ash."

Yes. *Now.* She freed her hand, and together they removed the last of his clothing, then he joined her on the bed again, and again he hesitated. "I don't know if I can…"

"*We* can," she whispered. Hands on his shoulders, she gently pushed him onto his back, then bent low for a kiss. His mouth was hot, his tongue bold. His hands, moving in heated caresses, were even bolder, rubbing her breasts, across her stomach, in hot, steady strokes between her thighs.

"Take me inside you, Ash." His effort to retain some bit of control tightened his jaw, making his voice thick and raw, and beaded sweat across his forehead. "I want to be inside you...."

She moved into place above him, seeking, guiding, sinking, taking him exactly where he wanted to be, where she needed him to be. He filled her, stretched her, made her feel more whole than she ever had before. He made her feel stronger, more alive, more womanly, more beautiful. For the first time in her life she *felt* beautiful, because of this incredibly beautiful man.

This incredibly beautiful and deeply loved man.

She closed her eyes on that last part. She had plenty of time ahead of her to think about loving him and losing him and living alone. Countless hours, endless nights. Tonight she wanted to focus on *this,* on the physical, on their bodies joined together, on the hunger and the arousal, the need, the sensation, the pleasure, the throbbing, the burning. She wanted to feel it all, wanted to make it all a part of her, a treasured memory that she could take out and relive when she had to make it through another lonely night.

His hands were on her thighs, moving restlessly, silently urging her to move, and she did, settling into an easy rhythm, taking him deeper, harder, feeding his arousal stroke by stroke, making him hotter, until, with harsh breathing and a harsher groan, he stiffened, went motionless for an instant, then filled her. She didn't stop, though, didn't give him a chance to catch his breath, didn't wait for the overload of sensation to become manageable, but continued thrusting against him, withdrawing, sheathing him again within her body. As he stroked her breasts, her thighs, any part of her that he could reach, he whispered soft words, erotic sounds, coaxing her, tempting her, encouraging her. Unable to resist the pure, sweet pleasure a moment longer, she gave in to it, too, and through it all, her gaze was locked on his face.

His sweet, beautiful and very much beloved face.

"It *was* Russell Bradley."

Dillon hadn't been sure before he spoke that Ashley was awake; she lay so still in his arms. But the instant she understood his words, the muscles all up and down her body tightened, and he knew she was totally alert and waiting for more. With a weary sigh, he told her everything.

"I was surprised when Russ offered me a job. I hadn't seen him in years. We lost touch when he joined the navy after high school and just happened to run into each other when he was visiting Atlanta. We'd grown up together, but you couldn't tell it by looking at us. He was wearing an expensive suit and gold jewelry, driving a seventy-thousand-dollar import and having meetings at his convenience with corporate CEOs, and I was strictly blue jeans, blue-collar. I was working as a mechanic— not exactly a high-tech, fast-track, big-money career. It was probably my tenth job in ten years, and I was barely getting by, so when he called a couple of weeks later and offered me a job in Asheville, I took it. I moved there, settled in, learned the business—"

Ashley rolled onto her side, her head pillowed on his arm. "Met Pris."

Without looking, he heard the lighthearted teasing in her voice. If nothing else, the past few hours had at least convinced her that he didn't find her lacking compared to his old girlfriend. "And met Pris. For the first time in my life, things seemed to be coming together. I was making good money, I liked my job, I had a nice place to live and a good—"

He broke off for a moment, rubbing the soft underside of her breast as he considered his next word. Just yesterday he'd insisted that he didn't have relationships, only affairs, sometimes only anonymous one-night encounters, but that wasn't entirely true. It certainly wasn't true of Pris. He hadn't been in love with her and didn't think he ever would have loved her, but he had liked and respected her. What they'd had wasn't exactly a romance—Ashley was very possibly the only romance meant for his life—but it had been more than an affair.

"I had a good relationship with Pris," he said at last, and Ashley patted his stomach.

"That wasn't so hard to say, was it?" she gently teased. "Next time we'll work on a harder phrase, something like 'I trust you.'"

Or maybe one like *I love you,* he thought grimly. Resolutely drawing back from even the idea, he picked up the threads of his tale again. "My life was stable, routine and perfectly normal...until the Catlin job came up."

"When did Bradley tell you that he intended to rob the bank?"

"That night last April after I'd already done it." He sighed again, hating this story, wishing he didn't have to tell it to her. But she deserved this much. After everything she'd given him, everything she'd done for him, she deserved to know the truth. "I know now that Russell had never intended for me to get so good at my job. I was supposed to just learn the basics. I *wasn't* supposed to become so familiar with the systems that I could recognize a problem. The problem with the one we were installing in the First American Bank and Trust of Catlin was that it wasn't sufficient to meet the bank's needs. Any fool who knew anything about alarm systems could bypass that particular system. There's not a bank in the country with such an inadequate security setup."

"You told your boss that, and he said—"

"'Prove it. Prove to me that it can be done. Show me how it can be done.' So I did. I made very detailed notes, just as he asked."

"The notes that were found in your room at the boarding house."

He nodded, his chin bumping the top of her head. "I can't believe I was such an idiot. I've been a screwup all my life, but this was particularly stupid, even for me."

Ashley pulled out of his arms and sat up, turning on the bed to face him. He liked that she was all soft from their lovemaking, especially liked that she was still naked but made no effort to hide herself from him. She sat unselfconsciously, her back straight, her legs tucked beneath her. "Come on, Dillon, don't be so hard on yourself. You were following your boss's orders. With ten jobs in ten years, maybe this comes as a surprise to you—" she smiled to take the sting from her words "—but that's what employees are supposed to do."

"Not when following orders leads to a crime."

Her smile faded and her expression grew serious and intent. "Your notes didn't convince him, right? So you asked, 'What do I have to do to prove this?' and he said, 'Break in and bring me proof. Bring me…'" She fell silent, no doubt replaying one of the previous days' conversations in her head, finding the little bit of information she wanted. "'Bring me five thousand dollars to prove that you were in the vault. If you can do that, we'll upgrade the system and fix the problem.'"

He nodded. That was exactly what he'd done. They had settled on that Wednesday evening for no particular reason except that the job had been finished that morning. The other techs had already returned to Asheville; only Dillon had remained behind. He had waited for the bank to close that evening, had gone to the café for dinner and had taken a leisurely walk around town, thinking all kinds of idiot thoughts, like what a nice little town Catlin was. Small-town America, Ashley had called it. A perfect place to settle down, if you could find a job that paid a living wage, and raise a family. He'd been thinking about Pris and how nice it would be to see her again, to make love to her again. About his job, how much he liked what he was doing, how good he had turned out to be at it and how grateful he was to Russell for giving him the chance.

Grateful. He gave a derisive snort at the memory.

"Russ said he would clear it with Bill Armstrong. A day or two later, he gave me the go-ahead. I made sure everyone had left the bank for the day, then I did exactly what I had told Russell I would. I circumvented the system, including the security cameras, let myself into the vault and took the five thousand dollars. I drove back to Asheville, where he was waiting for me in his office, and I gave him the money. I didn't stop at the boarding house to pick up my stuff. I knew that, as soon as Russ saw that I was right, we would be going back to work at the bank again, so I figured why bother.''

"What happened?" she asked when he didn't immediately go on.

"Armstrong was supposed to be at the meeting with Russ, but he wasn't. He was in Catlin. In the bank. Russ called him, told him that I was there with five thousand of the bank's dollars, told him to go ahead as planned and take the rest of the money, then notify the sheriff that the bank had been robbed.''

She was silent and still for a long time. Had he lost her with that last part? Had she been willing to believe everything he'd said until he'd implicated Bill Armstrong? She had known Armstrong all her life. Along with her ex-husband's family, the Armstrongs made up the upper class of Catlin society. It was one thing for her to believe that Russell Bradley, a complete stranger, was involved in the robbery. It was another altogether for Dillon to ask her to believe that a man she knew and probably considered a friend was also involved.

He waited uneasily for her response, for skepticism, a denial, an accusation that he was lying. When it finally came, it was better than he could have hoped for, provided he had been able to hope at all.

"So Bill Armstrong robbed his own bank," she murmured. "I always thought he was an insufferably arrogant man. So he's a crook, too. He and Bradley set you up."

He reached for her, pulling her down beside him again. "Hell, yes, darlin', they set me up. I made it so easy for them."

"Why did you run? Why didn't you stay and tell your story then? Seth would have listened. He would have investigated your claims right along with theirs. Running just made you look guilty."

"Stay and tell Seth my story? You think it would have been that simple?" Even though she was entirely serious, he laughed anyway. "And what would I have said? 'Yes, Sheriff Benedict, I *am* the world's biggest loser. I can't hold a job *or* a woman, I've spent most of my life in one sort of trouble or another and I have an arrest record going back to when I was nine years old. And, yes, Bill Armstrong and Russell Bradley *are* upstanding citizens and highly respected businessmen, but I'm telling you the truth when I say that *they* robbed the bank, not me. *I* only broke in—*they* took the money.' And you think he would have believed me? You think he wouldn't have slapped the handcuffs on me and sent me off to prison as quickly as he could?"

"He would have looked into it," she insisted stubornly. "When you disappeared, it was only natural for everyone to think you'd taken all that money. But if you'd had any faith in the system…"

He interrupted her with a quieting touch. "It's easy for you to talk about having faith in the system. You've never been in trouble. People have always liked and respected you. If you said something was so, they would believe you." He stared up at the rafters and the dried herbs hanging there. "When I was nine, one of my father's sons—Alex, the one whose name I share—cornered me on the playground at school and beat the tar out of me. When the principal broke it up, Alex said it was my fault. He said I had started it, that he had only defended himself. Keep in mind he was three years older than me, five or six inches taller and a good twenty pounds heavier. The extent of his injuries was a tear in his shirt. My shirt was torn, too. I also had a black eye, a bloody nose, two teeth knocked out, a busted lip and more bruises, bleeding and swelling than you can imagine. Do you want to guess who the principal believed? Who got suspended from school? Whose mother had to pay practically a week's salary to replace the little bastard's shirt?"

She didn't say anything. She just turned onto her side to face him, wrapped her arms around him and held him tightly. It was such a simple gesture, just an embrace, nothing more, but it made his chest grow tight and stirred a longing that left him feeling empty inside.

Closing his eyes, he breathed deeply and smelled her scents combined with his own. "We've lived different lives, Ash," he said quietly. "I've always had to prove myself. No one but my grandfather ever had much faith in me, and I learned not to have faith in anyone else. Yes, running made me look guilty, but I didn't see that I had any choice. In my experience, cops, more than anyone else, need proof, and all the proof, all the evidence in the bank robbery, pointed to me. Maybe Seth would have been different. Maybe he would have listened. Maybe he even would have looked for proof, but these are two intelligent men. I doubt they left even the smallest clue to implicate themselves."

"You're an intelligent man, too." Her voice was muffled against his chest.

"No, I'm not. But I'm smart enough to know when I've been beaten. If I thought there was a chance that I could clear my name and stay out of prison, I'd go into town tomorrow and tell Seth everything. But there's no chance at all that Russ and Bill Armstrong are going to let me do that. If I try, I'm dead."

Tilting her head back, she stared at him in the dim light. "And if you don't try, then what? You live the rest of your life as a fugitive. That is, assuming that they don't track you down and kill you anyway. You can't let them win, Dillon. You can't—"

Twisting toward her, he cut off her argument with a kiss. She made a frustrated sound that quickly turned into a soft sigh of submission. When at last he gave her a chance to catch her breath, she sighed again. "You're a wicked man, Dillon, trying to distract me like that."

"Like what?" He kissed her again, quickly, hungrily. "This?" He cupped her breast in his palm, teasing her nipple until it was hard and swollen. "Or like this?" Ducking his head, he drew his tongue across it, slowly, hard, creating an unbearably pleasurable friction. "Or maybe like this?" His caresses and kisses moved lower on her body, across her ribs, spanning her waist, following the curve of her hip. He settled between her legs, bracing himself on one arm while, with his free hand, he treated her to a series of lazy, intimate caresses that made her back arch, the muscles in her thighs straining.

"Dillon…" Her voice was barely a whisper, harsh and throaty. Erotic.

"Do you find this distracting?" He slipped one finger inside her, then another, feeling her heat and the dampness that had come from both her own body and his. Her body clenched and tightened, and she tried once more to speak, but the sound faded into a gasp, then a low, husky moan.

You can't let them win, she'd said, but she was wrong. He couldn't do anything *but* let them win. He couldn't do anything but leave, try to stay alive and hope that his leaving kept *her* alive. He couldn't do anything but sacrifice the rest of his life, all those years that he could have spent here with her.

Except for *this*. Tonight he could bring her pleasure. He could make love with her. He could forget about Bradley and Armstrong, could put them out of his mind and give her a few hours of normalcy, of intimacy, of love, and he could pray that it would be enough. For her.

And for him.

Chapter 9

Ashley woke up early Saturday morning, momentarily disoriented until she realized the weight across her ribs was Dillon's arm and remembered why she was in her own bed and not on a pallet on the floor. Twisting onto her side, she faced him, watching him sleep, committing every detail of his face to memory. The relaxed line of his mouth. The graceful curve of his lashes. The way his hair fell across his forehead. The shadow of his beard across his jaw. It made him look sinister, she'd told him earlier, but she knew now that she'd been wrong. *Wicked* was a much better word, much more accurate. Yes, indeed, he looked incredibly wicked unshaven.

Raising her hand, she drew one fingertip lightly across his lips. His muscles twitched and, without waking, he brushed her away, then turned his head to the other side. Blowing out her breath in a heavy sigh, she eased from the bed, dressing quickly in the clothing she'd discarded the night before. She added logs to the fire, put a pot of water on the stove to boil, then put on socks and shoes. Five minutes later, wearing her parka and carrying a mug of hot tea, she slipped silently out the door and made herself comfortable in the rocker on the porch.

The sun wasn't up yet, though the eastern sky was already lightening. Once the sun rose high, it would burn off the mists and heat the air to a comfortably warm spring temperature. It would finish the job of drying out the land...and Bessie's distributor. Unless Ashley's prayers were answered and the rains returned, there was little doubt that the van would be ready to go as early as this afternoon, ready to start Dillon on a journey that would take him out of her life.

She wasn't sure she was ready for that.

She felt like such a liar. She had told him right here on the porch last night that she understood that he would leave her, that she accepted the fact that she would never see him again. She had promised that she wouldn't ask for anything else beyond those few hours in her bed—no commitment, no future.

This morning her heart couldn't understand why he had to leave her; her soul couldn't accept never seeing him again. This morning, more than anything else in the world, she *needed* a commitment from him and a future with him. And she knew only one way to get them: if he turned himself in.

Or if *she* turned him in.

Drawing her feet onto the seat of the rocker, she tucked her skirt around her bare legs, then wrapped both hands around the mug for warmth. She could do it—could find some excuse for going into town today, could talk to Seth, could repeat everything Dillon had told her last night. Seth was no fan of Dillon's, but at the same time, he was no fan of Bill Armstrong's, either. He hadn't liked the banker before the robbery and liked him even less now. He'd taken a lot of grief from Armstrong about his department's inability to locate Dillon. If he had even the faintest suspicion that Armstrong had been ragging him about a crime that *he* had committed, Seth would certainly investigate, and he wouldn't stop until he either found evidence to support his suspicions or was positive beyond a doubt that Armstrong wasn't guilty.

Ashley could plant those seeds of suspicion.

If she dared. If she was willing to face the risks. If she was ready to accept responsibility for possibly sending Dillon to prison. If she told Seth, and he was unable to find any evidence implicating Bradley and Armstrong—evidence Dillon insisted would be too well protected to be discovered—then Dillon would remain the one and only suspect. Seth might not arrest him immediately, might wait until the investigation was complete and the other men cleared, but he would never allow Dillon to escape again.

But if she told Seth and he *was* able to put together a case against the other men... The rewards could be rich. Dillon could stay in Catlin. He could make a home and a life for himself right here. She could take that long look years ahead and see the two of them, living, working and raising a family together.

But what if *he* didn't share the same vision? What if she deceived him, turned him in, helped him clear his name and get the charges against him dropped and he still wanted to leave her? What if he returned to Asheville and to Pris or went home to Atlanta or headed out west anyway to try to put to rest memories of the worst time of his life?

He had never hinted or indicated in any way that he wanted to stay with her. Even last night when they'd made love, the closest he'd come to a declaration of emotion had been right after he'd removed her shirt. *You're sweet and lovely and delicate and tough, and you take my breath away.* As sweet as the sentiment was, it was a long way from *I love you.*

So those were her options. She could help him escape, thereby putting his life in danger, and never see him again. She could turn him in, and he might go to prison or he might be cleared of any wrongdoing. In that case, maybe he would stay with her, love her and never leave her. Maybe he would hate her for risking his freedom and betraying his trust, would leave her and never forgive her. Maybe he would be grateful for her help but would leave her anyway because, as he'd pointed out, she wasn't his kind of woman.

Every outcome but one would break her heart, but there was

only one she couldn't live with. She couldn't watch him take off again, damned to a shadowy existence, unable to trust anyone, unable to let down his guard even for a moment, always knowing that there were people looking for him who wanted him dead. He was an innocent man, and he deserved to live like one. He deserved a home, a wife, a family, a job. He deserved to live his life with dignity. The only way he could have those things was to stop running, to stand up to Russell Bradley and Bill Armstrong, to trust in Seth and the justice system to clear his name. Surrendering was the best action he could take, whether he believed it or not.

Besides, she *had* to tell Seth about Steven Vickers.

A few feet away, the door creaked as it opened, but wisely Dillon didn't step out. She could see him—mussed hair, a lot of bare skin, a sleepy, contented look—through the wedge of the open door. "You're up early," he said in greeting.

Summoning a smile from all the worry inside her, she let her shoes hit the floor with a thump, then got to her feet. Just in case there were curious eyes that she couldn't see, she didn't speak until she was in the doorway, her back to the world. "Good morning." After closing the door behind her, she set the tea down, shrugged out of her parka, then moved into his embrace. He smelled of heat, soft sheets and herbs, and he felt...

Her smile against his chest was just a little sad. He felt like the other half of her.

With his hands in her hair, he tilted her head back and studied her face, his eyes dark and intense, his expression thoughtful. After one moment and then another, she shifted uncomfortably and asked, "What are you looking for?"

"Regrets."

"Do you see any?"

"No. I don't think I do."

With a smug smile, she cupped her palms to his cheeks, then leaned forward for a kiss. "That's because I don't have any. Listen, Dillon..." Her smile quivered before disappearing. "I need to go into town."

He went utterly still for a moment, then, reaching up and catching hold of her wrists, he pulled her hands from his face and clasped them tightly in his. "Why?"

"To get some money from the automatic teller. To let Seth know that I'm okay so he doesn't come up here to see. To find out where the roadblocks are and how many there are."

He wanted to say no. She could see it in his eyes. No arguments, no discussions, no leaving, no way. But clearly struggling with that desire, instead he offered a cautious response. "You can get the money tomorrow on our—our way out of town." His falter was slight, barely noticeable—but *she* noticed. "The roadblocks don't matter, and if Seth comes up here, you'll just have to keep him outside, then send him on his way. You did it the other day. You can do it again."

"The bank, you may recall, is directly across the street from the sheriff's department," she gently reminded him. "I would really prefer to not park out front there and leave you hiding in the van while I get money from the machine. You're right, I probably can distract Seth if he comes up here again, but I don't want to take any chances. And, sweetheart, the roadblocks *do* matter. They're the biggest obstacle to your getting out of here safely."

He continued to look at her, his gaze still searching her face, but it wasn't regrets he was looking for this time. He was seeking some sign that he could trust her, and it made her heart ache to know that, if he offered his trust, she would simply turn around and betray it. Would it make a difference to him that the end result would, with God's blessing, be his freedom? Would he care that she was only doing what she believed in her soul to be right for him? She hoped so. She prayed so.

When he released her and turned away, she felt his rejection more strongly than ever before. She didn't move but simply stood there, staring down at the floor, a welcome numbness slowly filtering through her. Then, from across the room, with his back to her, he finally spoke, and she understood that it wasn't *her* he'd turned away from but himself. He'd sworn to never again do what he was about to do, and he wasn't happy that he was doing it now. He wasn't convinced that he wasn't making the biggest mistake of his life.

Neither was she.

"All right," he said, his voice quiet, self-reproachful and tentatively—very tentatively—trusting. "When do you want to go?"

"What about the key?"

Ashley looked up from the shoe that she was tying and grinned. "I'll take a quick look through the weeds, but if I don't find it, it's no big deal."

Dillon's scowl deepened in proportion to her grin. "No big deal? How are you going to drive Bessie without keys?"

"I'll hot-wire it."

"You know how to do that," he said skeptically.

She replied with such innocence that he couldn't help grinning, too. "Of course. Doesn't everyone?"

"*I* don't. Let me guess. Seth taught you."

"No. My granny. She was always losing her keys." The smile grew brighter until just looking at her made him hurt. He'd never known anyone with a smile like that. He wished he could capture it on film, for all those future nights when he would need some way to connect with her, when he would need something more than cold, distant memories to hold close. But he'd seen no sign of a camera, and it didn't matter anyway, because no flat, two-dimensional photograph could ever do her justice.

Besides, he would never forget.

"Your granny must have been a resourceful woman," he said quietly. "You take after her."

The compliment pleased her far more than it should have, but he understood. She felt the same things for her grandmother that he felt for his grandfather, and he couldn't think of any greater compliment in the world than being compared favorably to Jacob Boone.

She gave her shoelaces one last tug, then stood up. She had changed into a dress after this morning's bath, a cotton print with short, fluttery sleeves and a shaped neckline that curved above her breasts before dipping low in the center to reveal just a hint of cleavage. It was loose, flowing and thoroughly feminine…even with the ragg-wool socks and moss green hiking boots she wore. She looked beautiful.

"Dressing up for Seth?" he asked, making no effort to camouflage the jealousy in his voice.

"Dressing up for *you,* " she replied, coming around the table to take his hand.

"I'd rather you *un*dress for me."

For a moment she looked so serious, so wistful. He wondered if she was thinking about tomorrow, when she would take him to Nashville, or if she was considering all the time they couldn't have together, all the things they couldn't do together. Then the moment passed, and she shook off the somber mood and smiled. It wasn't a very good smile, more than a little on the sad side. "Maybe when I get back," she said quietly. Leaning forward, she pressed a kiss to one cheek, then the other, finally reaching his mouth.

Long before he was ready for it to end, she drew away and started toward the door. There she paused and looked back at him. "Dillon…"

He waited for her to go on. She fumbled with the doorknob, moved her purse from one arm to the other, met his gaze, then looked away a half-dozen times. At last, with a deep breath, she went on. "Stay away from the windows and lock the door behind me. I'll try not to take too long. Is there anything special you'd like from town?"

Disappointed because that *wasn't* what she'd started to say, he shook his head. He watched as she walked out, closing the door behind her, then did exactly what she'd warned him against. He went to the nearest window, stood off to one side and lifted the sheet there just enough to see out.

With such easy grace, she crossed the clearing to the patch of weeds, where only a moment's search yielded her keys. He liked the way she moved. Whether she was cooking or washing dishes, weaving baskets, nursing his wounds, brushing her hair or simply walking... He was fascinated by it all. He was fascinated by *her*.

He was afraid he was in love with her.

She climbed into the van, and through the glass he heard the engine crank and sputter before catching. It was badly in need of a tune-up. Given the time, the parts and the proper tools, he could have it running like new—or at least more smoothly—in no time. But he didn't have the parts or the proper tools, and he damned sure didn't have the time.

Letting the sheet fall as she turned the van in a tight circle in the clearing, he locked the door, then went to the chair where she did her needlework at night and slumped down, his feet stretched out in front of him.

Yes, he was in love with her. He wished he could deny it, wished he could write the feelings off as a peculiar mix of lust, gratitude and affection, but he would only be lying to himself. Granted, for his age he had little experience with loving or being loved, but he knew it for what it was. He could identify it by its very absence the better part of his life.

How many times in his life had he thought that maybe *this* would be the time he would fall in love? *This* would be a relationship, not an affair. *This* would be forever and always. Every new relationship had always held the possibilities; every new woman had always held the promise. But after a date or two or maybe three, he had always realized that it wasn't the right time or the right woman. He had even started to wonder if maybe there was nothing wrong with his timing or his choice of women, if maybe the problem was with *him*. Maybe, he'd thought, he just wasn't meant to fall in love.

Apparently he'd been wrong.

Blowing out a sigh, he reached into the basket next to the chair for her needlework. The fabric was white, rolled tight around the two long bars of the frame that held it. She had finished less than half of the scene, and the sections she'd done weren't always adjacent, but there was enough to get the general picture. It was a mountain scene, looking out across green valleys that rose into treetopped peaks, then dipped low into more distant valleys, with houses tucked here and there, fields being tilled, cattle grazing, kids playing. Clouds filled the blue sky, and high above, a brilliantly colored hot-air balloon drifted over the tallest peak. Like everything else she did, it was neat, impressive and beautifully done. She was an incredibly talented woman.

And he was going to miss her when he was gone, more than he had ever missed anyone, even his grandfather.

His finger hovering a trace above the fabric, he followed a line of trees from end to end, careful not to touch the stitches or the canvas. The shadings of green were so subtle that he couldn't actually tell where one color gave way to another, but he could easily see the depths and dimensions they created.

It was appropriate that she was putting so much time and energy into a mountain scene. He had meant it last night when he'd insisted that she belonged there on her granny's farm at the top of the mountain. Try as he might, he couldn't imagine her in any city, not even Raleigh, where he knew she'd once lived. She was as inextricably bound to this land and this place as Jacob had been to *his* land. The old man had been born on his farm, and he had died there. Sometimes—most of the time—it had been a real struggle for him to keep things going, but he'd never given up. He couldn't have, because losing his land would have meant losing a part of himself. Without it he would have withered away and died.

All his life Dillon had wanted to belong to something—or someone—that way. "Be careful what you wish for," the old saying went, "because you just might get it." Well, now that he had his wish, now that he'd found both a place and a woman he could belong to, he no longer wanted it. Ashley and her damned farm complicated things. They made him want to stay. They made him want to take his chances, face up to his troubles and try to make a life for himself here. But facing up to his troubles meant one of only two things, and he was neither ready to die nor willing to go to prison. That meant he had to get out, had to head west where no one knew him. Leaving Ashley behind meant his life wouldn't be worth living.

But it beat the alternative. Staying meant he wouldn't even have a life to live.

I love you.

That was what Ashley had been about to say when she'd stopped on her way out of the cabin. She had come within a deep breath of making a declaration to Dillon that couldn't be taken back. A vow that he might have appreciated at the time, but that probably wouldn't have meant anything to him later, after he found out what she'd done in town. He would hate her once he understood that she'd turned him in, and he wouldn't believe anything she'd ever said. He wouldn't trust her again.

He would *never* love her.

Maybe she should forget her plan. Maybe she should do exactly what she'd told him she would, then go back home. Fix dinner. Make love. Plan for the trip to Nashville. Say goodbye. Forever.

Forever. She was only twenty-nine years old. She couldn't even comprehend how long *forever* would be. She couldn't begin to understand what it would be like living *forever* alone, with unbearable loneliness, intolerable sorrow and the emptiness of never knowing where Dillon was, what he was doing or if he was even alive.

Only twenty-nine years old, and incredibly selfish. Her future, or lack of, wasn't the issue. It was *his* future at risk, his very life in danger. If he didn't mind living the rest of it as a fugitive, what right did she have to interfere? Taking him in and nursing him didn't give her that right. Making love with him last night didn't. Even falling in love with him didn't.

But he *did* mind living as a fugitive. He hated it, he'd told her last night. He was a good man who deserved a better fate than he'd been dealt. All he wanted was a normal life, and clearing his name could give him that. Even if he chose not to spend that life with her, she still wanted him to have it.

Scowling, she pulled into a parking space in front of the courthouse. Seth's Blazer was parked in the sheriff's reserved spot to her left. She hadn't been sure she would find him in the office this afternoon, but the dispatcher always knew how to reach him. She would have tracked him down if necessary.

Climbing out of the van, she slammed the door and turned not toward the courthouse but across the street instead. If something went wrong—if Seth didn't believe her, if Dillon somehow got away again—she wanted him to have enough money to get by until he was out of the area.

As soon as she'd withdrawn the daily limit from her savings account, she tucked the cash into her bag, then crossed the street once more. The courthouse, built of native stone, was closed on weekends, but there was a small side entrance that led to the sheriff's department on the first floor. She hurried up the steps, passing a state trooper who held the door for her.

Seth was alone, as she'd hoped. The dispatcher, who doubled as receptionist, desk sergeant and surrogate mother, sent her on back before returning her attention to the magazine in front of her.

When she walked unannounced into the small office at the back, her ex-husband was studying a large map that filled the available wall space between the filing cabinets and the window. Entire areas around her place had been marked off—as searched and done with, she fervently hoped. The last thing she needed was for a search party to show up at the cabin this afternoon while she was away. Practically everyone out there had known her all of her life; when they saw that her van was gone and that the padlock that secured the door when she left was also gone, most of them wouldn't think twice about letting themselves into the cabin to search it. And when the door wouldn't open because Dillon had locked it from the inside…

She grimly shook away the thought. "Hey, Seth."

He glanced over his shoulder, then turned to face her. "What brings you into town?"

"I needed some groceries." If it wasn't exactly the truth, it wasn't a lie, either. She *had* stopped at the grocery store and stocked up on milk, eggs and fresh bananas. She had also splurged on the best steaks in the whole meat department, a bottle of the finest wine the store had to offer—which, unfortunately, wasn't particularly fine—and one of Mary Lou's special German chocolate cakes in the bakery. If tonight *was* her last night with Dillon, she wanted it to be special, from the dinner straight through to the lovemaking. "You look tired."

"Twenty-hour workdays will do that to you." He gestured toward the chair in front of his desk as he sat down in the one behind it. "Everything okay up at your place?"

"Yeah." She rested her hands on the back of the wooden chair, but she couldn't bring herself to sit. She wanted to pace, but she couldn't do that, either, for lack of room.

Whatever she did in the next few minutes—pumping Seth for information about the roadblocks so she could help his prisoner escape or betraying Dillon's trust—was going to be very wrong. She wished she could just say goodbye and leave, but that would be wrong, too. So, drawing a deep breath, she chose the wrong that just might, with any luck, come closest to being right. "How is Tom?"

Seth's expression darkened. "Still the same. I'm worried about him, Ashley. I don't suppose you have any remedies that the doctors over there at Duke don't know about."

Her smile came and went. "I'm afraid comas are a little out of my field. Have you seen him?"

"I haven't had time. I've been staying here coordinating this blasted search." He gestured toward the map. "Do you have any idea how long it takes to search *one* acre of land up there? In places you could walk within five feet of a person and never know he was there."

"You think he's still in the county."

"He was hurt, and the weather's been terrible. He couldn't have gone too far." He shrugged. "I don't know. Maybe he's dead. Maybe we won't find his body until summer, when the hikers are out in force. Maybe we'll never find it."

She knotted her fingers together and fixed her gaze on her knuckles, turning shades of white, purple and red. "He's not dead."

"If his injuries from the crash didn't kill him, the lack of food coupled with exposure—'' Abruptly he broke off. She knew he was staring at her by the heat of guilt that was spreading through her. ''How do you know that, Ashley? How do you know he's not dead?''

Suddenly the idea of sitting seemed much more appealing. In fact, she was pretty sure her legs were going to give way if she didn't take her weight off them immediately. Sliding into the chair, she moistened her lips, then finally met Seth's gaze. ''If I tell you, do you promise to hear me out before you do anything? And do you promise not to tell anyone else, at least not right away? And promise to keep your deputies out of it. If you need to bring someone else in, let it be a trooper or someone from the State Bureau of Investigation, but nobody local.''

''Ashley—''

''Do you promise?''

''*No.* Now, what the hell's going on here? How do you know that Boone's not dead? Have you seen him? Have you talked to him? Did you—'' He stared at her a moment longer, then closed his eyes in an expression of dismay. ''My God, Ashley, you've been taking care of him, haven't you? *Haven't you?*''

The shout made her jump, made her muscles tighten and her stomach knot. In the years they'd been married, in all the years they'd known each other, Seth had never raised his voice to her. Even when he was angry, he'd always controlled it so carefully, had always spoken in an even, calm voice. The fact that he was yelling now didn't bode well for Dillon's immediate future—or hers. ''He was hurt, Seth, and half-dead. What was I supposed to do?''

''Let the son of a bitch die!'' he shouted, then automatically checked his voice. ''You could have gotten in your van, driven into town and told me—or is that too complicated for you?''

His sarcasm stung, and in response her voice sounded pouty. ''It was raining. Bessie doesn't run in the rain. You know that.''

He started to speak—more advice from the male point of

view regarding the unreliability of her transportation?—then made a dismissive gesture. "Is he at the cabin?"

She didn't answer. He didn't need her answer.

"How long has he been there?"

Again she said nothing.

"Was he there when I came up to tell you that he'd escaped?"

Guiltily she dropped her gaze to the desk top, to a bulletin featuring a photograph of Dillon. She reached for it, holding it in unsteady hands, studying the picture. It was recent, taken by the Sylvan County Sheriff's Department, she guessed. He looked grim, tough...and afraid. She had seen the grimness and toughness herself that first night, but she had missed the fear, blinded to it by her own. "Can I have this?"

"What do you want with a picture?" Seth asked derisively. "You've got the real thing hidden up there at your cabin." But he didn't protest when she folded the paper carefully so the photo was intact and slid it inside her purse. "Take the bulletin and give me some answers. Is he at the cabin?"

"Yes."

He shoved his chair back from the desk so hard that it banged off the back wall. Quickly Ashley stood up and moved in front of him as he came around the desk. "Please, Seth, you have to listen to me. You have to hear me out."

"I'll listen *after* he's locked up in my jail. Now, move out of my way or I'll move you—right into the cell next to his."

She didn't budge. "If you bring him in," she said, her tone intense, her words deliberate, "one of your deputies will try to kill him."

Shaking his head, he muttered a curse. "Come on, Ashley, you don't believe that. Yes, the men are mad as hell at what he did to Tommy, but—"

"I'm not talking about Tom—and just for the record, Dillon didn't shoot him." She drew a fortifying breath. "I'm talking about the deputy who did."

He stared down at her for a long time, his breathing loud and measured, then slowly returned to his chair. She didn't sit down right away, though, but remained where she blocked his exit from the room. "I'm listening. Start talking."

"Which would you like to hear first? How the bank was robbed? Or how he escaped?" The look he was giving her hardened, lending his eyes a cold gleam. Clearing her throat, she didn't wait for him to voice his obvious preference. "Tom and Dillon were ambushed at Sadler's Pass. The car went off the road and into the ravine. They were both injured, but..."

Seth's expression was skeptical. "Ambushed," he repeated dryly.

"There was a van blocking the road and three men who were shooting at them. One of those men shot Tom." Going on quickly before he could show any more doubt, she added, "It was a black van. Presumably the men would have gone down into the ravine to make certain they were dead, but a woman with kids stopped. She called for help on her car phone."

He considered her thoughtfully for a moment, and she suspected that her last comments had struck a chord. She would bet that they *had* received a call about the accident from a woman with children, that the woman *had* reported a black van and three men in the area. Still, he sounded far from convinced when he spoke again. "This is *his* story."

She nodded.

"And you believe him."

Another nod.

"Why?"

Because instinct had told her early on that Dillon wasn't guilty. Because even when she'd been his hostage, he hadn't hurt her, hadn't wanted her to be afraid, had been quick to reassure her that she would be all right. Because when he had been soaked, freezing and suffering from his injuries and exposure, he had been more concerned with *her* wet clothing, with whether or not *she* was warm and comfortable. Because handcuffing her that first night had filled him with shame. Because she'd started trusting him practically from the start. Because she'd started falling in love with him soon after.

"Because his story of being ambushed, considered along

with everything else, makes sense," she said at last. "Because all of his injuries weren't caused by the accident. Because, like Tom, he had been shot. In the back, Seth. Because..." She glanced hesitantly at the door, seeing through the glass that no one but the dispatcher was in the outer room, that she was still absorbed in her magazine, but she lowered her voice anyway. "Because I think it was Steven Vickers who shot him."

She told Seth everything—how Dillon had gotten the job with Bradley Electronics, how he had discovered the problems with the bank's system and pointed them out to his boss, how Russell Bradley had challenged him to prove his assessment by breaking into the bank, how Bradley and Bill Armstrong had then used *his* break-in to cover up their own. When she finished, she sat back quietly in her seat and waited for him to speak.

When he finally did, his expression was drained, his voice weary. If he was still angry, she couldn't tell. "When did he show up at the cabin?"

"About five o'clock Tuesday."

"So he was there when I came by the next morning."

She nodded.

"Why didn't you tell me?"

"Because he was standing right inside the door with Tom's gun."

That piqued his interest. "Tom was shot with a nine millimeter. We think it was his own gun."

"All of your deputies carry nine millimeters, don't they? Including Steven Vickers."

Looking pained, he didn't comment on that. Of everything she'd said this afternoon, that, she knew, was probably the hardest for him to accept. He had hired Steven himself, had trained him and fathered him along. It had to hurt to even consider the possibility that *his* officer had been bought off by the bad guys, that one of his own men had tried to kill an unarmed prisoner, that in the process he had almost killed one of his fellow deputies.

After a moment he shook his head. "Ashley, this is crazy. Steven's a cop. We've known him all of his life. He almost married your sister, for God's sake. How can you believe that he's part of this?"

"I don't blame you for not wanting to hear this, and I don't expect you to believe it. Just consider the possibility, Seth. Look into it—not because I'm asking you to, not because it might keep Dillon alive, but because *if* it's true, Steven has to be stopped. He has to be punished."

"It's *not* true. None of it is true. It can't be."

"Then who shot Dillon?" she asked gently.

"Maybe Tom did. Maybe Boone tried to escape after the accident, and Tom shot him." But she could see that he wasn't impressed with his own theory. Tom had suffered serious head trauma in the crash; Dillon had injuries of his own, both from the wreck and from his confinement in the Sylvan County Jail. Tom was taller, much heavier and far more muscular than Dillon. How likely was it that the badly injured deputy had shot his prisoner in the back, lost his gun to the wounded man and was then shot himself?

Not very.

"How is Boone now?"

"He'll be fine."

After another silence, he grudgingly asked, "You believe this guy?"

"Yes."

"Everything? You believe he thought he was just doing his job when he broke into the bank? That Bill Armstrong—bank president, former mayor, school board member, county commissioner—was behind the robbery of his own bank?"

Ashley stood up and paced off the length of the room, five feet, maybe six, then retraced her steps, passing her chair and ending up in front of the window. There was a small parking lot out back, enclosed with an eight-foot-tall chain-link fence and secured with a wide gate. The occasional impounded car went into the lot, and when prisoners were brought into the

jail, the deputy parked out back, then brought them through a
narrow door only a few feet from this office.

Right now the only vehicle in the lot was a Crown Victoria,
old and much used even before its tumble into a ravine. The
front left door was missing, and every window was either shattered or missing altogether. She couldn't identify a single body
part that hadn't been scraped, crumpled or accordioned; the
roof had been flattened until it rested mere inches above the
door frames. The only way the back doors could be opened
was with a crowbar, which meant Dillon must have escaped
through the window. Lucky for him he was so lean. If he'd
been bigger, taller or heavier, he wouldn't have been able to
wriggle through that small space. He would have been forced
to stay there and wait for Seth and his men to arrive. And if
his luck were bad enough and Steven Vickers had been the first
deputy on the scene...

Sighing, she turned her back on the badly damaged car and
faced Seth. "You sound just like him. That's the reason he
took off a year ago. He didn't think anyone would believe him.
Armstrong and Bradley are good citizens, and he's..."

"A punk."

His response weighed down her shoulders and made her sigh
again. "Maybe he was right. Maybe you would have been too
bigoted and narrow-minded to listen to him. Maybe you would
have taken the easy way out and locked him up without ever
considering other suspects. Maybe you would have been so
eager to solve Catlin County's biggest crime ever that you
wouldn't have cared that you were sending an innocent man
to prison."

"That's not fair, Ashley."

She smiled sadly. "Life *isn't* fair. Ask Dillon."

For a long time he sat silent, toying with a pencil on his
desk. Finally he tossed it onto the desk pad, sat back and met
her gaze. "What is it you want from me?"

"I want you to talk to him. To listen to him. To prove—"

"Or disprove."

She acknowledged his interruption with a nod. "To prove

or disprove what he says. And I want you to let him stay at my cabin until you have proof one way or the other. I don't want him locked up here. I don't want him where somebody can get to him."

"Why are you doing this? What difference does it make to you?"

Ignoring his questions, she moved away from the window. "Give me enough time to get home and talk to him, to tell him that you're coming. Thirty minutes should be plenty. And please don't tell anyone anything, especially Steven." She walked to the door, then turned back and finally answered those two questions. "I'm doing this because it's the only thing I *can* do. Proving his innocence makes all the difference... *He* makes all the difference in the world to me." She slid her purse strap over her shoulder and opened the door, then stopped once more. "Thank you, Seth."

The first hour and a half Ashley was gone passed at a relatively normal pace. Dillon knew it would take her close to thirty minutes to make the fifteen-mile drive down winding, narrow roads and another half hour to return. Figure another thirty minutes to get her money and talk to Seth, and she should be on her way home. Hell, she should *be* home by now, he thought with a scowl. She'd been gone at least two hours, maybe two and a half.

Maybe she'd had trouble with the van. Maybe she'd needed time to track down Seth. Maybe she had stopped at the store or gotten delayed by friends or acquaintances.

Or maybe she wasn't coming back.

Maybe she had gone to see Seth, all right, to tell him where his missing prisoner could be found.

No. He couldn't let himself start thinking that way. He trusted her. He *did*. There could be any number of innocent reasons why this trip was taking so long. He didn't have to automatically suspect the not-so-innocent ones. Ashley deserved better than that.

He stopped his restless prowling in front of the fireplace.

The fire was out, the ashes cold, sending a pungent smoky scent into the room. He had let the flames die soon after Ashley left. It was such a sunny, warm day outside. But inside, with the door closed and all the windows covered, it was gloomy and uncomfortably cool. Maybe he should build another fire to warm the place before she returned.

Or maybe they could warm each other in bed instead.

With a sigh, he settled his gaze and his attention on the mantel, where primitive pots shared space with carved boxes and one tall round basket. He picked up one box and lifted the lid to reveal a half-dozen metal buttons inside. Silver thimbles, some looking fairly old, nestled in the next box, and two thin gold bands sat on a piece of fluffy cotton in the third. Wedding rings. Hers and Seth's, or maybe her grandparents'? Feeling guilty and more than a little foolish, he picked up the larger of the two and slid it easily onto his finger. It definitely wasn't Seth's, he decided. Sheriff Benedict was a big man with big hands. This ring might fit his little finger, but definitely none of the others.

For a time he stared at his hand. Even in the cabin's gloom, the gold somehow gathered enough light to gleam brightly against the dark bronze of his finger. He'd never worn a ring of any sort, not once in his entire thirty-four years, but this one felt comfortable. Familiar. Right.

But it *wasn't* right. He wasn't anyone's husband and wasn't likely to ever be.

Returning the ring to the box and replacing the lid, he picked up the tall basket. Most of her baskets were woven with thin, flat reed or narrow bundles of sweetgrass, but this was made from some sort of vine, with a flat, round lid. Lifting the lid by its round wooden knob, he looked inside and grinned. She didn't have any money at all, she'd insisted, but she had lied. The basket was filled with bills, a few fifties and twenties but mostly tens, fives and ones, some rolled together, others crumpled and dropped in. He wasn't surprised that she kept a little cache of money around the cabin; it sounded like something she would do, exactly like something her granny would have done.

Hearing the uneven sputter of the van's engine chugging up the hill, he put the lid back on and the basket back where it belonged and went to the front window to look out. A tremendous feeling washed over him—relief mixed with shame. He shouldn't have doubted her. She'd given him no reason to think that she would betray him, and he regretted the lack of faith. Better than anyone else in his life, though, she would understand where the doubt had come from.

She climbed out of the van and slammed the door, then circled to the other side, taking a grocery sack and a small cooler from the back. He would like to go out to meet her, to greet her, but he went no farther than the door, opening the lock, staying safely out of sight of any prying eyes.

"How did it go?" he asked the moment she was inside.

"Okay." She didn't stop but went straight to the kitchen, setting her load on the counter there. Potatoes and a bottle of garlic powder spilled out of the bag, rolling until the backsplash stopped them. "I picked up a few things for dinner tonight."

"You saw Seth?"

"Yes," came her muffled answer as she opened the refrigerator and ducked behind the door to unload the cooler.

"Everything's on for tomorrow?"

Straightening, she closed the refrigerator, set the cooler on the counter and removed a cake from the bag, setting it aside out of the way. She finished unloading the remaining items, gathering them neatly on the counter, before finally facing him. "You really want to leave tomorrow, don't you?"

He studied her face in the yellow glow of the overhead light. She looked so serious, so unhappy, so... So filled with regret. Feeling an odd little quiver inside, he cautiously answered. "I don't *want* to leave at all, Ash. Don't you know that? But I have to. If I want to stay alive, if I want to keep you alive, I *have* to go."

"No, you don't. You don't have to go anywhere. If you stay, we can work things out. We can—"

He laid his fingers over her mouth. "No more arguments, please."

Last night she had let him stop her, had let him distract her. Not so this afternoon. She pushed his hand away. "*Would* you stay if you could? If you woke up in the morning and the bank-robbery charges were gone, if Russell Bradley and Bill Armstrong had disappeared, if you were a free man, would you stay here?"

His grin was crooked and felt phony. It *was* phony. There was nothing amusing about her question, nothing worth smiling about. She was talking about the one thing he wanted most in the world—to stay here with her. The one thing that he could never have, because the bank-robbery charges weren't going to be dropped, and Russell and Armstrong weren't going to disappear from his life. He was never going to be a free man again.

"Honey, you wouldn't be able to get rid of me," he murmured.

She considered his answer for a moment, seemed to grow a little unhappier; then flatly announced, "I told Seth where you were."

Dillon stared at her, certain that he must have misunderstood. But the words remained between them, emotionless and blunt, and her expression confirmed them. He took a step away from her, then another, not stopping until the table was at his back. "You...told...Seth...."

At last her grimness and regret gave way to other feelings—to fear and anxiety, remorse and sorrow. "I had to, Dillon. Can't you see that he'll help us? That he'll protect you? That he'll prove your innocence so that you can stay?"

He'd never felt such numbness. It was almost as if he were outside looking in, watching this little scene unfold between two other people...except for the sharp little ache of betrayal that was rapidly growing in his chest. "You told Seth," he murmured again, then his voice sharpened. "*What* did you tell him?"

"Everything."

She didn't elaborate; she didn't need to. She had waited until she'd gotten all the details herself and then gone running off to repeat it all to her precious Seth. She had played Dillon for a fool, had made him believe in her, had coaxed him and seduced him....

A sickening shudder rippled through him. Oh, God, was that what last night had been about? Seducing him into trusting her, into opening up and letting down his guard? All her talk about wanting him, about having just one night together, about not having a chance for a commitment or a future but settling for just one little bit of intimacy... Had it all been lies, all part of her plan to get away from the cabin alone this afternoon? Had there been any truth at all in anything she'd said or done in the past five days?

"He's coming up here to talk to you," she said uneasily. "He's going to let you stay here at the cabin while he checks out your story. He just needs to hear it from you."

He didn't believe her. He wasn't sure he could ever believe her again.

"I—I asked him to give me thirty minutes so I could talk to you, so I could make you understand...." Her voice quavered. "Dillon, you *have* to understand. This is *right*. It's best—"

"Right for whom?" he interrupted. "For Seth, who gets to singlehandedly capture the armed-and-dangerous bank robber? For you? This earns you points with him, doesn't it? Are you willing to settle for his gratitude, or are you hoping to get something more from him? Hey, maybe he'll sleep with you— he could go a long way toward easing that loneliness you were talking about last night, couldn't he? Maybe he'll be so grateful that he'll even let you back into his life."

Her eyes bright with unshed tears, she responded with more dignity than he deserved. "Right for *you*, Dillon. You haven't done anything wrong, beyond trusting the wrong people, and—''

He interrupted her again with an angry, mocking laugh. ''Damned right, sweetheart. Obviously I haven't learned my lesson yet. I trusted *you*.''

''You haven't done anything wrong,'' she repeated, becoming more agitated, ''and Seth can prove it. Now that he knows who to investigate, he can clear your name. You'll be able to stay here. You can have all the things you want—a job, a home, a family, a place to belong.''

''With *you*?'' he asked, his voice menacingly soft. ''You think I would stay here with you? You think I would trust you? You think I would still want you?'' He wanted to find some satisfaction in the hurt that flashed through her eyes, but he couldn't feel anything except his own hurt. Anger. Betrayal.

Her hand trembling, she reached out to him. ''Dillon, I love—''

He moved away so abruptly that the centerpiece of dried flowers in a pottery vase fell to its side and rolled onto the floor, the vase breaking with a hollow thunk. Detouring to the bed to pick up his shoes and socks, he went to the fireplace, sat down on the hearth and slipped his arm free of the sling, then began the task of putting on his socks, working quickly even though it sent sharp needles of pain through his shoulder.

He'd never been so clumsy—knocking the flowers over, fumbling with his socks, with his shoes and the laces. It was because his hands—his entire body—was shaking. Because he didn't want her to touch him. Because he couldn't let her say those words. He couldn't let her tempt him, torment him. He couldn't listen to any more of her lies.

He had thought when he'd come here that he knew all there was to know about betrayal, that his mother, his father, Russell Bradley and others had taught him everything. But he'd been wrong. They had never taught him how badly it could hurt. They had made him feel unwanted and unimportant, stupid, foolish and expendable, like a nuisance best dealt with harshly or an embarrassment best dealt with not at all. But they had never made him feel so lost, so hopeless, so disillusioned or so achingly sorrowful.

He felt all those things and worse as he tied his second shoe, then stood up.

Ashley stood up, too, from the floor where she'd knelt to pick up the vase. Her hands filled with chunks of pottery, she faced him. "You can't leave," she pleaded. "Seth is on his way up here right now. The mountains around here are still filled with search parties. You can't take the van, you don't know your way through the forest, and your shoulder isn't healed enough to risk that kind of travel. Please, Dillon, please wait."

"Wait for good ol' Seth to lock me up?" He made a derisive sound as he retrieved the handcuffs and keys from underneath the middle sofa cushion, then fished Deputy Coughlin's pistol from the bottom of a basket filled with bits of fabric left over from other projects and no doubt intended for one of her quilts. He tucked it into the waistband of his jeans, then started for the door. On the way he paused, the table between them. "You know, if any woman in the world could have persuaded me that she was worth going to prison for twenty-five years, it would have been you. I could have convinced myself that giving up half my life was more than a reasonable price to pay for spending the rest of it with you. But I would have been so wrong."

"Dillon..." Once more she reached out. This time he didn't jerk away. He stared at her hand for a moment, so strong and delicate, then deliberately turned his back on her. He refused to hear the soft, anguished cry she gave as he crossed the few yards to the door, refused to wonder if the tears that had filled her eyes earlier were spilling over now, refused to even consider how much she might be hurting. With each step he forced himself to concentrate on the hard, cold facts. She had lied to him. She had turned him over to the authorities, knowing that he would rather die than go to prison. She had betrayed him.

This was one betrayal he feared he might never get over.

Taking a deep breath, he unfastened the lock he had automatically secured when she had returned from town. He didn't want to do this, didn't want to head back out into the rugged mountains, didn't want to leave the cabin where, for the first time in his life, he'd felt a sense of belonging. But it wasn't the cabin that had given him that feeling of home, but rather Ashley, who had misled him, who was helping to send him to prison, who hadn't thought twice about risking *his* life and *his* freedom on the remote chance that she might gain what *she* wanted.

He hesitated before opening the door, aware that there was something he needed to say. *I'm sorry,* maybe, because he certainly was. He was sorry he had trusted her, sorry he had given her the chance to let him down, sorry that he'd made love with her and sorry that he'd fallen in love with her. Or he could try *Thank you.* For taking him in, for nursing him, for making him trust her, for seducing him into a moment of sheer idiocy, for reminding him once again of Russell's lesson—*Never trust anyone*—and for sending him to prison. Yeah, thanks for nothing.

I love you. Not *loved,* not past tense, not over and done with, but right now and in the future—with his luck, probably forever. But telling her now would serve no purpose but to underscore the futility of it. *Damn you* served no purpose, either, except possibly to vent a little of his anger.

Apparently he was wrong. There *wasn't* anything he needed to say. He simply needed to open the door and walk out of her life.

His fingers closed around the knob, and he twisted it, pulling the door open at the same time. He didn't take a single step, though, because the barrel of a pistol identical to the one secured in his waistband was pointed right between his eyes. He drew a small breath but otherwise didn't move so much as a muscle as Sheriff Benedict softly asked, ''Going somewhere, Boone?''

Feeling lower than he'd ever felt before, Dillon exhaled. ''Yeah,'' he answered just as softly. ''Straight to jail.'' Then he followed the sheriff's glance to Ashley, still standing beside the table, her hands clenched tightly around the shards of pottery, and he silently amended his response.

Straight to hell.

Chapter 10

"Where's the gun?"

Ashley watched as Dillon lifted his shoulders in the slightest of shrugs. "In my waistband."

"Get it, Ashley," Seth commanded, his own gun never wavering.

She remained motionless for a moment, unwilling to get so close, all too painfully aware that Dillon certainly didn't want her so close. But she had to cooperate, had to do whatever Seth said; otherwise, he might decide that in her custody wasn't the best place for his prisoner to be. Dropping the hardened clay on the table, she moved around between the two men, awkwardly lifting the hem of the sweatshirt Dillon wore, and pulled the pistol free. The entire time—only a moment, maybe a lifetime—he watched her with such an unforgiving gaze. When she moved away after handing the gun by its grips to Seth, she could actually feel it the instant she stepped out of his line of sight.

Seth came into the cabin, closing the door behind him before gesturing for Dillon to sit down at the table. He claimed the chair at a right angle for himself and directed Ashley to sit at the opposite end. "Ashley says you have a story to tell."

Dillon shifted his gaze slowly to hers, making her shiver. "Ashley lies," he replied sardonically.

"She says that breaking into the vault at the bank was part of a test of the new security system, authorized by your boss and the bank president." Seth waited a moment, but when Dillon offered no response, he went on. "She also says you didn't shoot my deputy."

Finally Dillon looked at him. "You've got the gun. Check the ballistics."

"While you're at it," Ashley added, "check Steven Vickers's, too." When Seth sent an annoyed glance her way, she simply shrugged, then watched as he picked up Dillon's—or rather Tom's—gun. He removed the clip, unloaded it, then pulled back the slide and ejected a single cartridge that hit the table, bounced, then rolled toward Dillon.

"I'll do that," he said grimly, glancing first at her, then at Dillon. "There are fifteen rounds here—one in the chamber, fourteen in the clip. That's the max this model will hold."

"Which shoots down—pardon the pun—your theory that Dillon shot Tom after Tom shot him, each firing the same gun," Ashley replied. Unless, of course, he believed that Dillon had just happened to be carrying with him a couple of shells of the exact type the sheriff's department used and had reloaded the pistol. She felt a tremendous sense of relief. All it would take to get Seth seriously started on a new investigation was an inconsistency or two like this. Now he knew that there had to be a second gun involved and—with no evidence to suggest that Tom carried a second pistol—also a second man. Now he wouldn't stop until he found out who shot his deputy…thereby proving that Dillon didn't.

Gathering the bullets, Seth reloaded the clip, pushed it back into place in the pistol, then looked at her. "How about making some tea? We've got some talking to do."

Without hesitation, she went into the kitchen and put water on to boil. Behind her Seth began asking Dillon questions and, judging from the time he was taking, probably making notes, too. She had been so sure of his ability to clear Dillon's name, but she had no idea how he would go about it. She supposed his first act would be to run ballistics tests on both the pistol Dillon had taken from Tom and whatever weapons Steven Vickers had, along with checking phone and financial records of everyone involved. She seriously doubted that Russell Bradley and Bill Armstrong had risked robbing the bank of nearly half a million dollars so that they could tuck the money away someplace safe for use in their retirement years. Surely they had spent at least some of it—part of it, maybe, to pay off the men who had tried to kill Dillon last week.

Of course, once the ballistics tests proved that it was Steven Vickers who had shot Tom, that would make things so much easier. The past day or two had proved that she didn't really know Steven at all, but she didn't imagine he would be willing to go to prison for the rest of his life—or to face death, if Tom didn't recover—without giving up his accomplices. Once he knew he'd been caught, *all* the money in Armstrong's bank wouldn't be enough to buy his silence.

Unless Dillon was wrong, and the bullet that had hit Tom hadn't come from the black-haired man in the Wildcats letter jacket. There had been three men, all of them shooting; Tom had lost control of the patrol car, and Dillon must have been scared as hell. Could he really have seen which one of the three had been responsible for Tom's injury?

As the water came to a boil, she added a half-dozen orange pekoe and black tea bags, along with a bag of mint tea, then set the pot aside to steep. Seth would be so grateful that she wasn't giving him chamomile, elderberry or ginger tea that he would forget he was one of those rare Southerners who didn't like iced tea, and Dillon... He didn't like her herbal teas, either—god-awful, he'd called them—and he wouldn't like this any better. Right now there probably wasn't a single thing associated with her that he did like, except the fact that he would soon be free to leave her.

This morning she had thought chances were good that he

would understand why she had betrayed his trust, that he would recognize the benefits as far outweighing the risks, that he would forgive her. Now she doubted that that was ever going to happen. She was going to have to live with his anger and hatred and without him.

But she had known the risks and had taken them anyway. She had no one to blame but herself—and Russell Bradley and Bill Armstrong, damn them.

She had to admit, though, that faced with the same decision, knowing what she knew now, she would take the same action again. Her living alone wasn't important. Dillon living free was.

When the tea was ready, she filled two glasses with ice and tea, placed them on a tray along with honey, sugar and spoons and carried it to the table. Immediately she retreated to the kitchen once more, busying herself with unnecessary cleaning and with preparations for a special dinner that she wasn't sure she could eat, before finally deciding to bake. She was on her third batch of oatmeal muffins when Seth called her name.

When she turned, he gestured for her to go outside with him. She picked up a paper bag holding the first two dozen muffins, then followed him out. He was standing at the top of the steps, staring across the fields, when she joined him.

"You're an idiot," he announced, sliding his arm around her waist and drawing her close to his side.

"I know."

"You live way up here where no woman should live alone. You eke out a living with crafts that require a ton of work for very little return. You don't have a telephone or any way to call for help if something happens. Now you go and fall in love with a wanted fugitive—and then you turn him in to the sheriff. You just can't do things the easy way, can you?"

She rested her head against his chest. "I never said I was in love...."

His chuckle interrupted her. "You forget, I've known you all your life. You've never speeded, never gotten a parking ticket, never even cheated on your taxes. Yet here you are, breaking every law in the book to protect a wanted felon. There's got to be some explanation for it.''

"I was his hostage," she murmured in her own defense.

"So he told me. And how long did that last? Twenty-four hours? Twelve? However long it took you to decide that a handcuffed prisoner who gets shot in the back while in police custody is deserving of your protection?" He paused, but she made no effort to answer. "Besides, honey, I saw you look at him. You never looked at me that way, not even on our wedding day."

Her eyes got teary, her voice thick. "It doesn't matter. He's never going to forgive me for this."

"He trusted you, and you let him down. You can't expect him to see past that right away to the fact that you had good reasons for betraying his trust. But he'll get over it someday. He'll come around and you'll be here waiting."

"I don't want to wait for someday. I've already waited all my life." She wiped away a tear that had slipped free, then sniffed. "Can you help him, Seth? Can you prove that he's not guilty of taking all that money?"

His shrug reverberated through her. "I think so. If it's worth anything, I believe him. We know at least two shots were fired up at Sadler's Pass—the one that took out Tom and the one that got Boone—and neither of them came from Tom's gun. And he's right about the woman who called in the accident. She did have two kids with her, and they did report seeing a black van with three men who left as soon as they arrived. Then there's the photo. While you were moping in the kitchen, I showed him some photographs from our files, including one of Steven out of uniform. Boone identified him as the man up at the pass."

"So what will you do now?"

He grinned down at her. "I've got so many things to do that I hardly know where to start. I'm going to do as you asked and leave him here for the time being...unless you've changed your mind. If you have, I can jail him over in the next county, where he would be safe."

Wondering if he'd made the same offer to Dillon, she shook her head. He probably hadn't. As much as Dillon hated the idea of going to jail, she was pretty sure he hated the idea of staying there with her even more. If Seth had given him the option, he would be leaving with him.

"Are there still search parties up here?"

"Maybe." Catching the chastising look she sent his way, he shrugged. "I'm coordinating the search for my department, the state police and SBI. As far we're concerned, this area has been cleared. But there are lots of private citizens out there looking, too, and most of them probably know that the Briggs brothers tracked Boone to the bluff out back." Releasing her, he leaned against the porch railing and faced her. "How is it they managed to miss his tracks right here?"

"Luck. A lot of rain. My own big feet. So you think some of them might be around."

He nodded. "Armstrong's reward still stands, you know, and every hunter and local boy who knows these hills could put that ten grand to good use. You be careful. Citizens don't operate under the same constraints we do. Some of these boys will be quicker to use deadly force than a cop. Stay inside and keep those sheets over the windows."

"We will."

"I warned Boone about trying to escape again. I also warned him about you." Grinning again, he lifted his hand to brush over her hair. "I told him that if he harmed one hair on your pretty little head, he would have to answer to me. I figured it was too late to warn him about breaking your heart."

"Gee, thanks," she said, hoping her dry tone concealed the ache in her throat. "You're such a good friend."

"It's just part of the job." Bending, he pressed a kiss to her forehead, then took the bag of muffins. "The Catlin County Sheriff's Department thanks you. Stay inside. Stay locked up. I'll be back tomorrow."

She waited until his Blazer disappeared in the trees below before reluctantly returning to the cabin. Dillon was lying on the couch, an open book resting on his stomach, but he wasn't reading. His gaze was fixed and distant. After a moment's hesitation, she crossed the room and sat down in the armchair, right on the edge of the seat. "I'm sorry," she ventured.

The look he gave her was cold and damning. "Not half as sorry as I am."

She clasped her hands together in her lap. "I—I don't know if he told you, but Seth believes you."

"And that's what matters to you, isn't it? Your precious Seth."

"No, Dillon, *you* matter. You're *all* that matters."

"Oh, that's right." He tapped the heel of his hand against his forehead as if remembering some great truth. "You *love* me. You love me so much that you can't wait to see me in prison."

Tears welling again, she had to clear her throat to speak and even then managed only a whisper. A plea. "Dillon, please don't do this. I only did what I thought was best—"

He sat up, swinging his feet to the floor, dropping the book, facing her with an intimidating scowl. "Who gave you the right to decide what's best for *me?*" he demanded. "We spent a few days together. We had sex twice. You think that entitles you to destroy my life?"

Aching inside and seeking only to ease the pain, she gave him a sorrowful smile. "You're the world's biggest loser, Dillon," she said softly. "You don't need me to destroy your life. You've been doing a fine job of that on your own."

With that, she stood up, went into the bathroom and closed the door. Sliding to the floor, she hid her face in her arms and, for what she swore would be the first and last time for Dillon, she cried.

Dinnertime came and went without notice. Ashley made no offer to cook. If he was hungry, Dillon was capable of fixing his own meal, but he tended to lose his appetite when things went really wrong.

He couldn't imagine anything being more wrong than his life was tonight.

You're the world's biggest loser, Dillon. They were his own words, but that didn't make hearing them in Ashley's voice any easier to bear. Neither did knowing that he deserved that insult and any other she might offer.

He'd thought the past eleven months had been miserable, but he was learning a whole new meaning for the word this evening. He should have insisted that Seth take him to jail. He would much rather take his chances with Vickers and the rest of them than spend one more silent, awkward, painful hour with Ashley.

It was time for bed. Earlier this afternoon, he'd had such plans for tonight. He'd intended to spend the entire evening making love with her, resting only when their bodies demanded it, saying the longest, sweetest, most intense goodbye anyone had ever said.

Instead, they hadn't spoken since she'd shut herself away in the bathroom.

Rising from the sofa, he walked past her chair, where she'd spent the past two hours working on her cross-stitch, and to the bed. He turned down the covers, removed his sling and shut off the lamp. After kicking off his shoes, he sat on the bed to remove his socks and sweatshirt.

That done, for a moment he simply sat there. He was more tired tonight than he could remember ever being, but it wasn't a physical fatigue. He would welcome that; he could crawl into bed, close his eyes and sleep until it was gone, until his body was well rested. No, this was a spiritual weariness, and all the rest in the world couldn't heal it.

But Ashley could.

There should be something shameful about wanting her after what she'd done, but he couldn't produce the shame. All he felt was the wanting. The need. The loss.

And the betrayal. It was still there, a painful emptiness centered somewhere in his middle, a place that throbbed at odd moments, that ached with the knowledge that she had lied to him, had misled and deceived him. It hurt in ways he had never experienced with an intensity that he hoped to never again experience.

But all the anger, all the hurt, all the disillusionment didn't change the facts.

He needed her companionship, her support and her faith. He needed to hold on to her. He needed to touch her, to draw strength from her. He needed to love her.

He *did* love her—although this evening a person would have trouble seeing it in the way he'd treated her.

Across the room, she put her needlework away, turned out the lamp and gathered an armful of quilts from the wooden stand. He watched as she spread them in front of the fireplace, each one adding its cushioning to the braided rug there. When she was done, she went into the bathroom, closing the door quietly behind her.

Dillon stood up and unfastened his jeans. Instead of pulling them off, though, he left the bedside and went to her pallet. Picking up each quilt, he folded them as carefully as she'd laid them out, stacking them over the arm of the couch. He was shaking out the next to the last when the bathroom door opened again. She came a half-dozen feet into the room before seeing him and stopping short.

She was wearing her nightgown and holding the wooden-handled brush in one hand. Ready to torment him, he thought, swallowing hard. That was all he needed—Ashley in that barely-there gown sitting in front of the fire brushing her long blond hair—to bring him to his knees. To make him beg for mercy, for relief, for sweet, swift death.

He folded the quilt in half one last time, added it to the pile, then bent to pick up the last one. Instead of folding it, though, he wrapped his hands tightly in the fabric. "I can't—" His voice was harsh, hoarse, the words unintelligible. After clearing his throat, he tried again. "I can't do this, Ash."

She remained exactly where she was. "Do what?"

"Waste our time like this. In another day or two, the sheriff is going to take me in. He's going to lock me up, and I promise you, there's not a judge in North Carolina who will let me out on bail, not after last week's escape and last year's flight. This may be the last time we have together for a hell of a long time, and I can't spend it being angry."

"Seth isn't going to arrest you."

"When he can't find evidence against Russell and Armstrong, he'll have no choice. I'm still the only one who's been charged. I'm still the only one they can take to trial. Someone has to pay—"

"But it won't be you."

His smile was a poor effort. "I wish I shared your faith." But he didn't. He just couldn't believe that, after a lifetime of things going wrong, now when he was in the worst predicament of all, fate was going to work in his favor.

"You're not nine years old anymore," she argued, "and Seth isn't a grade-school principal. This isn't two little boys pointing fingers at each other, saying '*I* didn't do it, *he* did it.' We're talking about points of law, Dillon. Evidence. *Proof.*"

"And what if Seth doesn't find evidence that the others are involved? What if he doesn't find proof that I was framed? *I* go to trial. *I* go to prison."

At last she came a few steps closer. "The evidence exists—unless Bradley and Armstrong committed the perfect crime. Do you honestly believe they're that smart, that good?"

"Maybe they're that lucky, because I'm sure as hell not." The words came easily—it was an old habit, putting himself down—but the moment he heard them, he wasn't so sure they were true. In the past five days, his luck had been pretty extraordinary. Three men had tried to kill him, but his only injury was as minor as a gunshot wound could be. The car he'd been riding in had rolled side over side into a deep ravine, ending up a bent and twisted wreck, but he had walked away from it. He could have easily died of exposure from the rain and the cold, but he'd found shelter. He could have been captured by one of the search parties, could have gotten hopelessly lost, could have stumbled onto a cabin owned by an unsociable, gun-toting hermit who didn't like strangers, especially those wanted by the law.

All things considered, he had been lucky the past week, and Ashley was the best luck of all.

"You really think this will all work out?" he asked hesitantly.

She nodded.

It was a gamble. If she was wrong, if Seth couldn't find any evidence linking Armstrong and Russell to the robbery, Dillon would surely go to jail. But if she was right... If she was right, he could have everything he'd ever wanted. He could stay here. Marry her. Have a family—children, grandchildren. Grow old. Be happy. Belong.

Blowing his breath out, he folded the last quilt and set it aside. "Do you realize—if Seth does find proof—what you're getting into? You're going to be stuck with me for a long time."

For the first time all evening, the tension that had kept her stiff and remote disappeared, and she slowly smiled. "It could never be long enough."

"You'll have to marry me."

"I guess I will."

"You deserve better."

Shaking her head, she closed the distance between them. "I've never known anyone better than you, Dillon. I've never loved anyone better."

All he had to do was reach out, lay his hands on her shoulders and pull, and she was in his arms, her soft body snug against his. He lowered his head, pressing his cheek against her hair, and closed his eyes, remaining that way for a long time, savoring the feel of her, the scent, the touch. After a while, though, he shifted until his forehead was resting against hers, until all he could see were her clear blue eyes. "If you're wrong..."

"I'm not wrong," she whispered.

"If you are, it'll kill me, Ash. Leaving here, leaving you, being locked up..."

"I'm *not* wrong," she repeated fiercely. "Trust me, Dillon. Trust Seth. Trust yourself. And pray."

"Oh, darlin', I've been praying since the first moment I saw you."

"For what?" Her voice was husky, teasing, enticing. "That God would deliver you from me?"

He chuckled. "Some part of me knew you were dangerous from the start."

"*You* were the one with the gun."

"And you were the one with the eyes of an angel, a gentle touch, more kindness than I knew what to do with and the loveliest breasts...."

Leaning back in the circle of his arms, she frowned at him. "You didn't see my breasts that first night."

"I got a glimpse when you were changing clothes, and it was enough to give me fantasies." Cupping her face between his palms, he stared hard into her eyes. "I do love you, Ash," he whispered. "Whatever happens...remember that."

Her eyes drifted shut as he bent his head to kiss her. It was a brief kiss, gentle, sweet, then he released her and backed away. It took her a moment to react, another moment to open her eyes, yet another to focus a decidedly bewildered look on him. By then he was already undressed and sliding underneath the covers that blanketed her bed.

"What...?"

"Don't let me interfere with your routine," he replied with a gesture.

She glanced down at the brush in her hand as if she'd never seen it before, then, damnably slowly she smiled. She sat cross-legged on the rug where her bed had so recently been made and unmade, turned slightly toward him and began drawing the brush through her hair with slow, steady motions.

Tempting and tormenting. Last night that was how he had described watching her brush her hair two nights before. Tonight it was no less of either. It made his body hard and his spirit weak. It heated his blood and sent a tremble through his hands. It was tantalizing, teasing and pure, sweet torture.

Gazing into the fire, she began talking, her voice soft, hypnotic. "I picked up this habit from my grandmother. Every night she sat right here and brushed her hair. Those were the only times I ever saw it down. Right up until her death, the first thing she did every morning was put it up in a bun, and the last thing she did every night was sit here and brush it out.'' She sighed contentedly. "She was a good woman. She believed in hard work, family, God and love. She always said she could tell all she needed to know about a person just by looking into his eyes. She would have looked into your eyes and seen your soul.''

As Ashley certainly must have done, Dillon thought, to find anything in him worth loving.

"She was a wonderful woman—beautiful. Tough. Resilient. My grandfather used to say that she had a kind heart, a strong back and a good head on her shoulders—a major compliment from a man of few words like him. Her life wasn't easy. They never had much, and they struggled for what they did have, and three of their eight children died before their second birthdays. But she had this tremendous faith, and she never lost it, not when her babies died, not when her kids grew up and moved away, not even when my grandfather died." She smiled dreamily. "I adored her. I admired her. I wanted to *be* her when I grew up.''

"I think you succeeded," he murmured. "You're a beautiful woman. You're tough, kind, strong, smart, and you have this amazing faith.''

She flashed him a smile that made his breath catch in his chest. "You think it's amazing that I have faith in you. It isn't. I knew the very first night that you weren't some desperate, cold-blooded criminal.''

He was starting to feel pretty desperate now, but there was definitely nothing cold about his blood. He was hot enough to burn. Still, he resisted leaving the bed and joining her on the rug, and he stopped himself from calling her over to him on the bed. "If you knew," he began, his voice thick and raspy, "then why were you afraid of me?''

"I did think you were dangerous," she admitted, then grinned. "Turned out I was right. You *are* dangerous…and wicked…and handsome…and sexy." Leaning forward, she laid the brush on the stone hearth, then gracefully got to her feet, unfolding, rising, stretching. Backlit by the fire, she came to him slowly, each movement fluid and smooth, pulling her gown over her head as she walked, dropping it to the floor.

Dillon had the presence of mind—just barely—to kick off the covers, which heated his already feverishly hot skin and did nothing to conceal his arousal. When she reached the bed, she didn't stop, didn't hesitate or fumble, but placed one knee on the mattress, moved over him, sank down and so smoothly, so easily took him inside her. Her body was fiery hot, tight, greedily drawing him deeper, until he could offer no more, until she could accept no more.

Resting her hands on the mattress, she leaned over him. There was no denying that she was aroused—her nipples were hard, her skin moist, her body where it held him damp—but her eyes were clear, true blue. Not hazy, not dazed, but sharp, piercing, honest. "I love you, Dillon, and I'm sorry I hurt you. I'm sorry I gave you reason to doubt me. I'm sorry I couldn't treat your trust with the respect and honor it deserved. But it'll never happen again, I swear to you."

He lightly stroked her hair. "You did what you thought— what might prove to be—best for both of us." He drew a breath that smelled of her unique scents. "I'm sorry, too. I said some things.…"

"You were entitled."

He shifted underneath her and felt her body move with him, adjusting, tightening. It sent a shiver up his spine. "One thing I said, that giving up half my life is a reasonable price to pay for spending the rest of it with you… That's true. If I have to go to prison—"

"You won't."

"But if I have to…" He broke off, unable to go on. The enormity of what he wanted to ask, the arrogance of believing he might deserve it, stopped him cold.

But Ashley apparently found it neither enormous nor arrogant. Bending lower, she pressed her mouth against his, rubbing, tasting, then drew back only enough to give the answer he needed to hear. "I'll be here for you, Dillon," she whispered. "Always and forever."

Chapter 11

He brought the subject up again late the next morning. Ashley was standing at the counter, spreading thick slices of bread with garlic butter, and Dillon was a few feet away, sharpening a paring knife—the closest she could come to a steak knife—on a whetstone with slow, even strokes when abruptly he said, "What I asked for last night…"

She gave him a sidelong smile. "What would that be? As I recall, we both asked for a number of things last night…and got them, too."

Clearly uncomfortable, he turned to look out the window, lifting the curtain just a bit. "If I get convicted… About waiting." After a moment of silence, he faced her again. "I wouldn't ask that of you. Twenty-five years is a hell of a long time. It's your entire life."

"Not quite," she said dryly. "You don't even know how old I am, do you?"

"You're young," he said with a grin. "You'll always be young. That's all I need to know."

"For the record, I'm twenty-nine. And also for the record…this is my home, Dillon. This is where I'll be living in five years, in twenty years, in twenty-five years. This is where I'll be if you're here with me, and this is where you'll find me if you're not.''

He started to touch her hair, but drew his hand back before he did. ''You're a beautiful young woman, Ash. It's easy to say you'll wait now. But what about a few months or a few years from now? What about when you get lonely? What about when you get tired of living alone?''

''For starters, I'm young, yes, but you're the only man who's ever called me beautiful.'' She softened the remark with a smile, then went on. ''I don't get lonely for just anyone. There are times I miss my parents, times I miss Seth. I *always* miss my granny. But those longings aren't interchangeable. Seeing Seth doesn't make me miss my folks any less. Seeing *anyone* wouldn't make me miss you any less. Living with someone else wouldn't make up for not living with you.''

''You would be wasting your life—''

She stopped him with a chastening look. ''Why are we even discussing this? Let's wait and see what happens. Even if Seth can't find enough evidence to arrest Armstrong and Bradley, he'll find enough to make you look less guilty. He'll create a reasonable doubt. We'll get a good lawyer, and we'll take our chances. Whatever happens, we'll deal with it—both of us, Dillon. You and me. Together.''

Rising onto her toes, she pressed a kiss to his mouth, then turned her attention back to the steak, wine and German chocolate cake she was fixing for lunch. Since this was the first bottle of wine she'd ever bought, she had bought a corkscrew, too, but it was nowhere in sight. Talking more to herself than to Dillon—''I know I bought it…I'm sure the clerk put it in the bag….now where could it be?''—she did a quick search of the kitchen, then sighed. ''It must have fallen out of the bag in Bessie,'' she decided.

''I'll check—''

She stopped Dillon before he'd taken even one step. ''Remember what Seth said. You stay inside.''

"He told us both to stay inside."

"Yes, but I live here. No one would be surprised to see me out there. You, on the other hand..." Patting his arm, she stepped into her old beat-up loafers, then left the cabin.

It was a beautiful day—bright, sunny, a slight chill in the air but not too uncomfortable. The air smelled of spring, of pines and wildflowers, of budding trees and shrubs. She loved spring and early summer in the mountains, loved the colors, the fragrances, the sounds. Birds' songs competed with streams tumbling over rocks and down cliffs and breezes rustling through the leaves, and the blossoms—redbud, dogwood, apple tree, honeysuckle, azalea and rhododendron—were heavenly. The next few months were a wonderful time to be living exactly where she was living.

She only hoped that Dillon could share them with her.

She hurried down the steps and across the bare ground to the van, opening the passenger door, leaning inside for a quick look. Sure enough, the corkscrew was lying on the floor, one corner of its cardboard package caught underneath the rubber mat. She pulled it free and was preparing to back out of the van and straighten when suddenly a face appeared through the driver's window opposite her. Her startled cry died unvoiced as she stared at Steven Vickers. He was wearing the green baseball cap of the Catlin County Sheriff's Department, but instead of his uniform jacket, he wore a Catlin High letter jacket.

And he was holding a gun.

Before she recovered enough from her shock to react, a hand closed around her mouth from behind, and powerful arms pulled her away from the van. She caught a glimpse of the man who held her reflected in Bessie's window, but he was a stranger. So was the man behind Steven and the fourth man approaching from behind the cabin. But the last man, bringing up the rear, was no stranger. She knew Bill Armstrong well. She had gone to school with his youngest daughter, entrusted her savings to him and been turned down by him for a loan when she had first returned to Catlin.

Everything Dillon had said was true. If she hadn't already believed him, this would have convinced her beyond a doubt.

Dillon. Oh, God, Dillon. They had come here to kill him, just as he'd predicted they would, and he had no way to defend himself because Seth had taken the gun yesterday. If he died, it would be her fault for confiding in Seth, her fault for convincing Dillon to stay, her fault for not getting up early this morning and sneaking him out of the county as they had planned. If he died, she would never forgive herself...but if he died, she realized with a chill, she was going to die, too. There was no way these men might let her live to testify against them.

Armstrong stopped in front of her, his expression harsh and cold. She had always thought he was a pompous and phony old goat, but this morning she realized that it wasn't arrogance in his eyes. It was evil, chilling, narrowly focused. "Is he in the cabin?"

She made no effort to reply with her mouth covered; after a moment's wait, he impatiently gestured for the man who was holding her to move his hand. "You bastard," she said softly.

"I'm not interested in your view of my character, dear. Is Boone in the cabin?"

She said nothing.

"Call him out." It was the fourth man who'd spoken, drawing her attention to him. Like the others, he was dressed casually, in jeans and a jacket, a hunting rifle cradled in his arms, but he didn't look like the others. His jeans were pressed, his jacket expensive leather, his hiking boots top-of-the-line. He was young, about Dillon's age, but he was far more polished, more elegant, more like Bill Armstrong.

So this was Russell Bradley, Dillon's old friend, former boss and betrayer. She couldn't imagine any two people less likely to be friends than these two. She couldn't imagine anyone less deserving of Dillon's friendship than this man.

"Call him out," he repeated, his voice soft, lacking all traces of his Georgia upbringing. When she still didn't respond, he shrugged, and the man holding her twisted her arm behind her back, forcing her wrist toward her shoulder. This time she couldn't control the cry as sharp little fingers of pain stroked through her arm, up into her shoulder and down her back.

Steven Vickers moved around the van, holding his pistol firmly in both hands. "Boone!" he shouted. "Dillon Boone!"

Inside the cabin, Dillon was leaning on the counter, idly waiting for Ashley to return, when his name echoed through the windows. His muscles went taut, and cold chills swept over him as he acknowledged in an instant that Seth Benedict was supposed to be the only one who knew he was here and that definitely wasn't Seth's voice. Moving to the nearest window, he raised the sheet a few inches, and his heart stopped beating in his chest.

Bradley, Armstrong, Vickers and the other two men from Sadler's Pass. God help him—God help Ashley—they were in trouble. They were dead.

His gaze lingered for a moment on Ashley. She looked frightened and in pain from the way the big son of a bitch was bending her arm, but other than that, she seemed unharmed. She wouldn't stay that way long, though…unless he figured out a way to help her.

As Vickers yelled his name again, Dillon let the sheet fall and gave the cabin a sweeping look. Seth had taken the deputy's gun, and Ashley didn't have one of her own, not that it would help if she did; he had never fired a gun in his life and wasn't about to start when she was standing between him and his target. The deadliest weapon available was the paring knife on the counter. Muttering a prayer of thanks that he was left-handed and still had full use of that hand, he slid the knife out of sight into the sling, then started toward the door. There he saw the walking stick, long, solid wood, hard wood. He hefted it, decided it could surely do some damage, then let it slide through his fingers until he was gripping it near the top. Taking a deep breath, he opened the door and, leaning on the stick, he feigned a slight limp as he walked across the porch to the top of the steps.

Russell smiled the big, friendly smile he used to hide his

black soul. "You're a hard man to find, Dillon. We figured you were dead somewhere out there in the forest until some of Steven's trackers finally picked up your trail again this morning. We never suspected that it might lead straight to Sheriff Benedict's lovely ex-wife."

A dozen agitated thoughts were racing through Dillon's mind as he listened. Where were the trackers now? Had Vickers sent them back home or deeper into forest to search for further tracks that didn't exist? If they'd gone back home, would they tell the sheriff what they'd discovered or trust Vickers to do it? How could he ever have trusted Russell, and did he get Ashley into this mess?

His fingers clutching the hickory stick tightly, he breathed deeply to make sure his voice was steady—to make sure he didn't plead—when he spoke. "You don't want to hurt Mrs. Benedict," he said, not shaky, not intense, just a quiet, careless warning, "because if you do, Sheriff Benedict will kill you."

"Sheriff Benedict won't have any reason to believe that it was us," Armstrong said.

"He knows everything. We had a long talk yesterday. Right now he's investigating each of you—" he gestured toward the three men in front, then made brief eye contact with each of the others "—and it won't take him long to find out who *you* are."

"All he knows is what you've told him," Russell contended. "He won't find anything to implicate us in either the robbery or the tragic events here."

Dillon shrugged. "He's got the gun I took from the deputy. Tests will prove that I didn't shoot him. The same tests done on *his* gun," he continued with a nod toward Vickers, "will prove that *he* did."

Vickers held up his pistol, a nine-millimeter semiautomatic identical to the one Dillon had taken off Coughlin. "You're right, Boone. Tests *will* prove that this gun was used to shoot Tommy. They'll also prove that Ashley was killed with the same gun. Then, presumably distraught over all that you'd done and over the prospect of spending the rest of your life—or dying—in prison, you turned the gun on yourself.''

"Seth won't buy that," she said scornfully. "How are you going to convince him that Dillon got hold of your gun when you *presumably* haven't seen him in almost a year?''

Vickers's grin faded, and his eyes turned cold as he looked at her. "Then we'll just have to take care of Seth, too.''

And that would leave them in the clear, Dillon acknowledged grimly. Not knowing who else might be part of Russell's scheme, Seth had proposed conducting his investigation quietly, completely on his own, at least in the beginning. If Vickers killed him and destroyed his notes, the only other person who could possibly speak out was Tom Coughlin...who had suffered serious head injuries...who was in a coma...whose recall of the shooting—provided he survived—could be easily discounted.

He and Ashley were screwed. He couldn't even try to bargain to save her life, because Russell held all the cards. Dillon had nothing to offer.

"Come on down here," Russell ordered.

Still using the stick as a cane, he slowly made his way down the steps. At the bottom, he stopped. "You people are crazy. You're willing to kill four people, two of them cops, for a lousy half-million dollars? That's nothing. It's certainly not worth dying for.''

"But that's the beauty of our plan," his old friend—his dearest enemy—replied. *"We're* not the ones who are going to die. And we never could have done it without you, Dillon. I knew the day I saw you in Atlanta that you would be perfect for it. You had never accomplished anything. You'd been in trouble all your life. You were a failure, a screwup. Yet you were smart enough to do what we needed you to do, trusting enough to not suspect what was up and honest enough to not rip us off. You were a perfect pawn.''

The truth of his words settled bitterly on Dillon's shoulders. So it had been an even more elaborate setup than he had suspected. From the very beginning, before Russell had even offered him the job, it had all been part of their plan. If only he hadn't lost that last job in Atlanta... If he hadn't accepted Russell's offer, if he'd had something or someone to keep him in Georgia, he could have avoided this entire nightmare. He never would have met Ashley, probably never would have known what it was like to love anyone the way he loved her, but at least he wouldn't be standing here preparing to die. He wouldn't be at such a damnable loss to think of a way to prevent *her* from dying.

She was looking at him, her face pale, her eyes bigger and bluer than ever. He wished he could hold her one last time, wished he could tell her how sorry he was and how very much he loved her. Then she smiled, just a faint little curving of her mouth, and he knew that she knew. She understood.

"Let's hurry up and get this done with," Armstrong snapped. "We've all got better places to be and better things to do."

Vickers stepped forward. "We've got to make it look like he killed her, then killed himself. Darrin, go inside and find her car keys. We'll say she saw a chance to escape, and he stopped her."

Ashley couldn't stand by silently while two people she'd known all her life planned the best way to murder her. "Right," she said sarcastically. "I was in town alone for two hours yesterday afternoon, but this morning I decide to escape. You guys are idiots. You think Seth or anyone else with a brain will believe that?"

Russell Bradley turned to look at her. His gaze was measuring, derisive and just a little bored. He was a far more dangerous man than she'd first thought, she realized. He truly had no qualms about murdering two innocent people, one a stranger, one whom he'd grown up with, whom he had considered a friend. He had no heart, no soul. "This whole incident will be quite a trauma for the county of Catlin," he explained patiently. "One deputy comatose and in critical condition, the sheriff dead, his unfortunate former wife murdered by the same cold-blooded killer who then ended his own life… Everyone will be in shock. They'll believe whatever they're told."

"You underestimate my friends and neighbors," she said coolly, but she wasn't sure she believed it. Three deaths and Tommy Coughlin near death… *Why* it happened could easily forestall any questions about *how,* and with Bill Armstrong—former mayor, everyone's banker and everyone's friend—there to smooth the cover story over, the *how* might very well never be asked.

"What do you think?" Steven joined them as the man named Darrin came out of the house with her keys in hand. "Ashley out here and Boone inside?"

"Sounds reasonable," Bradley replied. "Take care of him first. Be sure you make it look self-inflicted."

Ashley's heart rate tripled. "Bill, you *can't* do this," she pleaded. "You can't let them do this! You have your money. Please, Dillon will leave. That's what he was planning to do anyway. He'll leave the state and he'll never come back."

Armstrong looked at her without even a hint of remorse. "It's too late to bargain, Ashley. It was too late the minute he got arrested over in Mossville. Go on, Steven."

Switching the pistol to his other hand, Steven took hold of Dillon's arm as Darrin moved in on the other side. Terrified, trembling, barely able to breathe, she took a step forward before the other stranger blocked her way with his arm. "Dillon!"

He smiled at her, an accepting sort of smile that was underlaid with sorrow. "It's all right, Ash. Everything will be all right."

Tears blocking her throat, she watched, silently praying—pleading, screaming—for him to do *something* as he climbed the first step, the second, then the third. He stopped there, fumbled, then swung around, bringing the hickory stick crashing against the side of Steven's head. As the deputy staggered back, then fell, the stick continued its powerful arc, slamming into Darrin's arm, sending him to his knees and his gun flying through the air.

Ashley reacted instinctively, ducking underneath her guard's outstretched arm, diving for the pistol where it landed in a patch of yellow jasmine. The commotion of a struggle sounded behind her as the man came after her, grabbing her ankle just as her fingers closed around the rubber grips of the pistol, just as she rolled onto her back, clutching the pistol in both hands, pointing it only inches from his heart. It made him freeze where he was.

She had always thought that she was absolutely incapable of using a gun for self-defense; she had told Dillon as much his first night here. She would never shoot to protect her property and had doubted that she could do it to protect her life.

Well, she had been wrong. If she had any idea what to do to make this gun fire—if there was a safety, if it was on, if the hammer had to be cocked or if she could simply pull the trigger—she would do it. She would kill this man, and Russell Bradley and Bill Armstrong and the others. She would kill them and be glad to do it.

The sound of a gunshot boomed, making her jump. Scrambling to her feet, she risked a look at Dillon, who was standing at the bottom of the steps, his left arm around Russell Bradley's shoulders, holding the other man in front of him. The sun glinted off the newly sharpened blade of the knife he held at Bradley's throat. Steven Vickers lay unconscious on the ground, and the other man, Darrin, was sitting a few feet away, bent over in pain, cradling his right arm to his chest. Bill Armstrong had raised his rifle, taking aim on Dillon and Bradley, but he wasn't the one who had fired. It was either Seth, standing at the rear of the van, or one of the men with him.

Without waiting for an order, Armstrong threw his gun to the ground. "Thank God you got here in time, Sheriff. We tracked Boone to Ashley's cabin, and when we tried to take him into custody, he disarmed your deputy and his friend. He probably would have killed us all if you hadn't come."

Seth moved forward. "Your luck's run out, Bill. Dub Collins didn't like being cut out of the capture. He figured that he tracked the guy, so he deserved credit for catching him. To ensure that he got it, he came straight to my office when you sent him away." Slowly, his gaze shifted. "Ashley, you okay?"

"Yeah, I'm fine."

Turning toward his backup without taking his eyes off the men, Seth said, "Handcuff them all and read 'em their rights. Start with Mr. Armstrong."

"Wait one minute, Benedict—"

One of the men—an SBI agent, Ashley thought—stepped in front of Armstrong. He was a big man, backed up by a big gun. "Put your hands on the roof of the van," he ordered in a voice that demanded compliance. As the banker obeyed, another of the men took the pistol from Ashley and led the stranger away.

She started toward Dillon, but Seth, his attention already locked on him, stopped her a few feet away. "He's not worth killing, you know," he said quietly.

Dillon remained motionless. His fingers were wrapped so tightly around the wooden handle of the knife that his knuckles were white, and his breathing was audible, slow and measured. "That's what he was going to do to us," he replied, his voice just as quiet. "They were going to shoot Ashley in the back, to make it look as if she tried to escape and I killed her, then killed myself." He smiled faintly. "They were going to kill you, too."

Bradley wet his lips nervously. "Come on, Dillon, please don't do this. I've got a family—a wife, kids. Please don't… I'll tell them everything, I'll tell them how we set you up for the robbery, just please, *please,* don't kill me."

Seth glanced down at Ashley and, in a tense voice, murmured, "You could jump in here any time."

Her gaze stayed on the two men in front of them. "Frankly I think cutting his throat is too easy, too quick. I'd rather see him suffer." Then she sighed. "All right." Brushing Seth's hand aside, she approached Dillon. Pain etched thin lines around his eyes and mouth. In the condition he was in, the blows he had struck with her walking stick had probably hurt him almost as much as they'd hurt the two men. "I chose hickory for that stick," she began softly, "because my granny used to tell me that it was a good, strong wood for clubbing varmints that got too aggressive. Somehow I don't think she ever expected it to be used on varmints of this sort."

His gaze, very faintly amused, met hers, and she studied him for a long moment before giving him a knowing smile. "You aren't going to hurt him. You're a better man than that. You're a better man than he could ever be." She hesitated a moment, then reached for the knife. For just an instant, his grip tightened, then he let her pull it away.

He released Bradley, who moved away so quickly that he stumbled into Seth's arms, then Dillon tenderly touched her check. "I would have killed him if they had hurt you."

"I know, because *I* would have killed them if they had hurt *you.*" She drew a deep, shaky breath. "I almost got us killed, and I am so sorry. If I hadn't gone to Seth, if I had taken you to Nashville this morning—"

He stopped her with a shake of his head. "I don't think I would have gone. I don't think I could have left you." At last he pulled her into his arms, holding her tight.

Clinging to him, Ashley was just starting to get comfortable, to get over the delayed shakes and to begin to think about the future ahead of them, when Seth cleared his throat and, with such reluctance, said, "I hate to intrude...."

Without giving up one degree of their closeness, Ashley and Dillon both looked at him.

"I know you didn't rob the bank, Dillon—or at least it happened the way you said—but...there's still the matter of the charges against you. We can get them dropped, but it may take a little time. These men are going to jail for trying to kill you guys and for trying to kill Tommy, but beyond the one comment that Bradley made, I don't have anything yet to tie them to the robbery."

She stared at him. "What are you saying, Seth?"

Before he could answer, Dillon did, with a soft, resigned sigh. "He's saying that he has to arrest me."

Panic began growing dead center in her chest. "*No*. Seth, you can't do that. You know he's not guilty."

She tried to pull away, but Dillon held her tighter. "Ash. Listen to me, Ash." He waited until she'd stopped her struggle, until she was focused on him. "It's okay. He's just doing his job. Honey, you were right. We've got to get this cleared up. We don't have much of a future with this hanging over me, and I want—I *want* that future. Fifty years from now I want a bunch of blond-haired, blue-eyed grandkids and great-grandkids hearing stories about how their granny once helped an escaped prisoner hide from the police and how she saved their grandfather's life. I want them to know why hickory makes good walking sticks. I want them to know how to bake bread and make quilts, how to weave baskets and weave dreams. I want it all, Ash, and it starts with this. With clearing my name."

Tears filling her eyes, she turned once more to Seth, pleading with him. "You left him here yesterday. Why can't you do it today?"

"Because yesterday no one knew he was here but me," he replied miserably. "Today a lot of people know and a lot more are going to find out. I'm sorry, Ashley, but until the charges are dropped, I have no choice."

Dillon brushed her hair back. "It won't be so bad. You can get a lot of work done to make up for this past week, and when I come back, I'll be a free man, Ash, and…" He tilted her face up, dried her tears and gave her the sweetest promise she'd ever heard. "I'll be back to stay."

The dirt road climbed and twisted through the hills, passing trailers, log cabins and farmhouses. The pastures were lush and green, the fields newly planted or being prepared for planting. It was a warm April day, the kind of lazy day when wading in a creek or walking barefoot down a dirt road beckoned, when lying in the grass and watching butterflies, birds and clouds seemed a perfectly productive way to pass the time.

It was a perfect day, Dillon thought, gazing out the side window of the Blazer, for going home.

"You should have let me tell Ashley that you were being released today."

He glanced at Seth. The sheriff had called him yesterday afternoon to tell him that the robbery charges against him had been dropped, that the same charges were being added to the attempted-murder charges Russell, Armstrong and the others were facing. It had taken Seth three weeks, some serious investigating and, Dillon suspected, a fair amount of arguing with the district attorney to convince him to dismiss the charges. A statement from Deputy Coughlin—conscious and alert, although a long way from recovered—had been a major help.

Dillon had spent those three weeks in a jail a hundred and fifty miles from Catlin. Until the investigation was completed, until they were certain that Vickers had been the only deputy working for Bradley, Seth had thought he would be safer elsewhere. Dillon had appreciated the precautions, but it certainly would have been easier being in Catlin, where Ashley could have visited. As it was, he hadn't seen her since that Sunday morning, when he had told her he loved her, kissed her goodbye and left her in tears on the porch.

She had wanted to make the three-hour drive to visit him—Seth had even offered to bring her—but Dillon had refused. He hadn't wanted her to see him in jail, locked up like a dangerous animal. Somewhere along the way being free had become more important to him; being free when he next saw her had seemed tremendously important.

He'd had one other motive behind his refusal. They hadn't known each other long—only six days. Six frightening, intense, emotional days. He'd known that time, quiet and peace couldn't change the way he felt about her; nothing ever could. But he'd wanted to give her a chance to see if the same was true for her. Once her life had returned to normal, once the danger was gone, once she fell back into her usual routine, would she still feel the same? Would she still want him? Would she still love him?

Soon he would find out.

With a sigh, he finally responded to Seth's comment. "I wanted to surprise her."

"What are your plans now? You going to marry her?"

"If she'll have me."

"I don't think you have to worry about that," Seth said dryly. "What about work?"

He turned to the window again. "Her grandfather was a farmer. So was mine. I grew up on his farm. I think I'd like to give that a try."

"If that doesn't work out, I'm going to be hiring a new deputy soon."

Dillon gave him a sharp look, then laughed. "Right. With my background, I'd make a perfect cop."

After a moment Seth chuckled, too. "At least you'd bring a different perspective to the job." Taking his foot from the accelerator, he shifted down and turned into Ashley's narrow, winding driveway.

"Stop here," Dillon said abruptly. "I'll walk the rest of the way."

Without comment Seth brought the truck to a stop. Dillon climbed out, then reached in the back for the small nylon bag that contained his meager possessions. In jail he'd worn a prisoner's uniform, and Seth had brought him a set of new clothes this morning, so his old jeans and Ashley's sweatshirt were in the bag, along with the toiletries the sheriff had provided. He started to close the door but hesitated. "Thanks, Seth."

"For what?"

"Getting me out. Not locking me up in the first place. Not using these three weeks to convince Ash that she was making a big mistake. She listens to you, you know."

"Maybe...but she loves you." After a moment he leaned across the seat and extended his hand. Dillon shook it. "Be good to her."

With a nod, he closed the door, slung the bag over his shoulder and set off up the hill. The cabin came into sight first, looking much as it had for the past eighty or a hundred years.

Bessie was parked out front, as pathetically ugly as ever, and the door to the workshop was propped open to let in the warm afternoon air. No doubt that was where he would find Ashley, weaving a basket or dipping candles, molding soap or stirring up her sweet-scented potpourri. That was where he would find his welcome, if there was one. If Seth was right.

That was where he would find his future.

He crossed the clearing and stepped onto the stoop, then into the doorway, his tennis shoes making no noise on the weathered wood. The bright lights were on inside, and the worktable was clean except for a spool of thread, a pair of scissors and an assortment of needles and pins. The loom sat neglected, and the quilt frame, a quilt stretched across the bars, was un—

His startled gaze moved swiftly back to the frame and its quilt. It was unbleached muslin with an intricate pattern worked in browns, yellows and golds, old, heavily used and very much treasured. It was his grandmother's quilt.

He'd thought it had been lost forever.

A soft hum from that side of the room drew him through the doorway and closer to the frame. He saw her feet first, bare, slender, delicate, then a flash of leg, mostly covered by a long chambray skirt. Seeking courage and praying for the best, he stopped beside the frame and crouched down so he was closer to her level.

She was sitting on the floor underneath the frame, her head tilted back, using an impossibly small needle to replace old stitches on the back that had finally given way. For a moment she was totally unaware of him, then her humming gradually faded and her stitches slowed until the needle was barely moving. Finally she looked at him. Her hands dropped to her lap, and she simply looked.

God help him, she was beautiful, with the kind of beauty that made him ache just to see it. Looking at her made him feel weak. It made him feel humble. And it made him so grateful.

Her smile came slowly, starting in her eyes and making its way to her mouth, lighting her entire face, lighting his entire life. She didn't move toward him, though. She simply sat there and smiled that smile.

"How—" His voice was husky and quavered. "How did you find my grandmother's quilt?"

"I have them all. And the Bible. And the photographs." Her voice was as sweet and unconsciously seductive as he'd remembered in his dreams every night for the past three weeks. "I drove in to Asheville one day and looked up your old girlfriend. When the landlord cleared out your apartment, Pris persuaded him to give them to her. She knew they were important to you. She knew you would want them back."

He drew his finger along the pattern where it folded over the wood frame. "I can't believe you did that, that you went to so much trouble...."

"It wasn't any trouble," she whispered. "I was just repairing a few places on this one. I wanted to have it ready for you when you came back." Her gaze darted away, then back again. "You *are* back, aren't you?" she asked hesitantly. "You aren't leaving?"

He shook his head solemnly. "When Seth arrested me, I told you then that when I came back, it would be to stay."

On hearing that, she gave him the sort of welcome that he'd been dreaming about for weeks, launching herself out from beneath the wooden frame, throwing herself into his arms with enough force to make him tumble backward and take her with him. Laughing through tears, she covered his face with kisses. "I've missed you so much," she whispered. "I've been waiting and hoping and praying... Oh, Dillon, I love you."

Cradling her face in his palms, he kissed her, tasted her, savored her. She was so sweet, so special, so familiar—a part of his very soul. That was only fair, he supposed, since she already owned his heart.

Needing air, he ended the kiss—no, not ended, but interrupted, since he would pick up where he'd left off in a minute—and pushed her back so he could memorize every tiny detail of her expression. If he ever needed in the years ahead to know what pure joy was, he could recall this moment...or he could simply look at her face or his own. "How long would it take your family to get here from California?"

"For something special?"

"A wedding."

"Less than twenty-four hours."

He feigned disappointment. "That soon, huh? I kind of had plans for the next twenty-four hours…and the next…and the next…and they don't include anyone but you and me."

She smiled delightedly. "Of course, if we told them to come next week, they wouldn't show up early."

He returned to the kiss, then rolled her onto her back on the floor and leaned over her, resting his head on his right hand, using his left to unfasten the top button of her white blouse. "Next week," he murmured. "That should be enough time." He opened the next button, then the third, before a sudden intensity swept over him. "I love you, Ash."

She grew serious for a moment, then her expression softened and warmed. "I know. Oh, by the way, Pris gave me a message for you. She said to tell you that she wishes you the best."

He thought of all the things he had in his life now. The cabin. The farm. A place to belong. A bright future. The promise of children and grandchildren, of years of passion and years of pleasure. And Ashley. Beautiful Ashley who had taken him into her home and her heart, healed his body and his spirit, saved his life and his soul. She had undone all the harsh lessons of his past and taught him the tender lessons of love. She was every wish and every dream he'd ever had, all rolled into one. She was his life.

"I *have* the very best," he whispered before he kissed her once again. "I have *you*."

* * * * *

If you enjoyed this story, look out for One True Thing
*by Marilyn Pappano in Silhouette Sensation
in February 2005.*

SILHOUETTE

Passionate and thrilling romantic adventures

Sensation

NIGHT WATCH

Suzanne Brockmann

▼ SILHOUETTE

INTRIGUE™

Breathtaking romantic suspense.

His mysterious ways

Amanda Stevens

♥ SILHOUETTE®

Desire™ 2 in 1

Passionate, dramatic love stories

BEAUTY AND THE BABY
Marie Ferrarella

SOCIAL GRACES
Dixie Browning

New York Times bestselling author

DIANA PALMER

After Midnight

"No one beats this author for sensual anticipation."
— *Rave Reviews*

Published 21st January 2005

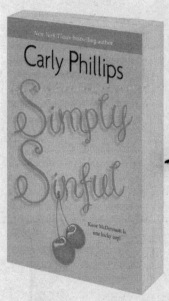